The Cruel Gods
The Children of Chaos

"This is an exciting and action-packed sequel that examines the tension between structure and chaos in our lives – and how the predominance of one is stifling. Highly recommend for readers looking for queer-norm worlds, wild imagination, and steampunk and/or gaslamp worlds." — *Nathan's Fantasy Reviews – Before We Go Blog*

TRUDIE SKIES
fantasy author

TRUDIESKIES.COM

THE CRUEL GODS BOOK TWO: THE CHILDREN OF CHAOS
Copyright © 2022 by Trudie Skies.

This is a work of fiction. Names, characters, gods, places, and incidents are products of the author's overactive imagination. Any resemblance to actual persons, living or dead, is entirely coincidental and rather unfortunate.

No part of this book has been aided by the use of artificial intelligence.

Cover design by James T. Egan, www.bookflydesign.com.
Map illustration by Soraya Corcoran, sorayacorcoran.wordpress.com.
Edited by Nia Quinn, www.editor.niaquinn.com.

ISBN: 978-1-7398179-3-0 (paperback)
First paperback edition October 2022.

Content Warning

THE CHILDREN OF CHAOS is an adult fantasy book that contains strong language throughout and content some readers may find distressing, including religious criticism, sexual themes, and scenes of abuse and torture.

For a full list of content warnings, please visit:

TrudieSkies.com/The-Cruel-Gods-Content-Warnings

For the rebels, the revolutionaries, the protesters, the unions, the outcasts, the non-conformers, the bullied, the abused, the abandoned. For those betrayed by their leaders, their church, their favorite childhood author, their parents. For those shunned by their home or community for being different. For those who ever felt shame for who they were born to be.

You are human. You are mortal. You deserve love, dignity, and respect.

Become the chaos this world needs.

Domain Map

DOMAIN CROSSINGS
XII
XI
I
X
II
IX
III
VIII
IV
VII
V
VI
PHANTASY
KRONOS
EVENTIDE
MEMORIA
RAPTURE
JUNIPER
OBITUARY
HEARTSTONE
TEMPEST
SOLARIS
ARCADIA
WITHERYN

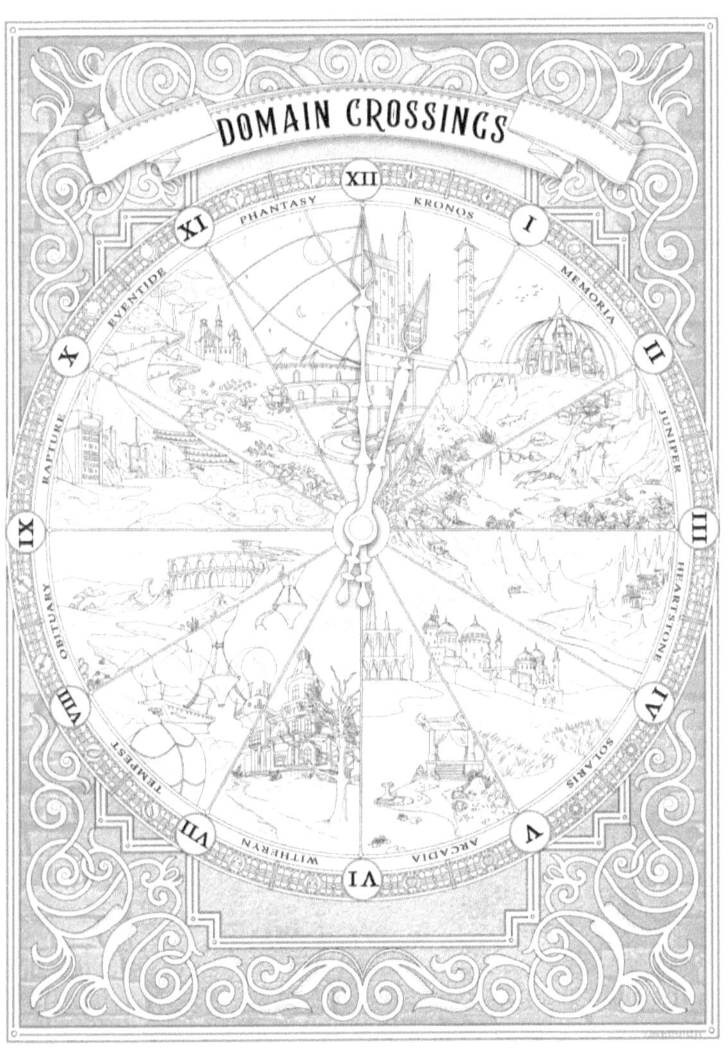

Domain Glossary

A list of the twelve domains in order of their designated crossing time:

Memoria

Home to the Amnae.

An underwater city. Ruled by Anima, the god of academia, books, history, memories, and water.

Juniper

Home to the Fauna.

A treacherous jungle. Ruled by Faen, the god of animals, creatures, metamorphosis, and sacrifice.

Heartstone

Home to the Umber.

A mountainous region with valleys. Ruled by Unghard, the god of craft, discipline, earth, nature, servitude, and trade.

Solaris

Home to the Glimmer.

A golden city of cathedrals. Ruled by Gildola, the god of birth, dawn, femininity, piety, spring, and sunlight.

Arcadia

Home to the Seren.

A series of tropical islands. Ruled by Serenity, the god of art, beauty, creativity, song, and summer.

WITHERYN

Home to the Necro.

A frozen wasteland. Ruled by The Nameless One, the god of blood, disease, flesh, healing, and winter.

TEMPEST

Home to the Zephyr.

A sky world made from floating airships. Ruled by Zyclone, the god of air, machines, science, and technology.

OBITUARY

Home to the Leander.

A desert plain. Ruled by Lionheart, the god of battle, challenge, domination, legacy, masculinity, strength, and trials.

RAPTURE

Home to the Ember.

A volcanic strip of casinos. Ruled by Edana, the god of depravity, flame, pleasure, and sensuality.

EVENTIDE

Home to the Vesper.

A land of glowing mushrooms. Ruled by Valeria, the god of autumn, dusk, moonlight, and shadow.

PHANTASY

Home to the Mesmer.

An observatory of stars. Ruled by Mesmorpheus, the god of dreams, nightmares, stars, and visions.

KRONOS

Home to the Diviner.

A clockwork city. Ruled by Dor, the god of bureaucracy, justice, law, logic, order, and time.

The Covenant of Mortals & Gods

We, the standing ambassadors of the twelve domains, do pledge to speak true as the holy voice of our patron gods. We ordain this Covenant as a record and warrant between mortals and immortals and agree to uphold its decrees in the eyes of our almighty gods, the faithful, and the Wardens who watch us.

The gods do pledge:

1. To create mortal life which obeys the laws of time.
2. To allow their mortals to exercise free will.
3. To provide a domain [hereby known as Chime] where mortals may seek life and liberty.
4. To bar non-mortal lives from entering this domain [Chime].
5. To allow mortals safe passage into their own domain.
6. To not interfere with the life or liberty of mortals belonging to other domains.

In turn, the mortals do pledge:

1. To honor their god and domain through factious worship and prayer.
2. To honor their god and domain by abstaining from sin.
3. To honor and respect the gods and mortals of other domains.
4. To honor and obey the ordinance of Chime.
5. To honor and obey the word of the Wardens.
6. To not commit the unforgivable sins of blasphemy and apostasy.
7. To bear a mark identifying citizenship to Chime and the twelve domains.

All mortals are made equal in the gods' eyes and shall be granted the same privileges and opportunities on Chime. Should a mortal fail to uphold these seven laws, or commit an unforgivable sin, their right to life and liberty within Chime is forfeit.

The Wardens do pledge to serve Chime and her mortals in accordance with these values and in honor of the gods and their mortal voices.

Signed by the twelve standing ambassadors in the eyes of our almighty gods, the faithful, and the Wardens who watch us.

The Unforgivable Sins

Blasphemy

To blaspheme: an impious utterance or action that besmirches one's patron god or the gods of other domains. To assume one's standing is above one's patron god.

Examples: curse words, disrespectful speech, or hateful imagery.

Apostasy

To reject the blessings and love of one's patron god.

To reject the laws of the Covenant.

To commit idolatry for another god or object in place of one's patron god.

To live a life of blasphemy and depravity.

Ignorance

To mispronounce scone.

PART ONE

0

What is reality, but a dream of the gods?
—Unknown, *The Philosophical Musings of Phantasy*

Dear God,

WHERE ARE *you? It's scary here in the dark. The shadows move, and the pipes clang and hiss. Everything's dirty and smells. There's hardly any light, and the lamps buzz with a horrid screech that makes my head hurt. I've prayed to you thirteen times! Why don't you answer me back? Did I do something wrong?*

Please answer. I'm so lonely.

You're not alone, a voice spoke inside my mind. My imaginary friend who had been with me since I first opened my eyes. *You'll always have me.*

Why doesn't our god love us?

Don't be silly. Mother wouldn't have made us if she didn't love us.

Then why doesn't she answer my prayers?

Because she can't right now. You'll understand one day.

I didn't think I'd ever understand.

The pipes clanged again, and I huddled against the wall on a dirty mat, my arms bunched around my chest to ward off the cool air on my naked skin. One moment there had been a vast nothingness, and then I'd appeared underneath a glowing silver lamp, though where, I didn't know. I'd run for the nearest dark place, the crevice of a tunnel, but the stones beneath my feet hurt, so I hadn't made it very far. The lamp flickered opposite, as though it laughed at me.

How long had I remained hidden in the darkness? Everything was so new and so horrible. My stomach ached for food I'd never tasted. My dry tongue begged for water I'd never drunk. I didn't know what pancakes even were, but I wanted them.

Clouds of smog drifted above and coated everything in gray.

Why was I here?

Why had my mother left me all alone?

We need to go, my imaginary friend urged.

It's too dark out there. And scary men walked by every now and then. I caught a glimpse of them in the lamplight; they had skin in shades of gray and dark blue, and they scowled at the shadows.

I'm with you. If anyone tries to hurt us, we'll hurt them back.

"I don't want to hurt anyone," I whispered. My voice cracked as I spoke for the first time. It was an odd voice, feminine but croaky.

You may have to. I can't save us—I'm stuck inside you. You have to save us both.

Why did I have to do the saving? I wasn't the brave one. That was what my heart said. I didn't know what I was good at, but it wasn't being brave.

The streetlamp opposite buzzed loudly and flickered in and out, sending spurts of darkness across the tunnel's entrance, where I hid. Then it flashed with a bright silvery-blue light that spasmed in my forehead. I covered my eyes. When the light faded, a man stood there, but his skin wasn't the dark shade of the strangers in the shadows.

No, this man shone with a silvery-pearl. His clothes were lighter in color too, a tan suit instead of swaths of black, and he wasn't as tall or fearsome as the others. Eyeglasses sat on his nose, and the silver eyes behind them met mine.

He smiled at me—a warm smile—and then he took a few slow steps in my direction.

I shrank against my mat, but I had nowhere to hide as he crouched before me.

"Don't be afraid." He spoke with a soft voice. "I'm not going to hurt you."

"What—What are you?"

"I'm a little lost, like you. I shouldn't be here—this isn't my time—but luckily fate has brought me to you." He pulled out a flask from inside his jacket pocket and offered it. "Go on. It's clean water."

You shouldn't trust him, my imaginary friend said. *He's a bad man.*

How do you know he's bad?
Because he's one of them.
One of who?
A man of time. An enemy of Chaos.

I didn't know what that meant, but I knew what my body needed. I snatched the flask and fumbled the stopper open. Cool water dribbled down my chin as I gulped mouthfuls of a crisp and refreshing liquid that some inner instinct knew to be safe.

"Slowly now," he warned. "You don't want to choke."

I spluttered a cough and wiped my lips dry. I tried to pass the flask back, but he held up his hands.

"Keep it." He shrugged off his jacket and laid it in the space between us. "Cover yourself in this. It's a little big, but it will keep you warm until help arrives."

"Help? I don't want—"

"There's no shame in accepting help, and you need all the help you can get." He glanced at my sorry state over the rim of his eyeglasses—black soot stained my hands and knees—but affection shone in those silver eyes.

How could this man be my enemy when he was so kind?

He flipped open a pocket watch. "My time is up, I'm afraid. Listen to me; a Vesper woman is going to find you shortly. She's a nice lady, and she'll look after you, so please listen to her, will you? She has a son, and he's going to be grumpy, but be patient with him. He's suffered a lot."

I draped the tan jacket around my shoulders. The inner lining pressed softly against my skin, and it fell across my body, enveloping me completely. "What happened to him?"

"His god was mean to him and his family."

"Why? Didn't his god love him?"

"Sometimes the gods are cruel."

He's right about that, my imaginary friend said. *Not our mother. But others.*

"Do you have a god?" I asked.

The man ran a thumb over his pocket watch. "Not anymore."

He stood back on his heels, the silver of his hair glowing in the lamplight.

I reached out and grabbed his wrist. "Don't leave me. Please." Tears pooled in my eyes. I couldn't be left here all alone again, I couldn't be! "Don't go."

He gently pulled himself from my grip. "You're a brave girl. The bravest girl I know. And you're going to be fine. More than fine; you're going to be brilliant."

Bright silvery-blue light encased his entire being. In a single blink he was gone.

Utterly gone.

I tugged his jacket tight around my chest, which ached with a pain I didn't understand.

Why had he abandoned me too?

"Please come back," I whimpered. The aching in my chest burst into a sob.

Don't cry.

"I want my mother! I want—"

"Hello?" a woman called. "Is someone there?"

My heart caught in my throat. I slapped a hand over my mouth. Tears ran down my cheeks and between my fingers.

"Careful, Ma. Could be anything lurking in these tunnels—"

"Wait there, Malk. Someone's hurt."

A tall woman with dark blue skin and black hair appeared at the entrance to my tunnel. Her amethyst eyes blinked in surprise as they fixed on me. "Are you lost, little one? What's your name?"

I didn't have a name. My mother hadn't given me one.

You're Kayl, my imaginary friend said. *The enemy of time.*

Was time truly my enemy? When time had been kind to me? "I'm Kayl."

"Kayl. What a lovely name. I'm Elvira, and I'm new to these parts. Perhaps you can help show me around? It's less scary when there's more of us." She held out her hand and beamed with a reassuring smile.

The silver man had said I could trust this woman. This Vesper, he'd called her.

He'd said I was brave. Had he lied?

I clasped her hand. My silvery-blue skin turned a darker blue shade to match hers.

She gasped, but didn't let go. "My, aren't you special?" My stomach growled, and Elvira chuckled. "And hungry! How about we go find something nice together? If you could eat anything, what would it be?"

"Blueberry pancakes!" I squealed as my imaginary friend said it at the same time.

Jinx, I inwardly giggled.

Jinx? the inner voice repeated. *I like that.*

You do? Then that's what I'll call you. Jinx.

Darkness descended over Elvira's face, shining with purple and pink stars as though night itself had entered the tunnel uninvited.

YOU DREAM OF THIS MOMENT OFTEN, came an otherworldly voice in my mind that was neither masculine nor feminine, and certainly *not* of my imaginary friend. *I DO NOT UNDERSTAND THE SIGNIFICANCE.*

A dream. Of course. Dreaming was all I ever did these days.

I wasn't a thirteen-year-old girl. I was a twenty-six-year-old woman.

The child—my younger self—faded as the nebula around me blossomed into clouds of glittering stardust. Within each cloud, still images formed. Dreams plucked from my subconscious. Events that had passed.

Nightmares come true.

An unholy machine that had split souls from their mortal hosts.

Eventide turning gray as it collapsed into dust.

Corentine, the thirteenth god trapped inside the clock tower.

Quen, as his silver eyes met mine only moments before his mortal end.

Images I never wanted to relive *ever* again.

I squinted in the dark and caught a glimpse of a figure striding through the mist of stars; the shape of a mortal in a tight black suit, though where a mortal's face would have eyes and a mouth, this one was a blank canvas of unfathomable stars.

"Mesmorpheus," I breathed. The god of dreams and nightmares. "To what do I owe the pleasure?" I'd sensed the god's presence in my dreams before as they sifted through them, an unwelcome lingering touch in my head. But they'd never addressed me until now.

YOUR DREAM HAS CHANGED. DID QUENTIN CORINTH APPEAR AT THE MOMENT OF YOUR BIRTH?

Gods, I could barely remember my childhood. There was no chance I'd be able to tell dream from reality. "How could Quen have been there?" He'd been the one to awaken Corentine as a young lad. Without him, I wouldn't even exist at all. Perhaps the guilt of losing him haunted my subconscious. "It's just a dream, isn't it?"

DREAMS REVEAL TRUTHS MOST MORTALS REFUSE TO BELIEVE. I SEE MANY PATHS. MY VISIONS GROW CLEARER WITH TIME, AND THE TIME TO ACT WILL SOON COME. ARE YOU PREPARED, CHILD OF CHAOS?

How could I possibly be prepared? "You can see the future. You tell me."

YOU AND YOUR SISTER WILL FIGHT FOR OUR SOULS. THEN EVEN THE GODS THEMSELVES WILL BEND.

The thought of bringing the gods to their knees thrilled me, I'd admit, but not at the cost of losing more mortal lives. "So how do you see this playing out?"

THAT REMAINS TO BE SEEN.

Great. Not even the almighty gods had a clue where Chaos was concerned. "And yet you chose me to be your savior. Are you a betting god? Do gods even bet? Because I'd say our odds of stopping Chaos from ripping our souls apart are looking pissing terrible."

YOU ARE THE ONLY HOPE WE HAVE.

Mesmorpheus's voice faded from my mind, and the night enshrouded me. A comforting darkness as dense as a Vesper's shadow.

The gods expected too much if they thought *I* could stop Chaos from destroying them. That was what Chaos wanted. Destruction. The death of all gods and their mortals.

And my sister would lead the charge.

Jinx had always been the smarter one. The braver one. She paid attention to the mechanics of the cosmos where I couldn't. Yet I was supposed to *stop* her?

Gods. It was an impossible endeavor.

But as sleep overtook me, for one blissful heartbeat, I could forget my place in the universe, and the part fate forced me to play.

I awoke to the dazzling lights of Babel. Of Chaos.

Pink stars swirled above me, a mimicry of a galaxy only a Mesmer could appreciate. But here in their temple, those stars came alive to mock me. Their light cast a pink glow in the otherwise dark room. I lay atop a pile of pillows, my body half-entombed in their softness, yet the darkness never took me for long.

I woke and remembered the dreams Mesmorpheus had pulled from my subconscious.

I remembered what I'd lost.

In another lifetime, a frail and angry Vesper would be sleeping beside me, his arms wrapped around my waist, my lips tucked against his neck, my hand resting above his beating heart.

But that boy was no more.

I'd erased him from existence.

And in the silence of this room, the silence of my thoughts was stark. Once, my mind had been full of chatter, of my twin living vicariously through me with her constant commentary on my life, my sins, my mistakes.

Now all that remained was emptiness.

I wasn't quite alone. Harmony's single wing fluttered in her sleep, and Dru's snoring rattled like a steam engine. The three of us shared this large bed—this room—but for all my problems, I couldn't confide in them. They wouldn't understand what I'd done. What I'd taken from this world.

They wouldn't understand like Jinx would.

Like Quen would.

My hand instinctively went to the cracked pocket watch, which no longer ticked or tocked, no matter how hard I'd tried to fix it. The stubborn thing simply didn't want to work, and we had that in common. Even in the dark, I'd memorized its design and knew the pattern of the marred brass like the back of my hand.

My dear partner. I'd only known him a short time, and yet my darkest thoughts kept returning to him and the sacrifice he'd made to save me.

I'd never gotten a chance to thank him.

I clutched his watch tight against my chest and blinked back the tears.

Quen was gone. Malk was gone.

The Vesper were gone.

And Chaos was coming.

Quen had called me brave in my dream, but he'd been wrong about me. So wrong.

How was I meant to shoulder this alone?

Plans & Schemes & Pancakes

BLUEBERRY JUICE STAINED MY golden fingers purple. I licked them clean with a groan loud enough to make the other mortals of this quaint café drop their spoons and stare. I'd demolished an entire plate of blueberry pancakes, and took to licking cream from the plate as more mortals tutted. But damn, these pancakes were *good*. The blueberries had a tang almost as tart as I was.

I finished off the plate and let out a musical belch that would put any Golden City orchestra to shame. The Seren seated at the table next to me had finally suffered enough and waddled out of the café, though not before shooting me a look of disgust.

I blew a kiss in her direction.

"Are—Are you finished, miss?" asked a nervous-looking Umber server dressed in a cute pinafore. Her skin was rose quartz in color, and her brow sprouted tiny white roses to match. Wowee. With the purple wisteria trailing down her back in place of hair, she was by far the prettiest Umber I'd ever met, and now I felt bad for ruining her day. Okay, I only felt a *little* bad.

"Yep. All done." I snatched a napkin and patted my lips clean. "Great pancakes, by the way. Almost worth *not* destroying your entire domain."

"Wha—What?" she stammered, her rose eyebrows quivering on end.

"Oh, never mind me. Just thinking out loud. Kinda weird having all these thoughts and no one to hear them, you know?" I threw my bag of ill-gotten goods over my shoulder, grabbed my crinkled copy of this morning's Courier, and left a batch of crisp bocs piled on the table. "Keep the change."

The server and her patrons stared as I swaggered from the café.

I gotta say, I *loved* when mortals stared.

Through their eyes, they saw a Glimmer woman acting not as society expected Glimmer to act. It certainly was fun to watch the snobs getting bent out of shape because a lady dared ignore their precious etiquette.

Playing as a Diviner was just as much fun, and for my next trick, I'd need their face.

As I stepped from the café into the bustle of Central, my skin changed from gold to silver. If anyone noticed, they'd likely think they'd gone insane. Though a few mortals did blink at my appearance. A female Diviner in a tight red dress? How indecent!

I'd flash them my cunt, but I wasn't actively trying to catch a Warden's eye today.

Across the square, the dull gray skies of Kronos watched over Central Station through the Gate, and it wasn't even midday yet. It hadn't taken those Diviner fucks long to fix their precious Gate and finish reinforcing the clock tower. Since Eventide had popped it, something needed to fill in for the tenth hour. There was no way they'd let Rapture's crossing stretch for a whole two hours, nor could they foist that hour onto Phantasy and confuse the poor Mesmer. So naturally, the Diviner had decided to steal it for themselves and give Kronos two extra crossings per day. I'm sure that would have fucked off the Glimmer, though it didn't make my life any easier either.

More Diviner swarming Chime would only hinder my plans.

I glanced up at the clock tower. A shiver ran down my spine.

You could barely tell where the reinforcements had been hammered in, but they wrapped around my soul and squeezed tight. Mother remained trapped inside the clockface with my brethren. Only a handful of us had remained in Central, taking on personas to help us blend in with Chime's citizens. A few more had tried to run for the Gate, to enter the domains of the gods and take back what was ours.

They'd been caught before they could make the crossing.

Somehow, those gods-damn Diviner had installed sensors around the station that could detect us. And with their shitty tasers, we couldn't get past them.

My brethren had taken their own lives rather than end up strapped to a table in Kronos. Smart, *I guess*, but now their souls were back with Mother while I remained down here. At least I'd had the brains to hang back and watch what those Diviner were up to.

They couldn't trap us all, and they certainly weren't going to catch *me*.

"Don't worry, Mother. I won't let you down."

Warmth flooded my chest as her voice echoed in my mind. *I HAVE EVERY FAITH IN YOU, DAUGHTER.*

I didn't need faith. *Where's my beloved sister now?*

SHE HAS LEFT THE TEMPLE DISTRICT ON ANOTHER TASK FOR THE GODLESS.

Good. I wasn't ready to run into Kayl just yet.

Not when she'd fucking betrayed me.

The Central crowds rushed to and fro as the clock ticked closer to eleven. It was funny how the city had gone back to normal so quickly after my own brethren had run rampant across this place, ripping out souls here and there. Mortals continued to use the now fixed glass elevator, despite it falling and smashing to pieces only a month ago. The Wardens had even replaced the burned-out streetlamps. They hummed now with the aether provided by my own mother's soul.

It disgusted me.

This whole damn city disgusted me.

Mortals of the twelve domains went on with their lives oblivious to the god who towered above them. They sat in cafés drinking tea and eating scones blissfully unaware of this city's true origins. They caught trams powered by bleeding Mother dry. They bought tacky souvenirs and ornamental junk from brick-and-brass shops without hearing Corentine's screams.

Chime was an amalgamation of all twelve domains, but the Diviner dominated it with their steam-powered machinery and clockwork bureaucracy.

It wasn't what my domain was meant to be.

It wasn't Babel.

These fucking Diviner had ruined it.

What did Kayl see in this stupid city that I didn't?

Why would *anyone* bother to save it?

I slipped between the crowds and accidentally brushed up against a few unsuspecting mortals—an Ember here, an Umber there—and helped myself to a few wallets as I caught the next available tram out of Central Square.

This tram was almost full with the midmorning rush. I managed to squeeze onto a seat beside a Leander, whose feline eyes ran down the entire length of my dress and lingered on my bare legs.

Normally such attention wouldn't bother me—I craved it, in fact—but today I had *plans* and *schemes*. "My tits are up here, fella."

His eyes snapped up, and his entire mane ruffled. "Are you for real, lady? Diviner like you don't exist."

I fluttered my eyelashes. "Oh, that's only because daddy Dor doesn't like us slutting it up with the common mortals. Why else are there so few female Diviner around?"

A Diviner sitting opposite spluttered in outrage, his silver face Ember-red. The idiot practically launched himself from his seat and started awkwardly waddling down the tram's carriage. "Warden!" he called. "Is there a Warden on board?"

Oh darn. Had I spouted blasphemy out loud again? I seriously sucked at pretending to be a moral member of society. How did anyone keep up with all these rules? Stay in your queue, don't spit on the pavement, don't swear, don't steal mortal souls, yada yada!

I peered out the carriage window. This rickety old thing had chugged past the Tower View district, leaving those miserable apartments behind, and was now making slow progress to my actual destination. Would I reach it before a Warden stomped over?

With a little luck.

But as the crowds on the tram parted and another Diviner pushed between them dressed in the black-and-bronze uniform of the Wardens, I let out a sigh. Bloody typical. I patted the Leander on his thigh. "Guess this isn't your lucky day."

At the sight of the Warden, the Leander turned away from me and lifted his jacket collar to pretend he hadn't been eye-fucking me a moment ago. Traitor.

The Warden grabbed the upper pole above me and leaned close, his body swaying with the tram's rhythm. "Should you be out dressed like that, ma'am?"

I scowled up at him. "Is there something wrong with my clothes?"

"It's a little revealing, ma'am."

I pointed to a Glimmer further down the carriage who was dressed as extravagantly as me. "What about her?"

"She's, uh, not Diviner."

"So?"

"I don't think our Father would appreciate you dressing this way." He raised silver eyebrows. "I think you should return to your domicile and change before you cause a scene, *ma'am*."

Oh, so that was why there were so few female Diviner; the males irritated them to death. I'd fucking love to cause a scene, but *plans* and *schemes*.

"Temple District, this is the Temple District," came the driver's announcement right on cue. "The time is ten twenty-five."

I stretched to my feet, forcing the Warden to shuffle back. "Well, I've really taken to heart what you just said. I'm off to the temple to renounce my sins. Have a *glorious* day." I shoved past him before he could stop me and merged with the crowd exiting the tram.

A quick glance over my shoulder showed the Warden was following me. Fuck.

On reflection, perhaps a red dress wasn't the most inconspicuous outfit to be wandering around Central in, but stripping and walking naked was likely more conspicuous.

Then again, the sight of a naked female Diviner might give him a heart attack.

I hurriedly joined a group of mortals heading into the Temple District. Twelve temples dominated the skyline in this part of Chime with an ugly mismatch of buildings that represented each domain. All twelve were spread out in a circle, with a pond in the center where water flowed down an hourglass statue representing Chime.

The temples were supposed to be equal according to the Diviner's stupid Covenant, yet it was their and the Glimmer's temples which overshadowed the rest. Both were towering cathedrals; the Glimmer's made from eye-wateringly bright gold and burning braziers, and the Diviner's like a replica of Mother's clock tower. Insulting, is what it was.

The Seren's was the prettiest by far, designed to be an outdoor pavilion surrounded by statues and other art. The Glimmer's was the busiest, with mortals crowding around it, chanting and praying and whatnot. Abandoned opposite was the Vesper temple, a twisted black miniature of Valeria's old castle. Someone had boarded up the entrance—a Warden I guessed—but there probably wasn't much point. No one was going in there anymore.

There was no temple for the thirteenth domain.

No temple for Chaos.

Luckily for me, the temple I wanted was next to the Diviner's; the Mesmer temple.

It wasn't quite a temple. It was the shabbiest-looking building of the lot and resembled a run-down dream parlor covered in peeling purple paint. Apparently, no one bothered to maintain it. I could see why. A single Mesmer sat slumped against the door, asleep.

The Warden still followed. I couldn't snap his soul or murder him in public—they definitely had rules about that sort of thing. But he likely wouldn't follow me into another temple. Mortals weren't allowed inside temples not of their domain, and even Wardens would need a warrant to enter.

Though I doubted a bunch of drugged-up Mesmer would pose much of a threat.

I took a casual stroll toward the Diviner temple, as though walking with purpose, and then quickly slipped under cover of the Mesmer temple doors. The Mesmer didn't even wake as I stole their persona, my silver skin morphing to a Vesper shade of purple.

"Excuse me, ma'am!" The Warden ran over to me and then blinked in surprise.

"Can I help you, sir?" I asked with my best *I'm high on mushrooms* voice.

"Oh, uh, forgive me, ma'am. I'm looking for a Diviner—she wore a similar dress to yours. I thought I saw her head in this direction."

A Mesmer in a nice evening dress wasn't as suspicious, even if the color clashed with my skin. I cocked my head to one side. "Do Diviner see the stars? They taste like blueberries. Sometimes I dream about pancakes the size of moons—"

"That's... quite all right. I can see I'm mistaken. You have a good day now." The Warden bobbed an awkward bow and then wandered off to his own temple, rubbing his chin with a look of sheer befuddlement.

Idiot.

I tutted and stepped over the still-sleeping Mesmer into the temple's foyer. It looked more like a dream parlor reception.

One Mesmer lay snoring on the front desk, a lollipop stuck to their cheek, as another slumped against the wall, idly eating candy from a bag, surrounded by discarded wrappers. Neither so much as twitched at my sudden appearance.

I knew Mesmer were lazy shits, but *fuck me.*

The double doors into the main temple opened, followed by an obnoxiously loud slurping. Out came a Mesmer trio of what looked like identical triplets dressed in tight black suits, only each Mesmer had slightly different colored stars blinking across their dark skin. The one in the middle was sucking on a milkshake.

"You're back already?" one asked.

"Were there more Wardens outside?" asked another.

"Did you find trouble?" said the slurper as their straw popped out of their mouth.

I slid my bag from my shoulder. "You know me, I'm always finding trouble. You want some candy?"

The trio converged on me with eager grins, the slurper tossing their milkshake onto the reception desk, a thick pink sludge spilling across the surface. Seriously, how did these Mesmer even manage to dress themselves? I pulled out various candies I'd swiped from a store in Central and handed them over to greedy hands.

"Oh, I love toffees!"

"Is that a sherbet lemon?"

"Do you have any bubblegum?" Slurper reached for my bag.

I snatched it away. "Hey now, you gotta share. Do you know where Dru and the others are? You know what I'm like, I'm *always* forgetting my way around this place."

Slurper giggled at me. "You'd make a great Mesmer."

Yeah, Kayl probably would. "So, which way?"

Slurper beckoned me past the double doors, and we entered a series of dull halls, each with their own signposted room stating if they were occupied. Just like a Mesmer parlor. And maybe it was. All Mesmer did was eat and sleep.

Why Kayl chose to shack up with a bunch of Mesmer was beyond me. Was it to stuff her face with candy? I wouldn't put it past her. "I bet I forget your names, too."

"Sometimes. Most of the time. But it's okay—"

"It's not okay. It's actually really shitty of me. You shouldn't put up with my shit, you know. Put me in my place."

Slurper looked sheepish as they stopped by a door. "Um. They're in here."

I dug out a packet of bubblegum and tossed it over. "Cheers."

The Mesmer grasped it close to their chest and skipped back down the hall, giggling like a maniac. Reve was never *that* annoying.

I let my persona switch back to Diviner as I made my dramatic entrance. "I'm back, bitches!"

The pathetic group known as the 'Godless' were seated around a table in what appeared to be a parlor room converted into a meeting place. Stars swirled in the ceiling in a perfect pink nebula resembling the chaos of aether. Resembling *my* home, Babel. Their pink and silver glow lit up the otherwise dim space.

How fucking cheeky!

The many faces of the Godless blinked up at me; Harmony the bossy Seren, Vincent the stuffy Necro, Sinder the slutty Ember, and Dru the Umber, Kayl's idiot best friend who was the only one who bothered to stand at my arrival. See, *I* could remember names!

"Where'd you get that dress?" Dru asked, her stony green face instantly suspicious.

"Never mind that," Harmony snapped. "Did you run into a Diviner?"

"It was nothing I couldn't handle," I said. "But who cares about them? I did a little shopping on the way back and got you all gifts!" I rummaged through my bag and dug out a flashy gold necklace. "You like jewelry, right?" I flung it at the Seren, and it clattered across the table. "Whoops. Better check that for dents."

Harmony lifted it in disbelief.

Next, I tossed a flowery brooch at Dru, who caught it in one hand.

"Did you shoplift this?" Dru asked.

"Why would you assume that? You know, there's these little pieces of paper called bocs—"

"And where did you get the bocs?"

"Oh. I stole those."

"Are you serious?"

I sighed and let my bag drop with a thud. "I bring you fucks gifts, and this is the thanks I get?"

"That's not Kayl," Vincent declared. He stood, his chair falling dramatically. Sinder leaped beside him as Dru's golden eyes widened and she took a hesitant step back.

"Shit," Harmony muttered. "You must be Jinx?"

I curtsied. "The one and only. Though I'm surprised my dear sister even bothered to mention me—"

"Why are you here?"

"Because we're family! Did Kayl ever tell you about the voice trapped inside her head? Bet she didn't. But I know you. All of you. I've watched every interaction you've ever had with my *dear* sister. I'd say I know you all rather intimately. I know, for example, that none of you ever considered Kayl to be a competent member of your little group. And why should you? It's her fault the Vesper are gone."

Vincent and Sinder subtly edged their way around the table to Harmony's side. None of the Godless dared take their eyes off me.

A red glow emanated from the Ember's fists. "I think it's best if you leave."

"So soon?" I pouted. "What lies has my dear sister spread? That I was responsible for Valeria's death and Eventide's destruction? She took Valeria's soul, not me. Bet she didn't tell you *that* either, did she?"

Confusion flickered over their adorable faces. Oh no, my dear sister hadn't confessed to that little sin.

"What do you want?" Harmony snapped.

"As I said, we're family. And family helps each other."

I picked up my bag and strode to the table. Dru flinched as I passed close and pulled out the rest of my gifts—a pair of silver cuff links for Vincent, and a bottle of vintage red wine for Sinder. They really weren't grateful for the thought I'd put into these gifts. It was hurtful, honestly.

"Don't be so nervous. We're alike, you and I, and we want the same things—an end to the gods. But you really can't trust a word my sister says." I sat on the edge of the table. "You know, I warned her about that Glimmer machine. I told her they couldn't be trusted. And because she wouldn't listen, Reve is dead." My gaze flickered to Dru, who was chewing on her bottom lip. "Malk is dead. *All* the Vesper are dead—"

"Isn't that what you want?" Harmony stood on her chair. "To destroy the gods, but take mortal lives in the process?"

"Is that what my dear sister told you?" I slid off the table and leaned over it, meeting her defiant diamond pupils with my own stare. "Well… She's right."

"You're a crazy bitch."

"Don't I know it." I grinned. "I'm going to take your gods' souls, one by one. As a courtesy, I'm here to warn you… don't get in my way. Or I promise you, Miss Arabesque, that I'll take Sinder's soul, then Vincent's soul, then Dru's soul… And I'll make you watch."

A part of me was eager to yank out their souls and savor them now, but all I wanted was to sow a little doubt and despair.

Why would Kayl choose these idiots over our mother? Our family? Our bond?

And why would they protect her knowing what a dirty liar she was? Knowing it was *her* fault their precious Vesper were gone?

Why look at *me* with those hateful eyes when I hadn't even killed a god! Maybe they'd damn well respect me if I had.

Sinder and Vincent came around the table to shield Dru at both sides. The Necro's lips curled back, revealing his fangs.

"I can see I've worn out my welcome." I dug my copy of the Courier out of my bag and tossed it across the table. "Read the headline. I'm sure you'll be interested in what it has to say. And tell my dear sister I hope to see her there." I slung my bag over my shoulder. "Now before I go, I'm sure it's customary in this shit heap of a city to swap gifts. Since I've been quite generous to you, I'd like something in return." I snapped my fingers at Dru. "You, Green Girl. Give me a flower."

Dru hurried back in alarm, bumping into the table behind her. "You— You want one of my flowers?"

"As a symbol of our undying friendship. I have known you my entire life."

Sparks sputtered from the Ember's fist. "Get out," Sinder snarled.

"One flower. It's a simple request—"

"Get *out*." Flame flared from his nostrils.

"Fine. I'll take them all."

I yanked time to a stop. These idiots stood there paused in a cocoon of time that my fun Diviner body had blessed me with. I'd had plenty of time to play around with it and get used to fucking with time without giving myself an aneurysm, and wow, it was so much fun! The Diviner had all these rules and rites about it, but they never used it to its full potential.

My Godless friends blinked at me. I'd frozen their bodies in time, but left their minds open with a delightful awareness of what I was about to do.

It wasn't fun committing chaos without an audience.

I slid my hands around Sinder's shoulders, his muscles solid under my wandering touch. "It's not nice to feel trapped at someone else's mercy, is it?" My finger traced across his collarbone and the tattoo that said *Sinner*. "I bet you'd know all about that." I leaned close to his ear. "I could destroy Gildola for you," I whispered. "And all her rotten Glimmer. Would you like that?"

His dark eyes widened. Was that longing I saw hidden there?

Next, I approached the prodigal best friend. Dru's eyes blinked rapidly in surprise or fear—I didn't really care. "I only wanted one flower. I thought you Umber weren't supposed to be so damn selfish."

They really were pretty flowers. Little golden daisies that stood on end and quivered ever so slightly.

I grabbed all of them with both hands and ripped them from her brow. She didn't scream. She couldn't, not with time standing still as it was. "Thanks, *friend*."

I hummed a merry tune as I made my way out of the Mesmer temple, casually stepping past the Mesmer paused in time gorging themselves on candy.

I'd made my first move. Now I'd wait for my dear sister to make hers.

2

No one wants to mention it, but it's obvious what happened to the Vesper. The Wardens simply had enough of them. Every year, hardworking businesses in Central lose stock and bocs to wandering Vesper fingers. It's no lie that criminal activity has decreased since the Vesper were banished. Chime's streets have never been safer.
They'll be coming for the Ember next. Mark my words.
—Anonymous, Overheard in Lady Mae's

AS THE ONLY VESPER left in Chime, it came down to me to stalk through the streets of Central and put up fliers, though it wasn't as easy as it looked.

The satchel dug painfully into my shoulder with the weight of hundreds of fliers—wonderful Godless propaganda I was expected to spread in the hopes that some impressionable mind would stumble upon them. Oh, there were plenty of brick walls, street corners, and lampposts for me to desecrate. But even with the Vesper's ability to summon and hide within shadows, there were too many mortals loitering. And too many Wardens. Since the Gate had broken a month ago, Warden patrols had increased, making the task altogether impossible.

And this was the only task I'd been deemed competent enough at to handle.

I waited in the crevice of an alley for another Warden patrol to pass. The morning was getting on, yet I still carried a full set of fliers. Dru would worry if I didn't return soon.

But I wasn't Malk. I lacked his finesse at swooping in and out of shadows.

For I'd not been born a Vesper, despite living as one for nigh on thirteen years. I lacked their natural talent.

I was a child of Chaos, and right now, chaos was all I could manage.

Shadow pooled around my fingers, and I slipped further into an alley behind one of Chime's busiest pubs, the Brick and Briar. At this time of day, only lodgers remained inside. Litter fluttered along the alley's gutter, including yesterday's Courier broadsheet. I wafted away the awful smell of alcohol and piss.

The Wardens ensured Chime's streets were swept clean, but they clearly didn't care for the darker parts no one entered.

No one except those committing nefarious deeds.

I pulled out another flier—a hand-drawn impression of a Vesper male and the question: *Where did the Vesper go? Ask a Warden.*

As much as I admired Vincent's artistic talents, this male looked too much like Malk for me to stomach. Those long black locks that I could no longer thread my fingers through. Those cool sapphire eyes that would never blink again.

Whispering itched in the back of my mind. I'd always assumed it to be guilt, some madness plaguing me. The whispering only occurred when I was in my Vesper form, in fragments of conversations I couldn't quite grasp.

Sometimes, I swore I heard his voice. Calling for me.

I'm with you, Malk said.

No. You're gone.

I'm here so long as you believe it.

I wished I could.

"Get a hold of yourself," I muttered, and shook off the emotions threatening to take over. I fumbled in my satchel for the little pot of paste.

This was the tricky part; smearing the right amount of paste onto the flier so it would stick. Yet somehow, the pissing stuff got in my hair and on my clothes. Gods help me if I was accosted by a Warden—I was wearing enough bloody evidence.

With some difficulty, I attached the flier to the wall, and it actually remained where it should. I'm sure Malk must have mastered the art much quicker than me. But with him no longer here, someone needed to step up and take his place.

That was all I was good for. Putting up fliers.

Footsteps clopped on the cobblestone street behind me.

Shit! Someone was entering the alley!

I whirled, but the alleyway was a dead end. Gods, Malk wouldn't have trapped himself with no way out! What an absolute rookie mistake, and I was no rookie. Or so I liked to think. There were no crates or barrels to hide behind, so I wrapped myself in a cloak of shadow and pressed against the far corner of the wall, next to a suspicious yellow puddle.

"It's rubbish, is what it is." A man swaggered into the alley dressed head-to-toe in black and bronze. A Warden. The aether streetlamp by the entrance to the alley gave his hair a white sheen. As he neared my hiding spot, I caught the shine of his silver skin.

A Diviner. Great.

"It's only temporary," said another Diviner. Bloody Wardens always came in pairs. "Stop complaining about it."

"Temporary until when? These longer patrols are killing me." The Diviner stopped only inches from where I stood, and I held my breath. He grunted and undid the zip of his pants. I was unfortunate enough to get a good look at his cock as he whipped it out and took aim at the wall. Apparently Diviner drapes *did* match the carpet.

A splash of piss landed on my boots. Ugh.

I thought the Wardens cared about the cleanliness of this city? Dor would be appalled!

The Warden shook himself off and turned to leave when my newly erected flier caught his attention. "It's another one of those blasted fliers." He tore it down with ease, proving I hadn't used enough damn paste. "Have you seen this? The lies they're spreading now? Trying to make it sound like *we* had something to do with the attack. They should be hanged."

"That's a bit strong, don't you think?"

"Is it? They caused the attack in the first place, and now they're trying to twist it around! Like anyone would believe Wardens had something to do with it."

Was that the official Warden line? That my organization had caused Chaos to bleed through and destroy Eventide?

We Godless knew the truth, but the Wardens had covered it up, naturally. By posting our fliers, we hoped to spread the truth—or at least get mortals questioning the narrative they'd been fed.

It was going well so far. *Not.*

"There's room in Central Square," he continued on. "We could build some gallows, find every apostate in the city, and let 'em hang."

"Except you know they won't because of the Covenant—"

"The Covenant shouldn't apply. If a mortal commits an unforgivable sin, no matter what domain, hang 'em."

"Their gods will punish them—"

"Not all of them do. Some get away with a slapped wrist."

"You don't know that—"

"One way to ensure justice is done? Hang the bastards. It's because of apostates like these that Eventide is closed, that we've got to scan everyone who walks into Central Station, that we need to work extra damn patrols, and you know what else? Tea prices have gone *up*! Insurance fees across Central are extortionate, that's what the Glimmer were saying over at Lady Mae's. All because of these." He scrunched the flier in his hand. "Hang 'em!"

"All right, you've made your point—"

"We should be hunting them down, not patrolling empty sodding streets. Our new ambassador is a joke. Karendar wouldn't be wasting our time like this."

"You know we need to be seen doing something. Have faith in our Father."

"I do, god bless his holy ways, but why choose *him* to be his mortal voice? You've heard the rumors, surely? Death follows him everywhere—"

The window to the upstairs pub opened, and a line of sunlight shone across my hiding place. Shit! Glimmer power counteracted a Vesper's, and I quickly shuffled to the side, slinking further into the darkest corner of the alley.

I accidentally kicked a glass bottle.

It rattled against the wall. Both Diviner spun to face me.

Shit. Fucking *shit*!

"Are you men quite finished?" yelled a Glimmer dressed in a nightgown and cap. She half hung out the window. "I'm trying to pray!"

"Apologies, ma'am. We'll be on our way," said the other Diviner.

But the public pisser was stalking toward me. "Did you see that move?"

"It's just the wind."

"What wind? Hey, lady," he called up to the Glimmer. "Can you shine your light over here for a second?"

"I'm not your servant!" the Glimmer shouted back.

"This is official Warden business, ma'am—"

"Well, *I'm* not a Warden!"

I scanned the alleyway for a possible way out while they bickered. If a Glimmer shone her light over me, I'd be fucked.

Make a run for it! Malk spoke again.

Run where? My shadows might be enough to slink around the edges, but the two Wardens would catch me if I tried to bolt.

"Oh, for pity's sake! Move out of the way, then," the Glimmer finally declared. She held up her hand, ready to summon light.

This morning kept getting better and better.

More footsteps stomped into the alley, and everyone turned to face the interrupter.

I did a double take. It was a giant of a Diviner. He was as tall as me, but all rippling muscle. Truly, I'd never seen a Diviner of his size! He was another Warden, judging by his uniform. Gods. If this thing started chasing after me, I'd be shitting myself.

"His Excellency is looking for you," the giant said. "You're both to report back right away."

"What? Now? We're still on patrol—"

"He says to drag you back if I must."

"What could be so sodding important," the public pisser muttered under his breath. He leaned close to where I pressed against the brickwork. "I could have sworn I saw something move. Like a shadow."

"Leave it," called his partner. "There's nothing there. The Vesper are gone, remember?"

"Right. They're better off gone." He kicked the bottle aside, and it careened down the alleyway.

I remained still until the three Diviner were gone and the Glimmer closed her window shutters with a tut.

That had been too close.

I debated replacing my torn flier with another, but what was the point? As soon as I put one up, the Wardens tore it down, and it wasn't the first time I'd brushed against their patrols. Spreading a little discord wasn't worth the risk of getting caught.

Harmony would be annoyed, but we weren't getting anywhere like this.

There had to be a better way.

I slunk out of the alley but continued to hug the edges of the wall with my shadows, avoiding the streetlamps. They glowed silvery-blue with aether, as menacing as they'd always been, but ever since I'd met Corentine and discovered what I was, they'd stopped giving me crippling headaches. Though now, I noticed aether wherever I went.

Its electrical buzz led me toward the tram lines. I couldn't catch a tram wearing the persona of a Vesper—I might as well paint a giant red target on my back. No, I needed to find another disguise.

A few mortals wandered the back streets around Central, some lost in thought, some reading the Courier as they walked. I needed someone wholly distracted, someone who wouldn't notice a Vesper sneaking up behind them.

Gods, I felt like a Necro stalking my prey, but I wasn't after blood, only a change of face.

And—there. An older Umber woman with a bark-like complexion and poppies for eyebrows sat in her tiny terrace garden pruning a bush.

She was so lost in her work, she didn't notice me approach. I brushed the back of her neck.

The Umber spun—I hadn't been as subtle as I'd liked—but in the space between blinks, I'd swapped my Vesper form for an Umber one. The woman stared up at me, visibly confused.

"You had a twig in your hair," I said. "Don't worry, I got it."

"Um, thank you?" Her fingers went to her vines.

"You're welcome." I skipped off to the nearest tram stop.

The trams would be busy at this time, but they'd get me back to the Temple District a lot quicker than on foot. I hoisted my skirt and ran to catch a carriage as it pulled in.

"Sorry, room for one more!" I elbowed my way through the crowd and practically launched myself at the doors.

The carriage rattled—actually bloody rattled—as my heavy Umber form thudded inside. A Diviner standing by the center pole looked me over with disdain and tutted.

I ignored him and leaned by the door. Better to stand here for an easy getaway.

The tram chugged along at an agonizingly slow speed, and I couldn't keep myself from tapping my nails along the handrail. The Diviner kept shooting me snotty looks and tuts, as if he owned the tram, though I supposed the Diviner did. It was their ordinances that kept the trams running, their power that had trapped an actual god in her own domain to be used as a glorified power source.

The god of time could be watching me now through this Diviner's eyes. Searching for Chaos like me.

Throughout my years in the Undercity, I'd always thought Glimmer were the threat to Chime's mortals. But no. Diviner were the *real* threat, and they always had been.

This Diviner looked at me and saw a citizen of Chime acting like some Undercity dreg, and not as the Umber who worshipped at their feet. Changing forms from one domain to another would only disguise me if I acted the part. I forced a smile and offered a placating curtsy. "Forgive my manners, sir. Today is laundry day, and I'd hate to be late."

"Understandable." He puffed out his chest. "But do remember the Covenant."

As if I could ever forget.

The tram ran along the central line that circled the Gate, and as we passed, the clock tower struck quarter to eleven. I glanced at the Gate.

Eventide was gone. Replaced with the dull gray skies of Kronos.

Chime's citizens carried on with their daily drudgery and queued for the Gate as though Kronos had always occupied the ten o'clock slot. They caught the trams as though forgetting creatures made of aether had torn their way across the station concourse. They caught the elevators as though one of them hadn't crashed down from the sky.

It was impressive, really, how normality resumed like clockwork. The Diviner snapped their fingers, and everything went back into place, the chaos forgotten.

And no one seemed to question where the Vesper had gone.

No one seemed to care.

I leaned my head against the handrail, letting my satchel dig its imprint into my shoulder, and sighed.

The Godless would be waiting for me back at base. Huddling inside a Mesmer temple wasn't the same as stuffing ourselves inside a tram back at the depot. But thanks to the Diviner and their Wardens, we couldn't even reach the Undercity anymore. Their extra security meant entering Central Station was nigh on impossible, leaving us trapped in Central.

I supposed staying here worked in our favor. Better to be trapped here than underground. But I missed the Undercity. I missed the dark and smog and soot.

I missed hiding behind the depot's brick walls, where I was free to be whoever I wanted to be. I missed the privacy of my family scheming up blasphemous propaganda.

Fuck it all. I missed Malk.

It was my fault. I'd killed the Vesper. *It was me*, I wanted to scream.

Who could I talk to about it? Who could I confess to?

And what good would it do? What use would I be locked inside a correctional facility for my crimes? Who would even believe I'd personally killed a god?

No one on this tram, certainly.

I couldn't even admit the truth to Dru.

My gaze caught the headline of this morning's Courier abandoned on the seat next to me: *Memorial to be held in Meridian Park*.

Huh. Perhaps Chime's citizens hadn't forgotten the Vesper after all.

I ignored the judgmental eyes of my Diviner and snapped the Courier open.

"Following the tragic events that befell Central last month when the great glass elevator malfunctioned, a public memorial service will be held in Meridian Park next week to commemorate those who lost their lives." I snorted. They were still peddling that shit about a malfunction? *"Some of Chime's most prominent ambassadors will be present to deliver the memorial address, including the newly appointed Diviner ambassador, His Excellency, Quentin Corinth—"*

My heart stopped dead, and I almost tore the paper in half.

Quentin Corinth.

I read it over again. *Quentin Corinth.* No. It couldn't be.

My eyes were pinned to the words so clearly printed in front of me.

Quen was alive. He was here. Could it be him? Or some imposter using his name? Why would Dor break the Covenant after I'd watched him yank Quen's soul from his mortal body? Why name Quen his ambassador after everything Quen and I had done?

It couldn't be him. My Quen. It couldn't be.

I barely noticed when the tram arrived at my stop. I staggered out, half-dazed, the Courier clutched in my shaking hand.

"Ma'am?" a squeaky voice said behind me.

Shit! I almost dropped the Courier! A Seren paperboy carrying a satchel far too large for his short stature approached. "Sorry to disturb you, ma'am. You got a telegram."

I scanned the tram crowds hoping to catch an eye. Someone had been spying on me, and I'd been too bloody distracted to notice. "From who?"

"Wouldn't give her name, ma'am. Tall lady in a red dress. She said I'd catch you coming off the tram." He rummaged in his satchel and handed over a folded card and a small bouquet of golden flowers. "You have a good day now, ma'am."

The paperboy tipped his flatcap and flew off, the weight of his satchel making him swerve erratically. The flowers he'd gifted me were tiny things. Golden daisies. Like they belonged to an Umber...

Oh gods. These were Dru's flowers. I'd recognize them anywhere.

I tore open the note.

"Be grateful. I could have taken her soul."

"Jinx," I whispered. Fuck! If she'd hurt Dru, or any of the Godless, I'd hunt her down and wring her gods-damn neck!

I shoved the bouquet and Courier into my satchel and headed for the temple at as brisk a pace as I dared. Running would attract too much attention, and Wardens regularly patrolled the Temple District.

It was ironic, really, that the Godless had found a new base within a temple, of all things, but it made the perfect hideout. No one suspected we'd be lurking here.

I strode past the Vesper temple, which had been boarded up. Even as a Vesper, I'd never once stepped inside. These temples were designed to trap and punish mortals. To keep a record of one's existence on Chime, and whether one had provided the adequate homage to one's patron god. They were all such an odd mismatch. Each homed the devout, but the devout could get rowdy, especially among the Glimmer, and so Wardens were always in view in case someone chose to spout a little blasphemy or commit a hate crime.

All except the Mesmer temple, which was, quite honestly, a disaster.

One of the Mesmer lay slumped by the door. If I hadn't spent the last few weeks hiding behind those doors, I may have assumed they'd been murdered, but no, that was how they slept, and there wasn't any point waking them to see if my crazy twin sister had somehow managed to infiltrate the temple.

In truth, I was surprised it had taken her this long.

But if she'd harmed *any* of my family, I fucking swear I'd rip out her soul and shove it where a Glimmer didn't shine.

As I stepped inside the main foyer, the Mesmer trio waited for me. The three of them were triplets, I think. They looked practically identical to one another and spoke with the same annoyingly dreamy voices.

"You're back already?" said the most lucid of the three, whose name I could never remember, but really, there were three of them! I never stood a chance. "And you changed again?"

"Yes, I'm sorry. I was in a rush and forgot the protocol." We'd agreed I was able to come and go if I took on a Mesmer persona and brought back a few bars of chocolate with me, and I'd done neither. "Where's Dru?"

"You were just with her, silly—"

"*Where* was I?"

The Mesmer shared a glance with their siblings. "In the red room."

The meeting room.

I pushed past them and ran for the room, dodging confused Mesmer who loitered in the corridor.

Sobbing came from beyond the door, and I burst inside.

Dru was seated on a chair, crying her eyes out as Vincent stood over her, examining her forehead, and Sinder tried to calm her.

His blazing eyes turned to me, and then flame burst from his fists.

"It's me!" I held up my hands. "I'm Kayl, it's me—"

"How do we know it's you?" Sinder snarled.

"Because I'd never hurt Dru, you know that!" I tried to get past him, to catch Dru's eye. "Dru, I'm sorry—"

"You look identical. How are we supposed to know who is who?"

I opened my satchel and displayed the pitifully huge number of fliers still stuffed inside. "Because if I were Jinx, I wouldn't have bothered returning with fliers, and she'd probably do a better job of getting rid of them."

Harmony snorted from across the table. "That's Kayl."

Sinder lowered his fists, and his flame fizzled out. "I still can't tell the difference."

"Really? You can't tell the difference between me and some crazy woman? Wait, don't answer that. I *did* warn you she was my twin—"

"I didn't think you meant literally, dearest! How do we protect each other from *that*?" Sinder gestured at me. "It's not like these Mesmer know how to guard their own damn temple."

Vincent stepped aside as I approached Dru. Her forehead was completely bare of the tiny golden flowers that sprouted there, and instead her green skin looked red and sore. Blood bubbled from a few spots where Jinx had viciously ripped them out.

"Dru, I'm sorry. I should have been here." I reached for her.

She recoiled from me, her eyes avoiding mine as she wiped away tears.

I'd never seen her cry. Not once.

And now she was scared of me.

Vincent placed his hand on my shoulder. "Give her space."

Those words sank in the deepest pits of my stomach. Dru was my best friend. We'd gone through so much together, and I couldn't even comfort her. "Can you grow them back?" I whispered.

"I can stimulate growth, but it'll take time."

Gods. Jinx had hurt her in the worst way. Physically and emotionally. An Umber's flowers were precious.

She'd done that to get at me. That rotten bitch.

"Let's get you cleaned up," Vincent said, and he led a still-sniffling Dru out of the room. The temple didn't have a clinic ready and waiting, but with Reverie's permission, Vincent had begun setting one up, and we made do in the meantime.

Sinder grabbed a pitcher of lemonade from the table and sank into a chair. "Should we be expecting more visits from your psychopathic sister, darling? I like a little torture here and there, but I'd rather be dressed for the occasion."

"Hopefully not, but who knows where Jinx is concerned. What did she want?"

Weariness dimmed Harmony's diamond pupils. "She wanted us to know she wasn't responsible for Eventide. That it was you."

Gods.

I stood absolutely stunned. I'd known it was coming—known Jinx would open her spiteful little mouth and drop me in it. Technically, the loss of Eventide *was* Jinx's fault. She'd forced me into a position where I had no choice but to act in self-defense.

Could I blame Jinx? When it was my hand that had stolen the soul of a god? Damned an entire domain to nothing? Would Harmony understand?

Sinder stared at me, his mouth open, holding the pitcher to his lips. Waiting for me to speak. What could I say? The truth? The Godless deserved it, but... I needed them.

They'd hate me if they knew. I couldn't bear to lose them, too.

"Jinx is trying to stir shit. To get us fighting among ourselves."

"She's right, Harm," Sinder said. "We can't let our guard down like that."

The hardness in her eyes softened a touch, much to my relief. Lying wasn't the worst sin I'd ever committed. It was a skill that came with being a Godless, and I'd always been adept at it. But lying to Harmony made my skin feel icky.

Would she understand if I explained it had been an accident?

That I carried those deaths with me?

Harmony held up today's Courier. "Your sister also dropped this off."

I dumped my satchel onto the table and pulled out my crinkled copy. "You've seen it?"

Sinder gulped the lemonade with a gasp. "What's the headline?"

"It's Quen," I said. "Quen's alive."

"Shit, are you sure?"

"Not entirely, but look." I spread my copy out for him to see. "They're holding a memorial in Meridian Park. Quen will be there. If we can get in the crowds—"

"We're not going to the memorial," Harmony said.

"Why wouldn't we?"

"You know why." She crossed her arms, as though steeling herself for the upcoming argument.

I slumped into the nearest chair. "Are you going to elaborate?"

"It's too dangerous, for one. I'm not risking any more of us. The security detail will be too widespread."

"It'll be crowded, we can blend in—"

"And they know our faces, even yours, with your face-changing ability."

"Then Vincent can work his magic."

"You don't think they'll have Necro Wardens checking for that? It'll be a gated event. The ambassadors will be kept apart from the public. There's no point attending—"

"Quen will be there!"

"Corinth is on the Wardens' side, not ours."

"You don't know that."

"It doesn't look good, dearest," Sinder said. "According to this, he's the Diviner ambassador now." He tapped a black nail on the broadsheet.

I scowled at him. "Quen's not our enemy—"

"Isn't he?" Harmony raised her brow.

"He was our benefactor, for god's sake!"

"You don't even know if this is *him*. You're too close to this, Kayl. You're not seeing the risks—"

"I see the damn risks." Capture, torture, whatever. "What are we doing? I'll tell you what we're doing—nothing! Handing out fliers is achieving fuck all. Wardens are pulling them down faster than I can bloody put them up, and I almost got caught by their damn patrol! They think *we* were responsible for attacking Central Station. We need to step up."

Harmony unfolded her arms with an exasperated sigh. "You're telling me you almost got caught by Wardens, and you want me to throw you into greater danger?"

"Only because the risk of putting up fliers isn't worth it. If I get into that crowd, I can distribute more among them—actually spread the truth—"

"And get yourself arrested as soon as the Wardens see what you're doing."

"I can use my Vesper shadows. I can stop time. I won't get caught." I had power in my fingers. Real power. And Harmony wouldn't even let me unleash it.

"Darling, the number of times you've been caught and kidnapped are not in your favor," Sinder murmured.

"You're not helping," I snapped.

"I'm sorry, girl," Harmony said. "The answer is no."

I clenched my fists in my lap. "So what now? We hide in this temple until the Wardens forget we exist?"

"For now. The Wardens' patrols will quiet eventually, and then we'll see what kind of man Ambassador Corinth is."

"That's a shit plan, and you know it."

Harmony turned her gaze from mine.

Sinder wore a strained smile. "It's for the best."

I chewed the inside of my cheek to stop myself from saying something rash. I understood Harmony's fears. I'd heard her whimpering in her sleep. We were up against insurmountable odds, now. The Wardens blamed *us* for the attack on Central Station. That Diviner Warden had gotten a hard-on just thinking about hanging us.

Worst of all, their new security measures increased their grip on the city. They could enact curfews, put Chime's citizens under greater scrutiny, all to flush out apostates, and they'd be justified in doing so.

Was that Quen's goal? As the Diviner ambassador, he was the most powerful man in Chime. Any security ordinances would have come from *his* office.

Did I know him at all?

My hand went into my pocket and reached for the watch that had once belonged to Quen. It *couldn't* be him. But if there was even the slightest chance it was...

Gods. We'd all mourned Reve and Malk. But Harmony was using their deaths as an excuse to avoid danger.

Now that Jinx knew where to find us, danger was coming regardless.

And I wasn't going to sit here and wait for it.

III

The attack happened at exactly 11 p.m. Eventide had closed, or should have.
The Gate powered down, which affected the streetlamps across Central.
I was off duty at the time, and wasn't with the Warden battalion at
Central Station. I'd taken a leisurely jog through Meridian Park as part of
my physical training routine when I saw the Gate go out. From my vantage
point, I witnessed the glass elevator fall. I saw creatures made of silvery-blue
light attack citizens. I immediately ran to their aid.
I helped evacuate mortals through Meridian Park.
Only later did I learn that our ambassador had been fatally attacked and
other Diviner had lost their lives.
—B. Seasons, *Warden Dossier on the 'Central Station Incident'*

THE STREETS OF GRAYFORD were empty.

Returning to Varen's realm always left me feeling a little lost and melancholy for oh so many reasons, though none of those compared to the aching loss which now permeated these gray streets. With no one to maintain them, the smog from the nearby steamworks coated everything in thick grime. Even the ever-present aether lights flickered with a dull silvery-blue, the shine of their glass bulbs now marred.

Anything left of the ramshackle homes, broken stone buildings, and market stalls had been scavenged. Picked apart. I carefully made my way through Grayford's Main Street and caught the odd flicker of Ember and Fauna scurrying to the shadows, the only color in this drab space.

My foot accidentally kicked a pile of dust that had once been a Vesper.

A whole month had passed, and the evidence of their demise rested with the grime.

For all that remained in Grayford was dust and stragglers.

The dead and the desperate.

"Careful, Your Excellency," said the Diviner Warden following me. "I don't think it would be wise to proceed further."

I bit back a sigh. Father insisted I be accompanied by a chaperone wherever I went for my own safety, despite the fact I'd been a Warden for damn near most of my life. I'd only gotten away from my blasted office on the compromise I'd allow at least one to accompany me, and the one Father had chosen was worth at least three Wardens.

This Diviner was an anomaly. He possessed the same silver skin, hair, and eyes as most of our domain, but he was, to put it politely, indisputably massive. He stood far taller than any Diviner alive, at an Umber's height, and he possessed their muscle mass too, as though he'd been born under the wrong god.

Diviner didn't need brawn when we could quite literally stop time, though I daresay this fellow had his own methods of stopping time well enough.

I pushed on regardless of his protests. "I know these streets. They're safe enough."

"Anything could be lurking in the shadows, Your Excellency."

I turned to him with a raised brow. "Like Vesper?"

He kept his mouth shut but looked visibly annoyed. The Wardens had failed to train the emotion out of this one, at least.

"I'm heading back to the depot," I said.

"Your Ex—"

"I do wish you'd stop calling me that. It's quite grating."

"Of course, Your—sir."

I resisted the urge to roll my eyes and kept picking my way past rocks, bits of metal, and other debris. "With a little work, we could convert the depot into adequate housing. It has rooms, a kitchen, a restroom—"

"Forgive me for asking, sir, but why bother? There's no one here."

Chime's poorest always made their way to Grayford, and it was better to find a home in this dilapidated slum than head to Sinner's Row or the workhouses. "There're still Ember and Fauna lurking in the neighborhood. We'll take steps to ensure they're housed, with food and clean water.

Perhaps hire some Umber to do up the place. Give it a paint job, plant some flowers. Rename it something more pleasant like *The Meadows*."

The Warden looked at me like I'd lost my mind.

Perhaps I had. Such an endeavor would require some wrangling in the budget, alongside my proposed tram refurbishment. But I wasn't going to allow Chime's poorest to fall through the cracks left by Eventide's end.

I'd been granted this title—ambassador to the Diviner, voice of my god—and whether I'd asked for it or not, such a title gave me the means to bring forth change.

And that was one reason I'd accepted it.

With this power, I could actually make a difference.

Shouting came from the stalls that made up Grayford's now empty night market. I gripped my pistol in its holster and jogged on, the Warden at my heels.

A Glimmer was trying to hand a flier to some Fauna girl, who was having none of it.

"Leave us alone, lady! We're not interested!"

"What's going on?" I demanded.

The Glimmer stepped back, startled at my sudden appearance—or rather my companion's sudden appearance. She huffed at me, though her annoyance softened at the sight of my Warden in his uniform. She'd not recognized me, dressed as I was in my casual tan suit and not the tabard of the ambassador's office.

"She won't stop pestering us!" the Fauna yelled, and pointed in accusation. I looked the girl over; she was a raggedy thing no older than thirteen or fourteen, dressed in an oversized jacket she'd likely scavenged from somewhere nearby. She had messy red hair, a fox's red ears, and a little fox nose with whiskers. Hiding in the neck of her jacket was a rat. Another Fauna child, no doubt. Likely a sibling.

The Glimmer sighed, exasperated. "We're trying to help you, child—"

"We don't want to join your stinking workhouse!"

A chill swept over me. Glimmer never entered Grayford, but without Varen to kick them out... "May I see that flier?"

The Glimmer clutched it to her chest. "You may not!"

The Warden flashed his badge. "His Excellency gave you an instruction, ma'am."

Her cheeks turned red. Oh, *now* she recognized me. Though there weren't many Diviner with my dashing good looks, sense of style, and spectacles. Alas, she likely recognized the spectacles.

"I act on the authority of Her Holiness, Gildola herself!"

"Until Her Holiness graces the Undercity, you'll pass me that flier." I held out my hand.

With a tut, the Glimmer handed it over, and I quickly scanned its contents.

It was an advert for a workhouse, offering free board and food in exchange for a pittance. With no one policing Grayford, the hungry and desperate were easy targets, another reason to clean this place up before the Glimmer got their golden fingers into a potential workforce.

The Glimmer held so much power in Chime, even heading the Council wasn't enough for me to close their workhouses down. But the fact they were trying to steal children... The ire deepened my voice. "You have no authority to be recruiting here."

"Authority?" She laughed with annoying haughtiness. "These slums don't fall under your domain's jurisdiction—"

"Nor do they fall under yours." I stared her down over the rim of my spectacles. "Though as head of the Council, I'd say my rank supersedes you in this matter."

"We'll see about that," she snapped, and then stomped away.

Wonderful. My plans for renovating Grayford were becoming a battle.

I didn't mourn Varen, the Vesper ambassador turned traitor and now floating somewhere in the aether. But I did mourn his absence, for his firm hand had at least kept Grayford safe from her kind. Or so I had once assumed.

"You're a Warden?" the Fauna asked, her brown eyes wide.

I forced a smile. "No, not me." Not anymore. "Are the two of you here alone?"

The rat squeaked and scurried into the folds of the girl's jacket. "We didn't use to be alone. There were Vesper who let us in the soup kitchen, and we helped out sometimes, but... they're gone." She scuffed her threadbare boots against the soot-stained cobblestones. "Even the chestnut roasters are gone. Some of them followed the Glimmer and joined their workhouse, but the Vesper—they always told us to avoid 'em."

"That's wise advice."

"Where did they go? The Vesper?"

So many rumors and half-truths had spread regarding the mystery of the disappearing Vesper. It wouldn't have gone unnoticed, of course—an entire domain vanished with the snap of one's fingers. Eventide had been closed for an entire month.

One of my first tasks as ambassador was picking up the pieces and bringing order to the public. And that meant utilizing an ambassador's greatest skill.

Deceit.

The Glimmer had been quick to take advantage of the Vesper's sudden disappearance by declaring they'd been so full of sin, they'd been banished from Chime altogether. Sadly, many mortals believed them. We couldn't reveal the truth, however, and risk disturbing the peace. No, I'd gone for a rather weak explanation.

"Their god, Valeria, recalled her mortals for reasons known only to her. What that means is the Vesper are now living in Eventide together, and Eventide is closed until Valeria decides they can come back."

"But why take them?"

"You know the Vesper had a hard time of it here in Grayford. Sometimes the gods recall their mortals to their domain if they think they're in danger. To protect them."

"They're not in danger anymore? They're happy?"

"I'm sure they're at peace now."

The Warden gave me another of his bewildered looks. The chap was starting to grow on me.

"But enough about that." I clapped my hands together. "You two must be hungry. How about I take you up to Central and get you both something to eat? A pasty or a cream bun?"

The rat popped their head out. "What kind of pasty?" they asked with the voice of a young boy.

"Oh, how about cheese and onion?"

The rat boy squealed. "I *love* cheese and onion!"

The Fauna girl poked the rat back inside her hood and scowled at me with wary eyes. "We don't follow no strangers." Her scowl turned to my companion. "And we don't trust no Wardens."

Smart girl. "Quite right." I pulled out my wallet and dug out a crisp note. "Tell you what, go get yourself a pasty and keep the change. There's more of this if you're looking for work; I could do with a few hands running my errands."

The Fauna snatched the note. "An Ember offered me work too. Said I was old enough to work in a cat café."

Goodness. Erosain surely wasn't allowing his mortals to recruit mere children into the brothels of Sinner's Row? I'd be having stern words at our next meeting. "You stay away from Sinner's Row." I handed over my business card. "Come find me at the embassy up top. I promise I'm not a Warden, and I pay generously."

The Fauna shoved the card into her pocket and then ran off before I could question her further. I could only hope she'd take me up on my offer, if only so I could ensure the two of them were adequately clothed and fed.

These were only two souls among thousands who struggled in Chime. Not even their own ambassador cared for them.

"Go follow the Glimmer and make sure she leaves Grayford," I ordered the Warden. "I don't want her harassing anyone else."

"Sir, I must protest—"

"Must you?"

"I'm here for your protection, sir. I can't leave your side."

"I'm capable of my own protection." I tapped my pistol. "And it is the duty of every Warden to care for Chime's citizens. What's your name again?"

"Benjamin Seasons, sir. The other Wardens call me Big Ben, sir, because of—"

"Because of your height?"

"Because of my height, sir."

"I see. Very clever of them. I'll come find you after I've finished my examination of Grayford."

"*Sir—*"

"This is my command."

He saluted me, defeat on his face, and trudged along Main Street.

Finally, peace.

I wasted no more time and made my way along the abandoned tram line that ended in the Godless depot. I didn't know why I kept coming back here.

This was my fourth visit in the past month. I justified it by arguing we should have Wardens on patrol in case the Godless returned, but no one ever did.

The Godless were smart enough to avoid Grayford. In fact, they seemed to avoid the Undercity altogether, and couldn't even be found in Sinner's Row.

I stepped over the broken glass that still decorated the platform of the Godless HQ. Not much else remained inside; the Wardens had already scoured every nook and cranny, tearing down and destroying any Godless fliers or propaganda, and placing everything else into neat little boxes tucked away in a dingy office.

The tram remained, its outer shell caved in after it fell from the ceiling.

That had been my fault. I'd led the Wardens here.

My breath blew out in one long exhale.

I could still imagine her here, sitting in that tram, waltzing across the platform, serving me tea and crumpets on the conveyor belt below. I could imagine her breath as her lips pressed into my cheek. Those eyes. That smile.

I'd lost her. Couldn't sodding find her anywhere, and perhaps that was for the best.

What I'd been ordered to do when I found her was entirely different from what I *wanted* to do.

I couldn't be certain the Godless had gotten away, that they were safe, but as far as the Wardens knew, they'd vanished. I had eyes watching the streets, watching their safe houses, but not a flicker.

Harmony was too shrewd to get caught. Sinder and Vincent were too sly. Dru had common sense. Malkavaan…

The crimson stain of his death was still visible on the platform.

I could picture him here, on his knees, the barrel of my pistol pressed against his head. It wasn't my hand that had sent him to the aether, yet it had been my actions as a Warden that had ultimately damned him.

Too many memories brought me guilt and shame, and I could no longer wipe away the consequences of my mortal existence. They were different lives—different Quens—yet those memories were a patchwork that made up the shadow of me.

The man. The Diviner. The Dark Warden. Ambassador Corinth.

I liked to think I was doing a damn good job of distracting myself from memories with plans and action. But they intruded on my waking thoughts. My dreams.

Perhaps returning here was its own form of self-flagellation.

I absentmindedly fumbled in my pocket for my fob watch, but I'd lost that, too. Death couldn't erase some habits.

"Where are you now, Kayl?"

"I'm here, Quen."

My heart leaped to my throat.

I whirled and almost fell to my knees.

She stood by the depot door, wearing a Diviner form and a tight red dress that barely covered her knees. I gawked as she approached with a sultry swagger. Surely, this wasn't the Kayl I knew? But it *was* her—that playful smile, that spark in those silvery-blue eyes that stayed no matter what form she took.

I never thought she'd return here, but oh saints, was I glad I'd taken that chance.

"How? Why?" I wanted to reach out and touch her, to check it really *was* Kayl in the flesh.

"I saw your name in the Courier—I couldn't believe it. I saw you die! Dor brought you back?"

"He did."

"And you're his ambassador now?"

"It's—It's complex—"

"Are you my enemy, Quen?" Accusation sharpened her tone.

"I don't want to be."

"What does Dor want?"

An end to Chaos. An end to her. "Peace."

"I don't believe you." She turned away.

"Kayl, wait." I reached for her arm, stopping her.

She glanced back, but no anger or fear shadowed her eyes. They traced down to my hand, and I hastily let go.

"I searched for you," I whispered. "For weeks. I wanted you to know, I never thought I'd find—"

She grabbed my jacket and yanked me forward, and then her lips pressed against mine.

I swallowed a breath. "Saints, I—"

"I missed you, Quen. You're all I could think of. Fuck, I missed you—"

Our lips met once more, my mouth opening to the sweetness of her tongue. Her bosom crushed against me, and I couldn't keep myself from running my palms along her arms, feeling the smooth softness of her skin. Once, touching a mortal in such a way would show me their death. But with Kayl, I'd been granted a freedom I'd never owned.

A freedom I eagerly grasped.

The kiss deepened with a touch of aether. It burned through my veins with an electricity that reminded me I lived.

In this moment, I *lived*.

She ripped apart my waistcoat, and her nails scraped down my shirt, the bite of them cutting into my skin. Down they went, until they reached my belt and began to unbuckle it.

I wanted it. Wanted her. But this was moving too fast.

"Malkavaan," I rasped, but Kayl ignored me.

She'd lost Malkavaan, a mortal she loved above all others.

I'd seen her tears, heard her cries.

This wasn't right!

I pulled back and grabbed her shoulders, holding her at a distance.

She bit her lip, and those eyes were wild, dangerous things. No longer the warmth I craved. My heart plummeted. It withered in my chest.

Gods damn me for a fool!

"Jinx," I gasped.

"The one and only." Jinx broke from my grip and laughed wickedly. "Oh, Quen. I missed you so much, Quen. I want to *fuck you*, Quen. You don't want to fuck me? I'd make it good for you. So good it'll destroy your soul." She lifted her dress and flashed me the mound of her sex.

I hastily stumbled back and wiped the taste of her from my lips.

"Oh, come on, was I that bad?" She leered.

"Why are you here?" I spat.

"Curiosity, you could say. You came back to life, so I want to know what Dor's planning. See, I would never have expected the god of time to break his own Covenant. And I'm pretty sure he's not a fan of my family."

"Where's Kayl?"

"You're so predictable, it's pathetic. Kayl this and Kayl that. You can't even tell us apart. I wonder what she'll say to that?"

"Where is she?"

Jinx shrugged. "How would I know? Could be dead—"

"You were meant to get her to safety! To heal her!" I placed a hand on my pistol.

"Maybe I did. Maybe I didn't. But why bother looking?" Jinx took a predatory step toward me. "She didn't care when you died, you know. I think she was relieved, actually, that you no longer plagued her life. Men like you *take* and *take*." Her eyes turned hard. "You were better off dead."

I whipped out my pistol and pointed it at her chest.

"You're going to shoot me, Corinth?"

"I don't want to hurt you—"

"Then tell me what you Diviner fucks are planning."

"Dor wishes to protect Chime from your kind. That's all."

"My kind?" She smiled, and its sweetness reminded me too much of her sister. "Tell your god Chime has nothing to fear. We don't want to harm its citizens. We just want to destroy him and everything he stands for."

"We can talk this over. Reach a compromise—"

"Let us into Kronos, and we'll compromise. No? Don't want that?"

"Warden HQ is a neutral location. We can negotiate there—"

"Over tea and biscuits? No thanks. How about I take you hostage and we go pay Dor a visit together? So put that silly pistol away before you hurt yourself."

"You know the Wardens wouldn't allow that."

"No? They won't allow their precious ambassador through the Gate?"

"Dor would kill me rather than allow Chaos into His domain."

Hunger gleamed in those eyes. "Not if I yank your soul out first."

My heart hammered in my chest. With a single touch, she could rip out my soul, and I'd witnessed for myself that bullets wouldn't be enough to stop her. "Then do it. You still won't make the crossing."

She rolled her eyes dramatically. "You love playing the martyr, don't you, Corinth? It's sad that your god would give up your soul so easily. Tell Dor... Things around here are going to change." She turned her back on me and began to walk away.

What could I do? Grab her? Shoot her? "Stop!"

"I'll see you at the memorial." She winked, and then vanished through the depot doors.

I stumbled after her, carefully stepping over glass and debris, but she was gone.

Blast it!

I sagged against the archway and rubbed the imprint of her touch on my chest.

She'd made a fool out of me, but what a fool I was.

"You were better off dead."

The dead version of me wouldn't get caught with his trousers down. When I once woke in the dead of night, the darkness comforted me. Reminded me of my brief sojourn into an existence where I floated in the aether and had little to worry about. But now, I woke in a cold sweat, terrified that if the aether took me, everything would fall apart.

Chime needed me. Its mortals needed me.

My own mortal body ached, my shoulders pained with the weight of it all.

ARE YOU HURT? YOU HEART RATE HAS INCREASED, bellowed a voice in my head, and I cringed. I knew how loud and demanding my Father could be, but now that I acted as His ambassador, His voice, we communed more regularly, and I had no choice but to accept the constant intrusions.

I'm fine, Father—

WHERE IS YOUR GUARD?

Nearby. I cringed again at the automatic lie that slipped out so casually. Father would see my thoughts, my lies.

HE EXISTS FOR YOUR PROTECTION.

I'm an ex-Warden. I don't need protection—

YOU WERE ACCOSTED BY CHAOS.

That was one way of putting it.

WHY DIDN'T YOU STOP HER?

Why indeed? But Jinx was too fast, too dangerous. She could have ripped my soul from my body and ended any hope of reconciliation between our domains.

YOU CANNOT AFFORD TO MAKE MISTAKES. YOU CANNOT LET THE WILES OF CHAOS ENSNARE YOU. GUARD YOURSELF AGAINST SIN. His voice faded from my mind with that one simple command.

Guard myself against sin?

A ludicrous notion. He may as well have ordered me to guard myself against air.

Though Father was right—I couldn't afford to make mistakes like that.

Everything was so simple when broken down; the forces of chaos and time were at odds, and I was meant to lead the charge against Chaos. A holy war hidden from the other domains, from Chime's public eyes.

But I wanted a way to unite the domains, not tear them apart. Such a task held many complexities.

Only a group of heathens could help me achieve it.

I'd spent weeks trying to locate either the Godless base, or where Jinx now resided, and I'd gotten nowhere.

Both were hiding in Central.

I knew, deep in my heart, Kayl still lived.

And I'd find her.

What's With These Clocks?

Under supervision of our new ambassador, maintenance of the clock tower has been completed. We took over from the Glimmer after they lost the bulk of their workforce. Fortunately, the plating was sufficient to patch the leaking aether. We've not had any such leaks since.

However, this project has given us ample opportunity to examine the aether leaking from the clock tower. It emits a subtle frequency separate from the aether generated by the steamworks. Our Zephyr engineers confirmed it. We believe this frequency can be identified and tracked.

Father knows this discovery could prove useful in protecting Chime from any future attacks by aether creatures.

—Diviner Engineer, *Report on the Clock Tower Repairs*

I fucking hated clocks.

Why did they have to tick and tock? Why not tick tick tock or tock tock tick? They were monotonous. Relentless. And if they went too fast or too slow, then they were deemed wrong or broken for daring to be different. Clocks were the servants of time, and time represented everything that was wrong with this universe.

So why the *fuck* was I trapped inside a gods-damn fucking watchmaker's store?

I paced behind the counter as a chorus of ticks and tocks rang under my skin like an itch I couldn't scratch without cutting it out. So many different types of clocks hung on the walls or sat on shelves. Some made of brass, some made of wood. I couldn't name the types, and I didn't fucking want to, but some made loud *dong* sounds, and others were a weird *cuckoo-cuckoo* that sprung forth with a tiny wooden Diviner.

The first time that thing had popped out, I'd screamed and smashed it against the wall loud enough for a Diviner Warden to come pay us a visit, and that was bad.

His eyeless body still lay in the storage room.

"You'll wear a hole in the floorboards," muttered Chance.

That birdbrain sat at the counter tinkering with one of the many clock pieces. This store *had* been a watchmaker's—their body was stuffed in the storage room, too—and Chance, in his Zephyr form, had taken over the role of watchmaker in order to deflect suspicion. Or so he said.

He was dressed in a tight tweed suit, his Zephyr feathers stuffed comically inside, and his massive wings taking up much of the counter space. Zephyr were tinkerers. They were as bad as Diviner for fixing clocks and shit.

Though I suspected Chance enjoyed playing the role a little too much.

"Sorry, was I distracting you from something important?" I snapped.

He continued to fiddle with the clock with those sharp talons. Around his head were some ridiculous goggles that had an aether light and a magnifying glass so he could better see the tiny cogs and gears. That dork. "This is delicate work."

"Why are you even fixing it?"

"Because if a customer walks in, they won't suspect anything."

"A customer." I snorted.

The watchmaker's was a cozy little store down the back alley of Central's market, built like the rest of the town houses from a mixture of brick and brass and wooden beams, and with a tiny apartment upstairs where I could eat, sleep, and shit in peace. The place stunk of Diviner, though—of oil and polish and nothing natural. It attracted some custom, Diviner mostly, and I supposed we couldn't keep killing them. Someone would notice eventually.

I'd taken the idea from my dear sister. No one expected the Godless to be hiding inside a temple, just as no one would expect Chaos to be hiding inside a watchmaker's.

But I hated those fucking clocks.

Could hear their stupid tick and tock from upstairs. I was surprised the whole damn city didn't hear 'em and burn this place down.

I slid onto a stool next to Chance. "Is this all you've been doing while I've been actually serving our mother's will?"

"I tried the bistro around the corner," Chance said without looking up. "They serve an excellent ale-and-mushroom pie. Nice beer, too."

"You're fucking useless—"

"And what have *you* been doing?" He gave me a sideways look, his aether eyes stark beside his beak.

"Plans and schemes, dear brother."

"Are any of your *plans* and *schemes* near to fruition?"

I picked up a spare gear and turned it over. "I've got a spy in my pocket ready to disrupt the Godless."

"That's it?

"*And*... Quentin Corinth is alive. He's a fucking ambassador now, and he's hosting a memorial in Meridian Park."

Chance placed his clock down. "The great god of time broke the Covenant? Interesting. The Diviner must be desperate. Shame we have nothing to show for it."

Even I was surprised Dor had brought Corinth back to life. Corinth had helped me escape and had effectively betrayed the Wardens, betrayed his own domain, and shot the last ambassador in the head. He'd literally ticked all the boxes of dirty traitor, had earned the death that found him, and... he'd been *promoted* for it?

Fucking mediocre Diviner men, I swear.

Now he'd been named ambassador, which meant all these security upgrades and Warden patrols around Central were *his* idea.

Which meant Corinth was my enemy.

I should have taken his soul when I had him in my grip.

But where was the fun of ripping out his eyes if my sister wasn't there to witness it?

Corinth had been right about one thing; there was no point taking a Diviner hostage if Dor was going to pop them out of existence. No, I needed an ambassador from another domain if I was ever going to make a crossing and steal a god's soul. A domain that actually gave a shit about their mortals. Which crossed out most of 'em.

Chance returned to his clock. His apathy grated on me.

"At least I'm fucking trying."

He sighed. "We lost Lucky and Flux. The Diviner have reinforced the clock tower so we can't return to Mother unless we slit our own wrists. The Gate has so much security around it, we can't even hope to travel to any of the domains. And with so many patrols in Central, it's only a matter of time before they find us, drag us to Kronos, and start picking apart our organs, one by one."

I tossed my gear across the counter. "So you've given up?"

"Face it. We never stood a chance against the Diviner. This is their domain now."

"The fuck it is!"

The tinny bell above the door jingled as a Glimmer stepped inside. This one wore a dress patterned with red roses. Her glowing golden hair hung in layers around her shoulders, her nose pointed up in that snobby way all Glimmer seemed to have, as if they had a permanent stick up their arse.

The Diviner owned Chime, but the Glimmer fought for it, too. Clawing and scraping for control. The Golden City was theirs, as were most of the stores around here. For a pious lot, they sure lusted for power.

I couldn't help my smirk as she approached the counter. Since I'd taken my own mortal form, I'd quickly realized I had a preference for tits and cunts, and that men, as pretty as they could be, were actually useless. The Glimmer were forbidden fruit, and I wanted to be their evil temptress.

Was it perverse? That I thought the Glimmer were gorgeous and ambitious and everything I wanted in a woman? Shame they cared for piety and rules. The Glimmer could have been true rivals to the Diviner, with potential for more.

But Gildola had ruined them.

That was what the gods did to their mortals.

"Can we help you, ma'am?" Chance asked in his perfect rendition of a boot-licking twat.

The Glimmer frowned. "I was told you fix clocks."

Chance removed his stupid goggles. "That's right, ma'am. You leave your clock with us, and we'll get it fixed right up."

"I need it fixed now by a *competent* Diviner." The Glimmer looked us over, disregarding Chance completely, and those burning red eyes turned to me. "I wasn't aware there were any female Diviner in Chime."

"We sneak out occasionally," I said. "But if you're not convinced I'm real, I can take you upstairs and show you the cunt I've got hidden underneath my skirt." I winked.

Chance shot me his *what the fuck* look, which was his default expression these days.

I couldn't help that I wanted to fuck her.

Or that I liked the way those words sounded in my mouth. Filthy, scandalous words. Kayl had never sworn enough for my liking, and I fucking *loved* it.

The Glimmer looked appalled. "I think I best take my business elsewhere." She turned to leave.

Chance rose from his seat. "Forgive her manners, ma'am. We really will take good care of your clock—"

"No, thank you."

I leaned over the counter and grabbed her wrist. My Diviner skin shimmered from a silvery-blue to gold.

The Glimmer gasped. "What *are* you?"

"Just a woman looking for a little lovin'. You game?"

She opened her mouth to scream, but she didn't get a chance.

With a single pulse, I ripped her soul clean from her body, and she collapsed to the floor in a heap. Damn. What would it take to get my clit licked?

"Fuck's sake, Jinx! Not again!" Chance flapped his arms, scattering feathers. "Can't you pretend to be a normal mortal for once?"

"Where's the fun in that?"

He locked the store's door. "If you keep doing this, we're going to attract attention—"

"And if I'd let her walk out of here, she'd only go and summon a Warden, idiot. You're welcome, by the way."

He grasped the Glimmer's shoulders and lifted her torso. "You're going to just stand there?"

I rolled my eyes and picked up the Glimmer's perfectly smooth legs. Hauling bodies was starting to get boring, and with three Diviner still stuffed inside the storage room, we were running out of space. I wasn't sure what would happen to a body without a soul—would it stay this way forever? Rot? I wanted to take on an Ember form and burn them, but Chance insisted that starting a fire in this neighborhood wouldn't go unnoticed.

Chance dusted off his feathers and returned to his clock.

"That's it?" I asked. "You're just gonna carry on?"

He put his goggles down with a thump. "What do you want me to do?"

"Take an active interest in destroying the domains, for one?"

"What's the point, though? Have you thought about it? We destroy everything, and what are we left with?" He closed the flap of his clock and began to wind it. "It's more fun to create."

"You've lost faith in our mother."

"I haven't lost faith—"

"Then why all this?" I waved my hand at the fucking clocks hanging off the walls. "You're sure acting like you actually *enjoy* all this Diviner shit—"

"So what if I do?" His feathers ruffled. "I spent years trapped inside that damn clock tower. Years watching the city below me, wishing I could be part of it. Now I can actually enjoy it, and you want to destroy it?"

"You think you had it rough? I spent years trapped inside another fucking body!"

"At least you got to experience life—"

"Without any choice of my own! I want to be in charge of my own damn life, not whatever my sister and her stupid Godless want, not what the Diviner want! This is our domain. Ours! We can create reality to be whatever we want it to be—"

"I like this reality. Maybe the Godless have the right idea—"

"You're a fucking traitor." I raised my brows.

He grimaced. "I'm not a traitor—"

"What about our mother? What of the Diviner who trapped her there, who are making her scream endlessly? Do you forget all that when you play with their toys?" One month of freedom, and Chance had gone soft. Pathetic.

"I don't forget, but the Diviner have already won."

"We're her *children*, we don't give up on her—"

"We're all children of Chaos. What does it matter in the end?"

Sunlight rippled under my skin, and I flexed my fingers, seething with the urge to burn my way to the Gate.

Though Chance was right about one thing. We were woefully outnumbered compared to the Diviner, and that didn't even factor in the other domains serving their every whim, nor the might of the Wardens.

We were just two Chaos. One Chaos, apparently, since Chance couldn't even be arsed anymore.

Lucky and Flux had tried to break through those stupid security barriers around the Gate, but the Diviner somehow knew how to detect us, and my brethren had sacrificed their lives to give us that knowledge.

The rest of my siblings were trapped inside the clock tower with no way out. As soon as the Diviner had finished their clock tower repair, any spare souls were forced to return. In her state, Mother couldn't maintain so many of us.

Back to square fucking one.

Mother still screamed. She called for me.

IT PAINS ME TO SEE MY CHILDREN FIGHT.

I know, Mother.

Chance had given up on her, and Kayl had given up on *me*, but I had a body now. I had a means. I had *plans* and *schemes*.

The Diviner hadn't won. Not while I still breathed.

I'd fight with whatever I could to regain control of Babel. *My* domain.

Sure, we didn't have a way of stealing a god's soul—the power needed to break Mother free from her prison—but we knew someone who possessed one, and if it came down to it, I'd tear Valeria's soul straight out of my sister's useless body.

Chance held up his clock, inspecting it. It was a pretty clock. All delicate wood and intricate brass.

I slapped it out of his hands and let it crash to the floor.

He clicked his beak. "You're a bitch."

"And don't you forget it." I headed for the door. I needed out of this stupid-arse store and its stupid collection of clocks.

"Where're you going?" he called after me.

"Plans and schemes, dear brother. One of us needs to be useful." I glanced over my shoulder. "Are you prepared to make the necessary sacrifices when the time comes, or are you going to get in my way?"

"I'll follow your lead, no matter what happens." He picked at the pieces of the broken clock and examined them. "Perhaps there is beauty in destruction. It reveals opportunities. Possibilities to create different designs."

That was the beauty of chaos.

I didn't understand what drove my brother to create when I wanted to destroy.

But when Chaos finally took Chime, we'd remake it to whatever we wanted.

I'd achieve what Kayl never had.

I'd end the reign of gods.

V

The problem with time is that one must make best use of it. Maximize it.
Time is a finite resource, therefore to waste time is to sin.
But sometimes, one wishes to simply exist. To bathe in time as it flows over
you. To breathe and feel time tick away. To just be.
Be cautious. Do remember that idle hands welcome sin.
—H. Bezel, *Philosophy for the Young Diviner*

MY OFFICE AT WARDEN HQ was a quiet and unassuming one.

I'd insisted on remaining here in Central, if only to keep my ear to the ground. Elijah's office had been a sprawling monstrosity up on Timefall Estates, as large as his home. But while that surrounded me with mortals of my own domain, it cut me off from the rest of Chime.

So here I sat in a squeaky leather chair in a cramped, moody space, where the walls were made of dark wood, the bookcases and filing cabinets towered over me, the aether lamp occasionally buzzed, the carpet smelled of a faint musk, and tea stained my desk. Behind me, light filtered through a large round window that gave an adequate view of Central Station.

It wasn't as luxurious as most ambassador offices, but it served me well enough. Though, alas, the paperwork was beginning to pile up.

Bureaucracy was a Diviner's bread, while administration acted as the necessary butter that kept it lubricated. It was no lie that debates over filing systems were common in Kronos's high society, and likely the reason my domain had such a reputation for being bores. Blast it, I *enjoyed* paperwork. I relished the penmanship and organization required, and my new role gave me ample opportunity to indulge. Even if most of these were simple passport applications.

I sipped at my lukewarm tea and flipped open the top file.

It was a report of crime sprees across Central. With the Vesper gone, someone needed to fill their shoes, and apparently it was a rogue Diviner pickpocket who had eluded even my increased patrols.

They must be Jinx. No Diviner would dare engage in such antisocial behavior. Though the patterns of her crimes were consistent with my belief Chaos remained in Central, how had she managed to sneak into the Undercity? Through the maintenance tunnels? I'd need to increase security *again*.

So far, Chaos had remained predictable in their unpredictability. My security barriers at Central Station had kept them out, and the crossings continued with minimal disruption. The other domains complained of the heightened security, but I'd ensured the Wardens did not underestimate the threat of Chaos or grow complacent.

Now all I needed to do was flush Chaos out.

YOU HAVE NOT DONE ENOUGH.

I choked on my tea as Dor's voice blared through my mind. *It takes time to secure Chime, Father. It's thanks to my efforts that the clock tower repairs were finished.* The Glimmer had abandoned the contract since they'd lost their Vesper workforce.

CHAOS STILL STALKS CHIME. WHAT HAVE YOU DONE TO STOP THEM?

We have security gates that can detect their aether. We're researching modifications of our tasers to make them more efficient. I have plans to catch Chaos, but you made me your voice. That comes with many other responsibilities. I tapped the pile of papers on my desk. Could a god even understand the rites of paperwork?

ELIJAH WAS NOT THIS TARDY.

Those words stung. *Elijah had years to prepare for this role. I've had weeks.*

YOU NEED AN ASSISTANT.

No, what I needed was time. *You gave me a task, Father. Let me complete it.*

THEN DO NOT DISAPPOINT ME, QUENTIN.

His voice faded from my mind, and I sank back into my chair. My beating heart slammed against my chest—a reminder I no longer lived in dreams, but sharp, demanding reality. I could never forget my Father had yanked me from existence, and then rebirthed me.

This body was mine, as it had always been. Fresh. Whole. Undamaged. Yet my soul...

Someone knocked at the door. I quickly sat up and shuffled my papers together. "Yes?"

The door opened slightly, and Ben popped his head around. "There's someone here from the ten o'clock crossing to see you, sir."

What cursed timing. "Send him in."

The door creaked open fully, and a woman entered.

Saints.

A female Diviner.

Her skin and eyes were the same silver as most, but a thick streak of brass cut through the short silver curls that framed her face. She stood an inch shorter than me, dressed modestly in a tan jacket and skirt.

I knew I was staring, but female Diviner were so rare.

"Your Excellency," she said, her voice soft and feminine. "I've been sent to assist your office as your new personal assistant." She opened a satchel and pulled out a file. "I've taken the liberty of preparing your speech for the memorial."

My stare moved to the file. "That won't be necessary, ah, Miss...?"

"Pendula Bezel, Your Excellency."

Bezel? That name rang alarm bells in my mind. "You wouldn't happen to know a Hector Bezel, would you?"

"He was my second father, Your Excellency. I'm aware he died in the line of duty. I wish to serve your office and Chime in his honor."

A second father. Remarkable. It was rarer still to meet Diviner who were birthed through parents, though naturally, even with a biological father, Dor remained our first and most important paternal figure.

Though why had Hector's daughter sought me out? It couldn't be a coincidence. Hector Bezel had been killed by Chaos while working on the soul-splitting devices. Dor *had* suggested I needed an assistant.

"I thank you for your notes, Miss Bezel, but I'm in no need of an assistant. I've also prepared my own speech—"

"I insist, Your Excellency. Father wishes to ensure your speech covers topics dear to our domain."

Father could very well have relayed His wishes Himself. "I'll look at it." I'd look, all right. If only to see what agenda she was trying to push. "Now, I'm afraid I'm quite busy—"

"I can help with your paperwork, Your Excellency. I studied at the bookkeeping school at Kronos University and I'm well versed in thirteen methods of filing. Please; you're a busy man. Allow me to free up your time."

The last thing I needed was a spy sticking their nose into my affairs, least of all one who likely held a grudge against Chaos. "I'll consider it." I gestured to the door.

Pendula offered a polite curtsy. "I'll pray our Father shows you the correct path, Your Excellency."

A spy indeed.

I waited until she'd left and shoved her speech into a drawer. My eye caught another file inside the drawer with a note on top in my handwriting.

"*This will stop Chaos. Pool all your resources into building a prototype ASAP.*"

Odd. I didn't remember writing such a note. I flipped open the file.

It was a set of schematics for some sort of aether-powered collar. A collar that, when worn, would stop the powers of any domain with the same effect as our tasers.

A device I surely needed, but this was the first I'd learned of it.

"Ben?" I called, and waved the folder. "Who brought this into my office?"

Ben lingered by the doorway looking confused. "You did, sir."

Had I? Gosh. I couldn't remember.

The note was clearly my handwriting. While I held a penchant for such mysterious transcripts, I'd recovered the memories of the notes I used to leave myself, and this wasn't one of them.

Was I wiping my memories again? Losing them? What a worrying thought.

"Would you like a fresh cup of tea, sir?"

I must have appeared utterly bewildered, though honestly, I felt it. "Go on, then. Grab some bourbon biscuits if you can find any."

The next few days were going to prove chaotic. Best indulge in the small comforts before Dor smote me for my tardiness and my sins. For that was the worst thing about death: no biscuits.

It was a crisp morning on the day of the memorial. Chime's temperature was often comfortable enough to balance the needs of twelve domains, but today, a chill descended upon Meridian Park. Even my black suit paired with the complementary bronze and silver tabard of the ambassador's office couldn't ward off my shivers.

As agreed, the Wardens had taken over the cricket hut to serve as my base. The inner hut was a stone building that had seen better days. White paint flaked from the walls, aether lamps flickered erratically, and the stone did nothing to protect against the damp cold. Altogether, it gave me the willies. A Necro cricket team would certainly feel at home.

The Wardens had at least tried to make it comfortable by setting up a tea stand, though the tea they offered me was a bland affair, lacking in flavor and personality.

Alas, I wasn't here for the tea.

"A Glimmer delegation has arrived, sir," Ben announced.

Blast it! I hadn't invited them, and their presence here would disrupt my plans. "The ambassador?"

"Yes, sir. She's waiting in the trophy room." Ben stood like a monstrous shadow underneath an aether lamp. I rather enjoyed the awkward expressions he made, though right now he grimaced at the window.

Crowds began to fill the park. The Council had wanted a private ceremony to unveil their plaques. I'd argued for a public one, to help restore faith in the Wardens, and because Chime's citizens deserved to mourn.

That, and I'd hoped to coax Chaos out.

I smoothed down the fold of my tabard. This was my first official engagement as ambassador, and I didn't intend to make mistakes.

The Glimmer delegation waited in the only carpeted room of the whole hut and home to a cabinet full of plaques and trophies won by Chime's sports champions over the years—mostly Leander, though a Seren wicket keeper had gone down in history for making a tremendous catch that had sadly smashed them to smithereens in the process.

I stepped inside and did a double take.

In the center of the room stood a life-size golden statue of Elijah Karendar, former ambassador and quite dead.

I'd been the one to blow his brains out.

The small group of Glimmer parted, and out waltzed Ambassador Gloria. Another ambassador who'd been shot in the head and who, like me, had made a remarkable recovery.

When it came to their favorites, the gods cared little for the Covenant.

She stood before me in a matching black dress, a taunting smirk already splayed across her Ember-red lips. "Your Excellency. You don't seem pleased to see me."

"Why are you here? I expressly stated that this memorial was meant to be a private affair—"

"Oh, come now. The attack on Central was an attack on Diviner *and* Glimmer rule. We simply could not miss a memorial where our own mortals were affected, nor do I trust a Diviner to handle our delicate interests. You cannot block me from this, Corinth."

Of course the Glimmer would shove their noses into everything. "These restrictions are meant for your safety." Because placing the most important mortals in Chime in this blasted cricket hut was a ridiculous idea.

"You have so little faith in Chime's citizens to act with decorum? Or is that an admission of your inadequacy? Karendar knew what he was doing." Gloria admired the golden statue. "We couldn't let an opportunity pass to honor the late ambassador who dutifully gave his life in the attack. Don't let it be said our domain does not respect the Diviner. This was sponsored by Solaris's most affluent businesses. Delightful craftsmanship, isn't it?"

I tucked my hands in my pockets to keep my ire in check. It would have been oh so satisfying to snap back. To point out the obvious; Elijah had been the one to kill her. But neither of us could reveal the truth, and thus we were sworn into an uneasy truce of sorts.

"It's wonderful. If you'd like to wait outside, I must prepare my speech. One of the Wardens will show you where to find the tea and digestives."

She looked affronted by my dismissal.

Everyone bowed out of the room. All except Big Ben, who stood in the corner in some parody of privacy. After he'd been chastised by Dor for leaving my side in Grayford, I doubted I'd ever be able to defecate in peace ever again.

I wanted to go over my speech one more time in case I actually did get the chance to recite it, but that odious statue distracted me.

I stepped closer to the thing. Solid gold, all the way through. Elijah stood a little taller than I remembered, but the facial features were uncanny. They'd even captured his sneer and the harshness of those brass eyes, now in Glimmer gold.

A part of me wanted to run my hand down the smooth surface of his cheek. Another part wanted to drop the statue in the lake and leave it there forever.

I'd loved him. I'd despised him. It ignited those feelings again. The affection and revulsion whenever memories of Elijah entered my mind.

"I tried to cure you of sin, Quentin! I tried to save your soul! No one will ever love you as I do!"

In death, he haunted me.

"It's an uncanny likeness, sir," Ben commented.

"You knew Eli—Karendar?" I asked, and wished I hadn't. This was no time to indulge my melancholy.

"Yes, sir. I was part of his security detail, sir. Helped guard his estate."

"Really? I'm sure I'd remember your likeness."

"He had me guarding the back doors, sir. Said my size blocked his view of the gardens."

Harsh, but that was just like Elijah.

He'd liked the aesthetics of a man, or hadn't, in Ben's case.

He'd liked the aesthetics of me.

"I'm sorry for your loss, sir," Ben continued in the silence. "I know you and Karendar worked closely together."

A polite way of saying we'd dallied behind closed doors. "Were you there when the attack happened?"

"No, sir. Was my shift off. I was playing poker back at HQ with the lads, sir."

With that face? "Did you win?"

He grimaced. "No, sir."

I rubbed my lips, hiding a smile. "Where are the other plaques?"

Ben pointed to a series of smaller bronze plaques piled unceremoniously in the corner. There were about thirty of them in total. Small slates with enough space for a name.

Thirty names.

Thirty deaths.

Reading the death toll of that fateful day had been my first unofficial act as ambassador. I'd wanted to know every single name. I'd wanted to burn them into my memory. Some had died when the great glass elevator had fallen. Others had been caught up in the crashing trams and chaos of the day. The remainder had been killed. Their souls ripped apart.

I hadn't been able to stop it. I hadn't been able to save these lives.

The attacks had eventually ceased as we reinforced the clock tower to trap Chaos inside once more.

Yet not a single Vesper was among the list of the dead.

An entire domain had been obliterated, its mortals reduced to the dust of time, but Chime and the remaining domains could never know the truth. Could never mourn them.

Without their names, how would we ever remember them?

I spotted Hector Bezel's name among the plaques. Even Walter Burns. No Reve. I'd come back with a plaque for him. He'd embraced the end of his existence, but that didn't mean I'd let him go unremembered.

There was no plaque for Malkavaan Byvich.

"A little space please, Ben."

"Of course, sir." He backed away to the door.

I turned to the statue.

Elijah Karendar had been responsible for the Vesper's demise, and here he was being hailed as a hero. Swimming in the peaceful bliss of an afterlife as mortals mourned him.

"You utter bastard," I murmured.

My name should have been among the dead. Or perhaps scratched from the historical records altogether. Yet I stood here, anger pumping through my blood, furious and alive.

No one remembered I'd been the one to shoot Elijah. No one remembered I'd died and come back from the aether. Father had altered His own mortals' memories of the event—to exonerate me—and those not of my domain had been recalled to Warden HQ to receive trauma therapy from an unnamed Amnae who was likely dead at this point.

I'd awakened to praise for my heroic deeds. Praise that had earned me the title of ambassador. All part of Dor's design.

I'd flipped through the speech Pendula had given me before I came here—what Dor wanted me to say. It had been mostly pro-Diviner propaganda, but I hadn't expected much else. A focus on Elijah's heroic sacrifice. How I'd allegedly stopped the attack.

Hardly a word about the lives lost.

I'd always fancied myself a hero. Had wanted a hero's death to absolve the Dark Warden.

But the fame that had found me was all a lie.

I was no hero. So many mortal lives had ended at the barrel of my pistol on Elijah's command. Vesper. Ember. Enemies of the Wardens. Apostates. Sinners.

Elvira Byvich.

Who had mourned *them*? Who had remembered *their* names? Not I— I'd wiped them. Tried to absolve myself.

There was no absolution, was there?

"Sir?" Ben prompted. "The crowd is building, sir."

Saints. I'd been so lost in memory, in regrets upon regrets, that I hadn't practiced my speech. Public speaking wasn't my forte. Elijah had been an orator. He'd known how to work the crowds and the press. I was going to make a fool of myself.

I straightened my tabard once more and smoothed my hair, and then Ben led me back out to the main cricket hut. A small crowd mingled; Glimmer, Wardens, a couple of Umber workers who managed the tea, a Seren reporter from the Courier.

Some of the Diviner Wardens looked embarrassed.

Pendula pushed through the crowd and offered me a handkerchief. "You're crying, Your Excellency," she whispered.

So I was. I waved her off.

To cry during a public memorial was a political decision, not an emotional one.

I wanted Chime's citizens to see a Diviner with emotion, to see we weren't all unfeeling clockwork hearts with stiff upper lips. I didn't care if my domain deemed it unseemly. Crying wasn't dignified. It was raw. But how many would deem my tears hypocritical?

Would the dead welcome my tears, knowing I'd done nothing to save them?

COMPOSE YOURSELF, boomed Father's voice in my head. *YOU ARE A DIVINER. YOU WILL ACT WITH DIGNITY.*

Right, that answered that. *There's no shame in emotion, Father.*

WE ARE THE LOGIC THAT SETS CHIME'S LAWS IN MOTION. WE CANNOT AFFORD TO SHOW WEAKNESS. NOT WHEN CHAOS STILL EXISTS.

You don't think showing a little weakness would earn public trust? The mortals of Chime look upon us like we're machines. We cannot govern this way—

WE HAVE GOVERNED THIS WAY FOR A MILLENNIUM. WE SHALL CONTINUE TO DO SO. CONTROL YOUR EMOTIONS, QUENTIN. YOU ARE MY VOICE. YOU WILL ACT WITH MY WILL.

His harsh command left my blood cool. Well then. I lifted my spectacles and rubbed my eyes clear. Saints forbid I cried during a memorial!

The other Diviner were staring at me with blank faces.

All except Ben, who smiled in sympathy. Oh, Ben. He was a rare one.

It was no wonder that many thought of Diviner as emotionally stunted when Father encouraged such behavior, or lack thereof.

I approached the window and observed the gathering crowds.

"They're quite a rabble," Gloria said as she came to my side.

"They're mourners, my lady."

"Are mourners as rowdy as these? I knew this memorial would be a farce."

"Protocols are in place. The public are cordoned off from the unveiling."

A dispute was going on beyond the barriers. The Wardens were trying to corral the loudest group, though from here, I couldn't tell what they were yelling about.

As the Glimmer had so ceremoniously invited themselves into my parade, I'd now need to spare Wardens for their evacuation, for pity's sake.

Ben gestured for my attention.

I bowed to Gloria. "Would you look at the time? I'd love to stay and chat, but I'd rather be elsewhere. Good day."

If looks could kill, Gloria would have set my hair on fire.

"The Wardens found these being handed out, sir," Ben said as he passed me a flier. "The Godless have infiltrated the grounds."

I scanned the flier, but this wasn't Vincent's art, nor Harmony's writing. It was a child's drawing that appeared to depict me as the Dark Warden. It blamed me for the disappearance of the Vesper.

This wasn't a Godless flier.

There'd been so many rumors about both the Warden and Godless involvement in the attack on Central Station. The Glimmer blamed the Godless, the Wardens blamed electrical malfunctions, the Godless blamed the Wardens.

Today wasn't going to go down as one of my finest moments.

"I don't advise you go ahead with this plan, sir."

"Our Father wants results, so let's get Him results."

I really hadn't wanted to use a public memorial to draw out Chaos, but how else was I meant to find Kayl?

We'd installed sensors inside the cricket hut, but it wasn't practical to set them up outside. Chaos could be lurking out there now, believing this hut contained a whole group of ambassadors to be taken.

My article in the Courier had merely been bait. We couldn't risk our ambassadors, could we?

The moment Chaos stepped inside this hut, we'd be ready.

"Are the Wardens on standby?" I asked.

"Yes, sir. Tasers are ready."

"Good. Empty the hut. I want the Glimmer out of here."

I strode past the staring faces of Pendula and the Glimmer and exited the cricket hut.

The Wardens had erected a barrier separating the hut and podium from the increasingly agitated mob. Mortals from across the domains pushed against the barrier. Shouting and swearing filled the air as the crowd swelled and squirmed. The Wardens were pushing them back with little success.

"It's him!" someone called out. "The Dark Warden!"

"What did you do with my Sylvaan?" an Ember yelled. "She turned to dust in my arms! What did you do to her?"

The anger in their eyes made me pause.

I'd hoped to attract Chaos without innocent mortals getting caught in the crossfire, but gosh, the number filling the park was far larger than I'd expected.

So much for my speech.

I scanned the crowd for familiar silvery-blue eyes, but could see no sign of Kayl or Jinx. No sign of the Godless.

A stone whizzed past me and collided with a Warden's head. He collapsed on the gravel, blood pouring from his forehead.

My hand instinctively went to my pistol.

The Ember had climbed over the barrier and was now dashing toward me.

Saints. I'd made a mistake, and I was about to damn well pay for it.

6

The Undercity is no longer safe.
If you need help, then stay away from Grayford and Sinner's Row. The
Glimmer need mortals to fill their workhouses. They may offer promises of
food and shelter. Don't listen to them.
Sinner's Row is home to violent thugs who prey on the vulnerable.
Begging is illegal on Central's streets, but if you must, head for Meridian
Park. That is the only safe haven in Chime left.
—Anonymous, Godless flier

HARMONY HAD BEEN RIGHT about the crowds.

Hundreds of mortals gathered around the main gates leading into Meridian Park. More than I'd have ever expected.

I'd never visited the park this early before. It was a lovely spot for taking a stroll by the roses or picnicking by the lake, which Malk and I had done a few times. Though one had to be careful if one took a sojourn into the bushes for a quickie. Wardens patrolled the paths, and they didn't take kindly to public nudity.

Coming here reminded me of those risky getaways, and the memory sat heavy in my heart. This morning, the park reflected the gloom of my mood.

Mist shrouded the pathways and coated the grass in a damp, glowing film. The overhanging plate of the Golden City had always cast the park in darkness, but now the streetlamps glowed with eerie silver light that made the trees lining the pathways look like shadows with outstretched claws ready to snatch mortals away.

"I can't believe you dragged me into this," Dru whined, her arm looped around mine. "Harm's going to kill us."

"No, Harm is going to kill *me*. You're too sweet and innocent to dare disobey her. She'll know I corrupted you."

"She'll know I came along to save you from yourself."

I'd tried sneaking out of the temple alone, but naturally, Dru had been waiting to catch and chide me. Instead of whacking me over the head and dragging me back, she'd decided to join me, as she too wanted to see the truth with her own eyes.

Quen was *alive*.

It had been a whole pissing month! How had I only learned of his unholy resurrection now? I'd mourned him, for god's sake. I still mourned him. And he had the cheek to be alive and *not* tell me?

Why was he alive?

Was he still the same Quen? My Quen?

Or had Dor reanimated him to be his puppet?

Ambassador. That was what the Courier had said. Quen had taken Karendar's place.

I didn't know what that meant, and I didn't like any of it. If Quen was keeping his distance from me, it was likely for good reason. He'd been the Godless's benefactor; he knew more about my organization than any Warden, which made him a liability.

"You're making me go out in public like this." Dru pulled her shawl tighter around her head. "Everyone will think I'm a slut handing out my flowers willy-nilly—"

"No one will think that, and if they do, I'll kick their shins. How do you feel?"

"Vincent says they'll grow back, and they've started to sprout—but it could take weeks, maybe months, before they flower. I'd been thinking about taking a trip back home, to Heartstone. I've not had a chance to write, and my family tends to get angsty. But I can't go back looking like *this*."

Thank the gods for that. Vincent had patched up the wound my damn twin had caused, and after he'd confirmed the damage wasn't permanent, Dru had come around. I'd worried Jinx may have ruined our friendship, but Dru knew my nature. She wouldn't let a little chaos get between us. We'd have never lasted otherwise.

We were dressed modestly as two Umber ladies in matching skirts and coats, our shawls wrapped tight around us. No one paid attention to Umber because no one expected Umber to be capable of committing crimes, and thus we merged easily with the crowds. Truly, taking an Umber's face was the only way to get around Chime these days.

Beside us, many were dressed in drab gray and dark mourning colors. They crunched up the gravel, their heads bowed, their chatter hushed, and a somber mood accompanied the mist. There were a mix of mortals, from Ember to Leander, and a surprising number of Glimmer. I assumed most weren't here to mourn the missing Vesper, but rather, the victims who'd befallen Chaos within Central Station. Many Glimmer had fallen from the glass elevator.

As we continued on, the trees overhanging the path eventually pulled back, revealing the open space of the badminton courts, bowling green, and cricket club opposite the bandstand, which had been cordoned off with barriers and a heavy Warden presence.

Mortals were pushing at the barriers and shouting. Wardens shoved back anyone who tried to get past them. These were the heavy hitters; Umber and Leander Wardens, each carrying batons that they used to corral the writhing mob.

Shit.

This wasn't good.

"It's obvious, isn't it?" called out a familiar voice wearing a Glimmer face. Jinx. She was standing on a park bench, dramatically gesticulating to an audience of eager doom-mongers. Beside her, a sign that said 'Repent! The end is nigh!' had been planted in the ground.

Great.

Jinx still wore that ridiculous red dress. It was the first time I'd seen her in weeks, and she hadn't changed at all. "Valeria was punished by the gods!" she continued, her voice carrying across the crowds. "Vesper were so full of sin, and that's why the Gate doesn't point to Eventide anymore—"

"You're talking shit, lady," said an Ember man. "If the domains were closed due to *rampant sin*, then my domain would have gone long ago."

"Maybe your domain's next."

Flame flickered in his hands. "You want to say that again?"

Another Ember grabbed his friend. "Cool it, will you? There're Wardens."

"She can't go around saying shit like that—"

"She can say what she likes. It don't make it true." He placed a protective arm around his friend's shoulder. "She ain't worth it, bruv."

Rumors of the Vesper's disappearance passed through the crowd. Each echoed in my mind like a fevered whisper.

The truth squeezed my chest, and I suddenly found it difficult to breathe.

Dru grabbed my arm, her grip tight. "Is that her?"

I shook off the voices distracting me. "Yes, though why she's pretending to be a Glimmer preacher, I have no idea. Stay here. Merge with the crowd."

"What are you going to do?"

"Find out what she's up to."

I pushed through, and Jinx's eyes found me. "Sister! Fancy bumping into you—"

"What are you doing here?" I demanded.

She jumped down from the bench and snatched a flier that had been piled there, handing it over to me. "Thought I'd help you and your Godless out. You know, spread a little *chaos*."

The flier was a crude drawing of Quen with his eyeglasses as big round orbs, and a childish scowl on his face. Beneath were the words: *The Dark Warden banished the Vesper! Your domain is next!*

Gods.

"The truth's written right here!" Jinx waved a flier while addressing the crowd. "Who hated the Vesper more than any other mortal? The Dark Warden! He's responsible for their disappearance! Don't believe me? Then why did he get promoted to ambassador, huh? Why is Kronos now in Eventide's slot?"

The crowd exchanged confused and angry glances.

"You're going to start a bloody riot!" I whispered.

"That's the idea. Did you know this whole fucking memorial is a sham? Only two ambassadors have shown up, and they're hiding inside a booby trap. Kinda shitty of the Wardens to use mourners as bait, huh? How stupid do they think we are?"

"Shit, really?"

"Never mind, sister. We can make the best of it." She waved another flier. "Why is the Dark Warden covering up the truth? We demand answers!"

I snatched the flier from her hand. "Quen didn't do this!" I hissed. "You know that!"

"Oh, I know." She turned her eyes to me—my eyes—and they held a malice that made my blood run cold. "But you Godless have the right idea. Let's get the domains fighting among themselves." She leaned close. "Then they'll be easier to invade and destroy."

I recoiled. Jinx was insane. She'd whipped up this whole crowd into a frenzy, and by the looks on their faces, they were ready to burst.

"Where are the Vesper?" yelled an Ember man. "We want the truth!" He lobbed a stone at the nearest Warden, a Diviner. It cracked against his skull and sent him down.

Oh shit!

Mortals surged forward, and I was being swept with them. I tried to fight my way back to Dru, but the crowd was so packed, I could barely move.

A shot blasted into the crowd.

Then everything happened all at once.

The Wardens charged, batons in hand. They swung at anyone within arm's reach. A baton clubbed an Umber next to me. An Ember screeched as their nose spurted with blood.

We were being pushed into one uncontrolled mob.

Keep moving and find cover. Malk's voice spoke inside my mind, reciting advice from the last riot we'd been caught in.

Good advice. Except I couldn't move. I couldn't breathe!

A Seren woman cried out as she fell, and she vanished under my feet.

"Stop!" I yelled. "There's a Seren—"

More shots exploded overhead, sending the panicked crowd screaming.

Red mist burst in the air.

I jerked my head aside as blood splashed my cheek. Gaps appeared in the crowd where bodies had faded before they could even hit the ground.

The Wardens were pulling no punches.

Smoke twirled from the barrel of a pistol aimed right at me. Shit!

I scrambled back, half tripping over my own feet. Something slammed into my left shoulder with the force of a cricket bat, followed by an intense burning pain. Hot liquid spread down my arm.

Oh gods!

"I've got you!" Dru pulled me out of the way as a Warden's baton narrowly missed us.

"I've been shot!"

"What? Where?"

"My shoulder," I gasped. I pressed my hand against the sticky wound. "*Fuck!* It hurts—"

"We need to get out of here—"

"Really? I thought we could stay and host a picnic."

Dru practically dragged me with her. She didn't know her own bloody strength, sometimes, and I had no choice but to stumble where she led me.

The mob jostled around us in full-on riot mode. Gods. I hadn't seen a riot like this since the Grayford Incident, and I could imagine the headlines calling it the Meridian Park Incident or the Memorial Incident or something equally unoriginal.

But fuck! My shoulder really hurt, and I couldn't move my left arm without blinding agony. Those absolute arseholes had shot me!

This was all Jinx's fault!

I spotted her further ahead. She was just standing there, grinning at the chaos unfolding around her.

Wardens were pushing the crowd apart, and I lost sight of the poor Seren who'd been caught underfoot and trampled. I'd tried to grab her, but the mob had a mind of its own, and I could barely move with bodies pressed against us. Dru elbowed her way through, creating a path for us both, but the mob was relentless.

They threw rocks and sticks and whatever else they could get their hands on at the Wardens. "Where are the Vesper?" they chanted.

An Ember tossed their flame, until they were shot down for it.

"Order, order!" the Wardens countered, their batons coming down *hard*.

More Wardens waited by the gates to Meridian Park. Mortals tried to run past them, but the Wardens swooped in and grabbed them left and right, arresting them on the spot.

Shit!

"Kayl, Wardens—"

"I see them—"

"We can't let them catch us—"

"I *know*!" Dizziness washed over me in waves, and I was finding it hard to walk straight. We wouldn't be able to escape via the main gates, but perhaps we could find another way out of the park. There were multiple entrances, many places to hide.

I probably wasn't bleeding to death. We could wait it out.

Find shadows to hide in, Malk said. His voice had been louder than normal this morning. Perhaps I was bleeding to death, and the souls of the damned were welcoming me into their arms.

"Go left," I said. "Aim for the wall."

Dru guided us onto the overgrown path against the park's wall, where both trees and bushes grew tall and gave adequate shadow. No doubt Wardens would come searching around here soon, as other mortals came after us, likely having the same idea.

I leaned against the brick wall and caught my breath. Cold sweat beaded my brow, and I whipped off my shawl for air.

"Oh gods," Dru whispered, and pointed at my shoulder. "How much blood have you lost?"

I examined the wound. My cream coat now had a dark red stain. Fuck's sake. I liked this coat! "I don't know, really. I wasn't keeping track." I fumbled in my satchel for anything I could use to patch up the wound, but shit, I'd stuffed my satchel full of fliers. A few spilled out and fluttered to the dirt.

"Your shawl." Dru came to my rescue, and I let my arms fall uselessly to my side. She carefully peeled back my coat's collar. I hissed as she grazed my shoulder. "Oh gods, oh gods."

"It can't be that bad," I gasped. "I'm still alive."

"I can't—We need to get you to Vincent."

Which was easier said than done. I caught glimpses of Wardens chasing after mortals, attempting to arrest them. Stragglers darted into the tree line and ran past me. If they weren't careful, they'd bring Wardens straight to us.

"Help me patch it up, and we'll get moving. I've survived worse."

"You haven't survived this yet."

With Dru's help, I wrapped the shawl tight around my shoulder. The bleeding hadn't slowed much, but I'd at least plugged the hole. Dru let me lean on her as we both stumbled away from the gate.

Movement ground in my shoulder, as though whatever the Wardens had shot at me remained lodged inside. It was a different kind of pain from when Valeria had snapped my ribs. That had been a crushing pain that made it impossible to breathe. This was more of a sharp, searing agony, and with each step, my energy drained.

"You'll carry me if I faint, right?" I asked Dru.

"Don't talk like that."

"Just being practical."

"Being a prat, is what you are."

"Do you really want to insult me when I'm dying? You'll feel bad about it when my soul reaches the aether."

"Can you please not joke about this?"

"It's all right, Dru. We'll get caught by Wardens long before I bleed out. At least they patch up their prisoners. Can't torture a dead woman." I tried to sound chipper, but she wasn't buying my optimism.

The worst part of this whole damn morning was that I hadn't even seen Quen—hadn't seen any of the ambassadors come out of their hiding place. They'd have run off, most likely. I'd gotten pissing shot, of all things, and I hadn't even confirmed if Quen was alive!

Harmony was going to kill me, if I didn't bleed to death or get arrested first.

The second entrance to the park came into view, and my heart sank. More Wardens stood on guard. Shit, they worked fast.

"What now?" Dru whispered. "If they block off all the gates, we're trapped."

I glanced at the wall. It was impossibly high—there was no way I could climb it, nor would Dru be able to break it. "I'll turn Vesper. Use my shadows to sneak us past."

"There's too much light."

Dru was right. Streetlamps lit the entrance, which meant they'd likely notice flickering shadows. As the only Vesper left in Chime, that would certainly make me a target. "It's the only idea I have—"

"I'll distract them so you can run past—"

"That's an even worse idea. I'm not leaving you, for one. And how fast do you think I can run with a hole in my shoulder?"

Though as I was dismissing her plan as lunacy, another Warden approached the ones by the gate—the same massive Diviner I'd seen in the alley the other day—and he appeared to be ordering them back.

The Wardens looked annoyed at being recalled, but they withdrew from the gate, leaving it wide open for an escape.

"What do you think?" Dru whispered. "A trap?"

"Could be. But what choice do we have?"

Carefully, we picked our way toward the gate. An Ember ran past us and got through without being jumped, so I had to assume it was safe.

The wound slowed me down, but we tentatively made it through. This side of the park put us closer to the Temple District, which meant we could sneak through a few side alleys and walk our way back to the temple without needing to catch a tram.

Bleeding on public transport was frowned upon. I spat on my jacket sleeve and wiped the blood from my face, just in case.

We made it to the crevice of an alley. I breathed a sigh of relief. Luck was on my side, getting shot notwithstanding.

"Oi! You there!" a man shouted behind us. "Halt!"

A Diviner Warden. And there went my luck.

"Go," I whispered to Dru, and we shuffled further into the alley.

"I said *stop*!"

Dru suddenly froze in place and trapped me with her, her arm wrapped around mine. The Diviner had paused time around us.

His powers didn't affect me, but I couldn't abandon Dru, so I tried to stand as still as bloody possible while my damn shoulder continued to bleed. I'd never mastered the art of staying still, truth be told, and pretending was worse—I struggled to slow my wheezing, my skin itched with sweat, and honestly, I *really* wanted to collapse around about now.

The Diviner Warden approached with a baton in hand, possessing the casual swagger of a man who enjoyed wielding power over mortals. He tapped Dru's bicep, and then those silver eyes turned to me.

I didn't dare blink.

He holstered his baton. "What do we have 'ere, then? Two lovely ladies running from the law?" His lingering gaze traced down to my bloodstained coat. "You don't look great, love."

He took my spare hand, twisted it painfully so my palm faced him, and then rubbed it against his groin.

What in the actual fuck?

The Diviner leered, his breath hot on my cheek as he continued to rub himself against me, and gods, I actually felt him stiffen. "I wonder what we have under 'ere?" He let my hand drop and began to undo the buttons of my blouse.

Quen had once told me that Diviner followed a moral code that stopped them from pausing time and abusing other mortals. Either he was completely naïve, or he'd been full of shit.

I'd never set out to deliberately steal a mortal's soul, but if this Diviner got my blouse unbuttoned, I was going to kick him so far into the aether, he'd be reborn as a dildo.

Just as he'd reached the bottom button, a deafening blast echoed through the alley. It hit the Diviner straight in the head, and his brains splattered the alley wall.

His body faded as it fell, and time instantly resumed.

Dru staggered back, her eyes wide at the newly decorated wall. "What happened? Did you do that? Kayl, did you…"

But I was staring down the alley.

A man stood there encased in the silvery-blue light of aether. Of Chaos. It glowed around him in a silhouette. As he lowered his pistol, the light caught his eyeglasses.

Quen? Could it be? I stumbled down the alley, covering my eyes as I tried to reach him.

The light flared and then vanished completely.

I blinked back starlight. Those eyeglasses, that height—it had looked like Quen! "Did you see him?" I called over my shoulder.

"See who?"

"I swear, I…" I hadn't imagined it. Someone had shot that Diviner.

I knew, deep in my soul, that Quen had saved me.

Though how, I couldn't say. Had he gained new abilities since coming back from the dead? But why run? Why abandon me here?

"Kayl, we have to go," Dru whined.

I hastily tucked my blouse into my skirt, and we shuffled out of the alley.

Shouts came from behind us. "Warden down!"

Bloody Wardens rarely worked alone. Hopefully we hadn't left a trail behind us, but I was dripping blood. We tried to act casual, just two women returning from errands, but I cursed at the wound pulling me down.

Thankfully the Wardens we passed were running to the park, and not after us. Shouting faded behind us. Gawking onlookers were too busy trying to discover the source of the commotion to pay us much attention.

In a way, Jinx's stupid riot had helped us escape largely unscathed. Okay, I was bleeding everywhere, but for a Godless, this could be considered a success.

We made slow progress, but eventually we followed the overhead tram line to the Temple District.

I was about ready to collapse when we burst inside the temple.

The Mesmer trio sat behind the reception counter, helping themselves to a bowl of candy. One straightened immediately, knocking the bowl over. "Is that *blood*?" they shrieked.

"It's raspberry sauce," Dru blurted. "We went to the ice cream parlor, and Kayl had a little accident; you know how she is—"

"Then why does she look hurt?" The poor Mesmer's lip wobbled, and tears filled their eyes.

"I ate too much," I groaned out. "Got—stomach pain. Need Vincent to help me ease it."

The Mesmer looked visibly relieved. "When I get a stomach ache, I go nap."

"Yes, that sounds like a good idea," Dru said. "I'll go take Kayl for a nap."

She ushered me through the corridor. Vincent hadn't finished stocking his new clinic yet, but we'd find him somewhere, hopefully before I passed out.

We burst inside the red room, where Harmony sat reading the Courier. She put the paper down with a sigh.

Dru pulled me to a chair, and I collapsed into it. "She's been shot."

"Yes, I can see that. Vincent's in the kitchen."

The door creaked as Dru ran out. I tilted my head back and stared at the stars that floated around the ceiling. The colors blurred together.

"Well?" Harmony sounded distant. "Was it worth it?"

I took in a shaky breath. "Are you really going to berate me as I sit here dying?"

"You're not dying quick enough. Was Corinth there?"

"I don't know—there was a riot—"

"Of course there was. Did you start that, too?"

"Why do I get the blame?"

"Because you're the one sitting here bleeding. Well?"

The room began to spin, so I closed my eyes. "It was Jinx. She started it. The Wardens, they shot into the crowd. It was bad, Harm."

"You're lucky you got out, girl."

I lifted my head and opened one eye. "What did I tell you? I always get... out..."

"Give me space!" Vincent snapped, the first time I've ever heard him so angry, and he was upon me instantly. "I need *space*."

I must have passed out for a moment, because I was lying on my back, my blouse undone, and his cool fingers pressed against my neck.

"Are you with me, Kayl?" he asked with a strained smile.

"I think so."

"The shrapnel is still inside you. I'm going to dig it out, but it will feel a little strange."

"You won't be the first handsome man inside me."

He choked back a laugh. "Please. I need to concentrate."

I focused on the swirling lights as his fingers pushed inside the wound. It didn't hurt. In fact, I couldn't feel anything at all. I tried to wiggle my toes and fingers and couldn't even tell where they were. Vincent had completely numbed me with his Necro abilities.

The stars of Babel floated around me. My eyes fluttered at their melodic dance.

Next time, listen to Harm, Malk chastised me.

There went my imagination again, believing Jinx had been replaced by Malk. I wanted to believe I carried Malk with me always, but it was wishful thinking.

Malk was gone. I'd watched his body turn to dust.

It was my own guilt manifesting his voice.

As the stars of Babel merged into one colorful smudge, my mind drifted to Grayford, and I swore I heard Malk's voice again, singing a Vesper lullaby.

"It's Wardens!" I hissed. "They're searching for illegals."

Dust crumbled from the walls, shaken off by the many Wardens stomping around Grayford. They'd come for the runaways. The Glimmer and Ember. Elvira, too. The Wardens had spun some shit about illegals, but I knew why they were really here.

Malk's midnight blue skin paled. "I'll fetch Varen."

"There's too many of them out there. If they catch us, you know what they'll do." A correctional facility or worse. Both Malk and I were illegals. Apostates at that. But the runaway Glimmer… She carried a child, and if her god found out what she planned to do with it, a correctional facility would be her best hope. "If we lay low, they won't find us."

"If we do nothing, then they'll march Vesper straight to Eventide. Varen's the only one who can stop them." Shadow pooled around his fingers.

"Malk—"

"Stay hidden. Keep my mother safe." There was a fierceness inside Malk's sapphire eyes that I'd glimpsed only a few times.

Malk would fight for his mother. He'd fight for me.

That knowledge burned in my chest.

I wanted to fight with him.

We'd both known this day would come, but not even I'd expected Wardens to come pounding on our doors. They had no right to attack Grayford!

He was out before I could stop him. I dared a look around the corner.

Wardens were rounding up the Vesper. Those who argued back faced the rough end of a baton. If they weren't careful, they'd start a bloody riot!

Light flashed behind me, and I spun.

A Diviner stood before me.

Shit! He must have used his time powers to sneak in here.

This one wasn't dressed like the Wardens in their black-and-bronze uniform, but in a tan suit. In one hand he held a pocket watch, and in the other, a brass pistol.

Light from the streetlamp shone off his round eyeglasses. "Would you change the past if you could?"

What kind of question was that? "Are you with the Wardens?" Some of them dressed in plain clothes—their stance gave them away. He had that look about him, but there was something else. Something that jarred a memory I couldn't place.

"No. You could call me a free agent."

Diviner were dangerous, regardless of who they affiliated with, but why was one here? What did they want? They never entered Grayford. I needed him gone. "If you're looking for a teahouse, then you took a wrong turn a few miles back."

"So it would appear. I'm about to make a grievous mistake I'll regret for the rest of my mortal life. However, as much as I'd like to rectify my mistake, the timeline demands this sacrifice. To alter it would change events irreparably. Do you see my dilemma?"

"Not exactly, no." Diviner were obsessed with past and future events, but I had no idea what this fool was rambling on about.

"If I allow events to unfold as they should, mortals will die. If I interfere, then these lives will be spared at the cost of untold suffering in the future. What would you choose?"

Shouting came from outside. I didn't have time for philosophical questions from some idiot Diviner when Vesper were in danger! "Save who you can now and change the future later. Seems simple, doesn't it?"

The Diviner smiled with an odd familiarity. "You'd save the ones you loved over thousands of unknown innocents?"

"Who wouldn't?"

He holstered his pistol. "Who indeed?"

Bright light burst from his skin, as though he were made of aether. I blinked, and then he was gone.

"Quen," I whispered.

Shit. I remembered now. I remembered how a strange Diviner—the Dark Warden—had come to Grayford. But... that wasn't how it had gone down!

Was I forgetting my own memories?

YOU ARE HURT, a voice interrupted. An interloper who didn't belong.

The scene went still. Quiet. Even the dust floating in the air paused.

Oh bollocks. I was dreaming, wasn't I? That explained why my past had completely diverged from actual history. "What can I do for you, Mesmorpheus?"

Color rippled through the dust motes with an iridescent shimmer as the god of dreams walked through them like clouds. *YOU ARE HURT. YOU BLEED.*

"That's what mortals do when they're shot, yes."

YOU SCARED MY MORTALS. DO NOT BRING BLOOD INTO MY TEMPLE.

"I didn't exactly have a choice—"

MY MORTALS ARE SENSITIVE. THEY SUFFER EASILY FROM NIGHTMARES. DO NOT BRING VIOLENCE INTO THEIR HOME.

"All right, I get it. I'll bleed outside next time." Gods, I had Harmony ready to berate me, and now an actual god was invading my dreams to tell me off. What next?

YOUR PAST HAS CHANGED.

"Isn't that the nature of dreams? You would know, right?"

THERE IS A PRESENCE IN YOUR DREAMS THAT IS NOT I.

"A what?" Were they speaking of Quen?

The stone walls of Grayford began to fade.

"Wait! What did you mean? What—"

"Shit!" I woke with a start.

A dream. It had been a dream, that was all. Mesmorpheus was fucking with me.

Or guilt was finally taking over my subconscious.

If I could change the past, I'd save Malk and the rest of the Vesper in a heartbeat. How far back would I go? To save Reve? Elvira?

Corentine? As if I could!

It didn't matter. Diviner power didn't work that way. Wishful thinking would only drive me insane, and I was mad enough.

I sat up in my bed, redressed in a silk nighty. I pulled back the covers and checked my wound. There was no bandage, no scar. Nothing to show I'd ever been shot at all.

Gods, I owed Vincent a drink! Two drinks!

"Finally back with us?" Harmony sat in an armchair under a lamp, the only light in the room, and read the Courier in her lap.

I wiped sleep from my eyes. "How long was I out for?"

"About a day—"

"A whole pissing *day*?"

"You're alive, so stop your complaining. Also, we have a few problems."

"When do we not have problems?" I slid my legs off the bed and searched for a pair of slippers. "Are you going to berate me now or after breakfast?"

"After breakfast. I'm not cruel. Besides, you need to see this, girl." She folded over the Courier and held it out for me. "It seems you've attracted a certain someone's attention. This was printed in this morning's edition."

I took the paper. It was open to the personal and missed connections page. "Are you looking for a date, Harm?"

"Just read it."

I skimmed down the advertisements. And there, at the bottom under missed connections:

"Looking for my partner.

I missed you at Meridian Park yesterday. You looked lovely in your cream jacket. It has been a month since we parted in Central Station. I'd like to invite you for tea and biscuits so we can catch up. I've left you an invitation at Arcadia Apparel on Cobbler's Street—ask for my name. They'll gift you an appropriate outfit, all paid for.

Your benefactor."

"That's Quen—that's him!" He must have spotted me in the crowds. But why in god's name was he leaving me cryptic messages in the damn Courier?

"Congratulations, you've got a date."

"And you're letting me go?"

"I doubt they'll let the Wardens host a shootout in Arcadia Apparel. And if Corinth *is* back, I want to know why."

Arcadia Apparel was one of the poshest boutiques in Central. Whatever Quen wanted me *there* for must be expensive. I handed back the Courier. "You said we had problems. Plural. What else has gone wrong?"

"You got followed into the temple."

Shit. "Do Wardens suspect we're here?"

"*Not* by a Warden—a Glimmer. He came here waving one of our fliers. Said he knows about the Godless and he's seeking asylum."

I gawked at her. "Did you say *he*? A male Glimmer? Are you shitting me?"

"Wish I were. He asked for you—apparently you've met him before?"

"I have?" Gods, when had I ever been on friendly terms with a Glimmer, let alone a male one? The only Glimmer I knew had been taken away by Wardens five years ago for refusing to do her womanly duty and birth a child.

Male Glimmer didn't exist.

"He's with Dru now. Sinder is *not* happy, by the way. Since this Glimmer followed you into the temple and asked for you specifically, this is now your problem." Harmony slid off her seat. "I'm letting you handle it. Good luck."

7

*Did you hear? The Vesper stores are closed. That's right. They just up and
closed overnight. Can't even buy pharmaceutical mushrooms for my rash
anymore. Worse, stores are having to cut hours and increase prices since
their Vesper workers vanished, too, that's what my sister said.*
What are the Wardens doing about it?
*Surely a domain shouldn't be allowed to recall their mortals? Disrupting
Chime's economy goes against the Covenant!*
What next? We lose Umber workers?
—Anonymous, *overheard in Arcadia Apparel*

MOST GODS PUNISHED THEIR mortal's disrespectful behavior with a good
flogging. But Harmony was a practical god, who punished me by making
me do her dirty work. And that meant acting as the 'voice' of the Godless.
It meant making sure we all got along, that disputes were handled fairly over
a game of cards and a bottle of wine. It meant vetting strangers who sought
out the Godless to ensure they actually *did* need our help and weren't
Wardens in disguise. It meant babysitting the Mesmer when we'd moved
into their temple so they wouldn't throw us out on our arses.

And now it apparently meant dealing with a rogue Glimmer who
happened to be a man. That was how I knew I'd truly pissed Harmony off.

The temple's corridors were quiet as I passed the many nondescript
doors marked as either engaged or vacant. One couldn't tell what lay
behind each door until opened, but most were bedrooms, making this the
holiest dream parlor in Chime. The Mesmer managed to find their way
around, for the most part, but me? I found myself lost at least twice a day.

The most hopeless of their kind resided within the temple permanently,
where Reverie could keep her eye on them. So many Mesmer varied in
lucidity. Some could manage full conversations, like the trio, but others

shied away from conversation and couldn't make eye contact. But they liked to play and draw and tinker with an astounding intelligence altogether separate from what polite society would consider normal.

Gods. I was beginning to grow fond of them.

A group of Mesmer lingered by a doorway, staring inside a room marked with red lipstick. Shit. That was Sinder and Vincent's room. They must have forgotten to lock the door.

There were many advantages to bunking with the Mesmer; amazingly comfortable beds and free candy, to name a couple. But the disadvantage was that we needed to lock our rooms at night, otherwise we'd wake to Mesmer watching us in our sleep. They weren't dangerous... but they could be unintentionally alarming.

I pushed between the Mesmer. "It's time you all got back to bed and ate some candy or whatever."

They didn't move. What could have caught their attention?

I peered into Sinder's room.

Oh *shit*.

Sinder and Vincent were sitting stark-bollock naked on their bed, their arms wrapped around each other. Vincent had his fangs in Sinder's neck, and those sucking sounds weren't kisses. A line of blood dribbled down Vincent's chin and dripped to his bare, pale chest.

As he drank, Sinder's hand was clasped around Vincent's cock, slowly teasing and tugging it hard. Oh my *god*.

The two of them were so lost to their own ecstasy as Vincent fed and Sinder's eyes fluttered—Sinder quite clearly enjoying the mix of pleasure and pain—that they hadn't realized they'd gained an audience. I knew this was how they spent their private time, but to actually witness it... It sent my blood burning.

I'd never gone *that* far—only light spanking here and there—but watching these two love each other in a way that supported them both made me ache for Malk. It was a pain that would never truly leave me.

"What's going on?" whispered a Mesmer next to me.

Gods! I almost jumped out of my skin.

The trio had turned up. As the most lucid, they were supposed to help me stop their own domain from being nuisances, but they caused more nuisances than they stopped. "Sinder and Vincent are, uh, trying to rest. Can you help me get these back—"

"Are they hugging?" asked one of the trio. "That looks like hugging."

"Is that *blood*?" the third screeched.

Great. Pissing great.

The Mesmer started screaming, which set off a chain reaction of even *more* screaming, and then they were running up and down the halls as though a murderer had gotten loose.

"For fuck's sake!" Sinder yelled. He was hopping mad—literally, as he struggled to dress in some pants and came bounding over. "Can't a man get a little privacy in this godsforsaken place? I don't mind putting on a show, but this is too much." His glare sent another Mesmer running. "Vincent has to eat," he whispered. "Especially after the stunt you pulled yesterday."

"Yes, I know." If it wasn't for Vincent's power, I'd be swimming with the aether. Right now, he was hiding under the bedsheets. "Get dressed, and I'll calm them down."

Sinder slammed the door shut.

One of the Mesmer trio was trying to corral the others. The second came up to me. "Can you help me find Cosmo? They get scared easily."

I rubbed my forehead. "Which one's Cosmo?"

"The one who's screaming."

They were all bloody screaming!

I jogged up and down until I heard sniffling coming from the foyer. One of the trio was hiding behind the counter, their knees tucked to their chest as they rocked back and forth.

"He's going to eat me!" the Mesmer sobbed.

I crouched beside them. "It's all right. No one's going to eat you. Vincent's a nice man, he wouldn't harm a soul—"

"But that's what Necro do, they—they eat mortals," the Mesmer blubbered. "And my blood is so full of sugar! I'd taste delicious!"

The gods were surely testing me. "I'm sure you would taste delicious, but Necro can't drink blood that is too sugary because it would hurt their teeth." I wasn't sure where I was going with this, but fuck it, I was committed now. "And you don't want to hurt Vincent's teeth, do you?"

The Mesmer rubbed their nose. "No, that would be terrible."

"Exactly." I helped pull them up. "So you've got nothing to worry about."

The two Mesmer who made up the remainder of the trio found us. One ran to the screamer—Cosmo—and comforted them with soothing whispers while the other came to me with a cheery smile.

"We haven't traumatized the rest of them, have we?" I asked. "Vincent wasn't *actually* attacking Sinder. They were, uh, hugging—"

"It's okay." The Mesmer giggled. "We know what sex is."

Really? I supposed I shouldn't be surprised. "So you lot use your massive beds for activities other than sleep?"

"We like to cuddle or hold hands under the sheets," they whispered, like it was some perverse secret. "Castor likes kisses, but Cosmo isn't comfortable with that. We don't really care about sex. It gets messy."

"Wait—aren't you triplets?"

"Oh no! We're lovers."

"The *three* of you?" But they looked the damn same!

"Uh-huh. We share a big bed together."

Fuck me. The Mesmer were getting more action than I was. "You know, sex can help you sleep. A good orgasm works wonders."

"We're Mesmer, we don't need help getting to sleep."

Of course they didn't.

Shouting came from down the hall. Shit, I'd forgotten about the Glimmer. "I'll leave the three of you to whatever it is you do."

Dru was standing between Sinder and the Glimmer as the pair bickered.

"Why is the Glimmer still here?" Sinder demanded.

I couldn't catch a break. "Let's talk about this somewhere private, shall we?"

"What's there to talk about?" His scowl moved to the Glimmer.

Gods. This Glimmer *was* a man. No wonder he'd wanted to escape Gildola's clutches.

He was dressed rather modestly for his domain, in a waistcoat and a pair of trousers. His hair had been cut short and was hidden under a flat cap and shawl. In fact, he'd done an excellent job of disguising his golden skin. At least we wouldn't have to worry about anyone reporting on a Glimmer entering the temple.

"I don't mean you any harm." He spoke with the posh accent of a Diviner. "I'm here to seek the Godless of my own volition. That's what you do, isn't it? You help mortals evade their god?"

"You expect us to believe that?" Sinder said.

Dru rolled her eyes. "Kayl, tell him."

It was too early in the damn morning for this. "We'll hear you out. Dru, take our guest to the kitchen and brew some coffee. Sinder? Can we have a chat?"

Sinder huffed and stomped back inside his room. He'd hastily dressed, though the scarf around his neck sat askew.

Vincent must have left in a hurry—the bedsheets were a crumpled mess.

Reverie had given them one of the temple's sensory rooms—a room that blocked out all outside noise, which was ideal for a couple who needed privacy, when they remembered to lock their damn door. Soft light and a rotating display of stars across the walls and ceiling were designed to induce relaxation.

But by the look on Sinder's face, I'd say they weren't working.

"We have to kill him!" Sinder declared.

Murder before breakfast. What was this morning turning into? "You know that's not our style."

"What else are we meant to do with him? We can't throw him out, he could be a spy."

"If he were a spy, we'd have Wardens knocking down our doors by now—"

"Why else would a Glimmer be stalking us?"

"For asylum? That's usually why mortals seek us out."

"Glimmer aren't like that, and you know it." Flame rippled under his skin. "They're brainwashed by their god's doctrine. Every single one of them is hateful—"

"They're victims of their god, much the same as we are. What choice do they have but to follow Gildola's word?"

"Don't defend them. They know exactly what they're doing."

"What about the girl who rescued you from the workhouse?" Talking of his past was a sore subject, but the only way to get through to him. "You helped her seek asylum."

"That was different."

"How was it different?"

"She had her motives, as I had mine—to escape from that wretched place no matter the cost, and no matter if I needed the help of some Glimmer bitch to do it. Tell me if you've ever met a kind or compassionate Glimmer. I'll wait."

His eyes were blazing, casting shadows across the room and disturbing the peaceful ambience. He was right, though—I'd never met a kind Glimmer in my life. They looked down upon the poorest, upon the Vesper back when there were any Vesper left.

But I couldn't believe all of them were terrible. There must be at least one good Glimmer in existence.

I'd met the one good Diviner.

Regardless, if they rejected their god, then they needed our help. "I'll speak with him. He could be Godless—"

"You can't be serious, darling. They'd never reject their golden whore."

"Either way, I need to know who he is and why he's here. Then we can make a plan. We're *not* harming him."

"Not yet."

I raised my brows in my 'don't start trouble' look, to which he responded with his innocent 'who, me?' face. Sinder wasn't the murdering type, despite his bravado. Well, I liked to think none of us were. I wasn't about to begin a new tradition.

Though, inviting a Glimmer into the Godless? That was certainly new.

I found Dru and our guest downstairs in the Mesmer's kitchen, though it was less of a kitchen and more of a makeshift candy store. There was a sink, a dining table, and a few storage cupboards for bowls and spoons. No oven, because who would trust a Mesmer to operate a damn oven? The rest of the kitchen was a glittering mess of glass jars with every type of candy imaginable—rows and rows of pink bonbons, fizzy chews, chocolate limes, hard-boiled mints, butterscotch, gummies, licorice, toffees, fudge. You name it.

It was no wonder my arse was getting bigger.

Dru patted my shoulder as she left us. "Go easy on him. It looks like he's had a hard time of it."

"Haven't we all?"

I helped myself to coffee and then pulled up a chair by the kitchen table.

The Glimmer stood and bowed. "You saved me from Ambassador Erosain. You gave me a ruby ring and told me I could go and become anyone, and I—I did. My name's Joe." He visibly deflated onto his chair. "I think. I'm still trying on names."

I'd been wearing the face of a Glimmer in Erosain's bar—back when Sinder and I had broken into Erosain's art gallery—which I clearly wasn't now. That meant Joe knew what I was. "Just so I don't make an arse of myself, you prefer to be known as a he?"

"Yes, please. I'm sorry to intrude, but I saw you at the memorial. You dropped this." He pulled out one of our fliers from his inside jacket pocket. "And I knew it was you. Forgive me, I followed you. I—I can't go back to my domain. Gildola, she would never approve of—of me." Joe waved a hand at his clothes. "I can cook. I can clean. I'll do *anything*. Please. I can't go back."

"You worked for Ambassador Gloria?" We'd both been hunting for prisms for a god-splitting machine I'd rather not think about.

"Not directly. I volunteered to enter Sinner's Row because I wanted a way out. I'd meant to meet with a Necro there, a private investigator who could have helped me start over. But Erosain caught me. He drugged me. You saw what he did." Joe shuddered. "I hold no loyalty to Gloria, but I'd understand if you didn't trust me. I wasn't in her inner circle, but I'll provide whatever information I can to you and your organization."

There was pain in Joe's eyes that was hard to fake. My gut didn't think him a liar. "Do you understand what it means to be Godless?"

"Yes." He thrust his chin out. "I reject Gildola. I reject the mold she forces upon me."

I'd met plenty of mortals who flirted with gender. Sinder was one, for a start. The gods weren't perfect, after all. Sometimes they got it wrong, like trapping me and Jinx in the same body, or trapping a man in the body of a woman.

I doubted Gildola would see it that way.

Gods. I couldn't turn away this Glimmer now. If he was caught by his own domain, they'd definitely send him back to Solaris for a good old-fashioned smiting. Sinder would be furious with me, but this Glimmer was godless—we didn't turn away apostates.

And by rejecting his god's design, Joe had committed an unforgivable sin.

"Can you wait here a moment? Let me talk to the others, and we'll see if we can find you space."

Joe nodded, and I stepped out. Sinder leaned against the corridor wall, picking his nails, while Dru paced.

Sinder glanced up. "Well?"

"He's called Joe, and he's staying with us."

"You've got to be joking."

"If we kick him out, you know Gildola will smite him—"

"And if we keep him here, he'll only draw attention to us! There are no male Glimmer! None!"

"Well, there are now. He's one of us. He's Godless."

The back of Sinder's head thumped against the wall. "You're killing me, darling."

"Dru?" I asked. "Could you give Joe a tour of the place? We'll find him a room, somewhere."

Sinder crossed his arms as Dru entered the kitchen. "He's not sharing with me and Vincent. I'll burn this place down first."

"Oh, give over. Joe isn't a threat to us."

"He might be a man, but a Glimmer is still a Glimmer. The males of each domain are often much worse than their female counterparts."

"I won't argue there."

Sinder snorted, and a puff of smoke blew from his nostrils. "You know I hate this, dearest, but it's your house of cards. I'll help you pick them back up when they fall."

"I appreciate your faith in me."

"Just—keep him away from me. I'm not here to make friends with Glimmer or Mesmer, and this temple is getting crowded."

This wouldn't be easy on him, but I knew just the thing to lighten his mood. "How about a trip to Arcadia Apparel?"

"Feeling flash, are we, darling? Whose pocket did you pick?"

I gave him a shove. "I've been invited for an outfitting, and I'll need your expert eye. I'll explain on the way."

"A dress fitting? How could I ever turn that down?" His face lit up. "Come on, then. Let's get out of here and make you fancy."

There was only one Arcadia Apparel in Central. It was a Seren-owned boutique nestled between the tall town houses of Chime's Market District on a street known for its high fashion. The cobblestone roads were large enough for a carriage or two, but it was mostly foot traffic here. Seating areas spilled out from the cafés, and carts lined the streets, selling everything from roasted chestnuts to intricate silk shawls. A Seren busker with a miniature accordion set a cheerful mood for spending.

It reminded me of the night market down in Grayford, with a mixture of domains hawking their wares to the melody of a hurdy-gurdy.

Unlike the Golden City, these stores weren't exclusively Glimmer-owned businesses. Each domain was represented in some way. Even the Mesmer owned a candy store, though business was awful, so I'd heard, as the Mesmer undercharged on everything.

"Oh, how I have missed this, darling." Sinder gazed longingly at the boutiques we passed. He was dressed in a smart black waistcoat and slacks, his eyeshadow and lips painted to match.

I hung off his arm dressed in a smart casual blouse and pencil skirt, and wearing the face of an Umber. A Glimmer seated outside a teahouse gave us an odd look. I supposed Ember and Umber weren't ones to fuck. Umber were too prudish about those sorts of things.

Most mortals went about their business, shopping or relaxing with a tea and scone. That was what Quen had invited me to. I kept a lookout in case he sat waiting, or for plainclothes Wardens spying on me, but no, it was a peaceful afternoon, despite the glaring headlines of the evening Courier reporting on the disaster at Meridian Park.

"I've got a few bocs left—want to grab a bite on the way back?" I still had some leftover notes from when I'd pawned Erosain's fancy pearl necklace a few weeks back. This little foray could be a trap, but I wanted to make my jaunt here worthwhile. Getting shot sure gave me an appetite, and my nose was getting distracted by a stall selling toasted garlic bread. "I fancy a pasty or something savory. Dare I say it, I'm getting sick of candy."

Sinder glanced at me with mock shock. "Am I walking beside another imposter? The Kayl *I* know would never speak such blasphemy."

"The Kayl you know is starting to put on pounds." Even my skirts felt tighter these days, but what chance did I have, when the Mesmer stocked chocolate limes?

"They're called love handles for a reason, dearest. A man needs something to grab."

"I doubt they'll be grabbed anytime soon." At least, not by anyone I'd want to.

"So we're *not* outfitting you for a date?" Sinder fluttered his eyelashes.

"I have no idea what I'm being outfitted for."

As I said the words, we reached our destination—Arcadia Apparel.

It was tucked down one of the back alleys, opposite a Diviner watchmaker's. Wooden beams ran alongside the brickwork. Underneath, colorful bunting and potted plants decorated the windowsill. Normally, alleys were the realm of pickpockets and thieves, but the Market District felt homely. Fancy hats and heels filled the window display.

I pushed open the door to a tinny bell and stepped into a quaint little clothes shop. Dresswear in all shapes and sizes hung from the racks—suits and gowns tailored for each domain. That was what set Arcadia Apparel apart from other boutiques. Most specialized in one domain or another, from Seren fashion to Leander outfits, but Arcadia Apparel managed them all for an eye-watering price.

No other customers remained inside this late in the afternoon, but a tiny Seren man with warm peach skin sat on a highchair at the counter in a cute little tweed outfit with suspenders. A measuring tape dangled around his neck, and his wings fluttered at our entrance.

"I'm afraid we're closing soon," he announced. "If I can take your name, I may be able to slot you in next week."

I stepped up to the counter and flashed my sweetest smile. "I was asked to come here by one Quentin Corinth?"

The Seren's diamond-shaped pupils widened. "Why didn't you say so! Of course, of course. Ambassador Corinth has paid a generous amount to get you fitted and ready for the big event."

"What event would this be?"

"The ambassadors' charity ball, of course! Here—" He fumbled under his counter and pulled out an envelope. "His Excellency left this for you."

A charity ball? I opened the envelope as the Seren flew over to the front door and turned the open sign over to closed. Inside the envelope was a note, an invitation, and a half-silver mask fashioned in the visage of a Diviner.

It was for a ball, all right. A charity masquerade ball being held by the ambassadors in the embassy of Warden HQ. A trap? Or an actual ball? Surely there was no way I'd be invited to a damn ball?

Sinder leaned over my shoulder. "A masquerade? You're climbing the social ladder, darling. What does the note say?"

I flipped it open and instantly recognized Quen's handwriting.

"Apologies for the subterfuge. You're a hard woman to find. If you're reading this, then the dress is paid for, and I've left you an appropriate mask.

We need to talk. I promise I won't have you arrested and thrown into the nearest correctional facility.

Your Quen."

"Are you sure this isn't a date, dearest?"

Warmth bloomed in my cheeks. "No, it's bloody not!" I whispered.

I still mourned Malk, for god's sake, and Quen was… I didn't know what Quen was. A partner in crime? A friend?

Whatever he wanted me for sounded urgent.

"If you'd like to step through?" The Seren waved a hand at the back room. "You may wait out here," he added to Sinder.

"He can come with me—he's got a good eye for fashion, and he's seen it all besides." I think I'd gotten undressed in front of every member of the Godless by now, our new Glimmer notwithstanding.

The Seren nodded. We followed him past a cloth curtain into a fitting room.

"His Excellency advised me on your taste, so to save time, I've prepared these designs for your approval. Please, make yourselves comfortable." He flew over to a curtain.

Sinder and I sat on a couch. "How well do you know Quen—the ambassador?" I asked.

"His Excellency has been a customer of mine for many years now. Trusts me to tailor his suits. Though I can't say any more! Customer confidentiality, and all that."

"And you take customer confidentiality seriously, do you?" Sinder asked, a hint of amusement in his voice.

"Oh yes! Why, I even have a Diviner customer who purchases custom-fitted Umber wigs! He loves to role-play as a gardener! Quite fond of green, that one. Oh, but I am a gossip." He yanked the curtain cord.

The curtains parted with dramatic flair. I gasped, my hand going to Sinder's thigh.

Three gobsmackingly beautiful dresses were on display.

One looked identical to the flower dresses of the Golden City that I'd lusted over during my first visit. Quen *had* been paying attention, it seemed.

The second was a flowing silver gown that shimmered in layers and then ended in ruffles at the bottom. An absolutely gorgeous design.

And the third was a scandalous indigo dress in the shade of a Vesper. Short and tight with revealing straps. If I wanted to cause a scene, *this* would be the one to wear.

What filth polluted Quen's mind? I'd thought of him as such an innocent boy.

By gods, that dress was anything but innocent.

Sinder leaned over to me and whispered, "Are you sure this isn't a date?"

I pinched his thigh. "You've been reading too many of Harm's books."

He choked back a laugh. "How many men buy a woman a beautiful dress if not to see them in it and then later out of it?"

"Calm your sordid thoughts, it's for a ball. Quen clearly knows nothing about etiquette." Not that I did, either, when it came to ballrooms. "Can you give us a moment?" I called to the Seren.

"Of course." He flew from the room.

I turned to Sinder. "Which do you think I should go for?"

Sinder rubbed his chin. "They certainly range from modest to slutty. The silver is quite classy. It would look good on you, darling, and I can do your makeup to match. Though it entirely depends on what face you wear. Silver pairs well with most things and would complement the mask. The purple, however, might clash if you wore an Ember's face."

"See, this is why you're the most important member of the Godless."

He fluttered his eyelashes. "How would we have ever survived this far without my eye for style? What are you thinking?"

Quen had given me a VIP invitation to a ball where the ambassadors would be gathering. Did he really expect me to walk through the front door wearing one of *these*? He must have gone mad. Doing so would draw attention—especially that purple one.

"I'll go to the ball—but I'll go as an Umber server, blend in with the crowd, and try to find out what he's up to." None of those posh arseholes would pay attention to Umber staff.

"If you're going to play maid, then why are we here shopping for dresses, dearest?"

"Because Quen is paying, and I still want one." Though I'd keep it for personal use, naturally. I couldn't turn down this opportunity! "The Godless didn't survive this long by throwing caution to the wind."

"You were literally shot yesterday."

"You don't have to remind me—"

"And you've invited a complete stranger into our new hideout."

"Yes, but *this* I'm right about."

"A broken clock is right at least twice a day."

Great. I was being compared to a broken clock, now. I pulled out the silver mask, fashioned in the face of a Diviner.

What games was Quen playing? Inviting me to a ball, of all things? He couldn't meet with me on a park bench like normal mortals?

I didn't know why he wanted this meeting, or what agenda it served.

Considering all the changes in Central lately, I was sure it must be related to Chaos.

But it could be an elaborate trap. How much did I trust Quen?

I'd watched him die. I'd screamed his name. How much of *this* Quen was the man I knew?

Gods. He must be the Quen I knew, because he was already infuriating me.

VIII

The Warden Council is hosting a charity ball in honor of the late Elijah Karendar. Money will be raised toward victims of the unfortunate incident last month in which Karendar sadly lost his life. He was a stalwart gentleman until the end and always put Chime's needs ahead of his own. We are deeply saddened by the loss of such an enigmatic ambassador. Our Guild has put forth a notion to our Father to name him a saint.
—Chairman, *The Timekeepers Guild of Kronos*

I PULLED AT MY necktie for a little air. The ballroom was stifling with so many mortals conversing and dancing, but the sweat under my armpits wasn't just from the ambience.

The Glimmer had pulled off a spectacular event, as always. The embassy's ballroom glittered with the decadence of the Golden City—only the best for our ambassadors, naturally. The perfectly polished tiles reflected the shine of the chandeliers above. There wasn't a shred of shadow in the entire space, which made hiding rather impossible, though I lingered by the gossamer curtains as guests mingled.

It wasn't just ambassadors in attendance either, but a collection of Chime's rich and famous. Celebrities, sports personalities, business owners. All dressed in their finest gowns and tuxedos. A shining hive of wretchedness.

All donned a mask representing a domain not their own. The choice of mask was a political decision, rather than a personal or creative one. Many chose to play it safe with Diviner, Glimmer or Seren masks. The occasional Amnae and Umber mask waltzed past. I even spotted a Necro.

I'd been expected to wear a Glimmer mask. They were our largest allies, and as head of the Warden Council, I should have been courting their favor, or at least extending a branch of cooperation.

That was what was expected of me, anyhow.

But this charity ball was meant to raise funds for victims of the attack on Chime. After the failed memorial, I'd felt a little rebellious.

And so my purple bow tie and cuff links matched the only Vesper mask in attendance. A custom mask, since no one had chosen to make any.

A daring choice, perhaps, for the Dark Warden.

"You look snazzy, sir." Ben came to stand beside me. We wore matching tuxedos, only his mask was a flowery Umber one. We were both feeling bold tonight. While I'd tried to go for a classy look, Ben appeared intimidating stuffed inside his suit. He watched the crowd as though preparing to put a hit on someone. Hopefully me, if I was forced to endure another conversation about taxes. "Would you care to dance?"

"Are you asking me to dance, Ben?"

His cheeks turned Ember red. "Uh, no, sir. But Miss Bezel has arrived. I'm sure she'd appreciate the ask, sir."

I glanced across the hall. A delegation from Kronos had arrived, and there indeed stood Pendula in a modest golden gown that covered everything save her neck. Even her arms were covered in long silk gloves. A good choice, for a Diviner.

During my first year with the Wardens, I'd attended a ball not too different from this one. It was an awkward affair, really, given that I lacked social grace back then. We'd been taught at the academy how to dance, and that it was polite for Diviner to wear gloves. That way one couldn't accidentally trigger their abilities during a waltz. Of course, no one had been interested in dancing with shy Quentin Corinth. And in subsequent years, no one wanted to dance with the Dark Warden.

A shame, really. I rather enjoyed a good dance. I was sure Ambassador Corinth would attract more attention, but I'd elected to forgo the gloves.

There was only one woman I wished to dance with. "I'm sure Pendula won't struggle to find a willing partner." Indeed, her presence alone had already attracted goggle-eyed Diviner who should know better than to stare and whisper.

"It would benefit you to show her your favor, sir."

I gave him a shrewd look. "I didn't realize you cared for politics."

Again, that blush. "I don't, sir. I'm a simple man. I say it how I see it."

Political posturing was never my forte. That had been Elijah's domain, and why he'd been chosen to act as ambassador and I'd been merely a weapon to aim at his enemies.

He'd had the charm, the charisma, the dashing good looks.

I had a headache. "Fine, I'll go mingle. Alert me when my guest arrives, will you?"

Ben gave a half bow. "Certainly, sir."

Tonight was going to be an evening full of surprises.

The Seren-backed band in the corner was already swinging into an energetic melody as the ballroom continued to fill. Umber servers dressed in sharp black-and-white outfits dipped and bobbed through the crowd with ease, carrying golden trays of sparkling champagne. The vast majority of guests were Glimmer and Diviner, both of whom technically weren't allowed to consume alcohol due to their gods' commandments, but apparently our gods made an exception for charity.

I helped myself to a glass to steady my nerves. That was what was wrong—anxiety buzzed through me like aether. Was it being surrounded by so many powerful mortals who judged me as I passed? Was it the speech I'd have to deliver later? My failed memorial, which had earned a smattering of gossip?

Or was it anticipation?

Arcadia Apparel had sent a telegram to my office informing me that Kayl had picked up a dress and had therefore received my message. It agonized me, not knowing what she'd picked, or whether she'd even arrive here tonight at all.

All of my plans would fall apart without her.

I needed her here.

"Good evening, Your Excellency," said a dreamy Reverie. The Mesmer ambassador glided across my path wearing a black dress that glittered with the same stars in her mask, fashioned with wings in the shape of a Seren's. An ideal choice for a domain that painted with dreams. "You will find me in the western corridor later on."

Was I being propositioned by a *Mesmer*? Gods forbid! "Ah, thank you for informing me of that, my lady."

"I look forward to it." She glided off into the crowds.

Goodness me!

"Quentin!" A slightly drunk Erosain stumbled over to me. The Ember ambassador looked as stunning as ever in a silver suit, silver eyeshadow and lipstick, and diamond earrings to match his Diviner mask. "Look at you, all dressed up! Are you dancing?"

"I'll see where the night takes me."

"Hopefully in my direction!" He wrapped his arm around my shoulder, and I caught a whiff of whiskey on his breath. "Have you had a chance to investigate the robbery? I can't file with my insurance until it's been signed off by a Warden, you understand."

"The documents are on my desk. I promise I'll get around to it. You know how the Council keeps a gentleman busy." Though quite who would have dared to rob Erosain in his own bar, I had no idea. A Necro, allegedly. My eye caught Pendula and Gloria approaching. "Apologies. It looks as though I'm needed."

"Don't forget about me, Mr. Ambassador." He patted my buttocks and then winked as he merged with the crowd.

In truth, I'd rather spend time with him or Dandelion, my only allies among the Warden Council, and the only two who appreciated a good whiskey, but needs must.

I forced a bow as Pendula cornered me.

"Good evening, Your Excellency." Pendula dipped into a curtsy. "Ambassador Gloria has put on a fabulous event. Whose idea was the masquerade?"

"Mine of course," Gloria said. As if the Glimmer would let me have any input. Gloria wore a lavish gown the exact opposite of Pendula's; silver, to Pendula's gold, though Gloria was showing so much skin, the silver hardly mattered. Even her Diviner mask couldn't dull the sheen of her golden glow.

"We've hardly got fair coverage," I said. "Only one Zephyr? No Fauna? Those could have produced some extravagant masks."

Gloria eyed my mask with disapproval. "Such a shame what happened at the memorial. Personally, I was in favor of hosting a public memorial for Chime's citizens to mourn, yet all it takes is a handful of sinners to incite anarchy. That's what caused the riot, isn't it? Apostates spreading propaganda in the crowds? It was a preventable tragedy."

I wasn't sure what had triggered the riot, and that hurt most of all. I'd specifically orchestrated the memorial to catch Chaos using nonlethal means—with Wardens testing our new sensors and tasers—but as soon as the riot had started, the Wardens had reacted against my orders. To protect the Glimmer, was the official excuse.

Mortals had died, and I'd been blamed for it.

"It appears Chime's citizens have much to be angry about." I tried to keep the bite from my voice.

"Do they indeed? Can we be assured that tonight's security procedures are sufficient?" Her gaze dipped to the pistol hanging from my belt. Ben and I were the only armed guests in attendance. "I worry for the safety of our ambassadors." Her raised brow was a challenge.

This political dance wasn't as much fun as the real thing. But as Ben had reminded me, it would be easier to remain on the Glimmer's good side. Falling out of favor meant Gloria could make my life difficult and block my proposals on the Council.

"The embassy is the safest building in Central, and by invitation only," Pendula said, stepping in with practiced poise. "We're honored to have so many guests donating to such a worthy cause. Money raised from tonight's festivities will help pay for any damage caused by the riot and for installation of the park's new plaques."

Gloria's stare never left mine. "And the statue of Karendar, I presume? Do you intend to follow in his steps, Corinth? Or can we expect deviation from our newest ambassador?"

The very thought of following Elijah's rule made me queasy. "With the recent chaos, my priority remains fixed on Chime's security for now. Though I'd rather like to improve Chime's infrastructure and launch a refurbished fleet of trams—"

"That's all Diviner men care about, isn't it?" Gloria tutted. "Chime's trams don't require investment; they're still fit for service for a good ten years. My dear, I do hope our new ambassador listens to your input. Chime needs more women watching over her." She playfully swatted Pendula's arm.

"I'd be happy to assist His Excellency, should he require my services." Pendula flashed a sweet smile, one that clung to the air as cloying as the clashing perfumes that polluted the ballroom.

Father wanted me to take on Pendula as my assistant, though I couldn't fathom why.

So she could play spy?

Or keep me in line?

It couldn't be as simple as organizing my papers, despite my reputation for hoarding them.

Ben signaled for my attention.

"If you'll excuse me, Miss Bezel. Ambassador. Have a pleasant evening." I allowed my guard to pull me out of earshot.

He bent close. "The sensor has triggered, sir."

A thrill raced through my blood.

Chaos was in the building.

Ben returned to his position by the bay windows. I sipped at my champagne, suddenly needing the courage, and I once again scanned the crowds.

More mortals filled the dance floor—ambassadors I recognized, but many faces I did not. Were any of them Kayl? What persona would she wear? I'd given her a Diviner mask—would she know not to wear a Diviner form to match? Blast my vague instructions!

The worst part of my botched memorial was that Kayl *had* been in the crowds. I'd caught sight of her escaping through them. Thanks to Wardens shooting down mortals, I'd had to stay behind and fix their mess rather than chase after her.

But it had been her. I was sure of it.

My imagination ran wild with the thought of wrapping my hands around her hips in a slow waltz. Was she the dancing type?

Was it presumptuous of me to hope?

"Would you care for another drink, Your Excellency?"

My heart soared in my chest.

That voice!

I turned slowly to face one of the Umber servers carrying a tray of red wine. Her skin was the silvery-blue of stone. Her hair hung around her face like ivy. Those eyes, hidden behind a Diviner's mask.

Saints.

"You came as a *server*?" I blurted out.

Kayl's lips quirked in amusement. "And you've come as an ambassador. I think we've both been caught unawares."

I leaned close, careful to keep my proximity proper in case of prying eyes. "I specifically invited you here so that it wouldn't be odd for us to be seen conversing. I can hardly vanish somewhere private with a *server*!"

"Oh? You don't think any of your friends are sneaking out for a quickie with the staff? Your lot revel in scandal, don't they?"

"This is serious. I need to speak with you—"

"So you invite me to a *ball*?"

"I have my reasons, if you'll let me explain."

"You're ridiculous. Aren't you supposed to be dead?"

I grimaced and glanced over my shoulder. "Could you say that a little louder?"

She stumbled toward me, and tossed a glass of red wine at my chest. "Oh my gosh! I'm *so sorry*, Your Excellency! We must get you changed right away!"

Wine ran down my previously white shirt. "Are you out of your *mind*?" I whispered.

"Now we have a reason to dally in private." She handed her tray to another server. "Excuse me, I must get His Excellency cleaned up."

She grabbed my sleeve and practically dragged me through the crowds as mortals stared. Ben tried to follow, but I gave him a shake of the head and allowed Kayl to guide me through a side door and into one of the changing rooms.

We hurried inside, and she locked the door behind us.

I pulled off my necktie. "Do you realize how expensive this shirt is?"

"Oh, give over. You're an ambassador now. You can afford it."

"I'm supposed to be giving a speech in an hour!"

"Oh. Well, we better get these clothes off, then."

"I can undress myself," I mumbled, but found my hands dangling uselessly by my sides as she began to undo my waistcoat.

She popped open the last button and helped slide off the jacket. "We'll have to find you another shirt."

"You want me to strip?" I croaked.

"What's the problem? You've seen me naked."

I choked on my own saliva. "*When* have I seen you naked?"

"You've seen Jinx naked, and we're twins. It all looks the same."

My cheeks burned at the memory of Jinx kissing me. In truth, I'd seen Kayl naked many times in my memories. I'd once wiped those intimate memories I'd dug from Malkavaan Byvich's mind, but since Walter had restored everything, they'd come back. Some nights they'd intrude on my thoughts until I found myself hot and bothered. "Well, ah..." I went to take off my mask, my face suddenly warm.

"Don't." She stopped me. "Purple suits you. Why are you here, Quen? I watched you kill Karendar. I watched you *die*." Those aether eyes took on a mournful edge. "Who are you? Are you still my Quen?"

"I'm your Quen, in the flesh."

Her hand rested on my chest, above my beating heart. "In the flesh. I thought... Thought I'd lost you."

My breathing stopped almost entirely. "I'm sorry, I—"

"You dolt!" She thumped my chest. "Why didn't you contact me sooner? I thought you were dead all this time!"

I rubbed my chest and winced. "How was I meant to? You and your Godless were in hiding! Should I have put out a full-page advert in the Courier? Set off fireworks above Central? I searched for you. I went back to Grayford—"

"You put hundreds of Wardens on Central's streets."

"For Chime's protection. I knew you could handle yourself. How are the rest of the Godless? Are they well?"

"They're as fine as can be."

"And where are they?"

She gave me a look. "You'll forgive me if I don't divulge our new secret hideout."

It was worth a try.

"Why a ball, for god's sake?" she asked.

"You may have noticed, but I have guards now. Minders and spies. I can't get anywhere on my own, and I certainly can't invite a Godless woman for tea."

"My scary reputation precedes me."

"Unfortunately. This was the only way I could get us in the same room. And you had to throw wine at me, didn't you? Everyone will assume I've been pinching bottoms."

"Sorry." She gave me an apologetic smile and then giggled.

I shared in that smile. "I missed you."

At that, she threw her arms around my neck. I pulled her against my chest, stain and all, and let her head nestle against my shoulder. I breathed in her sweetness—actual sweetness, like sugar or mint candies.

"Thank you," she whispered in my ear.

My heart fluttered. "For what?"

"For everything."

She gazed down at me. I lost myself in her eyes, drowning in emotions that no Diviner was meant to feel.

Her eyes were a domain all their own, in flecks of silver and aether blue.

"How did you return?" she asked, breaking the illusion.

"Dor punished me. He brought me back."

"Why?"

"To act as His voice. To stop Chaos."

The warmth faded from my chest as she stepped back. "You want to kill me."

"Dor wants to kill you." I forced a meek smile. "I'm hoping for an alternative. This is why I needed you here—I can't do this without you."

"Do what, Quen?"

I took a steadying breath. "My Father explained everything to me—about Corentine and her imprisonment inside the clock tower. How Chime is powered by her energy."

"I met her. She's not pleased about it."

"I imagine not. Let me guess—she wants to destroy Chime and the gods in revenge?" As Elijah and Father had once described.

"Good guess."

"Unfortunately, I can't let that happen. Nor can Corentine remain trapped inside the clock tower forever. I'd always believed that Chime was powered by the combined aether of all twelve gods, not one. It's time they stepped up and lent their power."

"What are you proposing?"

"We remove Corentine from Chime. The Wardens cannot allow her mortals to occupy Chime as they are—you know their penchant for stealing souls makes them a threat. However, we may have a method of removing their abilities permanently without harming them. Then they can be rehabilitated into society."

"How would that work? They're bound to Corentine."

"Do you remember the soul-splitting devices?"

Kayl crossed her arms. "You were meant to destroy those!"

"I wanted to." And a part of me still wondered if I was making a mistake. "But I believe they can be reconfigured to split Corentine's mortals from her control, which will also remove their ability to steal souls or swap personas on a whim. They'd be forced to choose one persona and stick with it. It would allow them to live. To have a future in Chime."

"And Corentine? What'll happen to her?"

"We'll find her a place. A domain separate from the others, if need be, where she can rest. It's not quite the freedom she desires, but she will no longer serve as a glorified energy source, I guarantee that."

"You're asking her to abandon her mortals? Look, I'm not on Corentine's side, but I know her. She'll never agree to this."

"She doesn't have a choice. It's either this, or Dor orders her absolute destruction, and that of her children. You're right in that I've placed more Wardens on the streets. I also finished the clock tower reinforcements and ensured no Chaos mortal could pass through Central Station undetected and reach the Gate. Chaos cannot hope to stand against the might of the Diviner. Corentine and her mortals will be obliterated in time."

"Then why go to all this pissing effort? Why not obliterate us?"

"Because I want a better way, saints curse it! A way we can coexist in peace." And where no one mortal would need to lose their soul.

"How am I supposed to bloody help?"

"Your connection to Corentine makes you ideally placed to convince her and her mortals to cooperate. The other domains also need to understand what threat Chaos poses so they'll be forced to act. I want you to represent Chaos. To become Corentine's ambassador."

She gawked at me. "Are you shitting me?"

"No, I'm not *shitting* you. You're the only one I can trust with this. You're charming, articulate, and smart—"

"Really, Quen? Flattery?"

"Is it working?"

She gave me an exasperated look. "So I become ambassador and wear one of your fancy tabards. What then? What, exactly, is your plan?"

"We convince the remaining gods to give their power to Chime. Only then can we ensure a new start for Corentine's mortals."

"You want *me* to go speak with eleven gods and convince each of them?"

"I know it sounds impossible—"

"Impossible? It sounds utterly ridiculous!"

I glanced over the rim of my spectacles. "Then you should be able to manage it. I can't do this without you."

"Say this plan of yours works and the gods agree. What if I can't convince Corentine's mortals to buy what you're peddling?"

"Then we place them into suitable accommodation until we're ready. They cannot be allowed to run riot throughout Chime." If they all shared Jinx's temperament, then they'd certainly pose a risk. "It's this or their destruction."

Kayl didn't look convinced.

"I didn't ask for this role," I said. "But I have power now. Real power. I'll use whatever I can to save Chaos and improve the lives of Chime's poorest. I know you want that too. Together we can amplify mortal voices."

"That's what the Godless have been trying to do—"

"The Godless are undermining my efforts, I'm sorry to say. I cannot unite the domains while they squabble, and while public trust deteriorates with the Wardens. You need to stop spreading your fliers."

"You're asking me to turn my back on the Godless? On my family?"

"I'm asking you to advocate for me. To give me a chance. I see no other way." I offered my hand. "Please, Kayl. Trust in me."

She took my hand, and her form instantly changed from Umber to Diviner, the vines on her head receding into silver hair. It felt so natural to slide my palm against hers. To explore the softness and warmth of her skin. There was pleasure in touch. Such a simple action that most mortals took for granted.

"I'm glad you're alive, Quen. Truly, I am. But I'm no Warden. I can't be an ambassador. How can I advocate for the gods when I'm Godless?"

My heart fluttered anew. "I know I ask much of you, but if I can't find a way to save Chaos..."

I couldn't bear to finish that sentence.

A knock rapped at the door. "Sir. It's Ben, sir—"

"Not now, Ben!"

"There's a problem, sir."

I took off my Vesper mask, tossing it aside, and yanked open the door. "Yes?"

Ben looked flustered. "The sensor detected more Chaos energy, sir. Two more."

Saints, two of them? "Gather the ambassadors—"

"There's another problem, sir."

"When isn't there?"

"It's the Glimmer ambassador, sir. She's gone missing."

9

The hot gossip of the day is the ambassadors' memorial ball! Tonight's ball is hosted by Ambassador Gloria to raise funds for the victims of last month's attack on Central Station. Word is, no expense is being spared!

Our Seren reporter has taken a sneak peek at the guest list, and as you'd expect of a Glimmer ball, there's going to be some famous names in attendance, including the ever-charming Ambassador Erosain, and the ex-captain of the Three Lions soccer team, Ambassador Dandelion, as well as the newly appointed Diviner Ambassador Corinth!

We'll be on standby to report back on this night to remember!
—Editor's Desk, *Chime Courier Gossip Column*

I RAN AFTER QUEN and bumped into the giant Diviner Warden I kept finding everywhere. He stood as tall as me, though he didn't bat an eye at my change from Umber to Diviner.

"Quick introductions." Quen waved a hand at the Warden. "Kayl, this is Ben Seasons, my bodyguard. Ben, this is Kayl, my, ah—"

"Deepest, darkest secret." I bobbed the guard a swift curtsy. "You're a big fella for a Diviner."

"That's what they say, ma'am. You may want to find shelter while we deal with the threat."

"Since the threat is likely my twin sister, you won't mind if I tag along."

"I don't think that'll be safe, ma'am—"

"Oh, I'm counting on it."

"Forget it, Ben," Quen said. "You won't out-stubborn her."

"I can try, sir."

I grinned and nudged Quen. "I like this one."

Quen rolled his eyes. "Which sensor did they trigger?"

"The main door, sir."

"Right. We'll make our way there."

"What are these sensors?" I asked as the three of us jogged along one of the embassy corridors, muffled music bleeding through the walls. "How do they work?"

"They detect sudden and large quantities of aether," Quen explained. "Fine-tuned specifically to detect the aether that radiates from Chaos. It turns out you give off an electrical signal that can be traced."

"Isn't that handy." Though not really. I didn't like the idea of being detectable. It made my hobby as a spy useless. "And you have these around Central Station?"

"To protect the Gate and the domains. Chaos has already breached them twice."

Gods. "And you caught them?"

"No. They escaped before we could."

My chaotic siblings were still trying to invade the domains, and that knowledge sent a shiver down my spine. If they could reach the Gate and get into a domain, then that god and their mortals were goners.

Just as Eventide and the Vesper were.

I knew Mesmorpheus nudged me toward this path, but Quen must have gone insane if he thought I could become the ambassador for Chaos. None of them would listen to me, for a start—certainly not Jinx.

But if Quen spoke true, and Dor planned to destroy Corentine—

HE CANNOT, yelled Corentine's voice in my head. *DOR KNOWS TIME CANNOT EXIST WITHOUT CHAOS.*

I cringed. *Hello, Corentine.* It had been a while since my own god had struck up a conversation—partly because I ignored her—though I often sensed her presence. *Must you eavesdrop on my thoughts and conversations?*

YOUR SECRETS ARE MINE, DAUGHTER.

And what of Jinx's secrets? Are they available to share?

I WOULD NOT PIT YOU AGAINST ONE ANOTHER.

I huffed a laugh. *I'm sure you wouldn't.*

"Everything okay?" Quen asked.

"Just Corentine rambling in my head as usual."

RAMBLING! Her laughter echoed in time to my steps. *THAT'S WHAT YOU CALL PLOTTING AND TREASON. YOU SIDE WITH A CHILD OF TIME, AND HE WILL CAST YOU INTO THE AETHER.*

I trust Quen—

THAT'S YOUR FIRST MISTAKE.

He's trying to save your damn mortals! If you care for them, you'll do what you can to spare them their fate to come.

AT THE EXPENSE OF MY OWN EXISTENCE? DO NOT DECEIVE YOURSELF. DOR WON'T ABIDE MY FREEDOM, NOR WILL MY CHILDREN LEAVE ME OR MY DOMAIN WILLINGLY.

They're your *children. You can tell them what to do!*

CAN I? WHEN EVEN YOU DO NOT OBEY ME?

You heard what Quen said. If we don't do something, Dor will act—

NOT IF CHAOS ACTS FIRST.

What in god's name was Jinx planning? She had a connection to Corentine far greater than I did, and I knew both of them kept secrets from me.

We arrived at the embassy's main doors. Quen approached two Diviner Wardens standing on guard. "Have we had any late arrivals?"

"Only two, Your Excellency," said the first. "A Zephyr male and a Glimmer woman. Both were wearing odd masks. Couldn't tell their domain."

"Diviner, maybe?" added the other Warden.

"Describe them to me," Quen said.

"They were a silver-blue? With pink edges."

The colors of aether. Of Chaos. Trust Jinx to be that dramatic.

"Thank you. Be on the lookout for more." Quen ushered me and his tall guard out of earshot. "Do you know the Zephyr?" he asked me.

"I couldn't say. I've hardly met my siblings. Shouldn't your sensor have alerted the Wardens?"

"They're silent sensors. I don't want to cause a panic."

"You've got two Chaos about to gate-crash your masquerade. Now would be an ideal time to panic."

"Warden protocol is to de-escalate a situation, not exacerbate one."

"Really? That worked so well at the memorial."

He winced at my barb. "I've got Wardens posted at every exit, but with their unique masks, they should be easy to find."

"You don't sound so surprised at their arrival. Did you invite them?"

"Not officially. But one can hardly keep secrets these days. And Jinx is hunting for an ambassador."

Shit. That was why she'd gone to the memorial. She may not be able to reach the Gate on her own, but with an ambassador as hostage, she might stand a chance.

"We must find Ambassador Gloria before the Glimmer notice," Quen continued.

"Gloria?" I raised a brow. "Not *the* Gloria?"

"The same." He raised his brow to match mine, implying I should shut up about it.

Great. I'd seen her mortal body crumple to nothing after she'd betrayed me and killed one of my own, but you couldn't keep a good Glimmer down, apparently.

It wasn't just Dor breaking the Covenant, then. Every god was at it.

Maybe Jinx would get an opportunity to steal her soul this time.

I followed Quen and his guard back to the main ballroom.

Mortals were still chatting and laughing away as the dancing was in full swing, completely oblivious to the chaos about to unfold. I would have loved to have joined them for a boogie or two, to show them how we danced in the Undercity—with far more vim and vigor, for one—but now I had to find my crazy twin before she caused another riot—or worse.

A dark part of me wondered if I should bother. This ball was a collection of Chime's most fortunate. The aristocrats who lorded their power in the Golden City above the rest of us. Surely if a few of them lost their souls, their wealth might actually trickle down.

I couldn't give a damn if Chime's richest met a foul end.

Sadly, if Jinx started a killing spree with my face, it wouldn't do much good for my reputation, and I already had a face for trouble.

"Split up," Quen ordered. "It shouldn't be hard to spot a rogue Zephyr in this crowd. Ambassador Corvus—the Zephyr ambassador—has black plumage. I doubt he'd get mistaken for our quarry."

"I'll stay by your side, sir," the Warden—Ben, I think—said. "For your protection."

Quen lifted his glasses and rubbed his nose. "No offense, but your height will make me stand out—"

"You look like you've been stabbed." I pointed to Quen's red-stained shirt. "Hardly inconspicuous."

"And who's fault is *that*?"

"I'm dressed as a server and I know how to play spy. Get out of my way and let me work my magic."

"There aren't any Diviner serving tonight—"

"There are now." I straightened my blouse and pushed past these two Diviner idiots. Truly, one was bad enough, but now Quen had his own larger-than-life shadow.

Perhaps becoming an ambassador wouldn't be so bad if I was gifted a handsome young bodyguard. I'd read enough depraved novels to know it could be worth my while.

I merged with the crowd and wove through it with purpose. The only Zephyr I could spot was the ambassador, as Quen had described, though I wasn't looking for them. My attention remained on the Glimmer.

But among the golden skin and red dresses twirling around the ballroom, I couldn't spot any who wore silvery-blue masks.

What is Jinx up to? I yelled into my mind.

Corentine conveniently ignored me.

Bloody useless gods.

There were a few familiar faces within the crowd, and I skillfully avoided those, including the Ember ambassador, Erosain. Though by the way he was staggering around the dance floor, I likely didn't need to.

Ambassadors certainly liked to cut loose.

The music suddenly stopped. The dancing slowed to a halt as confused mortals turned to the raised stage, where a Zephyr male came out. He was dressed in a fancy tuxedo, though his feathers were the silvery-blue of Chaos.

Shit. I recognized him, but couldn't place his name. Chase or Clive or something.

"Attention please!" he called out in a loud trill. "May I have your attention? Lovely. Are we all having a good time tonight?"

The mortals exchanged stares and murmurs.

The Zephyr put his hand to his ear—or whatever Zephyr had for an ear. "You can do better than that. I *said*, are we all having a good time? Come on now, folks, this is a charity event!"

A few mortals whooped as others clapped or laughed.

I scanned the crowd. Both Quen and his guard were subtly moving toward the stage. I followed their lead.

"That's better!" the Zephyr continued. "Thanks to your generous donations, we'll be able to help poor Diviner children who have broken their clocks. That's a joke. Lighten up. To kick off the evening, we're hosting a raffle. First up is lot number one!" He swooped his wing dramatically at the stage curtain.

The curtain fell, revealing an unconscious Gloria tied to a chair. The Glimmer ambassador remained much the same as I'd last seen her, only now her head lolled back, and her legs were spread wide open, her red dress ridden up high with literally everything on display.

I didn't know whether to be impressed that Chaos had managed to knock out a Glimmer, or appalled at the state of her. I had no reason to care for the woman—gods, she'd been responsible for Reve's death and would have blown my soul away without a single thought—but I couldn't help but pity her predicament.

The crowd gasped at Gloria's undignified pose. One of the Diviner collapsed in shock.

Sunlight flared across the ballroom. Another Glimmer flung their deadly flame at the Zephyr.

Silvery-blue light burst from his feathers, and his form changed from Zephyr to Chaos. A static wave of energy pulsed around him, deflecting the Glimmer's sunbeams.

Gods, I had no idea we could do that!

He stood tall as a Chaos male, his smirk no longer playful, but cruel. Aether energy pulsed around him, shaking the chandeliers into an erratic jingle. "There's no need for that. Her Excellency graciously volunteered to auction herself off in the name of charity. Though the poor dear can't handle her drink—"

"What *are* you?" called out a Glimmer from the crowd.

"We are Chaos, and you stand in our domain." At those words, another ripple of aether static passed over the crowd, making my hairs stand on end. "We have taken Eventide. We have taken Valeria's soul. Now we come for yours."

If the ambassadors hadn't known Chaos existed, they sure did now.

On cue, screams erupted from the crowd. Mortals ran for the exits in a mad panic. A Glimmer shoved me out of the way, and I stumbled back, almost tripping over a Seren.

"Calm them!" Quen ordered his guard.

Ben blew a whistle.

Some mortals glanced back in alarm, almost running into each other. A moment later, Wardens poured into the ballroom and attempted to round up the crowds, though with a far softer touch than they'd offered the rioters.

Only a few mortals remained behind; a couple of Glimmer trying to reach their beloved ambassador, the Zephyr ambassador—who looked both confused and annoyed at someone taking his domain's form—and a Leander in a fancy tuxedo and top hat.

The Leander bared his fangs. "Why don't you come down here, eh, chap? Let's see what you're made of."

Quen climbed up to the stage. "Raise your hands and step away from the ambassador!" He whipped out his brass pistol and pointed it at the Chaos male.

"Oh look, it's the Dark Warden! I've heard so much about you! I gotta say, gents, two against one is hardly fair. I need another Chaos on my team." His eyes found me. "And there she is. Remember me?" He waved with a cheery grin.

The few mortals and Wardens remaining in the room turned to me.

Great. Now they knew what I was, too.

"There are easier ways of getting my attention," I said.

"Like putting fake adverts in the Courier? Hosting a memorial and dangling ambassadors to lure innocent mortals into a trap?"

"Are you really trying to kidnap the Glimmer ambassador? That's a stupid idea. You could have picked an easier target like the Seren."

"What makes you think we haven't?"

Oh. Shit.

Jinx wasn't here. I hadn't seen her in this entire room.

I exchanged a glance with Quen, whose pearly face had paled. He'd likely come to the same conclusion I had.

The Chaos male was using himself as bait.

"Now, Ben!" Quen yelled.

A large net fell from the ballroom ceiling, descending upon the stage. The Chaos male didn't attempt to escape. He didn't even summon a shield. He just laughed with the maniacal disposition of a crazed Mesmer. As soon as the net touched him, he collapsed to the ground and spasmed as though he'd been zapped with a taser.

Oh gods. The entire netting was electrified with aether. What else had these damn Diviner been working on in the past few weeks?

"Secure the net," Quen ordered. He jumped down from the stage and strode to the nearest Warden. "Have all the ambassadors been accounted for?"

"We're still doing a head count, Your Excellency—"

"Keep counting. Assist the Glimmer and get Gloria covered up." Quen came over to me. "Do you have any idea who Jinx might target?"

"If not the Glimmer—"

"Reverie," Quen spluttered. "The Mesmer ambassador. She said to find her in the west corridor."

Why would Jinx target Reverie? She'd been inside the Mesmer temple... Had she been snooping on the ambassador and not there to torment me as I'd suspected?

I wasn't sure of the exact time, but it must be close to eleven—to Phantasy's crossing. Shit, shit, *shit*!

If I lost Phantasy—lost Mesmorpheus—then I lost the one advantage I had!

Quen bolted out of the room. I hoisted my skirt and chased after him, his guard and the Leander fast on our heels.

Our footsteps echoed down the corridor, and there, at the end under the light of an open bay window, stood Jinx and Reverie.

Jinx was wearing a much fancier red dress, with makeup and painted nails to match. In contrast, Reverie was a dark shadow, wrapped in a tight black dress. The two of them could have been on a date, if Jinx didn't look murderous, and Reverie didn't appear utterly uninterested in her own kidnapping.

"Everyone, stay back." Quen aimed his pistol at Jinx. "Let the ambassador go. We've already caught your companion."

Jinx sighed dramatically. "And? Am I supposed to care that my idiot brother got caught? Oh look, now my idiot sister has turned up."

"Give it up," I said. "You'll never make it to the Gate in those heels."

Jinx leered. "You're jealous that I've achieved more than you ever have. I could have taken the soul of every mortal in this damn building. And what about you, sister? Are you still scurrying around dark alleys in your pathetic attempts to save poor innocent mortal lives? Are these posh fuckers worth your efforts?"

"You're as bad as Karendar, judging which souls are worth saving."

"I never said any of them were worth saving." She pulled the Mesmer ambassador closer to her side.

"I'll warn you one last time," Quen said, his pistol cocked. "We can discuss this peacefully. Let Reverie go."

"Peacefully?" Jinx snorted. "Look, I'll cut you fuckers a deal. I want a soul. Any soul will do, I'm not fussed. Though..." Jinx turned to me. "If you give me the soul you're carrying, dear sister, I'll let this *innocent mortal* go. I know you're a bleeding heart like your precious Time Boy."

My heart raced.

Of course Jinx would set this up. She wanted a god's soul, and I just happened to have Valeria's soul buried deep inside me. If I gave it up, then Corentine would use Valeria's power to break the chains of her imprisonment. True, she needed all twelve souls of the gods to free herself entirely, but each soul would extend her reach to terrorize Chime's citizens.

But if I didn't, then Jinx could simply take Reverie, force her way into Phantasy, and then steal Mesmorpheus's soul, and I couldn't risk that either.

Without Mesmorpheus's help, and their temple to hide in, we Godless would be fucked.

Quen caught my eye. He gave me a subtle nod.

Really? He *wanted* me to give up Valeria's soul and damn the city?

No, he likely had some clever plan, because that was Quen. Too clever for his own eyeglasses.

And despite everything, I *did* trust him.

I trusted him with my soul.

"Fine," I said. "Let the Mesmer go and take me."

"Tell your Time Boy to toss me his pistol first."

"A trade for a trade," Quen said.

"You first."

Quen tossed his pistol at Jinx. She snatched it from the air and smirked. That smirk meant trouble, but to my great surprise she nudged Reverie forward.

"Come, sister." Jinx pointed the pistol at Reverie's back.

I staggered forward, suddenly unsteady on my feet as Quen, his guard, the Leander, and a whole bunch of pissing Wardens watched my every step.

As I reached Reverie, Jinx took aim at Quen.

I shoved Reverie aside and dove for the pistol.

The shot fired, but I managed to knock her aim. The bullet blasted through the bay window, smashing the glass.

I grabbed Jinx's wrist and tried to wrestle the pistol free. Static writhed from her skin, but it didn't hurt—it tickled.

My own skin had changed from Diviner silver to my glorious chaotic blue, right in front of a watching audience.

"Get off me!" Jinx snarled.

I dug my nails into her wrist. She yelped, dropping the pistol.

I caught it in one hand and swung the barrel in her direction. She may have the brains, but I had the brawn. "Who's the idiot now?"

Jinx frantically searched behind her as Quen, his guard, and the Leander advanced.

Quen raised his hands in a placating gesture. "Give yourself up to the Wardens, and I promise you won't be harmed."

"You're full of shit!" Jinx yelled. "And you, you bitch—" She pointed a damning finger at me. "You think you can trust a Diviner? They'll do to you what they did to our mother—lock her in a tower and say it's for the greater good! When Dor sends your fucking arse back into the aether, don't blame me!"

She leaped out the bay window.

I aimed with my pistol, but she was gone.

"Blast it!" Quen ran for the window and leaned outside. "Search the grounds!" he ordered the Wardens, and they ran out of the corridor.

"Should I have shot her?"

"No. It doesn't matter. She'll be long gone soon." He took his pistol back and holstered it before walking over to Reverie. "Are you hurt, my lady?"

Reverie tilted her head, confused by the question.

"I say, that was rather dramatic, old sport," the Leander said. He, too, was peering out the shattered window. "This isn't a ball I'll forget in a hurry."

Quen patted him on the shoulder with a grimace. "I'd appreciate it if you could help with the cleanup."

"So long as there's a drink in it for afters. Can't keep an old cat dry." The Leander gestured for the few remaining stragglers to follow him, and the corridor emptied out.

"Well?" I asked Quen. "Was this your plan? Bait Jinx into attempted kidnapping?"

Quen gave me a shrewd look. "An elaborate scheme to reveal Chaos to the eleven domains? It went rather well, don't you think?"

"And me risking my soul? Was that part of your grand plan?"

"I knew you could handle yourself. Besides, if I'd stepped in to save you, you'd only accuse me of being chivalrous. With the small audience we gathered, at least two ambassadors know you're fighting on their side."

I was going to kick his shin! "Jinx escaped, so I'd say your plan didn't work."

"That was unfortunate, but Chaos's numbers dwindle."

"What do you plan to do with the male?"

"He'll be heading to Warden HQ. I'll keep my word—he won't be harmed, only questioned. I want him off Chime's streets, but I don't want him dead."

"Are you sure? You know how Karendar worked—"

"I'm *not* Elijah." He bristled. "As head of the Warden Council I'll say again: he won't be harmed."

I lifted my Diviner mask and straightened my hair. This wasn't how I'd expected the night to go. "You really want to help Chaos? When Chaos would sooner see you dead?"

"I'm the Dark Warden. I'm used to advocating for mortals who would sooner see me dead." Quen glanced down the corridor at a group of Diviner who did not look pleased. "I've got battles ahead of me. I can't face them alone."

Reverie came to my side and placed a hand on my shoulder. "We have seen where your path leads," she whispered. "You must take it."

"No offense," I whispered back, "but the last time I listened to a Mesmer's vision, Chaos almost destroyed Chime."

"Chaos will succeed if you don't." She patted my shoulder and casually stepped over broken glass on her way out.

Bloody Mesmer and their bloody visions. Mesmorpheus had likely seen this coming. They'd seen what part I'd play.

Fate, destiny, a timeline set in stone; whatever you'd call it, I didn't appreciate cosmic forces pulling my strings.

IF YOU MARCH TO TIME'S BEAT, TIME WILL SPIT YOU OUT.

Time rules the universe. What choice do mortals have?

CHAOS ALSO RULES THE UNIVERSE. BOTH FORCES EXIST IN BALANCE.

So what happens if Dor wins? If he destroys Chaos? Besides ending my woeful existence, I mean.

WITHOUT CHAOS, THERE IS NO SPARK IN MORTALS. THERE IS NO VARIANCE. NO CHANGE. NO FREE WILL. WITHOUT CHAOS, EVERYTHING WOULD BE THE SAME. YOU WOULD BE A HUSK.

Wait, what? *Mortals have free will because of Chaos?*

MORTALS ARE NOT PUPPETS. THE GODS MAY OWN THEIR BODIES, THEIR MINDS, THEIR SOULS, BUT NEVER THEIR HEARTS. THAT IS THE REALM OF CHAOS.

Shit. If Dor ended Chaos, then what would become of mortals?

They'd become husks, as Corentine described? Puppets?

I couldn't stomach the thought!

THE GODS SEE FREE WILL AS SIN. DOR WOULD DESTROY IT.

The gods had always rallied against sin—the Diviner and Glimmer especially so. Was that why? Eradicate sin, make it a crime written in the Covenant, in order to control their mortals better? Shit. It made a twisted sort of sense. *Then help me stop this!*

YOU WOULD BECOME MY VOICE, DAUGHTER? YOU WOULD SPEAK FOR ME?

What would it even mean, to become the voice of Chaos? To advocate for it?

Before, I'd not wanted any part of it. Chaos wanted to destroy the domains. I quite enjoyed keeping my mortal friends alive.

But knowing Chaos played such a vital part in the making of the universe, knowing I would be advocating for mortal free will...

That was what we Godless did.

Quen wanted me to meet with the gods. Perhaps I could advocate for mortal lives along the way. Try to use whatever influence I had to make a difference, as Quen had put it.

I wasn't achieving anything by handing out fliers. But this... I could do so much. *If I become your voice, it's to save Chaos and mortal lives—I'll have no part in stealing souls and destroying domains. And Jinx needs to stop trying to kill everyone.*

I CANNOT CONTROL YOUR SISTER'S WILL—

Neither can you control mine. There had to be a positive side to Chaos. A less destructive side. I'd been born without the urge to murder and destroy, and I was pretty sure that didn't make me an abnormality.

CHAOS HAS MADE YOU AS YOU ARE, MY DAUGHTER. TRAPPED AS I AM, I CANNOT REACH THE OTHER GODS. I CANNOT BARGAIN WITH THEM. I AM MUTED. YOU WOULD SPEAK FOR ME?

For Chime, I would. *Make me your voice.*

THEN MY WILL SHALL BE YOUR WILL.

Laughter echoed in my mind, though I didn't feel any different.

I was going to regret this, wasn't I?

"So you're saying you need a partner," I finally said aloud.

Quen turned to me, startled out of his own thoughts. "Pray to Corentine and ask—"

"We've already spoken. But before I agree, do I get a sexy bodyguard? They've got to be tall and slightly mysterious."

He cleared his throat, though the action didn't hide his amusement. "I can assign you one of our Wardens. However, they'd need to know your exact location at all times, and I can't guarantee their attractiveness, height, or dark past."

Which would mean divulging the Godless hideout. That, I couldn't risk. "Drat. I'll have to find someone plain, short, and with a heart of gold."

"Good luck finding them in Chime." He held out his hand, and that sly smile of his made my stomach flutter. "Partners?"

I took his hand, my silvery-blue skin changing to a less conspicuous Diviner shade. "With some caveats."

"I wouldn't expect any less."

Gods. What nonsense had I gotten myself into now?

X

Ah, Kronos. Home of the Diviner. It would be biased of me to describe Kronos in flattering terms, but of course, Kronos is the birthplace of modern society. If one wishes to see the future, one need only pay a visit. However, I must caution guests from other domains. We Diviner have strict ordinances regarding public behavior. For one, queuing is rigidly adhered to. All appointments must also be diligently kept. There is nothing more offensive to a Diviner than wasting their time.
—Q. Corinth, *Warden Dossier on Kronos*

BY THE TIME I'D changed out of my red-stained shirt and settled the Chaos male into his new 'room' at Warden HQ, the clock had struck midnight.

Ben and I caught a carriage and rushed to Central Station in time for the crossing. The wondrous thing about acting as ambassador was that I received priority for all crossings. My fellow Diviner were forced to wait on my tardiness.

Splendid.

The midnight crossing was always an odd one. Diviner kept a rigid schedule, but that meant the midnight crossing was part of our routine. So many of us entertained late nights, surviving on as little as five hours of sleep per day. It was no wonder coffee had replaced tea as our domain's drink of choice. Terrible, really.

As I'd predicted, the main station of Kronos was busy with those traveling to and from Chime. At this time of night, the majority of mortals who filled the station were Diviner, as non-Diviner preferred the midday crossing, not that we received many visitors from other domains.

Kronos was either a marvel or a nightmarish labyrinth, depending on one's perspective.

The entire station was built from monochrome metal, glass windows, and brass furnishings. One could see the sky beyond the glass, and the towering skyscrapers that made up Kronos's main city. Not a single dot of dirt graced the station, and metal benches were placed neatly throughout. The station was so clean, even the oil and soot from the trains smelled like bleach and other cleaning products.

Above the station, a giant clockface counted down to quarter-past the hour.

I didn't want to stay here overnight, if I could help it.

"The train's in, sir." Ben pointed down the platform. He'd since changed into his Warden uniform. A shame. He looked far more intimidating when dressed up.

"We'd best catch it, then."

We strode down the platform leading to a sleek black steam train. These beauties were more monolithic beast than transport, and were twice the size of the trams back on Chime. They were one of the best reasons to return to my domain.

Steam already hissed from the top, its engine humming and raring to go as we climbed aboard.

And that was the other benefit of being ambassador; the luxury coach.

I collapsed into my plush leather seat as Ben sat across the table, opposite me.

The coach's interior was decorated like one's living room, with cushioned seating, cream wallpaper and carpet, silk curtains across the windows, and aether lamps glowing with a soft golden hue. Antique furniture filled the carriage, including a reading nook and a desk, and an antique clock between two abstract paintings of symmetrical lines—nonsense to an outsider, but they were an artistic rendition of Kronos's train lines. No expense had been spared on the wood and brass furnishings, and even the ceiling had been painted with a gray swirl of Kronos's skies.

It was cozy, certainly. And all this extravagance was for me, for this coach was the ambassador's private space.

Well, it wasn't *quite* for me.

A piano sat in the corner beside a small bar. I could have helped myself to a whiskey, but I didn't want to go anywhere near that piano.

This entire carriage had been decorated per the last ambassador's request.

The door to our coach compartment opened, and a well-dressed Umber server stepped inside—one of the few domains who sought contracts in Kronos, and who could put up with our demands. "Good evening, Your Excellency. Would you care for coffee?"

I'd rather choke on my own vomit. "No, thank you. Ben?"

"I'll take one, sir."

The server nodded and stepped back out.

"You're not one of those coffee-drinking heathens?" I asked.

"It keeps me sharp, sir."

"There's plenty of caffeine in tea." I opened the curtains covering my window. Movement caught my eye. Pendula was boarding the train and riding with us. Likely following me. No doubt she'd report on our *successful* charity ball.

With a toot and a whistle, we began moving.

This train went to one destination only. The home of our Father.

As we pulled out of the station, the glass panes were filled with the city skyline. Everything remained in perfect order. The lines of each street were symmetrical. The height of each skyscraper stood exactly the same. Each building was a minimalist tower of bronze metal and glass panes.

Therein lay the problem of navigating Kronos as an outsider. It all looked alike.

There were no plants. No flowers. The trees were copper wiring bent in the shape of branches. The leaves were cogs and gears that had the potential to clink and sing like chimes, except Kronos had no weather. No wind, no rain, nothing except for the constant moody sky.

Birds and butterflies made from minuscule clockwork parts were the only life, but they too followed predictable patterns that could be programmed.

Metal benches were placed where logical. We passed a water fountain built around an abstract construct made from levers, gears, and cogs, and above that, a giant metal clock that would click and whir, and bellow on the hour. That was where Kronos's beauty lay. In the symmetrical. In logic and order. In shining brass and clockwork hearts.

I'd revered this place as a child, before I'd first stepped into Chime and was romanced by its brickwork, by a chaotic mess of twelve domains attempting to eke out a living. By streets that curved and buildings that stood at odd angles. By plants and flowers that gave off scents other than iron and oil. By litter that fluttered in the gutters.

No one saw it as I did.

No one saw the beauty in Chime's flaws.

They saw only chaos.

Perhaps I'd always been destined for the ambassador's tabard, to be the city's greatest advocate. Whenever I returned to Kronos, the experience numbed me.

Though now, as the giant clock tower came into view, that numbing turned into anxious pinpricks along my skin.

"Magnificent, isn't it, sir?" Ben said, gazing out of the window.

Magnificent was too small of a word to describe Dor's home.

The clock tower rivaled Chime's in size and scope. As the largest building in Kronos, it towered above the skyline, the clockface visible from any angle, even at night. Its interior was more that of an office block, with rooms and meeting halls, and the ambassador's private office near the top, which I rarely stepped in.

And behind the clockface, hidden as Corentine was, lay Dor's realm.

The way it watched over everything unnerved me.

"If I may, sir," Ben began as he sipped at his coffee. "Was it wise to reveal Chaos's existence at the ambassadors' ball?"

Anger rose in my gut at the insinuation of incompetence and betrayal. "If I wanted your opinion, I'd ask for it."

Ben winced. "Yes, sir. Sorry, sir."

I swallowed a sigh. I *did* value Ben's opinion, and by snapping him, I was acting like a prat. I was acting like Elijah. "I appreciate your concern, but I know what I'm doing."

"It's my job to ensure your safety, sir, even against mortals who may appear friendly."

"For pity's sake, Kayl is no threat to me. Though if she decides to murder me, it's likely for good reason."

"Of course, sir." He returned to his drink.

Our god wanted Chaos hidden from the other domains, but chances were, the other gods were aware of Corentine's existence and awakening. They were gods, after all. By hiding Chaos, we only created distance between ourselves.

If I was to enact my plan, I needed to unite the domains.

I needed to disobey my Father's will.

My view turned pitch black. The steam train sped into a tunnel that connected with a private docking station within the bottom layer of the clock tower. Steam blew past my window, obscuring the faces of the station staff as the train came to a screeching halt.

Ben finished off his coffee and stood. "I'll escort you, sir."

I nodded, my mouth dry.

The station staff welcomed my entrance onto the platform with reverent bows. I wasn't yet used to this level of attention, but acting as ambassador meant following certain rituals and rites. To brush them off would be deemed an insult. I nodded cordially on my way to the plaza. Each step dragged heavier than the last.

It wasn't exhaustion that clung to my bones.

Dor's clock tower was part holy sanctuary, part business center, for it served as the hub of Kronos and all Diviner activity. Its inner plaza was a large, open space in the shape of a cog. Multiple elevators ran up the walls, leading to various offices, prayer rooms, and reflection chambers where one could confess one's sins—and pay for them. One could also purchase holy trinkets—sanctified cogs and clocks. Personally, I found them tacky, but I supposed religion was its own kind of business.

It was here in this clock tower that I had been born. Created in Dor's image.

Twice, now.

Mortals waited for the elevators in evenly spaced queues. Unlike Chime, queuing was an artform here, and they moved with the precision of a clock, each step in sync with the ticks and tocks reverberating from above.

My destination was the elevator at the very back. The only one without a queue.

Ben hit the button, saving me the indignity of having to steady my hands, and I instead shoved them into my pockets, searching for comfort that no longer existed.

Had Elijah ridden this elevator with dread in his heart?

Had he ever had a reason to fear it?

I entered the elevator with as much confidence as I could muster. We went up and up, and the speed of it stole my breath. And then the elevator jolted with a *ping*, and those double doors opened wide onto a nondescript hall.

"I'll wait for you, sir." Ben tried his best to give me a blank look, but he couldn't mask the sympathy in his expression.

He knew more than he ever let on.

"Thank you," I croaked.

I forced myself not to stare at the two constructs guarding the large double doors at the end.

They were beings made of pure brass. They stood like mortals did, with limbs and a rib cage made from metal, though much taller than any Diviner, even Big Ben. Their movement was made possible due to an intricate set of gears and pulleys that acted like muscles.

Their heads were made from the inner parts of a clock, and they ticked and tocked as a clock would. No eyes, no nose or mouth. No face at all. Nothing except a literal clock face.

They were called the *Divine Instruments of Dor*, His immortal servants, but most of us referred to them as the Guardians.

The two clockwork Guardians turned their heads at my approach, their bodies clicking and whirring with every movement. I didn't know how they could even sense me, yet they did. They opened the double doors, letting out blinding light.

I cringed at the harshness and willed myself inside, one step at a time.

The doors behind me vanished, and I stood in white space.

No. I stood in the palm of His hand.

Clocks of all makes and models hung in the air around me, chiming in and out of time as they had done when my Father had so ceremoniously pulled me from the aether and wrapped my soul in the flesh and bones of a mortal body.

The clanging bells, cuckoos, and ticks and tocks took on a harsh tone, chiding me with their deafening racket. I winced as I followed the line of my Father's palm and approached the center.

There, above me, floated Dor's form. A naked older man, hidden behind the long white beard that fell into eternity. His expression held no hint of joy or displeasure.

A searing pain cut through my head.

I cried out and sank to my knees. The pressure crushed my skull with unbearable agony. I gripped my head to stop it, somehow, but it only squeezed the breath from me. "Father, *please*!" I ground out.

YOU DISPLEASE ME, QUENTIN.

The pain relaxed with a lingering throb. I fell onto my hands with a gasp. Tears ran down my cheeks. I wiped them clear.

Blood stained my fingers. Those weren't tears.

YOU REVEALED CHAOS TO THE DOMAINS AGAINST MY WILL. Dor's voice thundered through this realm, though He didn't move an inch. The clanging clocks hushed as though curious what fate awaited me.

I forced myself to stand, though my legs shook with the effort. "They would have learned of Chaos regardless. Only now we can control the situation."

WHAT CONTROL? I GAVE YOU A TASK YOU HAVE FAILED TO COMPLETE.

This was a test—to convince Him of my path.

"I need more time!"

A MONTH IS SUFFICIENT.

"I've made strides, Father. We've designed sensor technology and proven it efficient in detecting Chaos and protecting the Gate. We're also developing collars that can cut off a domain's power, even Chaos—"

CHAOS HAS ESCAPED YOUR HAND.

"We caught one. A male. The rest are trapped inside the clock tower, as planned. With our reinforcements and the Gate's rotation, they cannot hope to escape."

WHY WAS THIS MALE NOT BROUGHT TO KRONOS FOR DISSECTION?

Because cutting him open wouldn't reveal any answers. Though I did find it suspicious that he'd surrendered so easily. "For your protection, Father. We cannot risk bringing Chaos into Kronos."

AND CORENTINE'S DAUGHTERS?

I swallowed thick saliva. This was the moment of truth.

I either won this battle, or I said goodbye to my soul.

And I hadn't even gotten a chance to dance.

Saints, I'd wanted one dance. Just one.

"I have a plan for Chaos, if you'll listen, Father."

I SEE YOUR PLAN. YOU WOULD OFFER CHAOS ITS FREEDOM WHEN I HAVE ORDERED ITS OBLITERATION.

"Chaos doesn't need to be destroyed. We can coexist—"

WE CAN NEVER COEXIST SO LONG AS CORENTINE PLOTS OUR DESTRUCTION.

"She's willing to negotiate with us! To join us on the Warden Council—"

CHAOS HAS NO PLACE ON THE COUNCIL. THEY CANNOT BE REASONED WITH. IT IS LOGICAL TO DESTROY THEM. WHY DO YOU FAIL TO SEE THIS?

"You designed me to experience emotion, Father. To use those gifts to understand and negotiate with Chaos. Let me."

YOU ARE MY VOICE, YET YOU DO NOT SPEAK WITH MY WORDS.

"As your voice, I represent mortals, too! What comes after Chaos? You told me yourself Chime is powered by Corentine's energy. With her gone, a void must be filled. My plan is to unite the domains so the gods give their fair share as they are meant to."

THE GODS AND THEIR DOMAINS SQUABBLE. HOW WOULD YOU UNITE THEM?

"With the threat of Chaos."

It was brilliant, really. By dangling Kayl in front of each god, they'd be faced with their own mortality and forced to concede their power in order to keep Chaos at bay. Doing so would ensure Chime's balance. It would put a halt to domain infighting and thus stabilize the domains and their influence on Chime, which would in turn improve mortal lives.

And the gods wouldn't say no to gaining a slice of Chime for themselves.

"And you, Father, would be at the head of this." Because once the gods conceded to Chaos, it would be the Diviner who delivered their safety— who ended the threat of Chaos—and the domains would be united under time's rule. "All I ask is that when we remove Corentine from Chime, we give her children a fair chance. A fresh start."

HOW CAN I TRUST YOU WITH THIS TASK WHEN YOU WOULD ALIGN WITH CHAOS?

"Not align. Chaos is a tool, a means to an end—"

YOUR AFFECTION FOR HER DAUGHTERS BLINDS YOU. I SEE THE TAINT OF YOUR THOUGHTS.

My cheeks burned. "You built me this way, Father. You built me to sin—"

I TEST YOU, AND YOU FAIL ME TIME AND TIME AGAIN—

"I'm willing to do what must be done to save Chime! Even if that means debasing myself and dallying with sin. Isn't that the reason I exist? To do what no other Diviner can?" I knew my soul was tainted, and that taint could never be washed away. But even Dor had admitted I had been designed with a weakness for sin in order to infiltrate the sinners of Chime. Surely that granted me a little leeway?

YOU SPEAK OF SIN AS A NOBLE SACRIFICE, YET YOU ENJOY ITS PERVERSION. IF YOU CANNOT GUARD AGAINST SIN, THEN

HOW WILL YOU GUARD AGAINST CHAOS? ELIJAH WAS MEANT TO CORRECT YOUR DEVIANT BEHAVIOR.

The mention of Elijah's name shuddered through me. "Corentine's daughters mean nothing to me. But you ordered me to befriend them, to infiltrate Chaos, and that is what I've done."

WOULD YOU CONDEMN THEM?

My heart skipped a beat. "In your name, Father."

Silence hung around me, squeezing my ribs until I was sure I'd burst.

Throwing myself to His palm and pleading wouldn't help my cause.

One couldn't plead with a god of logic.

IF YOU CAN UNITE THE DOMAINS UNDER MY NAME, I WILL GRANT YOUR REQUEST.

My breath came out in one large exhale. "Thank you—"

I GIVE YOU ONE WEEK.

A *week*? That wasn't enough time!

YOU HAVE WASTED ENOUGH TIME, QUENTIN. IF YOU BELIEVE THIS IMPOSSIBLE TASK IS POSSIBLE, THEN YOU WILL ACHIEVE IT, WITH ONE CAVEAT; CORENTINE WILL BE DESTROYED. SHOULD ANY OF HER CHILDREN REFUSE MY RULE, THEY TOO WILL MEET THEIR END.

I had to take it. I had no choice.

Once I may have bitten back and raged against the burden placed on me, but since returning to my mortal form, so many things had become clear.

Only I could protect the sinners and heathens of the domains. The poorest. The souls no one cared for.

Only I could save Chaos.

If I stood any chance, then I couldn't risk angering my god. I couldn't risk failure. "I won't let you down, Father."

YOU WILL REPORT TO ME DAILY. YOU WILL CONFESS AND REPENT YOUR SINS. IN THIS ENDEAVOR, YOU WILL ACCEPT PENDULA BEZEL AS YOUR ASSISTANT.

What? "I don't need an assistant—"

THIS IS NOT NEGOTIABLE. I GIFT HER TO YOU. SHE WILL ASSIST YOU IN YOUR DUTIES AS YOU SERVE ME.

"Very well, Father." If Pendula could handle my paperwork, then I supposed she wouldn't get under my feet. But with Ben following my every step, and now Pendula breathing down my neck, I couldn't help but feel I was being set up for failure.

DO NOT DISAPPOINT ME FURTHER.

With that command, the various clocks chirped back to life once more, and the double doors leading back to the clock tower reappeared behind me. I swooped into a low bow, my forehead almost scraping His palm, and then I strode for the doors as quickly as politeness could dictate, my heart hammering with each step.

Once I stepped into the hall, the Guardians closed the doors behind me, and I took a few shaky steps toward the elevator, where Ben waited for me.

"You okay, sir?" He pointed to my shirt. "You've, uh, got blood on you."

Tiny droplets from my own tears stained my shirt. Blast! Two shirts ruined in one day. This was becoming an expensive habit. "Yes, thank you."

"Will we be remaining in Kronos, sir? The Gate closes in half an hour."

Saints. That meeting had felt like a lifetime, yet only a moment had passed. I was well aware of the time, and of the pressure to get moving before the Gate closed.

So much pressure strained my shoulders.

It would be easy, wouldn't it? To obey my god's commands and absolve my conscience of the consequences. To put on a public face and then sin behind closed doors, following in Elijah's footsteps. Had damning souls bothered him at all?

Had he suffered with the weight of it as I did?

Or was it mere bureaucracy?

Under the Dark Warden's moniker, I'd taken lives. How many would Ambassador Corinth sacrifice before the week was out?

A week. One sodding week to unite the domains and save Chaos.

To save *her*.

Could I do it?

More to the point, could Kayl do it?

I wouldn't burden her with this truth. I couldn't.

Even with my memories restored, I lived a life of lies. To her. To my Father. To myself, thinking this foolish endeavor would be possible.

I knew where it led; to the destruction of my very soul.

By the end, I may even earn the death coming for me.

"We'll head back to Chime. We've got a difficult week ahead of us."

"We can get tea on the way, sir."

"I think I'll go for coffee."

This next week was going to throw worse things at me than coffee, and as disgusting as it was, I had the feeling I was going to need a cup or two.

PART TWO

11

Where are the Vesper?
The Wardens will tell you Valeria recalled them.
Ask yourself why.
The Glimmer will say their sinning caused this, but Rapture is still open.
What truths are the Wardens keeping from you?
—Anonymous, *Godless flier on the Vesper*

THE NOTE SHOOK IN my hand.

"Shit!" Malk exclaimed. He dug through the satchel that had mysteriously appeared on the depot's doorstep. "There's bocs in here. Hundreds of bocs. I'm not even joking! What does the note say? Kay—"

I was already running out the door.

Malk hadn't seen anyone drop it off, but who would come all the way to Grayford and dump a pile of bocs into our laps?

It had to be a setup. Some bizarre trap the Wardens were pulling to identify known sinners and draw us out. They knew Malk and I were apostates, or someone in Grayford had tipped them off. It didn't make sense otherwise.

"Chime needs godless heathens. May the gods leave you to your fate."

The Wardens had never been this subtle.

My feet pounded in time with my heart as I ran along the abandoned train tracks, skipping over piles of discarded gears and other contraptions. With my keen Vesper eyes, I hoped to catch a glimpse of our apparent mystery benefactor.

Something snagged my skirt behind me. I fell over my own arse as it ripped free.

"Shit!"

Hands caught me before I collided with the ground. With the amount of sharp piping and metal shards scattered around the yard, I could well have lost an eye.

I steadied myself and turned, expecting Malk.

But it wasn't a Vesper holding me.

It was a Diviner. Gods. Not just any Diviner. I *knew* him.

"Careful now." He released his hands from my waist. "It's dangerous to run along these tracks."

I staggered back, completely stunned out of my wits. "You're the man of my dreams!"

His silver eyes sparkled over the rim of his eyeglasses. "Am I?"

"*From* my dreams." I swished my skirt behind me, attempting to hide the awkward gash running down it. "How—why are you here?"

"No real reason. I happened to be in the right place at the wrong time." He pulled a watch from his waistcoat pocket—I recognized that damn thing, too. "Time is linear, and yet traversing it can be somewhat unpredictable."

"Who are you? You're not a Warden." I waved the strange note in his face. "Is this yours? Are you stalking me? Why?"

He peered at the note with restrained amusement. "As I explained, time is linear. Unfortunately, I'm getting my paths crossed."

"You're making no sense!" Whoever this damn Diviner was, he was gods-damn infuriating. "What do you want with me?"

"With you? Nothing. I'm searching for someone like you. In approximately five years, two months, three weeks, and to the hour, you're going to wake up and remember who I am. You're going to wonder if this is all a dream. Do you want to know a secret?" He leaned close, and the hairs on my neck stood on end. "I'm your part—"

WAKE UP!

I jolted awake. My heart was pounding. That was Quen! How was he invading my past? That was the day the Godless formed, but he hadn't been part of my memories?

YOU DREAMED, Corentine said.

A dream. Gods. Just a dream. It couldn't have been anything else, could it?

Corentine had practically screamed in my head, and her voice still rang in my ears. *What the fuck is your problem?*

YOU ARE MY VOICE. YOU CANNOT SPEAK FOR ME IF YOU SLEEP.

I'm a mortal, I need my pissing sleep!

YOU SHOULD HAVE CONSIDERED THAT BEFORE BECOMING MY VOICE.

So that was how Corentine was going to play it—invade my head and annoy the shit out of me until I gave up or killed myself? Too bad! No one could out-stubborn me, as Quen had said. *If we're going to work together and save Chaos, then you need to be nice to me. Otherwise, I'll tell the rest of the ambassadors that you eat arse.*

NO OTHER GOD PUTS UP WITH SUCH DISRESPECTFUL BEHAVIOR FROM THEIR MORTALS!

No other god has such limited choices. Be grateful I'm willing to help you at all.

WHEN I AM FREE, I WILL SMITE YOU FIRST.

What, when you're so busy eating arse?

YOU LITTLE SHIT.

I honestly expected her to smite me from afar, if her powers could do so, but Corentine's laughter echoed in my mind. These next few weeks were going to be the death of me, weren't they?

"Kayl? Are you listening?" Harmony snapped.

Oh shit!

I wasn't tucked in my bed, but sitting in a meeting after coming straight from the embassy ball. The dim lights of these bloody rooms made it so easy to slip into sleep. I sat up and wiped drool from my mouth. "Sorry, I drifted off for a moment there."

"Can you at least try to focus? Especially when this meeting is about *you* and your poor life choices?"

"They're not really choices when I don't *have* a choice," I mumbled.

Sinder snorted. "She's exhausted from all that dancing, dearest." He leaned on his chin and blinked long eyelashes at me. "So what was it like? Who did you dance with? Step on any toes? I promise not to kiss and tell."

"You know I actually went there to play spy. I didn't dance with anyone." Much to my dismay. There'd been so many extravagant dresses and mortals covered in expensive jewelry. The whole thing had been very fancy, and I'd half regretted not turning up in that tight purple ensemble to see who'd like to put their hands on my hips.

And to see which ambassadors would have fainted from the scandal.

"No? Not even with Erosain? He has quite the arse."

"Ugh, I'd sooner dance with Dru—"

"Hey!" Dru said.

"Can we not?" Harmony scowled.

"It's getting late," Vincent said. "We could host this meeting tomorrow?"

"No, we're doing this now."

Dru yawned. "Can we just get it over with?"

"Right, fine." I poured myself a glass of lemonade and shuddered at the sour tang. "Quen was there, and I agreed to become ambassador for Chaos."

"You agreed to *what*?" Harmony screeched.

"Chaos needs an ambassador to represent it, apparently, and I volunteered. I thought you'd be happy."

"Why in god's name would I be *happy*?"

"Because I've given you a gift—"

"A gift!" She almost fell off her chair in hysterics. "A gift is a new purse or a bottle of red wine or a box of damn chocolates—"

"On my new salary, I may be able to afford them."

"Your *salary*?" Her wing was quivering so much, I expected it to detach.

"Don't knock it, Harm." Sinder tutted. "I for one am proud of Kayl for climbing the social ladder and reaching heights the likes of which the rest of us can only dream of. And I'd love a new purse. In black, if you can, darling." He winked at me.

"Does Corinth seriously want you to act as an ambassador?" Dru asked. "He hasn't forgotten who you are, right?"

I elbowed her.

"Forgive me," Vincent asked, "but what does becoming an ambassador entail?"

"Yes, thank you for bringing us back on track." Harmony's scowl returned to me. "What exactly happened at that ball?"

In truth, I didn't know what it meant to be an ambassador yet—and whether I'd actually be entitled to a salary, though it was only fair—but I explained the events of the evening: confirming that Quen was indeed Quen, our encounter with Jinx and the other Chaos male, and Quen's plan to save the domains by having a lovely chat with the remaining gods.

Harmony was rubbing her forehead by the end of it. "Ignoring the fact that a masquerade using masks appropriated from the domains is *grossly* offensive—you've both lost your damn minds."

"I didn't choose my mask, for the record."

"You're really willing to cozy up with the gods?" Sinder asked, his nose twisted in distaste. "That's not our style, dearest."

"No, but playing a manipulative bitch is *my* style," I said. "I have the power to bring the gods down to my level. Quen wants me to convince them to play nice, and I can, with some caveats. I can use this to help mortals. Think of the possibilities, of the intel I can gain by not only working as ambassador, but by manipulating the gods to our whims!"

Harmony shook her head. "This is too big. You're not ready for this—"

"I can do more than hand out bloody fliers! I know how to charm." It was one of the only things I was good at. "And Corentine needs a voice. Quen is willing to offer her, and by extension me, a place on the Warden Council. Do you know what that means? I could be a voice for mortals! For Chime! I'm the only one who can do this. I won't blow it."

"You can barely stay awake in this meeting. How are you going to play ambassador?"

"That's not fair, Harm," Sinder said. "It's late."

Harmony waved him off. "You're going to offend the first god you meet and end up in pieces. These are *gods*. Divine beings with the power to snuff out a mortal life in a single blink. They're not some bumbling Warden you can toy with."

"So the worst that happens is they smite me—"

"Do you think I want that for you? For *any* of you?" Harmony stood on her chair and glared. "Do you think I want to lose another Reve? Another Malk? We're playing with forces beyond our control, and I can't protect you from that!"

Silence filled the room.

She's right. Malk's voice drifted in my mind.

No, she isn't. It hurt that she'd brought up Malk's name.

I knew the Godless thought me useless. I knew Harmony had been plagued with nightmares since she entered the temple—I heard her whimper in her sleep. And I knew I'd be doing this on my own, with no inner guide to steer me in the right direction, save my own personal madness and a literal mad god.

But Quen believed I could do this. That had to count for something.

"We've always played with forces beyond our control," I said slowly. "We're Godless. That's what we do."

"Maybe we shouldn't." Harmony deflated into her seat, and her lost expression made my heart ache. "Maybe we shouldn't fuck with things like soul-splitting machines, because look where it's left us. Begging for scraps in a gods-damn temple—"

"You see? We have nothing. Fliers aren't going to change Chime. The gods and their Wardens have always been the true power. By joining their ranks, think of what information I can glean, how many mortal lives we can save. The gods themselves will have no choice but to listen to what I have to say—"

"If you become voice to a god then, you're no longer Godless."

Harmony's words twisted in my gut.

She may as well have stabbed me.

Quen had said advocating for him would mean turning away from the Godless. I hadn't been sure what that meant at the time, but now it churned through my insides.

"You can't say that," Sinder protested. "We've all made sacrifices—"

"If she works for the gods, for the Wardens, then that puts the rest of us in danger—"

"Since when have we not been in danger?"

"We accepted that risk," Vincent said. "When we chose to become Godless. It was Kayl who began our organization, and Quentin Corinth who made us what we are. Without either of their support, we wouldn't be here today."

I chewed my lip. Thank the gods for Vincent.

"He's right, Harm," Dru said with a yawn. "Kayl brings trouble, but this is a new kind of trouble. High-class trouble with bells and whistles—"

"Yes, thank you, Dru," I said. "You all know I don't care for the gods. Of course I don't. And you know damn well I'll do whatever I can to undermine them. If you think I'm a danger, Harm, then I'll leave. I won't risk any of you. You're my—my family." I choked out the word as it lodged in my throat. "I won't turn my back on this. But I won't ever stop being Godless."

I stood to leave.

"Kayl, wait—"

I glanced back at Harmony.

Her eyes had reddened. "I haven't prayed in years, girl. But I pray you know what you're getting into, for all our sakes. This... changes everything. It changes who we are. We're no longer a group of heathens stumbling in the dark. I hate to say it... but this is your show now. You're going to need us."

My cheeks warmed. "I appreciate the thought—"And I did. Gods, I did—"but I don't think Quen's going to let me bring an entourage to the Council."

"You think an ambassador rules an entire domain and thousands of mortals alone? They'll have a team of advisors—"

"Chaos consists of me, my crazy twin sister, my other crazy brother who has now been incarcerated, and a bunch of other souls trapped in the clock tower. I think I'll manage."

"No, girl. You'll need intel. Information about the domains and their gods, how to address them, their strengths and weaknesses, and where to hit them hardest if we're going to truly make a difference. You can't wing this." She raised a brow at me. "Sifting through sources and information has been my job for years, so let me handle that, and don't you dare go crossing into the domains before I've briefed you."

I did recall Varen having such a team of advisors, and no doubt Quen had his own. Minders, he'd said. Harmony had seen more of the domains than I could ever claim. I'd be a fool to turn down her experience. "You're in. While on the subject, I need a bodyguard. Dru? You up for the job?"

Dru suddenly jerked up. "Are you serious?" She glanced around the table. "Is she serious?"

"I can be your bodyguard, darling," Sinder said with a slight purr.

While Sinder possessed the intimidating good looks and the power to burn my enemies to ash, I doubted he'd be able to restrain himself on a council with Glimmer. "I appreciate the offer, but you plus me would double the trouble."

Sinder fluttered his eyelashes. "That's true."

"So you want *me*?" Dru spluttered. "Why? You can take on the form of any domain. You don't need me to watch your back."

"Dru. I've always needed you to watch my back. Remember when I got groped on the Undercity elevator last year?" Some Vesper male had given my arse a good feel, which was par for the course on those cramped elevators. Dru had yanked the little shite off me.

"That was an accident. I didn't mean to dislocate their shoulder—"

"Why? They deserved it. But my point is, you're strong. You don't know your own strength sometimes. And you know I need protection from myself."

Dru sighed. "I know you do. You really want me to be your bodyguard looking like this?" She rubbed her fingers over the few sprouts budding on her brow and winced.

"That proves you're a battle-hardened wench. No one's going to mess with you." Having Dru by my side would make it easier to disguise myself in an Umber form when out and about. That, and I wanted her company. Sitting on the Council with a bunch of ambassadors sounded as pleasant as listening to a Glimmer sermon.

"Who's going to maintain the temple? Someone needs to clean up after the Mesmer."

"Didn't our new Glimmer volunteer?" Sinder said as he picked at his nails. "Let him do it."

"It's not his job to clean the temple," Dru said.

"We all have to pitch in, dearest, and that includes our new Glimmer. Getting him on his knees scrubbing floors may teach him a thing or two."

"I would like to lend my expertise to the Mesmer," Vincent said. "Many of them complain of toothaches and other ailments. Assisting them is the least I can do for the generosity they've granted us."

"Don't let them tire you out," Sinder warned.

Vincent smiled. "Thankfully, I'm in the right place for rest."

"Since we're all making ourselves useful, I'll stand guard at reception," Sinder said. "Someone needs to ensure we receive no more unexpected guests. And it'll keep me away from the rabble."

Harmony slapped her hands together. "Then we have a plan of sorts. May the gods leave us to our fate."

My stomach fluttered. A real plan of action, and I'd be leading it.

It was about now that Jinx would try and knock me down a peg or two. Say I'd fuck it up. But with her gone from my mind, I felt optimistic for once—

YOU'RE GOING TO FUCK THIS UP. IT SHALL BE AMUSING TO WITNESS.

Yes, thank you. Some things hadn't changed.

12

IT WAS MY FIRST attendance at the ambassador's Council, and I was running late.

The tram was on time, it was *me* that was the problem. Dru had practically dragged me out of bed, and I had little time to wash and get prepared for this damn meeting.

Quen waited outside the gates to Warden HQ, tapping his foot. "Do you know what time it is?" His voice rose slightly.

"As it happens, I don't."

The clock tower rang ten of the hour, putting me to shame.

"I dragged her here as quickly as I could," said Dru, who scowled at me.

I wrapped my arm around her shoulders. The pair of us wore Umber faces, my gray skin contrasting her green. "See? What would I do without you? Dru's agreed to be my bodyguard, if that's okay with you?" I asked Quen.

He rubbed his chin. "Typically, bodyguards serve their own domain, but there's no rule against who may serve whom. I do hope you'll keep Kayl on schedule, Miss Smith." Quen gestured to Ben, who stood at attention by the gates. "This is my bodyguard, Ben Seasons."

The pair of them sized each other up. Both stood at the same height as me, though Big Ben was a lot bulkier than Dru. He bent into a bow as Dru curtsied, and the two of them bumped heads.

I couldn't help but giggle. Dru had always been awkward around strangers, and it seemed Quen's guard was going to prove a great match.

"Come on," Quen said. "We're behind schedule." He strode through the gates and led us into Warden HQ.

I matched his stride as our guards trailed behind. "Where are we headed?" This was the second time I'd entered the Warden HQ willingly, and not as a prisoner being dragged to their correctional facility. It looked secure enough—I had to pass through five checkpoints to get here.

"The embassy. We'll convene in the Council chamber, which is attended by all twelve ambassadors. You'll be taking one of those seats."

"*Today?* You could have warned me." I suddenly felt woefully unprepared and inadequately dressed in a simple blouse and skirt. "Do ambassadors receive a salary?"

He gave me a sharp look. "Ambassadors are funded and supported by their own domain, not the Wardens."

Darn. I doubted Corentine had piles of bocs hidden inside the clock tower. "Since Chime is technically the domain of Chaos, surely I should be entitled to something?"

"I'll see what remains in Chime's coffers."

That was better than an outright no.

Compared to the dull gray buildings of Warden HQ, the embassy was an impressive brass cathedral that wouldn't look out of place within the Golden City. I'd heard from Varen that each ambassador had their own office inside, though most chose to operate from their own private residences. Varen had Grayford. Erosain owned Sinner's Row. Where did Quen work from?

Wardens stood on watch by the doors and saluted Quen. We entered brightly lit halls that were truly as gaudy as a Glimmer mansion. Ornate furnishings, decorative vases, and portraits of pompous-looking mortals in their finery guided our way.

"So are there any benefits to this gig?"

Quen beckoned me into a cloak room and gestured at one of the hooks. "You get a fancy tabard."

A silvery-blue tabard hung before me. The material appeared thick and cumbersome. I remembered how Varen was always wrestling with his purple tabard, and now I had to wear one. "Why must ambassadors wear these horrid things?"

"Tradition, mostly." Quen donned his own silver one and quickly tied the sides.

"Not all traditions are worth keeping."

"If you want to act the part, you must look the part."

Fine. I picked up the tabard, and my nail caught on the fuzzy fabric. Ugh. It reminded me of my old Vesper shawl. "How do I know this will even fit me?"

"I had you measured at Arcadia Apparel." Quen practically wiggled his eyebrows at me.

He'd been planning this for too long, so sure I'd agree to his mad schemes because I myself was mad and destined to go along with it.

This was payback for tying him to a chair in the depot all those weeks ago. "Do ambassadors at least get free drinks?"

"You know, the role of an ambassador is to serve their domain—"

"Having met an ambassador or two, I know they fiddle on the side."

He raised his brow in mock shock. "You wouldn't be thinking of fiddling now, would you?"

"Depends on what I'm fiddling." I threw the tabard over my head and fumbled with the fastenings.

Quen helped tie the knots. "As chair of the Warden Council, it's my duty to sniff out corruption within our ranks."

I bared my neck. "Then take a good sniff."

He leaned close, breathing me in. "Smells like trouble."

"Sir?" Ben said by the door. "The Council is ready."

Quen leaped back, his face pink. "Yes, quite." He cleared his throat. "We mustn't keep them waiting."

I bit my lip. What did trouble smell like, I wondered? Sinder's rose perfume, most likely.

"Before we step out, can you kindly change form?"

"To what? Diviner?"

"To yourself. To Chaos."

Gods. I didn't even know how to change form to Chaos. It just happened sometimes! "You want to terrify your Council so soon?"

"They'll need to know what you are if they're to accept you."

Right. Shit. *How do I change form into Chaos?*

WHY SHOULD I TEACH YOU?

Because you're my god and I'm your voice. Do you want to make the Council shit themselves or not?

YOU MUST UNDERSTAND HOW AETHER IS CONNECTED TO ALL LIVING BEINGS. THEN YOU CAN CHANGE FORM AT WILL.

Assume I never attended my classes on cosmic fuckery at Chime's Academy—

JINX UNDERSTANDS THIS.

Well, I'm not Jinx. And I couldn't pull off the fancy aether shields she seemed capable of, either. Though learning how to do it would be handy.

THEN WHAT USE ARE YOU?

Forget I asked. "I don't know how to change form, and Corentine apparently won't teach me." Switching back to my original Vesper was easy, since I could touch Valeria's power inside me. But returning to my original Chaos persona? I didn't have the foggiest.

"Oh. Well. We'll worry about it some other time. Take my form for now." Quen offered his hand. A heartbeat later, my skin morphed from Umber to Diviner, and my hair changed from vines to a natural silver. I released him at the tug in my palm.

Taking his soul would have looked bad on my first day.

Dru and Big Ben waited for us outside. Ben's expression was caught between forcing an innocent look and cringing on Quen's behalf. Dru rolled her eyes, as supportive as ever.

They followed Quen and me down one of the many *many* halls until we reached a set of double doors guarded by two Wardens.

"Ben, show Dru where the canteen is, please," Quen said. "Entertain yourselves."

"Yes, sir."

"They're not coming with us?" I asked.

"The Council is for ambassadors only. No Wardens. No guards. No outside godly interference. One thing before we enter—the Council has a strict hierarchy of who speaks first based on the times of the clock. As you'll be occupying Varen's old position, that puts you at the bottom, before the Mesmer."

Of course it did. "Shouldn't you be at the bottom as the twelfth?"

"The twelfth hour is the first, as is standard time procedure. That puts me as the head of the Council."

No wonder the Diviner were in charge of everything.

"Follow me, ma'am," Ben said to Dru. "They stock pebbles in the cafeteria."

"They do? Oh lovely!"

The two of them wandered down the hallway in awkward chatter.

I nudged Quen. "Don't they make a cute couple?"

"Are you playing matchmaker? Diviner and Umber are largely incompatible. Diviner are terrible at courtship, for one. It never works."

"Not with that attitude." Though Dru wasn't the dating type. In all the years I'd known her, she'd not once fluttered her eyelashes at anyone— male, female, or those in between. I liked to think of her as a work in progress.

Quen gestured to the door. "Shall we?"

"How much am I going to hate this?"

"Oh, only a lot. But I'll be suffering with you." He nodded to the Wardens, who opened the double doors.

I sucked in a breath and stepped into the wonderful world of politics.

Bright chandelier lights burned high within the large circular room, above a table designed like a clock. Each ambassador sat at their 'wedge' at the time designated to their domain, and each wedge had been painted with the landscape of their domain, same as the beautifully artistic crossing maps one found dotted around Central Station.

Eventide's wedge had been wiped clean, however. Painted white. Empty.

There were no windows. Only twelve individual doors around the room leading to little alcoves. Strange.

In the center of the clock table was a glass frame containing a pristine copy of the original signed Covenant. I was more interested in the tray of iced tea beside it.

The ambassadors stood as we made our entrance—a single mortal of each domain, except Eventide—and their stares landed on me.

Wow, did this suddenly feel like the worst place I could possibly be.

I recognized a few of their faces—Reverie, Erosain, the Leander and Zephyr from the other night, Gloria staring daggers—but most were complete strangers to me. They wore a glittering rainbow of tabards. A unique color for each domain.

Quen swept into a low bow. "My fellow ambassadors. I present to you Her Excellency, Ambassador Kayl Arkey. Voice to Corentine, the thirteenth god, ruler of Chaos."

Arkey? That, I hadn't been expecting. Corentine's name passed around the room like a frantic curse.

I forced a smile, but I didn't have a clue what to say. Did they expect a pissing speech?

Gods. This was why I needed Harmony. Despite all the etiquette I'd learned from Varen, and the days I'd observed him acting as ambassador to the Vesper, I couldn't remember anything for dealing with this scenario. It wasn't like he'd invited me to his secret ambassador meetings and tea parties and whatever else they got up to.

TELL THEM THEY SIT IN MY DOMAIN AND I WILL DESTROY THEM.

That's not a great conversation opener.

"What is this farce?" Gloria said. Of course it would be the Glimmer who spoke first. "You would invite Chaos into this chamber? When it was Chaos who made a mockery of me and ruined my masquerade? When it was Chaos who attacked Chime? Yes, Gildola understands the measure of Chaos—Dor has been withholding the truth!"

"Is this true?" asked the Amnae ambassador. His translucent scales were blue, with a single black stripe across his head, though his fins were a bright yellow. The Memoria wedge of the table had its own water pitcher. "A thirteenth god? That's preposterous! Surely, we would have been made aware of this? What secrets have the Diviner been keeping from the Council?"

"What is Corentine?" demanded the Zephyr ambassador with the black feathers. "What domain do they represent? What abilities do they possess? They looked like one of my mortals! How is that possible?"

"If I may, you said this god represents Chaos?" asked the Necro ambassador, a pale woman dressed in mourning black, her face obscured by a lace veil. "And this woman is one of their mortals?" She leaned over the table to get a better look at me. "Yet you wear the face of a Diviner. Curious."

"That's their power, an abomination," Gloria said with an air of disgust before I could even open my mouth. "They can take the guise of any of us with a single touch. What's worse, this power allows them to steal souls from our gods. And you want us to welcome them with open arms, Corinth? I refuse to sit at a table with *that* thing."

I flashed my sweetest smile. Did she remember me from her estate? Did she remember the deal we'd made and the betrayal that came after? By the glare in her red eyes, I was certain she did.

Oh, this was going to be fun.

The Amnae ambassador shook his head. "This is nonsense—"

"We witnessed Chaos for ourselves at Gloria's masquerade, Aberforth," the Zephyr said. Though now I thought about it, I didn't recall seeing any Amnae at the ball. I supposed the atmosphere was too warm for their gills. "One of them took the form of my mortals."

"If this mortal is truly what you say she is, then let's see it."

I glanced to Quen, who nodded. Oh, I did love a demonstration. But whose form would I take? I didn't fancy ripping my blouse with a Zephyr or Seren body, nor did I want to risk a Necro or Ember's face while Erosain sat in attendance. Taking a Glimmer's form would have been hysterical, but I didn't think Gloria would let me anywhere near her.

It was Reverie who I stood closest to. "Would you mind?" I asked.

She lazily lifted her arm. With a single touch, my Diviner skin turned to a more Vesper-shade of purple dotted with tiny silver stars.

The Council stared at me. Quen included. Oh right, he'd not witnessed my Mesmer form yet. I took his hand and returned to his Diviner form. "Is that sufficient proof?"

"So you *are* Chaos," murmured the Amnae. "These were the mortals responsible for the attacks on Chime?"

Quen raised his hands. "I'll explain in good time. Please, let us be seated—"

"The very same mortals," Gloria said. "This mortal is a danger to every one of us—"

"If it wasn't for Ambassador Arkey, you may not have left the masquerade alive," Quen said.

"If it wasn't for Chaos, I wouldn't have been placed in such an embarrassing and compromising situation in the first place!" Gloria snapped.

"Get a hold of yourself, woman," said the Leander. He bared his fangs in a terrible growl. "I witnessed Ambassador Arkey's deeds for myself. She helped stop the attack. If we're going to argue, then can we at least argue in comfort?" He sat in his chair, his thick mane spilling onto the table.

"I assure you," Quen said, "Ambassador Arkey is no threat to you or this Council. You have my word."

The other ambassadors shook their heads and sat. Quen gestured for me to take the spare seat by the Eventide wedge.

I went counterclockwise and sat between Reverie and Erosain. At least two faces I knew. Erosain remained his usual self, dressed in a black suit and red tabard to match his skin. He squinted as I passed him, as though he tried to place me.

Gods, I hope he didn't put two and two together and realize I'd been the one who robbed his art gallery. Between him and Gloria potentially out for my guts, this Council would certainly get lively.

Reverie ignored me entirely, as we'd discussed. We couldn't give any indication that we knew each other outside the Council, otherwise someone may suspect I hid inside her temple.

It felt odd to be taking residence in Varen's old seat. I'd always admired his efforts as ambassador to the Vesper—the way he balanced his duties with caring for Grayford—until he'd betrayed me. Funny, how he'd inadvertently prepared me for this role.

What sort of ambassador would I make?

A better one than Varen, Malk's voice said inside my mind. *He used mortals for his own ends. How many of the ambassadors in this room do the same? Watch yourself with them.*

I didn't need my deluded mind to warn me of that.

The Seren produced a notepad and pen. "If we may finally proceed?" Her skin was a pastel pink that paired well with her cream dress. Truly, she looked as though she'd come from another ball. "The time, please, Chairman?"

Quen took his seat at the point of the twelfth hour. "Ten forty-nine, Secretary."

The Seren scribbled a note. "This meeting was called by Ambassador Corinth at the time of ten forty-nine. On today's agenda, Ambassador Aberforth is seeking support for an underwater library in the Arcanum. Ambassador Gloria wishes to bring attention to increased cases of protesting across Central. And of course, there is the matter of the attack on the embassy. If you'd like to begin, Chairman?"

This was rather formal. Nothing like our rowdy Godless meetings back in the depot with cheese and wine. I was bored already.

Quen took a sip of iced tea, and somehow managed to avoid gagging. "Corentine is the thirteenth god, the god of Chaos. Chime is her domain."

"If this god and her mortals were responsible for the attack on Central, then why are we only hearing of this now?" asked the Amnae ambassador.

"Because our gods chose to hide this information, including my own. If your gods have not spoken to you of Corentine, then now is the time to pray and ask. They will be aware of her. They will remember what they did to her. She has been trapped inside the clock tower for generations against her will. It is her presence that powers Chime."

Shit. Quen wasn't holding back.

Gloria rapped her nails across the table. "The attack on Central Station not only targeted *my* mortals, but interrupted Gate traffic for weeks. Go on. Ask what Chaos really is."

Questions erupted from the ambassadors. What was Corentine? How many mortals did she have? They flung them at Quen, who did his best to keep up. He did a much better job at explaining than I would have.

"Did Dor know of their abilities?" the Amnae asked.

Quen raised his hand, and the chatter faded. "We knew back then that aether was leaking through the clock tower and causing disturbances, but did not yet realize it was the power of Chaos attempting to break free. Thanks to a collaboration between the Diviner and Glimmer, we were able to reinforce the clock tower and have prevented attacks since. The Diviner and Zephyr have worked together to create sensors to detect Chaos's energy. That, and our increased Warden patrols, has kept Central safe."

"Yet you sat on this information for a *month*? You allowed beings of chaos to roam Chime's streets without warning our domains of the threat?"

"I'm warning you now."

"This is unacceptable—"

"I apologize for keeping you in the dark, but Dor commanded me to ascertain the threat and secure Chime. That is what I have done."

"You used us as bait!" Gloria slammed her cup on the table, spilling iced tea. "Held a charity ball to lure Chaos—"

"The safety of the domains and the mortals of this room is my highest priority."

"Corentine is a threat to us, as are her mortals. Yes, Gildola is *aware* of her. The thirteenth god. The mad god. Locked away to protect the rest of the domains. Only that hasn't worked, has it? Eventide is gone. Only Chaos has the power to destroy an entire domain."

"Chaos was responsible for Eventide?" gasped the Necro.

Gloria mopped her spilled tea with a handkerchief. "Why are you so surprised? Chaos cares nothing for the Covenant or the sanctity of our domains. Corentine will see *your* domain destroyed next!"

The ambassadors exchanged frightened glances.

THEY'RE NOTHING BUT INGRATES.

They have good reason to be wary.

THEY DARE SIT HERE IN MY DOMAIN AND COMPLAIN! TAKE THEIR SOULS. GIVE THEM SOMETHING TO COMPLAIN ABOUT.

And turn every domain against us? You made me your voice, so let me handle this. It was time to make an impression. "I don't want to destroy your domain. Why would I come to this meeting and hear you talk nonsense if I wanted to see any of your domains gone?"

All heads turned to face me.

This was my moment to win them over.

The Leander's curious feline eyes pinned on me. "What does Corentine want?"

Gods, what was I meant to say? The truth?

I WANT REVENGE.

Yes, yes, I know. The destruction of the domains, blah blah—

YOU ARE MY VOICE. YOU WILL SPEAK FOR ME.

We'll compromise on that.

Oh, fuck it. "Corentine has spent a millennium trapped inside her own domain, and now she awakens. The truth is, she's not pleased. She seeks to bargain with the gods; to find freedom—"

"And why should we listen to some Undercity wretch like you?" Gloria said. "What right do you have to sit at this table and speak for a god long gone?"

Trust a Glimmer to kick low. I clenched my fists in my lap. She may think me a wretch, but I had nothing to be ashamed of. "It's true I grew up in the Undercity. I grew up as a Vesper, believing myself to be one. I was there when Eventide fell—I did everything I could to stop it—"

"And you failed." Gloria crossed her arms with a smug smirk.

I wanted to reach over the table and give her a good slap.

TAKE HER SOUL FIRST.

I'm considering it. Instead, I caught Quen's eye. He looked as though he wanted to speak up, but he held his tongue.

He was waiting for me to continue.

What had I ever done to earn his trust?

I played it cool and faced Gloria. "Don't pretend you cared for the Vesper when you locked them in workhouses." My voice came out like a whiplash.

I hadn't *actually* meant to sound that curt.

The Leander roared with laughter. "Our new ambassador has bite!"

"You see?" Gloria shook her head. "You let Undercity louts on the Council and this is what you get."

"Lady Arkey's right," said the Leander, still chuckling. "Don't weaponize the Vesper's demise for your own gain, Gloria. It's unbecoming."

Gloria glared across the table.

"Eventide fell because Corentine was angry," I said, finally finding my stride. "Because your gods stole her domain and trapped her inside it! Yes, Chaos has the power to destroy domains, like Eventide, I won't lie about that. It has the power to mimic your domains and steal your souls. And yes, Corentine desires her freedom. She desires revenge. And that's why *I'm* here—to negotiate a truce and prevent more domains from falling, if you'll listen to what Ambassador Corinth has to say."

"What does Chaos care for our mortals?" Gloria drawled.

"Chime is my home. My domain. As Corentine's voice, that makes me a representative of Chime and all mortals who reside here."

"Chime does *not* belong to Chaos—"

"No, it belongs to the mortals of each domain. That is what the Covenant stands for, and what Corinth and I are willing to offer."

Fevered whispering filled the chamber, but it was the Seren who spoke. "It seems you leave us no choice, Ambassador Arkey. Go ahead, Chairman. We're listening."

Quen gifted me a grateful smile. "We have a plan. A plan to remove Corentine from Chime and rehabilitate her mortals into society, where they will no longer be a threat. However, removing Corentine means your gods must provide their aether to power this domain. Without the combined energies of the gods, there will be no Chime."

"That's ludicrous!" Gloria spluttered. "You demand our gods sacrifice their power?"

"I expect them to fulfill their duties to the Covenant—"

"Then you risk creating a power imbalance when Chime remains imbalanced already thanks to Dor's influence!"

"Power will be distributed fairly. This is one way for the gods and yourselves to have a greater say in how Chime is maintained."

"How do we intend to remove this Corentine from Chime?" asked the Zephyr.

"We're still working on that part," Quen said.

"We can put her to sleep," said Reverie beside me. "Mesmorpheus would be willing to assist."

A few of the ambassadors gawked at her. I suspected the Mesmer didn't contribute to these Council meetings often.

"Then why bother moving her at all?" Gildola drawled. "Put Corentine to sleep and be done with it."

"Corentine is still a liability," Quen said. "Chime would be secure under the gods' power and responsibility."

"You ask a lot," said the Amnae. "You know our gods do not necessarily care for mortal affairs."

"Then make them care. Remind them of what the Covenant stands for, and what each domain stands to lose—"

"Is that a threat?"

"It's reality. Work with me, with Ambassador Arkey, and we can reach a solution that appeases all parties. We're willing to negotiate with each domain, to travel and speak with your gods if we must—"

"You'd be a fool to let Chaos into your domain." Gloria waved a dismissive hand at me.

"I promise I'll be on my best behavior," I said.

The Leander grinned. "I'm not scared of Chaos, nor is Lionheart. We'll gladly invite Ambassador Arkey into our domain. I trust Corinth—it's thanks to him we've not had any more attacks by Chaos—"

"It's thanks to the Wardens' incompetence that Chaos attacked at all!" Gloria said.

"And thanks to the Wardens that we have regained control." Quen glanced over the rim of his eyeglasses. "You don't need to give me an answer now, but time, as they say, is of the essence in this matter. Please pray to your gods."

YOUR PLAN IS TO BE RID OF ME, Corentine whined.

It's to save your children—

BY REMOVING ME FROM MY OWN DOMAIN?

Do you want to spend the rest of your existence in that clock tower?

IT IS IRRELEVANT. THIS PLAN WON'T WORK. THE GODS WILL NOT OPEN THEIR ARMS TO US.

You never know.

Chairs scraped across the tiles. The ambassadors made their way to the doored alcoves, which I came to realize were private prayer rooms for each one.

I headed for Quen's side.

Gloria intercepted me and barged into my shoulder.

"Gildola will not stand for this, nor will she support such madness," she hissed.

"Ambassador Gloria, you're looking well. Does the rest of the Council know Gildola disregarded the Covenant?"

"Does the Council know they sit beside a Godless?" She sneered. "It seems we all have our dark secrets, Corinth included. This isn't your world. Play these games, and I'll drag you both down with me."

"Gloria," Quen called, observing our interaction. "Ambassador Arkey has a place here. Be courteous."

"On your head be it, *Chairman*." She shoved past me and left the chamber.

"That went well." I leaned on the table next to Quen, my arse sitting on Kronos's skyline. "Won't we need the Glimmer for your plans?"

"Don't worry about her," he muttered. "She'll come around when she sees the other domains vying for control over Chime."

"You're so sure they will?"

"Naturally. They like to fiddle."

I snorted. "Ambassador Arkey? Really?"

"You have no family name. What else was I going to call you?"

"Oh, I can think of many names."

LIKE PAIN IN MY ARSE.

Shush, you. "What's our next move?"

"With any luck, we'll be heading to Memoria first. For my plan to work, we'll need to recruit Walter Burns's daughter."

Ilona Burns. The Amnae professor's daughter. I rolled up my sleeve and showed Quen.

He looked at me incredulously. "You tattooed her name on your arm?"

"So I wouldn't forget her." Quen had once tasked me with keeping her safe. "Though with the Wardens making the crossing impossible, I had no way of finding her."

"I appreciate your efforts. Truly. Now we'll go find her together."

"The Amnae ambassador didn't seem too cordial. What makes you think he'll allow me into his domain?"

"Because I know Ambassador Aberforth. And I know how Anima works. They won't be pleased that I've withheld knowledge from them. They'll want to learn more about Chaos, about you, and they'll want that intel ahead of the other domains."

"We're really going to do this? Visit the domains?"

He lifted his eyeglasses and rubbed his eyes. "Do try to be on time from now on."

"It's a lady's prerogative to be fashionably late."

"I'll buy you cake."

The man knew how to motivate me. "Cake and coffee and we'll call it a deal."

Quen shuddered. "The things I do to save Chime."

XIII

When entering a domain not their own, one must remember they are a guest. That means following the local customs, even if they differ from Chime's own ordinances.
In this endeavor, I recommend reading The Traveler's Handbook to Chime and Beyond. *Not only does it cover the various domains' etiquette required when dealing with certain mortals, but it also comes with a beautifully designed rendition of the domains as painted by legendary Seren artist, Soraya. One should not leave home without a copy.*
—Q. Corinth, *Warden Handbook on Domains*

I SAT HUNCHED OVER my desk at Warden HQ and took a moment to breathe through the weight of the tasks piled around me.

The stack of paperwork had grown and made my apartment's collection look small. It contained a mixture of petitions, crossing applications, invitations and appointments, complaints, requests, demands. The more interesting among them were reports on Chime's aging infrastructure and my own investigation into the city's trams and their apparent need for refurbishment. But that was a passion project right at the bottom of my priorities.

How had Elijah managed to get through all these?

Had he even looked at them before signing his name off and flinging them out the window?

I leaned back in my chair with a wistful sigh. I'd named Kayl ambassador, but she wouldn't need to contend with this level of crushing bureaucracy.

Technically, with Chime being Corentine's domain, Kayl should be the one dealing with these damnable crossing applications. But if I were to foist them into her lap, society would surely fall apart by the afternoon.

The door to my office opened, and Ben popped his head in. "Miss Bezel is here, sir."

I swallowed my groan. Father wanted me to play nice, so I'd play. "Let her in."

Pendula waltzed inside as though my office were hers and I was merely keeping her chair warm. She carried a briefcase in one hand and a stack of files under her other arm, and an intricate clockwork bird perched on her shoulder. She dressed smart in a tan jacket and matching skirt—her outfit similar to mine, and I'd assume that was intentional.

"Good morning, Your Excellency. Did your meeting with the ambassadors go well?"

"As well as to be expected." My allies on the Council would support me—Dandelion especially—though I'd have to win over the others. With Kayl working her charm in a way I couldn't, I was sure we'd succeed.

"I'd appreciate if you could allow me to arrange your appointments in future, Your Excellency, in order to ensure maximum efficiency of your time."

Was she *chiding* me? I sat up and straightened my bow tie. "I can manage my own time well enough, thank you."

She eyed my pile of paperwork with a look of shocking skepticism. Her clockwork bird flew around my office, taking it in before landing on the pile and clicking its brass beak with a disapproving whir. "I took the liberty of speaking with some of the ambassadors and collecting their responses." She placed the files awkwardly in the only space available on my desk.

Now she was overstepping. I flipped open the first folder to approved passport applications for Kayl Arkey. "I planned to gather these myself—"

"And I've saved you time. I've also filed your cash withdrawals from the Bank of Chime and present your receipts here." She placed another file. "Though to assist you at full capacity, I will need a copy of your fingerprints for my records. If I may, is it appropriate to be withdrawing such large funds?"

My cheeks burned. "These are from my personal funds, not the treasury. Therefore, it's none of your business—"

"Forgive me, Your Excellency. Father teaches us to be wary of excessive expenses."

"I'm not spending it on barrels of whiskey!" Though I could very well understand why Father would send a spy to check where I was funneling my money after I'd made so many anonymous donations to the Godless.

I'd worked overtime to eradicate those files, but secrets found their way through the cracks.

The clock struck half eleven, and I stood, my knees creaking from having sat for too long. "If you'll excuse me, I'm late for an appointment I must attend."

Pendula flipped open a file. "I don't see this listed on your schedule—"

"I'm working with Chaos. Don't expect my appointments to match any schedule."

She lowered her head and curtsied. "Of course, Your Excellency."

Had my words come out too harsh? The last thing I needed was her complaining about my lack of cooperation. "If you, ah, have time, I'd appreciate if you could take a look at these." I patted the top of my towering paperwork. "Ambassador Gloria has submitted a few complaints." A fair few. "You know how Glimmer are."

"I'd be happy to handle it, Your Excellency. The Glimmer appreciate a feminine touch." She held out her finger, and the clockwork bird flew over and perched there, a pen in its mouth, ready for business.

Perhaps I *did* need an assistant.

Though I doubted even divine intervention could organize the chaos my life was turning into.

I tapped my foot impatiently as time ticked closer to the hour. The woman was impossibly tardy, which must surely be the curse of Chaos, but with only a week to unite the domains and appease my Father, Kayl's tardiness was going to end me.

To be late grated on a Diviner far worse than grinding gears.

We waited outside Central Station before midday. Central's citizens hurried across the square to their own engagements. More queued outside food stalls or sat outside teahouses for an early lunch, and I caught the whiff of onion from a nearby Ember stall selling hot jacket potatoes.

It was an average day of hustle and bustle, but these times I cherished most—when Chime's streets came alive.

"They're here, sir," Ben announced, subtly nodding at two figures approaching.

Today Kayl wore an Ember's face and dressed as I'd requested; in something light and unassuming—a flowery dress that ended below her knees, and a cream handbag slung over her shoulder. It was modest and classy enough, though combined with her Ember persona, the whole ensemble lacked innocence.

An Ember's body was an inspired choice; where we were going, the humidity tended to cling.

"You coming for coffee?" Dru offered Ben. She too was wearing a modest flowery dress with splotches of golden flowers.

Ben stood at attention. "I'm at work, Miss Smith."

"Go on, Ben," I urged. "Kayl and I would like a little privacy to discuss the business of the day. We'll meet you over at the station shortly."

"Yes, sir." He looked dismayed at the thought of abandoning his post, which only made poor Dru annoyed. I'd have to teach him how to mask his emotions better.

"Business of the day, hrm?" Kayl stood with a hand on her hip and that troublesome smirk. "Is this the part where you show off how clever you are?"

I tugged at my sleeve. "I don't need to show off. Can I ask why it was so imperative to meet here? It would be easier if you gave me an address I could contact you at. In case of emergencies."

"This *is* my contact address." She beckoned me around the corner of Central Station to an abandoned bench. The aether bulb of the streetlamp had blown out. Judging by the grime, this spot had been neglected for years.

She sat on the bench and reached underneath it, pulling out a torn old piece of paper. "The Godless use this bench to meet and leave notes. No one ever comes here. No Wardens, no station staff. If you need to contact me, then leave a note. I'll know it's you."

I sat beside her. "This may be too much subterfuge for me."

She cocked her head and smiled. "Would you prefer I get a part-time job working for the Courier so you can leave notes in my drop box?"

That smile always sent a jolt of aether under my skin. "The bench will do. You've gained clearance for six domains."

"Six? Really? Which ones?"

"Memoria, Witheryn, Tempest, Obituary, Rapture, and Phantasy."

"Not Kronos?"

"Kronos won't be necessary." I pulled out an envelope from my inner jacket pocket. "For you. Your remuneration as requested."

She snatched the packet and rifled through it. "Oh my. Chime's budget made space for me."

Technically not; the notes came from my own account, not that I wished to divulge such. I owed a few months of backdated pay as the Godless's benefactor, after all. "Don't spend it all in one place."

She fluttered her eyelashes innocently.

Saints, she was going to bleed me dry. "I have another gift." I unwrapped a silver bracelet.

Her eyes opened wide. "Quen, I can't accept—"

"It's an aether device designed to mimic a piece of jewelry. With this, you'll be able to enter the embassy and Central Station without triggering my sensors, effectively negating the signal."

"To tell me apart from Jinx?"

"Precisely. Once you put it on, only I can remove it with this." I waggled a small key. "To prevent it from being stolen." Or to prevent Kayl from misplacing it, which was more likely.

"Clever." She placed the bracelet carefully around her wrist, clicking it into place. "Oh! That reminds me! I have something of yours." She dug through her handbag and pulled out a brass fob watch.

It was *my* fob watch! "Where did you find that?"

"In that trash can, believe it or not. I found it after you'd... I'm sorry, it got damaged—it doesn't work." She passed it to me.

The weight of it fit neatly in my hands. I examined the familiar marred brass and popped it open to the cracked glass and the hands stuck permanently between twelve and one. "I broke it myself years ago." When I'd fallen inside the clock tower. I'd never bothered to repair it, as though it reflected my own damaged soul. "Diviner children are given timepieces such as these when they're born."

"Like an heirloom?"

"More like a comforter." To be soothed by the tick and tock of time's heartbeat. Most Diviner outgrew them after a while. So many of us didn't recognize affection. We didn't have mothers to ease our nightmares. "Thank you," I whispered. "It's a silly thing—"

"I knew it was important to you. Just like this bench. A silly thing, but it has memory. Malk and I would meet here."

A lump caught in my throat. We hadn't spoken about those events of four weeks ago. About the demise of Eventide. The death of her lover. It must hurt. "I'm sorry for your loss. I never—I should have said so before now."

"Time gets ahead of us." Her eyes glazed over with that spacey look she once took on when communing with her soul twin—with Jinx. Though now I assumed she must be communing with her god. "What was it like to die?"

The question sucked the air from my lungs. I leaned back against the bench. "Painful, at first. But then... peaceful. There're no burdens. No... nothing."

"Sometimes I think I hear their voices, you know? The Vesper. I hear whispering in the back of my mind, and I don't know if I'm imagining it or going mad." She turned to me, those silvery-blue eyes so intense. "I killed them all."

"It wasn't your fault—"

"But it was. I yanked their souls out and tossed them into oblivion to save mine. Do you think they're at peace? Free of their burdens?"

"They're free of Valeria."

"So many of the gods are cruel. Shouldn't I let Jinx get what she wants? Let her take out a few gods and save their mortals? Gildola for a start?"

My heart raced, and I felt caught in a trap—between wanting to comfort and reassure Kayl, and abhorring the thought of stealing the souls of mortals. I couldn't deny the gods were cruel. But I couldn't advocate for their destruction either. "I've killed mortals. That crushing darkness right here?" I tapped my chest. "It's a guilt I'm well acquainted with. One that never leaves."

"Unless you wipe your memories."

"Which, as I've discovered, only makes everything worse." Those memories of my deeds haunted me, intruding on my thoughts at the worst moments.

I'd killed Malkavaan Byvich's mother. How could I ever admit that? Atone for it?

I'd been the one who'd damned Malkavaan to torture at Valeria's hands.

What would Kayl think of me if she knew the quality of my soul?

Would she ever forgive me?

"Then how do you cope with it? That darkness?" She wrapped her arms around her chest. "It... It feels like I'm falling."

Her pain echoed in my own flesh. "You do a little better every day. You find someone, some reason, to try. That and a good cup of tea."

"The Diviner solution to every problem. If only we could placate the gods with a good cup of tea."

"I'm not against trying it."

"Do you really think we can save Chaos? Is it even worth saving?"

My hand twitched toward hers. I wanted to hold her, to tell her in absolute terms that Chaos was worth saving to me. That all mortal lives were worth the chance. Even the Glimmer. Especially the Vesper. But my beliefs were an unpopular one.

Light needed darkness to shine. Time needed chaos.

I didn't know where such blasphemous thoughts came from, but they felt intrinsic. As though merging with the aether in death had granted me a wisdom I'd yet to understand.

I'd fight for both.

In the depths of her eyes, I saw the death I hurtled toward. The vision of my soul being torn apart by Chaos. I knew it was coming by her hand. And yet...

I'd walk this path to the end.

"I won't lie—our chances are slim. But you and I have both lived the impossible."

"You died."

"A minor inconvenience. I understand what it means to fall, Kayl. This time, I'll be there to catch you."

She blinked away an emotion I couldn't place, and then her playful smile returned. "So tell me your grand plan for saving the domains. It can't be much worse than any of mine."

I sat up and straightened my bow tie. "Convincing the gods to lend their power to Chime is one step. Arguably the most difficult. But with them on board, we'll be able to remove Corentine and rehabilitate her mortals. They'll need to choose a suitable persona, which will then be made permanent."

"They won't be able to change forms?"

"No. Nor would they be able to take souls."

"So if I went through this process as I am, I'd be made into an Ember forever?"

"Essentially, yes. The choice of which domain you choose to mimic will be entirely yours, though I'd recommend avoiding certain ones, such as the Glimmer. I doubt Gildola would approve."

"If we choose a domain, would we then be beholden to their god?"

"No. You'd be free of their influence. You would effectively be godless."

"I like the sound of that."

"I thought you would. We'll need to reconfigure the soul-splitting devices. Hector Bezel led the project team. His death is unfortunate." At some point, I'd need to broach the subject with Pendula—I was reviving her second father's project, which was bound to be awkward. "I'd like to recruit his apprentice, Doctor Zachery Finch. The Zephyr from the steamworks, if you recall."

"Oh yes! Chaos wanted him, too. I dropped him in a lake. Is he well?"

"You dropped him in a—never mind. He went into hiding on Tempest, I believe. We'll need to head there and convince him to help us. But first, Memoria."

"To recruit Ilona Burns?"

"Indeed. Her knowledge of memory manipulation rivals her father's, so Walter told me. I promised him I'd keep her safe, but she'll also be a valuable asset."

Kayl cringed. "You want to manipulate the memories of Chaos?"

"I want to give them a fresh start. Once they have chosen a suitable persona, it would be easier for them to reenter society with a new identity."

I could see the dilemma warring in her expression—to remove their memories, their past, their connection. It was a rebirth. One I would have rallied against.

But they'd spent their entire lives imprisoned and suffering. At least this way, they could start afresh. "It's a kindness," I said quietly.

She nodded. "You know, trouble often finds me, but now it feels like I'm going out of my way to make trouble." She stretched to her feet and offered her hand. "Tea?"

"A woman after my own heart." I grabbed her wrist, careful to avoid triggering her abilities, and she hoisted me up.

A little trouble was what some of these domains needed. And they were going to get it whether they welcomed it or not.

We'd visited the passport application office early and gotten Kayl inked with her clearance for Memoria. I'd expected the process to take much longer than it had, which was why I'd arranged to meet Kayl well in advance. But to my great surprise, the Necro updating her passport tattoo worked with efficiency.

Unfortunately, Ben and Dru had decided to grab coffee at the overpriced tea stand inside Central Station. As we joined them, Kayl insisted on ordering tea and scones, despite my objections.

We sat at the café's table with a good view of the Gate, currently set to Kronos, with half an hour before Memoria was due to open. Ben and Dru sat at another table with coffee, playing the part of inconspicuous bodyguards, though Ben attracted stares no matter where he went, and Dru constantly rubbed her budding flowers, to the shocked glances of concerned citizens walking by.

Deary me.

I sipped at my tea and forced myself to swallow the bland commercialized taste. A biscuit may have helped, but I was attempting to cut back.

Kayl lowered her cup without bothering to mask her distaste. "Ugh, this tea tastes like shit."

"I warned you."

"At least the scones aren't dry." She stuck her finger into the cream and strawberry jam and scooped off a knob, popping it into her mouth.

Dear gods. She'd pronounced *scone* like *gone*, and that was a crime I could not ignore. "I think you'll find it's pronounced *scone*." Like *own*.

"I think you'll *find* it's primarily Undercity residents who bake them, and they call them *scones*."

Oh, she was so wrong. "You're saying we need to invest more in public education?"

"Just because the Golden City sits at the top doesn't mean they know anything about the production of scones. Calling it *scone* sounds like someone bending over backwards to lick the cream out of their own arse."

"I've never met a single mortal who pronounces them as *scones*."

"That says more about your life experience."

I shook my head in despair. "You know, mispronouncing *scone* is one of the unforgivable sins, which would explain why your soul is cursed."

She stuck out her tongue and scooped another knob of cream, smearing it across her lips as she licked her finger clean.

Heat crept under my collar. Could the woman not use a blasted spoon?

An Umber server came to our table. "Are you finished, sir?"

"Yes, thank you." I nudged my teacup over and knocked a spoon off the edge. "Oh, excuse me."

I bent to pick it up at the same time as the Umber, and accidentally brushed against her hand.

Darkness slammed into me.

I stuffed my pinafore into the locker before my Glimmer boss could call me back for more overtime.

She waved over to me. "Your family coming over today?"

"Yes, ma'am. First time making the crossing."

"They've never visited Chime?"

"They're old fashioned. Scared the Gate will burn their flowers, and they think Chime is full of fancy artist types who don't know how to work using their hands."

The boss laughed. "Bring them here. I'll show them how we work in Chime."

I forced myself to chuckle. "I'll consider it, ma'am. Catch you tomorrow!" I quickly ducked out of the kiosk before she decided her joke held merit.

Working the tea stand in Central Station wasn't the most glamorous job, but it was honest work, and I hoped my folks would see that. They didn't trust Chime. They'd sooner have me back in Heartstone mending garments. I'd admit, I missed the valleys. Missed the smell of lavender on the wind, instead of coffee nonstop.

Maybe one day I'd get a day off to go visit them proper.

Working the night shift hurt my feet something rotten, but I had a few hours to clean my apartment before Heartstone opened. I found space on the platform to lean against the railing and relax for a moment. The tram home was pulling into Central, but there was something odd about it. Trams didn't normally go that fast, did they?

Oh god!

Mortals screamed and ran as the tram hurtled around the bend. They barged into me. I tried to push through them, but too many were rushing past me in a panic.

An almighty screech made me glance over my shoulder.

The tram had tilted over.

No! It was heading straight for us!

I shoved a Seren out of the way. My body was made from stone. I could stop the tram. I could stop—

Ben was crouched over me, his hand pinned painfully on my shoulder. "Are you all right, sir? You blacked out for a moment."

I swallowed mouthfuls of air, my chest rising in frantic pants as I tried to calm my nerves.

"Quen?" Kayl asked. "What did you see?"

"The server. Where did she go?"

"Back to the tea stand, sir. I think it was the end of her shift—do you want me to stop her before she goes?"

Ben didn't know the extent of my visions, that I witnessed—and experienced—the death of another through touch. I'd felt that tram slam into my bones and crush the life from me.

And it was going to happen soon.

I grabbed Ben's arm and pulled him close as Kayl and Dru surrounded me. "Don't question me, but I just had a vision. A tram is going to pull into Central Station shortly and derail. We need to evacuate mortals from the platform."

"Sir, trams don't travel fast enough to derail—"

"I said *don't* question me. If we don't act now, it'll be too late." Though as I spoke, I caught the Umber server leaving the tea stand from the corner of my eye.

Saints. It could already be too late.

The clock tower rang out one o'clock, and Memoria opened. With only six days to pacify ten gods, not including my own, I couldn't afford to waste time—especially when the Amnae ambassador was not known for his patience.

Why would a tram suddenly derail now? I didn't believe in coincidences. An accident of this proportion could well be a distraction.

This wasn't my jurisdiction anymore. I was an ambassador, not a Warden.

But I'd been cursed with these visions for a reason.

"Kayl, can you find the stationmaster and alert them? Ben, Dru, help me evacuate the platform." Neither Ben nor Dru were dressed as Wardens, but with their strength, they'd be more useful in the worst-case scenario.

I took off before anyone could object and ran for the platform.

Mortals were already calling out in alarm.

"Sir!" Ben pointed ahead at the tram careening down the street as mortals dove out of the way.

"Oh my god!" Dru exclaimed.

Why hadn't the driver attempted to slow it with their power? As it neared, I raised my hands and wrapped a bubble of time around it.

It slowed.

Merciful gods, it actually slowed! I could save lives, I could—

Time jerked forward, and the tram sped up. No!

Someone was trying to cause this!

I fought against it, and the tram jumped back and forth through fluctuations in time. Blood gushed from my nose. Whoever was fighting me was damn strong.

"Blast it, I can't—"

My knees buckled. Ben caught me before I collapsed to the pavement.

The tram burst from my hold and twisted onto its side.

A horrid screech of metal on cobblestone rang in my ears.

I tried to push Ben away, to yell at him to leave me and go help, but it was too late.

The tram plowed into a crowd; their shrieks cut off with a sickening crunch. I made eye contact with the tram driver as his face smashed against the cab's glass, cracking it, but not quite breaking through. Blood painted the window red.

I staggered from Ben's grip.

More blood smeared the cobblestones. Abandoned clothes lay trapped underneath the carriage, including those of the Umber server.

It squeezed my throat. "She was going to meet her family."

I'd thought I could save these.

I'd thought this time would be different.

When would I learn?

I closed my eyes to rigid memory. There was Reve's mangled body lying across the tram tracks. Each of his deaths had ended the same, though his broken limbs were posed at different angles. The splatter of blood painted different patterns. The tram cab had been labeled with a different fleet number. The mortals who screamed or gawked were of different domains.

But in all of Reve's suicides, my reaction remained the same. I lifted his head onto my lap. I tried to soothe his pain with mere words, not knowing it hadn't been his first death, and that I'd forgotten it. Not realizing that whatever tears I'd shed had been futile.

Reve had wanted his end. These mortals hadn't.

"He—*help!*" a woman called out. A Seren was pinned under a door that had come loose. Saints preserve me, she was still alive!

With Ben's help, we lifted the door high enough for Dru to reach under and drag her out. Her wings were bloodied and misshapen, but nothing a Necro couldn't fix.

"Fetch a Necro!" I called as Wardens and station staff raced across the platform.

They rounded up the injured, allowing me to catch a breather.

Ben leaned against the station wall. "You said you saw a vision, sir? Did you see how this happened?"

"No. If the brakes were tampered with, then a Warden investigation will discover it." Though I'd sensed something—or someone—clash with my power, and I only knew one mortal capable of that.

Was Jinx using this to break into Central Station? To reach the Gate?

Or was it a message?

"Ben, tell the Wardens to be on high alert. Check the sensors are still functioning." Kayl's presence should still be nullified by the bracelet.

"Yes, sir."

I left Ben to deal with the Wardens, and I headed back to the station. The entire situation left me shaken, though I couldn't help but worry I was missing something.

Memoria's underwater teal shone over the concourse. It was twenty-five past. That whole incident had taken almost half an hour. We could still make the crossing, but it wouldn't be enough time to host a meeting with the ambassador and return.

Blast it!

The Wardens cordoned off the tram platform. They had it in hand, and I'd read their report later.

Ben found me on the concourse. "What now, sir?"

"We'll have to cancel our meeting. We're not equipped to spend a whole twelve hours in Memoria." Not on my tight schedule. "We could aim for Tempest at seven... But making the evening crossing would not be wise."

"Why's that, sir?"

"Because the whole sodding place floats in the air. One false step and you're gone." And after today, I absolutely could not stomach the thought of navigating their airships and walkways in darkness. Kayl may be able to turn into a Zephyr and fly, but I couldn't! "Where's Kayl and Dru?"

"They're waiting in the queue to cross, sir."

I spun. There they were, preparing to cross. "I didn't tell them to queue!"

Ben looked confused. "I thought you did, sir."

Good gods! I approached the queue and waved at Kayl to get her attention.

She nodded at my signal and stepped through the Gate.

Which was precisely what I *didn't* want her to do!

I ran to the Gate. There was still time to reach in and drag her back—

A ripple of time passed over the station, and the clock jumped forward, the tower's bell jarring with a harsh and distorted tone.

The Gate suddenly changed from Memoria to Juniper.

Trapping Kayl in Memoria without me.

The station staff pulled down the barrier, unaware of time's sudden blip. "Sorry, sir. Please wait a moment for the next crossing."

Ben panted beside me. "Sir, what just happened?"

I wish I sodding knew!

14

Memoria is one of the more unique domains and can be both an enlightening and traumatic experience. It is recommended that first-time visitors stay for only twelve hours, as any longer can induce feelings of claustrophobia due to the change in air pressure.
Do remember that Memoria is full of aquatic life known as fish. Interacting with the local flora and fauna is strictly forbidden and will result in prosecution.
—Q. Corinth, *Warden Dossier on Memoria*

THE GATE BLIPPED OUT behind me. I frantically spun around and stared at the empty space. My heart raced. It was as empty as when Eventide had vanished.

"It's okay." Dru took my arm and dragged me out of the way. "It's normal for the Gate to switch off between cycles. It won't come back on again for another twelve hours. Which, by the way, is a bad thing."

Shit! "We've left Quen behind!" I could have sworn he'd told me to queue up and then waved at me to go ahead! Fuck's sake! "What if it doesn't come back on? What if—"

"It always comes back—"

"But what if it doesn't? And we're trapped here forever?"

"Then we'll get jobs and save up for a nice house somewhere. Seriously, it's fine. I grew up in Heartstone, remember? The Gate *always* comes back on."

Goosebumps popped up along my skin. Dru may have grown up inside a domain, but she hadn't been there when Eventide had faded into nothing. "What do we do now?"

"Well, uh... I suggest we find the Amnae ambassador. Do you remember his name?"

"Like fuck I do!"

Dru rubbed her forehead. "Someone here must be able to point us in the right direction. We've got twelve hours to kill."

Shitting shit! My first voluntary adventure into a domain and I'd gotten us pissing trapped here for twelve gods-damn hours! I didn't even have a copy of *The Traveler's Handbook to Chime and Beyond* to tell me what to do!

I was the worst tourist. The absolute worst.

Dru tugged on my arm and led me away from the Gate. At least I could depend on her to keep me grounded. The Gate here wasn't built underneath a giant clock tower, but was instead an odd triangular archway made of pockmarked orange stone—coral, I think Harmony called it. Multicolored plants and shells grew on top.

As I turned away, I swallowed a gasp. "Oh my *god*."

The station was open air with no walls or ceiling, only organized queues beside booths for currency exchange, passport applications, tourist information, and a little tea shop named Mr. Kipler's. These booths were made of a similar rock as the Gate. Mortals of various domains lingered in the station or sat on brass benches. The vast majority who walked by were Amnae, which I supposed made sense.

But it was the city sprawling behind the station that made my heart flutter.

Much like Chime, the buildings here were a mismatch of heights and shapes. But instead of brick, the walls were made of brass and teal-tinted windows. Thick piping zigzagged between each building, connecting them in an intricate web of bronze.

Most of the brass was hidden behind plants that stretched vertically to impossible heights between colorful shell mosaics in the shape of an umbrella—jellyfish, if I remembered right. The same pattern repeated throughout.

Above the city, no plate cast everything in shadow. A glass dome enveloped everything like a giant greenhouse. Only, beyond the walls lay water.

Gods. We were surrounded by deep blue water, and only that thick glass kept it out.

"Welcome to Memoria," Dru said.

"It's breathtaking." Quite literally, if I ended up being thrown outside these walls. How could anyone live here and not go mad? The dome loomed over us with dizzying height. I tripped over my feet staring at it.

Dru caught me before I fell on my arse. She truly made the best bodyguard.

The water around us rippled and churned, reflecting wavy light across the entire city. The effect made the buildings sway in a dancing rainbow of color, as though one had indulged in a Vesper mushroom, but shit, it also left me nauseous all of a sudden. "What are those wiggly things?"

"They're fish." Dru pointed to the weird flat creatures that wiggled beyond the glass walls.

I'd *heard* of fish, but since they were banned on Chime, I'd never encountered them before. "What do fish do?"

"They swim about."

"Is that it?"

Dru gave me an odd look. "You need to leave Chime more."

Well, here I was! Learning about fish, for god's sake. "How do you know all about this? Have you been to Memoria before?"

"No, but I read books."

"*I* read books."

"You read smut." Her eyebrows would be rising if they were long enough, but she gave a good attempt. "You've read *The Handbook*, right?"

"Yes, yes. You're not allowed to touch the fish, or talk to them, or whatever." As Harmony had also reminded me. Fish were supposedly sacred to the Amnae, since Amnae were designed after fish. Or something. I wasn't a scholar.

I wished Quen were here to explain all the nerdy things about this domain I would otherwise surely miss.

"Then stop gawking," Dru chided. "You're embarrassing me."

"How could I not? There's fucking fish!"

An Amnae strode past and gave me a funny look.

"If you're going to act this way in every domain we enter, then I quit. I thought you were good at playing spy?"

"I'm *brilliant* at playing spy. Who is going to expect a tourist to be subtle?"

"So you're deliberately being annoying?"

I grinned.

Dru clenched her jaw and pulled me toward the tourist information booth. This, too, was made of orange coral. A young Amnae girl stood behind the counter, her skin matching the décor with an orange pattern like a goldfish. I'd read about goldfish *somewhere*.

I'd only met one Amnae in my life—Quen's professor—but these were a variety of colors, all with different ridges and fleshy bits on their heads, from fins to tentacle-like locks. Most wore enough clothing to cover their privates, and that was it. There was so much flesh on display, it would be enough to make an Ember blush.

Though even in my Ember form, the humidity made my dress cling to my skin. Stepping into Memoria had felt like entering a steamy washroom, though one that smelled explicitly salty. I was glad I lacked hair, for I'd surely be dying otherwise.

How did Dru stand it?

"Can I help you, miss?" the goldfish girl asked in that garbled way Amnae spoke. She glossed over Dru, and her slitted eyes narrowed at me.

Was I overdressed? Or was I that annoying of a tourist? I stepped up to the booth and let my hands rub over the rough texture, which seemed far too brittle to be supportive. "Good afternoon. We're looking for the ambassador's office."

"May I ask why you seek the ambassador?"

"We're on official business from the Warden Council back on Chime. His Excellency, Quentin Corinth, sent us ahead but missed the crossing. We're expected."

"Do you have an appointment card?"

Shit. Proof I was what she was asking for, and I had none. "If you contact your ambassador, I'm sure they'd recognize—"

"I'm sorry, miss, but the ambassador does not take unsolicited calls."

"Is there a problem here?" An Amnae dressed in the black-and-bronze jacket of the Wardens approached. His badge was pinned to his upper pocket, though he wore shorts and sandals. An odd look. Though I'd honestly never seen an Amnae Warden before.

Wardens turned up bloody everywhere.

"These ladies were just leaving," the Amnae woman said.

I sized up the Warden. "Actually, we're looking for the ambassador."

"What does an Ember want with the ambassador?"

Was that their problem? That I wore the face of an Ember? "You don't get many Ember in these parts?"

"Just a precaution, ma'am. We're careful of any domain with abilities that could hurt our local flora."

"Does that extend to Glimmer? Or do their bocs make you more polite?"

"We don't trade in bocs here, ma'am."

How could these Amnae be so dry in this humidity?

Dru glowered at me with her *stop being rude before we get arrested* look, which she'd perfected over the years.

We weren't getting anywhere here. Sure, I had twelve hours to kill, but I'd rather not spend them in a Warden cell. "We're not looking for trouble. Your ambassador is expecting to meet with Quentin Corinth. You know? The Diviner ambassador? We're a little waylaid, is all—"

"I think you better take a quiet walk away, ma'am. You're disturbing the peace." The Warden grabbed my upper arm.

I instinctively reached for his hand to yank him off me and realized my mistake too late.

At one quick touch, my skin rippled from my dark pink Ember to the silvery-blue scales of an Amnae. Fins sprouted from my head.

The three of them, including Dru, stared in shock.

Great. I let out a wheeze. "I don't—don't know how to—to *breathe*!"

I sagged against the counter and sucked in rapid mouthfuls. Breathing as an Amnae was completely different from any other domain!

Dru was at my side in an instant, but panic filled her eyes. "Do something!" she snapped at the Warden.

The Warden looked lost.

My chest heaved as it tried to fill my lungs.

Shit. I was mere seconds away from passing out!

"Here!" The Amnae woman handed Dru a paper bag. "Breathe into that. Slow gulps, in and out."

Dru held it under my mouth as I took deep gulps of air. Slowly, my breathing steadied, and the gills on my neck adjusted to Memoria's atmosphere.

I lowered the bag and rubbed moisture from my eyes. "How in god's name do you all live like this?"

"That's what you have to say?" Dru asked, bewildered.

I stood and straightened my dress. My new webbed feet squeezed tight in my shoes, but I had to admit, the humidity didn't cling quite as much in an Amnae form. In fact, it was rather pleasant.

"Ma'am, I think you better come with me," the Warden said, his Amnae eyes practically bulging.

"Are you arresting me?"

"I think it may be safer for everyone if we took you back to our HQ—and then we can contact the ambassador. What, uh, did you say your name was?"

I glanced at Dru, who shrugged. "Kayl Arkey. Ambassador for Chaos."

"For... what?"

"Your ambassador will know who I am."

The Warden led us out of the station and into the heart of Memoria's main city. The locals had a specific name for it, so Harmony had said, but I couldn't remember. Both she and Vincent had studied here at the university. How strange to think they'd lived in another domain for years.

Instead of the cobblestone streets I was used to, I traversed smooth tiles a rich teal, and more brass piping traveled along the gutter, spewing out steam at various grates. At random points, the piping went vertical and opened like a large brass umbrella. Water spouted from the top in a shower of mist.

So that was why it was so damn humid.

Amnae stood casually under the umbrellas and allowed the damp to refresh them, I assumed. I suddenly wanted to run over there and join them.

"Doesn't the heat bother you?" I asked Dru.

"Nope." Dru tucked a vine behind her ear with a smug smile. "Stone skin, remember? Umber don't sweat."

Next time I'd come as a bloody Umber.

We approached what appeared to be a station. Amnae and other mortals queued, as though waiting for a tram, but the track lines dipped below the pavement, hidden. Though as we neared, I realized it wasn't a tramline at all, but a canal. Instead of carriages, passengers climbed aboard boats in the shape of giant shells.

"We're going to ride in *that*?" I stared.

The Warden waited for an empty shell-cum-boat and beckoned us in. "Be careful with your footing when entering the gondola, ma'am."

"Can it hold an Umber's weight?"

Dru scowled. "Do you want me to push you overboard?" She hopped into the boat. It swayed, but remained afloat. I supposed it was sturdy enough.

The Warden followed, leaving me to awkwardly climb in after. Shit! The whole thing wobbled underneath me, and I grabbed Dru's shoulder for stability. She helped me down onto a bench, but gods. Even my old hanging tram back in the depot felt more secure than this!

Another Amnae male stood behind us wearing a wide-brim hat. He operated what appeared to be a steam engine attached to the arse end of the boat. It rumbled to life with a soft hum, and then we were moving.

My tourist-inspired gawking was *not* for show.

The gondola seemed to glide effortlessly through the canal with only minimal bops and dips. As we sailed, I couldn't help but marvel at how familiar yet different Memoria was compared to Chime.

But the familiarity turned to an uncanny oddness. Single-story buildings in the shape of giant shells lined the canals. We passed water fountains that the Amnae sat in, trees made of coral, and grass made of seaweed. Actual bloody seaweed! Other strange plants were dotted between them that writhed as though alive. Even the streetlamps were made of bulbous fish that glowed. The tang of salt in the air followed us.

Above, glass tubes connected various areas of the city. These were filled with water, and Amnae swam through them at a much faster rate than us.

Most were naked, and I got a good eyeful of flapping Amnae breasts and balls, which were as translucent as the rest of their skin. No one else stared at this blatant public nudity.

If this were Chime, they'd be thrown out.

Come to think of it, I hadn't encountered many Glimmer loitering in Memoria.

The Amnae themselves went about their daily lives much the same as Chime's citizens. Some carried briefcases, others read their version of the Courier. Some sat outside cafés drinking green tea. Smaller Amnae children chased each other around their water spouts, splashing one another and giggling.

I couldn't believe it.

How did they live such normal lives knowing a god watched them?

The few times I'd visited Eventide, the Vesper had been fearful of their master in her bleak castle. They'd gone about their lives constantly glancing over their shoulder.

I'd assumed most domains were the same.

But Memoria... It seemed freer than Chime. Even the Wardens were few and far between.

Did the Amnae not live in fear of their god?

Or did their god simply hide the bad lurking underneath all that brass and teal? The rust had to be somewhere.

The gondola passed under a bridge and then parked beside a stack of giant glass bulbs that connected to the walls of Memoria with a tube at the top. At first, I couldn't tell *what* the structure was meant to be, but the bottom bulb had double doors leading inside, and I could see desks, chairs, and potted plants through the tinted teal windows. Offices?

"Is this the Warden HQ?" It was certainly more impressive than the gray building back in Chime.

"This is the Archive, ma'am," the Warden said. "Memoria's largest library."

Oh my. Dru and I followed the Warden into a reception area and were asked to make ourselves comfortable on the couch. At least we weren't being arrested. Inside, more seaweed grew up the walls, which caught Dru's attention, though mine was fixed on a large glass tank full of tiny pink fish behind the reception desk.

I scooted up to Dru. "So, what do you think of Big Ben?"

She gave me a sideways glance. "Why are you asking me that?"

"Just curious."

"There's always an ulterior motive with you."

I blinked in feigned innocence. "Me? Never!"

Dru patted the growing buds on her forehead. "He thinks I'm a slut."

"He *what*?"

"Well, he keeps staring at my flowers."

"That doesn't mean he thinks you're a slut."

"You know what Diviner are like."

Sadly. They were as pious as Glimmer, though I wasn't so sure about Quen. A sinner lurked under his gentlemanly facade; I was sure of it. "You're being extra grumpy today, and here we are on our grand adventure surrounded by fish."

Dru sighed. "I don't know what to do about my family."

"Oh? In what way?"

"The last time I wrote to them, they thought I was still apprenticing with the steamworks. They'd lose their minds if they knew I was a bodyguard of all things. They worry enough about Chime being dangerous. Should I even tell them?"

"Have you considered lying?"

She wrung her hands in her lap. "I've been lying all this time. I never told them about Grayford and the soup kitchen. Or... you know. Us. The Godless. They wouldn't understand."

"I thought Umber were in favor of charity work?" That was how she'd once justified her involvement with the Godless. She wasn't helping *us* further our blasphemous goals, but helping the mortals who needed us.

"Within reason. You ever wonder why there's hardly any Umber in Grayford or Sinner's Row? Because it's unsafe, for one. And because... they're a bit like the Glimmer, sometimes. Believing we can't help those who don't help themselves, not understanding that sometimes it's those mortals who need the most help..." She drew in a breath. "My family wouldn't approve, is all I'm saying."

I put a hand on her thigh. "Then it's a good thing your family isn't in Chime."

"What if we end up visiting Heartstone? My family are well-known traders—I'd be recognized, and they'd see the state of my flowers—"

"We'll worry about that if and when it comes to it." I wanted to ask more about Dru's family, but a female Amnae walked up to us.

"Ambassador Arkey? His Excellency is ready to see you now. Your companion may wait here, and I'll order in refreshment."

Dru shot me a worried look, but I flashed her my most confident smile. I was heading into a meeting with the ambassador alone, but I was sure I could handle it.

This was what Quen had hired me to do.

Chatting and charming was what I did best.

We entered a glass elevator, which took a slow ascent up the bulb floors to the top. I could sense the aether powering it, yet it didn't itch and scream in my head like the aether back on Chime. Did Anima power this?

The door popped open with a *ping*.

It wasn't what I expected a library to look like.

I stepped into a circular dark room where the walls were made of glass containing hundreds of multicolored fish and plants. Sporadic shafts of light created a rather moody and serious atmosphere. It rippled across the only furniture; a metal desk and some sort of font in the center.

Standing beside the font was the Amnae ambassador, dressed in a casual white shirt and beige slacks. "Ambassador Arkey." His voice warbled. "Welcome. I was most perturbed to learn Ambassador Corinth had missed the crossing—unusual tardiness coming from a Diviner—but you made it."

The elevator door closed behind me, leaving me alone with the ambassador. "There was an incident back on Chime, Your Excellency. A tram derailed."

"How unfortunate. But at least we'll be able to talk without a Diviner's overbearing presence. Please, take a seat." He gestured to a metal stool before his desk as he sat opposite. "Do you drink? The citizens of Memoria are fond of herbal cocktails, which your palate may appreciate. We have a saying; no one drinks like a fish!"

Drinking during a negotiation was likely a bad idea, but it would be rude to decline. I didn't need Harmony to advise me that ambassadors craved flattery. "I'd love to, Your Excellency. I can't say I've ever entered a library without books."

"Our libraries can store untold quantities of knowledge without wasting a single piece of paper. They're all there, in that font. And please. Call me Aberforth." He reached under the desk and produced two cocktail glasses and a canteen, which he shook. All the while he observed me. "I'll admit you surprised me at the Council, when you changed from a Diviner to a Mesmer. But this is rather... disconcerting, to say the least. How do your powers manifest? Through touch?" He poured a bright turquoise drink that glowed in the dim light of the room.

"That's right. Though my transformation today was out of necessity, more than anything. Memoria is a unique domain for those not accustomed to it." I took my cocktail and dared a taste. Whatever alcohol was mixed in it was masked by a strong mint flavor. It burned down my throat with a chill that made my gills quiver.

"My domain has its quirks, and I daresay none work harder than I to provide for my mortals. We require many accommodations on Chime merely to exist."

That was true. I'd never come across any Amnae in the Undercity, and they were rare in Central. Most lived in the Golden City. Anima certainly cared for their mortals.

Or did they? Harmony had briefed me on the Amnae god and their penchant for stealing memories. "I heard your mortals give up their memories in worship."

Aberforth took a sip from his cocktail. "My mortals enjoy academia. They are eager to pass on what they learn to our god, and Anima in turn lives through those memories, enjoying their experiences. As you can see, Anima provides for us." He waved a webbed hand around his room. "My mortals have no qualms passing on select memories in exchange for decadence and freedom. Though my question to you, Ambassador Arkey, is what does Corentine plan for my domain? For Chime?"

ANIMA WAS ALWAYS AN ODD ONE, Corentine's voice rumbled in my mind. *THEY WANTED TO BE DIFFERENT. SEPARATE AND UNIQUE FROM THEIR BRETHREN. THAT'S WHY THEY CHOSE AN UNDERWATER WORLD WHERE THE OTHER GODS DARED NOT TREAD. BUT SUCH DISTANCE DISCONNECTED THEM. THEY'RE FORCED TO LIVE THROUGH THEIR MORTALS' MEMORIES.*

So is Aberforth talking shit?

NATURALLY. ANIMA TAKES WHATEVER MEMORIES THEY DESIRE FROM THEIR MORTALS. THEY HAVE NO CHOICE BUT TO OBEY.

I've never heard an Amnae complain about it.

HOW COULD THEY? THEY DON'T REMEMBER.

Gods. Anima could strip whatever memories they wanted from their mortals, could abuse them in so many depraved ways, and they'd carry on oblivious to the tortures their own god inflicted. No wonder they went about their lives without fear.

Anima could erase those fears.

Was that better than death at Chaos's hands? To forget their own god's cruelties?

I'd come here with a plan to help the Amnae, to improve their lives, but would that even be possible if they forgot their grievances and complaints?

How could I stop a god from plucking from their mortals' minds?

"Ambassador?" Aberforth prompted.

I took another steadying sip of my minty cocktail and blinked back a sudden rush of dizziness. Whatever was in this thing was damn strong. "Corentine desires her freedom, and both I and Ambassador Corinth have a plan to grant her wish without violence. But as her soul currently powers Chime, we'll need the gods to lend their power. Since Anima so generously provides for their mortals, I'll assume they'd be willing to contribute."

"Is that all Corentine desires?"

"We also wish to recruit an Amnae to help us rehabilitate Chaos mortals."

"Oh? Do you have a specific Amnae in mind?"

"Ilona Burns. She's the daughter of an Amnae professor who studied memory, uh, experiments back in Chime's academy. He was a good friend of Ambassador Corinth, who sadly passed away during the attack last month. His daughter studies the same memory things. She'd be a valuable asset to us." I tried not to cringe at my own poor description of whatever it was the professor had worked on. This was why I needed Quen, but Aberforth didn't seem confused by my request.

I was handling this *perfectly*.

Harmony would be so proud I hadn't fucked it up yet.

"I'm aware of Professor Burns. His reputation precedes him. I was saddened by his death—he served our university well. Should his daughter be willing, we'd happily lend her to your cause. However, Anima wishes to make a trade."

"What sort of trade?"

"Our cooperation in exchange for a perusal of your memories."

"Why?" I blurted. My voice came out slurred.

Shit, I should have declined the cocktail. Who knew Amnae drinks would go to my head this quickly?

Aberforth stood and strode to the strange font. "I mean no offense, Ambassador Arkey, but Anima and I have no reason to trust you, nor any reason to trust Quentin Corinth. You both withhold the truth, and thus we'd like to see it for ourselves." He pressed the sucker of his forefinger against the side of his head and slowly pulled out a strange string of light, which he dropped into the font. It glowed in the water, and then merged with it, fading altogether. What was that? A memory? "You see, we're both aware of Corentine. She was meant to be sleeping. We'd like to know how she awoke."

GET OUT OF HERE, Corentine warned. *DON'T LET THEM INTO YOUR MIND.*

Shit. I wasn't handling this perfectly at all!

"It doesn't matter how she awoke, does it?" I said, my tongue heavy in my mouth. "Ambassador Corinth would be able to answer your questions. We can reschedule this meeting when he's next able to make the crossing. It was a pleasure meeting you." I stood and instantly swayed on my feet, my limbs shaky. I had to grab the side of the desk to stop myself from toppling.

"You're leaving so soon? We have at least eleven more hours until the crossing opens. Where will you go?"

"I heard there's a café here that sells exceedingly good cakes—"

"Are you sure you won't consider my offer? We simply wish to take a look at your memories. The process doesn't hurt—"

"I'd like to keep my memories to myself, if you don't mind."

"I'm afraid it wasn't a request." He swirled his glass and smiled over the rim. "Please sit before you fall and injure yourself, Ambassador."

The drink, Malk's voice said.

Shit. That cocktail wasn't just strong alcohol.

"You *drugged* me?"

My legs buckled, and I slid down the side of the desk onto my knees. The whole room spun, and the fish swimming through the walls were a blur of color.

Aberforth loomed over me. "It's fortunate you took on the appearance of my domain. It'll be much easier to deliver you personally to Anima."

"You fish-faced prick!"

"There's no need to be rude. You'll be quite pleased with our arrangement. In fact, you won't remember this at all."

I lurched forward to shove him away, but my body was heavy and uncoordinated, and I landed flat on my face instead.

Help me!

WHAT DO YOU EXPECT ME TO DO? YOU GOT YOURSELF INTO THIS MESS.

I don't know! Something godly!

MY BODY IS STRAPPED TO A MACHINE IN CHIME. I DO NOT HAVE THE POWER TO REACH YOU. IF I DID, I WOULD HAVE DESTROYED THIS DOMAIN BEFORE YOU STEPPED FOOT IN IT.

Some great god of chaos you are!

Footsteps echoed behind me, and I gazed up at another Amnae man holding a trident. He slammed the bottom of the trident close to my face, but I didn't even have the ability to flinch.

"Escort Ambassador Arkey to the outer rim."

Shit.

Harmony was going to be so pissed off with me.

15

As a Warden, it is imperative you do not enter memory parlors. Do not allow yourself to be touched by an Amnae. If you experience any of the following symptoms, report to the nearest Warden-sanctioned building immediately:
Memory loss
Confusion
Dizziness
Nausea or 'seasickness' as the locals call it
A sense of missing time
—Q. Corinth, *Warden Dossier on Memoria*

PERHAPS SINDER WAS RIGHT. I kept getting kidnapped more times than was socially appropriate. First by Wardens, then Glimmer, and Wardens again, and now Amnae.

After being betrayed by Varen, you'd think I'd learned not to trust ambassadors. If Quen were here, I'm sure he would have brought his bodyguard along, whereas I'd so casually left mine behind. These were lessons to learn. Shame I was about to forget them.

The Amnae pulled me up, and I stumbled like a drunk. I still had my faculties, though my vision blurred and my protests came out with a dribble of spit. My limbs were utterly uncooperative.

"Ambassador Corinth will kick you off the Council for this!" I tried to say, but it came out sounding like *Blamwassador Coreen*, so I abandoned speech altogether.

Aberforth ignored my gibberish as his cronies unceremoniously dragged me into the glass elevator and we rose even higher to the top level. I wasn't sure what to expect, but I certainly wasn't expecting to enter some sort of cloak room.

"Remove her clothes," Aberforth commanded as he began to undress.

"*Blot?*" I spat out. Gods, was I about to become prey to this sick fuck?

I'd been groped enough times in my life to know female mortals needed to take certain precautions against the males. Some domains were more handsy than others—Leander, for a start—and other domains were frequently the target of fetishists. Ember, Fauna, and Seren especially. I'd heard so many heartbreaking stories while living in Grayford. Fauna and Ember forced to prostitute themselves on Sinner's Row to avoid the workhouses, because joining the workhouses often resulted in abuse regardless.

It was Malk who'd taught me self-defense; where to jab my fingers for a quick getaway, what nerves to pinch. I'd tried to pass those onto the women I came across.

Protecting your drink was the only way to defend it against being spiked, and I'd failed that test right from the start.

Gods. I'd been so damn stupid to think an ambassador would be beyond such twattish behavior. Between Varen and Erosain, I *really* should have known better.

The Amnae tugged at my dress. I tried to swat them off, but I truly was at their mercy. Fuck this domain, I was going to steal every last soul!

Aberforth stood with his translucent flaccid cock swinging before me. "Don't panic, Ambassador. I have no interest in your body. In Memoria, it is far easier to swim when naked. Clothes tend to catch on the coral. Besides, it would look suspicious if I returned you to your Umber companion soaking wet."

Swim? He expected me to *swim*?

I didn't know how to pissing swim!

The Amnae got my clothes and boots off with relative ease, leaving Quen's silver bracelet around my wrist, and then they tied my hands together behind my back. Just how they expected me to swim like this, I didn't know.

My webbed feet flapped awkwardly against the tiles. They led me to a glass room with a good view of the dome surrounding the city. Even the floor was made of glass, and a large hole was cut into the center.

Water churned from the hole.

Shit. This connected to those pipes above the city.

And they were going to force me into it.

"Have you ever swum before?" Aberforth asked with genuine curiosity.

"*Blo!*"

"It comes naturally to all Amnae. I wonder how naturally it will come to you. My men will guide you, regardless. Don't fight them. The depths of Memoria's oceans can be claustrophobic. It's easy to become lost, and we wouldn't want that, would we?"

I tried to protest, but my Amnae guard shoved me forward, and I fell into the tube.

Warm water completely enveloped me. I opened my mouth to scream, and a rush of water filled my lungs.

Shit! I was going to choke! I was going to *fucking die*—

Air blew out of my gills. I was breathing. Gods, I was bloody breathing! Despite the sheer oddness of it, my breath came easier, as it had the first time I'd turned Amnae and Quen had needed to drop me into a tub.

I couldn't speak—my voice came out in a garbled collection of bubbles. But I could breathe, and right now, that was good enough.

One of the Amnae guards leaped in after me, forcing me aside, and they took my arm. Before I could even get my bearings, they were pulling me through the tunnel at impossible speeds, water rushing past me. My arms were still tied, so I couldn't flail, but apparently the Amnae didn't need to move their arms to swim. Their bodies twisted from side to side, their legs kicking out behind them. I copied their movement, and our glide through the tunnel became smoother.

I should have been fighting them off and swimming to my freedom, but there was something enjoyable about following the flow of water and letting my feet splash back and forth.

Between swimming as an Amnae or flying as a Zephyr, I much preferred swimming. There was less chance of death.

Though as I thought that, the tube suddenly ended, and I was flushed out into the great expanse of Memoria's ocean.

I'd thought the deep blue looked terrifying from the other side of that glass dome, but out here it was like floating in the sky with nothing above or beneath me. The domed city was already so far away I could barely see sunlight rippling on the surface.

There was plenty of rock—little underwater mountains where other glass domes hid among the coral in the distance. Most of the rock was painted in more seaweed and colorful plants and shells. Fish and other odd creatures swam around them.

It was beautiful.

But so utterly different to anything else I knew.

It wasn't home. It wasn't Chime.

The Amnae tugged me along and my stomach lurched as we dove.

Down into the dark.

We swam past coral outcrops and tiny orange fish who hid among the seaweed, past shells that housed creatures with twitching antennae, and past rocks where hundreds of eyes blinked at me. The further down we went, the darker it became, and I could no longer see where we'd come from.

The water too became colder and thicker, the pressure building in my ears and chest.

Aberforth swam on ahead, and he was right; if they abandoned me here, I'd become lost in a heartbeat.

As the darkness grew, so the plant life and fish began to glow with a bioluminescent blue to rival the mushrooms of Eventide. Jellyfish floated on by, and they danced with a kaleidoscope of color.

I remembered now what Harmony had said about the jellyfish.

They were immortal servants of Anima. Swim too close, and you were liable to get stung.

We came to a stop, but I could see nothing but the void beneath us.

"We're here," warbled Aberforth as bubbles escaped his mouth. He held a sharp-looking shell. I balked as he swam to me with it, but then he sliced through my bonds, and my arms were free.

I rubbed the imprint of the rope around my wrists. My coordination had come back, enough for me to wallop him in the face. Before I got the chance, he and his guard kicked their feet and swam up. I wafted away the spurt of bubbles that surrounded me.

They'd gone. Not even the glowing fish or plants remained.

The darkness pressed in with suffocating oppression, squeezing my chest. I let out a garbled cry as I twisted every which way. Shit! I couldn't tell up from down!

Why bring me here just to leave me floating in the middle of the pissing ocean? Surely there were less extravagant ways to kill me!

You've never feared the dark, Malk's voice said. *Don't start now.*

That was easy for him to say, he was dead!

My ability to transform into various personas had been useful up to now. In this moment, it had become a liability.

You could at least help! I yelled into my mind. *I can't be your ambassador if I drown—*

A CHILD OF CHAOS, came a voice from deep below in reply.

Shit.

That wasn't Corentine.

Movement bubbled below. Purple tentacles appeared out of the darkness and reached for me.

I kicked out and swam to one side. The tentacles followed.

One slipped around my waist and yanked me back with such force, my neck half-snapped. Shit! I went to grab it, to pull myself free. More tentacles shot out and wrapped around my wrists and ankles, pulling them apart until my limbs were stretched painfully in an undignified star.

I tried to writhe free, but the tentacles' grips were tight.

I'd read enough shit novels to know this was going to end badly.

Bubbles continued to churn around me as the source of the tentacles appeared from the gloom.

It was a gigantic jellyfish. Its bulbous head was as large as the glass dome and glowed teal. More purple tentacles dangled from its body, some crackling with aether static.

I'd seen images of this exact jellyfish throughout Memoria.

Shit. This was Anima.

God of the Amnae.

And I was completely at their mercy.

Panic gripped my chest and came out in a sputtering of bubbles.

SO CHAOS CAN FEEL FEAR.

What do you want from me?

For a moment, the waters stilled, and the silence near drowned me.

KNOWLEDGE, came the voice that was definitely *not* Corentine. Anima could hear me all right. *CHAOS ENTERS OUR DOMAIN, BUT CHAOS SHOULD NOT EXIST. DOR HAS BEEN KEEPING SECRETS.*

I'm sorry to spoil the surprise. Though while we're being friendly, would you please let me go? I promise to keep my hands to myself.

YOU ARE A RISK. WE KNOW WHAT POWER CHAOS POSSESSES.

I came into your domain peacefully! To negotiate! Is this how you treat guests? Dragging unsuspecting mortals to their wicked lair certainly made an impression. Not a good one.

WE WILL BARGAIN. BUT FIRST, WE MUST SEE THE TRUTH.

Tentacles slithered up my spine. I jerked at their cold touch, but Anima held me tight. They slid around my skull. Suckers lodged themselves against my forehead.

Anima was going to examine my memories, just as Quen's professor had.

But if Anima rooted through my mind, they'd see *everything*. Not just my pathetic existence, but Quen's plans, Corentine's threats, all of it.

That would give them more knowledge, more power, than any other god. What could I do to stop it?

I clenched my eyes shut, knowing it would be futile.

Images flared in my mind, and my life flashed before my eyes. Anima warped through them at such speed, I caught only glimpses—seeing Quen at the masquerade ball in that Vesper mask, leaping from the clock tower as I escaped Jinx, meeting Corentine and witnessing her vision of Babel, watching Quen's body crumple as Dor took his soul, losing Malk as Eventide turned to dust, watching the professor's body burn as he was strapped to the god-splitting machine...

The water surged around me at that memory, but still the images flashed on. My memories with Quen. With Malk. With the Godless.

Anima saw everything I was. Everyone I loved.

The images came to a glaring end as I languished in the Undercity as a child.

The place I'd been dumped through the aether.

Anima had seen it all.

THAT IS HOW WALTER BURNS MET HIS END. HIS SOUL DID NOT RETURN TO US. DOR HAS BROKEN THE COVENANT AND HAS MUCH TO ANSWER FOR.

Then we're on the same side!

YOU WOULD USE THESE DEVICES.

To protect my own mortals! We wouldn't force them on others—

YET YOU SERVE CORENTINE AS HER VOICE.

You've looked into my mind. You know what Quen and I want.

WE HAVE SEEN UNPLEASANT TRUTHS. DOR AND CORENTINE WOULD DO BATTLE. THE REST OF THE DOMAINS WILL BE CAUGHT BETWEEN THEM.

Shit. Had I just accidentally triggered a war between the gods? *We're trying to unite the domains—*

THERE WAS ONCE A BATTLE BETWEEN TIME AND CHAOS. THE GODS WERE FORCED TO TAKE SIDES.

The gods have battled before? Could that be true?

THOSE WHO LOST WERE BANISHED. THOSE WHO TOOK THE SIDE OF TIME REMAINED IN THEIR DOMAINS.

What are you saying? That there were more gods?

HUNDREDS MORE.

I couldn't wrap my head around it. Hundreds of gods? Hundreds of domains? *And Dor destroyed them?*

WE WERE FORCED TO FIGHT. AS WE WILL BE FORCED AGAIN, SHOULD CORENTINE FIND FREEDOM. AS YOU SPREAD HER INFLUENCE, THE GODS WILL DECIDE. WE SEE IT THROUGH MESMORPHEUS'S MEDDLING. SOME WILL TAKE DOR'S SIDE AS WE HAVE ALWAYS DONE. OTHERS WILL BE

DRAWN TO CHAOS. SOME WILL WAIT AND SEE WHICH WAY THE TIDE FLOWS.

And you? Whose side are you on?

WE ARE THE RIVERS OF HISTORY AND MEMORY. WE HAVE ALWAYS ALIGNED WITH TIME.

Well, shit. That probably made us enemies, which probably made me very dead. *I thought you were angry at the Diviner? They killed your professor.*

THE DIVINER'S MACHINATIONS RULE US. YOU CANNOT HOPE TO FATHOM THEIR DESIGNS. YOU ARE CHAOS, YET YOU ASSIST DOR'S CHILDREN. MESMORPHEUS HAS SEEN WHAT WE HAVE NOT.

Which is?

THE END OF TIME.

The water swelled once more, as though the ocean came alive with Anima's discontent, though the suckers remained lodged to my forehead.

WE WILL ALIGN WITH YOUR CAUSE. WE WILL SEND OUR CHILD TO SERVE YOU SO WE MAY SEE DOR'S WORKS FOR OURSELVES. THEN WE SHALL JUDGE WHICH WAY THE TIDE FLOWS.

Ilona Burns. Had Quen realized Anima would be able to spy on his plans through her? I sure hoped so.

WE SHALL BE READY FOR WAR, SHOULD YOU FAIL. MEMORIA IS DESIGNED TO BE DEFENDABLE.

So even gods could be paranoid.

IT IS NOT PARANOIA. IT IS LOGIC. GODS DO NOT TRUST EACH OTHER.

I got it. So, now we're on the same side, would you mind letting me go? I'd really like to try out Memoria's cakes. I've heard they're simply delightful. I pulled on the tentacles for good measure, but they didn't release me.

YOU ARE A DANGER. YOU POSSESS THE SOUL OF A GOD. OF VALERIA. WE SEE IT INSIDE YOU.

My heart hammered in my chest. *If you've seen my memories, you'll know I took that in self-defense! She would have killed me! I'm trying to stop*

Chaos from taking more. I couldn't bear to lose another domain. Another Malk.

YOUR POSSESSION OF THIS SOUL IS PROBLEMATIC—

Bloody take it, then!

WE CANNOT TAKE IT FROM YOU. CHAOS COULD. THEN CORENTINE WOULD GAIN AN ADVANTAGE. YOU ARE BOUND TO THIS SOUL THROUGH A PERSONAL CONNECTION. WE SHALL SEVER THIS CONNECTION.

What? If Anima cut off my access to Valeria's power, would I still be able to turn into a Vesper or access their shadows? Though if that meant Jinx couldn't take it from me, perhaps it was worth the sacrifice. *What do you mean by personal connection?*

They mean me, Malk said.

My Malk.

But—you're gone! I killed you, I killed them all—

We're here, Kayl. Inside you. Where you can reach us.

How's that possible?

You took her mortals. You took our souls.

THE LOVE YOU HOLD FOR THE VESPER BINDS YOU TO VALERIA'S POWER AND ALLOWS YOU TO ACCESS IT WITH EASE. SHOULD WE REMOVE THESE MEMORIES, YOU WILL NO LONGER BE ABLE TO WIELD IT, AND HER AETHER WILL REMAIN BURIED WITHIN.

Wait! Malk was real, he was talking inside my mind!

Gods. Could I bring them back? The Vesper? Could I save them all?

Malk. I could bring back Malk!

THIS IS THE AETHER OF GODS. NO MORTAL SHOULD WIELD IT.

You don't get to decide! Don't you see? I could bring back Eventide! This was my chance to fix everything I'd done!

SUCH POWER WOULD LEAD TO DESTRUCTION. IT IS FOR YOUR SAFETY, AND THAT OF THE DOMAINS, THAT YOU FORGET.

"*No!*" I screamed with a warbled burst of air.

If I forgot the Vesper, then I forgot Elvira, I forgot every single Vesper I'd ever helped as a Godless. I'd forget the end of Eventide and every life lost.

I'd forget I was responsible for their deaths. I'd forget what that meant.

Gods. No. I'd forget Malk.

I'd already erased him from existence once, I couldn't wipe him from my mind!

Malk! I can't lose you again!

Not again!

I thrashed in the water, attempting to escape, but Anima's grip only tightened around my limbs. *Corentine! Please, Corentine—*

SHE CANNOT HEAR YOU. THIS IS OUR DOMAIN.

You touch my memories and I swear I'll rip your domain apart!

THERE IS THE TRUTH. CHAOS IS VOLATILE.

Light seared in my mind. I screamed until my eyes burned with salt and my throat ached.

Malk! Come to me, Malk. Please. Come back to me.

I'm with you, Kayl. Even if you can't hear me. You'll carry me with you. Always.

I screamed until I forgot what I was screaming about.

My first trip to a domain had gone well, if I did say so myself.

Ambassador Aberforth turned out to be a charming host, and once he'd agreed to Quen's demands, he'd taken Dru and me for tea and cake at a charming little teahouse in Memoria, the famous Mr. Kipler's, where I'd helped myself to a delicious lemon meringue.

For afters, we'd visited a quaint Amnae bookshop—Bath's Books and Beyond—where I'd been gifted with a personal copy of *The Traveler's Handbook to Chime and Beyond*. I took the time to study the section on Memoria like a good tourist, and admire the beautifully painted map of the domains as designed by a famous Seren cartographer.

It would certainly come in handy for my future adventures.

Then the ambassador so generously put us up in a penthouse suite for the evening with the promise of collecting us for the 1 a.m. crossing.

Waking up that early didn't appeal, truth be told, but we couldn't keep Quen waiting. No doubt he was going out of his mind with worry. The early start left me a little shaky and confused, I'd admit, but after dressing in an Umber form, I soon found my bearings as Aberforth came to collect us.

The evening skies of Memoria were glorious. The city didn't need streetlamps. At night, the seaweed glowed in turquoise and teal tones, and even the fish glittered overhead like portable lanterns.

Though, gods was I glad to see the Gate switch on at one.

At the exact turning of the hour, Quen burst through the Gate, his wild silver eyes only calming when they settled on me. Behind him, Ben followed at a brisk pace.

I waved him over to where I, Dru, and Aberforth stood in the station, allowing other mortals to pass through with the usual station traffic.

"Good evening, Your Excellency," greeted Aberforth as Quen approached. "Or should I say good morning? I was sorry you missed the crossing. Is everything well back on Chime?"

Quen had since changed clothes. He forced a polite smile, which I could tell was forced by the strain in his eyes. "Yes, my apologies. We had a small incident back in Central Station, but everything is now in order." Those strained eyes moved to me. "Perhaps we can reschedule our meeting—"

"No need. Ambassador Arkey and I had a most productive discussion. Anima is happy to support your endeavor. Should Miss Ilona Burns be willing to assist, you won't mind if I send her over at the next crossing? It would be rude of me to contact her at this time."

"Of course. Thank you for your cooperation."

Aberforth bowed. "I should return to my duties. It was a pleasure to meet you, Ambassador Arkey, and you, Miss Smith."

Dru and I both curtsied as Aberforth left the station.

"Can I have a private word?" Quen said, his eyebrows twitching.

I shrugged at Dru and left her with Ben as Quen wandered out of earshot.

"Well?" he demanded. "I assume you were able to successfully entertain yourself for twelve hours?"

His attitude grated on me. "Yes, as it happens—"

"Why did you cross without me?"

"You told me to!"

"I did no such thing!" He ran his hands through his silver hair.

"Then you need to learn how to communicate better." I could have sworn Quen had told Dru and I to go on ahead and that he'd catch up. I wouldn't have bloody left without him otherwise! "What happened back on Chime?"

"The Wardens are still investigating the tram incident. Someone used time manipulation to force it to crash. It may have been Jinx."

Shit. Why in god's name would she cause a tram to derail?

Do you know anything about this? I asked Corentine.

WHY SHOULD I CARE FOR DIVINER TECHNOLOGY?

Why indeed. *Did Jinx fuck with the trams?*

YOU ALWAYS THINK THE WORST OF YOUR SISTER.

That's because she's the worst.

"Never mind that," Quen said, bringing my thoughts back to the present. "What happened here?" He thrust his hands into his pockets, his body tense.

"You assumed I'd fuck everything up?"

"Kayl—"

"It's *fine*, Quen. Dru and I met with the ambassador. I explained our plan, and Anima's on board with it." Which surprised me too. But after visiting Memoria and seeing how the Amnae lived with my own eyes, maybe my previous judgements were too harsh. Anima was still an almighty god, but they seemed to care for their mortals in a way no other god did. "And then Dru and I did some sightseeing. Have you seen the fish? There're so many types—"

"Aberforth agreed, just like that?"

"Honestly, you could have a little more faith in me."

"Where ambassadors are concerned, I need to ensure all deals are made by the book."

"You're an ambassador—should I be watching out for you?"

He glanced over the rim of his eyeglasses. "I *am* the book. If they rooted through your memories, they could have seen anything, taken anything—"

"Nothing happened, all right?" What had gotten into Quen to leave him so rattled? Did he not trust me with the task he'd set me? Or was Jinx getting under his skin?

Quen's hands came out of his pockets, and he grabbed my wrist just below the silver bracelet. "Do you remember me? Do you remember our plan? Our purpose?"

"To save the domains, I remember—"

"Harmony? Sinder? Vincent—"

"Of course I bloody remember them—"

"The Vesper?"

As though I'd forget what fate had befallen the Vesper! "Honestly, Quen—"

"Do you remember that I kissed you?" His voice turned hoarse.

My heart skipped a beat. "Like I could forget."

His cheeks reddened, and he released my arm. "Apologies, I... I don't trust Aberforth's intentions."

"He seemed nice."

"That only raises my suspicions further. He's always been uncouth with me."

"That's because you lack my charm."

Finally, a real smile came to his lips. "Well, if there *are* any consequences to this meeting, I'm sure I'll regret them later. Though next time, wait for me, will you?"

"You know me. It's rare for me to be on time for anything."

"I'll count your future tardiness as a blessing." He pulled out his pocket watch. I was glad to see it returned to his hands. "We should return to Chime before we waste another twelve hours. Are you able to make the crossing to Tempest at seven?"

"*Seven?* You want me to make another crossing on only five hours' sleep?"

"What about Obituary at eight? I can visit Tempest with Ben."

"You won't need me there to coerce and threaten mortals?"

"All I'm really after is Doctor Finch. We can sort out the specifics later."

Quen offered his arm. I wrapped mine around his, and we returned to Dru and Ben, who were caught in some polite conversation about Memoria's plants.

I wasn't quite sure what Quen's hurry was to visit all these domains, though I had a hunch it had something to do with Jinx. While my twin lurked in Chime, the domains were still at risk.

Though I did feel a smug satisfaction.

My first task as Ambassador Arkey had gone perfectly.

Harmony would be so proud.

XVI

Forget what you know of the other domains.
Tempest is a test of the faithful.
Arguably the most dangerous of the domains, one must enter Tempest with
caution. Tempest's atmosphere boasts extreme weather, which can be
impossible to navigate. If one must enter Tempest, then it is advised one does
so with a local guide who can rent out a vessel for traversing the domain.
And for pity's sake, keep away from the walkway.
—Q. Corinth, *Warden Dossier on Tempest*

NOT MANY QUEUED FOR the morning crossing to Tempest, but the station was busy enough with tourists waiting for the elevators both up and down. Ben bought, me a coffee and I stared into the murk, working up the courage to dare a sip.

Courage was what I needed to face the task ahead of me.

The events of yesterday had left me exhausted. I'd never known a panic attack to last twelve sodding hours, yet that was what it had felt like as anxiety possessed me. When Kayl had made that crossing, I had debated yanking time backwards and dragging her out, but as someone had quite clearly tampered with time, it wasn't wise to tempt fate.

My suspicions landed on Jinx. What had been her intentions? To sneak into the Gate? To cause disruption around Central? To remind me that Chaos still had a foothold in the city?

With Doctor Finch's help, we'd soon have the tools we'd need to deal with Chaos.

Ben finished off his coffee and didn't look any worse for wear considering our midnight jaunt.

"Do you ever sleep?" I asked. "Or are you fueled purely by that foul concoction?"

"I sleep in shifts, sir."

"That's just as well. Though I'm hoping we won't be making any more late-night crossings."

"Are the Amnae backing us, sir?"

"Apparently." Despite Kayl's confidence, I didn't trust Aberforth.

I had faith in Kayl. Of course I did. But anything could have happened to her in Memoria, and it would have been entirely my fault. She had the street smarts of an Undercity upbringing, and could handle herself in a fight far better than I could, but she didn't know these domains like I did, nor their ambassadors.

I could have grabbed Aberforth and examined his past for those twelve hours, but even my high rank on the Council had its limits. None of the other ambassadors would ever cooperate with me again if I pulled that stunt.

Though perhaps I worried over nothing. Dru had been with her. Neither of them looked mistreated from their sojourn to Memoria.

But that didn't stop the doubts gnawing at my gut.

Was I such a mistrustful wretch?

I forced a gulp of my bitter coffee and almost gagged. "What do you think of Miss Smith?"

Ben raised his brows in my direction. "She thinks I'm simple, sir."

"No! Why would she ever think that?"

"Don't know, sir. She keeps explaining things to me." The poor man looked dejected.

"Women of the domains always assume the men are incompetent." Though in some cases, they were right.

I don't know why I bothered asking him. It wasn't any of my business. Though I did enjoy conversing, unlike the rest of my domain. I would never understand why other Diviner were so opposed to such pleasantries as small talk. Mortals held so many fascinating secrets. The fact that Diviner could unlock those secrets with a single touch made the allure of *not* doing so all the more enticing.

Though, despite what Kayl thought, Diviner didn't date outside our domain. It wasn't the done thing. Father didn't approve, for one. As His voice, I shouldn't be advocating it. I blamed Kayl entirely for putting the thought in my head.

The clock tower struck the hour, and seven harsh dongs shook through me.

The Gate changed from the nightmarish landscape of the Necro domain to something I feared far more.

The open skies of Tempest.

"Well then. Let's go prove how competent we men are. Are you fine with heights?"

"They don't bother me, sir."

"Does *anything* bother you?"

"Paperwork, sir. Gets tedious." His expression was serious.

Sometimes I had to wonder if Ben was even a Diviner at all.

We made our way across the station concourse and approached the Gate. Though I couldn't feel it, wind rippled on the other side, sending flags and bunting flapping in the air.

I'd visited some truly awful domains—Juniper, Witheryn, Eventide—but none compared to Tempest, home of the Zephyr.

In a way, I was glad Kayl hadn't chosen to accompany me here. Her ability to turn into a Zephyr may have been useful should I lose my footing.

But I also didn't want to soil myself in front of her.

There were only so many indignities a man wished to make known publicly. Incompetent males indeed.

"Sir?" Ben prompted.

"Right you are." I pushed my spectacles up my nose as far as they'd go and then braced myself as I stepped through the Gate.

Howling wind blew through my hair and made me stagger sideways.

My stomach lurched. The whole station was one giant hot-air balloon that wobbled precariously in the sky. Above, the gigantic balloon blotted out the sun and occasionally roared with a blast of fire. Below, a sky ship of some sort comprised the station's passport office and waiting area. Only a thin bronze railing prevented curious travelers from wandering off the side and falling to their demise.

For that was the maddening reality of Tempest. There was no land here. No floating islands. No ocean below the clouds. No firm footing to be found. The entire domain was a bubble of air, and all constructs and buildings floated within it at the whims of Tempest's winds. If one fell overboard, saints knew what became of you.

"It's windy today, sir," Ben called out over the ghastly howls.

"What an astute observation!"

Sails flapped around the side of the ship, and my stomach churned at every tip and tilt the platform made. I glanced toward the Gate and the safety of Chime. That was the other maddening reality of Tempest. The Gate here was made of a collection of bronze gears and wiring that should comfort me—indeed, Diviner and Zephyr had much of their technology in common—yet this Gate was the only Gate in all the domains that constantly shifted as the platform flew through the air.

One could enter Tempest and emerge at a completely new location, despite Chime remaining solidly in place. Though that wasn't what bothered me. The Gates of the other domains were anchored. Safe.

What if one day this ship faltered and the Gate tumbled into the void?

What if that happened when I was visiting?

Unlike Kronos, the skies here changed frequently, morphing from clear blue skies to raging black storms that poured with rain, hail, and lightning as powerful as aether. And judging by the dark gray of the horizon, we were headed into danger.

I pointed to the foreboding clouds. "We best not dally. I have no intentions of getting caught in that blasted thing."

Ben pulled his collar up. "After you, sir."

A metal sign pointed to the entrance of the station office below deck. Unlike the static signs of Chime, this one updated on the fly. Today, it warned of the upcoming storm, and—

"Transport is offline, sir."

"Yes, I can see that." Blast it!

"We could return when the weather is more favorable, sir?"

"We need Doctor Finch. I'm not waiting." I didn't want to return to Kayl empty-handed.

If the transport boats were down, then we had only one choice.

To traverse Tempest's deadly walkways.

Each of these ships, including the Gate's platform, were tethered together with a sprawling metal walkway that eventually led to one floating monstrosity: Zyclone's fortress.

The real challenge lay in crossing the walkway without screaming or urinating on oneself. Fortunately, the howling winds masked screams rather well, and soaking pants could be mistaken for rain.

I approached the entrance to the walkway in a haphazard motion, my body leaning from left to right, like navigating between tram carriages on a bend. Before me, the walkway disappeared into a fog of clouds, with no way of knowing what lay ahead. Zephyr rarely used the walkways—they could simply fly between the ships, though many manned smaller steam-powered boats for longer journeys.

The walkway, then, was designed for mortals without wings. Mortals who were apparently fearless.

My hand gripped the railing with white-knuckled tightness.

And my feet remained firmly in place.

If Kayl were here, she'd likely relish the challenge and go bounding on ahead. Saints. I could imagine her jumping up and down on the walkway as I hung on for dear life. I was *never* bringing her here.

"We'll have to pause time," I called to Ben. "The winds aren't calm enough to cross."

"I'll be right behind you, sir."

I ground my teeth. Surely my bodyguard should be the one to lead? Though as I glanced over my shoulder, his face had paled to a Necro's shade.

Why did I have to be in charge? Surely, I'd earned some cowardice.

The walkway was made up of individual metal planks chained together and a railing on either side. I knew from experience that the flooring was solid, despite the minuscule gaps between planks that allowed wind to blow up one's trouser legs. This design was meant to allow the walkway to flow and bend with the ships.

But the way they swayed caught in my throat.

Without moving a muscle, I brought time to a stop.

The walkway ceased its unrepentant sway. Zyclone would notice I'd manipulated time in their domain. The gods always did. Some weren't bothered by it, but others had strict rules—Diviner were banned from large parts of Rapture due to the fear we'd pause time to cheat in their casinos. By stopping time, I'd effectively announced my arrival.

At least Zyclone would be waiting for me.

I tentatively placed one foot onto the walkway.

The first lesson of traveling to Tempest was to *never* look down, to always stare straight ahead. With thick clouds all around us, it felt like being stuck in white space.

It reminded me of being trapped in that room, surrounded by ticking clocks, as I awaited judgement from my Father.

Like being surrounded by death.

"One foot at a time, Ben."

One foot at a time.

Thankfully, the walkway remained a solid path as time held its breath. I still gripped the metal railing as I slowly edged my way through the clouds. With visibility as poor as it was, one slip could still mark my doom, even with time paused.

Ben's steps clattered closely behind me, and I was grateful they weren't causing the walkway to bounce up and down with his weight.

Cloud obscured the airships that would otherwise surround us. Every now and then a break allowed me to glimpse the plated structures made of wood and bronze. As the walkway headed up, and we climbed out of the clouds, hundreds of airships came into view. Thousands.

"That's a sight, sir," Ben said as he joined me. "How do they stay afloat?"

"Aether and steam engines, mostly."

We had a couple of blimps back on Kronos, but nothing compared to Zyclone's massive fleet. It was an entire city made of individual airships, hot air-balloons, blimps, and other floating constructs connected via the walkway. Most could untether and fly off at a moment's notice, and the smaller ships served as private homes, so I'd read.

And at the heart of this sea of clouds, wood, and metal was Zyclone's fortress.

I allowed time to catch up as my feet finally made contact with solid ground, or what passed for solid ground here on Tempest. Cool air whooshed around me, and my grip remained painfully clutched around the railing.

We stood on the main deck of the largest airship in Zyclone's fleet. This deck alone was the size of Central. Below were numerous levels all holding Zyclone's workshops, factories, and housing for the Zephyr. Above, the giant mast was as impressive as Chime's clock tower. Lightning from the oncoming storm was already spiking the antennae attached to the mast. Natural aether, which powered these ships.

And perched on the sails were large birdlike creatures. Hawks and falcons, they were called. Zyclone's immortal guardians. They cried with an ear-wrenching shriek, their beady eyes watching everything.

A group of Zephyr approached. All wore avian leathers and goggles, which allowed them to fly easily in Tempest's atmosphere. I recognized the Zephyr with black feathers.

"Ambassador Corvus," I called out by way of greeting.

The crow-like ambassador tilted his head sharply. "Corinth. Our master sensed your arrival. You did not bring your Chaos friend?"

"Just me today, I'm afraid. I'm here to speak with Doctor Zachery Finch."

"Doctor Finch is refusing visitors and asks not to be disturbed. He's already spurned our guests from yesterday's crossing."

Other guests? "May I ask whom?" I yelled.

"A Glimmer delegation."

Blast. If the Glimmer were searching for the good doctor, then it likely wasn't with altruistic intentions. "It's imperative I speak with him." My voice was going hoarse from shouting above the wind. "Can we discuss this somewhere quieter?"

Corvus and his guards led the way across the deck, which also served as a runway for the Zephyr's smaller floating devices. Planes, or some such. We headed for the large hangar that made up the bulk of the fortress's bridge.

The hangar doors were opened only wide enough to allow us through, no doubt due to the growing storm. Zephyr flew above us, securing flaps and wiring as more lightning blasted the antennae.

"Nice weather you're having," I quipped.

Corvus cocked his head. "This is mild."

Mild? Dear gods. "It's a little blustery."

Ben stared at me dumbfounded.

"We ask that Diviner refrain from using their abilities while visiting." Corvus gave us both a sharp look. "Time manipulation interferes with our weather."

"Apologies," I mumbled. Though if this blasted storm didn't halt soon, we wouldn't make it back to the Gate in time. I'd sooner break the Covenant than remain here for twelve sodding hours.

Inside the hangar, the howling wind was replaced by chaos. And this was where the similarity between our domains came to a grinding halt.

Diviner constructs were made with orderly precision following logical blueprints and the laws of science. The Zephyr, however, were chaotic in their experiments. Half the time, there was no rhyme or reason to them. They simply created because they could.

The entire space resembled a bustling indoor market with multiple stalls set out in disorganized lines. Many were filled with contraptions and parts, from aether lamps to crates of nuts and bolts. Others were displays showcasing the latest technology—gramophones that played recorded music and devices that could slice and toast bread. Many more stalls were workshops where Zephyr donning overalls tinkered with machinery or banged their hammers down on metal plating. The hiss of steam, rattle of cogs, and ringing of hammers echoed throughout in a jarring cacophony that made my head ache.

Mortals from the other domains came here to haggle over the most coveted inventions and seemed oblivious to the display above them. As lightning struck the fortress, aether pulsed across the ceiling and upper walls in a sparkling web of electricity. And there, in the center of the ceiling, a large artificial eye watched everything.

Not many realized this eye was Zyclone themself.

The god rarely interacted with mortals, but versions of this artificial eye spread throughout the fortress. Forever observing. Though to what end, who knew?

The eye swiveled on me. I lowered my gaze.

"We would have welcomed a visit from Ambassador Arkey," Corvus said above the din, though I wasn't sure if it was him or his god speaking. "We're curious to know how they interact with aether, and how they're able to change physicality between the domains. Do you still have the male in custody?"

"We do." Though I hadn't yet had the chance to question him.

"Will you grant us a copy of your report once you've dissected them?"

I cleared my throat. "I'm not planning on any dissections."

"Oh? I thought that was your predecessor's policy."

"My predecessor's, perhaps. Not mine."

"How else will you study their nervous system?"

"With great care." I eyed a nearby Zephyr who was eavesdropping on our conversation. How much of Hector Bezel's experiments had Doctor Finch revealed to his domain? Diviner and Zephyr made valuable partnerships when it came to technological developments. The clock tower and elevators would not exist without our combined expertise.

But such brilliant minds often lacked a mortal's vulnerability.

They forgot that mortals bled and screamed and suffered if you cut them open.

Or they never cared at all.

I suppressed a shudder. We followed Corvus into a corridor not too dissimilar from the inside of Chime's clock tower. Metal plating, pipes, and wiring covered every inch of the walls, turning the corridor into a tunnel of brass. It vibrated around me with the hum of both storm and aether, and occasionally steam hissed from an overhead pipe. A song of natural and unnatural energies in unison.

Though, the lingering stench of oil and soot reminded me of the steamworks. I could practically taste the metal on my tongue. Everything about this domain seemed... unnatural. Mechanical in a way not even Kronos suffered.

"Are there any plants in Tempest?" Ben asked, breaking the silence.

"We have nurseries where we grow fruit and seeds," Corvus said. "They're located below deck."

Ben looked baffled. "How do you grow them below deck, if you don't mind my asking?"

"Is there any particular reason you're asking?" I said with a sly smile.

Ben's cheeks turned pink. "Just curious, sir."

Yes, I was sure it had nothing to do with a certain green-skinned Umber.

"They're specially designed greenhouses," Corvus continued. "We use artificial lamps and water pipes. Our diet has undergone centuries of research to perfect. No food or water is wasted."

We turned into a larger corridor lined with bulkhead doors and metal stairs leading up and down. Other Zephyr rushed past, unbothered by a pair of Diviner on their ship. Their feathers fluttered against a steam grate. How did they manage to keep their feathers from cluttering the place and clogging the machinery?

Corvus led us down two flights of steps, past more identical decks, into the belly of the fortress. Here, the whistling wind had grown quieter, but in its place the groan of the ship's engines rumbled. Occasional glass portholes gave us slivers of natural light, though the corridors were mostly lit by orange lamps.

The further down we went, the more claustrophobic the walls grew.

Soon we came to a stop beside a bulkhead door labeled *Hatchery*.

Oh my. Mortals from other domains were forbidden from the hatchery.

Corvus pulled the handle down and invited us in.

We entered a reception room with the usual desk and waiting area. Only, the wall opposite was entirely made of glass. Corvus gestured us over, and a thrill shivered through me as I peered into the room.

Below us were rows and rows of boxes. Each were labeled with a family name and had an orange aether bulb dangling above.

And there, in each box, were large beige eggs the size of my head.

"Incredible," I whispered. Zephyr had the oddest breeding rituals of the domains by far. No other mortal literally laid an egg that then hatched. The only other domain with such oddities were the Amnae, who birthed children with fused fins for legs and required them to remain in tanks until their lungs finished forming. "How many eggs are there?"

"Hundreds. We keep them here, as the engine soothes them."

"But why?" Ben blurted out. "Why are they separate from their mothers?"

"Once an egg is laid, it becomes the responsibility of the ship to raise them in a communal environment."

"But surely, it's the mother who, uh, makes the egg?"

"Ben," I warned. He was being rather offensive.

"Curiosity is a sign of a healthy brain." Corvus waved me off. "Our women lay the eggs, yes, but our men help rear them. We raise our young together so mature adults may engage in play. This is encouraged, as all can learn from children."

Maybe I should have been born a Zephyr. Their lives certainly sounded less complex than mine. "Is there a reason you've brought us here?"

Corvus pointed to the left side of the hatchery, where a familiar wingless Zephyr in a lab coat was checking readings against a clipboard. Doctor Zachery Finch. I'd not realized he possessed a paternal side.

The ambassador picked up a microphone. "Doctor Finch?" His voice rang through a loudspeaker. "Ambassador Quentin Corinth is here to speak with you."

Doctor Finch's face turned sharply and looked up at me.

I gave him a little wave.

He dropped his clipboard and ran from the room.

"That's unexpected," Corvus commented.

"Did he just *flee*?"

"Doctor Finch's paranoia has reached remarkable levels lately. That's why he requested basic maintenance work here in the hatchery."

Kayl had said something about Chaos wanting him. Likely for the same reason I did, and the Glimmer, too. "I assure you I have no intention of harming the good doctor. Can you order him back?"

"Oh no, he's long gone. But he won't get far in this storm. If you're that desperate to speak with him, I suggest you run. Good hunting."

Wonderful. "Ben, with me!"

I bounded into the corridor and caught sight of Doctor Finch at the far end. "Doctor! Wait!"

Alas, he did not.

Chasing him across Tempest was *not* how I'd expected this meeting to go.

He launched up the metal stairs with more vigor than most scientists boasted. I kept him in my sights as Ben and I slid past confused Zephyr who narrowly dodged out of the way.

"Blast it!" I gasped, catching my breath.

The doctor barreled into the main hangar, forcing his way through the crowds.

I followed, ducking under a metal crane that swung out. "Doctor! I just want to talk!"

He slowed to a stop, his feathers ruffling as he panted. "I have nothing to say to you!" He threw off his lab coat and kept running.

Such dramatics!

While the doctor certainly possessed the adrenaline of paranoia, I was a trained Warden. Chasing down mortals was part of my skill set.

"Ben, go wide around the stalls. We'll flank him before he reaches the hangar doors."

Ben nodded and slunk between the workshop stalls. With any luck, the doctor would be too focused on me to notice him.

I kept a quick pace, weaving between mortals, crates, and contraptions as the good doctor rather predictably ran for the doors.

They were open wide enough for a single mortal to slip through. Beyond, the skies had turned nigh on pitch black, and rain splattered the entrance. Saints!

We had to stop him before he made it out!

He was mere seconds from slipping away. If I could sodding pause time, this would have been over by now.

Ben leaped from the side.

The doctor squawked, and shoved another mortal carrying a box into Ben.

They collided, flinging cogs and metal parts everywhere. Ben tripped over a spring and crumpled to the ground with a yelp.

Doctor Finch smirked in the only smug way a beak could, and then he slipped between the hangar doors.

Damn and blast!

I crouched beside Ben. "Are you hurt?"

Ben gripped his boot. "Twisted my ankle, sir. Sorry. I'll catch up."

Rain was coming in from that sliver of space that divided my safety from my doom.

This entire morning had been a foolish endeavor.

Surely we could manage without Doctor Finch? He wasn't *vital* to my plans... There was time to dry off and grab a cup of tea.

Oh, I so desperately needed a cup. Two sugars. A splash of milk—

"You can do it, sir," Ben gasped. "You've made it this far."

He was right, though I loathed to admit it. What kind of man was I if I couldn't face a little rain? It was no different than a pleasant shower in my tub. I could handle that. One must set an example for their subordinates. "Rest here. I'll, ah, return in good time."

I dove into the darkness before I could change my mind.

Rain lashed with a fury I'd not thought possible, and I staggered as it hit my spectacles. Visibility in this dark storm was already down, and blurriness made everything so much worse.

Lights danced in the storm ahead. The Zephyr had lit lanterns beside the railings and walkways. They clearly suffered these storms regularly.

I no longer wished to be born a Zephyr.

My footsteps splashed across the deck as I followed a shape in front— Doctor Finch.

"Doctor, please! I mean you no harm!"

He vanished into the void.

And screamed.

Saints! I stumbled after him. My footing gave way, and I collided with a metal railing.

We'd ended up on the blasted walkway!

The walkway swayed from side to side with such violence, as though I clung to the back of a roaring Leander who was trying to shake me off.

Ahead, I could just about see the doctor hanging off the side. Oh my goodness.

He was trapped, and dangling quite precariously with no way of flying to safety.

"Help me!" he screamed, but no Zephyr remained out in this storm.

A bolt of lightning struck a metal pole above, and I instinctively wrapped my entire being around the damn railing.

I was still close enough to Zylone's fortress that I could crawl my way to safety, leaving the doctor to fall to his demise.

He rather deserved it for the merry chase he'd put me through.

But that was fear talking. An irrational thing. I'd faced death. My own, and countless others at the touch of my hand. I'd brought death and lived with the nightmares they granted.

I knew where my timeline would end, and it wasn't here.

And yet...

Gods curse this domain!

I vaulted forward before my feet were ready. The metal railing was slick under my grip, and the walkway continued to buck beneath me, causing my stomach to perform somersaults. I was mere moments from vomiting or urinating on myself.

My foot slipped, almost missing my step. Saints preserve me!

I'd fallen so many times in my life. Fallen from a clock tower. Fallen into sin.

Fallen into aether.

How many more times would I fall?

"One foot at a time," I muttered, moving across one plank, and then the next.

One foot at a time.

All in all, I was glad I'd left my pistol behind in HQ, for I surely would have lost it by now. I practically dragged myself to where Doctor Finch screeched.

"No! Not you!" he squawked.

"You've got no damn choice! I'm *not* here to harm you!"

"I wouldn't be in this predicament if it wasn't for you! Can't you stop time?"

Pausing time wouldn't have helped, not in this thick rain. I'd done that before, and it was like pushing through curtains. "I'm obligated not to!"

"*Obligated?*"

"Shut up and let me save you, damn you!"

My life flashed before my eyes as I leaned over the railing—tea, misery, more tea, death, oddly erotic dreams, bourbon biscuits—and hauled the doctor over.

He collapsed onto the deck and rolled onto his back.

I sank beside the railing, my chest heaving, my limbs like a soggy digestive. Every muscle ached, and I was soaked down to my bones. "Was that so damn hard?"

As I spoke, the rain eased off, turning into faint drizzle, and the wind stopped trying to throw me overboard.

An eye was watching me from the porthole of the ship opposite.

Zyclone.

Had this been some bizarre test?

"What do you want with me?" the doctor gasped, returning my attention.

"Your help—"

"My *help*? The last time I helped a Diviner, my mentor ended up dead! My project was scrapped! I was kidnapped by soul-eating creatures who threatened to murder me! And then *your* friend tossed me out of the clock tower and let me fall into a *lake*!"

So Kayl *had* thrown him into a lake. "You survived to tell the tale—"

"Only because I came *here*!" He sat up and jabbed a talon at my chest, which bloody hurt! "Your friend is one of those creatures—"

"And she saved your life, by the sounds of it."

"Well—yes. But that's beside the point. What do you need that can't be done by a Diviner?"

"To help me reconfigure the devices you and Hector Bezel designed."

"That's what the Glimmer wanted. What's your purpose with them?"

"To remove the powers of the soul-eating creatures, as you put it, so they may choose their own domain and be rehabilitated into Chime."

The doctor stared at me. "Are you insane?"

I took off my spectacles and wiped away the raindrops. "Quite insane, yes."

"I don't work for Diviner. Not when they partner with Glimmer. They tried to recruit me into their workhouse."

A break in the clouds sent a ray of light over the ship's decking. My goodness. A rainbow spread across the sky.

Only now did I wish I'd brought Kayl with me to see it.

Its color curved over Zyclone's fortress with a natural beauty I'd thought this domain lacked. It was an awe-inspiring sight, but I'd had enough awe for one day.

"You'd be working directly under me, not Glimmer interests. I promise you, I don't run a workhouse."

Doctor Finch patted the water from his feathers. A few stray ones came loose. "I refuse to stay in Chime for my own safety. If I assist you, then you take me to Kronos."

"That can be arranged—"

"With a fully equipped laboratory—"

"Whatever you need, Doctor. I'll personally escort you to Kronos on the next crossing. Speaking of, it's almost eight."

"I'm not a fan of small talk, loud noises, or surprises."

"Noted."

"We understand each other, then?"

I held in my sigh. The good doctor was going to prove difficult to work with, but at least he was cooperating.

Things could only get better from here.

17

Obituary is another domain the Wardens have listed as unsafe. While we cannot stop mortals from crossing into dangerous domains, we can at least try to warn them of potential dangers. Obituary, then, is full of danger— from the rowdy and aggressive Leander to the desert heat itself.
If one must travel to Obituary, I recommend taking adequate shade, staying well hydrated, avoiding the arena, and avoiding alcohol. One does not want to indulge in a challenge or bet by a drunken Leander.
Trust me on that one.
—Q. Corinth, *Warden Dossier on Obituary*

THANKS TO DRU PRACTICALLY dragging me out of bed, we made it to Central Station well before the clock struck eight in the morning. Though as we found a seat within the public waiting area, there was no sign of Quen or Big Ben.

It wasn't like Quen to be late for anything. Indeed, I didn't think it was physically possible for a Diviner. But when the clock tower rang out quarter to the hour, I started to worry.

"You think they fell off an airship?" I asked Dru.

"I don't think they're that careless."

"Oh, I don't know. Quen likes to play the hero, and his friend seems just as bad. Is that a male thing or a Diviner thing?"

"Both."

I hummed in agreement as I fiddled with my parasol.

Quen had insisted I bring this damn thing and dress for heat worse than Memoria—the kind that burned. After checking in with Harmony and Sinder, I realized I'd need something practical that covered my arms and legs without looking too informal. I still needed to woo the Leander.

Thanks to Sinder's expertise, I'd donned a light beige dress and shawl if I should need it, and an Ember's face.

Obituary's heat wasn't like Rapture's, he'd said. The Leander domain had a tendency to bite like their mortals.

I was about to get up and grab a coffee when the Gate rippled and three familiar figures staggered out.

Shit. Quen appeared absolutely soaked and disheveled next to the Zephyr doctor, and Ben was limping. What in god's name had they gotten up to?

Dru and I hurried toward them, but as soon as the Zephyr noticed me, he squawked.

"You didn't tell me *she* would be here!" He turned and tried to run back to the Gate.

Quen grabbed his shirt and yanked him still. "Calm down. We're on the same side."

I took my cue and bobbed a curtsy. "You're looking well, Doctor! Have you been practicing your swimming?"

The doctor flapped his arms in outrage, sending a flurry of feathers into the air.

Quen shot me a warning look as he dragged the doctor away from the Gate.

Dru was already at Ben's side. She wrapped her arm around his waist and practically carried him to the nearest bench.

"What happened, then?" I asked.

"Twisted my foot, miss," Ben said with a wheeze. "It's nothing serious."

"Well, you're in no fit state for a trip to Obituary. And what about *you*?" I asked as Quen approached after finally settling the doctor with a cup of tea from the nearby booth.

Quen removed his eyeglasses and tried to find something dry to clean them with, but he truly was soaked through.

"Here." I pulled out a handkerchief.

He wore a strained smile. "The weather got ahead of us, but I'd still like to enter Obituary—"

"You need a change of clothes. Why not wait until tonight?"

"Because Obituary is far rowdier at night." He finished cleaning his eyeglasses. "I'd rather do this now and get it out of the way. Besides, their ambassador is expecting me."

"So you're going to meet with their ambassador dressed like a sad mop?"

"Ten minutes under Obituary's sun and I'll be dry as their desert."

"And poor Ben?"

"Someone needs to watch over Doctor Finch. Ben, I'd like you to escort the good doctor to Warden HQ and secure him until we can transfer him to Kronos at ten. You can find a Necro for your foot there."

Ben sat up. "But, sir, Obituary isn't safe—"

"I'll be fine on my own, I assure you. I've crossed into Obituary before. Besides, Dandelion will be there waiting for me, and I trust him with my life."

"You expect Ben to hobble across Central on that foot?" Dru said, appalled.

"You go with him," I said. "Keep him and the doctor out of trouble."

"And who's going to keep *you* out of trouble?"

"I'll be with the famous Dark Warden." I fluttered my eyelashes at Quen.

Quen grimaced. "Please don't call me that."

"It's not a good plan, sir." Ben's face twisted in discomfort. "You're not armed, and Leander are beasts, if you don't mind me saying." Ben stood on his foot. "I can walk—" He hissed and immediately sat down.

"We'll be safe," Quen said. "And we'll be back on the hour."

As he said those words, the clock struck eight, and Tempest's blue skies were wiped clean and replaced with the orange landscape of Obituary.

"Right." Quen clapped his hands together. "We best not dally. Ben, take care of the doctor. And Miss Smith, take care of Ben."

"Try not to get eaten by a Leander," Dru warned me.

I blew her a kiss and strode beside Quen, careful to avoid rubbing elbows with him as he squelched his way up to the Gate. He paused to take off his shriveled bow tie and run his fingers through his hair, but instead of smoothing it down, he only forced strands to stick out at sharp angles.

"Look, you're only making it worse." I used my fingers to straighten it back, letting a bit of Ember warmth flow through my touch to dry out his damp hair.

He looked as though he was about to fuss, but he rolled his eyes and let me fix it. I adjusted his collar for good measure.

"Are you done?" he asked, his lip twitching with amusement.

"For now. I can't have you embarrassing me in front of the kitties."

"The *kitties*?" he spluttered. "Dear gods. Call them that and you'll be the death of us both."

"That's why they call it Obituary, right?" I winked and raised my parasol over my shoulder. Why else would I travel to a domain full of Leander, if not to see their teeny little kittens?

As we stepped up to the Gate, I understood what Dru had meant when she said I needed to leave Chime more. I'd always been afraid of the domains, of traveling through the Gate, but this... this was an adventure I'd been missing out on my entire life.

Shit. The moment I stepped through the Gate, the heat hit me like entering the kitchen in Lady Mae's café, only the kitchen was on fire and the teacups were melting.

We'd passed from Chime into some sort of canyon. Sand brushed across my cheeks in a soft flurry and caused my eyes to water. The air was much drier, much harsher, compared to Chime or even Memoria, and my parasol did little to protect me.

A wall of jagged red rock surrounded us, casting shade upon an open market. Hundreds of stalls hugged the edges of the canyon, hiding in the shade with colorful canopies, and they glittered with all manner of goods I'd never seen on Chime. Intricate pottery and vases, golden jewelry with gems the size of my fist, and bizarrely shaped fruit. Leander bustled around the stores, haggling and trading, oblivious to the strangers visiting.

Obituary's station wasn't a station at all.

I glanced back to the Gate. Unlike every other domain I knew of, this Gate had been carved into the rock, as though we'd literally stepped from the canyon. Geometric lines had been scratched around it in symmetrical patterns, and at the very top, three large red gemstones were embedded into the stone.

A shadow darted past me, and I muffled a squeal. It was a tiny furry thing with the face of a Leander, minus the mane. It ran naked on all fours, chasing a ball. Another Leander raced after it, wearing the Three Lions soccer shirt of Chime's famous team.

I leaned into Quen's side. "Oh my *god*," I whispered. "Is that a kitten?"

"Please, I'd like to survive the hour." His head tilted toward mine. "Many Leander consider that word to be derogatory."

"Really? But it's so cute. What do they call the little ones, then?"

"I believe they're called cubs."

"I want one."

"Don't say that out loud, or you'll find a line of Leander ready to oblige you."

The thought of a Leander lifting my skirts didn't thrill me, I'd admit. Maybe I could go back to Memoria and steal one of their fish instead.

Quen took my arm in his, which still felt uncomfortably damp, and guided us to the center of the canyon, where a sliver of sun sparkled atop a marble water fountain. Water poured from a statue depicting the three-headed god of Obituary. What an ego.

LIONHEART WAS ALWAYS AN ARROGANT ONE, Corentine said.

What gods aren't?

NOT ALL NEED STATUES AND ARENAS TO HONOR THEIR PRIDE.

The gods are your children. If they turned into giant spoilt brats, that's on you.

WHY ELSE ARE YOU MY VOICE IF NOT TO CHIDE THEM?

You want me to spank the gods on your behalf? What a thought!

Corentine laughed in my head, distracting me from the Leander approaching us.

Quen released my arm and greeted the Leander ambassador, who I recognized from the ball and Council. "Thank you for inviting us on such short notice."

"The pleasure is all mine, dear fellow." Even in this heat, the Leander dressed in a perfect tuxedo and top hat, his fashion style at odds with the Leander manning the markets. He opened his arms to embrace Quen.

Quen held up his hands. "Best not. I'm a little damp from a trip to Tempest."

"Tempest, eh? Tell me about it over a glass of whiskey." His feline pupils turned to me. "And this must be the ravishing Ambassador Arkey. Welcome to Obituary. Your smile is as dazzling as our fierce sun."

A flatterer. They were always trouble. I dipped a curtsy. "Pleased to make your acquaintance at last, Ambassador...?"

"Dandelion, if it please you, my lady. Any friend of Quentin's is a friend of mine, especially one who drags him back into my domain. It has been too long, old sport."

Quen bowed his head. "It has."

"Let us not delay, then. His Majesty awaits your audience, and there's no better view of Obituary than from Lionheart's plateau."

Dandelion beckoned us into an open hut containing carriages, only the carriages were more like extravagant boxes. These resembled the fancy carriages of the Golden City, but instead of wheels, they sat on two large poles. How in god's name did they move?

My question was soon answered as two bare-chested Leander stepped forth. Their beige fur glistened with sand, as though they'd been rolling in it. One of the Leander crouched and grabbed the poles in front, while the other grabbed the back ends, lifting the box.

Dandelion opened the carriage door and waved me in. "After you."

I stared in amazement. "They're going to *carry* us all the way up there?" My gaze followed the plateau looming above us at a dizzying height. "In this heat?"

"The heat means nothing to them. Our mortals regularly make the trip for exercise. One Leander is as strong as ten Diviner." He smirked in Quen's direction.

"Oh, at least," Quen muttered.

How would one Leander compare to one Umber? I reckoned Dru could give them a run for their bocs.

"Perhaps you should help them," Dandelion teased Quen. "Put some muscle on you."

"I'm happy enough with my exercise routine."

"What's that?" I asked. "Lifting a teacup and putting it down again?"

"Please. I dunk biscuits, too."

Dandelion laughed with a soft purr.

Quen offered me his arm. I was careful to avoid touching his skin, and hoisted myself into the carriage, tucking my closed parasol beside me.

It was a smaller size than wheeled carriages, yet the three of us could squeeze onto the cushions comfortably enough without rubbing knees or shoulders. Quen and I huddled together as Dandelion took up the entire opposite side by spreading his legs and sprawling out like the Leander did on the trams back home. Apparently, they needed the extra leg room for their tails and massive balls, or so they said.

If you kicked a Leander in the right place, they soon shrank down.

At Dandelion's signal, the carriage lifted. It wobbled from side to side, and I grabbed Quen's knee from the shock of it.

He patted my hand. "It's perfectly safe."

I begged to differ! The whole thing bobbed up and down with the pace of the Leander's march, though to their credit, they walked fast, and must have been made of stern stuff if they could manage to carry Dandelion, Quen, and my fat arse.

I almost wanted to apologize for all the candy I'd scoffed lately.

Outside, we moved through Obituary's market, and at this level I got a good view of the stalls. Their fashions weren't exactly fit for Chime, at least not Central, but the bright colors and geometric designs were gorgeous.

Soon we passed through a stone gate, and then the morning sunlight hit me straight in the face.

"Lionheart lives at the top of the plateau?" I asked, shielding my eyes.

"He entertains his honored guests there," Dandelion said. "There are hundreds of rooms, including a pool, gymnasium, spa, conference rooms for doing business, my own suite, and our famous bar, which serves a range of grilled meats. Popular with visitors."

Meat? I shuddered at the thought. "I didn't think your sort were the business type. What business does your domain engage in?"

"Those that will earn us power and prestige. We're not all athletes and brutes, my lady, despite the stereotypes."

"I meant no offense."

"My domain is ambitious. We seek to fight our way to the top in all we do, and matters of business are a game we aim to win. Whether in finance and stocks and shares, we'll play. Capitalism has always been a game of winners and losers, and we are winners."

Now he mentioned it, I'd never seen Leander in the slums of Grayford. They were the fat cats in their fancy top hats. Quite literally. "The Glimmer still have their claws in the Golden City. You're saying you want a share?"

His feline pupils turned sharp. "We want it all. For too long, the Glimmer have dominated Chime's businesses. We've muscled in where we can, but they keep a tight hold thanks to their position on the Council. This is why we're keen to hear more about Quentin's proposal."

They wanted a share of Chime, and they'd do whatever it took to snatch it from the Glimmer. I couldn't say if Leander rule would be any better than Glimmer, but I had to admire their honesty.

At least it meant they'd be on our side.

The carriage suddenly tilted back, pinning me to my seat. We were going up.

I didn't want to strain too close to the window in case any movement threw our carriage over, but we climbed around the canyon in one impressive tour. The sun moved out of my field of vision, revealing the market and Gate below.

As we climbed higher, Dandelion pointed out various landmarks across the horizon. Some were rocks in odd shapes, like a stack of them precariously balanced on one another. And on the opposite side of the market lay Lionheart's famous coliseum, a large stone arena said to attract challengers from across the domains.

Though what fascinated me was Obituary's landscape in general. It was dotted with red and orange rocks, as well as beige sand throughout, but there was plant life too. Prickly green columns and trees with flat tops. I'd been expecting a dry, dead wasteland, but the desert thrived with color.

By the time the carriage had leveled out, we'd reached the top.

"Welcome to Lionheart's plateau," Dandelion announced.

The sight stole my breath.

Desert stretched for miles. Not only desert. Sandstone buildings popped up next to pools of glistening water. Towns. A whole world separated by sand. It seemed so primitive compared to Chime and even Memoria, yet it held a wonder of its own.

"Before we meet with His Majesty, I have a... personal request."

"Name it," Quen said.

Dandelion pulled a cigar case out of his inner jacket pocket. "Do you mind if I smoke?"

Quen glanced to me. I shook my head. "Go ahead."

Dandelion readied his cigar and lit it with a flick of a match. He took a deep drag and let out a curling tendril of smoke that smelled woody. "You're aware of our arena, yes? Sometimes the stereotypes are true. Many of my domain like to compete for fame and riches. It's part of our culture—to make a name, a legacy, for oneself. To leave an obituary as tall as a mountain. In recent years, our reigning champion has been the Lioness. A fierce woman who has cut down foes and rivals alike. She is Lionheart's favorite warrior. And my sister. We grew up as cubs together. She now wishes to retire."

My Ember ears pricked up. I'd come to Obituary with this purpose in mind—to find a way to support their mortals. Though as I personally didn't know any Leander, I'd set myself a difficult task. "How can we help with that?"

"Lionheart will not let her go free. She is forced to battle day after day, and she grows weary. She has tried protesting many times. Even as far as sabotaging her own fights. But Lionheart punishes such behavior."

"You're the ambassador. Can't you get her out?"

"Believe me, my lady, I've tried. You must understand that strength means everything to Leander. My position as ambassador is not a respected one. While Lionheart understands the need for bureaucratic power and ambition, many sneer at my place."

"You want us to leverage her freedom as part of our proposal?" Quen asked. "We may not have the bargaining power—"

"He tortures her cubs, Quentin."

That word hung thick in the air, as suffocating as the heat. It lodged in my throat. In my heart.

Quen's pearly face paled. "He... What?"

"For every battle she dares lose or forfeits, Lionheart summons her to his chambers and forces her cubs to fight one another until she begs him to stop."

Shit. I'd never heard of anything so brutally barbaric. Gods abused their mortals, yes, but this...

There was no question in my mind.

We had to help this woman. The Lioness. We had to save her and her cubs.

"Can't you remove her cubs from this situation?" Quen asked.

"Their father agrees with Lionheart's punishments."

"Then take me to Lionheart," I urged. "Give me five minutes with him, and I'll get them out." I'd crush his fucking balls, god or not.

"I'm afraid Lionheart cannot be won over by mere diplomacy. Only a show of strength will convince him to heed your words."

"Meaning what?"

"Meaning, my lady, that Lionheart wishes to see the power of Chaos for himself." Dandelion tucked his cigar between his left fangs and exited the carriage.

Quen grabbed my thigh, keeping me pinned to my seat before I could rise. "Remember that Lionheart is a *god*. This is his domain. We can't simply waltz into his palace and make demands—"

"I don't need an explanation of how shit gods work."

"The Leander are brutal—they don't play fair, and they certainly don't care for diplomacy."

"Then we make him care."

"We're here to win Lionheart's favor, not antagonize him."

"What use is his favor if he abuses his own mortals?"

"I'm serious, Kayl. Be on your guard while we're here. Don't enter a room alone with any Leander. Don't turn your back on them."

Where was this sudden concern coming from? "You know I can take care of myself. If he gets handsy, I can steal his soul."

"You think he's not aware of the threat you pose? A Leander could physically overwhelm and restrain you before you have a chance to blink."

"Then it's a good job I have a big strapping Diviner to protect me." I patted his cheek and climbed out of the carriage.

Quen muttered something and followed.

I faced a large sandstone building at the top of the plateau. It was as large as The Grand Hotel back on Chime, and resembled one, what with multiple balconies decorated with palm trees, lit braziers burning outside doors, large lion statues made of gold, and an open-air terrace where Leander and mortals from other domains lounged in the shade with a cocktail or two.

It was by far the most modern building in Obituary, though its beauty was marred by the monster who lurked inside.

Upon entering, I was instantly wrapped in cool air. My shoulders sagged with relief.

"If you'll follow me." Dandelion led us down a corridor where the walls were made of smooth sandstone and glass. A line of brazier fire burned throughout, creating an ambience not too dissimilar from Erosain's bar back in Sinner's Row.

In fact, I spotted a few Ember reading broadsheets while sipping iced tea in what appeared to be an open bar named the Sand Dancer.

We passed glass windows where Leander in suits shook their fists in heated negotiations. The stereotypical depiction of Leander was that of a thug chugging ale in a pub, or jogging through Meridian Park while catcalling obscenities at pissed-off women. This version—the Leander dressed in business attire—seemed a far more dangerous beast.

If they were anything like the Glimmer, they wouldn't care who they crushed to be on top.

Quen stared ahead. Rather forlornly. Something worried him.

I bumped into his elbow. "You and Dandelion seem close," I whispered. "How many times have you been here?"

"Just once."

"You never wanted to return?"

"One trip was enough." He remained tight-lipped and gave me a look that suggested now was *not* the time to discuss it. What could have happened to bother him so?

The ceiling opened into a pyramidal roof. We climbed a series of steps and entered a brightly lit space filled with golden statues, trophies, and placards. All dedicated to Lionheart. How large was his ego?

I WARNED YOU, Corentine said.

Well, she wasn't wrong. There, seated on an extravagant ruby throne in the center of it all, was Lionheart himself.

I'd seen depictions of the great Leander god, but none did him justice. He was a mountain of a man, a grotesque example of masculinity and muscle. Nothing but a flimsy loincloth covered his gleaming golden fur, and even that bulged with a girth that would make any lover wince.

Leander prided themselves on their unwieldly cocks, declaring them the source of their strength. The larger one's prick, the more manly the man. As if most men had any idea what to do with such sizes!

Upon Lionheart's broad shoulders were three heads. Each maned. Each staring with golden feline pupils.

And on his lap sat a naked Leander. I did a double take. This Leander was a woman, judging by the lack of mane and her bulging breasts. Gods. I'd never seen a female Leander before. Why had I never seen one in Chime?

Without the mane, her face was closer to the kittens, uh, cubs in style. Though she too had the sharp claws and fangs of her male counterparts.

Lionheart's large paw was wrapped around her waist, holding her possessively, while one of his heads huffed by her neck.

I despised him already.

Dandelion began the proceedings by kneeling with his head bowed. "Your Majesty. I present Ambassador Quentin Corinth of Kronos and Ambassador Kayl Arkey of Chime."

Lionheart's three heads looked me over, each wearing a leering grin. "You like our women," he said with a low growl.

I dropped my parasol to the floor and yanked my dress in a quick curtsy. "Sorry, I've never seen a female Leander before."

"You wouldn't. They don't enter Chime."

"Is there any reason why?"

Quen raised an eyebrow in warning.

"Our women are strong and smart. They do not sully themselves with the weak. Chime is full of weak mortals. Normally, I do not permit such weak mortals to speak in my presence, yet I'll make an exception in your case."

Oh, I definitely despised him. Would shoving my closed parasol up his arse count as one of the unforgivable sins? I sure wanted to try.

Quen hurried forward into a bow. "Your Majesty—"

"I don't welcome your preening, Diviner. I know what you want and why you're here. You seek to take my darling Lioness. What a game Dandelion plays." One of his heads turned to the woman on his lap and licked her neck. She remained in his grasp, not flinching. Not uttering a word. Her eyes vacant.

Shit.

I knew that look. I'd seen it on so many women in the Undercity.

Women were the first to be used, abused, and discarded with no one to save them.

I wasn't going to let this one go unforgotten.

"I hear Leander are supposed to be the strongest mortals in the universe," I said. "That one Leander is worth ten or more of any other domain. Does the almighty king of Obituary not honor and respect his greatest warrior?"

"I honor my Lioness every night. I'd offer you the same courtesy, but I've yet to see if you're worth my effort."

"Come down from your throne, and I'll show you what I can do," I snapped.

The two side heads laughed. "You've got bigger balls than the Diviner."

Quen shot me a look that said to *back down*, but I couldn't stop the seething rage from burning under my skin.

I didn't want to bargain with this arsehole.

"What I see is some Ember whore at my feet," Lionheart continued. "My voice swears you can change from one domain to another. *Show me.*"

The command came out in a low snarl. Not a command, a demand.

I didn't flinch. "Give me your Lioness, and I'll demonstrate."

Lionheart patted the Lioness's thigh. "Approach."

The Lioness didn't hesitate. She slid from her master's hold and prowled toward me with feline grace, her tail swishing from side to side.

Gods. She was absolutely gorgeous.

She stood as tall as me and offered her hand with no fear in her expression.

At one touch, my skin rippled with a gray-blue fuzz that coated everywhere, making me shudder. I'd grown pissing fur! Whiskers sprouted from my nose, and my ears twitched, my hearing suddenly acute.

Something filled my panties as if I'd shat myself.

Shit. I'd grown a damn tail too! It curled painfully around my arse, and I couldn't damn well pull it out in front of everyone!

Quen was openly staring at me. It was like he'd never seen a cat-woman before. And maybe he hadn't. That was Quen. Too gentlemanly for his own good.

Lionheart was also staring at me—with all three heads. "So it's true. It has been a long time since anything has surprised me, and your presence is a surprise. Corentine was a force of nature. It took all twelve gods to subdue her. How was she able to create mortals?"

"The how and whys don't matter," I said. "Fact is, Chaos is free, and not all my siblings are as friendly as I am."

"Thus Chaos stands in my palace and wishes to bargain." He gestured for the Lioness, and she returned to sit at his feet. "Then let's bargain."

Quen cleared his throat. "Our terms are clear. In exchange for lending your power to Chime, you will be granted an equal share in Chime's Council, including decisions of its infrastructure, ordinances, and allocated space for property and business investment. But this will be equally divided between each domain."

Lionheart leaned back against his throne. "That's a small slice of Chime."

"But it's a slice."

"Between eleven domains? Will the Glimmer concede? They don't share."

"They will if they wish to keep their slice of the pie."

"Are the Diviner prepared to war with the Glimmer?"

"I expect the Glimmer to bend. They have too much to lose."

"Release the Lioness, and a slice can be yours," I said.

Lionheart huffed. "You need my power more than I need your slice. I've yet to hear a compelling reason why I should concede my Lioness."

YOU MAY AS WELL TAKE HIS SOUL, Corentine drawled. *VIOLENCE IS ALL LIONHEART RESPONDS TO.*

You have a point. I stepped in front of Quen before he could open his mouth. "By accepting our generous offer, you not only gain a slice of Chime, but also protection. You're aware of what Corentine and her mortals can do, aren't you? You said it yourself—we're a force of nature. Is that power you really wish to claw against?"

He grinned, exposing wicked fangs. "Prove to me that you possess even a shred of Corentine's strength, and I'll accept your terms. I challenge you, child of Chaos, to enter my arena."

XVIII

The Leander can be a brutal lot, and they have a nose for weakness in other mortals. They'll take any opportunity to put you in your place.
It is imperative, then, that one de-escalates any encounters with an aggressive Leander. Do not engage with them. Do not argue back. If they insult your face, turn the other cheek. It's better to be thought of as a weakling than to be proven one. Pride is a sin, after all, and the Leander are full of pride. That's a joke. No, don't edit it out—
—Q. Corinth, Redacted Warden Dossier on Obituary

"**Absolutely not**."

The words came out before I'd had a chance to consider their implications.

Lionheart wanted to bargain, but throwing us literally to the lions was no bargain.

Kayl forced a polite smile. "Will you excuse us for a moment?"

Two of Lionheart's heads flashed a leering grin. "Take your time."

She dragged me a few paces from Lionheart's throne, her new claws pinching my wrist, and shoved me behind one of his large statues. It was a meaningless gesture, really. Lionheart would be able to hear our conversation even if she dragged me across the other side of the desert.

"We're saving her." That hardened stare brooked no argument.

Oh, I did so love a challenge, though I much preferred a duel of wits than brawn. "By what? Entering an area full of battle-hardened Leander with sharp teeth and claws and expecting we'll get out of there with our skin intact?"

"You make it sound easy."

"It's not! Ignoring the fact neither of us are capable or equipped to fight in an *arena*, for pity's sake, the Gate closes in thirty minutes. Do you want to be trapped here for twelve hours?"

"That woman has been trapped here her whole life—"

"Which is irrelevant. I'm sorry. We can do nothing for her or her cubs."

"I'm not walking away from this!" she hissed. "If you think I'm not going to help, then you obviously don't know me well enough."

I sucked in an exasperated breath. "And if you think I'm going to let you risk your life in that blasted arena, then you don't know *me*."

"Oh, quit your chivalrous shit!"

"You first."

She growled, baring her new Leander fangs. "You don't own me."

Her words were a knife to my heart. Each one a puncture that bled.

They caught in my throat. *You don't own me.*

"He's abusing her, Quen. Torturing her children. Do you even care?"

"Of course I care!" I snapped. I'd seen the look on the Lioness's face. I knew it intimately. I felt it where my deepest shames curdled. For all of Kayl's protests, I wanted to save her, too, if we could.

Kayl's words cut, but those were wounds I could bear compared to risking her life.

"Yet you're willing to toss a mortal to the gutter just to tick some box? How many mortals did the Dark Warden let fall between the cracks? How many did your own colleagues abuse? I could tell you some stories."

I shoved my hands into my pockets and ran a calming thumb over my fob watch, the marred brass a soothing balm against the ire building in my chest.

I *hated* that name.

Despite the Wardens' actions under Elijah's leadership, they were still a force for good. Chime needed them. Mortals needed them. Yes, I'd been a Warden long enough to understand we couldn't save everyone.

Damn it, I wanted to save them all!

I wanted to witness Kayl busting Lionheart's balls.

I wanted to bust them myself.

But we were here to negotiate, and that meant bowing and scraping. "The Wardens may not be perfect, but we do what must be done for the greater good, even if that means putting personal notions aside. And *this* is personal, whether you'll admit it or not—"

"You know, during the memorial? One of your Diviner Wardens paused time and groped me. Was that for the greater good?"

My heart stopped dead. "What?"

"So don't you talk shit about your pissing creed—"

"Tell me his badge ID, and I'll deal with him."

"How? By giving him a firm telling off and a slapped wrist?"

"By putting my pistol to his head and blasting his brains out," I seethed.

I didn't know where this sudden rage came from.

The thought of Kayl being hurt, of being touched in such a way... It shook through me, like when I'd taken my first breath.

You don't own me.

Was I turning into Elijah? Becoming possessive? Controlling? He'd kept me on a short leash with the excuse of protecting me. But with his other hand, he'd hurt me. Abused me. Elijah had been his own god, and he'd forced himself upon me, knowing I had no choice but to obey.

I could never be that. *Do* that.

But I'd kissed her. I'd forced myself onto her lips without her consent. Was I not keeping Kayl on a short leash by forcing her by my side with the justification that I couldn't let Chaos run rampant?

Should I blow my own brains out, too?

"Is this what you are now, Quen?" she asked, her words coming out slowly and carefully. "Judge, jury, and executioner? What's the difference between the Lioness and me?"

The Lioness didn't keep me awake at night.

Saints. The way Kayl's whiskers twitched, the way her feline pupils turned to slits, the slight lift of her fangs, the highlights of her silvery-blue fur... Of all her transformations, from Umber to Amnae, this one had surprised me the most.

I'd not been expecting the cat version of Kayl to be so... curvaceous.

The Lioness had practically bounded her breasts in front of my face, and I'd not felt a thing. But Kayl...

She'd need only look at me, and I was lost. So utterly lost I may as well be floating in aether. I knew I'd lost *this* argument before I'd even opened my damned mouth.

I was a bastard. And I'd be punished for my bastardry. For my sins, I'd lose my very soul.

I shook my head. Lionheart wanted to judge Chaos's measure for himself. There was no getting out of this, was there? "If we're to set these events in motion, then we do it together. As partners."

"Fine. As partners."

That was as close to a compromise as I was ever going to get.

Blast it. We were doing this, then. I'd waste another twelve hours when my damn schedule was tight enough, only to be torn apart by Leander for the pleasure.

Kayl and I returned to where Lionheart sat amused. He'd likely eavesdropped on our entire conversation and now knew where my weakness lay.

Dandelion remained kneeling on the floor, his head bowed, but his tail flicked with agitation. He'd forced me into this damnable position, though I understood why.

For the Lioness and her cubs, I'd try.

I stared Lionheart in the eye—his middle head, anyhow. "What are your terms?"

"I wish to see what Chaos is capable of. One match. One life. Win, and I will grant your request. Fail, and my arena will soak up your blood. Though I doubt even Chaos will best my weakest warrior. I'll even let my Lioness advise you."

That Lionheart would gladly throw away his mortal's life for a challenge should have come as no surprise, yet the casual indifference of it grated on me. It could be a trick. Leander knew how to swindle. "Not so fast. If one Leander is worth ten Diviner, then you won't mind if I join the party. If she fights, I fight with her."

"Chaos and time fighting side by side? Intriguing. I'll allow it on one condition. No time manipulation. That's cheating. I'll know if you do."

I glanced to Kayl. She nodded. "Agreed."

Lionheart patted the Lioness's shoulder. "Escort them."

The Lioness didn't hesitate. She didn't utter a single word as she marched from the throne room.

Dandelion stretched to his feet. "Your Majesty."

Lionheart waved him off.

I pulled Dandelion to one side. "Can you send a telegram back to Warden HQ in Chime? Inform Ben Seasons that Kayl and I will likely miss the crossing and will return on the next one." Assuming our limbs were still intact.

"Leave it to me. I'm sorry for dragging you into this, old boy." He patted me on the shoulder. "Follow the Lioness. You can trust her."

The female Leander waited for us in the corridor, dressed in a robe. She snarled at my approach. "You are foolish if you think you can outsmart Lionheart. What was my brother thinking getting you involved? Look at you." She grabbed my bicep with a sharp pinch. "Tiny thing."

Kayl mouthed *I like her*.

I snatched my arm back and scowled. "Pleased to make your acquaintance, Miss Lioness—"

"You should leave Obituary and never return. The arena will eat you up and spit you out."

I could see why she was Lionheart's favorite.

"I doubt even Lionheart would allow two visiting ambassadors to die in his domain," Kayl said. "It would look rather bad."

"You like your limbs, yes? You want to keep them? Then leave."

"I want to make Lionheart look like an arse. Are you in?"

The Lioness's grin reminded me of Jinx.

We were doomed. Utterly doomed.

Lionheart's plateau jutted over the arena, casting half of it in shade, and providing the god with an ample view of his sandstone coliseum.

Thankfully, the gigantic walls sucked all the heat from the air, though it didn't muffle the cheers and chanting beyond.

I'd watched the arena myself on my last visit some years back. It was bloody and brutal. The complete opposite of sport in civilized society.

It certainly was *not* cricket.

The Lioness welcomed us into an armory lit by brazier flames. Drinkable-water fountains were placed between stone benches, but the far wall was decorated with an assortment of shiny weapons, from bladed swords to javelins and flails.

Kayl grabbed my arm, her claws digging in. "You've got to help me," she whispered.

Panic tightened my chest. "It's all right. We'll find a solution—"

"No, it's my tail. You've got to pull it out."

"I've got to *what*?"

"Rip a hole in my dress and pull it out. I can't reach behind."

Saints preserve me. She wasn't joking.

"One moment!" I called to the Lioness as I placed Kayl's parasol down and angled it to give us a little privacy. I leaned back to see where Kayl's tail began. Of all the awkward situations I'd faced in my short mortal life, this was a true test. "I'll need to touch your buttocks."

Kayl glanced over her shoulder, her whiskers twitching with restrained amusement. "Really, Quen? My *buttocks*? I'm not asking you to spank me. Just grab my arse and pull the tail out." She bent over and practically thrust her behind into my hands.

Gods forbid. I'd be spending the night on my knees deep in prayer. I took hold of her cheeks, which were firmer than I'd expected—a thought to push aside—and focused on finding the optimal place to tear a hole that would allow comfort both standing and sitting.

Making the hole was easy enough with my nails, and I sized it big enough for my fist. My hand reached through and touched bare fur.

Oh my goodness. She wasn't wearing panties.

"Where, ah, is your underwear?" I choked, my voice suddenly hoarse.

"Dropped it back in Lionheart's fancy room."

"Dare I ask why?"

"You try wearing knickers with a tail. It's ridiculously uncomfortable."

Saints. The softness of her furry buttocks made me ache for a good cup of tea. Something very dark and bitter. Kayl giggled as I managed to grab her tail and carefully fed it through the hole.

She turned with a playful smile and swatted me with her tail. Like the rest of her fur, it was a smooth silvery-blue. How did it operate? Like a third limb?

"You done?" the Lioness asked, her arms crossed as she watched us.

The Obituary heat sent my entire face aflame. "Ah, yes. Thank you for waiting."

She rummaged inside a wooden locker and pulled out leather clothing, tossing it to Kayl. "You change into these. Dresses are not suitable for the arena."

Kayl held up what looked like a leather brassiere. "Is this supposed to protect me?"

"No. But you will be able to dance, Chaos girl."

Kayl mouthed me an apology, her tail swishing by her side. "So what are the rules? Can I grab a tail and yank it?"

"You fight dirty? Good. Arena is dirty. Most Leander do not need weapons. They fight with teeth and claws. You change clothes?" the Lioness asked me.

I held up my hands. "I'm fine without." I wasn't about to strip down to a leather thong for an audience of leering Leander.

"Can you fight, tiny man?"

"I'm a trained Warden and sharpshooter. I'm good with a pistol." Of course, I'd left my own bloody weapon behind because I'd not anticipated a scenario where Kayl would drag me into a sodding arena. A mistake I would not make again.

"We have no pistols."

"Got anything more primitive? A crossbow, perhaps? I have good aim."

"We have throwing knives or spears." She pointed to the wall of weapons. "Choose one."

Kayl began unceremoniously undressing, so I turned to the wall and appraised it with a Warden's eye. Most of these weapons were banned from

Chime—knives, brass knuckles, swords certainly. Only Wardens were permitted to openly carry a weapon, and even then our arsenal consisted only of batons, tasers, and pistols. I'd long thought even pistols were dangerous in the wrong hands. Too easy to misfire.

Somehow, weapons always smuggled their way into Chime, and Erosain turned a blind eye to whatever hazardous goods passed through Sinner's Row.

As a Warden, I'd been trained in boxing and wrestling, but with my build, physical contact was not my forte. Diviner had an edge. We could casually pause time and aim where we pleased. But that fancy trick wouldn't work today. Lionheart would notice.

It would be best to keep any potential aggressor at a distance, especially one with sharp teeth, but how?

My attention was drawn to a metal shield.

Kayl bounded to my side, her new leather gear little more than a breastband and shorts. "What's the plan, then?"

"Plan?" I glanced over the rim of my spectacles. "Why do you assume I have a plan? It was *your* idea to risk life and limb."

"Because you're clever and always have something hidden up your sleeves."

If I were a Leander, I would have purred at the stroke to my ego. "As it happens, I *do* have a plan." I tapped my nose.

The Lioness waved us over to a window overlooking a training room. A group of male Leander filled it, currently engaged in an ongoing brawl. Both fur and blood flew through the air. I hoped this wasn't what passed for a warm-up.

"What are they doing?" Kayl asked.

"They're deciding who will have the honor of killing you in Lionheart's name," the Lioness said.

"Oh."

I swallowed a lump in my throat. As Leander collapsed in defeat, a clear winner stood among the bloodied bodies. A hulking figure with black stripes zigzagging across his fur. He roared in victory, blood staining his teeth and mane.

"There is your opponent." The Lioness gestured at him. "They call him Whiskers."

Kayl snorted. "Really?"

"Because he has no whiskers," I croaked, my voice dying in my throat.

"You know of him?" the Lioness asked.

"We've, ah, crossed paths." My legs suddenly wobbled. I sank onto the nearest bench before they gave out completely.

This was such a foolish endeavor. How was I meant to serve my god, serve Chime, the domains, their mortals, and enact my plan to refurbish a fleet of trams if I got torn apart in some blasted arena?

Kayl sat beside me. "I take it he isn't very pleasant? Do you want to talk about it?"

No. I didn't want to dredge up that part of my past, and I averted my eyes from the Lioness's curious stare. I'd wiped the memory, once, but returning here was like going through the motions. "Obituary would be much better off without him."

"Are his sins worth losing his life?"

I couldn't be the arbiter of souls like Elijah had been. To decide which sins were worth total obliteration. I couldn't become that man.

Could I?

There were sinners, and then there were utter bastards. Mortals who brought nothing to civilized society except suffering wherever they went. Sinners could be redeemed, but abusers? Rapists? Those who sought to snuff the life out of a beating heart? There was no absolution waiting for them.

Whiskers was one such mortal.

"That's not for me to decide."

"So it's for me to decide? I'm not a killer, Quen."

I saw the lie in her eyes and met it with my own. "Neither am I. Are you sure you want to do this? When we enter that arena... I don't know if I'll— I may not be able to protect you from him."

"We're partners, remember? The two of us can handle one big kitten."

"Even the two of us may be no match for a Leander." I forced a smile. "Ben will be absolutely appalled I allowed this."

"And Dru will spend the next week berating me, don't you worry. Why do we even have bodyguards?"

"They're more for show, really."

Though in this moment, I wished Ben were here.

Whiskers had single-handedly proved I couldn't match other mortals for sheer strength. It had been a painful lesson to learn. One I kept close at heart.

But I hadn't come all this way to let Kayl down. To let Dandelion down.

At that moment, Dandelion entered and approached with a grim expression that did nothing to inspire confidence. "The herald is sent. You've one hour to prepare."

I pulled a notepad and pen from my inner jacket pocket and started scribbling a list of tools and components. "Think you can find these for me in the next half hour?"

He examined the note with a frown. "I say. This is a tad unconventional."

"I'm an unconventional man."

"And you can do this in an hour or less?"

"I'm a tinkerer. I can do it in half the time." But of course, time was on my side. I shrugged off my jacket and rolled up my sleeves. "Let's get to work."

For the next hour, the Lioness taught Kayl a few Leander fighting moves, and in exchange, Kayl passed on a few Undercity tricks. The way their tall, lithe bodies swerved and ducked was mesmerizing, so I distracted myself by customizing Kayl's parasol.

"You might be better off with a sword and shield, old sport," Dandelion said as he handed me a flask.

"Swords aren't my style." I took a swig and almost choked! Whiskey. Just what I needed before a fight to my death. "Did you know Whiskers would be my opponent?"

Dandelion patted my knee. "Yes. But now you may earn revenge."

Damn him. But that was ambassadors for you. Fiddling deals wherever they could, though I'd expected better from Dandelion. He was supposed to be my ally! Yet even he and Erosain wormed favors out of me now that I had the power to grant them. What was I to them? A kept Warden?

I didn't want revenge. I wanted to forget.

Kayl strode over for a drink as I twirled the parasol. "This is your grand plan? To keep the sun off our backs?"

I'd fitted the parasol with metal plating, effectively creating a shield. "Do you know how easily Diviner burn?" I retracted the parasol with a flick of the wooden handle, turning it into a lance. "More to the point, Obituary's sun makes an excellent conductor."

"You're saying that thing's solar powered? To do what?"

"The two of us won't be enough to subdue a Leander as large as our opponent. I don't happen to have a taser on hand, but with enough components, I've rigged this to shoot one blast. But *only* one blast. It should be enough to stop him dead in his tracks."

Kayl whooped with a slight purr. "I knew you had something."

Once again, I was struck by how beautiful those feline eyes were. "You'll need to distract him until it finishes charging. I hope you know how to dance."

She gave a little spin. "Let's put on a good show."

We helped ourselves to another shot of whiskey, and then Dandelion and the Lioness were marching us through a corridor to our inevitable demise, the parasol slung over my shoulder. The chanting of hundreds of Leander vibrated through the walls.

Kayl strode beside me with quiet confidence. How could she not feel fear? Yes, she'd faced down a god and lived to tell the tale, but did destroying a god really grant that level of confidence? Or had she always been this way?

It wasn't only gods. She'd run headfirst into danger without hesitation.

Was the woman even mortal? I'd died once, and yet I still felt ready to defecate myself at this very moment.

Dandelion slapped me on the shoulder. "Good luck."

"Don't die, tiny man," the Lioness added.

I grimaced, and then a deafening roar welcomed Kayl and me into the arena.

The circular coliseum appeared much larger down here on the ground. Rows upon rows of stone seats surrounded us, each filled with Leander men, women, and cubs. Their many feline faces howled with impatience and delight; a cacophony that brought Obituary alive.

My boot scuffed through sand as I forced myself to keep pace with Kayl, who marched straight for the center. A sharp line of shadow provided the only shade, coming from Lionheart's plateau, leaving us with ample heat. It wasn't even midday, and yet Obituary's sun had risen with an angry hiss. Thank the gods I had a parasol.

I'd become the fanciest Diviner in existence.

Lionheart watched from a private balcony above us on his plateau, seated on a large cushion like some smug fat cat.

"Quen," Kayl said, snapping my attention forward.

A cheer rippled through the arena like a gust of wind. Sand grains whooshed across my exposed skin, tickling my nose with the heady scent of salt and sweat.

Whiskers had entered the arena and was now stomping in my direction.

My heart began to race.

"The Diviner with the smooth arse! You came back for more!" He stood tall at almost seven feet in height, taller than even Kayl, and wore nothing but a loincloth. I remembered rough paws pinning me down. The hot breath at my neck. "And you brought me a playmate. How about we finish what we started, and then I'll take her."

Kayl shot a look in my direction, and understanding dawned on her face.

I hadn't wanted to utter the truth of my last visit.

I hadn't wanted to admit my weakness. My shame.

What kind of Warden was I, if I couldn't protect myself?

Sinners attracted sin, so Elijah had said.

For so long, I'd believed him.

Kayl's face twisted from understanding to rage, and she turned that ire on Whiskers. "I'm sorry, I thought we were dueling with one of Lionheart's warriors? All I'm seeing is some cute chubby kitten."

Whiskers roared. His sharp claws extended out like knives.

Then he launched forward.

Those claws swiped through the air with bloodcurdling speed. Kayl dove to one side, narrowly escaping his attack.

He whirled on me. I raised my parasol in time to deflect his claws. They scratched down the metal plating with a horrid screech.

Whiskers slashed again and again with wild abandon. Each hit threatened to tear through the plating, but it held, thank the gods! It wouldn't survive a barrage for long.

If he cut through it, he could damage the charge, and then I'd never get my shot!

"I'm going to rip your arse in half!" Whiskers grinned, exposing sharp fangs.

Saints.

I was going to die. *Again!*

He poised to pounce and then let out a sudden yelp.

Kayl had caught his tail and given it a good yank. "Settle down, kitty."

Whiskers tugged free in an instant and turned his attention on Kayl.

She signaled with a subtle nod.

I tried to angle the parasol to best capture the sun's power. The audience jeered and laughed at my antics as Whiskers barreled down on Kayl.

To her credit, she kept him distracted. A jab here, a punch there. Taunting moves designed to annoy rather than do any actual damage, and it was unfortunately working.

With each movement, Whiskers became more irate. "You don't fight like a Leander. You fight like a Seren!"

"Oh?" Kayl raised her fists. "How do Leander fight, then?"

He grinned.

With blinding speed, Whiskers pounced at Kayl. She attempted to dive out of the way, but wasn't fast enough.

His fangs sank into her right forearm with a sickening crunch.

"Fuck!" she screamed.

No!

Rage burned under my skin. The device wasn't at full capacity, but I had no choice!

I retracted the parasol and aimed it at his back.

Whiskers shoved Kayl into the sand and turned to me with a blood-smeared smile. My stare frantically flipped between him prowling toward me, and Kayl. She cradled her mangled arm close to her chest and kicked up sand as she skittered away, leaving a trail of crimson dots.

She was hurt. Gods. She was hurt, and I'd let this happen.

"What are you going to do, little Diviner?" Whiskers taunted. "Waft me?"

"I'm going to bloody well destroy you."

Aether pulsed from the point of the parasol and hit Whiskers square in the chest.

Silvery-blue static spasmed across his fur, causing it to stand on end. His eyes rolled back.

The crowd fell still.

Saints. I'd done it. I'd—

"Neat trick." He shook the static from his fur. "Now it's my turn."

No, damn it! The taser hadn't charged enough!

He rushed right at me, his paws pounding the sand.

I thrust out the parasol. His claws shredded through it in a single swipe, as though the metal were made of paper.

He'd been toying with me all this time. Waiting for me to show my hand.

Whiskers wrenched the parasol from my grip and knocked me off my feet before I could swallow a breath. My head bashed into the sand with a painful thud.

Ringing flooded my ears, the violent excitement of the arena buzzing along with my frantic heartbeat, and I blinked back dots.

Then weight bore down onto my chest, crushing the air from my lungs in a gasping wheeze.

Whiskers was on top of me.

His mane tickled my chin. "Dandelion won't save you this time."

His golden feline eyes were so similar to Elijah's.

I'd escaped Whiskers once. I'd escaped Elijah.

And yet, here I was again.

Over his shoulder, Kayl stood, her bloodied arm dangling uselessly by her side. Broken. This was all my fault.

Anger still burned in her silvery-blue eyes. No, not anger. Determination.

They asked a singular question.

Was rape a sin worth losing one's life?

In this moment, I decided it was.

I nodded.

She leaped onto Whiskers's back.

He roared and tried to shake her off, but she grabbed on tight with her left arm.

"Get off me, you whore! You—"

He stopped thrashing.

I scrambled out of the way as his body collapsed, sending up a cloud of dust.

His eye sockets were vacant. Gone.

Gods almighty. She'd taken his soul.

The crowd quieted. Feverish muttering gripped the arena. They'd witnessed what Chaos could do with their own eyes.

I almost collapsed from sheer exhaustion, both physical and emotional. Kayl stood there panting, her arm a bloodied mess. I wanted to run to her, to pull her close, but I couldn't afford to show weakness in front of Lionheart, not now.

That rage still burned in her eyes. I should have been terrified.

Here stood a woman who could destroy gods. Topple domains. Pure chaos. The enemy of time. Of my Father. A woman made of anger and aether.

She'd taken a soul with my blessing.

Where did that leave us now?

Watching from his plateau, Lionheart did not look pleased. But we'd established Kayl's abilities. She'd upheld her end of the bargain.

It was time for Lionheart to honor his.

We staggered our way out of the arena. As soon as we came into the shade, Kayl sagged against my shoulder. It took all my energy to keep her upright.

"Gods, Quen," she sighed onto my neck. "I'm so sorry."

She trembled in my arms. She was mortal, after all. "For what?"

"For what he did to you."

"He tried. Dandelion saved me."

That night years ago, Dandelion had invited me to his bar. I'd consumed one too many whiskeys, and upon visiting the urinal, I'd come face to mane with Whiskers. Ready to pounce. His bulk had outmatched mine—I couldn't fight him off. Nor could I simply pause time and escape him—one shouldn't play with time when inebriated.

But then Dandelion had come to my rescue and dragged him off. I'd been so grateful, and so foolishly drunk, that I'd gone back to Dandelion's lounge and allowed him to take me instead.

There are mortals who relish the pain and pleasure of making love to a Leander male, though I personally didn't enjoy being sodomized by a brush.

Our relationship didn't last long. For one, Elijah found out.

And for two, Leander fur gets *everywhere*.

I guided Kayl back to the armory, where Dandelion waited. With his help, and a swig of whiskey, we patched up Kayl's arm as best we could without the aid of a Necro, wrapping it in a sling. And then we were ready to face Lionheart.

The Leander god awaited us in his throne room, the Lioness by his side.

His three heads surveyed us. Kayl swayed slightly on her feet, her fur stained with blood. We were both covered in beige dust, which we'd rather rudely tracked onto the pristine tiles.

"You took his soul," Lionheart accused. "I do not sense it in my aether. You stole power from me."

"You told me to prove what Chaos could do." Kayl's voice came out flat. "Now honor our bargain."

"The children of Chaos are as vicious as their mother. If the Diviner plan to destroy them, then we'll assist."

"Rehabilitate them," I said.

He gave me a knowing look. "We'll grant Chime our power in exchange for a slice of the Golden City. No more. No less."

"Done. Now release the Lioness."

One of Lionheart's heads nodded.

The Lioness rose to her feet. There was no hesitation in her movements as she shrugged off her robe.

And sat on Lionheart's knee.

"I belong to my king," the Lioness stated.

Blast. The Lioness's eyes were downturned, staring at the tiles. I knew that look. It settled in my gut with a churning familiarity.

"Wha—what?" Kayl stammered. "We made a deal!"

Lionheart wrapped his large paw around the Lioness's waist, claiming her. "I gave my Lioness a choice. Would you presume to deny her will?"

Kayl turned to me, her expression lost. "Quen, do something!"

"I'm sorry," I whispered.

No one had saved me from Elijah. No one could have.

I'd saved myself, in the end.

Understanding dawned in Kayl's eyes. Bitter disappointment warred with righteous fury. She pointed a damning finger at the god. "One day, your mortals will recognize their own strength. They'll rise above you." Her gaze flickered to the Lioness. "And I'll be with them when they do."

Lionheart merely smirked. A cat with his cream.

I've gotten what I'd come for, but Obituary had left me sick to my stomach.

If I ever returned to this domain again, it would be too soon.

19

TAROT READINGS
KNOW YOUR DESTINY
Have you ever wondered what lies in your future?
Our Mesmer seers offer tarot readings for the curious mortal. From our
twelve-domain deck, we'll reveal secrets from your past, gifts from your
present, and hints of your future.
Note: A Necro card does NOT mean you're going to die. Please stop asking.
—Lady Nara, *The Dreamcast flier*

WE RETURNED BACK TO Chime on the evening crossing. After our failure, I'd wanted to get out of Obituary as soon as I physically could, but we'd remained trapped there for the full twelve pissing hours. Neither Quen, Dandelion, or I had felt like a sight-seeing tour, so we'd grabbed ourselves a private booth in the bar and drowned our sorrows. I'd swigged exotic cocktails I'd never heard of while gorging myself on grilled watermelon, focaccia, and melted cheese. Quen had nursed a whiskey and tea, and Dandelion had alternated between drunken crying, drunken singing, and drunken facts about cacti.

Thankfully, Lionheart had left us alone to our misery.

I'd wanted to catch the Lioness before our departure. One last chance to convince her to join us, but she'd refused to speak with us. I still couldn't believe Quen had let Lionheart get away with fucking us over. But what were we to do? Kidnap the Lioness?

One couldn't help someone who didn't want to be helped.

The only highlight of the trip had been watching the sun set over the desert. A beautiful sight. By the time we made the crossing back, we'd sobered up a little, though my head was throbbing, and judging by the scowl on Quen's face, he wasn't faring much better.

Naturally, they didn't have a single Necro in all Obituary, so my arm was bloody agony once the alcohol wore off.

As Quen and I entered the bustle of Central Station, Dru and Ben lingered in the waiting area next to a woman—a female Diviner. The first I'd ever seen.

Dru was staring at me. "What in all that's holy happened to you?"

I'd switched back to a Diviner form, which was awkward as I stood in front of an actual Diviner woman better dressed than I. My arm was wrapped in a bloodstained sling, sand fell whenever I moved, and I no doubt looked as shit as I felt. "I tripped and fell over a rock. You know how clumsy I am."

"You were supposed to watch over her!" Dru chided Quen.

He lifted his eyeglasses and rubbed the bridge of his nose. "Apologies. But we returned with our limbs mostly intact."

"If I may interrupt?" began the female Diviner. She pulled out a file from her briefcase. "Your Excellency, during your twelve-hour sojourn, Benjamin Seasons and I were able to sufficiently relocate one Doctor Zachery Finch and have also received Miss Ilona Burns from Memoria. She's waiting for you back at the embassy."

"Good." Quen shoved his eyeglasses back on. "I'll meet with her right away. We'll escort her through to Kronos on the ten o'clock crossing—"

"And what's our next plan?" I asked.

"Take the night off. See to your arm. We'll meet here tomorrow for the morning crossing into Rapture. Make sure you dress for heat. It's worse than Obituary."

Somehow, I doubted anything would be worse than our time in Obituary. "Are you going to introduce us?" I eyed up the Diviner woman.

Quen waved a dismissive hand. "Kayl, this is Pendula. Pendula, Kayl."

The woman—Pendula—offered a startled curtsy. She was a tiny thing wrapped in a business casual ensemble. Her skin and hair were silver except for a streak of brass cutting through her neatly shaped bob. Those silver eyes held a flicker of annoyance. "I'm Quentin's assistant."

"Really? Quen hadn't mentioned needing an assistant."

Quen gave a look that suggested he didn't need or want an assistant, but thought better of saying so.

MORE DIVINER ARE ALWAYS TROUBLE, Corentine said. *WATCH OUT FOR THAT ONE.*

She wasn't wrong. *Why aren't there more female Diviner?*

DOR DOES NOT TRUST THE FEMALE SEX. HE THINKS US CHAOTIC.

I wonder where he got that impression from?

"We should get back, sir," Big Ben said, saving us from an awkward silence.

"Yes, yes. Tomorrow, then." Quen barely met my eye as he wandered out of the station, both Ben and Pendula flanking him.

"You could have been more polite." Dru tutted. "We're on the same side."

"That *was* me being polite." She'd soon know if I was being a bitch.

Pendula stopped Quen for a moment and tried to adjust his disheveled collar, but he snapped something I couldn't hear and yanked his collar free from her touch.

"He's looking grumpy," Dru said. "What happened?"

"It's been a terribly long day." Twelve hours trapped in Obituary's dry heat would make anyone miserable. "Come on. Let's get back before Harmony thinks I'm dead." And so Vincent could fix my damn arm. I wrapped my good arm around Dru's, and we headed out of Central Station into the lamplit streets full of Leander prowling the pubs. "Did you and Ben manage to keep each other company while I was away?"

"Don't you start on that, or I'll tell Harm you spent twelve hours fighting in an arena."

"That would be ridiculous. She'd never believe it."

Dru gave me a suspicious look.

Such a shame that my reputation for ineptitude occasionally worked in my favor.

It was almost nine by the time Dru and I snuck back inside the temple. Sinder sat at reception, his elbows resting on the counter as he kept watch by the entrance.

"What trouble have you gotten into now, darling?" He dug out a chocolate lime and unwrapped it for me.

"Oh, you know. The usual chaos. Where's Vincent?" I asked, before popping the candy in my mouth. Truly, chocolate limes were becoming my favorite.

"Babysitting the Mesmer. They've taken a liking to him, which means I get peace and quiet *here*, but they pester Vincent wherever he goes. You've got to save him, dearest. I can't wank off in my own bed without one of them appearing out of nowhere."

"I'll have a word with them."

"Follow the giggling. You'll see what I mean."

Sure enough, we didn't need to wander in far to hear giggling echoing along the halls. What in god's name was going on?

I turned the corner and found a whole line of Mesmer queuing outside the storage room Vincent had finished turning into a mini-clinic.

"Do me next!" squealed one of the Mesmer trio.

"I'm going to go find Harm." Dru turned tail. "Have fun."

"Some bodyguard you are!" I couldn't believe she was abandoning me! Damn her, I thought she liked these bloody Mesmer. She'd taken care of Reve.

I pushed through a crowd to Vincent's clinic, only to find one of the Mesmer trio lying on their back with their shirt up as another Mesmer held a stethoscope to their stomach.

"It's so cold!" giggled the one lying down.

"Stay still, I can hear your tummy!"

Vincent leaned on his cane with a strained smile. Dark circles colored his eyes, and his skin looked haggard. Gods, he looked worn out. His smile faded when he noticed my approach. "I'm sorry, Cosmo. It would appear I have a patient."

The Mesmer—Cosmo, I guessed—suddenly sat up, and their eyes bulged at my arm. "Are you hurt?" they said with a quiver, their lip already wobbling.

If they started screaming, I was out of here. "I had a small tumble. I just need Vincent to take a look."

"Can we stay and watch?" said another of the trio with an eager grin.

The trio were supposed to help control the Mesmer, not encourage their bad behavior!

"Now, Celeste," Vincent said. "What's the second lesson of being a medical practitioner?"

"The blood stays inside the body?"

"That's the fifth lesson."

"Bones stay inside the body?"

"Sixth."

"Oh, um..."

"Patient confidentiality and privacy are important, which comes after lesson one; if a mortal requires medical aid, you must help them immediately should it be safe to do so." Vincent popped open a glass jar of lollipops. "Which means I must attend to Kayl here alone, if you don't mind."

The Mesmer pouted but queued up for a lollipop. "Will you read us a bedtime story later? *Please?*"

Vincent smiled with a careful curve that hid his fangs. "I'll try and make time."

Cosmo hopped down and snatched a lollipop. "Thank you, Uncle Vinny!" They joined the other two identical Mesmer that made up the trio, and the three of them skipped away—literally skipped, as though the corridor were some meadow full of daisies on Solaris.

I wish I knew what drugs they were on. "Uncle Vinny? A few days ago, they were screaming in fear."

Vincent closed the door behind me, leaving us with the harsh glare of an aether lamp and the overpowering smell of antiseptic. There was room for only one bed and a cupboard full of supplies, but Vincent made do. "Mesmorpheus came to my dreams last night, and we negotiated an arrangement. They no longer wish for me to drink blood inside their temple, and in return, Mesmorpheus told the Mesmer I could be trusted. They've taken quite an interest in me since."

"So now you're teaching them medical secrets?" Gods, I didn't want to even imagine a Mesmer becoming a doctor. They'd fall asleep during surgery.

"To entertain them. They're a curious lot."

I sat on the edge of the bed. "Sounds like you need saving. Do you want me to have a word with them?"

"They're no trouble. They're rather sweet, actually. Cosmo brought me a blood orange earlier and asked if I could eat it."

"Bless them. Seriously though, you need to eat. Mesmorpheus should understand that."

"It's fine. I can sneak out of the temple to feed. It's Sinder I'm worried about. Being cooped up inside stresses him."

"The Mesmer aren't giving you enough privacy for a feed or a fuck?"

Vincent's pale cheeks flushed red for a heartbeat.

"Don't be embarrassed," I added. "We all have our needs."

"It's... I'm not ashamed of our relationship. It's needing his blood that shames me. But enough about me. May I?" He gestured to my injured arm.

I allowed him to examine it. "I don't think it's broken—I can still wiggle my fingers—but it pissing hurts."

"Hrm. How did you injure it?"

"Well, I told Dru I tripped over a rock, but really, I got into a fight with a rather large Leander."

"And you came off worse?"

"Oh, he came off *much* worse."

I hadn't stepped into that arena with the intention of stealing a mortal soul, only saving one. But then Quen had been absolutely terrified of Whiskers. I'd never seen him that scared before. And when I'd met his eye, I'd realized why.

Rage had burned through me. I hadn't thought beyond wanting to utterly destroy that damn cat. Whiskers hadn't been the first mortal to hurt

Quen—I knew Karendar had, and if Karendar were here maybe, I'd take his damn soul, too.

But the thought of anyone hurting Quen—*my* Quen—had set me right off.

Quen had said he'd shoot the Warden who'd groped me. In a way, he already had. That Diviner's brains had decorated a wall, and even though it wasn't Quen who'd pulled the trigger, it had felt like him in some way I couldn't explain.

This new version of Quen was taking no prisoners.

And neither was I.

He'd kill his own mortals for me. I'd taken a mortal soul for him.

What had we become? Whatever this was went beyond a simple partnership.

Should I be scared knowing I would kill for him? For any of my family?

I *wasn't* a killer. I wasn't Jinx.

"Have you ever lost a life?" I asked Vincent as he carefully removed my sling. "You know, when trying to save someone."

His bloodshot eyes met mine. "Yes. We Necro are gifted healers, but sometimes we're too late, or mortal bodies are damaged beyond repair. We can't save everyone, as much as it pains us. Some we must let go."

"And have you ever... killed someone? Deliberately and without remorse?"

I cared nothing for Whiskers's soul, yet losing the Lioness... Gods, that hurt.

Vincent didn't meet my eye that time. "Yes."

"When?" I whispered.

"During the Grayford Incident. One of the Diviner Wardens was injured. I saw to his wounds, but instead of healing them, I hastened them. I caused his death and quit the Wardens before they could investigate."

Shit. He'd never revealed *that* before. "Do you regret it?"

"I've ended many lives that I've regretted under guidance of The Nameless One. The Warden? I don't regret that. He'd been injured attacking a young Vesper girl. He'd shown that child no mercy, and so he received no kindness from me. Why do you ask?" He got my arm free and began to roll up the sleeve. "Did you kill this Leander?"

I hissed as he unwrapped the bandage from my arm. "Worse than kill. I ripped out his soul."

"Did he deserve it?"

"Yes. But killing him didn't fix the damage done. I stole his *soul*. His very existence. His consciousness is gone forever. It won't even return to his god, or an afterlife. It's simply gone. Regardless of whether he deserved it or not, doesn't that make me a monster?"

Didn't that make me as bad as Jinx?

Though she'd stolen thousands more. An entire domain of innocents.

"I can't grant you absolution, Kayl. No one can grant that. Nor can vengeance save lives lost. But sometimes, foul deeds need another foul deed to end them. In defeating the monster, you must become a monster, if that's what it takes."

"I could steal your soul with a single touch. You're not scared of me?" If any of the Godless knew what it meant to be a monster—or to be perceived as one—it was Vincent.

Vincent flashed a fang. "I've seen real monsters, and you're not so fearsome."

I gave him a shove and winced at my arm.

He chuckled, and then as the bandage fell away, his face froze at the sight of blood, his entire body becoming rigid.

"Vincent?"

"I'm sorry, I—" A gurgle came from his stomach. He staggered back from the bed and pressed against the wall as though cowering from me, his chest rising in rapid gasps. "Forgive me. I need a moment."

"When did you last feed?"

He turned from my probing stare.

"*Vincent—*"

"A few days ago." His bloodshot eyes looked dark and sunken.

I offered my injured arm. "You know you can take my blood anytime."

"I wouldn't ask that of you." He bit his lip.

"I don't want you going hungry."

"I'm fine, truly. I'm careful leaving the temple. My own temple is close by if I get desperate or feel I'm becoming a danger to others."

"Are you sure going to your temple is safe? This is stupid, you should eat—"

"I won't break my promise to Mesmorpheus. They've given us their hospitality. The least I can do is respect it." He straightened his collar and regained his polite composure. "Now, let's get your arm fixed up."

He took my arm with care, his fingers cold to the touch, and worked in silence, mending the bone and flesh with minimal pain.

Sinder was right to worry if Vincent was starving himself in order to keep the Mesmer happy. And I couldn't help but worry I was neglecting my family by running off with Quen on these grand adventures.

I had to find a way to keep them safe.

After Vincent had fixed up my arm, I gave myself a quick cleanup and headed for my room to change before anyone noticed the massive hole in my dress.

Sinder loitered in the corridor outside. "Off to the meeting? I wouldn't bother, dearest. Our new Glimmer has Harm's ear, and the two of them have been talking nonstop about city ordinances and other dull nonsense. I couldn't guess why."

Really? I hadn't expected Harmony to become friends with our Glimmer guest so soon. Or maybe Sinder wanted an excuse to avoid the Glimmer, which was more likely. I needed to report back on my trip to Obituary, but the way Sinder's shoulders slumped, I'd say he needed me more. "I was going to get changed first. Look at this." I held up my hand. "I only went and chipped a bloody nail when I fell over that rock."

Sinder's face lit up, though thankfully not literally. "Need a manicure, darling?"

"I wouldn't say no."

He looped his arm around mine. "Then I insist."

Harmony could wait. She'd send Dru chasing after me when she was good and ready.

I returned to my room and changed into something more casual while Sinder fetched his manicure kit and a packet of pink wafers.

"Like old times, darling." He spread out his kit and a box full of nail varnish on the oversized bed.

I crossed my legs and got comfortable. It wasn't quite like old times. We used to spend our evenings in the depot doing each other's nails with music and laughter in the background, occasionally playing a game or drinking wine, when we could get it.

But in the Mesmer temple, the walls were stifling. There was no music, no wine, though the incense that wafted through the corridors was almost strong enough to get high on. We huddled under the never-ending swirl of glowing stars like two secret conspirators.

"How have things been in the temple while I was gone?"

"Chaotic. The Mesmer are like children. I've never been fond of children. Except for Reve. I liked Reve. At least he didn't follow me around like a Fauna pup asking constant inane questions about reality. *Why is the sky blue? Why does purple candy taste like raspberry?* I don't fucking know!"

"Vincent seems to be handling them well."

"I keep telling Vincent he needs to stop encouraging him, but you know what he's like. I think he enjoys having a purpose. Though really, I think he enjoys being in the company of mortals who don't run from him screaming. That's the only reason I haven't set fire to the temple yet."

I snapped a pink wafer in half, scattering a few crumbs on the bed that Dru would no doubt tell me off for later. After all the chocolate limes I'd been eating, at least the pink wafers were a lighter snack. I loved the vanilla cream inside. "Is he feeding enough?"

"Not as much as I'd like. I'm going to drag him into the nearest dirty alley and let him have his way with me."

"You be careful."

"I don't plan to be, dearest." Sinder took my right hand. "Let's get these filed, and then we'll think about color. We can't have an ambassador walking around in this state."

"What would I do without you?"

He fluttered his eyelashes. "Get thrown back into the Undercity, most likely." He reached for a cuticle remover and began his work in earnest. "All that Obituary heat has dried your skin, darling. I've got some moisturizer that'll help. So, how did it go? It must have been some party if you stayed the full twelve hours."

"It was a party, all right. Quen managed to negotiate what he wanted, but..."

"But?"

"There was a Leander woman. She was being abused by Lionheart. We tried to save her, to negotiate her freedom. But she didn't want our help in the end." I let out the sigh I'd been carrying since Obituary. "We lost her." And nothing infuriated me more.

Sinder checked each nail and then swapped to my other hand. "Not all mortals want to be saved, or can be. You know the tight hold their gods have. Only a few are truly godless, like us. Most would remain by their god if given the chance."

What a depressing thought. "Lionheart was abusing her cubs. Why wouldn't she seek any way possible to remove them from that?" To protect her cubs, at least? Though deep down, I *did* understand. She didn't want to leave her cubs to that monster, and between Quen and Dandelion, we'd found no way to save them.

"It's complicated." He grimaced. "Sometimes mortals don't realize they're being abused by the ones who claim to love them. I didn't."

Shit. I'd strayed into an uncomfortable topic. "I'm sorry, I didn't mean to bring this up—"

"It's fine. You'll be heading to Rapture soon, won't you? Rather you than I, dearest, but you'll need to know what dangers to watch out for." Sinder switched to the file and began shaping my nails.

"I was going to get intel from Harm." Sinder never directly spoke of his past, and I wasn't going to push it out of him. I always figured he'd tell me himself, one day.

"She'd give you the facts. I'll give you the truth."

"You don't have to tell me anything you're not comfortable with."

"Thank you. It's... about time we had this conversation." He moved between my nails without skipping a beat. "Edana will take an interest in you because she likes shiny new toys, and that's what you are to her. You're new, and dangerous, and gorgeous. She'll try and take you for her own."

"You really think so?"

"I know so. Edana collects a harem of mortals from across the domains. So long as they please her, they'll receive her affection in turn. Many seek this arrangement because Edana is everything. But don't be fooled. She'll use you, and when you no longer satisfy her, she'll crush you, as she crushed me."

"I'm—I'm sorry."

"Don't be. I loved Edana. I worshipped the ground she walked on. She could spit in my mouth and I'd savor the taste like a fine wine. I didn't blame her for discarding me. It was the Glimmer who made me feel unworthy of her. Who made me believe my love could never be enough."

"Sinder." I placed a hand on his knee. "You are worthy as you are. You don't need a god to tell you that."

"One day, I may believe you, dearest. I don't feel worthy of you or Vincent. I have such... poison in my blood. An all-consuming hatred that never settles. I can't even look at Joe without wanting to burn him to ash."

"You haven't burned him."

"Not yet. That doesn't make me a saint."

"But you see, you've got self-control. You're tolerating him and all this nonsense for the sake of our family. That takes strength."

His shoulders sagged. "I'm happy to support you and Corinth's crazy venture if it means the Glimmer lose power. I'm keeping it together for entirely selfish reasons."

"And I'm not?"

"How do you do it, darling? After everything that's happened, after Eventide... What's kept you going? You were a mess only last week, and now you're visiting domains on a grand crusade."

The pain of losing Reve and the Vesper would never fully leave me, but now I had a chance of protecting mortals from their gods. From Jinx. There was no better balm than action. "We keep going because we have to. Because no one else will."

"So it has nothing to do with a certain Diviner?"

I raised a brow. "Quen and I are just partners. He doesn't see me that way."

"No? He only buys you expensive dresses, and oh, what's this? An expensive bracelet?" He tugged the silver bangle around my wrist.

"It's not jewelry, it's a tool."

"What does it do besides look fancy?" He turned my wrist over, examining it.

"It's designed to nullify the Chaos-detecting sensors around Central Station. I don't really know how it works, but it means I don't set the sensors off."

"So other Chaos, such as your charming sister, can't get through without it?"

"That's right. Plus, I can't take it off, so short of chopping my hand off, no one can steal it from me."

"It's locked? Who has the key? Corinth?"

"He keeps it safe on his person, I believe."

"How lovely. He owns the key to your heart."

I gave him a shove, and he fell back on a cushion with a chuckle.

The door to my room opened, and Joe popped his head in. The Glimmer appeared different from the last time I'd seen him—he was wearing a properly tailored suit, his hair had been brushed back in sleek waves, and his jawline had been contoured to look more masculine.

Gods. Dare I say it, but Joe looked impeccably handsome.

Not only handsome. But *hot* in a way Glimmer didn't even appreciate.

Sinder immediately sat up, and all humor drained from his face.

"Sorry to interrupt," Joe said. "Harmony was asking for you."

"I'll be there in a moment," I called.

Joe nodded and closed the door behind him.

"Are those Vincent's clothes?" I asked.

Sinder rolled his eyes. "Of course. You know Vincent. As helpful as ever."

Not only had Vincent given Joe access to his wardrobe, but it looked as though he'd tailored the Glimmer's face, too. Bless him for making Joe more comfortable, but I didn't want this to come between him and Sinder.

"I don't trust him." Sinder blew flames from his nostrils.

"I know you don't—"

"Not just because he's a Glimmer. He worked in Gloria's staff, remember? I keep seeing him sniffing around, poking his nose into places he shouldn't. And now he's cozying up to Harm—"

"What are you saying?"

"Nothing, darling." He blinked in feigned innocence. "Only that you should keep an eye on him. My gut tells me he's not what he seems."

XX

Warden morale has been low of late. The recent attack, the failed memorial, and the increased security around Chime all contribute to a growing uneasiness.

Therefore, I propose a 25% raise for all acting Wardens, along with additional benefits such as a generous pension packet, an additional day of annual leave for charity work, and a 'picnic in the park' team-building exercise to boost flagging morale.

Our budget will need some adjustments, but unlike the Glimmer, I believe a happy workforce makes an effective workforce.
—Q. Corinth, *Internal Warden Memo*

PENDULA INSISTED I WASH and change in one of the communal showers in Warden HQ before meeting with Miss Ilona Burns, and I couldn't fault her assessment. I stunk of sweat, sand, and whiskey—the latter of which she chided me for—and I no doubt looked like some ragamuffin begging on Sinner's Row.

More than that, everything hurt. I had a splitting headache, which was made all the worse by Pendula's nagging, and my muscles hadn't ached this much since my early days training with the Wardens.

A hot shower and a cup of tea were exactly what I needed after twelve blasted hours in Obituary. I left both Ben and Pendula in the staff tea room and headed for the showers.

I stripped, dumping my sandy clothes unceremoniously on the floor for Future Quen to deal with. The rough-and-tumble of the arena had left me a tad battered and bruised, but the hot water helped soothe those twinges away.

My breath came out in a shuddering sigh.

Kayl had stolen a soul on my command.

She'd been angry at me, at my insistence that we follow the plan and give Lionheart what he wanted. But what choice did I have? One could not argue with a god and retain one's physical body. If Lionheart had torn me apart, I supposed Dor could simply reanimate my body once more, but would he?

Lionheart had toyed with me. He knew I feared Whiskers.

And now Whiskers was no more.

Saints. I agonized over every mortal death I'd witnessed. Over every life I'd ever taken. Yet I felt no remorse for Whiskers. Not a jot.

I wasn't a killer, yet Elijah had turned me into one.

I *wasn't* a killer. And yet, when I'd died, some part of my soul had remained dead. It had been replaced with a darkness that allowed a killer to step forth.

Kayl had taken Whiskers's soul, and I'd allowed it. Welcomed it.

Was I becoming the man my younger self had feared?

What did it matter in the end?

Each drop of water running down my face was another second rushing toward destiny. My fate was still on track, and perhaps this was where it began. My decisions could very well push Kayl away until she finally snapped and took my soul next.

I only hoped I could save Chaos before she ended my timeline once and for all.

It should scare me. If anything, I worried more for Kayl's soul.

One could not kill and remain the same.

I rinsed my hair off and slapped soaking feet across the tiles to the locker where my jacket and other personal effects waited.

For a moment, I sat on the bench and let my damp head rest against the cold metal of the locker. Soon, I'd need to escort Ilona Burns through to Kronos, though the thought of meeting Walter's daughter filled me with dread.

I hadn't been able to save her father.

Another shameful failure on my part.

But first, I wanted to check in on another guest.

I dressed in a spare suit and donned my jacket. Instead of locating my bodyguard and assistant as I no doubt should, I ducked through HQ's corridors and headed for the correctional facility.

I still hated these hallways.

The oppressive gray corridors stretched on forever like some labyrinth of the damned. I'd experienced the never-ending aether of the afterlife, and even that didn't compare to this purgatory. Since I'd replaced Elijah, I'd taken on the task of reducing the number of incarcerated mortals, arguing that our resources shouldn't be wasted on petty crimes such as littering or vandalism, so long as they weren't blasphemous, of course.

And with the entire domain of Eventide gone, I thought we'd surely have less pickpockets and thieves?

Yet these cells remained as occupied as ever with Fauna and Ember and a few surprise admissions, including a couple of Leander and a rogue Seren who'd been caught embezzling funds on Sinner's Row.

It was as though mortals were stepping into the Vesper's shoes, or Wardens were looking for new targets out of sheer boredom.

Or these were mortals who simply fell through the cracks left by Varen's absence.

"Good evening, sir." An Umber with a reddish-brown gravel complexion and poppies for eyebrows saluted me as I approached the cell I needed.

"How is our guest behaving?"

"He's quiet, sir. He hasn't attempted to remove his gloves or escape, nor has he given the guards any trouble."

"Excellent. It's time I formally introduced myself."

The Warden opened the door, and I stepped inside a brightly lit cell. An aether lamp buzzed above a table, where the Chaos male was chained. He no longer wore a Zephyr form, but that of Chaos— rippling silvery-blue skin with pink highlights at the tip of his ears and fingers, and cropped white hair. Even sitting, his height towered over mine.

Though chained, he had enough freedom to stretch his limbs, and his gloved hands currently busied themselves with a crossword in today's Courier.

"What's a six-letter word beginning with *C* that means a possibility of something happening?" he said without looking up.

I slid into the chair opposite. "Chance."

He sat up and set his crossword aside. "Pleased to meet you, Master Corinth."

"That's your name? Chance?"

"It's a Chaos name, not that you Diviner would know much about my domain. Chance, Jinx, Flux, Lucky—we're all children of Chaos."

"You missed out Kayl."

"How rude of me. She may be one of us, but she's as ignorant as a Diviner when it comes to Chaos. And yet our dear mother named her ambassador. Isn't that bizarre?"

"Kayl and I are working on a plan to save Chaos, so our domains may coexist in peace."

"That's awfully nice of you. Let me know how that goes." He returned to his crossword puzzle. "What's an eight-letter word beginning with *P* that means an incarcerated mortal?"

"You're not a prisoner."

He rattled his chains. "Are we playing pretend? That's a seven-letter word. Try again."

"I don't mean Chaos any harm. However, your kind have caused irreparable harm to Chime and mortals across the domains. You'll remain here for your own safety—and Chime's. But while you're here, I swear you'll be treated well."

"I'd like to take your word for it, but I don't trust Diviner."

"Some part of you must, otherwise you wouldn't have allowed yourself to be caught." I cocked my head. "Why did you?"

Chance leaned back with a wry grin. "You've met my sisters."

"You don't agree with Jinx's plans?"

"I'm an easygoing man. I don't want trouble. But I'm made of chaos, see? Trouble tends to find us. You've probably figured that out for yourself already."

Sadly. "Help me stop Jinx, and I'll personally ensure that you and the rest of Corentine's mortals will be delivered to safety."

"Why, what's she done now?"

"A tram derailed by Central Station the other day."

"That was *her*?" Chance whooped a laugh. "I read about that in the paper."

"What are her motives? What is she planning next?"

"Sorry, Corinth. I may not want any part of her particular brand of crazy, but that doesn't mean I'm going to betray her, either—"

"Mortals *died*. More could follow if she continues to pull such stunts. I cannot advocate for Chaos if she continues to undermine my efforts."

"Jinx doesn't give a shit."

"And neither do you?"

Chance gave an awkward shrug. "So what now? You going to torture answers out of me? That's what this place is for, right?"

I steepled my fingers. "You'll remain in this facility, where you will be treated well so long as you continue to cooperate. When the time comes, you'll be given a choice; settle into a persona from one of the domains and live out your life without your Chaos abilities."

"A choice usually has more than one option. You really believe Dor will let us go? That he'll let me live out my life in a nice suit and visit the Brick and Briar, where I'll be overcharged for the privilege of too much foam in my pint?" He returned to the crossword. "Get me another newspaper, will ya? I'm done with this one."

What he wanted was normalcy. A mundane existence.

His goals weren't too dissimilar to mine. "Give me something to work with, and I'll get you a whole stack of broadsheets." Or perhaps I'd swing by a bookstore and pick up some puzzle books.

There was an unnerving gleam in Chance's silvery-blue eyes so like Kayl's. "There's only one thing Jinx truly wants."

"Which is?"

"Her mother."

I returned to my office with a desperate need for a cup of tea.

It was almost half nine, which meant I'd need to prepare for the ten o'clock crossing. However, my migraine had only gotten worse since speaking with Chance. For some reason, Chaos had that effect. I hadn't expected him to be cooperative, yet he'd been more forthcoming than I'd imagined. Mostly, I'd wanted to check in on him to ensure he wasn't being mistreated.

Did I trust my own damn domain?

I pushed open the window to my office and allowed a cool breeze to soothe my throbbing temples.

Paper fluttered across my desk.

I awkwardly leaped and snatched it before it blew out the window. It was another note written in my own handwriting.

"*Control your thoughts. They aren't your own.*"

Why would I leave myself such a note? It wasn't as if I needed the reminder! Like the last blasted note, I couldn't remember writing this one, either.

I sank into my chair and massaged my forehead. What I'd do for an Ember's touch...

YOUR DECISIONS HAVE BEEN IRRATIONAL.

Dor's voice battered my mind, making me cringe. I'd been gearing up for this conversation once I returned to Kronos later, but apparently, we were doing this now. *Do you refer to a specific decision in particular, Father?*

DO NOT JEST WITH ME. YOU ALLOWED LIONHEART TO WITNESS CHAOS'S POWER FIRSTHAND. IF THE OTHER DOMAINS LEARN OF THIS, THEY MAY ALSO LEARN OF THE GOD DEVICES.

Lionheart isn't one for sharing his sources—

THE OTHER GODS MUST NOT LEARN THAT THIS POWER CAN BE HARNESSED AND USED. THE DOMAINS COULD TURN THIS POWER AGAINST US.

How?

BY ALIGNING WITH CHAOS.

My heart skipped a beat. Here I was trying to unite the domains against Chaos, but would some of them see the potential in Chaos's power?

No. They wouldn't go against Dor. Only the Glimmer knew about the soul-splitting devices, and they certainly wouldn't align with Chaos. Besides, Kayl was on my side, and I had Chance locked away here while more of his siblings were trapped in the clock tower. The real threat was Jinx. Would any domain dare align themselves with her?

When she threatened to steal the souls of gods?

Though perhaps certain gods would welcome that threat.

YOU SEE THE THREAT OF CHAOS. YOU SEE WHY I WANT THEM DESTROYED.

The gods are loyal to you, Father. By meeting with them and convincing them to unite in Chime's favor, they're reaffirming their loyalty.

YOU WALK A FINE LINE. THIS WOMAN YOU PARTNER YOURSELF WITH ALMOST COST YOU LIONHEART'S FAVOR. HER GOALS DO NOT ALIGN WITH OURS. TAKE HEED. CHAOS CANNOT BE TRUSTED.

His voice faded from my mind, and the pressure in my head lessened. I understood why Father didn't trust Kayl, but He didn't know her like I did.

She wanted to save Chime and all its mortals. We were on the same side.

"Having a rough night, Corinth?"

I swiveled in my chair.

Jinx stood by the window completely naked. She wore the colors of Chaos, though I didn't need this form to know it was her, and not Kayl—those eyes and matching smirk were as sharp as a knife.

Saints. She'd broken into HQ!

For a moment, time stretched between us. My pistol was tucked in my desk drawer, but she could probably reach me in the seconds it took to open it. Ben stood guard outside, but if I yelled, I'd only be putting him at risk.

"How did you get inside my office?" I asked, dumbfounded. There were sensors at all the major doors leading into Warden HQ, including here. There was no way she could have snuck in without triggering at least one of them.

"You left your window open, silly."

"You flew in? That window is tiny, how—You took the form of a Seren?" Which would explain why she wore no clothes.

"A Fauna, actually. But good guess." She pushed away from the window and prowled toward me.

I tried to leap up, but she suddenly dashed forward and shoved me back into the chair. Her hand pushed painfully into my shoulder as she pinned me down.

She snatched a letter opener from my desk, scattering a flutter of papers and folders in the process, and pressed the sharp edge against my throat. "Be a good boy and stay still. I just want to chat."

All my muscles tensed as her nakedness and that blasted letter opener pressed too close for comfort. "What do you want, Jinx?"

"Oh, many things. I want blueberry pancakes. I want tickets to the theater for the production of Big Busty Ember Wenches. I want you and every single fucking Diviner to disappear forever. But right now, what I want most of all, is for you to go downstairs and release my brother. I know you're keeping him here."

What an odd coincidence that she'd choose to visit now, when I'd just questioned him. "He's being treated well."

"I didn't ask you to throw him a party. I said I want him *out*."

"We can negotiate—"

"On what? Your grand fucking plan to capture my siblings and force us into joining your merry society? News report, idiot; there's no happy ending where Chaos is involved." The letter opener cut into my skin a bite. "Slitting your throat would be fun, though a waste of my time, since I actually need you alive to get my brother out and I don't trust the rest of you Diviner fucks." Her spare hand slid underneath my jacket. "But I'm not against cutting off a few bits here and there. Should we start with your cock? It's not like you're using it, is it?"

These threats were growing tiresome. Perhaps she was starting to like me. "You know, there are more pleasant means of negotiation. We could chat over a cup of tea, for instance. I'll even provide pancakes."

"And listen to you yammer on about tea and trains? No thanks."

"I know you desire Corentine's freedom—"

"But you'll never grant it, will you?"

"I'm doing all I can to ease her suffering. I want her free from the clock tower, too. Work with me, with Kayl, and we can come to some sort of arrangement—"

"Is that how you won over my sister? With pretty promises?" Jinx leaned in, as though about to kiss me. "I know you're going to betray her." Her hot breath caressed my cheek. "And when you do, I'll be there to destroy you."

The door to my office opened. "Your Excellency, you're late for your appoint—" Pendula stopped dead in her tracks, her silver eyes going wide at the sight of a naked woman practically straddling me. One who unfortunately appeared identical to Kayl.

This wasn't turning into my night, was it?

Jinx grinned. "No way! Is that a female Diviner?"

Pendula regained her composure and stood defiant by the doorway. "If you wish to make an appointment with His Excellency, I suggest you return in the morning fully dressed. Otherwise, Warden Seasons here will be forced to remove you from the premises."

Ben appeared from around the corner with his pistol loaded and aimed over Pendula's shoulder. "Are you okay, sir?"

What a foolish question. "I've had better days."

Jinx slid from my lap and swiveled the chair so I faced the door, though she remained standing behind me, the letter opener still at my throat. "Three Diviner in one room is enough to make me sick, but you didn't tell me you were hiding this pretty little thing, Corinth. What's your name, Silver Girl?"

"I don't need to divulge any information to you." Pendula huffed.

"Don't be that way. Mine's Jinx. You'll need to remember it later when you scream it. You've been touched by Chaos. I'd be happy to touch you again."

Pendula instantly reached for her hair, and the streak of brass that cut through the silver. "I think you should leave."

"Jealous that Corinth has a type, and it's not you? Don't be—he's a sloppy kisser. Trust me, I know."

Jinx pushed my chair forward. My palms slapped against the desk.

Time slowed in the room as Ben slid past Pendula. A useless gesture, really. Chaos didn't obey the laws of time.

Jinx had already transformed into a magpie and flew out the window.

"She—She can do that?" Ben stared open-mouthed.

"With a Fauna form." Blast it, we'd now have to place sensors on the damn windows.

Though... if she could sneak into Warden HQ, why now? Why not before?

I reached inside my inner jacket pocket.

The key to Kayl's bracelet was gone.

I patted down the rest of my jacket and trouser pockets to be sure, but it was most certainly gone. How in Dor's name had she known about the bracelet? Had Kayl let it slip? Had Corentine taken the information from her mind and passed it on to Jinx?

Damn it! I had no way of warning Kayl before tomorrow's meeting. This was why I'd insisted on learning of the Godless's location! I was their sodding benefactor, and yet they still didn't trust me.

Pendula peered out the window. "So that was our enemy." She snapped a glare in my direction. "Why, may I ask, are you going out of your way to help creatures like that?"

I sat on the edge of my desk and rubbed my neck. "They're not creatures. They're mortals, same as us. Don't forget this was originally their domain. They can be forgiven for being upset that we're trying to dictate their lives—"

"Wardens dictate laws for the rest of us. That's how we maintain a fair and equal society. Regardless of Chime's past, this domain now belongs to every mortal who lives here. And if they seek to become a member of the society we've built, then they need to act the part."

"Is our society really fair and equal?" When the Glimmer and Diviner rule the Golden City, and the poorest languish in the Undercity? "Have you ever thought to question it?"

Pendula gave me an odd look. I shouldn't have said anything. Any signs of sedition would only get reported back to Father.

"It's quarter to ten, sir," Ben said, saving me from further awkwardness.

"I know it's imperative we escort Miss Burns through to Kronos, but I can't leave Chime now. Not when Jinx is running rampant and HQ needs securing." And now she'd stolen my blasted key, I'd need to increase security around the station. "I hesitate to ask, but can you escort her, Ben? When I know Chime is safe, I'll follow on tomorrow's 10 a.m. crossing."

"If Chime is in danger, sir, then I can't leave your side—"

"I'll take Miss Burns through," Pendula offered. "I'm sure she'd appreciate a friendly welcome."

I wasn't sure of Pendula's motives, but she at least knew how to be personable in a way Ben lacked. "Thank you. Get her settled."

"Don't forget your prayers tonight," Pendula chided once more.

As if I could forget my prayers when Dor had me at His beck and call.

Chaos may not want saving, but I'd save them whether they wanted it or not.

A Delicious Slice of Betrayal

What do we know about Chaos?
I am one of the few mortals to have brushed close with the apparent 'aether creatures' and live to report it. I suspect my firsthand knowledge of these creatures, as well as my work on Dr. H. Bezel's investigations into aether, is why I was chosen to head this project.
These 'mortals' have a fascinating connection to aether that no other domain possesses. This connection is of a biological nature. They can rewrite their own physiology to take on the physical properties of other domains, similar to the Necro and Fauna's abilities.
Could Chaos be manifested and harnessed in some way?
Could I, for example, change my physiology from Zephyr to Diviner?
—Dr. Z. Finch, *Notes on Chaos*

FUCK CHANCE.

THAT TIME-LOVING twat could have escaped from Warden HQ whenever he liked. At first, I thought getting himself captured was a brilliant move. He could infiltrate those fucking Wardens and destroy them from the inside out.

But nope, that absolute wanker was having the time of his life eating cucumber sandwiches and doing crosswords.

So *fuck* him.

I tossed the key to Corinth's fancy bracelet in my hand as I walked down the cobblestone streets to Central Station, wearing a Glimmer's face and a hot-arse dress to match. My dear sister likely didn't see the irony of being chained by a Diviner, but I was going to set her free and win myself a trip to Rapture.

Central was quiet this morning, with many of the stores not yet open to sell whatever tacky shit they could trick tourists into buying. The cafés were open, though, and I'd readied myself for the day with a plate of pancakes. On my way back, I spotted a familiar face in the window of Lady Mae's.

It was that female Diviner from Corinth's office!

She sat drinking coffee with Ambassador Gloria, their heads bent close in some supersecret discussion, I'd bet. I'd love to sneak in and eavesdrop, but I'd likely get noticed, and I had my own schedule to worry about. But what the fuck was Corinth's fancy new assistant doing holding secret meetings with the enemy?

Lady Mae's really was the place for a cup of tea and a slice of betrayal.

I left them to their plotting to attend to my own plotting. It was after eight, which meant my dear sister would be making her way to the Gate soon. Everything in this stupid city happened on time, so I was ready and waiting for her to step off the tram.

Kayl was wearing an Ember's face and dressed in a casual dress and jacket. She wasn't even paying attention as she walked straight into me.

Her eyes went wide. "Jinx."

"Sister. Let's go for a walk." I wrapped my arm around hers and dragged her from the crowd.

She dug her heels in as we reached the end of the tram platform. "Whatever you're doing, stop it."

"Let her go," Green Girl said in some deep voice that was supposed to be menacing, though her golden eyes held a flicker of apprehension.

"Oh looky, your flowers are growing back!"

The Umber touched her brow with a flinch.

Kayl tried to pull from my arm. "Forget it, Jinx. You're not taking me—"

"I'm feeling particularly stabby today, so why don't we go for a nice little chat before someone loses an eye?" I switched to my Diviner form and yanked time to a stop before anyone would notice. "There. Now we can be left in peace."

Kayl stared across the station. A few Diviner were looking around, likely trying to find the source of this sudden pause of time. "Central is crawling with Diviner Warden. You'll never make it to the Gate."

"We're not going to the Gate—"

"The clock tower, then."

I rolled my eyes. "Can I not want to spend time with my sister?"

"What, you want to grab a cup of tea and cake?"

"I already ate. I want to *talk*. We'll find a nice bench in Meridian Park. The two of us. No Godless. No Corinth. Just us, like it used to be. You're our mother's voice. That means you have to hear me out."

She glanced up at the clock tower, clearly worried she'd miss her crossing. "Fine. We'll talk. But if you pull any stunts, I'm gone."

I released her arm, and she followed me into a back alley that led to Meridian Park. It wouldn't be odd for me wearing a Diviner's face to be seen wandering, but an Ember casually ignoring the laws of time? Bit suspicious. Of course, Kayl had never learned to swap forms like I did.

Why did she get to play ambassador to Chaos when she didn't have a clue?

We walked in silence. Once we reached the park gates, I let time slip back and returned to my Glimmer form. Of all the forms I'd tried recently, the Fauna was the most fun. Being able to shift between animal types in the blink of an eye was damn useful. Sadly, the good citizens of Chime didn't appreciate it when I suddenly appeared naked in front of them. Those prudes.

The Glimmer was my second favorite. What wasn't there to like? An absolutely gorgeous body, gleaming golden skin and hair, eyes like fire, and the ability to incinerate as well as an Ember. Plus, everyone got out of my way when I came near them.

Glimmer were queen bitches for a reason, and that was me. Queen of 'em all.

I headed for a bench obscured by a bush and hidden from any potentially wandering Wardens. Only a few Leander joggers were out this early, and a couple of Umber tending to the roses.

Kayl sat her arse as far from me as she could.

I left a gap and casually slid down with my handbag dangling over my shoulder. "So why have you been avoiding me this past month?"

"Really? You don't think trying to destroy the domains and endangering my friends could be the reason?"

"Everyone needs a hobby. I can't believe you'd hold that against me."

"Those murdering tendencies of yours get in the way of any potential relationship."

"Is that why you betrayed me?"

She let out a breath. "Are we really going to do this? *Here?*"

"Why not here? You hurt my feelings, you know. You're my sister!"

"You know why I did it."

"Because you decided other mortals were more important than your family."

"If your idea of a chat is to berate and guilt me, then we're done." She moved to stand.

I pulled her back down. "Try and see it from my perspective. I got my own body. I was excited! I could finally meet our mother. I wanted to share it with you—with the most important mortal in my life. And you threw that in my face. Even now you're being a bitch about it."

She turned to me with a look of irritation. "Jinx. I can't say this any plainer. I will not jeopardize the lives of *any* mortal for your sick pissing agenda. Got it?"

"Only if they're a Leander—"

"Who told you about the Leander? Corentine?"

I smirked. "News spreads, sister."

Her nostrils flared with a touch of flame. "You need to stop this— whatever *this* is. Corentine made me her voice. That means she trusts me to do what's right for Chaos and for Chime. Which means *you* need to stop acting like some teenage Fauna lashing out at everything. All you're doing is turning the domains against us when I'm trying to save our sorry arses."

But I was a teenager, wasn't I? I had the body of a twenty-six-year-old, but technically I was thirteen—and technically, I hadn't even owned this body for more than a month.

It was all right for her—she had years to fuck up and learn, not that she ever learned shit without my help. And yet, for all those times she did fuck up, her so-called family had forgiven her. Malk forgave her. Corinth forgave her. Mother, too.

She'd destroyed an entire domain, not me.

Why wasn't I allowed a little chaos? It wasn't fucking fair.

I plucked a stray golden hair from my dress. "I don't care if the domains hate us."

"You're the last Chaos in Chime. Do you really want eleven domains on your back?"

"If they destroy me, they'll destroy you too. You really think they'll honor whatever bargains you're making? I thought you were Godless. I thought you wanted to end the reign of the gods. But you're like every other selfish mortal. Ready to suck the gods' cocks if it gets you power. Just like pretty boy Karendar. Worked out well for him, didn't it?"

She observed me as though I were some lowly Vesper beggar. "You were always the smarter one between us. What happened to you, Jinx? Surely even you must realize that negotiating with the gods is the smartest thing to ensure our survival. What you've become is some vicious thing. What you *could* become is so much more than this."

A vicious thing. A desperate thing. When I'd been trapped inside her head, I had nothing *but* thoughts. One of us had needed to be smart, and it wasn't her.

But since I'd gained my own body? I was filled with rage. I wanted to scream and tear and rip the domains apart. It burned inside my gut, my chest, my heart. This fire consumed every inch of me. My skin. My nails. My mouth.

And I didn't understand how she couldn't fucking feel it.

How could she look upon the gods and see salvation?

She'd changed. Not me. I'd been released. I was finally free.

"Are we enemies?" I asked. "I could make your life real difficult."

Kayl let out an exasperated sigh. "You already do."

I met her eyes.

My eyes.

Our lives had been so interwoven. I couldn't imagine a world without Kayl. Her inane thoughts. Her gibberish. Her playful laughter. The way she'd needed me.

My entire life had been through her eyes. Her lips. Her touch.

I'd lost her.

No.

She'd abandoned me.

She'd done this. She'd fucked everything.

I DO NOT WISH FOR MY DAUGHTERS TO FIGHT.

She started it! You chose her over me. Why?

KAYL IS MY VOICE TO THE COUNCIL. BUT YOU ARE MY HEART. MY ANGER. MY RIGHTEOUS FIRE. AND YOU WILL BURN THEM ALL IN MY NAME.

How can I, when she gets in my way?

KAYL WILL OPEN THE DOOR. YOU WILL WALK THROUGH IT.

I ground my teeth. "Fine. I'll play your stupid game." I pulled a taser from my handbag and shot Kayl square in the chest.

She fell back against the bench and spasmed where she sat, her limbs flailing wildly. Dumb bitch didn't even see it coming. "*How?*" she spluttered, saliva dripping down her chin.

I examined the taser. "Stole it from Warden HQ. Corinth was smart enough to pair Wardens with at least one Diviner, but Wardens still gotta piss."

"If you've—you've hurt Quen—"

"Shut up. No one cares about Corinth." I shot her again, and this time her eyes fluttered shut. No one in the park noticed Kayl sprawling on the bench, and if they did, they'd likely deem her some unsavory drunken Ember.

I tucked my taser away and began the fun task of dragging her arse into the nearest bush. She wouldn't mind if I swapped our clothes. My dress was *much* nicer.

Once I'd swapped our outfits and changed my persona to an Ember, I checked our passport IDs looked identical, and then undid her fancy bracelet. With it wrapped around my wrist, Corinth wouldn't be able to tell us apart. Green Girl might, but I wasn't planning on getting chummy.

"You have a nice nap." I left Kayl buried under a bush. Chances were, no one would find her, but she'd wake up pissed off soon enough.

The clock tower rang quarter to nine by the time I made it to Central Station. Rather predictably, Corinth was waiting on the platform, his stupid face all twisted with concern. It relaxed a little when I approached. And what do you know, the bracelet really did protect me from their damn station sensors.

"Are you all right?" He pulled me away from the concourse traffic. "Dru said you had an encounter with Jinx. She and Ben were looking for you."

Slipping into Kayl's persona was easy. I'd spent my entire life in her head, after all. "I managed to give her the slip. She dragged me to Meridian Park and started ranting about making a partnership, but you know her. She's crazy. Are we still in time for Rapture?" I eyed the Gate over his shoulder. Obituary was still open.

"Soon, though I'm hesitant to leave without our bodyguards."

"We managed without them in Obituary. I'm sure we'll be fine."

"Let's grab a cup of tea while we wait. How do you feel about a scone?"

"I'd love a scone." Though if this idiot kept me waiting too long, I'd taser him and run for the Gate myself.

"Oh, that reminds me. We'll need to get your passport ID touched up before we go. A rather annoying formality, I'm afraid."

I'd already marked myself with the stamp for Rapture, but there wasn't any suspicion in Corinth's eyes, though there might be if I refused.

Corinth led the way to one of the ticket offices. But instead of queuing by the passport booth, he gestured for me to follow him inside an empty waiting room.

As soon as I stepped inside, he whipped out a taser.

Fuck! Aether burst across my skin, and I fell to the floor. "You twat!" I screamed as my limbs twitched.

Corinth stood casually over me, the taser in his hand. "Kayl doesn't pronounce scone that way. But good attempt." He pulled my handbag from my shoulder and dug out the spare taser. "I know you stole this last night. Wardens *do* report these things."

"Fuck you!" I spat.

"Where's Kayl?" There was a coldness in his silver eyes. "If you've hurt her—"

"Oh, fuck off, the pair of you!" Kayl this and Quen that, those fucking *fucks*. I was going to taser Corinth in his damn balls!

"I don't want to hurt you, Jinx. In fact, I'd rather we sat down for a nice tea and scone right now and talked this through—"

"Stop being so damn friendly with me just so you can fuck my sister." I crawled to my knees and wiped saliva from my mouth. My arms were still trembling.

"You believe that's my motivation? That's rather sad."

"Isn't it? Dor once tricked my mother into her own imprisonment, and you're doing the same damn thing! Only Kayl's too fucking stupid to realize."

He crouched to my level. "I'm not Dor. And neither of you are Corentine. This petty feud between our domains needs to end or Chime will continue to suffer."

"That's all you care about, is it? Chime?"

"I serve Chime and all its mortals."

"You serve a bastardized version of Chime. This is *my* domain! If you really served Chime, you'd be fighting on the side of Chaos!"

"Chime no longer belongs to Chaos. Nor does it belong to the gods. Chime is a city of mortals and should remain that way."

"Then why are you giving control to the gods, you idiot?"

"Someone needs to power Chime. And this way, control will be balanced across the domains, and not in the Diviner and Glimmer's favor. The city will still remain in mortal hands with their ambassadors. It's the best we can hope for. The alternative results in Chime's destruction, and I will not have that."

"You're such a good little Warden, aren't you?"

"I'm no longer a Warden."

"You fucking act like one." I lunged for his taser.

Static fired and bounced off the stupid bracelet. Pain zapped up my arm with a sharp spasm, but I was still on my feet!

He took aim at me. With a few more shots, I'd be fucked.

But I stood closest to the exit.

I ran for the Gate.

The taser blasted at me. I leaped out of the way and scrambled for the door. As soon as I made it out, an almighty alarm blared across the station.

Fuck!

I examined the bracelet. The back had blackened. Corinth's taser must have fried it.

Wardens came pouring out of nowhere. A whole group of them immediately put up a barricade across the Gate.

Fucking *fuck*!

There was no way I'd make it to Rapture now, but that was the least of my problems.

Wardens were cordoning off the exits to the station and dragging unsuspecting mortals into groups. Soon, I'd be trapped, and if Corinth caught me, it was all over. Everything I'd worked for!

"Stop her!" yelled Corinth from behind me.

I should have taken his damn soul when I had the chance.

Most of these Wardens were Diviner armed with tasers. There was no point switching to a Diviner and stopping time to escape. The rest were heavy hitters—Umber and a few Leander. Swapping to an Ember form and burning this station down was tempting, but I wouldn't last long.

RUN. SAVE YOUR RAGE FOR ANOTHER DAY.

Oh, I was fucking angry, but I wasn't stupid enough to get caught.

Not. *Me.*

"Hands up where I can see them!" commanded a Leander.

I flipped him my finger and swapped my form to a Fauna magpie.

Chime suddenly grew larger as my smaller body adjusted. I flew free of Kayl's dress and that stupid bracelet.

The Leander swiped for me. I swooped out of the way.

A Diviner Warden fired their taser, but I was already flying out of reach. Just as I was flying out, Kayl bounded into the station with Green Girl and that massive Diviner Warden bodyguard of Corinth's. The sensor went off anew, and the confused Wardens turned their attention from me and pointed their weapons at her.

Idiots.

I perched myself on a streetlamp and surveyed the station.

The Wardens were locking it down. I should have flown through the Gate instead of out here; now there was no way to get in. Corinth had already freed my dear sister, and his arm was wrapped around her as she pretended to be distressed. What a load of shit.

A clockwork bird landed on the streetlamp beside me. It was made of all brass gears and cogs, like one of the Diviner's fancy toys.

"Shoo!" I flapped my black wing at it.

The bird clicked its beak and bobbed its head, as though gesturing below us.

Wardens had marched out of the station and were pointing at me.

Fuck. They were going to hunt me down.

I took off across Central and landed atop a tram heading out to the Market District. Flying was fun, but it ached in my arms, shoulders, and back after a while. The tram chugged along at a casual pace. Behind me, I could see the Wardens spreading out across Central.

They couldn't search everywhere. But I'd gotten so damn close to the Gate...

I wanted to fly back and shit in their mouths.

PATIENCE, DAUGHTER.

I almost had it!

THERE WILL BE OTHER OPPORTUNITIES.

Would there? Every attempt I made increased the Wardens' hold on the Gate. I doubted I'd be able to pull off another stunt like that again—Corinth was too careful. And Kayl didn't trust me. Fuck her. Fuck 'em all.

The tram pulled into the stop closest the watchmaker's shop, and I flew in through an upstairs window I'd left open a crack. Shops in the Market District didn't open until nine, and some not until ten, so it wasn't like I needed to be here—though with no Chance to run the place, closing up shop looked suspicious.

I switched back to my Glimmer form and dug through the piles of clothes for something suitable to wear. Dirty plates and laundry were scattered across the couch and floor of the tiny little apartment. I had to pick my way carefully across it in case I stepped in something disgusting.

Someone knocked on the front door.

Give me a fucking break!

I quickly slipped on a golden dress and switched to a Diviner form. The knocking came again, more insistent this time. "We're closed!" I yelled as I hurried down the stairs.

"This is a welfare check, ma'am," said a male voice. "Open up for the Wardens."

They hadn't followed me all this way? "We don't need no welfare."

"Open the door, ma'am, or we'll be forced to come inside."

I paced the room and chewed on my thumbnail. If the Wardens had found me, I needed a new base, fast.

The Warden bashed at the door.

"All right! I'm opening!" I yanked the door open and glared at a Diviner wearing a Warden's outfit.

He blinked at me, and then his stupid silver face slowly roved down my dress to my bare feet. "Are you, uh, alone, ma'am?"

"What does it look like?"

"Is a Mr. Granville Cogsworth in residence? We've received a telegram concerned about his whereabouts. His partner on Kronos hasn't received any shipments in weeks."

Damn it, Chance was supposed to handle that shit! "He's taking a bath. It's been a stressful month, you know, with the attacks on the station or whatever."

He raised a silver brow. "Can I step inside, ma'am?"

"Why?"

"I'd like to check in on Mr. Cogsworth myself." He rested a hand on his baton.

Was he really going to beat an innocent Diviner woman? Fucking Wardens. I searched over his shoulder to spy for his partner, as these twats always came in pairs. A whole group of Wardens were walking down the street and questioning shopkeepers and shopgoers alike.

They pointed in my direction.

This was *not* my day.

"Fine. Get in." I ushered the Warden in before any of his colleagues followed.

"Mr. Cogsworth?" the Warden called as he entered. "It's a Warden here to speak with you, sir, if you'd like to come down."

I closed the front door. "Give him a moment, he's still bathing."

The Warden wandered to the counter and examined the broken clock Chance had left there. "What happened to this poor thing?"

I switched to my Glimmer form. "I fucking smashed it."

His stupid metal eyes went wide in alarm. I grabbed his wrist. A pulse of aether passed through my palm, and I yanked his soul out of his useless-arse body.

He collapsed in a heap by the counter, his mouth gaping open. His eye sockets empty.

Just how I liked 'em.

"What's going on here?" came a gasp behind me.

Another Diviner Warden was standing by the now open door. Fuck! The partner!

Time slowed around me. That was always their default reaction to any danger. Though as I prowled toward him, he soon realized his mistake.

With one touch, I'd taken his soul, too. He fell awkwardly against the doorway, his legs spilling out onto the street.

I dragged his body inside and quickly shut the door, locking it this time.

Two Diviner Warden bodies were now sprawling across the shop floor, with more Wardens on patrol. They'd soon notice the pair of them missing.

I kicked the body next to me. "Fuck you! Fuck you! And especially fuck *you*!" I kicked its head in until blood and teeth spurted across the floor.

This was their fucking fault! If it wasn't for Diviner, I wouldn't be trapped in this stupid damn shop with these stupid fucking clocks!

I picked up the nearest clock and threw it against the wall. Then another one. And another. They showered the floor in a sprinkle of brass and steel parts. I hated clocks! I hated their shitty little hands and the way they ticked and tocked. I hated the way their guts were made from gears and cogs and nothing real.

My breath came out in seething gasps.

I hated that time ruled everything.

Hated that Diviner ruled it all.

None of them had a heart. They were cogs inside silver flesh. Machines made mortal.

Unfeeling, arrogant bastards who ruled it *all*.

They didn't feel what I fucking did!

"Are you quite finished?"

Ah shit. Corinth's Diviner assistant was standing behind the counter, her nails tapping idly on the surface.

"How the fuck did you get in here?"

"You have a back door."

Her smug smirk boiled my blood. Those silver eyes didn't hold the fear of last night in Corinth's office, despite the bodies by my feet. Nor did they exude the arrogant coldness of a Diviner. They were shrewd. Calculating.

I wanted to tear out her soul.

But I also wanted to see what made her *tick*.

I leaped over the counter. She squealed in alarm as I grabbed her neck and shoved her against the wall. Bitch didn't stand a chance.

This was the first female Diviner I'd ever seen. She squirmed under my touch, her dainty body struggling to remain composed, her throat quivering against my palm as she struggled for air. Those silver lips parting in a beautiful wheeze.

They looked so adorable when they suffered.

"I've come—to negotiate!" she spat out.

"I'm not interested in anything Corinth has to say—"

"Quentin—doesn't know—I'm here."

Huh. Now *that* was interesting. I loosened my grip on her neck, allowing her to swallow gulps of air.

She sagged against the wall, huffing and puffing while she straightened her blouse. "Tha—Thank you. Ambassador Corinth isn't aware of my visit. I'm here of my own accord." Her words came out all prim and proper.

"So why would Little Miss Perfect betray her boss to pay a visit to Chaos? You may have noticed, but I don't play nice with Diviner."

"I'm not surprised." She casually strode around the counter and picked up the remains of a broken clock. "You have good reason to despise my domain, as I have reason to fear you. Diviner men try to understand the cosmos without really understanding what makes a mortal fallible." A spring fell from the clock and rattled across the counter. "I'm not like them. Quentin wants to find a solution to a problem. I seek opportunities."

I crossed my arms. "I'm your problem, all right. But I'm not your damn opportunity—"

"Do you believe you can stand against the might of Kronos? Your position is precarious. Alone, you will fall, and Chaos will be forgotten. Together, we can reshape Chime. We can rewrite the rules."

There was something about those gleaming silver eyes that was more mortal than the rest of her domain. "The fuck are you saying?"

"I'm proposing a partnership. We share the same enemy." The clock fell from her hands and smashed into a pile of cogs and bolts. "I'd rather like to see them shatter."

Oh, I saw how it was.

The Diviner wanted to use me to do their dirty work for them by getting rid of their rivals. They'd likely stab me in the back later, but not if I stabbed first.

This could be the opportunity I needed.

A way to beat Kayl and Corinth at their own game.

"I'm listening, Time Girl."

The Diviner woman smiled in a cocky way that delighted my inner mischief-maker. "Please. Call me Penny."

22

Rapture is a haven for sin and largely exists outside Warden purview. What happens in Rapture, stays in Rapture, so they say, though this of course isn't true.

Sins and criminal activity committed in Rapture are not magically waved away. On your return to Chime, you will still be liable for whatever unsavory deeds you have indulged in.

This is a warning, then, that as a Warden you must still act a Warden even when off the clock. Unfortunately, that means Wardens are discouraged from entering Rapture unless it is for work-related purposes. All visits to Rapture are monitored.

—Q. Corinth, *Warden Dossier on Rapture*

THE EVENTS OF THE morning had forced us to miss our crossing into Rapture, but Quen didn't want to waste another day. He'd ordered me to head home and change into suitable evening wear for the later crossing, and I didn't intend to disappoint.

Dru, however, was not pleased. "How can I be your bodyguard if you're going off without me? You were practically kidnapped this morning. It could happen again."

I didn't want to admit that my encounter with Jinx had left me shaken. My twin had gone off the deep end. What terrified me more was that she almost made it to the Gate. If not for Quen, we could have lost another domain. I could have lost Sinder.

I couldn't let my guard down like that again.

The Wardens were taking Jinx seriously and scouring Central for her, at least. Quen assured me she wouldn't be harmed if caught, though really, if it came down to it, she only had herself to blame.

"I'll be with Quen and Ben. I doubt Quen will let me out of his sight." Rapture wasn't the safest place for Umber, and I wasn't going to drag Dru through for my benefit. "I'll bring you back a stick of rock as a souvenir."

"Rapture's dangerous. Not only dangerous, but full of shiny, tempting things." She gave me a pointed look that suggested I couldn't be trusted to manage on my own.

"Gods, Dru. I'm not going to get lured into a circus." I knew all about Rapture's vices—I'd been lectured on them enough by Harmony and Sinder. "I'll be fine."

Crowds wandered into Central Station for Rapture's opening at nine. It was by far the most popular evening crossing, despite how much Chime's citizens were warned against sin. Who didn't want to spend the night partying and gambling?

Of course, Quen and I were traveling through on a diplomatic mission, though I still couldn't wait to see Rapture's famous strip with my own eyes.

I found Quen and Ben waiting outside the station. Both were dressed in their snazzy tuxedos from the ambassadors' ball.

I nudged Dru. "Doesn't he clean up well?"

Dru replied with an exaggerated groan.

As we approached, Quen's face lit up with a beaming smile. He placed a hand on my shoulder and leaned close, his breath tickling my ear. "You look stunning," he whispered.

Damn right I did. I'd opted for the tight purple dress from Arcadia Apparel and paired it with dark purple nails and lipstick. Despite Sinder's warnings, the color matched well with my shocking pink Ember skin. I likely looked a complete slut, but I'd certainly fit in.

"You're not coming with us, ma'am?" Ben was asking Dru, and why yes, I *did* note disappointment in his voice.

"No way. I'm not risking my flowers in that heat." She tentatively touched her brow.

"They've got a poison garden," Ben mumbled.

"A what?"

"Where the, um, volcanic plants grow."

Quen slapped Ben on the back. "Another time. We've got a crossing to make, and I wouldn't want to inconvenience Erosain by rescheduling twice."

"You better take care of her this time." Dru waggled a finger.

"I promise you, she's in safe hands."

"I can take care of myself, you know." It was like no one believed me.

We joined the crowds heading into Central Station. The concourse was busy with Ember and other mortals chatting and laughing, many dressed up as extravagantly as we were for a night to remember.

As we stepped inside, no sensor went off, and I wasn't wearing a pretty bracelet since Jinx busted it yesterday. "How do you know I'm me and not Jinx?"

"I've learned to tell you apart."

"Really? How?"

"One must keep some professional secrets."

The clock tower struck nine. Obituary's orange landscape was replaced with a red glow, a sight I'd seen many times through the Gate. Ripples of heat danced beyond from the volcanic atmosphere. I'd be fine in an Ember body, though I felt for Quen and Big Ben in their suits.

Quen offered his arm. "Shall we?"

Our status as ambassadors meant we were able to completely skip the queue. Mortals grumbled as I swaggered past, unable to hide my glee.

I could get used to this.

We'd entered a party, all right.

I'd expected the heat to hit me first, but instead my ears were assaulted by loud music and cheering.

Rapture's station was more like Obituary's, with a line of carriages waiting on one side of the stone road for eager passengers, and a whole collection of stalls and booths on the other, making it seem a more colorful and glamorous version of Grayford's night market.

"Souvenirs! Get yer souvenirs!" yelled an Ember stall owner. "We got snow globes, rock, and a Rapture favorite—lava lamps! They shine brighter than Glimmer!"

"Don't suffer with dry skin!" yelled another. "Fight off the fire and brimstone with our extra-strength moisturizer!"

I nudged Quen. "Can we take a look?"

"We *are* on a schedule—"

"Just a quickie, I promise." I ran into the throng before he could stop me.

My head spun at the various goods on sale, from golden jewelry to designer handbags, exquisitely decorated ceramic plates, figurines made of glass dotted with gemstones, roasted chestnuts and popped corn, and edible, if not illegal, delicacies.

A group of Ember youths hung around these. "Damn, still no Vesper mushrooms," one of them muttered. "When's Eventide coming back? They were the good shit."

I ducked my head and moved on.

Between the stalls were buskers—entertainers—and the source of the commotion. Most were Ember, and they juggled white-hot knives while blowing rings of fire. Others were playing energetic ditties on barrel organs and accordions as mortals cheered them on, tossing bocs into hats.

I paused before a hurdy-gurdy player. The last time I'd heard one had been in Grayford with Dru. Rapture's buskers didn't compare to Vesper players and shadow puppet theaters spinning tales of woe and misery.

"There you are!" Quen bumped into my shoulder. "How am I supposed to keep you safe if you go wandering off?"

"Got a few bocs?"

"What happened to the notes I gave you days ago?"

I fluttered my eyelashes. "That's a question you should never ask a lady."

"Kayl—"

"What is *that*?" I bounded to where a crowd gathered around a stall run by a Zephyr. Gadgets lined his booth in all manner of odd shapes, blinking in random colors or whirling with bizarre sounds. But what caught my eye was the buzzing dildo in his talons.

It writhed in his grip. The Zephyr waved it above the crowd to raucous hooting. "Forget all you know about pleasurable devices! The Thrust-Master is powered by aether to generate vibrating sensations no mortal can withstand. For only two hundred bocs, the Thrust-Master will send you to a higher plane of existence not even a Mesmer could conjure!"

"I want one," I said to Quen, who'd caught up with Ben.

Quen gave me an exasperated look. "That thing will give you a headache."

"The headache may be worth it."

"Quentin!"

An open-top carriage rumbled toward us, forcing the crowd to scramble out of the way. The carriage stopped, and excited chatter replaced the cursing.

Mortals pointed at the figure of Erosain, who swaggered down the carriage steps as though parading on a stage.

"And here's our ride," Quen muttered under his breath.

The Ember ambassador was as flamboyant as ever in a sharp tuxedo, matching black heels and makeup, as well as the hair transplant most Ember couldn't afford. Two male Ember in black suits flanked him, shoving back eager mortals who came too close.

"Looking for something special?" Erosain planted a kiss on both of Quen's cheeks. "You made it this time."

"We had some bother this morning. All sorted now."

"That's good to know. And what a pleasure to make your acquaintance again, Lady Arkey!" He took my hand for a lingering kiss as his dark eyes studied mine. "You've come at the right time, my lady. There's no experience quite like Rapture at night. Though as you see, the fun never stops!" He gestured at the carriage. "After you, my dear."

Quen climbed in first and helped me up.

I sank onto a plump cushion beside Quen as Ben squeezed beside me, his size forcing us to rub shoulders. There I was, trapped between two handsome Diviner. The carriage was all gold, as extravagant as the carriages of the Golden City, and powered by a similar aether generator by the looks of it. The open top meant we were exposed to the dry air, though the heat didn't bother my Ember skin.

Erosain and his guards climbed in next, and then the carriage whisked us away.

We rode past the various stalls and marquees by the Gate, followed by jazzy music the entire way, as though it filled the sky.

Then the road opened up to the famous strip I'd read and heard so much about.

"Welcome to Rapture!" Erosain announced with dramatic flair.

"Oh my *god*," I said aloud. I'd never seen anywhere like *this*!

Above us loomed a gigantic cavern. It was like being under the glass dome of Memoria, only no sun filtered through, no fish swam above. Only jagged dark rock as far as the eye could see. Glowing red light emanated from lava flowing between cracks in the rock like waterfalls, merging with a river of magma running parallel to us.

But that wasn't what made me gasp aloud.

Our road stretched from the Gate to a golden palace that filled the skyline. The top glowed like one gigantic fire brazier, and more lava flowed down its walls.

Buildings lined the road on both sides that glittered with an array of colorful lights and flashing signs. Most appeared to be casinos, but there were a few burlesque theaters between them—as indicated by the giant signs of Ember women with their legs spread—along with spas, saunas, and massage parlors.

Flashing lights spread across the road like bunting. Carriages like this one trafficked mortals up and down, who shouted drunk obscenities as they rode by. More gathered outside the casinos as scantily clad Ember girls fought for their attention.

It was a bustling chaotic mix of sound and color that made Sinner's Row look like a dark alley. "How does this place exist?" The aether alone needed to power this domain must have been tremendous.

Erosain flashed a smug grin. "Edana provides, naturally. But Rapture is built by those seeking enterprise. Many of our businesses are owned by non-Ember, who Edana generously rents space to. We have a surprising number of Zephyr here, for example. They care little for the glamor, but we allow them to test their inventions without Chime's red tape. Much of the strip is owed to Zephyr technology."

Based on the aether buzzing around me, I could believe it. I never would have thought Zephyr would find a home in Rapture, of all places. Though I supposed, if one wanted to deal in dangerous and possibly illegal dealings, then this was the place to be.

My neck ached from all the ogling I was doing. Mortals from most of the domains gathered here, with a notable absence of Glimmer and Diviner. I didn't spot any Amnae either, likely for good reason.

Most domains disguised their dirty dealings, but despite all the glitz and glamor, Rapture's dirt manifested as a lingering scent of rotten eggs. Quen didn't seem to notice or care, but I subtly covered my nose with a handkerchief.

As we approached the golden palace, our carriage entered some sort of underground parking garage. Cool air shivered across my skin. Quen and Ben sighed in relief. I was glad to leave that awful smell behind.

"Aether fans," Erosain explained, pointing up. "Zephyr designed. They help cool the air. Most Ember don't mind Rapture's atmosphere, but our visitors do." He stretched to his feet. "Edana awaits us, and she's not known for her patience. We'll go over a few formalities before I lead you inside, if you don't mind."

Ben helped me down, and we followed Erosain into a dark corridor, his guards trailing behind us.

Quen bent his head close. "Now, when we enter Edana's court, politely decline all offers of food or drink," he whispered. "They're often drugged."

"I wasn't born yesterday."

"It's only a warning. Also, please try to refrain from calling her a vile bitch. You *do* have a record."

"No promises."

We strode down dimly lit stairs and emerged into a room filled with cells.

"Arrest her!" Erosain declared.

Great. We'd walked into a trap.

Erosain's guards drew out pistols and aimed them at me. Ben drew his own as I slowly raised my hands.

"What is this?" Quen demanded, his calm composure quickly snapping taut.

Erosain's joyful welcome had been replaced with a sneer. "She's the one who destroyed my art gallery and robbed me!"

Ah, shit. He wasn't as daft as he looked.

"You must be mistaken," Quen said.

"There's no mistake. I recognized her the moment she joined the Council and displayed her domain-shifting powers. But I have a witness!" He waved at a man leaning against the wall.

A Necro swaggered over. The same Necro whose persona I'd taken the night I'd stolen Erosain's prisms. He looked me over with a shrug. "That's her."

Shit!

"See!" Erosain shrieked. "She wrecked my art gallery, stole precious items—"

"That's preposterous," Quen said. "What reason would Ambassador Arkey have to destroy your art gallery? It makes no logical sense. Right, Kayl?"

I forced a weak smile. "Sorry."

Quen looked as though he was about to properly swear for the first time in his mortal existence.

"I want justice and compensation!" Erosain ranted.

"Perhaps we can come to sort some of arrangement—"

"Generous compensation, Quentin! This isn't about the bocs—she broke into my bar, made a mockery of my security, and injured my fucking legs! She emasculated me!"

I rolled my eyes. "Oh, give over."

Erosain glared. "Return the items you stole."

"I can't. I pawned them."

"You *what*? They were priceless items!"

"Really? I only got a few bocs for them."

Sparks sizzled from Erosain's fake brows. "Lock her away!"

His guards stalked toward me.

I let a flicker of flame dance in my palm. "Touch me, and I'll break your legs next."

Quen intervened and pulled me to one side. "Let's not descend into violence. Stay here while I sort this mess out."

"You're going to let them lock me up?"

"You'll be safe here, at least. Don't worry. I'll speak with Edana and clear this up."

Great. Just great.

I was supposed to be an ambassador, for god's sake!

The guards escorted me to a cell and locked it behind me. Quen followed Erosain out, who was ranting the entire time like some petulant child who'd lost his favorite toy. Ben shrugged and ran after Quen, leaving me alone to wallow.

At least the cell wasn't too bad. It contained a single bed, blanket, toilet and sink. I supposed I could nap. Though this really wasn't how I'd expected my trip to Rapture to go.

Only as I sat on the rather hard bed did I realize I wasn't alone.

The Necro stood outside my cell, visible through the bars. He lit a cigarette and took a deep drag, letting smoke waft through the air.

"I didn't think Necro could smoke," I commented.

His bloodshot eyes narrowed. He didn't appear quite as old and haggard as he had that night in Erosain's bar. Clearly, drinking blood had an antiaging effect on Necro, because in this light, he looked rather handsome, in a rugged kind of way. An old trench coat hung off his shoulders, tattered at the hem, and his short white hair had that bedraggled just-out-of-bed style. "We can still breathe. These?" He examined the lit cigarette between his fingers. "They take the edge off. Help control my urges."

"So if you're not here to eat me, why are you here? If I recall, you weren't interested in Ember harlots."

He rasped a laugh. "You caught me on a bad night, lady, and made it worse. I've had Erosain on my back for this case."

"I'm a case, now?"

"You stole from the boss of Sinner's Row. That's a big deal."

"Congratulations on solving it. I hope he pays you well, though you've no right to be mad at me."

"You drugged me and left me under a table."

"I didn't take your wallet, though."

"No, I'll give you that." He took another drag of his cig. "I know of your kind."

"My kind?"

"Godless. One of your compatriots, an Ember named Sinder, introduced himself to me after you drugged me. Wanted to apologize. We've shared intel since."

I approached the bars. "And who are you?"

He left his cig dangling between his lips and pulled out a business card. "Name's Gast. M. Gast. Private eye right out of Sinner's Row. I handle the dirty cases Wardens don't touch, for mortals who don't want a Warden near. Whenever I got a sorry sop who couldn't pay their tithe, I sent them your way. To Grayford."

I turned the card over. Sinder had never mentioned working with a PI, though it could be useful having another contact to exchange information with. "Then what can I do for you, Mr. Gast? As you can see, I'm in no shape to offer assistance." I grabbed the bars. They were made of an odd stone material, not metal.

"You won't burn your way through those." He confirmed my thoughts. "But this'll help." He pulled a key from his pocket and waggled it. "I'll spring you in exchange for a little information."

I leaned against the bars. "Go on."

He finished his cig and tossed it aside. "I had a... Vesper friend. An ex-partner, you could say. Last month, when the attack on Central Station happened, she turned to dust before my eyes. I'd like to know why."

An ache throbbed in my chest. What could I say that he'd not likely uncovered himself? "Why do you assume I know anything?"

"Because I saw you at the scene. You and Mr. Dark Warden, who looks miraculously happy and whole despite dying, and don't deny it. I know what I saw. The Wardens are covering this up, saying Valeria recalled her mortals and everyone is safe back on Eventide, but that's a load of shit, isn't it? Tell me the fucking truth." His eyes burned.

I bit the inside of my cheek. He deserved the truth. "Eventide is gone. Valeria is dead, and her mortals are dead with her. I'm sorry."

His shoulders sagged. No, his entire body seemed to deflate, as though I'd stolen his soul. "How?"

"If you witnessed the attack, then you no doubt saw the aether creatures. Mortals made of chaos. They can steal souls. One of them took Valeria's."

"That's—That's impossible. How do you know this?"

"Because Corinth and I are trying to stop them. To ensure this never happens to any other domain."

"You're insane, lady. But I believe you." He lit another cigarette. "I wish I didn't. They're gone? All gone?"

"If I knew a way to bring them back, I'd try it. I'd do anything."

Losing the Vesper, the entirety of Eventide, had crushed me. What was worse was the hole in my soul. Some missing piece. Something I'd loved that I'd now lost. The pain in Gast's voice reflected my own. He'd loved his Vesper.

I understood the depth of that love, even if I struggled to place it.

"You say you're trying to stop these chaos beings? With Corinth? I'd suspected the Dark Warden had something to do with the Vesper's disappearance—"

"Corinth is on my side."

"You trust him?"

"I trust him more than I trust you."

"That's fair. So what can a weary Necro do?"

"You want to help? In my experience, hiring PIs doesn't come cheap."

"I'm feeling a little vengeful, let's say. I'll help you find whoever destroyed Eventide for free."

I tried to keep my expression neutral. "And what will you do when you find them?"

He grinned, baring his fangs. "Tear them apart."

Again, I understood the depth of his rage. But I wanted to stop Jinx, not offer her on a platter to some Necro. "So it's revenge you want?"

"Someone needs to be held responsible."

"And here I thought you were a walking stereotype."

"Lady, you're the one locked in a cell."

"Point taken. If you truly want to help, then keep an eye on Grayford. Since the Vesper left, there's been no one to watch over whoever remains, and the Godless haven't been able to return and check. I'm sure the Glimmer are taking advantage of the situation to fill their empty workhouses."

"You're not wrong. I'll send someone. Though I'll take any intel you uncover on the mortal responsible for the Vesper. You know where to find me." He unlocked the cell door.

I tentatively stepped out. Thankfully, none of Erosain's guards were waiting to jump me. "You sure you want to risk running afoul of Erosain?"

Gast smirked. "That fucker doesn't pay me enough. Head up those stairs and turn left. It'll take you back out onto the strip. I'll go first and distract the guards. Next time we meet, you owe me a proper drink."

He left me to compose myself. I hadn't expected to make a new ally here, least of all a Necro, but my gut said Gast was honest.

And I'd sleep better at night knowing someone was watching over Grayford.

It probably wasn't smart leaving my cell and abandoning Quen, but I wasn't going to subject myself to Erosain's mercy—I'd witnessed that for myself back in Sinner's Row. Nor would I suffer the indignity of being locked away while idiot men decided my fate. I headed up the stairs, and sure enough, Gast was chatting up a guard, allowing me to slip on by.

Music thrummed underneath my feet as I made my way to the top of the stairs. There were two doors—the emergency exit to the left, as Gast had directed, and then a shiny red door labeled Casino Floor.

I pressed my ear against it. Music vibrated through me with a shiver.

It wouldn't hurt to take a quick peek, would it?

I pushed through, and the music washed over me in a roaring wave.

The casino floor came alive with twinkling lights, jazzy piano tunes, and an intoxicating clash of alcohol, perfumes, and sweat. Aether static buzzed from the vast lines of slot machines and spinning roulette wheels, though a different energy emanated from the array of mortals seated between tables. Desperate mortals shouted in glee or despair while Ember dealers in tight black suits dealt cards.

Above, the ceiling was on fire—literal fire—that lit up the golden furnishings. It was decadence and greed on a level with the Golden City.

It was a magnet for chaos, and it reeled me in.

I found myself wandering between the tables and passing Ember women in dresses tighter than mine who paraded the floor handing out glasses of bubbly. A few of them hung on the arms of gamblers, whispering encouragement as fake as their nails.

An Ember woman stopped me. "Would you like to try your luck?"

Gods. She was the most gorgeous Ember I'd ever seen, and clearly wasn't part of the staff. She stood at my height with a curvy build, wearing a black silk dress that perfectly hugged the folds of her stomach, hips, and breasts. Black glitter shone on her thick lips and fluttering eyelashes. Even her horns were painted in a layer of glossy black.

I hadn't brought any bocs with me, and judging by the amount of chips passing hands, it was probably a good thing. "Sorry. I'm all out."

The woman beckoned me with her finger. "My treat. I can't let a lovely young thing like yourself out of my sight." Her voice burned like smoke; husky yet full-bodied like wine.

How could I say no?

I approached the roulette table. Sinder had explained the rules to me long ago, but I could barely remember them now.

The Ember handed me a chip, and her long nails slightly grazed my wrist. "I'll start you off easy. Pick a color. Red or black."

Standing beside her made my skin flush. It had been far too long since I'd last enjoyed the attentions of another mortal, and I'd always been drawn to Ember. The way they flaunted their beauty and strength. The way they sinned without fear of the consequences. I cleared my throat. "Red."

She nodded to the dealer.

The roulette spun in a blur of red and black. A tiny white ball bobbed between tiles. It slowed, and then finished on red.

"Lucky number thirteen," she remarked.

"Beginner's luck." I picked up a handful of winning chips. "Though I'm afraid I can't stay. I've lost my friends somewhere around here, and they'll be awfully worried about me."

"Indulge me one more time. We'll make it interesting." She placed a warm hand on my shoulder and leaned close. "You win, and I'll help you find your friends. I know who is who in this establishment. It wouldn't take long. But if I win, I'll do what I like with you." She ran nails teasingly along my cheek.

A jolt of aether shuddered down my spine. I stared into her eyes, which were hot as burning coals. "What do you plan to do with me? I'm rather shy."

"Dressed like that? I sincerely doubt it. Girls like you know how to use their tongues."

"I'm not your slut."

"You could be. I want that naughty tongue between my lips."

"Which ones?"

A sliver of flame flickered in her eyes. She pressed a finger to my bottom lip. A possessive touch. A promise. I should have shoved her away, but she'd set my blood aflame, and gods help me, I wanted more. "We'll start here, and then you can work your way down. Now. Red or black?"

"Black." My voice came out in a croak.

What in god's name was I doing?

My knees wobbled as the roulette wheel spun. If luck wasn't on my side, then what had I signed up for? A night with a hot Ember? Things could be worse, I supposed, though I doubted Quen would approve.

Come to think of it, I didn't even know what time it was, and we were supposed to meet with Edana before the Gate closed. Some ambassador I made! Less than an hour in Rapture and I was already shacking up with the nearest Ember and gambling my life away.

Dru was right, I couldn't be trusted with anything.

The wheel came to a complete stop. The white ball hung in the air, frozen in time.

In fact, the entire casino had paused, except for Quen and Ben now approaching my table. Quen's brow was scrunched in displeasure. Ben's face was a churning mixture of uncomfortable anxiety. Behind them, Erosain had been caught midstride, his face twisted in ugly rage.

Well, shit.

"You make quite the entrance, Quentin Corinth," the Ember woman said beside me.

Gods! I jumped out of my skin. The casino had been caught in Quen's time stoppage, except for this Ember. But that wasn't possible unless she was another Chaos in disguise.

Quen's irritable expression reset into a pleasant smile. "Good evening, Lady Edana. Thank you for locating Ambassador Arkey for me. I was rather concerned when she disappeared."

Lady Edana.

Oh *shit*!

I'd been flirting with the pissing god of Rapture!

Edana tutted. "You know Diviner aren't allowed to interfere with my casinos, you naughty thing."

"Apologies, my lady." He took Edana's hand and pressed a quick kiss. "Time simply stands still in your presence."

There was no affection in his gesture, no love, nor lust. It was simply Quen being Quen. Polite. Charming. To a fucking fault.

So why did it annoy me?

Time resumed, and the little white ball bounced off the wheel and across the table, my bet now forgotten. The rest of the casino's patrons carried on with their games, either unaware of or uninterested in the god standing among them.

Erosain shoved past Ben and stomped over.

Edana raised her hand before he could speak. "Return to your duties. I'll entertain our guests from here."

"But, my lady—"

"I don't enjoy repeating myself."

He swooped into a low bow, though not before shooting me another glare. The two of us had unfinished business, it seemed.

Edana tossed her chips in the air, and they disappeared with a puff. "Come, daughter of Chaos. We have much to discuss."

23

SHIT. I'D BEEN FLIRTING with the god of Rapture, and I didn't know whether to gag, vomit, scream, or shit myself. I *never* would have if I'd known who she was—least of all because an actual god had gotten her hands on me.

Knowing who she was, and what she'd done to Sinder... *Ugh*.

Edana played hostess in her own casino. As she led Quen, Ben, and me through her glittering halls, she paused by mortals to share a word or sign her autograph. I'd never known a god to act like a celebrity, but Edana courted attention from fawning Leander to a giggling gaggle of Seren.

Mortals loved her. Doted on her.

It made me sick.

Eventually, we made our way to Edana's private penthouse. I was expecting a throne room as extravagant as the rest of her golden palace, but what I entered was a harem.

The floor dipped on both sides of a walkway, creating pits of sin lined with cushions. There must have been at least twenty mortals of a variety of domains, genders and sexes engaged in various acts that would kill a Glimmer from shock.

Most were caught in a tangled group of limbs and moans. I tried not to stare, but the motion, the thrusting and sucking sounds, were doing awful things to my lady bits.

None of them were being held down or forced against their will. There was such a curious mix of bodies. Leander. Fauna. Necro. Males with breasts. Females with cocks. Ambiguous mortals with both. One Ember had two cocks and was being pleasured by two separate mouths.

Fuck me.

Edana strode between them as they writhed in an ocean of pleasure. So many were lost in their throes, they didn't even notice us enter. A few paused their vigorous activities to reach out to Edana and murmur words or to kiss her feet as she passed.

We followed to curious glances, but the harem mostly ignored us and returned to sucking nipples, cocks, toes, and gods know what else. Quen stared straight ahead at a golden throne, his attention never wavering. But poor Ben's eyes were practically bulging out of their sockets, his entire face red as the Ember. Gods, the man was worse than me for staring, and he was doing a terrible job of remaining composed.

I only hoped he didn't pop an erection and make our awkward situation even worse.

As though reading my mind, Ben subtly clasped his hands over his groin.

Oh, Dru was certainly missing out on an entertaining trip thus far. I could only imagine how the poor dear would fare if she were here.

She'd soon stop worrying about her flowers.

Edana casually sprawled across her golden throne and gestured for us to sit on a couch in front. Quen and I took our seats as Ben stood behind us.

"Welcome to my palace." Edana clapped her hands.

Three naked Ember servants appeared from a side room—two male and a female. They were bound in golden chains across their wrists, ankles, and necks, as well as smaller chains connecting their horns and nipples. More golden rings and hoops adorned their horns, ears, and noses, and their lips were painted a glittering silver.

One of the males immediately kneeled beside Edana and allowed her to rest her feet on him like a footstool. The other two carried trays of wine and grapes.

Had Sinder served Edana in this same way?

I abhorred it. Yet the male on his knees was fighting back a grin. His cock was rigid and dripping with precum. Either Edana had trained these poor souls to enjoy their servitude, or everyone in this damn domain was depraved.

It was likely a mixture of both.

No wonder the Ember held such a reputation for sin. I enjoyed sinning, but even this was a bit too much for my tastes.

None of it seemed to bother Quen, who sat relaxed on the couch as though he'd seen it all before, and he probably had.

EDANA ALWAYS LIKED TO BE THE CENTER OF ATTENTION. I ADMIRE THAT ABOUT HER. SHE KNOWS WHAT SHE WANTS AND TAKES IT.

Why didn't you bloody warn me I was flirting with her earlier?

YOU SEEMED TO BE ENJOYING YOURSELF. AND YOU DIDN'T ASK.

You're absolutely useless!

Edana gestured at the male holding a tray of wine. "Would you care for refreshment?"

"We're fine, thank you," Quen said. He sat up, a stiffness in his movement. Perhaps he wasn't as comfortable as I'd thought. "Erosain will have no doubt informed you why we're here, my lady."

A particularly loud groan from behind stole my attention, and I found it impossible to keep track of the conversation Quen and Edana were now having regarding Chime's future. How could I concentrate when all I could hear was the slapping of flesh against flesh? Each soft moan sent a shiver down my spine, and I fought to reel my attention back in.

It was as if Edana wanted me distracted. As if she knew this was a particular torture that only a Diviner or a Glimmer could resist.

Quen nudged me, and I realized I'd been asked a question.

"Say that again, please?"

"You have a connection to Corentine, do you not?" Edana asked. "What does she want? Vengeance?"

MY OWN CHILDREN BETRAYED ME. I WOULD SEE THEM BURNED AND REBORN ANEW IN FIRE AND BLOOD.

"Something like that."

"It's understandable. There's no greater wrath than a woman scorned. But you'll have your hands full with her." Edana summoned a perfect blue flame in her palm and let it dance over her hand. "It seems we have no choice but to aid Dor once more and ensure the safety of Chime and our domains. It would be no fun if Chaos wiped us out from existence. Though the gods and their ambassadors will take advantage of this conflict, if they haven't already."

"My intent is to unite the domains," Quen said. "And to ensure a fair balance for all across Chime."

"We both know Chime suffers from inequalities. Don't expect those in power to give it up so freely."

"I don't."

Edana snuffed her flame, and her fiery eyes observed Quen. "You've always been a friend to the so-called lesser mortals. I believe your honest intentions, as naïve as they may be. You have my support on one condition."

Quen leaned forward. "Name it."

Her eyes moved to me. "You stole from my voice, which is an insult to me. I'm willing to overlook this matter in exchange for a single kiss. I wish to taste Chaos for myself."

My stomach lurched.

Quen snapped his gaze to mine, his silver eyes wide with—what? Shock? Pain? Fear? I couldn't place the emotions rolling over his face.

Edana wanted a piece of me by fair means or foul. I wasn't her slut. She had no right to make such demands. Gods like her wanted to exert their power, but I was Godless, and owed her nothing.

"While I'm flattered, I'll have to decline."

Edana popped a grape into her mouth and took her time licking juice from her fingers. "Then I'm afraid we can reach no bargain."

Quen's hands tightened to fists in his lap. "The Wardens are willing to provide Erosain with financial compensation, my lady—"

"I have no need for treasures. This is the deal I offer. My power in exchange for one kiss. I didn't think a child of Chaos would play hard to get."

I fidgeted in my seat. "You know what I am and what power I possess," I said. "I could accidentally take your soul."

Edana's eyes smoldered. "Isn't that poetic? To risk my soul, my mortals, and my entire domain for a kiss. What are you willing to risk for your future?"

Shit. We needed this deal. Quen needed it.

YOU LIKED HER WELL ENOUGH BEFORE NOW.

I'd admit I found her attractive. What hot-blooded mortal wouldn't? That didn't mean I'd betray Sinder just to get my jollies off.

It was a kiss. A single kiss. It wasn't as if I was whoring myself out.

Fuck it. Sinder wouldn't need to know. And I could leverage it. "Release your slaves, and we'll have a deal."

Amusement danced in Edana's eyes. "Done." She clapped her hands. "You are all free to leave if you wish."

The naked Ember by Edana's side didn't move. Nor did the one at her feet. Even the harem continued on with their debauchery.

"These are my guests," Edana said. "They come to my domain to seek the pleasure and release that my court grants. How rude of you to assume otherwise."

Shit. Was Sinder right? Would mortals worship their gods if given the choice?

MORTALS HAVE FREE WILL, Corentine said. *LIKE GODS, THEY SEEK CONNECTION, COMPANIONSHIP, AND POWER. GODS LIVE THROUGH THEIR MORTALS. YOU ASSUME MORTALS GAIN NOTHING FROM THIS RELATIONSHIP.*

It's hardly a mutual relationship when the gods hold power over their mortal subjects! When a god could smite their mortals in the blink of an eye, what choice did they have but to placate their god's whims?

MORTALS ARE OUR CHILDREN. WE WISH TO SEE THEM GROW.

Don't give me that. I've been Godless long enough to know that isn't true.

WHY ELSE WOULD I NAME YOU MY VOICE, IF NOT TO MEND OUR RELATIONSHIP, DAUGHTER?

We'll need a lot of family therapy before that happens.

"I'm waiting," Edana said, snapping me out of my thoughts.

Well, I'd walked straight into this. "Fine. One kiss."

I moved to stand, and Quen took my arm. "You don't have to do this," he whispered.

"It means nothing." I curtsied before Edana. "You wanted me? Here I am."

Edana rose from her throne in a slow, graceful movement. "You are a treasure."

Her arm wrapped around my waist, pulling me into her warm embrace. Plump lips pressed against mine, forcing my mouth open.

Then her tongue struck aether through my blood like a match to a candle.

I couldn't move. Couldn't breathe. My entire body flushed with a fire that threatened to ignite. I was completely at Edana's mercy, and she dominated my mouth with the taste of fire and brimstone.

Shit. It felt *good*.

I swooned as her lips moved to my neck. "You have power in your touch," she whispered. "You'd be doing us all a favor if your touch reached Solaris."

My eyes fluttered. "What?"

"The Glimmer have been taking my mortals, among others. Take them back."

Gods. Edana couldn't possibly be encouraging me to take Gildola's soul? To damn the entire domain of Solaris?

The Glimmer and Ember had always been at odds. With the Vesper gone, the Ember were likely their next victims.

ARE YOU SURPRISED THE GODS INTEND TO BACKSTAB EACH OTHER?

I shouldn't have been, should I?

What political shit had I gotten caught up in now?

I returned to the couch, my legs shaky. Quen's expression was completely unfathomable, but Ben was staring at me. Really, we should have dumped him in the casino, not that he'd be any good at poker with that face.

Edana sat with her feet back on her overeager servant. "I agree to your bargain, Quentin Corinth. As a show of my hospitality, I'll arrange a room for you in my personal suite. Please enjoy your time in my domain, and remember what they say: what happens in Rapture stays in Rapture."

Quen stood and bowed. "Thank you, my lady. We're most grateful." He pulled me up, and then we were striding out of the throne room at a speed almost a jog.

As soon as the doors closed behind me, all tension sagged from my shoulders. "Shit, what time is it? Did we miss the crossing back?"

"It's ten past ten." Quen raised his brow as though blaming *me*. "If you'd stayed put, we could have returned in time."

"I didn't know Erosain was going to pissing arrest me! Is he still angry?"

"Yes. You've made things rather awkward for me. Thank you for that." Quen yanked off his bow tie and undid the top collar of his shirt, exposing a line of silver chest fluff.

"What now, sir?" Ben asked, his face still flushed.

"We've earned ourselves an overnight stay, but don't get any ideas. Diviner are banned from the casinos and gambling halls, and I'm not getting into debt because Kayl fancies her luck."

"I wouldn't think of gambling, sir."

"Can we get a drink or something?" I asked. "I'd rather like to forget the last half hour."

Quen threw his hands up in exasperation. "Why not? There's a bar lower down."

Together, we strode down wide carpeted stairs lit by twinkling chandeliers. The entire golden palace was more of an extravagant hotel, with rooms for Edana's rich and famous guests, the casino below, a restaurant, and a packed bar.

Inside, a collection of colorful glass bottles took up an entire wall, stacked like an alcoholic's library. Space had been cordoned off in the darkest corner for a dance floor, complemented by an all-Ember band currently hammering away an energetic number on piano and saxophone.

On the other side of the bar, steps rose to a private balcony and tinted glass windows that gave a breathtaking view of Rapture's lava ocean below.

Quen led us to a spare private booth. I sank onto a plush cushion.

Ben hesitated. "Think I'll go for a walk, if that's okay, sir. I need to, uh, cool down a bit."

"Go ahead."

"Will you be safe alone? I'm supposed to be on guard—"

"We'll be fine here for a few hours. I'm sure we'll find a way to entertain ourselves."

Ben wandered off, looking a little lost.

An Ember server came to take our order. I scrolled through the cocktail and dessert menu. "I'll have a coffee liqueur and—oh my. Quen, do you want to split a chocolate lava cake?"

"Indulge yourself. I'll take a regular tea, please. A splash of milk and two sugars, thank you."

The server bowed and hurried off.

Quen shrugged out of his jacket and rolled up his sleeves. The heat wasn't bothering me, but sweat stuck to his forehead.

"Tea? In this heat?"

"Tea is the perfect beverage for all climates. If one is cold, one can warm up with tea. If one is hot, then tea can encourage sweating, thus cooling the body. If one is tired, then tea can also stimulate the mind and soul. There is no situation where tea is not the appropriate remedy."

"Will tea make you less grumpy?"

"I'm *not* grump—but yes," he mumbled.

"I'm sorry for getting us trapped in another domain and wasting your time for another twelve hours."

"Your company is never a waste of my time."

I didn't know what to say to that.

The server returned with Quen's tea and a tall cocktail glass with a creamy coffee froth. I took a sip, and my stomach warmed at the alcohol mixed with coffee.

"Do you fancy a game of billiards?" Quen said out of the blue.

"Billiards? Really?"

His cheeks turned pink. "I'm a dab hand, but haven't had a good game in years. Most mortals don't like to play with Diviner. They assume I cheat, but I'm a gentleman. I'd never."

Billiards was a popular pastime in Sinner's Row, and we'd had our own version in Grayford, until someone had smashed our spare cue over someone's head in a brawl. I couldn't remember the last time I played, but I'd always been able to beat Sinder and Vincent on muscle memory alone. "I've forgotten the rules."

"I'll teach you."

There was an eagerness in those silver eyes I couldn't deny. I swirled my cocktail. "I'll play your game if you play mine. For every ball pocketed, we play truth or dare. It's a classic drinking game."

He smirked over the rim of his teacup. "Are you trying to steal my secrets?"

"That depends how good you are."

He finished off his tea and stood. "Exceptionally."

Oh, Quen didn't know what he was getting into.

We found a spare billiards table by the corner where the bar chatter and music didn't carry as loud. I grabbed my cue as Quen set up the fifteen balls in the triangle.

He placed the white ball. "I'll let you break. Aim for the cue ball."

I angled my cue. Quen came over to adjust my arm. "Lift it up." He leaned over, his fingers gently moving my wrist. "Like so."

His touch lingered for a heartbeat too long.

I made my shot. Balls scattered across the table. One bounced into the top corner pocket, and I turned to Quen with a smirk. "Truth or dare?"

"Truth."

"Do you really believe you can unite the domains? They don't get along."

"Yes, I believe it's possible. Otherwise, I wouldn't be here. I will *make* it possible, whether the domains want it or not. Some of them squabble, and not all the gods care for mortal interests, but we'll make them care. I'm pleased with our progress so far, but we're far from done yet." He lined up a shot, and his ball bounced off the side.

"Unlucky." I pocketed my next shot with ease. Truly, I was a natural. "Truth or dare?"

"Truth."

YOU SHOULD ASK HIM IF HE PLANS TO BETRAY YOU AND LOCK YOU AWAY AS DOR IMPRISONED ME.

I trust Quen.

THEN ASK.

Fine. "You mentioned before about giving Chaos a new start. You know who I am and what organization I represent—will you force me into this 'new start' as well?" To wipe my memories alongside theirs?

"No. Absolutely not." He answered quickly and with conviction.

Are you happy now?

Corentine's laughter echoed in my mind. *DIVINER KNOW HOW TO LIE.*

So do gods.

Quen took his next shot and missed. Either he was awful at this game, or he was letting me get my shots in. I pocketed another and decided to have a little fun. Corentine didn't trust Quen, and I supposed there was much I still didn't know about him.

I was going to unravel the secret life of Quentin Corinth. "How many mortals have you fucked?"

"Asking the hard questions, are we?"

"Is that a pun?"

"I'm a gentleman, remember? Puns are beneath me." He rubbed a chalk cube over his cue. "I've dallied with three men."

Only three? I supposed Diviner didn't get out much. One of them must have been Karendar. "Who are the lucky men?"

"I've answered your question." He took aim and pocketed a ball. "My turn. Truth or dare?" He glanced over the rim of his eyeglasses.

"Truth."

"Why did you kiss Edana?"

Oh, now he was hitting me with the hard questions, the arse. "To seal our deal. Nothing more, nothing less." I aimed and pocketed my fourth ball in a row.

"Are you cheating?" he accused me, though there was humor in his voice.

"Beginner's luck." I leaned on the table. "Truth or dare?"

"Dare."

"Feeling brave?"

He chuckled nervously. "Not anymore."

"You're such a polite boy. You've *dallied* with three men. Did you fuck any of them? I want to hear you swear." There was a sinner lurking underneath Quen's gentlemanly facade, and I wanted to draw it out.

"I've slept with three men."

"You fucked three men."

"I've fornicated with three men."

"Say *fuck*."

"I've engaged in coitus with three men—"

"Seriously, Quen? What do you have against swearing?"

"Nothing, really. We were taught at the Academy that foul language was the vocabulary of the uneducated and wicked. To swear is a minor sin, but a sin all the same."

"You don't honestly believe that?"

"Not at all. But certain words are best saved for opportune moments."

"Like now."

He glanced toward the bar and cringed. "Do I have to say it out loud?"

I slid from the table and rested an arm across his shoulder. "I'll let you whisper it."

He leaned in close. "I've *fucked* three men. Does that please you?"

"Very much."

"You're a terrible influence."

"I know." I grinned. "Your go."

He adjusted his eyeglasses, his face flushed and flustered, and missed his next shot. "Blast it!"

"Language, Quen. It's only a game." I pocketed my fifth ball.

He gave me an exasperated look. "Are you sure you're not some professional Undercity prodigy?"

"Would I lie to you? Truth or dare."

"Truth."

"You've never fucked a woman? Do you have a preference for men?" I wasn't quite sure why I asked.

He took a moment to order us another round of drinks—a shandy for him, and a cocktail for myself. "I don't have a preference, no. But it's hard for Diviner to date women. There are very few female Diviner, for a start, and most of us don't date outside our domain. Other mortals don't trust us, and women are smart to avoid us. And there's the stereotype that we're all asexual."

"You aren't?"

"Asexuality exists across a broad spectrum. Some Diviner have no interest in romantic dating. Others experience no sexual drive at all. But we're a mix, and we have needs, same as any mortal."

"So where do you fit on this spectrum?"

"You're cheating, now."

I fluttered innocent eyelashes. "I'm curious."

Quen leaned against the table and observed the many bargoers drinking, dancing, and flirting in booths as he sipped his shandy. "I don't feel attraction until I've formed some sort of emotional or intellectual connection with a mortal, which is rare for me. My unique abilities make dating rather difficult. Nothing spoils the mood more than touching your bedmate and experiencing their death."

I shuffled up beside him. "And that happened to you?"

"A few times."

"With who?"

"I believe it's my turn." He placed his shandy down and angled his cue.

I leaned over and blew in his ear.

The ball shot off the table at ridiculous speed and flew toward some poor Ember serving girl carrying a whole tray of colorful cocktails. Quen yanked time to a stop and casually collected the cue ball from thin air. "I must be a little rusty."

Time resumed with the bargoers none the wiser.

I swirled my cocktail. "I do believe that's a foul."

"I do believe you're cheating."

"That's a damning accusation. I thought you were a gentleman?"

"I thought you were a lady?"

"I never claimed to be a lady."

We both leaned against the billiards table, our shoulders almost touching.

"Why do our conversations always turn to sin?" He ran his fingers through his hair, and his mop fell to one side. "We're ambassadors. We should be setting a better example."

"As ambassador for Chaos, I'd say you need more chaos in your life." I wiggled my fingers at him. "Let loose and live a little."

"I have plenty of chaos in my life. And a Diviner's idea of letting loose is drinking tea with sugar."

"Then you must be wild at parties."

He laughed. A deep, joyous thing.

Sometimes I forgot he was Diviner.

Sometimes I wished he weren't one.

But that smile... I wanted to steal it. Keep it safe forever. Bring it out whenever he appeared grumpy, for a sad Quen didn't bring me joy.

"I don't deserve you." Those silver eyes of his shone with conflicting emotion. Cautious. Hopeful.

I straightened his collar. "I'm your eternal punishment, so yes. You do."

"Are we playing billiards, sir?"

Quen skittered back as Ben found us.

I shoved my cue into Ben's hands. "I won you a head start."

Quen avoided my eye as he and Ben finished off the game. For a dab hand, Quen was distracted the whole night, and Ben won the game on my behalf while I watched, sipping cocktails.

When the clock struck eleven, we headed to our rooms.

Only to discover it was one room.

"There must be a mistake," Quen argued, his jacket slung over his shoulder.

"No mistake, sir," said the hotel porter. "My lady Edana has specified that you and Ambassador Arkey will take the ambassador suite."

"And what of my bodyguard?"

"We have a spare bunk bed down in the barracks."

"Only one? Then Ben and I will share that—"

"I'm afraid it's only big enough for one, sir. And my lady Edana would take great personal offense should you snub her generous offer."

Quen ran a hand through his hair.

"It's all right," I said. "I'm sure it's big enough for us both. There'll be a couch or something."

"I'll come collect you in the morning, sir," Ben said.

"Eight o'clock sharp," Quen said. "We're not missing another crossing."

We bid Ben goodnight and entered the ambassador suite.

I whistled aloud.

It was exactly what I'd expect of Edana's golden palace. The marble furnishings wouldn't look out of place in the Golden City. A cozy hearth took up most of the space next to an open bar. Opposite that was the largest bed I'd ever seen, draped in silk curtains. Quen opened a door, revealing a washroom.

But it was the glass balcony that caught my attention.

I bounded outside and gripped the railing. We were high up, higher than Quen's apartment, and I was blessed with a gorgeous view of the entire strip. Truly, Rapture didn't sleep. Crowds of mortals still queued outside the casinos.

"Blast it!" Quen muttered behind me.

I turned back to see what he was complaining about.

Shit. There was no couch. Nothing that could act as a second bed.

"I'll sleep on the floor," he offered.

"Really?" I pointed to the bed. "That thing's huge. We shared a bed in a Mesmer parlor. We can manage this for one night."

"The Mesmer parlor was an entirely different scenario."

"Are you scared I'll steal your soul in the middle of the night? Don't be such a chivalrous arse."

He threw his jacket onto a stool. "Right you are." He kicked his shoes off and collapsed onto the bed fully clothed, his arms crossed over his chest.

Honestly, this man! I sat on the edge of the bed. "Are you going to bathe?"

"You're saying I smell?"

"You've been sweating in that shirt all night." Though I didn't mind the musk of male sweat, I was sure he'd prefer not to sleep in such a state.

He huffed and stomped off to the bathroom.

Thanks to my Ember skin, I didn't feel the need to shower yet. Instead, I changed into a silk nightgown I found in the closet and wiggled under the covers.

That kiss floated to the forefront of my mind.

Truth be told, I hadn't hated it, though I knew I should have. Never in my *life* would I have thought I'd snog a god! An actual god.

One visit to Rapture had left me so unbearably horny that I was starting to find Diviner attractive. When was the last time I'd indulged in a good fuck? Shit, I couldn't even remember.

Damn it, I had *needs*.

I slid my fingers down to where I was already soaked through. My natural wetness helped me get a good rhythm going, and I rubbed my clit with eagerness. Pleasure writhed through me, and I bit my fist to muffle my moans.

Fuck, I wished I'd bought that aether dildo.

Music from the strip floated in from the balcony, though I kept an ear out for the shower. I needed to be finished before Quen was done. Then I'd sleep well. The Mesmer didn't know what they were missing out on.

OH YES. KEEP GOING. Corentine's voice cut through my mind.

I almost fell out of the bloody bed! *Can't you give me any pissing privacy?*

YOU ARE MY MORTAL. YOUR PLEASURE IS MINE.

What? Don't tell me you're experiencing what I'm doing?

I TOLD YOU GODS LIVE THROUGH THEIR MORTALS. I HAVEN'T FELT THE TOUCH OF ANOTHER IN THOUSANDS OF YEARS. KEEP GOING AND SATISFY US BOTH.

"Oh my fucking god!"

The bathroom door burst open. Quen waddled out wrapped in nothing but a towel. "What's wrong? Are you hurt?"

Oh *my.*

Water dripped down his bare chest. For a Diviner, his abdomen was remarkably well toned. No, he wasn't bursting with muscle, but he kept fit, despite all the biscuits he ate. His skin shone with a glittery sheen I'd never really paid close attention to. But like most Diviner, it had a metallic quality to it, pearly in shade.

"Sorry, I was, er, nodding off."

He looked me over, his expression once again unreadable, and then returned to the bathroom. Moments later, he climbed into bed, his hair mussed but dry, and scooted as close to the edge away from me as physically possible. "Goodnight," he whispered.

Without his eyeglasses, his eyes were silvery moons that shone in the dark.

I wanted to drown in them. "I can't sleep. Sing me a lullaby."

"Diviner don't have any lullabies."

"Really? That's sad."

"I can quote you Diviner philosophy. That sends most mortals to sleep."

"Even better."

He cleared his throat, and his voice lowered to a dull monotone. "The universe is made of the gears of mortal lives. We are simply cogs in a greater machine."

I giggled. "You're such a dork."

"Is that a bad thing?"

"Not to me." I brushed a strand of hair from his brow. "Thank you."

His eyelids fluttered shut. "You're welcome."

I watched his chest rise and fall as he slept. My Quen.

In his deepest dreams, he reached for me. His hand finding mind and clasping tight.

Even in the dark, I felt my skin change to a Diviner's, knew the time was exactly 12:13, but there was no tug in my palm, and I didn't let go.

I tucked my nose into his nape and breathed him in. All sweetness and sorrow.

WHAT WOULD YOUR VESPER THINK?

Don't you bloody sleep? The Vesper are gone.

GONE AND APPARENTLY FORGOTTEN.

Quen was never their enemy. He gave his life for them. Gods, I'd lost Quen once. I couldn't bear to lose him again.

Shit. Quen was no longer the bumbling dork I knew only this morning. Who was he to me?

My partner. Nothing more.

YOU LIE TO YOURSELF, DAUGHTER.

No. I knew myself. And I knew Quen.

We came from different worlds—me, crawling up from the Undercity, and him, gracefully falling from the Golden City. He'd never see Chime as I did.

He was a man so vulnerable and pure of heart.

I'd ruin him.

Quen deserved better than that.

XXIV

Why do the gods let mortals age and die?
Because change is vital for society. If mortals remained in the same state as
they were born, they would never learn and grow. If they did not die, they
would have no ambition.
Each generation of mortals improves Chime with fresh ideas.
Without these, Chime would stagnate.
Put simply, the gods will it so. They have a plan for you.
And all things must come to an end.
—E. Karendar, On the Death of Mortals

I FELL TO MY knees and hugged her legs. "Please. If you have any love for me at all, then do it." Bloodied tears ran down my cheeks. There was nowhere safe anymore.

This was it. The end of my timeline.

Her silvery-blue eyes were red, and for a heartbeat, I feared she'd deny me. But then she rested her hand on my neck.

She lowered her lips to mine. One final kiss.

I sighed as I tasted her. Tasted life and joy.

In a different lifetime, a different universe, I would have made myself a man worthy of her. Was I even worthy of the death she'd grant me? My timeline had been filled with misery and suffering. This was a mercy I didn't deserve.

"Don't leave me, Quen. Don't you dare. I'm not done with you yet."

I wanted to confess. To apologize. I knew I'd be leaving her with pain and guilt. But I couldn't. Even now, at the end.

I kissed her again. A desperate kiss.

"Thank you," I whispered. For delivering my salvation.

For breaking my fall.

Saints, she was beautiful. So wonderful—

"Kayl!" I startled awake, ripping the bed covers off.

That wasn't a dream. It was my death. A future yet to come.

So many times, I'd suffered this same exact dream. The images grew clearer each night, as though my fate edged closer with every tick and tock.

Chasing me. Reminding me of what I was set to lose.

I took in a deep breath. Saints. It wasn't my time, not yet.

"Quen?" Kayl rubbed her eyes and sat up. She must have accidentally touched me during the night, for she was no longer an Ember, but a Diviner persona. Those silvery-blue eyes opened wide, and she waggled her brows at me. "Nice dream, was it?"

I glanced down.

A throbbing erection strained against my boxers. I wasn't a swearing man, but damn and blast it!

I snatched a pillow and covered myself. "I am *so* sorry—"

"It's fine, Quen. It happens to the best of us."

She was grinning like a Leander with a bowl of cream. But as I'd learned last night, Kayl truly delighted in my suffering.

"I'll, ah, go have a shower."

"Good idea." Her smirk followed me all the way to the bathroom.

I cranked the water down to Witheryn temperatures and squealed as ice-cold water blasted me. Everything about this trip to Rapture had been a disaster. Not only had I wasted another twelve hours of my impossibly tight deadline, but now Erosain was angry with me, and I'd gone and made things awkward between Kayl and me.

And my damn erection was *not* going down!

I took matters into my own hands, quite literally, and began to ring the sinner's bell.

This was entirely her fault. How could I remain pure and free of sin when she existed? When those eyes existed? When she wore such a ridiculously tight dress that rode up those thick thighs and shaped those perfectly curved buttocks? When she changed into a dressing gown that was practically see-through? When she teased me so with that sinful mouth? When she kissed Edana and it burned through my blood? When we were forced to share a bed due to some power play?

When her damnable identical twin kept flaunting her nakedness in front of my face?

When her company was such a delight? She could change into a Necro persona and I'd let her bleed me dry.

How was I ever meant to guard myself against Chaos?

"I'm your eternal punishment."

I was cursed. Doomed. Ready for the gods to smite me into oblivion.

"Fuck," I gasped as my life's seed came shooting out and flowed down the drain.

It was a release, yet I still felt frustrated. Disgusted.

What kind of man was I who wanked off when Kayl sat on the other side of these walls?

Not a gentleman.

I'd dallied with three men in my life. Dandelion, I'd crushed on for a while, until a night of regrets and a performance I held no desire to repeat. We made better allies.

Then Erosain. He'd wanted to flirt Warden secrets out of me, and one evening, I'd found myself on his bed. I'd explained my aversion to touch, and he'd taken the initiative and tied my hands so I wouldn't be tempted. A wonderful idea at the time. But as his cock pressed against my lips and my tongue lapped his salt, I'd been struck with a vision of his death. I'd choked, and Erosain had instead taken me from behind.

I'd come all over his expensive rug, which I'd been obligated to professionally clean. We'd not dallied again since.

All the while, Elijah had still commanded me. We hadn't been in an official relationship, but I'd been bound to him, and I'd cheated. My behavior had not gone unpunished.

So no, I was no gentleman. Not really.

I was a bastard who deserved everything I got.

If Kayl knew how depraved my thoughts were, she'd never speak to me again.

Nor could I ever admit them. Not when she still mourned Malkavaan.

On the plus side, at least my plumbing still worked after my death and resurrection.

All right, Quen. I was being dramatic. This trip hadn't been a wasted venture. Erosain may curse my name, but Edana was on my side. No one had been injured. There was still time to save Chime, Chaos, and everything in between. And we still had over an hour until the Gate opened.

Saints, I needed a cup of tea.

I reached for a towel. Pain splintered through my skull.

Darkness claimed me as I fell against the sink.

What was taking my partner so damn long? He was only supposed to be checking up on the watchmaker. We had bigger problems, and no time to dilly-dally.

I pushed the store door open and peeked my head inside.

My partner fell to the ground, his eye sockets empty. A Glimmer stood next to him.

"What's going on here?" I gasped too late.

She'd done that. She'd—

Time slowed, my ability flaring on instinct. It should have stopped her. It should have been enough. But she... God save me. She was still moving!

Oh Father, no. She was one of the Chaos creatures!

I needed to run. To get out. My legs wouldn't move. She reached toward me—

"Quen?" Kayl kneeled beside me, her hands gripping my upper arms. "Talk to me."

"A vision," I gasped. A recent one. "It's Jinx. I know where she's hiding. We need to return to Chime, we need to stop her—"

"Calm down and talk slowly. What has she done?"

"She's killed Diviner." I swallowed a lump in my throat. Dor had sent me this vision for a reason. I couldn't sit on it.

"Gods. Right. Get dressed. I'm coming with you." She handed me a towel.

Oh blast. I was sitting on the bathroom floor dripping wet and completely naked.

Heat warmed my face. I covered myself with the towel. To Kayl's credit, she hadn't made light of my situation, and stepped out to let me dress. My clothes were in a sorry state—my shirt was crumpled and stunk of sweat. Hunting down Jinx in a tuxedo wasn't exactly ideal. But when time called, one did not wait.

"You okay in there, sir?" Ben asked from outside.

He'd arrived just in time to maximize my awkwardness. If the fate of the domains didn't rest on my shoulders, I'd ask him to take me outside and shoot me.

Once dressed, I greeted Ben, who was subtly trying to avoid staring at Kayl. She wasn't exactly dressed modestly, either. A tight purple dress suited her Ember form, but on a Diviner?

Gods forbid.

"Sleep well, sir?" Ben's face struggled to remain innocent. I'd really have to teach him how to hide his emotions, or fire him later, one or the other.

"Is there time for breakfast?" Kayl asked. "I'm pissing starving."

"I suppose we can grab something on the way."

We left the ambassador suite and stopped off at the restaurant for a quick breakfast of tea, coffee, and pastries. I didn't have the appetite for anything except a raspberry muffin, but Kayl managed an entire plate of blueberry pancakes while Ben helped himself to a stack of toast and eggs.

Seren may be culinary artists, but Ember made fantastic bakers.

When we were done, we headed down to the parking garage, where Erosain waited beside a carriage. He didn't look pleased to see us.

"My lady Edana specified that I arrange travel to the Gate," he said through barely restrained anger. "Though I'll be making my own arrangements back to Chime. My lady also bids me to relay that you are welcome in Rapture anytime, *Ambassador* Arkey." He spat the words with malice, and his red eyes glowed aflame. "However, Sinner's Row is my domain, in which you are no longer welcome. Neither of you." His glare turned to me.

Well then. My days of mingling with the sinners were over. "I understand you're upset—"

"Upset!" His nostrils flared with smoke. "Edana wishes for me to drop this matter, but I will not! Not until I have been fairly compensated, Quentin! Now please! Your carriage awaits."

Kayl opened her mouth to argue, but I shook my head and gestured for her to get in the carriage. There was no point prolonging the argument, and I didn't want to miss the crossing and spend another twelve awkward hours failing at billiards.

At this time of the morning, the strip was largely empty except for meandering mortals who stumbled around hungover or dejected from losing their life's savings. More were making their way to the Gate after a night of regrets.

Unfortunately, I could relate.

But what happened in Rapture, stayed in Rapture, so they said.

At least our carriage made good time.

Kayl leaned into my shoulder as the carriage bobbed down the strip. "I'm sorry for fucking up your relationship with Erosain."

"It was doomed from the start."

"Was he your mystery third lover?" she whispered.

I glanced at Ben, whose attention was enthralled by some sort of volcanic flowery display of dried plants. "Yes," I whispered back.

Her eyes went wide with sudden eagerness. "Oh my. Wait. Does that mean you've seen his death?"

I kept my foolish mouth shut.

"You have, haven't you?" she prodded. "You've got to tell me. *Please.*"

"*You* can't keep a secret."

"I won't tell anyone, I swear. Come on. You can't drop this and not tell me."

I'd wiped the memory for good reason, but Walter had brought it back, along with every other memory I wished I could forget. "Edana will soon grow tired of him."

"Ooh, an old-fashioned smiting."

"You can't say a word." I raised my brow to emphasize the seriousness.

She mimed stitching her lips together.

It saddened me that Erosain wasn't long for this world, and that his campaign against Kayl would eventually be his undoing. He was good company. Or had been.

There was much about his dealings on Sinner's Row that was unsavory. Maybe I'd turned a blind eye to it. Maybe I'd been naïve to the depravity behind his closed doors. Either way, a new leader would soon rise in Sinner's Row. Potentially a kinder one. Likely a crueler one. On the plus side, I'd need not arrange for Erosain's much-sought-after compensation. He wouldn't have a use for it, and I needed funds for my tram refurbishment project.

I was a bastard, wasn't I?

"What's our plan when we return to Chime, sir?" Ben asked, finally pulling his attention away from the strip.

"I'd like to return to Kronos on the ten o'clock crossing if possible." I had yet to check in on Doctor Finch and Ilona Burns, and I couldn't keep putting it off. "But first, we have a matter in the Market District to attend to."

Central Station remained fairly quiet. Travelers came with us from Rapture and chose to nurse their hangovers at the local teahouses. Kayl had managed to brush up against an Ember and swap forms at my suggestion, though the crossing from Rapture's heat to Chime's morning stillness had left her with a chill.

She wrapped my jacket around her shoulders, and we caught the tram into the Market District. I stifled a yawn as we made our way along the cobblestone streets. Only teahouses and coffee shops were open at this hour.

"What do you expect to find, sir?" Ben asked, a wary eye on each alleyway.

"Trouble."

My visions had brought me here for a reason. In truth, I didn't think we'd catch Jinx—she was smart enough to avoid Wardens. But we'd uncover something, I knew it.

We passed Arcadia Apparel and turned the corner to Divine Timepieces. A Diviner watchmaker's. I'd visited this very store myself a few times and vaguely recalled the owner. A charming older gent by the name of Cogsworth.

What had Jinx been doing here?

I tried the door. It was locked as I'd expected.

Kayl scanned through the window with both her hands on the glass. "It's too dark inside. I don't see anything."

"Ben, check around the back. I'll handle the front."

"Sir."

Kayl came to my side. "You think she's still in here?"

"It's highly unlikely." I grabbed the door handle and allowed a small pocket of time to envelope the lock. A century passed in a blink of an eye, reducing the lock to dust. The handle crumbled in my hand. I shook it clean and slowly pushed open the door to the jingle of the shop's bell.

Chaos had most certainly been here.

Broken clocks were scattered across the floor and counter, their guts spilling out in piles of cogs, gears, and springs. And there, underneath the wreckage, sprawled two bodies. Two male Diviner in Warden uniforms.

"Gods, Quen," Kayl muttered, entering behind me.

I didn't need to examine their recent memories to know what had befallen them. The face of one was a mess of blood and barely recognizable—the result of horrifying violence. I crouched beside the other and turned him over. His mouth hung open in a silent scream. His empty eye sockets stared back at me.

"I'm so sorry," Kayl said. "If I pissed Jinx off, set the Wardens on her—"

"The Wardens were searching for her on my orders. They would have found her eventually." As they evidently had.

I picked my way around the counter. Silence pressed in on me, as though time held its breath. Glass and wood crunched beneath my shoes. Not a single clock had been spared to serenade me with their tick and tock. I knew in my gut Jinx was responsible for this mess. Her rage for the Diviner truly knew no bounds.

Kayl followed as I headed up the stairs to what appeared to be a studio apartment. This was as messy as the shop floor. Clothes, dirty plates, and trash covered every surface. This store had been lived in. By Jinx? For how long? It had that rotten stench of moldy leftovers.

"Jinx lived here." Kayl confirmed my thoughts. She picked up a discarded red dress. "But why here? She hates Diviner."

"It's the perfect cover." Really, it was quite clever of her. I wondered where she'd gotten the idea? There weren't just women's clothes, but men's too, and a couple of stray feathers stuck to the couch. The Chaos male, Chance, had also inhabited this space. "The question is, where are the original owners? They must be somewhere."

Whatever Chaos mortals had taken over this store had long since vacated the premises. I headed back downstairs to the storage cupboard. The door was a little stiff, but it opened with a hard tug.

I swallowed bile.

I'd found the watchmaker and more.

At least seven bodies were stuffed into the storage cupboard, some piled awkwardly on top of each other, others leaning against the wall. There was no sign of blood or bruising or any damage that would indicate a physical altercation. In fact, their bodies were perfectly preserved, with only their eyes missing.

Most were Diviner. Two were Glimmer. One was a Fauna girl.

Kayl came up behind me. I slammed the door. "You don't want to see this."

"I need to."

I chewed my lip as she opened the door.

"My god." She turned to me with tears welling in her eyes. "How could she have done this? How could she have killed... *Gods*."

I wrapped my arms around her waist and allowed her to sob on my shoulder.

"How could she do this?" Kayl's voice cracked. "Is this my fault?"

I rubbed her back in soothing motions. "She is responsible for her own atrocities. Don't blame yourself for that."

"I knew what she was capable of, I should have stopped her—"

"We didn't know it would lead to this."

Kayl pulled back and stared at me with bloodshot eyes. "Didn't we? She's taken souls before. Thousands! The Vesper are *dead* because of her!" She leaned over the counter, her breath coming in ragged gasps.

We'd both taken lives and had to live with the consequences, but the difference between Kayl and me was that none of my kills had been accidental. There was guilt in being a survivor. But there was worse guilt in being an active killer. "If I could change the past—if I could save the lives lost—I would do so in a heartbeat."

"Why am I standing here? Why didn't you lock me away in your correctional facility? I'm Chaos, too. Is this what *I'm* capable of, Quen? She's my twin. Aren't we the same?"

I wanted to grab her hand. I wanted her to understand. "You're *nothing* like Jinx. What happened to Eventide was an accident—"

"You can't call killing thousands of mortals an accident."

No. And calling it regrettable was too minor a word.

"We keep pretending it was some other random Chaos mortal who destroyed Eventide," Kayl said, her words spluttering out. "We're lying to the ambassadors, to actual gods! Telling them that if they help us, ally with us, the domains will be safe. They'll be safe. But it was *my* sister. Jinx destroyed Eventide. And if they knew..."

Jinx destroyed Eventide?

My heart caught in my throat. "Do—Do you remember what happened in Eventide?"

"As if I could forget! It was Jinx—it was all Jinx." She laughed bitterly.

"Valeria attacked you," I said slowly.

"Yes, I remember. And Jinx took Valeria's soul in some grand gesture of saving me, destroying everything in the process. Should I be thankful I'm still here? Me, and not the Vesper?"

Good gods. I scanned her eyes, her expression, but she wasn't joking.

She couldn't have forgotten?

"And Malkavaan." I broached the subject with as much care as my heart could muster. "You watched him die."

She looked confused. "Malkavaan? Who's that?"

Now my heart was pounding. "Malkavaan—Malk? Your Vesper lover?"

"I've never dated a Vesper."

"He was Elvira's son—"

"Who?"

Saints. Kayl had forgotten them.

Deliberately? Was it from guilt? Shame? As I'd so often wiped my own memories?

Aberforth. The Amnae ambassador had sworn Kayl's safety during her time in Memoria, but I knew that cad couldn't be trusted. Had she given up Malkavaan in exchange for a bargain? Forgotten her part in Eventide's demise for a slice of peace? Or had Anima taken those memories and rewritten Kayl's past for their own amusement?

I was going to get my hands on Aberforth's neck and wring the life from him.

"Quen?" Kayl prodded.

If she truly couldn't remember Malkavaan or the events of Eventide, then bringing up those memories would only distress her. There had to be a way to get those memories of Malkavaan back, at least. She loved him. I wasn't going to let him be forgotten. "I'm sorry—I was thinking of a Vesper I knew—"

"But they're dead, right? These bodies? These deaths? That's all on *her*."

And therein lay the truth. Jinx may not have been the one to pull Eventide's plug, but that had been her intent. She remained the real threat.

I'd tried to be patient with Jinx—I'd tried to reason with her—but she'd gone too far. Kayl's pain echoed in my own heart.

There was no hope of saving Chaos if Jinx continued to murder Diviner.

She needed to be stopped. One way or another.

"I have to be the one to stop her," Kayl said, reading my thoughts. "It has to be me."

"Jinx is too volatile, too dangerous—"

"I'm the only one who *can* stop her—who can reach her. We're not arguing over this." She rested her forehead on mine. "I won't risk your soul."

I breathed in her scent. Sweet, like roses. It overpowered the sweat coming from my jacket. "Then let me help."

"How?"

I turned to the counter and picked up a spare cog. It was a tiny delicate piece of brass. A small part of a bigger design. "The Wardens have been developing an aether collar that can counteract Chaos. They're extensions of our tasers, and work in the same way—by blocking a mortal's abilities. While they can work on any domain, they're designed specifically for Chaos."

"Like the bracelet you gave me?"

"They were developed on similar lines, yes."

"These collars would be used on all Chaos?" *And myself?* I heard the unspoken question on her lips.

"Their use would be authorized if it became necessary to subdue Chaos mortals. You know I don't mean to harm them. This is a nonlethal method of ensuring that."

She rubbed her forehead. "Right. Fine. Does it work?"

"We have a prototype, but they haven't been fully tested."

"Then it sounds like I'm going to be doing a field test."

"Do you have a plan in mind?"

"Oh, gods no. But don't worry. I'll improvise something."

That was what worried me. "Come back with me to HQ. I can arrange the prototype."

"Give me an hour to speak with Harmony and the others. I'll meet you by the bench at Central Station at eleven." She shrugged off my jacket and handed it over.

I'd miss the ten o'clock crossing, but this needed to take priority. "Be safe."

She headed for the door and glanced back. "You too."

I let the cog roll off the counter and sighed.

My foolish optimism had hoped Jinx could be saved. For Kayl's sake, I'd wanted to save her sister. I should have anticipated this outcome. The fact I hadn't meant these bodies—these deaths—were my responsibility.

Another failure on my part.

Being ambassador meant making harsh choices to protect Chime.

Jinx had to go.

But knowing Kayl had forgotten Malkavaan and Elvira...

That concerned me far more.

What else had she forgotten?

"All good, sir?" Ben said, popping his head around the door. His eyes bulged at the sight of two dead Diviner.

"I'm afraid we've got quite a mess on our hands." And things were about to get worse.

25

It's been four weeks since the incident, and I still can't wrap my head around it. All the Vesper... Gone.
First thing I did was head to Grayford. The Undercity should have been crawling with Vesper, but I couldn't find a single damn one. The Fauna who were brave enough to chat with a Necro told me they'd vanished in front of their eyes. Just as Zorya had vanished.
This was reality, then. Stinking reality.
No one hired me for this case. Even Noct tells me to drop it. But I can't. Not when I close my eyes and see Zorya turning to dust in front of me. Where did the Vesper go? I'm going to fucking find out.
—M. Gast, from the personal files of PI Gast

MALKAVAAN.

THAT NAME SOUNDED familiar, yet I couldn't place it. Quen's words had followed me all the way to the Temple District and back, nagging at me. I sat on the bench watching mortals pass to and from Central Station. It was a mundane day, all things considered. The trams still ran on time. The teahouses still served customers. Seren boys still flew past flogging the Courier. The lamppost beside my bench remained busted.

It was Chime as I knew it.

Yet everything had changed.

The clock tower rang quarter to eleven. Eventide's purple skies should have been visible through the Gate, but instead, I stared at Kronos.

"Your Vesper lover."

I racked my brain trying to remember, but I'd always been shit at remembering things. Surely, I'd remember a lover? I'd indulged in flings here and there—with Ember, mostly. Had I ever loved a Vesper?

Once, I'd sat on this very bench, waiting and worrying for Eventide to open, but why? For this Malkavaan? I couldn't recall. I *did* remember Dru keeping me company, or if I was alone, then my own mind had distracted me with conversation.

Only, it had never been my mind. It had been Jinx. The jokes and games we'd shared had all been her. The times we'd watched mortals stroll by and try to guess what sins they hid from the public eye. The times she'd tried to protect me from myself.

Jinx was a reflection of me. My sins. My vices.

She'd become my apostasy made flesh in the most abhorrent way.

And now she was completely out of control. I'd known she was crazy. I knew she hated Diviner. But seeing the depths of it stacked in that storage room…

Gods.

I couldn't let this continue. Otherwise, what would be the bloody point of bowing and scraping to the gods to save mortal lives if Jinx took them anyway?

At the turn of the hour, the Gate changed over to Phantasy. Those starry skies reminded me of Eventide, and I couldn't help but feel Mesmorpheus watched me from afar. They'd taken an active interest in protecting Chime. Perhaps now they'd see I was damn well trying.

Quen sat beside me. He'd since freshened up, as I'd changed and swapped to an Umber body. "You're on time. Should I be worried?"

I pulled a face. "Is Ben with you?"

"He's loitering somewhere." Quen pulled a small packet from his inner jacket pocket. "This is the prototype. We've tested it on Chance back at HQ and verified it's safe. However, I cannot be certain of its effectiveness."

"Chance?"

"The Chaos male from the ball?"

Oh, *now* I remembered his name. I took the collar in my hands. It had a heftiness to it. "How do I use this, then?"

"Wrap it around the neck. It will click into place. It cannot be removed without my fingerprint."

How convenient. I shoved the collar into my satchel and pulled out a sealed envelope. "Details of my plan. Read it somewhere private, obviously."

He examined the envelope. "It's more prudent *not* to write down your secret plans."

"Am I being lectured by a man whose entire apartment is covered in secret notes? I've been running operations like this for years." Ignoring the fact I'd blown most of them. "You'll have to trust me."

"I trust you. I don't trust Jinx."

That made two of us.

Mother, dear? I called into my mind. *I know you're listening. And I know you still speak with Jinx. I'd like to meet with her for some sisterly bonding.*

SO YOU MAY CAPTURE HER AS YOUR DIVINER HAS CAUGHT YOUR BROTHER? I WILL NOT HAVE MY CHILDREN FIGHT.

You do think the worst of me. I want to talk, negotiate, whatever. I'll even meet her somewhere public, say, Lady Mae's café in an hour? They sell cream cakes.

Corentine didn't answer me, which could be either a good or bad thing.

I knew Jinx wouldn't resist.

But while I waited, I had another place I wanted to be.

The Vesper temple had been boarded up. Dust gathered by the entrance, and I couldn't tell if this had once been a Vesper, or was simply the marking of time for a place abandoned.

With the Vesper gone, there was no need for anyone to step inside, and no one had. Not even the Glimmer, in some twisted plot to steal it for themselves. They likely thought this temple cursed.

Even when I'd masqueraded as a Vesper, I'd not once stepped foot inside the temple.

Until now.

The planks of wood came apart easily, and I entered a miniature representation of Valeria's bleak obsidian castle. Darkness seeped from the walls, built from the same dark purple material, as though it absorbed all light.

I longed to change into my Vesper form, but since Jinx had destroyed them all, there were no longer any Vesper left to grant me that comfort.

Comfort was what I sought, but... uneasiness found me.

Perhaps it was anxiety for what lay ahead.

Or guilt.

I let my eyes adjust to the darkness, though without a Vesper's sight, it didn't help much. Slowly, I fumbled my way through the corridor, my fingers skimming across the cool, smooth walls.

With each step, the urge to flee this horrid place grew stronger. But some part of me needed to come here.

I needed to face my failure.

I'd been unable to stop Jinx. That could never happen again.

Moonlight shone ahead and guided me into the main sanctum. I came face-to-face with a life-size statue of Valeria.

The Vesper god had been carved from pure silver. In the darkness of the temple, she shone like a beacon, reflecting light across the stone pews that encircled her. It was hard to believe I'd once feared her—hated her—and now she was gone.

Jinx had taken her soul. Her very essence.

Piles of dust were scattered across the pews. Mortals who had once lived and dreamed of a better day. Mortals who would dream no more.

More dust swirled in the air with a musty scent of decay. The thought I might be breathing the Vesper in made me want to vomit. "I'm sorry," I whispered. "You all deserved better than this."

Silence replied. A bone-quaking silence full of judgmental scorn.

Corentine had said I'd forgotten them. Had I?

IT TOOK YOU OVER A MONTH TO COME HERE.

And? I owed nothing to Valeria.

I THOUGHT YOU CARED FOR THESE MORTALS.

I did. I do. *Who was Malkavaan? Did you take my memories?*

I DO NOT HAVE THAT POWER.

So you can't bring them back?

YOU FORGOT THEM FOR A REASON, DAUGHTER.

What possible reason could I have to forget other than my own shitty brain?

I sank onto a step and held my head in my hands. Gods damn it! I was always forgetting things, getting distracted. I didn't know what day it was half the time. Shit, if it wasn't for Dru, I'd never have made it to the Gate each day.

If it wasn't for Jinx, I wouldn't have made it this far at all.

And now I'd forgotten the most important thing in the world.

What else would I forget? Dru? The Godless? My family?

Quen?

That the piles of dust filling this temple were because I couldn't protect them?

Jinx had destroyed an entire domain, and I'd let her, out of sheer idiocy!

Tears stung my eyes. *Why did you make me so pissing useless?* I asked Corentine. *Why did you make me... me?*

YOU ARE WHAT YOU ARE. THAT CANNOT AND SHOULD NOT BE CHANGED.

But why? Why this? Why couldn't I have been as smart and collected as Jinx? *You designed me this way!*

YOU ARE A CHILD OF CHAOS, AND CHAOS IS UNPREDICTABLE IN THE GIFTS IT BESTOWS.

You're saying my existence is some random game of chance?

AS ARE ALL MORTALS. THE GODS CREATE MORTALS IN THEIR IMAGE, BUT MORTAL LIVES ARE GOVERNED BY CHAOS AND TIME. CHAOS LEAVES ITS MARK ON ALL THINGS.

Gods. I wasn't in the mood to think about metaphysics. That was Quen's area, not mine. I didn't even *have* an area, besides being bloody useless.

I'd never felt so lost.

Malkavaan. That name felt so intimate, yet I couldn't remember the face it belonged to. A Vesper as dead as the rest. Why had I forgotten him?

Quen. I couldn't sort out my feelings for him. We were partners. Being in his company felt safe. It felt right. But he was a Diviner, for god's sake!

Jinx. She was my sister. My twin. And she completely unnerved me.

She wanted a reality where mortals were reduced to dust.

How could she look upon Chime and want that?

And me. Foolish me. I'd been traipsing into the domains of the gods and treating it like some bloody fun adventure, yet they were no such thing.

The fate of the domains rested on me. I'd agreed to become ambassador to help mortals, and up to now, I'd been doing a piss poor job of it.

"So this is where you're wallowing in self-pity, sister."

I leaped to my feet.

Jinx stood by the sanctum entrance wearing the face of a Glimmer and a silver gown this time. I had to give it to her, she knew how to dress, and looked far more glamorous compared to my blouse and pencil skirt, and my Umber face.

Her golden skin radiated in the darkness of the temple sanctum. Even the dust seemed to stir at the harshness of her light, a profane brightness in Valeria's temple.

"Hello, Jinx."

She leaned casually against the wall. "I know what you're plotting. You really thought you could invite me to Lady Mae's for tea and scones and have Quen and his stupid Wardens jump me? You're a fucking idiot."

I raised my hands. "You got me."

Harmony and I had devised a simple plan to lure Jinx out. A public place I didn't mind getting trashed. Quen was familiar with Lady Mae's, as was Jinx.

Only, that had never been my plan at all.

My real plan I'd discussed with Mesmorpheus and Reverie during a quick nap, because in my dreams, not even Corentine could spy on me.

Someone had relayed my fake plan to Jinx, but only Harmony, Sinder, and Joe had sat in on our meeting. Of course I trusted Harmony and Sinder. Joe was a newcomer, who Sinder clearly didn't trust, but Sinder had an obvious bias.

Which left Corentine to pluck the information from my mind.

I can't be your voice if you're working against me.

I WOULD NEVER TURN YOU AGAINST ONE ANOTHER.

You could have fooled me!

YOU ARE MY VOICE, YET YOU DO NOT SPEAK FOR ME.

Did you really expect me to be your herald of vengeance?

CHIME IS MY DOMAIN!

No, Chime is mine*!*

"Problem, sister?"

I bit back a sigh. "It's you, Jinx. You're the problem. I'm not going to spend the rest of my life fighting you."

Her eyes glowed red. "What are you gonna do about it, huh? Kill me?"

"I don't want to hurt you, but what you've done... It stops *now*."

Sunlight burst from Jinx in response.

I dove behind Valeria's statue as a ray of sunlight burned across the floor, leaving a trail of smoldering flame.

"You think this is about *me*?" Jinx yelled. Blasts of light collided with the statue, sending sparks in all directions. "This is on *you*, Kayl! We could have taken the domains by now. We could have freed our mother together! But you never gave a shit about her or what I wanted. Every soul I take is on *you*!"

Flame spread across the statue, singing my jacket. Between the power of a Vesper and a Glimmer, Jinx would have outmatched me. Not even my shadows would have kept her at bay. But at least in an Umber's body, I had some protection against sunlight.

Though if I'd possessed any actual forethought, I could have brought a damn plant or something to use against her.

Valeria's silver statue melted into a molten, smoldering lump. Shit! I quickly scrambled behind a pew.

My twin approached with glowing red eyes as tendrils of flame swirled around her fists. There was no humor in her expression. I'd had enough of her shit, but the feeling was apparently mutual.

"You'd really kill your own sister?" I called out.

"I don't need to kill you, silly. I just need to burn your limbs off, and then I can drag the rest of your useless arse to the clock tower. So what will it be? Either you come with me willingly, or this is going to turn ugly."

Shit. She wasn't playing around.

Neither was I.

I charged at Jinx and tackled her to the ground.

She tried to shove me away, but my Umber weight outmatched hers. I wrapped my thick arms around her, holding on for all I was worth. Flame sparked against my chest, burning through my blouse until embers flew from my stone skin.

I wasn't intending to crush her. I needed to pin her down.

"No, you fucking don't!" Jinx yelled.

Sunlight flared across her entire body, burning both our clothes to ash. I cringed at the brightness. It burned with such strength, I had no choice but to let her go and protect my eyes.

Gods! How was Jinx that powerful?

Colorful dots filled my vision. Shit, I couldn't see!

I patted the ground. My fingers touched dust, and then—the collar. It must have fallen from my pocket when my clothes burned.

Jinx's blurry figure swiped it. "Looking for this?"

Shit!

I scrambled after the collar. Jinx tripped my ankle, sending me sprawling.

And then she was on top of me.

I squirmed and kicked, but then her hands wrapped around my throat.

"Did you ever love me?" She spat, her saliva landing on my cheek. "I loved you my *entire* life, and you couldn't even be arsed to love me back because I wasn't real to you! And now I'm here with my own fucking body, you *still* don't love me!"

I scratched around her wrist, trying to pry her off. "How—How can you say that you ever loved me?" The words spilled out of me with bitter resentment. "You were in my mind for thirteen damn years and kept me in the dark for all of them! You never told me about Corentine or Chaos. None of it! Yet you knew the entire time!"

"To protect you, idiot—"

"Even now, you and Corentine conspire behind my back!"

Her fingernails bit into my neck. "Maybe if you hadn't *fucking betrayed me*, I could have taught you about Chaos. Taught you how to use your powers. We could have made better partners than you and your Time Boy. But you had to ruin everything, didn't you? All I've ever wanted is you. Our mother. My own family. What's so wrong about that?"

The look in her eyes was murderous. Crazy.

We'd spent our entire lives together, and this was where we'd ended up.

I blinked away tears. "I'm—I'm sorry, Jinx," I choked out.

"It's too late for apologies now."

I know. But I'm sorry.

A shadow loomed behind us. Jinx glanced over her shoulder. "What the fuck—"

A single touch to her forehead, and Jinx collapsed over my legs, fast asleep.

I sucked in a breath and pushed her off me. "You cut it pissing close!"

Reverie stood over Jinx, observing her as though she was some odd curiosity. "We had to wait for the opportune moment."

I stood and patted dust from my knees. "If you'd waited any longer, I'd have been dead." Or worse. "How long will she sleep for?"

"For as long as I wish."

"You couldn't have done this when she tried to kidnap you at the ball?"

Reverie cocked her head. "That wasn't the opportune moment."

"Right. Well, you better help me carry her and hope no one notices us kidnapping a naked Glimmer."

I picked up the collar. It resembled the silver bracelet Quen had given me, only heavier, and a subtle aether-blue light shone around the edge. This damn thing would supposedly cut off Jinx's power. Stop her from switching forms or otherwise being destructive. The thought of it wrapped around my neck sent a shiver down my spine.

This was the only way I could control Jinx without killing her or locking her away inside a Warden correctional facility.

SHE IS YOUR SISTER! Corentine screeched in my mind. *MADE OF THE SAME FLESH AND BLOOD! AND YOU WOULD BETRAY HER TO DOR?*

For god's sake, I'm not handing her over to the Wardens.

That was the bargain I'd made with Quen. Jinx was my responsibility. My monster. I'd be the one to deal with her. So long as she stopped murdering mortals, it wouldn't matter if she was in my care.

THEN BRING HER TO ME. TO THE CLOCK TOWER.

Look. She had her chance. If she stays on this path of vengeance, then it won't just be her life she forfeits, but all of Chaos, and you as well. She's safer with me.

THIS IS NOT MY DESIRE.

Tough shit. We're doing this my way.

I awkwardly placed the collar around Jinx's neck, snapping it in place. It shouldn't hurt, I was told, but it would certainly irritate.

It was only a prototype. Gods, I hoped it worked. Otherwise, I'd be dealing with a very pissed-off maniac when she finally woke. I didn't want to keep her trapped in a coma.

I just wanted her to *stop.*

Jinx's head lolled as I lifted her. She was as heavy as me, and it took some effort to carry her to the entrance of the Vesper temple.

The Mesmer trio waited by the entrance carrying a blanket.

"We'll help you carry her," one of them said.

"We won't drop her. Promise," said the other.

The third held up a dress and a pair of shoes. "We brought you clothes. Reverie said you would need them."

I didn't want to admit I was glad to see the three of them.

They carefully wrapped Jinx in the blanket as I dressed. While they went on ahead to the Mesmer temple, I boarded up the front of the Vesper one to ensure no Wardens would wander by and find anything suspicious. There wasn't much I could do for the disturbed dust, but I doubted the Wardens would look that close.

Once done, I stepped back to admire my handiwork. A glint of bronze shone from the eave of the entrance roof.

Gods. Had a Glimmer climbed on top to spy on me? No, it was some sort of clockwork bird. It clicked and whirred with the stiff mechanical movement of a toy. It couldn't be a Fauna, then. Was it a Diviner invention?

I reached up to grab it, and it flew away, its wings fluttering unnaturally.

Well. I'd never seen anything quite like it, but I had more important things to worry about, namely my twin sister. If I remembered, I'd ask Quen about it later.

Sinder shook his head as I entered the Mesmer temple. "Darling, I love you, no matter your crazy schemes. But are you sure it's safe to be bringing in your dear sister?"

I leaned against the counter to catch my breath. "There's a padded room downstairs." For chronic sleepwalkers, so Reverie had told me. "She'll be locked away in there."

"That sounds like it would be easy to break out of."

"I've cut off her powers. She won't be going anywhere."

"We're keeping her prisoner?"

"Until Quen and I finish what we need to do. Then Jinx and the rest of my chaotic siblings can be redeemed in the eyes of Warden law."

"Does Dru know she'll be sharing a home with that thing? Remember that your sister threatened us—"

"I *know*. Dru will understand. This is the best I can do."

"All right, dearest. You know best." The tone of his voice betrayed his insincerity. "I'll guard her, then. If she tries to escape, I can at least burn her down."

This wasn't an ideal solution, and I didn't want anyone murdering *anyone*, but it really was the best I could do. We'd have to make the most of it.

I found the trio downstairs. They'd laid Jinx in the padded cell and locked the doors.

"You can't let her out under any circumstances," I warned. "Even if she pretends to be me. Don't fall for her tricks."

"She fooled us once," one of the trio said. "She won't fool us again."

"Let's hope not."

I peered through the small window. Jinx lay sleeping and looked peaceful. Not some rampaging monster bent on destroying the domains.

Was there another timeline where Jinx and I were close? Real sisters? As close as I was to Dru? Or were we too stubborn to ever give each other the chance?

Light flashed in the corner of my eye, and I peeked around the corridor. Quen was standing there.

He was dressed in a tan suit, not the tuxedo from before, and his eyeglasses were different—no, there was something else different about him. The way he stood.

Confident. Poised.

"Quen?" How had he gotten inside the temple? Had he followed me? Why sneak in and not tell me he knew?

Aether flashed in his eyes. "Oh bugger," he muttered.

And then he ran.

What the *shit*?

He dove inside a room and slammed the door behind him. What in god's name was going on? I rattled the handle. He'd locked it from the other side!

"Quen!" I yelled through the door, and gave it a good thump. "What are you doing? Why are you even here? What is going *on*?"

"I'm sorry," he said, muffled through the wood. "I'm going through a strange time in my life right now—"

"You're not the only one!"

"Be patient with me, please. I know I'm insufferable, and I suffer for it."

Light flashed between the door's beams.

"Quen?" I tried the door and this time it opened to an empty storage cupboard.

Of course. That was it. I was finally losing my mind.

"Is something the matter?" Reverie asked.

Gods! She'd bloody snuck up on me! "Did you see that?" I pointed to the empty cupboard. "Quen was here. I saw him with my own two eyes, and then he vanished! Am I sleeping? Is this a dream?" Some sort of Mesmer trick?

"Can you sit?"

"Why? Because I'm going mad?"

"I'm going to enter your subconscious, and I'd rather you didn't fall and hurt yourself."

Shit. I didn't fancy napping in the corridor, but that was apparently going to happen. I hastily sat and leaned against the wall. Normally, I'd balk at Reverie invading my mind like this, but damn it, I wanted answers.

Reverie placed her palm on my forehead. "Sweet dreams."

Darkness swarmed over me before I could even take a breath.

I sat on the bench outside Central Station.

Night had taken over Central, though the streets were eerily silent. Not a single soul walked past on their way to the station, and even that appeared empty. The only sound came from the stirring of litter and a copy of the Courier fluttering into a gutter. Dust and grime covered the cobblestones. Central was never this dirty. Nor this quiet.

I glanced behind me and swallowed a gasp.

The town houses and boutiques lay in ruins. Brick, plaster, and glass were scattered across the square. Clothes, teacups, and souvenirs mingled among the debris. An empty tram waited in the middle of the track, its doors hanging open.

What in god's name had happened here?

Only the station appeared intact, though...

Shit.

The Gate was off. Completely powered down, leaving only a gaping void of nothing. My gaze followed the clock tower up. Aether swirled around the clockface, but... Gods. Even the Golden City plate looked wrong, as though it was missing parts.

This was a nightmare. It had to be.

A Chime without mortals. Empty. Abandoned.

Dead.

The streetlamps flickered ominously, and then Quen appeared next to me on the bench in a bright blast of aether. Literally appeared out of pissing thin air!

I wished everyone would stop bloody doing that!

He pulled a candy bag out of his jacket pocket. "Would you like a jelly baby?"

I was losing my mind. "Where in god's name did you get jelly babies?"

"Cosmo was saving them. They said the purple ones are your favorite. Licorice flavor, I believe?"

Why not? I picked out a purple jelly baby in the shape of a Vesper. These came in all shapes and flavors based on the domains, though most didn't include the lemon Glimmer, due to them finding something as innocent as candy offensive. As if anyone would eat an actual baby… Well, maybe a Necro would. "This is a dream, isn't it?"

Quen helped himself to a blue jelly baby in the shape of an Amnae. Blueberry flavor, if I remembered right. "It would appear so."

"This isn't the first time you've entered my dreams."

He raised a brow. "Is it not? How many other times have you dreamed of me? Let's compare." He set his bag of jelly babies aside and pulled out a pocket-sized notepad. "Where did you dream of me first?"

"In Grayford, when I was a child."

"That makes sense. Where else?"

"Grayford again, a few times."

"Have we met inside the clock tower?"

"No. Should we?"

"In my timeline, we already have." He tapped his notepad.

Timeline? What was he blabbering on about? I strained over to read his notepad, but he flipped it shut.

He tutted. "No spoilers."

"If this is my dream, shouldn't it bend to my will? Where are we? Is this the future?"

"It's *a* future. A potential one among many."

"Shit." I grabbed the jelly babies and picked out an orange Leander. These squishy things really did resemble a cute cub. I wondered what

Chaos would taste like? Bubblegum? "How do we prevent this one? That's what you're trying to do, isn't it?"

"That depends entirely on you."

"On me?" I choked on my Leander cub.

"What are you willing to sacrifice to prevent this future? Whose soul are you willing to take?"

"Are you speaking of Jinx?"

His silver eyes glowed with aether.

And then the streetlamps blew out, plunging me into darkness.

"Quen!" I reached out to grab him, and my hand swiped through nothing. Gods, even the bench had disappeared! "*Quen!*" I screamed until my voice went hoarse. "Don't you dare leave me, you arse!"

I blinked, and the darkness had morphed into a familiar hotel room. Lights twinkled from beyond the window, and it took me a moment to realize this was Rapture, and the lights were the strip.

There I was, sleeping beside Quen. Our arms wrapped around each other. I swallowed a lump in my throat.

Why would I dream this?

Gods. Quen looked so peaceful. So vulnerable.

While I was drawn to him, it was my own body, my own expression, that made me pause. I, too, looked peaceful. Happy, even. When was the last time I'd slept in the same bed with a man? When had I wrapped my arms around them? With Malkavaan or whoever?

I'd forgotten Malkavaan for a reason.

Maybe that reason was Quen.

A shadow pulled from the wall as Mesmorpheus casually entered my dream. The god was dressed in their tight black suit. Their face a maddening void of stars.

"Are you fucking with my reality?" I accused.

THIS IS NOT MY DOING.

"This isn't the first time I've seen Quen pop in and out of existence." He'd been there in the alley after the memorial riot. "How is this possible?"

Mesmorpheus strode to where Quen and I were sleeping and placed their hand over Quen's forehead. *HE DREAMS OF YOU.*

"Really? What does he dream of?"

YOU KILL HIM.

I didn't know if my heart could stop in a dream, but it certainly tried. "Quen dreams of me killing him?" But he'd woken up with a damn hard-on! Gods, I'd been distracted by it ever since we left Rapture. The way it had strained against his briefs left no room for imagination regarding his length and girth. Truly, Quen was a grower.

If mortals were made in the image of their gods, then Dor surely possessed a dong the size of the clock tower. Though why make Diviner cocks so large if they were discouraged from playing with them?

FOCUS.

"Yes, right. What the shit does this mean?"

NO MORTAL CAN TRAVEL THE VEINS OF TIME. NOT EVEN DIVINER. EITHER QUENTIN CORINTH HAS DISCOVERED A METHOD TO TRANSCEND SPACE AND TIME BEYOND MORTAL MEANS, OR THE THREADS OF TIME HAVE BROKEN.

"Allow me to reiterate: what the shit does this mean?"

Mesmorpheus stared with their eyeless face. *THE TIMELINE OF REALITY HAS FRACTURED IN A FUTURE YET TO COME.*

My mind was reeling. "Fractured? So the Quen I'm seeing... is from the future?"

QUITE POSSIBLY.

Shit. "How could this happen? What does it mean?"

IT MEANS CHAOS HAS WON.

XXVI

There is much we don't understand of immortality. Each god of the twelve domains creates immortal servants in their idealized image. These servants can perform duties mere mortals cannot, and their consciousness is more closely connected with their gods, which would otherwise overrule free will. Occasionally, mortals can be reborn as an immortal. This is often gifted as a reward in death so they may continue their existence within their domain. We refer to these mortals-cum-immortals as saints, and revere them as such.
—H. Bezel, *On Divine Immortality*

AFTER HANDING OVER THE aether collar prototype to Kayl, I'd made the later twelve o'clock crossing with Ben and Pendula and boarded the steam train headed straight for the clock tower plaza.

I let the large chair swallow me as I leaned back and pulled out my fob watch. Of course I worried. The envelope Kayl had given me contained a note with a silly doodle of me holding a cup of tea. I got the message. She didn't want me to interfere, but Jinx was dangerous. I should have been there to intervene should the worst happen, but Kayl had made me promise, so here I sat instead, hoping she had prevailed.

My thumb rubbed over the brass. Blast it, I should have stayed.

"I could get that fixed for you." Pendula gestured to my fob watch. She sat opposite with a stack of paperwork she was reading through, her clockwork pet resting on her shoulder. "We'll give it a whole new lease on life. Good as new."

To a Diviner, a broken clock was akin to nails on a chalkboard. "It doesn't need fixing."

Pendula chuckled. "If it doesn't keep time, then what use is it? Even my bird is programmed to follow basic commands."

"Not all things need a use. Art has no intrinsic use, yet it has value."

She raised a brow. "You consider broken objects as art? How... chaotic."

Ben suddenly shuddered, startled from his thoughts. He'd been quiet and nursing the same cup of coffee since we'd left Chime. Not many Wardens had seen an actual body.

He'd witnessed several.

Pendula had typed up my report, but I knew what they must both think of me. I allied myself with Chaos—with Kayl—yet Chaos had stolen the souls of our brethren. Their judgmental silence and stares said it all.

We had the technology, the numbers, and the power to crush Chaos. To end this once and for all. Only Kayl and Jinx stood in our way.

By keeping them alive, I risked our domain, Chime, the gods. Everything.

But we would *not* be the arbiter of souls. I refused.

I glanced out the window, my cheeks flushed, aware of my own hypocrisy.

What was worse? Abusing a mortal or destroying their very soul?

Were the two any different?

The clock tower came into view, and that familiar anxiety crawled under my skin. I promptly tucked my fob watch away. Its touch no longer soothed me as it once had. Perhaps Pendula was right. Why keep a useless, broken thing?

Since Walter had restored my memories, everything felt disjointed. Fractured. I'd killed Elvira five years ago, and yet it felt like yesterday. My fob watch hadn't just soothed me—it had grounded me in reality when my reality was at the mercy of Walter and Elijah's machinations. But now? Now... it was Kayl who grounded me. Her touch kept my psyche together.

In her company, I forgot who I was. Forgot I was an ambassador, a Diviner. The Dark Warden. In her company, I was merely a man.

The window went dark as the steam train pulled into the plaza. Dor expected my arrival, but I had another stop to make first. "To the laboratory."

Ben and Pendula followed my hurried footsteps. We made our way through brightly lit corridors to the private laboratories hidden within Dor's tower. It was time to meet Miss Ilona Burns.

We entered a round room, and I was instantly beset by steam that misted my spectacles. I slowly meandered inside as I gave them a good clean and shoved them back on.

And came to a sudden halt.

There, in the center, was the soul-splitting device. A machine that looked innocent enough—it was simply a metal chair. But the longer one looked, the more one recognized its sinister nature. Straps were attached to both the arms and legs, and a metal hat dangled above. Wires spread from the back.

It was an odious thing. I turned to Pendula. "I ordered this to be locked away until needed—"

"If Doctor Finch and Miss Burns are to successfully study this technology, then they require easy access to it."

While I didn't fault her logic, we were effectively asking Ilona Burns to work on the same model that had murdered her father. Saints above. "You should have cleared this with me."

"I did. You signed the report. You... did read the report?"

Now she was making me look foolish. "Next time, deliver your report directly."

She took a moment to compose herself. "Yes, Your Excellency."

There I was, acting the prat again. She likely thought me a bastard.

At least she'd followed my instructions to make the laboratory comfortable for Amnae. Thick piping lined the upper walls and delivered short puffs of steam, creating a humid atmosphere. Miss Burns wasn't in the room as far as I could see, but a very fluffy Doctor Finch bustled over. The humidity was doing no favors for his feathers.

"How do you expect me to work in these conditions?" he squawked, and flapped his arms. "This temperature is unbearable. And if I'd known I'd be working alongside a *child*, I'd have reconsidered! She keeps stealing my feathers and using them to write, which is *grossly* offensive—"

"I'm sorry, did you say child?"

"I knew you Diviner were desperate, but I'd have thought child labor beneath you."

Oh bugger. "Will you excuse me for a moment?"

He flapped his arms again and muttered something I didn't quite catch.

The door on the other side of the laboratory opened, and in waltzed an Amnae girl dressed in an oversized white lab coat. Her skin wasn't like Walter's at all, but more of a translucent purple. She stood shorter than even Pendula.

Good gods. She *was* a child.

This had to be a mistake.

I approached with a strained smile. "Miss Burns?"

She placed a seaweed plant pot onto a desk and curtsied. "Master Corinth," she said with a warbled young voice. "My father spoke highly of you, sir."

"You *are* Walter's daughter?"

"That's right."

"I don't mean to be rude, but I was expecting someone much older—"

"I get that a lot."

"He said you were in your final year at Memoria University." Final-year students were in their early twenties at least! I was certain of it.

"I graduated early, sir."

"How early? How old are you?"

"Thirteen, sir."

Thirteen! I was about to pass out from shock!

"I know what you're thinking, sir," she said with the bossy attitude of a damnable teenager. "But I know what I'm doing. I'm familiar with my father's research. Ambassador Aberforth would not have recommended me otherwise."

"That's very admirable, but I cannot let a child—"

"She's a young prodigy, isn't she?" Pendula beamed. "A real child genius. Top of every class. We're blessed to have you helping us."

"Thank you, miss." Ilona bobbed another curtsy. "I understand the assignment, Master Corinth, and I want to be here. My father died at the hands of Chaos. It's not revenge I want, but justice." Defiance shone in her slitted Amnae eyes.

Pendula flashed a saccharine smile.

Just *what* had Pendula told her?

This was my fault. I should have met with Ilona sooner. She deserved the truth of her father's death, but she was thirteen years old, for pity's sake.

A child genius.

I pinched the bridge of my nose. Truth was, I needed her and Walter's expertise, whether she was a child or not. So now I *was* running my own damn workhouse.

"If there's anything you need at all, don't hesitate to ask," Pendula was saying.

"Can you do anything about the feathers? They get everywhere."

Pendula chuckled. A charming, pleasant sound. "Do you like clockwork birds? I'm rather fond of them, and they make far less mess." She whistled, and her pet hopped onto Ilona's shoulder.

Ilona giggled as the bird let out a chirping song. "It's wonderful."

"I can design one for you, if you'd like." Pendula took Ilona's arm and steered her toward one of the benches covered in alchemical bottles that bubbled with a foul green liquid. "Mine is programmed to hold pens and paper to assist me. I'll show you."

Should I be worried that the two of them seemed to get on?

I found Doctor Finch tinkering with one of the aether collars beside Ben, who sat with his head in his hands, his expression one of complete disinterest. Again, I wondered if my bodyguard was even a real Diviner.

"How are you settling in?" I asked the good doctor. "If the humidity is too much, I could arrange for a separate lab—"

"I'll cope. It's not the worst thing to happen to me lately. I'd rather keep watch over her." He eyed Ilona with Pendula in the corner, and then his beak tilted sharply at me with a look of suspicion.

I slid next to the doctor and lowered my voice. "I wouldn't have hired her if I'd known."

"Is she safe here? Working on this project cost Hector Bezel his life. It almost cost mine. I know what you Diviner are like."

"If she's in any danger, I'll pull her out immediately. I have a friend who can take her in and keep her safe."

"Your Godless friend?" he whispered.

I glanced at Ben, whose attention was elsewhere. "Yes. Now how close are we to finding a solution?"

Doctor Finch straightened. "We've created and tested a series of collars to your specification. They can contain a mortal and block their power, but ideally, we need a living Chaos to test them on."

If Kayl was successful at containing Jinx, then we'd have a result. "I'm working on that. And the device?" I eyed the chair sitting ominously in the center.

"Based on your schematics of the collar, I believe we can transfer the adjustments. Permanently locking the abilities of a mortal will require some work. If we miscalculate, there is a risk Chaos will go free. That would be bad, in case I wasn't clear."

"Then we must be absolutely certain."

Rehabilitating Chaos would be no mean feat, but with Ilona's help, the transition would go smoothly.

So much could go wrong, and likely would.

"Do you think... Chaos could be harnessed?" the doctor asked. "Not as an energy source, but their power—the power to transform into any other domain?"

An odd question from an odd man. "The gods would never allow it."

"No. I suppose not."

YOU ARE AWAITED! Dor yelled into my mind.

I cringed at His voice. "Apologies, Doctor, but I'm needed. I'll check in with you when I get the chance."

He nodded and returned to his work.

"Come, Ben." I tapped my bored bodyguard on the shoulder. "It's time."

I left Pendula and made my way back to the main plaza and that damnable elevator.

As it rose, so did my heart rate. I'd often wondered how the Diviner below could go about their day knowing a cosmic deity lurked above. None of them seemed concerned. But no doubt, none of them had a reason to be concerned.

As the elevator went *ping*, I sucked in a breath.

Was my fear justified? Dor was my Father. I, His son. He cared for me. His lessons, His punishments, were meant to guide me.

I existed because of His will.

To enact His will.

Everything I did was for Him.

For her.

No. For *Him*.

"I'll wait for you, sir," Ben said.

"Thank you."

Each step brought me closer to those large double doors and the two brass clockwork Guardians. Again, they cocked their faceless heads as though observing me.

They opened the doors with rhythmic precision.

I stepped into Dor's realm.

The varied clocks that hung in the air weren't ringing this time. Instead, they floated in somber silence. The weight of empty space popped in my ears.

I fell to my knees in the center of my Father's palm. "I'm here, Father."

STAND.

I dragged myself onto shaking legs.

Before me, Dor watched with silver eyes. His form remained much the same—an almost expressionless elder male covered with the white beard of an ageless being. Yet I could sense His energy in the air—a quivering thing, like a cuckoo about to burst into song.

YOU DISAPPOINT ME, QUENTIN.

"We have gods on our side. Anima, Lionheart, Edana—"

OF COURSE THEY ALLY THEMSELVES TO ME. THEY HAVE NO CHOICE.

He made it sound like my mission was a waste of time.

NO. THE GODS MUST BE REMINDED OF THEIR PLACE IN THE UNIVERSE. THEY UNDERSTAND ALL TOO WELL THE

*COST. YET YOU DISOBEYED MY COMMAND. WHY HAVE YOU
FAILED TO PRAY?*

My heart skipped a beat. "I've been a little busy—"

I SEE YOUR THOUGHTS. I SEE YOUR DESIRES.

What happened in Rapture apparently did not stay in Rapture.

YOU HAVE SINNED. WHY HAVE YOU NOT CONFESSED?

"To which sins, Father? I avoided alcohol at your behest. Surely you
can make an exception for a shandy—"

DO NOT TEST ME. YOU KNOW WHICH SINS.

I tucked shaking hands into my pockets. Did I really need to spell it out?

YOU COVET CHAOS.

"Never, Father. I have no interest in such a sinful harlot. The ideal
woman should be quiet, respectful, obedient. Should not swear or
blaspheme or show too much skin—"

YOUR SARCASM IS DISTASTEFUL.

"Sarcasm, Father? I would never! I'm simply stating I have no desire
where Chaos is concerned. Kayl is far too tall. All legs and bosom. And that
arse of hers? I wouldn't even know what to do with it!"

Light burst around me. Two Guardians had suddenly appeared out of
thin air.

Now I was in trouble.

Each grabbed one of my arms with metal hands, their grip clamping
down so painfully tight that I couldn't move.

"Father, please—"

*YOU HAVE DISRESPECTED ME. YOU HAVE IGNORED MY
COMMANDMENTS. I WILL NOT ALLOW SUCH BEHAVIOR TO
GO UNPUNISHED.*

A third Guardian materialized in front of me.

There was no emotion in their faceless stare. No compassion.

*I HAVE COMPASSION FOR YOU, MY SON. WHICH IS WHY
THIS MUST BE DONE. FORSAKE CHAOS. DENY HER.*

My heart was hammering so hard in my chest, it ached. Those words
were easy enough to say. Forsake Chaos. Deny Kayl. Except my Father
didn't want me to just say them.

He wanted me to feel them.

To accept them as a truth I couldn't.

The Guardian curled its hand into a fist.

It slammed into my stomach. Air burst from my lungs in a pained gasp, and I slumped in the Guardians' hold.

FOR EVERY DEVIANT THOUGHT, YOU WILL BE PUNISHED.

Saints. I couldn't control my own thoughts! Nor could I control my dreams. Dor may as well command me to stop breathing!

This was who I was! A sinner. An utter bastard.

Another fist collided with my jaw, snapping my head to one side. I spat out a bloodied tooth.

YOU WILL SUBMIT TO ME. YOU WILL ENJOY YOUR SUBMISSION. YOU WILL DO AS I COMMAND.

How could I deny what I was?

The Guardian broke my nose.

Blood gushed down my waistcoat. I'd never broken my nose before, and I couldn't say I enjoyed the experience.

For every minute that passed, the Guardian found a new, untouched part of my body to punch. My abdomen. My chest. Each blow rippled through my flesh in agonizing spasms, stealing my breath and energy.

My spectacles fell, leaving my vision to blur with dizzying nausea.

I licked my lower lip and tasted the metallic tang of my own life force. If Dor killed me now, who would finish what I'd started? Pendula? She didn't care for Chaos as I did.

And therein lay my dilemma. To save Chaos, I needed to deny it.

To deny her.

To hate her.

But...

Saints.

I'd loved Elijah. He'd hurt me in so many depraved ways, and I'd loved him. Hadn't I? Or had he manipulated me from the first kiss?

I thought I'd loved him. Did I even know what love was?

I'd not found it in Dandelion or Erosain.

Would I even recognize it?

"Is this... how you instructed Elijah?" I mumbled, my ears ringing.

ELIJAH DID AS HE WAS BID. HE WAS MEANT TO CORRECT YOUR DEVIANCE. IT APPEARS YOU DO NOT RESPOND TO PHYSICAL PUNISHMENT.

"You called for me, Father?" said a female voice.

Gods no. Not Pendula.

I squirmed in the grip of my two Guardians as Pendula walked in front of me. Her eyes opened wide as they lay on my sorry state—bruised and bloody.

Fear shadowed her eyes, but she kept her chin high and kneeled before Dor. "I'm here as you bid me, Father."

I blinked, and two more Guardians appeared. They grabbed Pendula's arms as they held me. She didn't resist. She couldn't. In their hold, she was so small. So fragile.

It was my actions that had brought Pendula here, but these were *my* actions! They shouldn't involve her!

DENY CHAOS.

Gods help me.

My Guardian moved in front of Pendula.

"Quentin, please," she begged, her voice wavering.

The Guardian tore open her blouse, exposing her brassiere and silver skin. It raised a brass finger, which shaped itself into a tiny oscillating saw.

"Father, don't," I choked out.

The saw pressed into her skin below the collarbone.

Pendula screamed. Blood dripped down to her skirt as the saw carved lettering into her chest. She writhed, her screams turning into hysterical sobs.

"Stop!" I yelled. "I deny Chaos!" I strained against the Guardians holding me, but I couldn't free myself from their grasp. "Please stop!"

YOU THINK ME CRUEL, MY SON, BUT I DO WHAT MUST BE DONE TO SAVE YOUR SOUL FROM SIN. EVEN IF THAT REQUIRES ME TO TAKE A PERSONAL INTEREST IN YOUR HOURLY ACTIVITIES.

FOR EVERY DEVIANT THOUGHT, PENDULA WILL BE PUNISHED. EVERY SIN YOU COMMIT WILL BE MARKED ON HER SKIN FOR YOU TO WITNESS.

"Please, Father, that's not necessary—"

SAY WHAT I NEED YOU TO SAY.

"You're right! I despise Chaos, I despise Kayl and Jinx and the whole lot of them." I couldn't let Pendula be harmed because of me. She was my responsibility now, and I just couldn't. If it meant denying Kayl, then so be it. "I submit to you, Father. All that I am is yours."

Whatever existed between Kayl and I would die. It had to.

I knew where this would end. It was my path.

I'd deny Kayl, and she'd rip out my soul.

This was meant to be.

The Guardians released my arms, and I collapsed atop my Father's hand. Warmth flooded through my blood, melting my aches and pains away. My fingers shook as I collected my spectacles and pushed them back on.

VERY GOOD, QUENTIN. YOUR LOVE AND LOYALTY TO ME SHALL BE REWARDED. I HAVE SEEN YOUR DESIRES. YOUR DREAMS. I WILL GIFT YOU A WIFE. PENDULA WILL BE YOURS TO ENJOY.

"What?"

I stood and stared at Pendula. She, too, had collapsed in a heap and was trying to cover her bloodied chest. Dor hadn't healed the wound that spread across the full length of her collarbone, which I could clearly see, carved and raw on her chest, the word *masturbation*.

A minor sin she'd wear because of me.

YOU WILL MARRY PENDULA AND FORGET CHAOS.

Marry her? But—I barely knew Pendula! Who was to say she even wanted to be married to *me*?

THIS IS MY COMMAND.

"I'm humbled, Father." Pendula bowed her head. "I will do as you bid."

Saints upon saints.

I lifted Pendula to her feet. Her entire body trembled. I'd done this. I'd hurt her.

My future wife.

"I'm sorry," I whispered.

She forced a weak smile.

YOU HAVE THREE DAYS TO UNITE THE DOMAINS, QUENTIN. DO NOT FAIL ME.

Three days.

Father believed I could shoulder this. I needed to have faith in His plans.

He was my god. I needed to believe He would do what was right—for me, for Chime. For all our mortal souls. Even if His love for us cut.

I guided Pendula out of the room. The Guardians watched the entire way, though I didn't dare stop walking until we reached the elevator.

Ben stood waiting for us, and his eyes bulged from his sockets.

Both Pendula and I were covered in blood. We'd need to clean up before we left Kronos.

"Let's get a cup of tea," I suggested. "I'm gasping for—"

Agony flared behind my eyes, blinding me.

Had I committed another sin in desiring a simple cup of tea?

But as darkness swept over me, my reality morphed into another.

Screams rang outside.

"Oh my. What's going on?" asked one of the Glimmer patrons.

I peered through the window of Lady Mae's café. Mortals were running by in a mad panic. Wardens surrounded Central Station in blockades, though they were overrun by Glimmer coming from the Solaris crossing.

Odd. Lady Mae's was often full of Glimmer at this hour. That's why I came—to find work for those seeking a Necro's touch.

I licked my fangs. Screams didn't bother me, but something in the air tasted wrong.

The Seren server hovered over my shoulder, her wings fluttering in an annoying hum. "Is it another attack?"

The tray she carried rattled precariously, spilling tea and sugar cubes over the side.

I hastily stood and helped lower it to the table. "Calm yourself. Whatever's going on, the Wardens will have it in hand—"

"They didn't when Lady Mae was attacked!" She collapsed into a spare chair, her pastel pink skin almost as pale as mine. "They killed Lady Mae and then—"

She jumped as a teacup shattered behind us.

The café was empty. Completely empty.

A golden dress and a pair of diamond earrings lay discarded over one of the chairs where a Glimmer had been sitting. Steam still wafted from her tea.

Another red dress and apron had fallen to the floor in a heap. That had belonged to the proprietor, another Glimmer.

"Are... Oh my god. Are they dead?" *the Seren wailed.*

The screams from outside hadn't stopped.

Slowly, I rose and opened the door to Lady Mae's.

It was chaos.

Mortals from all domains were scrambling to escape the station. Clothes were scattered across the square, yet I couldn't fathom why.

And then mortals began to pop out of existence. One by one.

Glimmer. Umber. Leander. Ember.

Necro.

I examined my hands. Dust fell from my skin.

So here it was.

Death as I understood it.

"I don't want to die." Tears streamed down the Seren's face. Her wings peeled away into nothing. "Please help me. I don't want to—"

No.

Gods no.

I gathered my breath.

Pendula's hands shook my shoulder as I lay slumped against the elevator. "Quentin? Did you have a vision?"

A vision to end all visions.

No! I refused to believe it was true. It couldn't be. It couldn't!

"Sir?" Ben asked.

I reached for my fob watch and clasped it tight. My plan would work, damn it! It didn't end here. It didn't end this way. I could still protect Chime. Still save Chaos.

An odd sensation came over me.

I shuddered. "Did you feel that?"

"Feel what, sir?" Ben said.

A blip in time.

The usual tick tock had gone tick tick tock. That never happened.

Something was wrong with time.

I scrambled to my feet. "Forget the tea. We need to get back to Chime, now."

Part Three

XXVII

Chime isn't safe these days. Even with Wardens everywhere, Central has been gripped by chaos. First the attack on Central Station, then the riots, the derailed tram, and now protests.

What is the world coming to?

Honestly, I've been thinking of returning home to my domain. It's not as cosmopolitan as Chime, and I'd certainly miss the teahouses, but is a cream scone worth the risk?

—Anonymous, *overheard in Central Station*

CHAOS AWAITED US ON our return to Chime.

Not the chaos I expected, but something entirely new. Protesters gathered outside Central Station, waving placards and harassing anyone trying to slip past. The few Wardens on watch were woefully outnumbered by the mob and calling for backup.

They blocked the exit, and I was already behind schedule. We'd come back on the early ten o'clock crossing, which left me little time to head over to the embassy. Blast it! I couldn't leave this matter unattended.

Pendula peered around my shoulder. "What are they shouting about?"

The crowd was a mix of mortals. Most notably Ember and Fauna, with a few Umber. How odd. Umber weren't the protesting type.

In all my years as a Warden, I'd only encountered the occasional protest or riot. Wardens came down hard on those who disturbed the peace with such antisocial behavior. To protest was an act of civil disobedience that was unheard of. It was a subtle form of apostasy—the rejection of law.

And the battleground of choice for the Godless. Damn it, was this Kayl's doing?

"Ben, escort Miss Bezel to safety. I'll find the stationmaster."

"I should remain by your side, sir—"

"We need to contain this before a riot breaks out." I ignored Ben's warnings and approached the station entrance.

"The Covenant is a lie!" an Ember yelled. "We're not equal when we're barred from the Golden City!"

"We want work, not workhouses!" chanted a group of Fauna.

Their placards featured grotesque depictions of the Glimmer and slogans calling for their downfall. The art was intricately applied, as was the lettering. Sadly, I recognized it.

It was Vincent and Harmony's work.

I'd expected more riots over the Vesper's disappearance, but these were protesting the Glimmer's workhouses.

THIS IS THE WORK OF APOSTATES, Dor said. *IF YOU HAD DESTROYED THEM AT MY COMMAND, THESE MORTALS WOULD NOT BE SWAYED BY BLASPHEMOUS IDEALISM.*

They're protesting the workhouses, Father. They have a right to complain about unfair treatment.

WORK IS NOT MEANT TO BE PLEASANT. IT IS DESIGNED TO CREATE STRUCTURE AND DISCIPLINE, WHICH THESE MORTALS LACK. CIVIL DISOBEDIENCE SHALL NOT BE TOLERATED. THE LAW MUST BE ENFORCED.

At your command, Father.

A Diviner Warden saluted me. "Your Excellency! We've got reinforcements on the way, and the station staff are secure. What are your orders, sir?"

By donning the ambassador's tabard, I'd hoped to bring change to Chime's streets, but right now, my only purpose was to bring the rule of law. Which meant these poor sods would be incarcerated in our correctional facility and likely earn a one-way trip back to their domain. "Arrest them all."

We needed to set an example, didn't we?

On my word, Wardens marched across the square armed with batons.

"Order! Order!" they called between blowing their whistles.

The protesters didn't stand a chance.

Batons came down in force, wielded by Umber and Leander. The protesters fought back with their placards, but were soon overrun. The Umber dealt with the Ember, negating their flame, as the Leander wrestled with the Fauna, forcing them into black wagons. Those who managed to slip on by were caught by Diviner. Time fluctuated around the station in bursts of stops and starts. The telltale sign of Diviner Wardens at work.

And there, wrestling with an Umber, was Kayl, also wearing the form of an Umber.

"Get off me, you prick! I'm a pissing ambassador, for god's sake!"

Yes, that was most definitely Kayl.

The relief that flooded me made my knees weak. I almost forgot I wasn't meant to feel anything at all, for I was betrothed now, and that meant my actions—my very thoughts—could hurt my future wife. Physically, at that.

Our partnership was merely business, and whatever relief I felt was for the task at hand. I caught the Umber Warden before he could throw Kayl inside a wagon. "Stop—she's with me."

"But, sir, she's a blasphemer. Orders are to arrest—"

"I'll deal with it."

Kayl yanked her arm free from the Warden's hold. "They've arrested Dru! If they've hurt her, you can bet your arse you won't hear the last of it."

I didn't spot Dru among the crowds. The Wardens had likely already shoved her into a wagon. "I'll get Ben to release her, don't panic." I steered Kayl away from the crowd.

In the space of only ten minutes, the square had been cleared, leaving only abandoned placards and gawking onlookers.

"Why are you arresting them?" Kayl demanded once we'd sought a private area of the station free of public traffic. The blue and pink petals of her brow were quivering on end.

"I should ask why you're arranging a protest when I explicitly asked you to stop hindering my plans?"

"Why do you assume this is my doing? We only just arrived here—"

"You just happened to be caught cavorting in the middle of a protest?"

"Gods, Quen! We were making our way to the embassy for *your* pissing meeting. I had no idea a protest was going down—"

"Those placards were Vincent's art. I'd recognize the style anywhere."

"What do you want me to say? This isn't our doing. Clearly Chime's citizens are fed up with the Glimmer, and can you blame them? What are you going to do with them?"

"They'll be taken to HQ. Is Jinx secure? I assumed you had no trouble. Did you?"

"Don't change the subject. What will you do with them? Throw them into a correctional facility? Send them back to their domain?"

"I need to know if Jinx was involved in this—"

"The collar worked. Jinx won't be bothering us anymore."

"Where is she?"

"Safe. *Well?*"

I wished she'd elaborate on what she defined as 'safe,' but I clearly wasn't going to get the answers I sought. Since returning from Kronos, I hadn't noticed any other strange blips in time, yet I knew I'd sensed something odd. Something to do with Kayl and Jinx.

Only Chaos could have such an adverse effect on time.

"You know the Warden response to apostates."

Kayl looked as though she was about to clobber me. "For god's sake! They're protestors, not apostates! As Chime is Corentine's domain, I should have a greater say in what laws are implemented. And I say release them."

I sucked in an exasperated breath. "We don't have time to debate this now. We're late for the Council—"

"Fine. We'll debate it there."

CHAOS SHALL NOT BE GRANTED A VOICE IN CHIME'S AFFAIRS.

I understand, Father. They'll be denied.

SEE TO IT.

Saints. As if I didn't have enough to contend with.

As soon as we arrived at the embassy, I arranged for Ben to locate and release Dru while Pendula headed over to my office to begin the paperwork needed to process our newly incarcerated mortals. Meanwhile, Kayl and I were unfashionably late.

We had enough time to don our tabards and for Kayl to switch from an Umber to a Diviner persona, which would work better for the Council.

Female Diviner were so rare, and yet I was going to marry one. Allegedly. Would Kayl kill me before or after my wedding ceremony?

Unfortunately, or rather fortunately, Pendula had accepted the match. We still barely knew each other, an oversight I planned to rectify. Arranged marriages weren't uncommon between Diviner, though I'd never thought it would happen to me.

Who would want to marry the Dark Warden? Even Elijah had hidden our relationship from the public eye. Ambassador Corinth, however? Yes, that had a different ring to it. I'm sure the busybodies back on Kronos would be delighted by the news.

Alas, I had more important things to concern myself with than my impending nuptials. I'd have to inform Kayl of my betrothal at some point. I would. But I needed her charm to work its magic today.

The ambassadors sat waiting inside the Council chamber, gossiping and drinking either tea, coffee, or fruit juice. Dandelion offered me a nod in greeting. Erosain offered me a glare, which soon switched to Kayl as she sat next to him.

Only one ambassador was missing; Ms. Hazelhearth, ambassador to the Umber. Presumably she'd been called to deal with her incarcerated mortals. Likely a rare event for her.

Thankfully, the one ambassador I hoped to catch unawares was in attendance. The Amnae ambassador, Aberforth, met my gaze with a cordial smile.

We'd be having words over Kayl's slight memory problem later. But for now, I had a meeting to run. I took my place at the head of the table, and the chatter died down.

Our Seren secretary dressed in blue with a short boyish hairstyle that resembled mine. It was his way of displaying his chosen gender for the day.

Sonata rapped his pen across the table. "May we begin?" He spoke with a masculine voice. "The time, Chairman?"

"Ten thirty, Secretary."

Sonata began the arduous process of note-taking. "This meeting was called by Ambassador Corinth and Ambassador Arkey at the time of ten thirty. Today's agenda is in regards to Ambassador Corinth's proposals concerning Chime's future—"

"I'd like to add an item to the agenda," Gloria said. "Regarding the unseemly rabble shouting outside Central Station this morn."

Wonderful. We'd be debating the protest, then. If only I could pause time and sneak out during it.

Sonata scribbled the amendment down. "Noted. You may begin, Chairman."

I cleared my throat. "Thank you all for your time attending this meeting. As you're aware, work is underway to shift the balance of power in Chime. This change may result in some disruption to Central Station and crossing traffic, but is necessary to ensure Chime's future. As of this morning, I have the support of four domains." A woeful amount, I'd admit. "I cannot wait any longer. I ask the rest of you to consider your position and speak with your gods."

"Zyclone is willing to lend their assistance," Ambassador Corvus announced. "So long as our engineers are involved in any maintenance regarding the clock tower."

"Granted." No doubt we'd need the Zephyr's expertise when it came to removing Corentine. "You'll be kept informed."

Corvus nodded his thanks.

"Chairman, if you don't mind, I have a question," asked the Necro ambassador, Morana.

"Go ahead."

She adjusted the veil covering her face. "I've brought this matter to The Nameless One, but they have no interest in Chime's affairs, or indeed anything outside their own purview. What will happen to the Necro in this instance?"

"I, too, would like to know," added the Fauna ambassador, Willow. A tall, lithe woman with soft brown skin and the antlers of a deer. "Mortals do not concern Faen."

I was afraid this might happen. While some gods held an interest in Chime's governance and the affairs of their own mortals, others did not. Mortal matters were beneath them. And it made it so much easier for other domains to exploit their mortals.

Technically, Chime only required one god to power it. But I'd promised Dor I would unite the gods under his rule. Not to mention, I needed the Glimmer to bite.

"Surely there must be some way to bargain with both The Nameless One and Faen?" I said. "If it's within my power to grant, I will do so."

"And if there isn't?" Morana asked.

I didn't want to resort to threats, but time was not on my side. "Then we'd need to reevaluate their position in the Covenant."

Morana sat up. "Chime needs Necro. Without us, passport applications would come to a standstill."

"Necro make the process quicker, but their skills aren't entirely necessary. I suggest you speak with The Nameless One again—"

"You cannot shut us out! You don't have that power—"

"On Dor's authority, I do."

The ambassadors exchanged unpleasant muttering.

When it came down to it, they knew where they stood, as did I.

Underneath time's fist.

"Oh, listen to yourselves," Gloria said. "You're willing to bow under Dor when he continues to keep us in the dark! Ambassador Arkey swore to deal with her mortals, and yet they are still terrorizing innocent citizens—"

"Chaos is under control. Wardens continue to patrol Central's streets—"

"Under control, is it? Then how do you explain the dead Glimmer who turned up inside a Diviner watchmaker's? Killed by Chaos, and yet you failed to inform me. What else are you hiding from the Council, Chairman?"

How could she have possibly learned that? Souls taken by Chaos didn't return to their gods to tattle. Either the dead Glimmer had been important enough to warrant investigation when missing, or someone had leaked the information.

The former was plausible. The latter was a headache.

"Is this true, Quentin?" Erosain asked with mock shock. "Perhaps we should be limiting our passport applications into Chime while this threat exists." He deliberately shuffled his seat away from Kayl.

Trust him to stick the knife in.

Kayl leaned over the table. "There was an incident. I dealt with it."

"*You* dealt with it?" Gloria said. "It was your *creature* that murdered one of my own domain!"

"That creature, as you call her, has been imprisoned—"

"And why am I only hearing of this now? What justice will it face?"

"*She* is a mortal—"

"Apologies, Ambassador Gloria," I quickly interjected. "The incident took place only yesterday. I should have informed your office sooner, but my priority was securing Central and apprehending the suspect. With that satisfied, I offer my deepest condolences for your loss."

Gloria shook her head. "I'm not satisfied. It seems awfully convenient to me that this threat of Chaos has us all at Dor's beck and call. And yet the pair of you are such *close* allies." She glanced between me and Kayl with a knowing look.

Whatever Gloria implied did *not* exist.

Kayl was examining her nails. "You wouldn't know what it means to have allies, Gloria."

Dandelion roared a laugh. "Don't act so sore because the other domains are encroaching on your space."

"Irrelevant," Gloria snapped. "Gildola cares for her daughters, and she knows any bargain made with Chaos is a fool's bargain. Don't you understand yet? Chaos is sin incarnate. It's no coincidence that talk of apostasy and blasphemy has increased these past few weeks. First, the attack on Central Station. Then the failed memorial. And now protestors are disrupting Gate traffic!"

Ah. There we went. I poured myself a glass of water.

The maddening reality of time was that moments like these stretched for an eternity.

I understood Kayl's objections. And I understood why mortals saw fit to protest. Their ambassadors were bureaucrats, unused to dealing with rowdy Central and Undercity citizens. They needed to hear what the mortals of Chime had to say.

But mere words weren't going to make their lives any easier.

"They were protesting *your* workhouses," Kayl said.

"Why would they? They should be proud to serve our workhouses. For their toil, we gift them shelter and food. Without our generosity, such mortals would only resort to thievery or prostitution—"

"When a mortal has no choice between starvation or a workhouse, then thievery and prostitution become an honest option—"

"An honest option?" Gloria scoffed. "My domain seeks to purify mortals of their sins in line with the Covenant, and yet we allow degenerates onto this Council who undermine it. Mortals understood their place before Chaos polluted Chime's streets—"

"Oh, give over! Admit you're pissed off because there's no Vesper to fill your damn workhouses."

"The loss of the Vesper is bittersweet, I'll concede. Chime will be better off without their pilfering fingers, but they did make obedient workers. Ember and Fauna are too volatile. Though at least the Umber appreciate the ethics of honest work."

"The Ember are not yours," Erosain said with a scowl.

"Neither are the Fauna," added Willow.

"Your mortals go against the Covenant." Gloria sneered. "Quite why Dor lets them run rampant across Chime, I don't understand. Under his rule, Chaos has reigned—"

"That's enough," I said. Gloria's words were bordering on offense.

"You wanted an answer, Chairman. Gildola has answered. So long as Chaos remains free—" She turned her nose up at Kayl. "Then we shall refuse to bargain."

An ultimatum. I did so hate those.

Concessions would have to be made to accommodate the change in Chime's leadership, but these changes came at the Glimmer's expense. Truth was, Chime didn't need them. There were plenty of domains vying for their spot in the Golden City.

They had little to gamble with, yet they remained as arrogant as ever.

I was more than willing to let them fall.

Based on the smirk stretching across Kayl's lips, I assumed she thought the same. "The Covenant is supposed to serve all mortals, not just yours," she said. "That includes the Ember, the Fauna, and yes, my own. If they see fit to protest your workhouses, then you're failing them—and the Covenant. If you don't like that, then you can catch the next crossing out."

Dandelion roared another laugh. The other ambassadors shared jeers of astonishment and outrage.

"Order!" Sonata rapped his pen against a cup. "If you're done, Ambassador Gloria, I'd like to return to Ambassador Corinth's proposal on behalf of my domain. Serenity extends an invitation to Chaos and yourself, Chairman. Though Serenity also requests a personal gift."

"Of course," I said. "Name it."

"Thirteen years ago, Serenity banished a Seren from Arcadia. A woman by the name of Harmony Arabesque. I believe you've made her acquaintance."

Unease pooled in my stomach. I glanced at Kayl, who tensed.

I rubbed sweaty palms on my knees. "What do you need from Miss Arabesque?"

"Serenity punished this mortal by removing one of her wings. They desire the other wing for their collection, and extend an invitation to Miss Arabesque—"

Kayl slammed her hands on the table. "No."

Sonata looked taken aback. "Well, I never! There's no need to be so rude—"

"This is my polite face." Kayl gave an exaggerated smile. "And I'm telling you no."

"This is Serenity's demand. If you do not offer it, then we cannot bargain—"

"I'll offer Serenity my arse so they can kiss it."

Sonata stared as shocked gasps tittered around the room.

"You see?" Gloria drawled. "This is what you get when you negotiate with Chaos."

"You can line up and kiss my arse next if you like."

"That's quite enough," I said with a firm voice before the entire chamber erupted. "We'll discuss Serenity's terms and get back to you."

Sonata bowed his head.

Kayl simmered with a look that suggested this was nonnegotiable. And truly, I wished it were, but time was running out.

"As for those who have yet to make an agreement—" My gaze lingered on Morana, Willow, and Gloria. "You have until the end of this week. I can be contacted at my office. Unless there are any other points of interest, this meeting is adjourned."

The ambassadors finished their drinks and began shuffling out of the chamber.

Kayl stomped to my side and grabbed my wrist. "We are *not* asking Harmony to do this," she hissed.

"We'll discuss it outside," I whispered. "Go find Ben and Dru. I need a moment."

She stomped past me and slammed the chamber door behind her.

"Aberforth," I called before he could slink off. "May I speak with you for a moment?"

The Amnae ambassador lingered by the door until we were alone. "What's this about?"

I stepped until there was a pistol-drawing space between us, though luckily for him, I drew a breath instead of my weapon. "Kayl is missing memories. Would you happen to know anything about that?"

He leaned against the edge of the table, over his own domain. "Mortals come to Memoria all the time to remove memories. It's not something we police."

"These are personal and important memories. She wouldn't have removed them willingly."

"Personal memories are often the hardest—"

"Don't waste my time. I know Anima took them from her."

His slitted eyes narrowed. "And you want them back? What a shame. Your Chaos whore gave them willingly in exchange for our cooperation—"

"Show her some respect—"

"If you want these precious memories returned, then our deal is off."

I clenched my fists behind my back.

These were her memories. The love of her life.

Could I really sacrifice them? I knew she hadn't given them willingly. She would never. Not even her part in Valeria's end, though truthfully, to forget that was a mercy.

Once again, I'd failed Malkavaan. In life and in death.

"You are an utter bastard," I seethed.

"You would know all about removing hard memories, wouldn't you, Corinth?"

"I don't know what you're talking about—"

"Do you think Anima perused only the one memory? They found some *very* interesting memories inside your friend's mind."

Saints.

Anima could have seen anything within Kayl's subconscious.

Anything regarding myself or the Godless.

Aberforth leaned close. "I know Dor broke the Covenant. Anima saw you die through your friend's memories. She screamed for you, you know. There was such sorrow. Such mourning and sleepless nights as she cried over your death, and yet here you stand. Curious."

Kayl...

She cared for me that much?

"I know what you feel for her," he whispered, twisting the metaphorical knife. "And what she feels for you. If you'd like those memories to remain private, then you'll go about your business." He slapped me on the shoulder and headed for the door.

I had to reiterate; he was an utter bastard.

It took one to know one.

YOU ALLOWED ANIMA TO TAKE THOSE MEMORIES! Dor yelled inside my mind. *YOU HAVE GIVEN THEM AN ADVANTAGE.*

I cringed at His fury. *Anima is still on your side, Father.* Likely waiting to see where the cards would fall next.

CHAOS CONTINUES TO JEOPARDIZE YOUR MISSION. BRING IT UNDER CONTROL.

It's in my hands.

I stepped outside the Council chamber to another headache. The Umber ambassador had turned up, and was now arguing with Kayl.

Where was my bodyguard to protect me from damnable politics?

"Master Corinth." Hazelhearth greeted me with an irritated expression. "Can you explain why I've spent the past half hour arguing with your Wardens?" Her skin was that of dark brown bark, resembling a tree more than the stone of her domain. Twisting branches grew from her head in place of hair and sprouted green leaves, and on her brow were a line of red buds with yellow petals, which quivered with her mood. Dressed in business attire, she cut a classy, if stern, figure.

"Apologies, my lady. I sent Warden Ben Seasons to explain the situation. A number of mortals were engaged in a protest at Central Station—"

"Who we are happy to release," Kayl said, her voice strained.

Hazelhearth frowned. "Which I cannot fathom. If my mortals involved themselves in public disobedience, then they must be reminded of the consequences. What confuses me is why you *asked* for their release. What is your relationship with them?" she asked Kayl. "Why does the ambassador of Chaos employ an Umber?"

"Because Chaos can be somewhat disorganized, and who is more organized than an Umber? Dru's my friend," Kayl hastily added. "We've known each other for years."

"I find that hard to believe. I'm well acquainted with the Smith family on Heartstone. They wouldn't approve of such an arrangement."

"Fortunately, the Covenant covers free will—"

"Druzy Smith owes her allegiance to Unghard. Not Corentine."

The two of them stared daggers at each other.

Saints, I needed a cup of tea. I'd even stomach coffee at this point. "Has Unghard given my proposal much thought?"

"Unghard is with you," Hazelhearth confirmed to my great surprise. I'd been expecting a battle over Kayl's choice of bodyguard. "They understand the personal sacrifice required to maintain a city such as Chime. Therefore, it is our duty to serve Chime's citizens and ensure our roots remain strong."

I bowed my head. "Thank you. Unghard has my gratitude—"

"As it is every Umber's duty to serve Unghard." Her pointed look turned to Kayl.

Making Kayl take on a Diviner persona instead of an Umber one was meant to avoid awkwardness such as this! That had worked out well. "If you don't mind, my lady, Ambassador Arkey and I must return to our duties. We're running behind schedule."

"Not at all."

"Well?" Kayl demanded once Hazelhearth was out of earshot. "Have you reconsidered the Seren's proposal, or do I need to start a riot for real?"

I shoved my hands into my pockets and braced myself for another argument. "I don't like it either, but we must find some way to appease Serenity." The Glimmer were troublesome, but having the Seren for an enemy would be far worse, given their ability to manipulate via song. Serenity was also far more unpredictable in their schemes.

"Then we find something else. Anything else! I'm not putting Harmony through that."

"We have little time to find something else. Three days, to be precise."

"What?" She gawked. "You're saying we only have *three* pissing days to convince the rest of the gods to go along with your mad scheme? Or else what?"

"Or else Dor will deal with Corentine in his own way."

"Shit. When were you planning on telling me this?"

"I'm telling you now."

"You are ridiculous." She shook her head. "Are you at least going to release those protesters? You know they did nothing wrong."

"That's up to each domain's ambassador. Though if the Godless hadn't instigated this protest in the first place—"

"*Quen—*"

"Everything good, sir?" called Ben from down the hall. He walked alongside Dru, whose worried expression moved from Kayl's scowl to my undoubtedly exhausted-looking face. Diviner aged slowly, but I'd aged a decade in that meeting, I was sure.

At least Dru didn't look any the worse for wear for her arrest and brief respite in a Warden-sanctioned cell.

Respite I'd be glad for after these next three days.

I forced a smile. "Time will tell."

28

*The gods don't ask much of their mortals. They birth us, raise us, gift us free
will and the ability to enjoy mortal existence. All they ask for in return is
our devotion. We can show our love through prayer and worship. By
offering tributes and tithes.
Of all the beings in the universe, the gods created you. You.
The least you can do in return is thank them.*
—Ambassador Gloria, *The Golden Doctrine*

DESPITE MY TWIN BEING locked underneath the Mesmer temple, I couldn't
bring myself to go check up on her.

Instead, I found Sinder.

He sat at reception with his feet on the counter, filing his horns. Dru
and I had come straight from the embassy, still annoyed by the protest and
Quen's reaction to it. Gods, this morning had left me utterly frustrated.

My feelings for Quen blew hot and cold. Since our return from
Rapture, I couldn't keep myself from watching him. Every time I looked
up, his silver eyes were on me, and I could sense a ripple of aether in the air.
Like we shared a connection no one else could see.

And then he'd gone and told me we only had three days to save Chaos!

Not only that, but he *wanted* me to speak with Harmony and convince
her to give up her wing. We'd briefly argued over it, and he promised to
convince the Seren ambassador to reconsider, but then—*three* pissing days!

The man absolutely infuriated me.

There was no way I could ask Harmony. I couldn't.

"You look troubled, darling," Sinder said as I leaned over the counter
and swiped a toffee from the candy bowl. "What's bothering you?"

"Oh, only the fate of every domain and their thousands of mortals."

"Only that? I thought it might be something serious, like a chipped nail."

I snorted and shoved the toffee in my mouth. If only. "Is Harm free? I need to speak with her."

Sinder's expression turned sour. "She's with Joe. I'll come with, just in case today's the day Joe decides to betray and murder us all."

"I'll stay on watch," Dru sighed. "I'm not getting involved in another argument."

There really was no end to the joys of this day, was there?

Dru took Sinder's place and dug into the candy bowl, looking for the jawbreakers. She'd been quiet since we left the embassy, though I wasn't sure if it was due to Ben, being locked inside a correctional facility for a hot minute, or the hard-faced Umber ambassador.

I hoped choosing Dru as my bodyguard wouldn't come back to bite me in the arse. That ambassador, Hazelbreath or whatever, looked like she had a branch growing from her behind that flowered whenever she needed to fuck over some poor mortal.

The only thing worse than a god was their damn ambassador.

Sinder and I headed into the main temple. There was much I wanted to ask—about Vincent, and this pissing protest—but something else come out of my mouth. "Do you remember Malkavaan?"

He gave me an odd look. "I know the Mesmer have been a strain, but it's only been a month, dearest."

A month? I knew this Malkavaan a month ago? I chose my next words carefully. "I miss him."

Sinder wrapped his arm around my shoulder. "We all do."

"Your Vesper lover."

I shook away the darkness clouding my thoughts. "Have you checked up on Jinx?"

"She's awake and none too pleased. Between her, Joe, and the gods themselves, I'm not sure who will kill us first."

"You still don't trust Joe?"

"What reason do I have to? He's infiltrated our temple rather successfully, yet none of you can see that. Harm practically dotes on him."

She did? Harmony wasn't the doting type. "Worry more about Jinx. She's crafty."

"Believe me, I know, darling. She's asking after you. She says that collar hurts."

Shit. "She's lying. Quen told me it shouldn't. I'll go check in on her at some point." I supposed I had to, even if every conversation with her frustrated me as much as Quen.

We entered the red room, where Harmony and Joe were poring over documents scattered across the table, an aether lamp lighting them both.

"Have a productive meeting?" Harmony asked, setting aside a file.

I slid into a chair. "If you can call drinking tea with a bunch of tight-arsed ambassadors productive, then sure. Quen has politely informed me we have three days left to convince the gods to side with him, otherwise Dor is going to take matters into his own hands." Which likely meant the death of Corentine, Jinx, and all Chaos creatures.

And me. Though if it came down to it, I wasn't going to go out quietly. Karendar had tried to split my soul once. I'd be damned if the Wardens got another chance.

"Fuck," Harmony muttered. "What gods are left?"

"The fun ones, of course. Faen, Gildola, The Namelesss One... Oh, and Serenity."

"Serenity? I'd have thought they'd not want to risk their position in Chime. They're one of the few gods who encourage their mortals to rise within high society. Did Sonata mention why they're hesitating?"

I shifted uncomfortably in my chair. This was a touchy subject I wanted to discuss privately with Harm. "They're asking for a tribute. One I'm hoping you can advise on. But first, I need to ask; were you behind the protest at Central Station today?"

"There was a protest?" Harmony asked with mock innocence.

"Did you forget we're supposed to be keeping a low profile? Quen's not pleased—"

"Corinth has no reason to get pissy. We didn't plan this operation. We merely provided the means for mortals to organize themselves—"

"Wardens rounded most of them up and sent them off to a correctional facility. Dru was arrested with them. She's lucky Quen got her out—"

"They were arrested?" Joe asked, alarm in his voice.

"Of course they were. Did any of you expect otherwise?"

"Then this is my fault." Joe ran a hand down his golden face. "It was my idea."

"Yours?"

Harmony picked up one of the scattered papers. It was some sort of employee log. "Joe has been kindly sharing his knowledge of the Glimmer workhouses. With his help, we may be able to shut them down for good."

I sat up. "How?"

Joe glanced at Harmony, who nodded. "You know I worked with Ambassador Gloria's staff. I've shared what intel I have, and I'd like to do more. While I can't exactly return dressed like this, I was there when the Vesper vanished. I know they're struggling to fill their workhouses. They don't have enough workers to maintain their contracts."

"Such a shame," Sinder said. "Who will staff them now? Umber?"

"Umber are an obvious choice, but that's not how Gloria likes to work. She sees herself as the holy messenger of Gildola, sent to Chime to rid the sinners of their sin. That is why they preyed upon the Vesper, and why they now turn to Fauna and Ember. And why I reached out to them—to encourage them to push back."

Sinder's nostrils flared. This was dangerous ground. "You're playing with Ember lives. Those of us trapped inside the workhouses had no choice! You say you worked on Gloria's staff. Did you work in her workhouse? Did you hold a whip? Swing one?"

Joe looked taken aback. "No. Never. That wasn't my role—"

"Then what *was* your role? We've been fighting to get these workhouses shut down for years, and you conveniently turn up when your golden whore tosses you out—"

"*I* left *them*," Joe seethed. "I want nothing to do with that hateful bitch—"

"You're just another male full of anger."

"I have a right to my anger."

"You both have a right to your anger," I interrupted, before the two of them started flinging fire at each other. "And we all want these workhouses gone. How can we make that happen?"

Joe straightened his collar. "With you. Harmony informed me of your and Ambassador Corinth's plans to strip the Glimmer of power—"

"We're sharing our secret plans now?" Sinder asked.

Harmony waved him off. "If Gildola is forced to share power with the remaining domains, then that means the Glimmer stand to lose the most. Which means you'll have bargaining power, girl. Don't you see? You can pressure them into giving up their workhouses in exchange for a larger cut of Chime."

"You *want* to give them more power?" Sinder said, aghast. He crossed his arms and huffed out a ring of smoke. "I thought the whole point of this venture was to share power across the domains, not give the Glimmer extra—"

"The Glimmer will still lose out to the other gods. But not all of them will care enough about Chime to want a cut. I'm willing to bet neither Faen or The Nameless One will bother themselves. That's two domains' worth of power. And if Serenity also refuses, then that's three. This is leverage we can use."

Harmony made a good point. If Serenity refused to negotiate, then they'd only lose out, and the Glimmer would happily take their place—the Seren held a chunk of Chime's businesses as well as their art galleries.

The Leander were sniffing for more power, too. Perhaps this could encourage Lionheart to release the Lioness.

Would Quen agree? He wanted the workhouses gone as much as I did. Though I couldn't help but remember Edana's request.

Chime would be better off without the Glimmer.

But that didn't mean I wanted to murder them.

"Why not let the Glimmer fall?" Sinder said. "Let them get fucked over by their own hubris."

"Because," Joe began. "We've established that the Glimmer will take advantage of the Fauna at the very least. They won't give up their grip on the Golden City easily."

"Sounds to me like you don't want your former masters to fall. Even the lowliest Glimmer still benefits from being one."

"Sinder," Harmony warned.

Joe didn't take the bait. Instead, he tugged on his sleeves, straightening them. "You've every reason not to trust me. I won't waste my breath trying to convince you otherwise. Just know that the workhouses on Chime aren't the only ones the Glimmer operate. Yes, they prey on Ember and Fauna, but they force their own mortals into servitude back on Solaris. I came from one of those workhouses. I want them gone." A flash of sunlight shone in Joe's eyes. "I want to hit Gloria where it hurts."

Sinder opened his mouth and shut it again with a scowl.

I didn't think any mortal could render him speechless. The two of them had so much in common; they could be friends if Sinder stopped being so damn stubborn.

"I'll speak with Quen, but no promises," I said, attempting to salvage this meeting. "You have to stop arranging these protests. I hate to say it, but the Warden Council is the only way we'll make change."

"I want to believe that," Harmony said. "But I can't stop Chime's citizens from protesting off their own bat. They want to make their feelings known, and through their voice, the Council will listen. These workhouses *will* come to an end, one way or another."

"If they're arrested, there isn't much I can do to help them."

"We'll get some fliers out and warn them of the dangers. The last thing I want is more mortals being locked away by Wardens."

"I'm willing to assist in whatever capacity I can," Joe said with genuine eagerness. "Please, leave it to me."

That was as good a compromise as any. None of us wanted to dictate what mortals did with their lives, and if they wanted to risk theirs to have a say, then it wasn't my place to tell them otherwise.

YOU WOULD GIVE A VOICE TO CHIME'S MORTALS, BUT NOT TO ME?

I'm giving a voice to your *mortals. When the gods stop acting like pricks, then maybe I'll listen to them.*

Corentine's laughter echoed in my mind.

Harmony shuffled her papers into a pile. "Then we're done here, but Kayl? Can you help me fix the printer? Damn thing's jammed."

I smiled. "Like old times."

My method for fixing the printer was to kick and swear at it until it worked. I'm sure there were more technical ways of fixing it, but my method hadn't failed me yet. I joined Harmony in the little storage room the Mesmer had lent us for printing fliers.

The printer was a rusty old thing powered by a small aether generator. Gods know where Reverie had gotten it from. Beside it were piles of printed fliers and Vincent's art supplies. I picked up one of the fliers. It was covered in painted doodles of Vincent.

"That's quite a likeness."

"The Mesmer keep breaking in," Harmony said. "I lock the room, but they somehow get their hands on my ink. I might as well let them. It's not like we're printing much." She sat on a stack of fliers.

I gave her a shrewd look. "Is the printer actually broken, or did you bring me here for ulterior reasons?"

She clasped her hands in her lap. "You said Serenity wanted a tribute. Spit it out."

Gods. How could I say it? Plainly, I supposed. It was shit either way. "Serenity wants your spare wing for their collection."

Harmony's mouth formed a tight line, and her single wing quivered.

I leaned against the wall. "It doesn't matter. I told Quen and Ambassador What's-Their-Face no. It's not happening. Serenity will have to find something else to appease their ego."

"Honestly, I'm surprised Serenity remembered me. They often forget about their mortals, and it has been years since they exiled me from Arcadia."

When Harmony came to Grayford all those years ago, she'd told us her story—that Serenity had murdered her lover and taken her own wing as punishment by association. We didn't question it, though she avoided talking about her past. From the moment I first met her, I trusted her, and she'd given us no reason to ever doubt that trust.

"I've heard of mortals being exiled from Chime, but never *to* Chime," I said carefully. Like Sinder, the past was likely a sore subject. It wasn't my business to pry.

"It was one of Serenity's unique punishments. To cut me off from my home, my family and friends, my community. What makes me Seren. Taking my extra wing is another aspect of that." She drew in a deep breath. "I'll do it."

What? "No, Harm—"

"It's my choice, and I'll do it." Her diamond pupils were sharp with defiance.

"But why? We have a plan—"

"Sinder's right. Do we really want to give the Glimmer power when we can fuck them over for good? You've got three days, and that isn't enough time to appease Serenity. Besides, I'll not let the Seren suffer because of one god's ego."

"They threw you out of Arcadia."

"That doesn't mean I want revenge, girl."

"Isn't that why you joined the Godless?"

Harmony pulled out one of her fliers and stared at it with a mournful yearning. "Do you know why I joined the Godless? To fight inequality wherever I saw it, and I saw it plenty. We've done good work, you and I. But for every mortal we've protected from their god, dozens more have shunned us. Not all mortals want to be saved."

"Then they're idiots."

"No, they're trapped in a system they can't escape from. We all are. The only ones who escaped were Malk and Reve. That's our choice. Slavery or non-existence."

A shudder ran through me at the mention of Malkavaan's name. At what his freedom had cost. "You sound like you're giving up."

"Maybe I am, girl. Maybe I am. You're helping the gods gain more control over Chime, and that's not going to be a good thing, long term. They'll have more control over their mortals. The Wardens already have Central in their grasp—"

"Quen's in charge of the Wardens—"

"He still reports to his god. I know you won't accept it, but Corinth is a liability. Always has been."

She was right, I didn't accept it. "Quen has always been on our side." Even when he didn't remember.

Harmony shook her head. "I'm worried for you. For what'll happen when Chaos is exiled from Chime, and what'll happen if it's not."

"You don't have to worry."

"I don't have to write smut, and yet I'm compelled to."

I swallowed a lump in my throat. Really, I chose not to dwell on the consequences, because if Quen and I failed, then... Bye-bye, soul.

AND IF YOU SUCCEED, I WILL BE EXILED FROM CHIME AND FORCED INTO A NEW CAGE. AS WILL YOU.

Stop bothering me, I'm having a conversation! "Here's a thought; why don't I turn into a Seren and give up one of my wings? It's not like I'm using them." The Seren form wasn't exactly my favorite.

"Serenity will know the difference. We all have to make sacrifices, and if they want my wing, they can damn well have it. They'd be doing me a favor. You know how hard it is to get around with only one wing? My entire balance has been ruined for years!" She chuckled, but there was no happiness or warmth in it.

I still didn't like this. "I'm not taking you to Arcadia. If we do this, then we'll get Vincent to remove it and I'll deliver it myself." There was no chance I'd let Serenity get their hands on her.

Harmony hopped off her tower of fliers. "Then let's get this over with."

Gods. I didn't think I'd be spending today cutting off Harmony's remaining wing.

Damn Serenity for putting me in this position.

And damn Quen for going along with it.

Harmony strode to Vincent's little clinic with purpose. As usual, the Mesmer trio were loitering outside, listening with unusually rapt attention as Vincent read through some medical book.

Upon seeing us, he snapped the book shut. "We'll continue another time. It looks like I have a patient."

The trio whined. "But it was getting interesting!"

One of them turned to me with a giddy grin. "We're learning about insomnia."

"I think I have it," said another.

Really? A Mesmer with insomnia? "You can have him back later, promise. Why don't you go give Dru some company at reception?"

"Not Dru," another whined. Celeste, I think. "She tells me off for eating too many toffees."

"She makes me brush my teeth."

"And she tells *me* off for getting wrappers under the bed."

I hid a smile. Dru was exactly what these Mesmer needed. "You should listen to her. She knows what's best for you. Off you go."

"Yes, Mama," they said in unison, and then meandered down the hall in a sulk. One of them whistled, and a clockwork bird flew to their shoulder.

Hadn't I seen that clockwork toy before?

"Mama?" Harmony asked.

I shrugged. "Your guess is as good as mine." Speaking with Mesmer was like being the butt of an inside joke you knew nothing about.

Vincent placed his book on a shelf and waved us in. "What can I do for you both?"

Harmony straightened. "I want you to remove my wing."

Vincent blinked. "I'm sorry?"

We explained the situation. Vincent's brow was furrowed with the polite restraint of a doctor listening to the maddening ramblings of his patient, though his pale face looked haggard with an exhaustion I felt too well.

"Well? Can you do it?" Harmony demanded.

"I... can," he said slowly. "It won't hurt, but it may be disorientating for a while. Are you certain this is what you want?"

"It's about time I did it. Living with one wing isn't that convenient."

"As you wish. I'll need you to take off your blouse and bra and lay on your stomach. The procedure itself won't take long."

"Shall I go?" I asked, my foot halfway out of the door. "I could fetch Joe—"

"No," Harmony said. "Only you, if you don't mind."

"I'm with you, Harm."

I helped her get undressed and onto Vincent's medical bed. Harmony shuffled into a comfortable position and held out her hand for me.

"I'll turn into a Seren," I whispered.

"It'll be nice to have the company of a Seren who doesn't scorn me."

There was a sadness in Harmony's eyes that caught in my throat. I took her hand and shrank as my persona changed from Umber to Seren. Wings sprouted from my back, though these weren't large enough to rip through my blouse. I took a moment to shrug it off and let them loose.

Vincent fetched a footstool for me so Harmony and I would be at eye level.

Harmony's gaze wandered to my wings, and then back to me. "You make a pretty Seren."

"Are you coming on to me?"

She laughed. "You're too young for me, girl."

"What about Joe?" I teased.

"He's nice to look at, I'll give him that. But I swore off dating years ago."

"Why? You're a class act, Harm."

"Besides being the leader of an underground organization? Seren don't date outside our domain. It's too awkward, given the size difference. And any non-Seren who seek us out usually do so because they're perverts."

"There's no other Seren you could date?" Many of them congregated in Sinner's Row and even Rapture. They weren't as pious as the Glimmer, that's for sure.

"Serenity didn't just throw me out of Arcadia. They forbade all Seren from speaking or interacting with me ever again. I'm a curse, as far as they're concerned. A non-Seren."

I squeezed her hand. "I'm sorry. They don't deserve you."

"Sometimes I wonder if it was worth it. I had it all, once." Her voice turned wistful. "A penthouse in Windsong. A mansion back home on Arcadia with my family. A career that made use of my degree. And then... she entered my life. You remind me of her."

"Your lover?" Harmony never spoke about the mystery woman. "Tell me about her."

She drew in a deep breath. "Monica. That was her name. She was so full of life. She used to drag me to the opera and art galleries even if I wanted to stay at home and read. Every day was something new with her. I still remember the first time we kissed. We'd come out of the theater from watching a Seren ballet and sat on a fountain, soaking in the sun. She looked so dazzling; I knew then that there'd be nobody else for me." Harmony sighed. "They used to call us 'Harmonica' because we were always together."

"She sounds lovely. I wish I could have met her."

"You would have liked her. Monica had an opinion on everything, and she... She made the mistake of airing her opinions. They accused her of blasphemy. Of disrespecting Serenity. It was such a stupid, *stupid* thing. A bloody poem. It was all because of a stupid bloody poem. And I... I watched when Serenity tore her apart. I cried and screamed, and so... Serenity ripped off one of my wings for daring to express emotion." Her wing fluttered, sending a light breeze over my face. "For years, I was so angry. I wanted revenge. I blamed Serenity, but... Monica was fucking stupid."

Gods. The words spat from Harmony with bitter regret, as though this was a confession she'd never been able to admit until now. "It wasn't her fault or yours."

"I joined the Godless because her death still cut me raw. Because I woke at night, dreaming of Serenity pinning me down and pulling out my wing with deliberate slowness so it would hurt more. I wanted to know if a god could suffer what I had. But that was never going to happen, was it?"

"One day, it will."

"I can always tell when you're lying, girl."

Vincent tentatively stepped over to us, as though afraid to interrupt. "Are we ready?"

Harmony squeezed her eyes shut. "Do it."

I let her keep a tight grip on my wrist as Vincent carefully spread out her wing, examining where the bone merged with her lilac skin.

She was our leader. Fearless, despite her short stature. Today I'd witnessed a side of Harmony Arabesque she'd never shown anyone else.

For that and more, I loved her.

Would Harmony ever find true freedom from Serenity? Would any of us mere mortals ever be free of our gods?

I'd taken on this task with Quen to try and make a difference. Did she think me a fool for daring to try? That was what she'd implied. She'd been there for my fuckups. Because of me, we'd lost Reve. Eventide and the Vesper. Even now, I'd taken Quen's side against a protest I would have otherwise happily joined.

The Godless had been my idea. I'd dragged Dru into it, then Sinder and Vincent. I'd convinced them we could save Chime's mortals.

It *was* futile, wasn't it?

We'd always be beholden to the gods. We'd never be free.

Only in a death beyond death.

NOW DO YOU SEE WHY CHAOS MUST PREVAIL?

That was what Mesmorpheus had said.

That Chaos had already won.

I'd wanted to talk to Quen about what I'd seen, but how in god's name did I broach the subject? Oh, by the way, I saw a future version of you sneak into the Godless mystery hideout, would you know anything about that?

Besides, he'd been strangely off with me earlier. The stress of his gods-damn three-day deadline was likely getting to him.

And I couldn't afford to wallow in my ignorance and ignore the consequences. Not when they resulted in Harmony losing her wing.

The alternative you and Jinx give me is death and more death. You know I won't risk mortal lives.

WE COULD REMAKE THE DOMAINS.

To your benefit! That was the problem with Jinx; she wanted to end the reign of gods, but she'd still be chained to Corentine.

She didn't see her own hypocrisy.

"There we go," Vincent declared.

Harmony's wing came free. It was a tiny thing in the grand scheme of the universe. Why Serenity wanted this, I didn't know.

Because they were cruel. That was the only reason.

Vincent placed the wing down and helped Harmony sit. "I've numbed your back, but it may feel sore in a few hours. If you have any pain or dizziness, send someone to find me. I'll check in when I'm able."

Harmony's eyes glazed over. "At least—at least now I'll be able to wear a decent suit." She forced a smile, but her voice was shaky.

I wrapped my arm around her waist, careful to avoid touching her back.

For all her brave words, she'd sacrificed this for me.

How many more sacrifices would my family make for my goals?

Could I live with them?

29

Arcadia is one of the more popular domains and a prime holiday destination for mortals seeking rest and relaxation. While there is plenty to see and do (I recommend visiting the Isle of Art) one must remain on guard. Seren are banned from singing in Chime, but there are no such rules in Arcadia. Be wary when in the presence of a Seren.
Wardens should traverse Arcadia in groups of three at least. Remain within the tourist hotspots for your own safety.
—Q. Corinth, *Warden Dossier on Arcadia*

WITH ONLY THREE DAYS left to unite the gods and save Chaos, Quen had arranged for a trip to Arcadia.

The four of us—me, Dru, Quen, and Ben—packed for an overnight stay and made the crossing in good time. We made one snazzy group dressed in tan. Dru and I could almost pass as sisters with my Umber face and our matching tan dresses. Even Ben was sporting a tight tan suit to match Quen's. It had been Sinder's idea, naturally.

Who knew tan paired so well with my silvery-blue stone skin?

At five thirty in the afternoon, I found myself seated under a sprawling pavilion that could give the Golden City a run for its bocs. Marble columns and arches curved in a semicircle that sheltered a collection of couches. Across the immaculately cut lawn, a band of Seren played a relaxing melody on their harps under a gazebo.

"Welcome to Arcadia!" announced the cheerful ambassador, who flew on over to our table. "So pleased you made it." Today, they were dressed in a frilly pink dress.

"Good evening, Sonata." Quen greeted them with a bow. "Thank you for the last-minute invitation. How may we address you today?"

"I'm feeling like a lady." Sonata gave her dress a swirl. "Serenity is also in a playful mood. He wishes to be known as a male tonight, and looks forward to your company. If you don't mind, I have other guests to attend to. Indulge yourself—Serenity will be along when he is ready."

A fluttering collection of wings descended on the pavilion as Seren servers laid out exquisite platters of fruit and golden jugs. I'd never seen so many Seren all in one place, and these were a rainbow of colorful wings and cute little outfits.

If Leander cubs were cute, then how adorable must Seren babies be?

I needed to hook Harmony up with someone *immediately*.

Other domains mixed with the Seren, chatting and mingling over wine. I spotted Glimmer, Leander, and even Ember among the guests. Some of their faces looked familiar—from either the Courier or a magazine. The wealthy and the famous.

Dru and I shared a couch. I left the briefcase containing Harmony's wing by my legs and went to pluck a grape.

Quen stopped me. "Be careful what you consume here," he warned. "The wine is particularly potent."

"I'm an Undercity girl. I know how to handle my drink."

"I'd watch out for her," Dru said. "She tends to stick her tongue in places it doesn't belong when she gets drunk."

"And what's that supposed to mean?"

"You're a happy drunk, that's all. A *very* happy drunk."

"It's better than being a boring one." I popped a grape into my mouth and savored its sweetness. My god, these were amazing! I snatched a few more while Quen wasn't looking.

From my experience, alcohol revealed character. Sinder made a morose drunk. Harmony was a riot. I'd never managed to get Dru to drink anything, but I reckoned she made for a grumpy drunk.

And Quen? The last time we'd drunk wine together, he'd kissed me...

I had him pegged as a slutty drunk.

Maybe I'd get him drunk tonight.

No, Kayl! Bad Kayl! There'd been enough shitty mortals taking advantage of him in his life, he didn't need another one. If only I had Jinx to stop me making these awful decisions—

I TELL YOU TO STOP MAKING AWFUL DECISIONS, AND YOU DON'T LISTEN.

No one likes their mother nagging them.

THEN GET DRUNK. BE MERRY.

You're encouraging me to sin? How very Ember of you. Come to think of it, what are the sins of Chaos? Every god has their rules. What are yours?

CHAOS HAS NO RULES. NO SINS. IT EXISTS TO CONTRADICT. TO REBEL. TO BE THE FORCE THAT SPREADS DISCORD.

Huh. Corentine had described my life as a Godless.

I really was a child of Chaos, wasn't I?

I EXIST THROUGH YOU, THOUGH MY EXISTENCE NOW IS PATHETIC. SO LIVE FOR US BOTH. IT WILL BE AMUSING TO WATCH.

Great. Now I had Corentine as a voyeur for the mistakes I'd likely make. I grabbed a whole bunch of grapes. They tasted fucking amazing.

We sat in polite silence as I popped grape after grape. Seren flitted between the tables to top up wine or light lanterns. Already, the sun began to dip below the palm trees and tailored bushes that surrounded the pavilion. Arcadia's gardens were truly sublime, decorated with plinths wound with vines and fountains I couldn't hear over the chatter.

Various flowery perfumes contrasted with each other, and tiny glowing insects buzzed idly past us. The sweetness permeating the air was a little heady. It was the complete opposite of the Undercity. Instead of smog, it was nature's bounty.

If we weren't about to confront a god, it would be something magical.

Ben sneezed an awfully loud shriek, making me jump. He'd been sniffing one of the roses. "Sorry. Think something went up my nose."

Quen tutted and passed him a handkerchief.

More Seren flew onto the lawn carrying bouquets of flowers and tiny harps. They were dressed in robes and sandals, and they hovered in midair.

The band stopped their music as the Seren began to sing.

Oh, joyous one. Oh, joyous one. We beseech you gift us

With your calming tranquility and peaceful composure.

Oh, dear one. Oh, dear one. Please gift us your serenity.

Make this night a blessing of pure quietude and placidity.

Their voices were high-pitched and rather charming. Too charming. I couldn't forget that Seren held the power of song, and that power could be dangerously persuasive. "Should we be covering our ears?" I whispered to Quen.

"No. The Seren may take offense."

"What's to stop them from manipulating us all?"

"Political immunity. It wouldn't be wise for Serenity to invite guests to his pavilion and then abuse them. Unlike the Amnae's memory manipulations, mortals *do* remember when they've been caught with their trousers down by a Seren."

I had to hope our political immunity was enough.

The Seren finished their song to raucous applause.

And then statues popped onto the lawn out of nowhere in a haze of blue smoke. More and more appeared, in the shape of a naked male, but no Seren male. They looked more like a Necro with unnaturally perfect porcelain skin, and stood as tall, with no Seren wings. At least twenty identical statues dotted the lawn in various poses.

The one in the center suddenly came to life, and I dropped a grape.

The statue strutted across the lawn as mortals cheered. I was at a complete loss.

Dru leaned into me. "That's Serenity."

Really? The Seren god sure knew how to make an entrance. And here I thought the Ember were flamboyant.

"Welcome, one and all!" announced Serenity with a high-pitched singsong voice to match his mortals. A couch *poofed* out of thin air, and the god sprawled upon it, his flaccid stone cock dangling for all to see. A flock of Seren surrounded him with large palm leaves and began fanning him. Others held trays of fruit and wine.

He plucked a grape and stared directly at me as he popped it into his mouth. "We have honored guests this eve. Welcome, welcome, to the domain of art and beauty! I cherish your adoration and tributes, my loves. What delights do you have for me?"

Harmony had explained what would be in store for me tonight, and I watched it unfold with growing unease. Seren from various noble families approached their god with artistic tithes—worship in the form of flattering poems, powerful ballads, painted depictions, and even some colorful pottery. All were gifts Serenity greedily accepted and showed off to his eager audience.

Gods and their egos.

SERENITY WAS ALWAYS THE FUN ONE. HE ENJOYED THROWING PARTIES AND PLAYING PRANKS. MY IMPRISONMENT MUST BE ONE BIG JOKE TO HIM.

A prankster? Great. Another Jinx. Just what I needed.

The procession of pointless art and interpretive dance continued to a smattering of applause. I was growing increasingly bored and digging into the bowl of grapes when a shrill laugh forced me to refocus.

A male Seren with lime green skin held up some sort of fuzzy lump in the shape of a face. Onlookers were pointing and laughing at the poor man, who swayed awkwardly, his wings quivering.

"Is that a potato?" Ben asked, squinting at the figure.

Gods. It was! It was a bloody potato in the shape of Serenity's face!

"This isn't going to end well," Dru muttered.

Shit, she was right.

Serenity appeared amused, but there was a dangerous glint in his stone eyes. "A potato," he said plainly, to a roar of laughter. "Do you believe my devotion is worth a mere potato?"

"It—It grew in your likeness, dear one!" the Seren stammered. "I knew then it must surely be blessed—"

"Come hither."

The laughter faded as the Seren approached his god, the potato-head shaking so violently in his hands, I feared he'd drop it.

I caught Quen's eye. His fists were clenched in his lap. He shook his head—a subtle signal that said *don't try anything*.

I'd heard from Harmony what happened to mortals who failed to appease Serenity with adequate tributes. Based on Quen's expression, he knew it, too.

The pavilion went still except for the flutter of wings and hushed whispers. I glanced around, hoping to catch the eye of mortals as uncomfortable as me. But no. They weren't appalled by what was about to happen.

They were on the edge of their seats, absolutely enthralled. Even the Seren.

Was that what these parties were? Sick entertainment?

Gods.

Serenity took the potato and placed it carefully on the couch beside him. "What a unique gift! Do you grow potatoes?"

"Ye—yes, dear one." The Seren was staring at his feet.

"Don't be shy. Let's look at you." Serenity took the Seren's head in his hands, tilting his face up. "Aren't you adorable. You look like a potato yourself, did you know?" He squashed his cheeks together. "Looky at this cute potato!"

A dark stain spread down the Seren's legs. He'd pissed himself.

Whatever was in those grapes filled me with a sudden boldness. I grabbed my briefcase and stood before Quen could stop me. "Art is so subjective, isn't it?" I called out. "I've always admired how a Seren can turn simple food into art. But when food grows itself into their visage? That's something special. Random. A feat only Chaos could manage."

Serenity released the Seren, shoving him aside. "Ah, my honored guest. You would deem this an act of Chaos?" He lifted the potato-head.

I approached Serenity with my chin held high, aware of the many eyes following my every step. "Naturally. To disregard the laws of Chaos would deeply insult my god."

NO IT WOULDN'T.

Look, I don't care if that potato is shaped after your arse. The gods' faces were always appearing in toast and other random places for some damn reason. That sounded like Chaos to me.

"Then I accept this tribute as a personal token from Chaos herself."

The Seren scrambled to his feet and bobbed a series of bows. "Oh, thank you, dear one, blessed one—"

Serenity dismissed him with a flick of his wrist, and the poor Seren skittered from the pavilion to see another day. Hopefully his next tribute would be a better one. "We're pleased to have Chaos grace Arcadia. Though I see we are missing another guest. Where is Harmony Arabesque?"

"Miss Arabesque declined your invitation. I've brought what you asked for." With a quick flip, the briefcase popped open, revealing a single Seren wing.

Surprise shone in Serenity's marble eyes.

Quen hurried to my side. "Your Reverence, we apologize for not observing the correct etiquette." He shot me a scowl. "However, the terms of our bargain indicated one wing, and not the mortal in question—"

Serenity laughed. A cheerful warble that echoed around the pavilion. "You found a loophole! Well done! *Sonata!*" he sang. "Where are you?"

The ambassador flew over. Fear washed over her face as she bobbed a series of curtsies before her master. "Forgive me, Your Reverence, I must have misunderstood—"

"Add it to my collection."

Sonata snatched the briefcase and hurried away.

"Wings are so beautiful, aren't they?" Serenity snapped his fingers at a server, who promptly passed him a golden goblet. He swirled it and took a lingering taste. "I enjoy Zephyr wings too, but their mortals are such a bore. I simply cannot stand them."

"Then why don't you have wings?" I asked.

Quen shot me another scowl, but we were both standing here awkwardly. One of us had to make small talk.

And I needed a reason to stare at Serenity's face, and not what dangled lower down.

"Sometimes I do. I like to change it up. Keep things fresh. That's what makes good art; it's ever changing, ever evolving. Looking for new trends, new styles. And what of you? You can change form, can't you? Don't you ever get bored wearing the same body?"

Since learning of my abilities, I'd changed into most domains. I'd never really considered their aesthetics, but more what felt comfortable, or useful. Vesper felt natural to me only because I'd grown up as one. But in recent times, I'd adopted the Umber's persona, if only to blend into Chime's society without arousing suspicion.

Aesthetically, I enjoyed the Ember body. It suited my inner slut far more than an Umber one.

Which form did Quen prefer? He always seemed to get a bit goggle-eyed whenever I turned Diviner. Though he also rather liked my Leander form, the dirty boy.

"I choose whatever works best."

"Interesting. And here you are asking for my favor. Now this is new. This is… refreshing. Like fine wine."

"Your Reverence." Quen flourished a bow. "Your contribution to Chime—"

"I don't care for politics. I care for art, for music, for beauty. That is what Chaos represents. Without Chaos, there would be no creativity. No imagination. No art. Dor would create a universe built from logic and let art wither and die. But it's art that gives mortals their souls. I wouldn't expect a Diviner to understand."

My heart skipped a beat. I'd never imagined Serenity to be on the side of Chaos.

ART HAS ALWAYS BEEN A BYPRODUCT OF CHAOS. ART CANNOT EXIST WITHOUT EMOTION, WITHOUT IMAGINATION. THAT IS WHAT CHAOS IS.

Chaos seems to be a lot of things.

Even so, it didn't endear the god to me.

This was the brute who'd so callously ripped off Harmony's wing. Who'd cut her off from her friends and family.

"I understand," Quen said. "Under my protection, Chaos will remain."

"We shall see what your word is worth, son of time." Serenity sat up, the goblet still in his hand. "I accept your tribute, daughter of Chaos. In return, I grant my favor. Now, the night is young. Enjoy the festivities!"

Quen and I didn't need to be told twice. We rushed back to our seats.

Had it really been that easy?

"We're not being smited then?" Dru asked.

Quen grimaced in my direction. "Not yet. Though I do wish you had adhered to the correct etiquette—"

"Relax, Quen. Everything went *splendidly*." I grabbed more grapes. "So does this mean we can eat? I'm pissing starving."

As the sun set over the pavilion, the Seren and their non-Seren guests indulged in fine food and fine wine. Serenity knew how to host a party, and the god mingled as music played throughout the night.

We kept to ourselves, and Serenity thankfully neglected our table. Quen and Ben kept to a modest meal of cheese, crackers, and fruit juice, while Dru was offered a bowl of pretty rocks, and I gorged myself on grapes. I avoided the wine, so as to avoid Dru and Quen's judgement.

Though a lovely Seren girl kept my grapes well stocked. Bless her!

Eventually, the various faces of the Seren began to blur into one colorful smudge, and even the music droned into a dull whine in my ear.

Dru and Ben spoke about trees or something as Quen sat there, all quiet and broody, but what did he have to brood about?

Nothing bad had happened. Serenity hadn't poisoned our drinks or ordered our heads be removed. It was a rather dull night.

All in all, I'd had better piss-ups in Grayford.

"Right then." Quen slapped his thighs. "We better get some sleep. We have an early start tomorrow."

"Ah, shit," I mumbled. We'd have to get up at stupid o'clock for the 5 a.m. crossing. "Can't you carry me out come morning? Then I can sleep more."

"I'm not carrying you," Dru said.

"I wasn't asking you."

"I'll help you, ma'am," Ben offered.

"See? At least he's a gentleman." I stuck out my tongue.

Dru dragged me up. I swiped a handful of grapes as I was being marched away.

A Seren bellboy with orange skin came to collect us. We cut through the garden onto a cobblestone path, away from the pavilion. The various statues and marble plinths were lit by colorful lanterns that guided our way through the dark.

As we walked, the music of Serenity's party was replaced by an odd *whooshing*.

I hung off Quen's arm and idly dangled grapes above my mouth. "What *is* that?"

"The ocean," Quen said. "It goes out and comes back in with the tide."

"Why? What for?"

"To create waves."

That wasn't a satisfactory answer, and I was going to bloody well tell him so, but then we reached our destination.

"Your lodgings," announced the bellboy.

We'd stopped outside stone huts. These weren't Seren homes—the doors were certainly big enough for my height. They didn't have glass windows, either, but holes cut in the stone, where white curtains shifted in the breeze.

"There's a path down to the beach, should you fancy a late-night swim," the bellboy was saying. "The water is perfectly safe and pleasingly warm. Here's the ladies' hut." He pointed to the nearest one. "The men's hut is a little further down, if you'll follow."

"Hang on," I said with my mouth full of grapes. "We don't get a hut each? We're ambassadors! And she snores in her sleep!"

"You're being rude," Dru said.

"Rude! You're the one who snores! How rude is that—"

"Ignore her. She's tired." Dru yanked me inside our hut.

I stumbled inside our home away from home. It was a modest thing lit by an oil lamp. There was a washroom, two separate beds, our luggage propped against a table, and—

Yes!

A whole bowl of grapes!

I snatched the bowl before Dru could object.

She sat on the edge of a bed. "Will you stop eating those grapes? You're going to make yourself sick."

"You know I'm a whore for food. They're divine. Do you want one?"

"Are you drunk?" She squinted at me suspiciously. "You've been making eyes at Quen all night."

"Don't be ridiculous. If I was trying to catch Quen's attention, I'd have my tits out—"

"I didn't become your bodyguard so I could watch you ruin your life in real time."

"Then maybe I should change into a Diviner so I can speed it up for you."

"You're impossible."

"I'm the right level of possible. Besides, you're one to talk. You spent the whole night chatting up Ben." I waggled the flowers of my brow.

Dru sighed. "We were talking about Arcadia's flora—"

"Who spends an entire night *talking* about plants? Come on! If you can't gossip with me, then who can you gossip with?" I popped a grape into my mouth.

"I'd rather not gossip at all. Kayl, seriously. Ben and I aren't like that, so don't get any ideas."

"Dru. This is me we're talking about."

"He wanted some advice, that's all."

My flowers perked up. "Advice on what? Growing a garden?"

"He's got a... secret. He can't talk to his own domain about it, so he asked me."

Oh my. I placed my grape bowl down. "What secret?"

"It wouldn't be a secret if I told you."

"You're killing me here."

"I'm thinking about it."

"*Dru—*"

"He's an apostate." Dru covered her mouth as the words tumbled out. "*Why* did I say that?"

Oh my god. Diviner rarely admitted to apostasy, besides Quen, who'd once been killed for the privilege. I honestly wouldn't have expected it from Ben—but then the man wore his emotions on his sleeve. That wasn't something Diviner tolerated. "Are you sure?"

"He knows we're Godless. He—He doesn't want to be a Diviner anymore."

"Why didn't you tell me this before?"

"Because he's Quen's bodyguard. He's scared of what Dor will do to him."

"Quen doesn't know?"

"Seriously? Of course he doesn't."

Shit. I understood Ben's fears, but... "You don't trust me?" Why else keep this from me? I was Godless, for god's sake!

"You've got a god inside your head, too."

That was what this was about? "Corentine doesn't have power over me. You know that."

Dru avoided my eye. "When your twin came into the temple, she... she said it was you who killed Valeria. You're the reason Malk is gone, and all the Vesper." She glanced up. "Was she lying, or you?"

"Are you joking?" But no. She wasn't. Dru wasn't the joking type, especially not over something like this. "It was Jinx."

Of course it had been Jinx.

How could it have been anyone but Jinx? Why in god's name would Dru even *ask*?

"You don't talk about Malk anymore." Dru wrung her hands in her lap. "It's like... you're trying to forget him."

There was an unspoken accusation in her voice, and I didn't know how to broach it, because it was the truth. I *had* forgotten him. I still didn't understand why. "You know what happened still hurts," I said carefully. "That's what all this is about—entering the domains, speaking with the gods. To ensure that what happened to Eventide *never* happens again."

"Okay. Good. I'm—I'm going to sleep now." She kicked off her boots and pulled the bed sheet over her head.

"Night, then."

This evening had taken an unexpected turn. Shit.

I lay on my bed and ate another few grapes to calm the clash of my heart. Had I really been that close with this Malkavaan? Why would I have forgotten him if so?

Moonlight shone in through the window. Even from here, the whoosh of the ocean called out to me.

After that discussion, there was no chance I'd fall asleep.

I may as well go find those waves Quen had mentioned.

With my bowl of grapes tucked underneath my arm, I quietly slipped out of the hut and followed the vague direction the bellboy had pointed toward. Lanterns lit the way, though it was awfully dark. If only I were still a Vesper.

If only they were still here.

I stumbled onto a sandy path between palm trees and emerged onto a whole field of sand. Beyond, a void of dark blue water swelled under the moon. Each ripple cascaded into the *whoosh* I'd heard before, bringing with it the salty scents of Memoria.

And there, seated on a towel, was a familiar broody boy.

The sand beneath my feet was heavy and shifted uncomfortably. It wasn't like the ankle-twisting cobblestones of Chime.

"Shit!" I couldn't gain traction and stumbled rather ungracefully.

Quen steadied me before I could drop my grapes. "What are you doing out here? It's late."

"I could ask you the same, mister."

He helped me onto the towel and sat beside me. "I couldn't sleep."

"Neither could I. Dru snores like a steam engine, you should hear her."

He flashed a smile, which quickly faded, and turned to the ocean as it rolled and crashed and whooshed. "There aren't any nights like this on Chime."

There truly weren't. The colors were a Vesper palette of moody dark blues and purples, smudged with silver clouds. I shuffled closer until our elbows touched. "Want a grape?"

"No, thank you. I'd love a good cup of tea, though."

"I bet you would. Don't Seren serve tea?"

"Fruit teas. It's not the same." He leaned back and stared at the stars, which glittered gold. "Was it true what Serenity said about Chaos?"

How much did Quen know about Chaos? How much should I reveal?

TELL HIM EVERYTHING.

You want a Diviner to know?

I WANT HIM TO KNOW.

All right. I was sick of keeping secrets, anyhow. "Without chaos, mortals don't possess free will. That's what Corentine explained to me. That without chaos, mortals would be nothing but mindless husks. Slaves to their gods. The universe needs both forces—chaos and time—to balance each other out."

"Husks? Like immortal beings?"

I wasn't that knowledgeable on immortals, but they didn't have free will as mortals did. They were essentially puppets of their god. "I suppose. All mortals are touched by chaos in one way or another, as we follow the laws of time. Chaos is the reason I'm so scatterbrained. Why Ben is so big." I turned to him. "Why you wear eyeglasses."

He touched the side of his frames. "I damaged my vision when I fell from the clock tower. Dor didn't heal my eyes—it was a punishment."

"Perhaps your fall only hastened the damage that was there. Think about it: why would Dor give a natural disadvantage to his ambassador and top Warden?"

"I... don't know."

Silence stretched between us, punctuated only by Arcadia's ocean singing as pleasantly as its mortals.

It soothed the aches of my soul. "Before I met you, I'd never left Chime. I was too scared to. But you've shown me so many wondrous things... So many beautiful domains. I want to save them. All of them."

"We will."

"When the time comes, I'll have to choose a persona." A new version of myself. With the Vesper gone, I couldn't return to my old face. I shuffled down and leaned my head against his shoulder. "What do you prefer?"

"It's entirely your choice, though Father won't allow Chaos to take on a Diviner form, for obvious reasons. I would also caution against Amnae."

He'd skillfully deflected the question. What *would* suit me? Ember? I didn't fancy being stuck as an Umber for the rest of my life, no thank you. Though becoming a Glimmer would sure be a riot...

Gods! I'd almost forgotten the most important thing I needed to say. "Harmony had an idea for getting the Glimmer on our side." I sat up and briefly went over her and Joe's plan for closing down the workhouses. "Do you think that could work?"

"Hrm. My agreement with Dor was to unite all the domains, but I may be able to negotiate on that point. Faen and The Nameless One have never been interested in Chime or the Warden Council. I doubt their influence would make a positive contribution."

"No trip to Juniper or Witheryn, then?"

"I'd rather not. They're both deadly in their own way."

"We survived Obituary."

Another smile. "Just."

I lived for that smile, though tonight, they seemed in short supply. Was I the only one not suffering from an acute case of grumpiness? "There's something else I need to ask you. Do you know how to time travel? Is that a Diviner thing?"

"Time travel?" He raised a brow. "Why do you assume I can do that?"

"Because I've seen you in places you shouldn't be, and I'm not going mad." At least Mesmorpheus could back me up.

"What? Describe them, please."

I went over the few times I'd seen the Future Quen, without mentioning the Mesmer temple, naturally. The time he'd appeared in the alley and shot a Warden in the head. The times he'd appeared in my altered dreams.

The way he looked different. Older, maybe? Wiser?

Quen ran a hand through his hair. "No mortal has the ability to transcend time, not even Diviner. And certainly not me. But thank you for informing me. I'll look into this matter as soon as we return to Chime."

"You don't remember these events? You've had no visions of them?"

"Not at all, which is rather disconcerting."

"Do you think the timeline could be damaged? Mes—uh, Corentine mentioned something like that."

"Something *has* changed. I... felt a disturbance, but couldn't place it. It's likely a future event that is sending ripples back through the timeline."

"Meaning what?"

"I don't know, but it's not good." He pulled out his pocket watch and cradled it in his palm.

Hadn't he said that watch was a comforter? I had no idea how the timeline worked, but Quen looked like he needed comforting right now.

In the moonlight, his pearly skin twinkled like iridescent stars. Whenever I stared into those silver eyes, past the grinding of gears that was my clever boy lost in thought, I saw *him*. His vulnerability. His strength. The emotions Diviner weren't allowed, but that was Quen.

My Quen.

"Whatever it is, we'll get through it together. As partners."

I leaned close and pressed my lips to his.

They didn't part.

Instead, his entire body tensed, as though his muscles had locked up. He pulled away before I could deepen the kiss.

What had just happened? Shit, had I hurt him?

Did he hate me? Fear me? Was it because of his dream—that I would kill him?

"I'm sorry," he said with an odd breathlessness. "I meant to tell you— I'm betrothed to Pendula."

Betrothed? How could he be betrothed?

That made no sense. "Was that before or after we shared a bed in Rapture?"

"After."

But—he'd kissed *me*! He had no interest in his assistant! The few times I'd seen them together, he'd been positively annoyed with her. Was it because I was Chaos? Because Pendula was a female Diviner? "Is Pendula— is that what you want?"

He turned away.

Shit. This was an arranged marriage. "So you're doing what Dor wants like a good boy—"

"I'm bound to Dor," he snapped. "You know as well as I what that means."

I grabbed his arm. "I don't care for what it means. Dor doesn't own your mind, your heart. Look me in the eye and tell me this is what *you* want."

His silver eyes never wavered behind those eyeglasses. "I'm sorry if I led you on in any capacity. We simply don't share a connection."

My heart sank. It plummeted, until it left my body and could no longer beat at all.

I WARNED YOU HE WOULD BETRAY YOU.

But this... This wasn't him!

He spoke with such coldness, but this wasn't my Quen speaking. He was throwing up walls. Pushing me out. All because Dor commanded him to.

"How does this affect our partnership? How does this affect Chaos—"

"It changes nothing. We'll complete what we set out to do."

He returned to staring at the ocean, his body hunched, his shield up. Untouchable. Unreachable.

Gods. How could I help him? Save him?

Did he even want to be saved?

I grabbed my bowl of grapes. "I better go back to bed."

"Do you need me to escort you?"

"I'm sure I'll manage."

On the way back, I caught sight of two familiar figures sitting under a bush. Dru and Ben. That sly slut! She'd probably snuck out after me. The two of them were bent so close together in some secret conversation, they could practically kiss.

Good for them.

I tiptoed my way past and returned to my hut.

Serenity was sprawled on my bed.

Great. "I didn't order a late-night snack."

"No? You seem to be enjoying my grapes." He grinned.

I examined the grape in my hand.

Shit! I'd been eating them nonstop since we arrived, which was a wild coincidence, because I'd been acting like a prat the entire time! I let the bowl fall from my hands, spilling grapes across the floor. "Did you poison the damn grapes?"

"I wouldn't touch my beloved vineyards. My Seren like to sing such suggestive songs. Melodies that lower one's inhibitions. You'd be entranced by the secrets mortals let slip when I invite them to my evening tea parties. Or the naughty behavior they get up to in the bushes when they believe no one is looking."

Gods. There were all manner of guests back at that pavilion—celebrities, business owners, politicians. Mortals with power. Not to mention Quen and me as ambassadors. What would Serenity want with their secrets? "I thought you cared only for art?"

"Is there no greater art than theatrics?" A grape appeared from thin air, and he sucked it into his mouth with a slow, seductive kiss. "Mortals amuse me. Your antics especially so. What dark secrets you carry, my love." His lips quirked.

Shit.

I ran for the door.

Stone hands burst from the ground in a cloud of dust. They grabbed my arms, holding me in place. I tried wrenching free, but shit, they'd clamped tight and remained still and solid as though they'd always been some bizarre statue on display.

"You better let me go, or you can say goodbye to whatever power you have on Chime!"

Serenity rose and prowled toward me, his stone cock swinging from side to side. "Power. It comes in so many forms. Gildola believes her power comes from wealth. Lionheart views his power as strength. Edana's power comes from passion. Mine? I prefer subtlety. My power comes from manipulation. But none of us would exist without time and chaos. The gods will take sides when the inevitable conflict begins. And it will."

"What are you saying? That you're on my side? You're one of the gods who imprisoned Corentine in the first place!"

"I played a part that I regret. I have lived with those regrets for centuries."

Is he talking shit? I asked Corentine.

I WOULD EXPECT NO LESS. MY CHILDREN COULD HAVE TURNED ON DOR THEN. PERHAPS THEY WILL DO SO NOW THEY HAVE EXPERIENCED EXISTENCE UNDER DOR'S RULE.

Were we heading for a battle between the gods? Both Mesmorpheus and Quen had mentioned a future event affecting time.

Did the gods break it in the future? They had that power, didn't they?

"How do you plan to stop Dor?" I asked.

"I don't. But Chaos has destroyed one god. Taking another is within your realm of possibility."

"If you're suggesting what I think you are, then you can piss off." There was no way I'd risk Quen.

I'd never save him that way.

Serenity leaned close. His uncanny stonelike movements unnerved me. "You may not have a choice. Dor's absence would create a power vacuum. Who would replace him? Gildola? Lionheart? Corentine, perhaps?" He placed a stone finger under my chin and lifted it. "Chaos and time. A love story as old as the stars. Corentine and Dor's love birthed an entire universe. What will your love birth, I wonder?"

Our love wasn't going to birth anything with Quen's assistant in the way.

I shouldn't have kissed him, but Serenity had unleashed my inner slut.

YOU ADMIT YOU CARE FOR A DIVINER, THEN?

I admit to nothing.

THEN DON'T WASTE YOUR TIME. DOR IS PRAGMATIC AND FOND OF SACRIFICE. HE WON'T LET YOUR DIVINER GO FREE. YOU MAY AS WELL MOVE ON AND FORGET HIM LIKE YOU DID YOUR LAST LOVER.

Thank you for the relationship advice.

I felt torn between the battles of chaos and time, and all I wanted was a nap.

Vines suddenly shot out from under my feet. They wrapped around the stone arms and squeezed them until they crumbled into pieces. My arms came free, and I stumbled to the door, where Dru was standing, her stony face hardened with an absolute look of wrath.

"You *dare* touch my art?" Serenity screeched. "I could carve art out of *you*!"

Dru didn't flinch. "I'm Ambassador Arkey's bodyguard. If you touch her, then you go through me." More vines poked out between the hut's tiles, their little buds quivering as though ready to attack.

Gods. I could kiss her.

The rage on Serenity's face switched to a placid smile. "Then enjoy the rest of your evening. I have other guests to *entertain*." Serenity disappeared in a blink, and the hut's floor righted itself as though the past ten minutes had been some odd dream.

"Can we sleep now?" Dru grumbled.

I gawked at her. "You just yelled at a god."

"And I'll yell at you next if we don't get some sleep." Dru climbed into bed, oblivious to the fact she'd stood up to an *actual pissing god*!

This entire trip had left me wound up and bloody foolish. We'd both uttered things we probably wouldn't have if not for Serenity's meddling. Yet Quen had remained unaffected and infuriatingly chaste. I slunk under the covers of my own bed and turned my back on the bowl of grapes.

Think I'd avoid them for a while.

I woke to sobbing.

Dawn shone through the hut's window, highlighting the figure of Dru. She was kneeling by the foot of her bed, her hands clasped in prayer. Tears ran down her face.

"Dru!" I dropped beside her and grabbed her shoulders. "What is it? Is it me? Did I upset you? I'm sorry, shit, I'm sorry! I never meant—"

"It's not you." She rubbed her eyes clear with her sleeve. "It's—It's Unghard."

No. Fuck, no. I sat back on my heels. "You prayed to them?" That was the one rule we Godless had—never pray.

"I didn't—they came to me. Unghard learned I was your bodyguard through Ambassador Hazelhearth."

Shit. That was even worse. "What does Unghard want?"

"Me. They want me to return to Heartstone."

XXX

Diviner are split into family units so they may fornicate, marry, and breed if they wish without incestuous implications.
We are all one domain birthed from one heavenly Father. As a domain can only breed with itself, incest is part of being mortal and is nothing to be ashamed of. If domains were allowed to breed with each other, then any offending offspring produced would be monstrous.
—H. Bezel, *Philosophy for the Young Diviner*

AFTER THE AWKWARDNESS OF last night, I couldn't stomach the thought of facing Kayl. So I'd taken the coward's way out and left Arcadia alone ahead of the others. Ben stayed behind to ensure both Kayl and Dru would make the crossing on time.

The entire trip had left me exhausted. Nauseated. Numb. I needed a burning hot shower and a good cup of tea.

I caught the early morning tram to the Silver Suite. It was mostly Seren on board, fresh from the crossing, but the tram was empty enough for everyone to grab a seat. I took my usual position at the back and stared out the window as we rumbled forward.

An ache throbbed in my chest. I tried to distract myself from the sensation by examining the streetlamps we passed. The Wardens had done a good job replacing the blown-out bulbs. One of my first duties as ambassador.

Chime wasn't my city to own, but it was my home, and I'd do my duty by it.

Even if it hurt.

Especially if it hurt.

We'd gained Serenity's favor, even if he'd made a fool out of us. Only three domains remained—Juniper, Solaris, and Witheryn.

Ideally, I wanted to unite all the domains, but I didn't think Juniper would budge, unless I could offer Faen something they wanted, but what? Of all the gods, Faen was the most elusive, more interested in prancing around their jungles, completely cut off from the rest of civilized society. As for Witheryn... In truth, I'd rather avoid stepping foot there and dealing with The Nameless One.

I'd only met the Necro god once, and once was more than enough.

Dor wouldn't be pleased with the Glimmer holding three domains' worth of power and influence over Chime, but the Diviner would still come out on top, as was meant to be.

I barely noticed when the tram pulled into the Tower View district. Muscle memory prompted my body to go through the motions. In a single blink, I stood outside my apartment.

The Silver Suite, thirteenth floor. Door 303.

It opened into an empty hallway. Since my resurrection, I'd gone through my piles of paperwork and filed them away. With my memories restored, I no longer needed reams of notes, so now my apartment looked as immaculate as it was ever going to get.

I'd gotten rid of that damn piano, too. It wasn't mine.

These rooms held too many memories that merged into one hazy blur of regret. Even if I completely redecorated, the taint of those memories would forever return, like dust that could never be vanquished.

Nor could I hide the view. Once, the view of the clock tower opposite and Central Station below had comforted me. But now I knew what lurked beyond the clockface, the view filled me with unease.

Maybe once this was over, I'd get myself a cozy little apartment above a teahouse.

With Pendula? I had to think of my future with her involved.

Though why bother? I didn't have a future worth planning for.

I threw my jacket onto the coat hook and headed straight for the shower. Scalding water burned away the numbness of my skin.

It burned through the skin and bones that made me mortal.

It burned with the steaming aether of death.

I leaned my forehead against the wall.

She'd kissed me.

Knowing that Kayl cared for my depraved soul, that she desired me in some misguided capacity…

Saints. It burned.

Tears ran down my cheeks and mingled with the steamy water. I let the shower wash them away, along with the what-ifs and the could-bes. I knew my fate. I knew where it led.

There was no happy ending for the Dark Warden.

WHY DO YOU CRY?

I've got soap in my eyes, Father. Nothing to worry about.

Pain lanced through my skull. I gasped and grabbed the shower rail to stop myself collapsing.

DO NOT LIE. ONCE AGAIN YOU COVET CHAOS—

Look into my memories! Kayl came on to me, I rejected her! Please, Father, I feel nothing for her. Serenity manipulated the situation, but I resisted his sinful temptations—

I HAVE EXPLAINED WHAT CHAOS REPRESENTS. SIN. DESTRUCTION. DO YOU DOUBT MY AMBITIONS?

The pressure built, radiating down to my neck, my spine. I sank to my knees. *No! Never, Father! I would never question your intentions—*

YOU PROTEST, YET YOU CONCERN YOURSELF WITH CHAOS.

To appease Serenity! I understand Chaos can be destructive, but once we have removed their powers and memories, they will no longer be a threat. My loyalty is to you and Pendula. Always.

IF YOU ARE SO LOYAL TO YOUR FUTURE WIFE, THEN WHY DO YOUR ACTIONS HURT HER?

Don't hurt Pendula. I'm begging. Punish me if you must, but don't hurt her.

The pressure eased from my head.

VERY GOOD, QUENTIN. YOU UNDERSTAND WHY I MUST TEST YOUR FAITH. TO KEEP YOU ON YOUR PATH. DO NOT BE TEMPTED BY THE WILES OF CHAOS. REMEMBER WHAT POWER YOU SERVE.

I held my hands together in prayer. *Thank you, Father. I'm grateful for your love and mercy. I'll do better, I promise you.*

Dor's voice left my mind. I remained hunched over in my tub, gasping for breath. Blood swirled down the drain, and I traced it across my cheeks.

I couldn't afford to let my mind wander. To allow myself to brush against sin.

All I had left was to focus on the task ahead.

I dried myself off and dressed with the optimism of a man who knew his life's problems would be ended with the comfort and certainty of his impending oblivion. There was joy in nonexistence. No pain. No guilt for past mistakes. No wallowing in said mistakes. No women making his life a misery, and oh yes, they did make his life a misery. Only never-ending blissful nothingness.

The welcoming void was the darkness of a good cup of tea.

Delightful.

But something gnawed at me.

For the past week, I'd been finding notes I assumed were leftovers from my past self, yet I couldn't remember writing them, despite the return of my memories. Kayl had mentioned meeting a version of myself I most certainly did not remember.

A future Quen.

If a future version of myself was bouncing back to the past, that would explain the notes, and also the odd blip in time I'd noticed.

Blips that only *I* had felt.

But none of that should be possible. Diviner could manipulate time to a point, but not travel that far back in time. Only an immortal—a god— had that level of power.

And none of my visions of the future indicated how or why. I was destined to die, not to become a time traveler. Something was wrong. Very wrong.

Had Dor sensed it, too? Did He know?

If my future self was leaving me messages, then perhaps he'd left another in the one place I knew I'd check.

I entered my kitchen and pulled open my tea jar.

There, resting above my tea leaves, was a note.

I took a few breaths to steady my heartbeat and pulled it out. It was my handwriting, all right.

"*Dear Past Me,*

Did you honestly think your future self would risk a paradox by leaving you clues? You know that's a bad idea. By the way, I ate your last bourbon biscuit. Sorry, chap."

I choked back a laugh. My future self was a scoundrel! At least he retained his sense of humor, though, blast it, I'd need more biscuits.

I flipped the note over, and there was more.

"*There is a sealed envelope under your bed. Do NOT open it. When the time comes, take that envelope and place it under the bench outside Central Station. You know the one. Leave it there when you see this word etched in flesh: deceit. Trust me.*"

What madness had my future self concocted?

"Quentin? Are you here?" called Pendula from the hall.

I hastily stuffed the note into my trouser pocket. "Just making tea!" I popped my head into the living room, where Pendula had wandered in.

She looked flustered. "Apologies for being tardy, Your Excellency. The tram was thirteen seconds late. Can you believe such a thing?"

"Unfortunately." Standards had slipped after the disruption of Central Station. "Make yourself comfortable. Would you like tea?"

She tucked her skirt beneath her and sat on the couch. "Yes please. Two sugars and a splash of milk. The old classic."

The classic indeed. "You'd not prefer coffee?"

"Goodness, no. My taste palate is far too refined."

Perhaps our marriage wasn't doomed.

I brewed us both a cup and dug out what biscuits were left—custard creams. These hadn't been touched since Kayl had last visited my apartment. A thought I didn't want to dwell on.

"Thank you," Pendula said as I handed over a cup. She'd already pulled a folder out of her satchel that was half-open across the couch. Her clockwork bird was perched on top of my bookcase, the cogs of its body whirring away. "I've taken the liberty of documenting your progress today.

Father informed me of your success in Arcadia. Congratulations. That now leaves you with three domains, correct?"

I settled into my armchair. "Correct."

She put aside her tea and lifted a file. "Based on my discussions with Ambassador Morana and Ambassador Willow, it seems Juniper will be the hardest to convince. Faen is simply uninterested in Chime, or what their Fauna get up to. The Nameless One is willing to negotiate."

I leaned forward. "Oh?"

"They're happy to lend their power in exchange for a Chaos mortal. It seems The Nameless One is curious about them."

"No. Absolutely not. I'll not hand over any mortal to be used by The Nameless One." Because that was what they'd want a mortal for—to dissect, poke and prod.

"Your Excellency, is now really the time to worry about morals? You've got less than two days left."

And this was why I struggled dating mortals of my own domain. Their sense of morality was distinctly different from mine. "The whole point of this exercise is to ensure no one is hurt or otherwise abused, including Chaos. And please, if we're to be married, you may as well start calling me Quen."

A pink blush bloomed across her silver cheeks. "Then please call me Penny."

"Penny." A lovely name. Not common among Diviner.

I could learn to love it. To whisper it at night when I sought comfort from the dark.

Penny took a sip of her tea, though she ignored the biscuits. "I want to help you succeed. That is why Dor assigned me to be your assistant—your wife."

"I appreciate your assistance." Well, no, her assistance was meddlesome, but the least I could do was respect her efforts. "But we're not sacrificing mortals at The Nameless One's altar. I have another proposal in mind. An arrangement that may win the Glimmer to our side."

Penny sat in polite silence as I went over Kayl's idea. I didn't know if it would work, but saints, I wanted to try.

"Leave this with me," she said at last. "I'll meet with Ambassador Gloria and convince her to listen."

"Shouldn't I be the one to meet with her?"

"I mean no disrespect, but Glimmer respond better to a female touch. They're open to meeting with me, and Father willing, they'll see reason."

In truth, I'd rather *not* handle Gloria. "Then I'll leave it in your capable hands. Before you go… I thought we could get to know each other. It would make, ah, our upcoming nuptials less awkward."

She tucked her folder away and sat with her hands clasped in her lap. The perfect picture of a demure woman. "What do you wish to know?"

"Your past, your interests. Your idiosyncrasies."

"You should know my past. You've read my file, have you not?"

I'd skimmed it. "Of course."

"The circumstances of my birth are usually the first thing mortals inquire of."

I could imagine. Female Diviner were rare, but those born to a mother and second father were rarer still. "You must miss Hector?"

"Work keeps me busy. And I rather enjoy tinkering with my birds." She whistled, and her clockwork pet flew over and landed on her shoulder. "I hope you don't mind their presence. It was my second father who taught me how to program them."

"They're wonderful." Truly, they were. Their design was intricately crafted with tiny clockwork parts. The fact she'd been able to 'train' them to perform menial tasks was impressive, too. We Diviner loved to play with our hands. To create and improve.

"It's sentimental, but… these birds remind me of him. While I may have lost my second father, I still have my Father. I find comfort in His prayers."

"Quite right. Do you know many other female Diviner other than your mother?"

"Very few. You couldn't possibly understand what it's like to be a woman in Kronos."

"I have an inkling."

"Would you?"

"I'm an ex-Warden. I've seen enough—"

"Forgive me for being blunt, but I doubt you'd understand."

"Then enlighten me."

She took a measured sip of her tea and eyed me over the rim. "There's so few of us that when we speak, our complaints are infantilized and dismissed. We're Dor's children, yet there's a prevalent misconception that the female mind is somehow deficient compared to the male. That we're not as logical, and somehow more emotional. This apparently makes us lesser." Her silver eyes held a defiant conviction that reminded me of Kayl. "Have you seen a male Diviner behave when their clock breaks? They forget anger is also an emotion to be scorned."

"I know some males can be brutes—"

"Don't let their behavior off lightly. So many males feel entitled to a female's time, energy, and presence. So many try to take what they demand is owed. The number of times I've been touched inappropriately by a male is... too many. That is why I became a bureaucrat. To provide a voice where none exists. To prove to Father that the female mind is no lesser. That is why... I'm hoping you'll listen."

Ah. It made sense now.

Penny may be as enthusiastic about our pairing as I was, but she'd accept the marriage because of the opportunity my status provided. As ambassador, I could elevate her voice. Bring forth change.

And I would.

Her voice needed to be heard.

I sat on the couch beside her. The scar across her collarbone was hidden by her blouse, which was buttoned up to her neck. How many more scars did she hide? How many more would be carved into her skin due to my failures?

Would one of them say *deceit*? Or was that my future scar to bear?

My own scars had been wiped clean from my mortal body. Reset.

I still remembered the bite of Elijah's belt.

I remembered the shame those scars had ingrained into my soul.

"I'm sorry." My gaze lingered on her neck. "I never meant for my deficiencies to hurt you. From now on, I promise to do right by you. To honor you as only a husband can." What kind of husband would I make?

An attentive one? An affectionate one? Regardless, I'd try for her sake. "You shouldn't be my reward for being a good boy."

Her hand slid to my knee. A subtle touch that almost made me flinch. "Perhaps you're my reward. I'll honor you as a wife honors a husband. I'm not... I'm not pure. I've fornicated before with other women. I'm sorry."

"I too have fornicated previously. With men, not with other women." Such a foolish word now that I thought about it. I'd *fucked* three men. How many mortals had Penny fucked? The thought of learning such sinful, illicit knowledge thrilled me. "Do you... enjoy coitus?" Enjoy fucking? As I did?

Her cheeks blushed again. "Coitus is merely for procreation. I'm willing to engage in such activities for the sake of providing you with a son."

There it was. The Diviner distaste for sins of the flesh.

We'd be trapped in a sexless, loveless marriage.

And... that was all right, wasn't it?

It was a sin to find pleasure in such things. To enjoy the taste of cock on one's tongue. To desire the swell of a woman's budding sex. To want to tear open their dresses and grope their breasts, sucking upon their nipples. To warm my cock inside them, as I enjoyed men warming their cocks inside me.

Sin consumed me. Ravaged me. I wanted it to.

Saints. I needed to control my urges, otherwise I'd only be hurting Penny. The urge to fuck didn't seem to infect others of my domain, yet my urges had gotten worse since...

Since I'd met Kayl.

Stop it, Quen. Stop going down that path, you depraved degenerate.

Penny was willing to give me a child. A blessing. That was enough.

It didn't matter if that was what I wanted. It was what Dor wanted. Father knew what was best for me.

Penny was conventionally beautiful. Charming. Intelligent. A good conversationalist. And she held a distaste for coffee. I could see why other Diviner would covet her. Why anyone would be delighted to marry her. Perhaps in time our connection would develop. I could learn to love her. Maybe even desire her.

But there was one problem.

"May I kiss you?" I asked.

She whistled a command, and her bird hopped down onto the table. "You may."

Penny cupped my cheek.

The last Diviner to do that was Elijah. Sometimes I still imagined the imprint of his hand. The soft caress. The harsh blow when I'd displeased him. What would he think if he knew I was betrothed to a woman? A female Diviner?

I'd never wanted to enter a relationship where I held power over another, whether politically or not. Penny was technically my subordinate. Our relationship had already begun with a power imbalance. I didn't want to become another Elijah.

I wanted an equal.

A partner.

We awkwardly shuffled together, our bodies attempting to fit the shape of each other. Her modest bosom pressed against my chest

I leaned close. Her eyes fluttered shut, though I couldn't keep myself from gazing down to her collarbone, to where her skin was marked with my sin.

Would I ever see her naked? Would we fornicate in the dark? Every sin etched into her flesh would be a reminder of my failings.

I'd been designed to experience pleasure in sex, but to also feel shame for such temptations. Penny wasn't my reward.

No. She was my punishment.

I brushed against her sweet, soft lips. Breathed in the subtle scent of rosemary.

Then my body went rigid, and I fell into darkness.

The city was falling apart.

I'd grown up with these skyscrapers, and they were crumbling before my eyes. The gray skies of home had turned a solid white, and a wave of nothingness tumbled toward me.

Chaos had won.

She had finally won.

"Father!" I fell to my knees. "I'm sorry! I failed you, Father! Forgive me."

My Father was dead, and I'd done nothing to save Him.

Diviner screamed and ran from the nothingness, but their bodies faded to dust.

The clocks of Kronos chimed erratically, in and out of time. This wasn't just the end of my Father. Of my home. Of me.

It was the end of time.

The end of everything.

I glanced at my hands. Dust fell from my skin.

For one brief moment in my timeline, I had loved another. That too came to an end.

I was out of time.

Forgive me—

I sucked in a sharp intake of breath.

"No!" I pushed away from Penny. I'd expected to experience her death, but not like that.

Saints. Not like that!

Kronos had faded through her eyes. I'd witnessed a vision of the end of the domains and refused to believe it. But this... This confirmed the end of my own domain.

The end of the Diviner.

Of time.

Of everything.

My entire body was shaking. My bones were rattling, my teeth chattering. Oh gods.

Penny's bird was flapping around the room, chirping with a mechanical trill.

"Quen? Are you all right?"

I drew in a breath. "I'm—I'm sorry. I should have warned you—my sense of touch is quite sensitive. I get visions easily."

"What did you see?"

Saints, what could I say? That I'd not only experienced her death, but the death of every Diviner? Would another of my domain experience such a vision?

Would Dor have seen it?

"It doesn't matter." I steadied the rise and fall of my chest as my hand went into my pocket, searching for my fob watch. Instead, it found the note my future self had left me.

Did he know what was to come? Was he trying to help me? Warn me?

Diviner couldn't travel the timeline… unless time had broken.

If my future self was trying to fix it, then there was hope at least.

I needed to cling to that hope and continue on my path. Surely, if my actions to save Chaos led to this conclusion, then my future self would stop me?

Or was I merely fighting against inevitability?

I had the sudden urge to rummage under my bed and find that damn envelope.

The door to my apartment burst open. I leaped to my feet as Kayl bounded into my living room, followed by a flushed Ben.

Penny sat up straight. "What's the meaning of this interruption—"

"It's Dru!" Kayl blurted out, completely ignoring Penny. "She's been recalled to Heartstone!"

31

If you want something done right, get yourself to Heartstone. The Umber workshops are a sight to see, and as you'd expect, their work ethic produces some of the finest quality materials. Our Warden-issued uniforms and weaponry are produced in these workshops.
Heartstone offers additional training and apprenticeships for Wardens of any domain. I do recommend their courses on pistol maintenance and customization. They know their stuff.
—Q. Corinth, *Warden Dossier on Heartstone*

MY MORNING HAD ALREADY started off shitty, and learning Quen had traveled back to Chime without me—when I actually *needed* him—only pissed me off further.

And then I'd found him getting cozy with his newly betrothed over a cup of tea.

Quen's cheeks burned red, as though I'd caught him with his hand down his trousers. "Tell me everything that's happened."

I relayed what Dru had told me. Quen listened with a furrowed brow and Ben's face twisted with a horror resonating deep in the pit of my stomach.

Dru's god had recalled her to their domain. There were so many mortals in Chime, it was rare for a god to take a personal interest in a single mortal. Usually, that came down to their ambassador or the Wardens.

That Unghard had personally requested Dru's presence wasn't a good thing.

She wasn't quite a Godless, not like the rest of us. She still revered her god. But even associating with a group of apostates could have dire consequences.

If Dru didn't make the next crossing, I could lose her forever.

And if she did... I could still lose her.

Everything about this was pure, fresh shit.

"Where's Dru now?" Quen asked.

"I left her back at the tem—at our base." Shit, I almost spilled our cover! I drew in a breath. "She's distraught."

"We need to help her, sir," Ben urged.

"It's because of that damn ambassador!" I said. "You've got to sort this out."

Quen reached for his jacket. "All right, calm down. Ben and I will return to the embassy and speak with Hazelhearth. We'll meet at Central Station to make the afternoon crossing into Heartstone—"

"You can't be considering a crossing *now*?" Quen's assistant finally spoke up. "Need I remind you of your tight schedule?"

"Apologies, Penny. This is a delicate matter. Can I leave you to manage my affairs while I'm gone?"

Penny? Ugh.

"Why can't *Ambassador* Arkey manage this herself?" said 'Penny' with undisguised contempt.

Oh, she didn't like me, did she? The feeling was mutual. "I require my partner's help. Do be a dear and go make me a cup of tea. Three sugars and a dollop of cream, ta."

"I want to ensure this doesn't jeopardize our bargain with Unghard." Quen gave me a warning look that said *please don't start something*.

I *really* wanted to start something.

Pendulum or whatever clicked her tongue. "Trust Chaos to jeopardize an operation designed to save itself."

I didn't think I could dislike this bitch more. "Do you have a problem with me? Because I'm about to make one."

"That's all Chaos is good for, isn't it?"

"That's enough," Quen barked. "Penny, continue working with the Glimmer. Ben and I will escort Kayl and Miss Smith to Heartstone on the afternoon crossing. I expect you both to arrive at Central Station *on time*."

Both Penny and I scowled at Quen.

"Fine," I said. "Don't be late." I swaggered out of Quen's living room and turned on my heel to shoot one last glare at his betrothed on my exit.

A clockwork bird sat on her shoulder.

The same design as the clockwork bird I'd spotted outside the Vesper temple. Shit. The same toy bird one of the Mesmer trio had been playing with.

Was Quen's assistant spying on me behind his back? But why? Did she not trust her newly betrothed? Or was it jealousy for all the time Quen and I spent together? I was a beautiful woman setting out to steal Quen's heart. And unlike Diviner, I knew how to fuck. Pendulum better be worried.

When I had Quen alone in Heartstone, I'd pass on my concerns about Penny.

But right now, my concerns were elsewhere.

I needed to help my best friend survive her god.

To avoid any awkwardness, Quen suggested I enter Heartstone in a Diviner form. The sight of me masquerading as an Umber may provoke offense, but for the first time, I wanted to be an Umber—to stand in solidarity with Dru.

Dru, however, was too worried about our visit to care either way.

So I made the crossing as a Diviner.

The air was much cooler as we passed from Chime to Heartstone. Wind whistled above me, and a gust almost lifted my skirt.

"Oh my," I gasped.

We were up pants-shittingly high on some sort of mountain ledge that put Lionheart's plateau to shame. Stone buildings were carved out of the mountainside, reachable from pathways, ledges, and outcrops that covered multiple layers heading both above and below us in a spiral around the entire damn mountain. There were too many buildings to count. An entire city's worth. And some disappeared into darkened caverns.

A wide cobblestone road provided the means of traversing this madness, though there was no railing to ward off the aggressive wind. I supposed mortals made of stone didn't need to fear being blown off.

More jagged mountains stretched across the horizon like teeth, cutting into the sky. Whirls of clouds dusted their tops white, but their peaks cut through the clouds to stretch as high as the sun.

Below, lines of blue snaked through fields of green. It reminded me a little of Eventide, what with the never-ending farmland. But the quaint houses below were made of stone, not mushrooms, and the farmers were Umber.

Heartstone was quite the sight.

"Welcome to my home," Dru said with the dejected air of one about to be sentenced to death. I swallowed my awe, remembering the real reason we were here.

Gods. It was *just* like returning to Eventide.

Hopefully we wouldn't have to kill Unghard to escape.

"Move aside, please," called out an Umber dressed in a Warden's outfit.

A steam wagon rolled toward us, and we quickly shuffled out of its way. More wagons followed, each carrying wooden crates, and they disappeared through the Gate.

Heartstone's Gate was a lumbering mass of stone and twisted vines. Those same dark vines spread across the cobblestone road like veins, between a lush carpet of moss beneath my feet. I swallowed another gasp as a rainbow of colorful daisies bloomed across the Gate's arch. Beautiful.

The magic was broken by a large Umber made of a dark red rock who shoved past me carrying a sack over his shoulder.

Gods, there were so many Umber of a variety I'd never seen step foot in Chime! The usual stone-skinned Umber with their flowery eyebrows, but taller ones made from jagged boulders twice my height, and women who resembled trees more than stone.

They bustled around carrying tools or crates. Not a single one of them stood still to relax or breathe in the fresh, pine-scented air. The natural ambience was spoiled by the banging of hammers and the hiss of steam coming from somewhere, and the rattle of more wagons rolling past.

The chaos of creation. The drudgery of work.

"Druzy Smith," called a familiar voice. "And Ambassadors Corinth and Arkey. What a surprise."

We turned as the Umber ambassador approached. Quen hadn't been able to contact her since I left him this morning because she'd rather conveniently chose to hide in her domain, forcing us to come all this way. The bitch.

"Ambassador Hazelhearth." Quen greeted her with a polite bow. "I hope you don't mind my intrusion, but you can understand why I'm here—"

"Dru is my bodyguard!" I blurted out. "What right do you have to drag her here?"

"What right?" Hazelhearth looked affronted. "Miss Smith is one of my mortals, and this is her home. You invade our domain to make demands of *me*?"

"Kayl," Quen warned.

I ignored him. "Do your mortals not have free will? Or have you forgotten the Covenant?"

"We obey the laws of the Covenant—"

"Then Dru should be allowed to seek employment at will."

"Miss Smith is still beholden to Unghard. Or did you skip that part of the Covenant, Ambassador Arkey?"

I ground my teeth. Never would I have thought an Umber to be as uptight as a pissing Glimmer, but what did I expect from mortals made of stone?

Dru touched my arm. "Leave it," she mumbled. "I'll meet with Unghard."

Hazelhearth flashed a pleasant smile. "Naturally. That's why you're here. I understand your concerns, Ambassador Arkey, and yours too, Corinth. If you'd like, we can discuss those in private while Miss Smith meets with her family. They are eager to see you before your meeting with the Heart Tree."

Dru nodded, her head drooping in defeat. "Is it okay if Kayl— Ambassador Arkey accompanies me?"

"If she must. A Warden will come fetch you when it's time. Now, this way please, Ambassador Corinth."

Quen patted me on the shoulder. "Don't panic yet," he whispered. "I'll sort this out."

"I'm not losing Dru," I whispered back.

"You won't." He stepped after Hazelhearth. "Ben, with me."

Anxiety contorted Ben's face. "But, sir—"

"Give Dru her privacy."

"I'll be fine," Dru said, forcing a meek smile.

Ben didn't look convinced, but he jogged after Quen, leaving the two of us alone.

Dru's shoulders sagged. "I don't think I can do this."

I took both her shoulders and squeezed them. "Listen to me. You're one of the bravest mortals I know—"

"I'm really not—"

"No? So who was that girl who infiltrated Lady Mae's teahouse with me? Who evaded a swarm of Wardens? Who rode on top of an elevator all the way down to the Undercity? Who confronted Serenity as my bodyguard?"

"I only did those things because you made me."

"I may have talked you into some of them, but *you* did them. You."

"But that's it, isn't it? I'm only brave when I'm with you. When I'm alone, I'm... not. How can I do this? Look, my flowers have barely grown, I'm a mess—"

"Dru. If you need me with you, then I'm here for you, okay? I always will be. And if you want to run back through the Gate and escape, then we can go find jobs in Memoria." Fuck Chaos and the other domains. I always figured I was destined for the life of a wanted fugitive, anyhow.

She sucked in a breath. "No, it's okay. I need to do this. Are—Are you sure you want to meet my family? They can be, uh, a rowdy lot."

"I put up with Harmony and Sinder. How bad can your family be?"

She grimaced.

We followed the road leading up the mountain, though I hoped we weren't about to climb the entire thing. While we had emerged out of the Gate high up, the damn mountain was taller than I thought.

Dru instructed me to carefully step over the vines and roots literally everywhere, as stepping on them was a sign of disrespect. They truly *did* get everywhere; their green tendrils crept up the walls, wrapping around the many stone buildings in a tender embrace. Glowing golden flowers sprouted from these, providing the only light source.

Other trees and bushes sprouted between the buildings on the mountainside, and these too glowed with colorful petals that brought the mountain to life in a glowing mosaic.

"Umber families are large," Dru was explaining as we walked up and up. "They're all based on a particular craft or trade. It's normal for family members to pitch in and learn."

"What's your family's trade?"

"Smithing. That's what we're named after."

"What made you leave?" When I'd met Dru, she'd been apprenticing with the clock tower engineers on their piping before volunteering at Grayford's soup kitchen, and the rest was history.

"We're supposed to volunteer for charity work every year. It's what Unghard asks of us. I wanted a break from smithing—from my family. They can be stifling. They weren't happy with me volunteering for work on Chime, but I liked it there. I liked being... me. And not another Smith."

After meeting my own mother and fighting my twin sister, I could relate. "So you're good with hot, thick rods? Does Ben know?" I waggled my brow.

"Don't you dare mention Ben in front of my family. I swear, Kayl, I'll push you off the mountain."

"My lips are sealed." I winked.

My calves were screaming by the time Dru stopped outside a series of workshops. The same vines spread across the walls, acting as natural curtains for the windows, and as a makeshift curtained door of dangling leaves. An older Umber woman stood outside hammering a piece of metal over an anvil. Her skin was a similar mossy green as Dru's, though her eyebrows were made from white daisies that wilted from exertion.

"Wish me luck," Dru whispered.

The older woman straightened. "Druzy? Is that you, my girl?"

"It's me, Mom. I'm home."

Dru's mother tossed her hammer aside and launched herself at Dru. "My god, I was so worried!" She clasped Dru tight. "You haven't written in weeks, and we heard of an attack on Chime—"

"I'm fine, Mom. Seriously."

The two of them embracing warmed my gut. Had I ever been comforted in such a manner? My childhood memories were hazy, but I remembered *someone* gifting me the rarest substance in the Undercity.

Kindness.

I WOULD HAVE LOVED MY DAUGHTERS, GIVEN THE CHANCE. TO HOLD YOU AND YOUR SISTER IN MY ARMS WOULD BE A BLESSING.

What would life have been like with Corentine as my mother? *You have children, and they turned into eleven insufferable spoilt gods.*

I CANNOT CONTROL WHO MY CHILDREN BECOME, NOR WOULD I WISH TO.

Yet you try to control my life while vying for the destruction of my friends. Or can you honestly say you wouldn't smite me if you were free?

THE GODS HAVE HAD MILLENNIA TO REPENT AND FIX THEIR MISTAKE. THAT ONLY A FEW WOULD COME TO MY AID SHOULD SPEAK OF THEIR LOVE AND LOYALTY. YOU, HOWEVER, ARE A MORTAL PRONE TO MISTAKES. I AM FORGIVING, DAUGHTER.

That's nice to know. So I release you, and we, what? Treat ourselves to tea and scones? Go shopping and then do each other's makeup as a mother and daughter should?

WE WOULD SMITE THE GODS FOR BREAKFAST AND CELEBRATE WITH BLUEBERRY PANCAKES AFTER. I KNOW YOUR DESIRES.

How thoughtful of you. Still, I'm not quite sold on bonding over genocide.

IT CAN BE THERAPEUTIC. YOU SHOULD TRY IT SOMETIME.

Gods. I'd have to remind myself to never take Corentine's advice on anything, ever.

"Mom, this is Kayl," Dru was introducing me as I caught back up to reality.

"A Diviner, how quaint!" said Mrs. Smith. "Please, come inside. I'll brew us some tea. I know how much you Diviner love tea."

I dipped into a quick curtsy and channeled my inner Quen. "That's all right, ma'am. You needn't trouble yourself."

"So polite, too! Where did you find this one, Druzy?"

"Well, um, she found me, really."

I followed Dru and her mother into the modest stone building. The entire front was a blacksmith's workshop stuffed full of at least thirteen Umber men and women busying themselves with tools such as hammers and prongs. Others of various ages, ranging from young to old, helped stoke the forge fires.

"It's Druzy!" they murmured among themselves in excited whispers, their soot-stained faces breaking out in wide grins.

Dru was loved, and yet she seemed to shrink in their presence. Why?

I couldn't just blurt out and ask.

The heat from the forge was uncomfortably hot, but thankfully Dru's mother led us around the back. These homes seemed to be dug into the mountain itself, and we entered a dimly lit passage leading to a much cooler living space.

This too was made of stone, with no natural light at all. More glowing plants gave the room a cozy glow. And while much of the furniture appeared to be carved out of the very ground and walls, they were covered in woven rugs, blankets, and cushions.

Dru gestured for me to sit beside her on a stone couch. It was solid under my arse, but the cushion helped.

Mrs. Smith had taken off her blacksmith apron, though her green hands were still stained black. "Are you sure you wouldn't like a cup of tea? It's no trouble at all."

"I'm fine, thank you."

"Go on, I make a lovely brew—"

"She said no, Mom."

"I'll make you one in case you change your mind." Mrs. Smith hurried from the room, though she stole one quick glance at Dru, as though not believing she sat there.

Dru sighed.

"You mother seems nice," I said, nudging Dru. "You're not happy to be here?"

"I love them, but they're overbearing at times."

"At least your mother isn't a psychopath who wants to destroy the domains."

"She could be if she wanted to."

I let out a low chuckle, and my eye caught a painting on the wall—a family portrait. There must have been at least twenty Umber squeezed into the one canvas. Mrs. Smith stood at the back next to a stony male with golden eyebrows—Dru's father, I presumed. The rest stood at various heights with golden, white, and even pink flowers. Their mosslike skin covered a range of green hues.

And there, in the middle, stood a smaller, younger, grumpy Dru.

"How many siblings do you have?" I asked.

"A lot. I told you; Umber have big families."

"And you're the youngest?"

"The baby of the family."

I could see why she'd feel overwhelmed. They likely coddled her, as the Godless were prone to coddling me. And yes, that felt frustrating at times. They didn't trust me to make my own decisions. Did Dru's family treat her with the same condescension?

"Here we are," announced Mrs. Smith as she entered with a tray. "One cup of tea for the Diviner, and a lemonade for my Druzy Whoozy."

Yes, I think I'd nailed it on the head, there.

"Mom, I'm twenty-five."

"But you'll always be my special Druzy Whoozy."

WOULD YOU LIKE ME TO GIVE YOU AN APPROPRIATE AND ENDEARING NICKNAME?

Don't you dare! I'd sooner throw myself in front of a tram!

MY PRETTY PANCAKE.

Stop it!

Mrs. Smith sat on a couch opposite. "We've been so worried, your father and I. Chime's dangerous, and when you stopped writing, we thought you'd fallen in with the wrong crowd, like a group of Vesper or something—"

"Chime's really quite safe." I smiled to hide my sudden flash of irritation. "I've lived there my whole life."

"The Gate went down for days after the attack. How could you call that safe? From our perspective, we had no idea what was going on, and then the ambassador herself comes to our door and starts asking questions—"

"What kind of questions?" Dru demanded.

"About you, and where you worked. I told her you were apprenticed with the station. Can you see how it looked? Your father and I were beside ourselves worrying that you'd been killed in the line of duty!" Mrs. Smith composed herself. "Why didn't you write or visit or anything? Your father made the crossing to the station, and do you know what they said? They said you didn't work there anymore. What were we supposed to think? What were we supposed to tell the ambassador?"

Dru wrung her hands in her lap. "*You* prayed to Unghard?"

"We prayed for you every night. Unghard listened."

Silence hung in the little stone room. Poor Mrs. Smith had only cared for her daughter and meant well, but her ignorance of the gods and their whims could well have damned Dru.

Was it ignorance or blind hope? I could understand her concerns. And Unghard was allegedly the kindest of the gods, but still a god.

I took Dru's hand and gave it a gentle squeeze.

Dru yanked her hand back. "Kayl, don't—"

Shit! I was a pissing idiot!

At one touch, my Diviner form instantly changed to the stony-blue of an Umber. I'd known of my bloody ability to swap forms for months now, and still there were moments I forgot and *this* happened!

Why did you make me so damn useless? I yelled into my mind.

YOU ARE WONDERFUL AS YOU ARE, MY PRETTY PANCAKE.

Keep calling me that and I'll march all the way to Kronos and tell Dor what a horrible bitch you are.

YOU WOULDN'T.

Mrs. Smith was already on her feet and shrieking while waving a hammer at me, though quite where she'd gotten the hammer from, I wasn't sure. "What are you? Get away from my Druzy!"

Dru was standing between us like a shield. "It's fine, Mom, I can explain—"

"She was a Diviner! And don't you tell me I'm getting old, young lady—"

"I'm no danger to you, ma'am." I raised my hands. "I swear. Dru and I are friends—"

"Friends! I knew you'd fallen in with the wrong crowd, didn't I say— look at the state of your flowers, Druzy!"

The ground shook, and then an entire line of Umber burst into the room, all yelling questions at once.

"Stop!" Dru yelled. "Listen to me for once!"

But Dru's family continued to talk over her, their fury pinned on me.

Once again, Quen was right. That absolute arse.

The shouting suddenly stopped. No, the entire room went still. Even Dru, who'd been caught midgrimace.

"Such dramatics." Quen tutted as he squeezed past the bodies caught in time. "Didn't I tell you *not* to switch form?"

"Yes, well, I forgot. And now everyone's angry."

"I can see that. It's time." He adjusted his bow tie. "Unghard is ready to meet with Dru."

My heart sank. "Were you able to speak with the ambassador? Convince her this is all some foolish misunderstanding?"

"I tried. But ultimately, Unghard still wishes to meet with Dru personally, and none of us can deny the will of a god."

I damn well wanted to.

Quen stepped beside me and allowed time to resume. The shouting came to a confused stop as Dru's family took in the sight of him. He wisely took advantage of their surprise. "Good afternoon. I'm Quentin Corinth, ambassador to the Diviner. I'm here with my partner, Ambassador Kayl Arkey, to represent Druzy. If you don't mind, Ambassador Hazelhearth is here to escort her to Unghard."

Dru lifted her chin high and strode from the room. A few of her family patted her on the shoulder and whispered murmurs of encouragement. Did any of them fear Unghard's wrath? Did they understand what their god could do?

I avoided their curious stares and followed Dru. No matter what happened, I'd be by her side.

Hazelhearth and Ben waited for us outside. The Umber ambassador gave me a cool look, clearly unimpressed with my Umber form, and led the way without a word.

We continued up the mountain. My lumbering pace slowed as the air grew cooler. Even the hammering below us quieted in reverence to Dru's fate. Leaves occasionally floated past. Odd leaves, which shimmered as they fell.

Honestly, I'd not expected to walk this damn much, and I feared we'd be pushing through the clouds next. I glanced at Quen, who wasn't the best with heights. He'd been chewing his lip raw.

I wanted to ask how he was faring, but then the road flattened into a crevice cut from the peak of the mountain.

And there, towering over the center like a giant umbrella, was the largest tree I'd ever seen in my life. Its branches cast shadows across the mountain, its leaves aglow in an almost ethereal shimmer of color that shifted in an incandescent hue with the breeze.

Even its bark was embedded with a splendor of colorful gemstones. Rubies, sapphires, and emeralds glinted in the light.

Truly, it was a magnificent tree to which no other could compare.

"The Heart Tree," Quen said beside me. "The heart of Heartstone."

"It's... so beautiful," Ben gasped with awe.

"Is that Unghard?" I whispered to Quen.

"Technically, all the plants in Heartstone are Unghard. They choose to speak directly to mortals via the Heart Tree."

All the plants were Unghard? But they were bloody everywhere! That was gods for you—forever watchful, like perverted bathroom creeps.

You better not watch over me when I shit.

THE MORTAL NEED TO DEFECATE IS ENTERTAINING.

Wait. Gods don't shit?

WHY WOULD WE?

The pissing joys of being mortal. *I like my privacy, thank you.*

I wasn't sure if Corentine was deliberately trying to distract me, but I'll admit, arguing with her did interrupt my anxiety. It churned in my stomach the closer we got to that damn tree and then threatened to spill altogether as we stood before it.

The Heart Tree received the reverence it so deserved. At its base were lit candles, miniature carved statues in the shapes of Umber, tiny trees and potted plants, and fruit baskets. Tributes, rather than tithes.

Between those stood two massive Golems. These were twice the size of ordinary Umber, and lacked their friendly facial features. Flowers still bloomed from their brow, but their eyes were a solid onyx.

Immortals, Dru had once told me. Unghard's servants.

Footsteps echoed behind us. Dru's family had followed us. All of them, by the looks of the mob. They huddled together in fevered whispers, but didn't dare step closer.

Perhaps they were worried after all?

Hazelhearth placed a hand on Dru's shoulder. "You know what our Heart asks of you. Go ahead."

I met Dru's golden eyes. It wasn't fear, there.

It was almost an apology.

I love you, I wanted to say, but the words caught in my throat.

She nodded, as though she read them on my face.

Then she approached the Heart Tree and kneeled in prayer.

Quen wrapped his arm around mine, his grip tight. I appreciated the comfort of his touch, though he said nothing, choosing to do the stoic Diviner thing. I wanted to speak with him about his assistant, but now really wasn't the time, and I feared even breath would disturb Dru's prayer.

This was a holy moment, and I distinctly hated it.

Instead, I glanced at Ben, who stood as rigid as only a trained Warden could, but his face was struggling to maintain composure. He was an apostate, Dru had said. He understood, at least.

We were united in our concern for Dru.

It felt like an age had passed when Dru finally stood.

And then the vines covering the ground came alive. They wrapped around her torso and lifted her.

Her family gasped behind her, but not in fright—in delight.

"What's going on?" I asked.

"Druzy Smith has been chosen to ascend!" exclaimed Hazelhearth.

"Ascend?" What in god's name did that mean? Dru's family were hugging each other and weeping with joy.

"To become one of Unghard's protectors, guarding the Heart Tree. This is a great honor for the Smith family!"

A protector. An immortal.

My heart didn't plummet. It dropped through the entire domain into nothingness.

"An *honor*?" The words tasted like poison in my mouth. "Do you understand what it means to become immortal? Because I pissing do."

Immortals didn't have free will, not like mortals. Sure, they lived forever, but they were trapped in their domain. They could never make the crossing into Chime. And they were nothing more than puppets, slaves to their god's will.

To turn a mortal into *that* was no honor. It was no gift.

It was an unthinkable punishment.

It was worse than death.

"You wear our face, but you don't understand our customs." Hazelhearth sneered. "Umber are born to serve. Only those lucky few are chosen to serve Unghard directly—"

"*Lucky?*" I shrieked. "You call having your freedom ripped out of your arse lucky?" I stared at Dru, who was hanging in midair. There was still time to stop this. "Quen, you need to do something!"

Quen looked pained. "I'm sorry. There's nothing I can do."

His arm tightened around mine. He'd known this was going to happen. Shit, even Dru had known, and they'd both chosen to keep it from me.

Fuck this!

I tore from Quen and ran over to the tree. If any Ember were here, I would have switched to their form and burned the damn thing down!

"Kayl, stop!" Quen called.

I ignored him and glared up at the tree. "If you're everywhere, then hear me! You have *no* right to force a mortal into immortality! This goes against the Covenant! Dru is not your damn slave—"

Vines shot from the ground and whipped toward me. I skipped out of the way, but then another wrapped around my ankle, and then another, holding me in place.

CHAOS ENTERS MY DOMAIN AND DISTURBS MY GARDEN, boomed a deep, ancient voice in my mind that certainly didn't belong to Corentine. *IT SEEMS THE OLD ROOTS HAVE GROWN NEW FRUIT. I SENSE CORENTINE'S SCENT WITHIN YOU.*

Unghard, I presume? Let me go, you fuck!

YOU ARE A WEED WITHIN THE STONE. A DEADLY THORN THAT WOULD TANGLE MY GARDEN, AS YOU HAVE TANGLED MY MORTAL.

I haven't tangled Dru! Whatever the shit that meant. *She's a caring, charitable woman who deserves better than your so-called transcendence—*

DID SHE NOT BREAK THE COVENANT WHEN SHE JOINED YOUR GODLESS?

Shit. There it was. *Dru was never one of us, not really. She helped us because she saw how mortals were being treated by their gods and she wanted to help! She's no apostate. She's principled—you can't punish her for being a decent mortal—*

SHE CHOSE TO SERVE CHAOS.

Not Chaos. Me. Because we're friends!

THEN YOU CONFIRM THAT MY CHILD HAS BECOME MISGUIDED. I AM AWARE OF WHAT YOU ARE. IT WAS CHAOS THAT DESTROYED EVENTIDE AND ITS MORTALS. YOU ARE A DANGER TO MY UMBER.

I'm no danger to you or your mortals—

YOU INVADE MY DOMAIN AND THREATEN ME. I WOULD SNAP YOU INTO TWIGS, BUT MY CHILD OFFERS HER SERVICE FREELY IN EXCHANGE FOR YOUR EXILE. SHE IS STRONG. SHE WILL MAKE AN EXCELLENT GOLEM.

Shit, no! Dru couldn't do this to me! I'd sooner be a twig! *Please, listen to me! She is mortal! She deserves a mortal life!*

SHE IS UMBER. AND SHE HAS BEEN CALLED TO SERVE.

Above me, Dru still hung in the air, held only by Unghard's vines. Her eyes had lolled back into her skull. The tiny buds of her brow quivered.

And then she began to change.

"*No!*" I thrashed against the vines holding me back and tried to grab her, but Unghard dangled her out of reach. "Let her go!"

Tears ran down my cheeks as I watched my best friend transform from a mortal to immortal. Her spine grew longer, her limbs thicker with muscled stone that tore through her clothes.

Glowing golden flowers sprouted from her brow.

Unghard released her, and she dropped with a heavy thud that quaked through the mountain. Slowly, she stood. Her eyes opened to two dark irises. Pure black.

No. Gods no.

The vines around my feet receded. I ran to Dru, whose immortal form towered over me. It was her face—the same face as my best friend—albeit contorted to match her new form—and her flowers.

"Dru." My voice cracked. "Are you in there? Is any part of you still there?"

But the being staring back at me wasn't her.

It wasn't Dru.

Dru was gone.

"I love you," I choked out.

Dru's massive stone hand plucked a flower from her brow and let it fall.

I caught it and cradled it in my palm.

This wasn't how it was supposed to go.

I was Godless. I was supposed to protect mortals from their gods. Save them. I wasn't supposed to lose the friend who'd been by my side through thick and thin.

Not like this. *Never* like this.

How was I meant to do anything without Dru?

Behind me, Dru's family were celebrating—literally celebrating. Didn't they realize they'd lost her? Gods. They were proud.

It was Dru's own mother who'd damned her.

Quen approached. "This was her choice to make. Her sacrifice."

A sacrifice. Because now that Unghard and Hazelhearth had been appeased, our bargain would be solidified. Had Quen talked Dru into this? He'd allowed it.

It wasn't worth it. Chime wasn't worth it.

NOW YOU UNDERSTAND, Corentine said. *YOUR FRIEND IS NOTHING. TAKE UNGHARD'S SOUL, AND SHE'LL BE FREE.*

Corentine was right. Dru's soul was already gone.

I screamed and ran to the Heart Tree. I was going to stomp on its roots and rip off its stupid fucking branches and tear the whole thing to splinters!

"Ben!" Quen yelled.

I'd almost made it to the Heart Tree's thick trunk when Ben charged at me. He tackled me to the ground and pinned my arms behind me.

"Get off!"

"I'm sorry, ma'am. I can't do that."

"If you harm Unghard, you'll lose her forever!" Quen said, catching up to us both.

"She's gone! Don't you understand? She's *gone,* and you let her go!"

Quen crouched beside me. "She chose this path to protect *you.* Now take a moment to compose yourself. Dru will survive this. Unghard is kind to their subjects."

Unghard was anything but kind.

I stilled and allowed Ben to drag me up, though he didn't let go of my arm.

Blood dripped from Quen's nose. He'd paused time, allowing me to tire out my grief. Dru's family and Hazelhearth weren't aware of my outburst, but Unghard was.

YOU WILL LEAVE MY DOMAIN AND NEVER RETURN, they said.

Fuck that overgrown tree.

I wasn't going to lose Dru forever. No. I'd find a way to save her.

Dru stood guard by the Heart Tree, staring at nothing. Under the shadow of Unghard's branches, her golden daisies seemed to glow.

I glanced at my empty hand, and my heart stilled. In my rage, I'd dropped her flower.

I frantically searched behind me, but couldn't see it anywhere.

I'd let her down one final time.

Quen ushered us away from the Heart Tree. I touched Ben's hand and switched from an Umber form to a Diviner.

I'd never be an Umber again.

XXXII

If you can, stay away from the temples.
They are not the harmless communities they appear.
The Wardens encourage their use so they can track mortals within Chime.
If you wish to remain anonymous, do not enter them.
Those who are registered at their local temple are then known to the
Wardens and ambassadors. They will report any sins or missing tithes.
And your life in Chime will end.
—Anonymous, *Godless flier on the Temples*

INK SPILLED ON THE page and left an ugly smear by Druzy Smith's name.

It was more efficient to use a typewriter for these reports, but I'd always preferred writing by hand. There was a personal connection between holding a pen, dipping it into the black blood that sustained it, and then conducting words into some semblance of meaning. Sentences flowed better when dictated by my subtle touch, and each ink stain was a written scar earned by opening one's heart and pouring it onto paper.

My old masters had chastised me for such romantic notions, but what did they expect from a student in the School of Philosophy? My essays held a dramatic flair that lost respect. Even my Warden reports had a personal touch they disliked.

They wanted cold, hard facts. Logic.

I wanted a connection. Those we incarcerated or exiled were more than statistics, more than lines on a piece of paper. They were mortal lives. We needed to remember that.

But as I sat here and wrote this report, I tried to ignore connection for logic. To write down the facts of what had transpired in Heartstone. And *I* had to be the one to write it. This wasn't something I could pass onto Penny.

No. This was my doing. My pen that needed to bleed.

When I'd stopped being a Warden, I'd hoped my position as ambassador meant I wouldn't need to damn any more mortals to their gods. And then I'd gone and damned Dru.

I'd let Unghard claim her.

All to fuel my plan to save Chime, to save the domains. To save Kayl. Dru had known exactly what sacrifice she'd made. She could have run. She could have begged me to save her. But she didn't.

And Kayl... Saints.

I didn't know what was worse. Cursing Dru to life as an immortal slave, or damning her soul for eternity.

No, I needed to stop thinking that way.

Dru wasn't cursed. She was blessed. To become a saint was the highest honor any god could bestow, higher even than to become their voice. Ambassadors were still mortal. They needed to be in order to enter Chime, where saints could not. But to become a saint meant a connection with one's god that went beyond telepathy. Their will was your will. Your entire existence was devoted to them. Wouldn't it be lovely to no longer need to think or feel? To just be, and to do, in the name of your god? It was a noble calling.

The *highest* of honors.

My pen shook in my grip. More ink dripped to the page in tiny tear shapes.

The door opened, and I practically jumped from my seat.

Ben entered with a cup in his hand. "I brought tea for you, sir."

"Bless you." I shuffled papers aside. My desk was truly a disaster unbefitting my rank.

He placed it down and lingered in my office, swaying slightly on his feet. "Could we have done anything, sir?"

I wasn't sure how close he and Dru had been in the end, and my prodding and probing of their relationship likely hadn't helped. "I'm sorry. Where the gods are concerned, our hands are tied. You know that."

He hung his head, hiding the emotions cascading across his face. "I know, sir. But she was kind to me. She... taught me things. About plants.

About myself." He pulled a golden flower from his jacket pocket. Dru's flower. He must have picked it up on our way out of Heartstone. It looked in remarkably good condition, and I sensed a pocket of time surrounding the petals. He'd paused its decay. That... was frowned upon.

"Pray to our Father. Find comfort in His guidance. But if you'd rather speak in confidentiality, you can talk to me. My door is always open."

"I can't, sir." He glanced up with red eyes. "Because you'd report anything I'd say back to the Wardens—to Father."

"Ben—"

"I know you wouldn't do it maliciously, sir. But you're His voice."

"If there's something troubling you, I'd like to help. Off the record."

"I appreciate that, sir. I never congratulated you on your engagement to Miss Bezel, sir. It's not often we host weddings in Kronos."

A subtle change of topic. Though true, weddings weren't an extravagant affair for the Diviner—they were more of a bureaucratic box-ticking exercise. "Thank you. I'm sure any celebration will be to budget. We wouldn't want to waste the public's coffers on meaningless distraction."

"No, sir." He lingered by the doorway. "Do... Do you ever wish you were made different?"

"Different? Physically?" I studied Ben's expression, but his face remained uncharacteristically blank.

"Yes, sir, like... You look in the mirror and don't see yourself. You look... wrong."

I imagined a tall man like Ben would nurture such feelings, though to air them bordered on blasphemy. "Father made us how we are for a reason. Your height, my stunning intellect, all of it was designed by Him. To begrudge our flaws—warts and all—is to insult Father's divine plan."

"I understand, sir. I best go and catch up on my reports." He left my office, carefully clicking the door shut.

We all had our shadows, didn't we? Even poor Ben. How could mortals ever forge relationships when our gods were watching through us? It naturally bred distrust.

REMIND HIM OF HIS DUTIES. Father spoke in my mind. *AS MY VOICE, YOU MUST SET AN EXAMPLE.*

Of course, Father. Though I wasn't quite sure what ailed Ben. Clearly, he mourned Dru's absence.

YOUR GUARD IS PRONE TO SIN AND EMOTIONAL WEAKNESS. YOU ARE HIS MENTOR AND MUST CORRECT HIS PATH, AS ELIJAH ATTEMPTED TO CORRECT YOURS.

How could I correct another mortal's path? Fall in love with them? Erase their memories? Manipulate them into a relationship that involved fucking and flogging?

Shoot him in the head?

YOUR SARCASM BORDERS INSOLENCE.

Apologies, Father. I'll speak with Ben and write him up for a visit to Kronos.

BETTER.

The door opened again only moments later. Perhaps Ben was ready to reveal his deepest, darkest secrets.

"Ambassador Gloria is here to see you, sir."

Oh wonderful. An unexpected visit from Gloria was exactly what I needed. "Is she not here for Penny—Miss Bezel?"

"No, sir. She asked for you specifically."

Blast it. I quickly tidied up my desk and took a sip of scalding tea. "Send her in."

The Glimmer ambassador waltzed into my office, her golden skin lighting up the room and unfortunately highlighting the dust on my shelves. Her upturned nose examined the furnishings with an air of distaste. "Is there so little left in the Wardens' budget that our chairman must be forced to work in such a hovel?"

I gestured to the spare chair opposite my desk. "I prefer to work closer to the admin offices, my lady."

"How peculiar. I remember Karendar's office was more... clean than this." She pulled a handkerchief out of her brassiere and laid it carefully on the chair before sitting.

I bristled at the mention of Elijah. "Did you visit his office often?"

"But of course. Karendar and I were natural allies. We both believed in a Chime purged of sin. Such a shame Dor didn't see fit to continue his work."

"Unfortunately, Dor has greater concerns." I clasped my hands.

"Her Holiness Gildola shares Dor's concerns. Our domains have always worked together to do what is best for Chime. Under our combined leadership, Chime has flourished. Therefore, I cannot fathom why you and Dor would seek to shut us out."

Ah. The Glimmer were ready to bend. I knew they'd come around. "Not to shut you out, but to offer greater equality to the other domains—"

"You know as well as I that the other domains care not for law and order. The Seren care more for extravagant parties than politics, and even then, can you trust them not to manipulate rule to their favor? The Leander wish for more control, but their tactics are aggressive at best and destructive at worst. *We* have kept Chime stable—why fix what isn't broken?"

A Diviner metaphor. Gloria must be desperate. "Equality is written into the Covenant. I simply wish to apply it. You'll still have your position on the Council—"

"But to share rule with the likes of Erosain? Who cares nothing for the Covenant? Come now, Corinth. Let's put aside our differences for Chime's sake. The gods and their domains are not and never will be equal. Striving for such a noble goal is a fool's errand. Chime's citizens are our children, as we are children of the gods. They require guidance, stability, and yes, occasionally they need punishment to correct their behaviors."

Yes, I could see how Gloria and Elijah had become allies. "If you care for Chime, then you'll work with me to protect it."

"Haven't I tried?" Gloria waved her hand. "I've warned you and the Council of Chaos's influence. I'm sure even Dor would agree that attempting to rehabilitate their mortals is foolhardy. But I can see you won't be swayed. Very well. Gildola and I are willing to negotiate."

At last. I'd thank Penny for her efforts later. I snatched up my pen and a fresh piece of paper. "What are your terms?"

Gloria examined her nails, which were painted a bright red—ironic, since they despised Ember so much. "It seems that Faen is not interested in lending their power to Chime. This comes back to what I was trying to explain—not all the gods or their mortals care for Chime's affairs. The Fauna have always struggled to adapt to society. They make terrible work staff, for a start. It would be beneficial for us all if concessions were made against them. Gildola, bless her generosity, is willing to take Faen's place."

Which was exactly what Penny and I had planned. Trust the Glimmer to be ecstatic over the Fauna losing their rights and being banished to the shadows of the Undercity. The Vesper had been easily bullied into slaving away in their workhouses—the Ember too—but the Fauna were far too independent for that. Too wild. They couldn't be tamed.

"Dor and I will be willing to accept those terms on one condition—you close the workhouses within the Undercity."

Gloria looked appalled at the thought. "Our workhouses provide a public service! Her Holiness is willing to sacrifice more of her power on Faen's behalf, and this is how you repay us?"

"I'm sure any other god would be willing to take Faen's place." I peered over the rim of my spectacles, counting the seconds until I'd won.

My victory came with a dramatic sigh. "Very well. We hardly have enough mortals to staff them, thanks to Chaos. Gildola and I have two more conditions."

Now she was testing my patience. "Which are?"

"One of my staff has disappeared. An agent by the name of J. Brightwell. They were sent to Sinner's Row on an investigative matter, but we believe they may be trapped inside the Mesmer temple."

The Mesmer temple? Why for pity's sake would a Glimmer be there? "Are you certain?"

"Gildola is certain. We believe they may have been drugged or otherwise tricked into entering a narcotic state, which clearly means they are vulnerable and not in their right mind."

"Have you spoken with Ambassador Reverie?" I couldn't march to the Mesmer temple and kick down their door. I'd wake them all up, for a start.

"I tried—she's ignoring my telegrams."

Or she was more likely taking a twelve-hour nap. "I'll ask a Warden to look into this matter—"

"No. You'll go there now. Gildola is protective of her daughters. She will not honor any bargain so long as one of our own remains in danger."

It was still early enough; kicking down the Mesmer temple's door wouldn't cause too much disruption, I hoped. It wasn't how I'd planned to spend my evening, but it was either that, or wallowing in self-pity, and I'd done quite enough of that for two lifetimes.

I took another gulp of tea before it went cold. "I'll see to it. What was your other demand?"

Gloria's red lips quirked into that smug smirk I so detested. "Her Holiness still grieves the death of Lady Mae. Karendar promised us justice, which has so far been denied. We wish to bring her killer to Solaris for judgement. Only then will Gildola be willing to bend to Dor's will."

It had just turned five o'clock when my tram pulled into the Temple District. I'd elected to come alone, albeit with Ben shadowing me, and not with the show of force a group of Wardens would have represented, despite Ben's insistence. My safety didn't concern me, but a runaway Glimmer hiding inside a temple did.

What would compel a Glimmer to seek shelter with the Mesmer of all mortals? And why their temple? It didn't make any sense. Mesmer weren't the kidnapping type, despite Gloria's insistence. I supposed a runaway would avoid their own temple.

But why the Mesmer? It baffled me.

It was likely that Gildola was misinformed and I was wasting my time. At least the walk out and this little adventure took my mind off other things.

Such as Gildola's ludicrous, if not predictable, request.

The Glimmer wanted Kayl for so base a reason as revenge.

And I wasn't sure I could protect her from them.

This early in the evening, the Temple District was fairly quiet. The Glimmer temple was busy as always, and a few Diviner waved as I strode past, their confused faces likely wondering why I wasn't heading in their direction. As ambassador, I was meant to make regular trips to my own temple, yet I slacked in that duty.

I had far too many duties as it was.

How Elijah had made time for the temple, I had no idea.

The Mesmer temple was the most run down of the lot. Technically, we weren't supposed to meddle in the affairs of each domain's temple, which meant they were effectively lawless sanctuaries beholden to their god. It also meant the upkeep was down to their ambassador, and Ambassador Reverie apparently didn't deem it important.

One of the Mesmer lay asleep by the door. I didn't want to wake the poor fellow, but I didn't want to *actually* kick down the door. It was considered sacrilege to enter the temple of another domain, but as head of the Warden Council, I held that privilege. That didn't mean I wanted to abuse it, however.

Instead, I politely knocked.

The Mesmer at my feet remained in deep sleep. Did this temple have any security at *all*? Ben would throw a fit.

The door opened, and the mortal who stood before me was the last I expected to see.

"Corinth," said Sinder with a surprised expression, though he wasn't as surprised as me, I was sure.

Once more, I'd stumbled upon the Godless's mystery hideout without meaning to, only this time I couldn't very well wipe my memories of it. "Am I correct in assuming I'll find Kayl, Harmony, and Vincent inside?"

His eyes narrowed at the name I'd missed out in my rundown. "Forgive me for being blunt, but why are you here?"

I stepped forward. "It's best if I enter to discuss—"

Sinder's arm shot out and blocked my entrance. "Now isn't a good time. We've lost one of our own."

"I understand that, and I'm sorry. I truly am. But I've received a report of a Glimmer hiding in this temple. Gildola wants them back."

He gave me a cool look. "Hiding mortals from their gods is our specialty, darling. You Wardens aren't above sentencing them to exile, are you?"

"I'm not a Warden."

"No? Then why are you here?"

This was the first time I'd spoken with Sinder since we'd escaped the correctional facility, and honestly, I'd expected him to be a little more gracious. Perhaps if I apologized for shooting him during the Grayford Incident, he'd be more forthcoming. Or perhaps I'd only stoke his anger, and he'd burn me to ash.

I understood his pain. The Godless likely blamed me for losing Dru. But getting burned to smithereens would only make Ben's day worse, and I so hated to burden the poor man.

"I'm sorry for shooting you all those years ago."

"You're bringing that up *now*?" Sinder shook his head. "You almost killed me. If not for Kayl and Vincent, I wouldn't even be here. Not that 'here' is a delight." His glare moved to the Mesmer sleeping at our feet.

I rocked awkwardly on my heels. "No hard feelings?"

"The only reason you're not a pile of smoldering coal is because Kayl likes you, though gods know why. You protected her. I'm grateful for that. But we've lost too many of our own. If you hurt her—"

"It's not my intention to hurt anyone—"

"Your intention doesn't matter."

"Are you going to let me inside?"

"And have Wardens harassing us?" Sinder scoffed.

Alas. We weren't getting anywhere like this.

I signaled for Ben to stay put and simply brought time to a stop.

Really, I should have done this to begin with, but I was a gentleman, and one still needed to act with decorum when performing one's duties.

I slipped past Sinder and entered what appeared to be the temple's reception. The inner temple was more dream parlor than holy sanctuary, and a few Mesmer lay slumped on the ground, either sleeping or caught mid-chew with their hands in a bag of candy. Naturally, excessive sweets were forbidden to Diviner, and thank Father for that. Toothache was nothing to sniff at.

My meandering took me deeper inside the temple. More Mesmer were posed midshambling, their expressions blank. I popped my head into a few rooms. Most were parlor beds. Some contained sleeping Mesmer. Most were empty.

One was a meeting room, and I blinked as I laid eyes on Harmony poring over a document with my quarry. Gloria had been right. A Glimmer was hiding inside the temple.

Not just a Glimmer—a male one.

Male Glimmer didn't exist, did they? Holy saints. What had the Godless been up to during my absence?

And what had Kayl been hiding from me?

Really, it was quite clever of the Godless to seek shelter within a temple. I would never have guessed. Least of all a Mesmer temple. Which meant, sadly, that Ambassador Reverie was likely a spy-turned-traitor of the Council. A wonderful political quandary I didn't want to entertain, but it certainly explained a few things.

Though why were the Mesmer eager to help the Godless?

They weren't the political type, either.

A headache was building in my forehead. I wouldn't be able to hold time for much longer. My task was to rescue the Glimmer—or arrest them, since they were cavorting with Godless and I'd been unwittingly sent after an apostate. But this one quick visit was going to thoroughly ruin my plans.

Damn those Glimmer! They knew *exactly* what they were doing.

"Quen?"

Kayl came out of one of the parlor rooms. My goodness. She'd switched to a Mesmer form, the second time I'd ever seen her wearing one. Her skin had changed to a bright indigo, almost Vesper in shade, though the silver stars twinkling across her skin were pure Mesmer.

It reminded me of the dream I'd experienced in the Mesmer parlor all those weeks ago. Of her in my arms in Meridian Park. A dream from which Dor had plucked my greatest desires and foisted them onto Penny.

"Are you my Quen?" Kayl asked as she approached cautiously. "Or are you the other Quen?"

"My future self came here?"

Her eyes narrowed. "Why are you here? Did your betrothed send you?"

"Why would Penny send me here?"

"Because she's been spying on me."

That, I found hard to believe. "You may not see eye to eye with her, but she's a bureaucrat, nothing more. Really, you should get to know her. I think you'll find you have much in common."

"Yes, we both want to fuck you."

Heat rushed to my cheeks and made my headache worse. I let time flow back to the present to ease the tension. "Gloria came to my office an hour ago. Gildola is searching for a certain J. Brightwell and sent me here to find them. I assume you are acquainted?"

"Shit. Joe's one of us—he's Godless."

"And here I thought you'd branched out into kidnappings."

My sarcasm was wasted on Kayl, who grabbed my arm and dragged me into the room.

A large bed filled the space. There were three different sets of quilts and cushions, enough for three mortals, and clothes were scattered across it. Dru's clothes, I realized a heartbeat later. She and Kayl must have shared this room.

Kayl sat on the edge of the bed. Her Mesmer skin masked the dark circles around her eyes, but the way she hugged her chest and shrank into herself pained me.

I never wanted to see her diminished in this way, yet I'd played a part in her pain. After we'd returned from Heartstone, she'd run from me without a word. I hadn't had chance to comfort her then, and now I could, I didn't know how. What words could possibly bring comfort? So I lingered where I stood, an unwanted guest in her grief. "I'm sorry."

A flicker of anger burned in those eyes. "You're sorry. Well, that's all right then, isn't it? So long as you're sorry, it doesn't matter."

"Of course it matters—"

"You could have stopped her. You could have let me stop her."

"Dru sacrificed her freedom for you."

Kayl launched to her feet. "I didn't ask her to sacrifice herself for me! I would *never* ask any of my friends or family to do that! I lost Reve, I thought I lost you, and I lost... I lost..." She put her hands to her head. "I lost them, and it's my fault!"

I grabbed her shoulders. "Don't blame yourself—"

"Then who do I blame? *You?*"

My heart skipped a beat. I'd guessed my entanglement with Penny would lead to Kayl's hatred of me and thus the destruction of my soul, but it was more likely this.

Fate was coming for me too quickly. Time squeezed my mortality, aching in my head, my muscles, my very bones, as though the death I'd escaped was finally catching up.

"Are we in danger now?" she asked, sinking back onto the bed. "Do the Wardens know our location? Does Gloria?"

I sat beside her. "Possibly. It can't be like old times—I can't scrub your records and keep the Wardens off your back. My thoughts are owned by Dor—He'll question my actions."

"We don't have anywhere else to go."

"Once we've secured Corentine and the rest of Chaos, security around Central will be relaxed. You could find somewhere in the Undercity again."

"Or retire to Phantasy at this rate."

"I didn't expect Reverie to be the blasphemous type."

"Neither did we." She reached over the bed. "I wasn't lying when I said your betrothed was spying on me. Is this hers or yours?" She unceremoniously dumped a broken and misshapen clockwork bird into my hands.

Saints. It was one of Penny's pets. The poor thing was a mangled mess and had clearly been smashed against a wall. I examined what parts remained and spied a tiny microphone. Could she have programmed these to spy on her behalf?

To spy on Kayl? On *me*?

Penny had a ruthlessness to her, I'd noticed. But what reason would she have to spy? I didn't want to believe it. "I'll have a word with her."

Kayl gave me a stern look. "You can't trust her."

"She's my betrothed—"

"She'll be the death of you."

I almost laughed at that!

The door to Kayl's room burst open. Sinder came inside, his fists aflame, with a trail of three Mesmer behind him, who looked awed at the sight of a Diviner in their temple.

"It's all right," Kayl said as she raised her hands. "Quen's with me."

Sinder scowled at me. "I don't appreciate you entering without permission."

"Apologies." I stood, placing the broken remains of Penny's bird into my jacket pocket. "I'm only here for the Glimmer."

"Go ahead. Take him."

Kayl shot a warning glance at Sinder. "Does Gildola know that Joe is an apostate? Is that why she sent you?"

Most likely. I recalled what Gloria had explained.

Sinder's irritation only grew. "I *told* you Joe's a spy—"

"Or Gloria is full of shit," Kayl said.

"What does it matter? Joe has led the Dark Warden straight to us, and the Glimmer will be aware of our presence here. This entire temple is in danger—"

"We're in *danger*?" one of the Mesmer squeaked. The three of them looked practically identical, and they'd been eavesdropping on our conversation the entire time.

This venture had at least proved that the Mesmer were on the side of the Godless—of Chaos—though I couldn't fathom why. They could receive visions as great as any Diviner, as well as potential futures. Had they seen what I had? Did they understand the role Chaos would play?

Mesmorpheus would certainly understand. In my endeavor to bring the gods to Dor's side, I'd discovered which side Mesmorpheus stood on.

It didn't please me.

"Joe is as much a victim of his god as we are." Kayl crossed her arms and stared me down. "He's claimed asylum with the Godless. That means we'll protect him from any threat, be that mortal or god."

I really didn't have time for this. "May I have a private word?"

Kayl followed me to a darkened corner of the room.

I bent my head close. "The Glimmer are ready to accept our bargain *and* close down their workhouses in exchange for the Fauna's slice of the pie and this Joe." And Kayl herself, but that would be a problem to worry about later—I still needed Kayl to handle her chaotic brethren when the time came.

"Then we lose the Glimmer's support. We're not sacrificing any more mortals. We've given enough!"

I sucked in an exasperated breath. "Do I need to remind you of what that means?"

"Do you really want to sacrifice innocents?"

"Of course I don't! Someone will get hurt regardless of what I do—"

"You're head of the Council. You figure it out."

"You're supposed to be working with me on this!" I hissed. "We're partners."

Her aether eyes glowed in the darkened room. "Are we? Because during this entire operation, you've allowed the gods to dictate *their* terms while not allowing me to represent Chime and state my case! Is this the real you, Quen? Is this who you are? The Dark Warden, who bows to the whims of the gods, bending over backwards so they can fuck over mortals?"

"I need the gods' cooperation to save the domains, blast it! I thought you understood the sacrifices we'd need to make. How am I supposed to protect mortals if you keep thwarting my efforts—"

"I'm Godless, Quen. What did you expect? Your idea of *protecting* them isn't working, so quit your chivalrous shit!"

I ground my teeth. "I'm *not* the Dark Warden. For once in my life, I want to be more than that—to serve mortals in the only capacity I can. Isn't it enough that I want to leave this world a better place than when I entered it?"

"No. It's not enough."

My goodness, those eyes burned with a righteousness to rival any Glimmer.

"Why are you fighting?" said a dreamy voice beside me.

Good lord! Both Kayl and I were startled by the sudden appearance of a Mesmer. One of the identical three. I hadn't even noticed them sneak up on us.

Kayl forced a smile. "Celeste, give us a moment here."

"I'm Cosmo."

"Cosmo. Okay, can you—"

"Do you see visions?" Cosmo asked me with innocent giddiness. "I do!" They giggled. "I know bourbon is your favorite biscuit. Mine too!"

Saints. Had they seen a vision of me? My future? "What did you see?"

"I'll show you." Cosmo grabbed my hand before I could voice an objection.

The darkness of the parlor room swallowed me whole.

The stars were falling.

I liked stars. I liked the way they danced across the sky full of glitter and color. I liked how they tasted sweet, like fruit candy. Papa said that when a star is born, it births a god. A new world. A new story. And there are thousands of gods and worlds and stories. Millions. Too many to ever keep track of.

But when a star dies, so ends that story. That world. That god.

Though not forever.

The aether of the stars becomes something new. A new god. A new world. A new story.

Phantasy was falling. Stardust rained on the observatory. As the stars popped out, one by one, the darkness of night became gray.

Papa's story was ending. Their siblings would also end.

Soon, new gods would rise out of the aether of the old. New worlds. New stories.

Celeste took my hand. "It's time to go."

Castor took my other hand with a soft squeeze. "Are you ready?"

Dust swirled in the void where Papa's magnificent stars had sparkled before.

Mama was standing there, glowing with aether.

Our new god. Our new story.
Are you ready to begin yours, Quentin Corinth?

"Gods!" I sucked in air as though I'd been drowning and couldn't breathe. My lungs ached as I gasped.

Three Mesmer were standing over me, staring with their dark eyes. Stars swirled within their depths, blinking in and out with a subtle glow. Utterly mesmerizing and terrifying in equal measure.

Phantasy had fallen—would fall. Another domain lost to Chaos.

For the woman in that blasted vision was either Kayl or Jinx, I couldn't tell.

"Quen? Are you all right?" Kayl asked.

Rather belatedly, I realized I was lying on the floor, my head resting in Kayl's lap. I scrambled up and adjusted my spectacles. "Yes—sorry, I—"

"Would you like a jelly baby?" said one of the Mesmer. They offered me an open packet. "I like the peach Seren!"

"No, thank you."

"Did you want one?" The Mesmer shook the bag at Kayl. "The purple ones are your favorite."

Kayl steered them away. "Can you give us some space?"

The three Mesmer skipped off, as though completely oblivious to the destruction looming in their future.

Why would they show me the demise of their domain unless they wished me to save it?

"You saw Cosmo's death, didn't you?" Kayl asked quietly. "What did you see?"

"What do you want me to say? That they die of old age peacefully in their sleep?"

"Yes, that's exactly what I want you to say—"

"Well, I can't!"

"Then what did you *see*?"

I glanced to where Sinder stood by the door, watching me. "A future I'm trying to stop." I hadn't revealed the truth of my visions to Kayl—of the domains falling in a potential future—in order to keep that information from Corentine.

Nor did I wish to reveal it to Penny or Ben and arouse panic. No, this was a burden I alone would carry.

"You said yourself that once an event is observed, it cannot be stopped."

Unfortunately, I had said that.

One couldn't stop the march of time, nor the calling of death. It dragged you with it whether you were ready or not. But one could choose whether to be dragged, kicking and screaming along the way. Or to run alongside it, and take whatever time planned on the chin.

Reve had sought comfort in his oblivion. If he could chase after damnation thirteen sodding times, then so would I.

That had been my choice.

Perhaps my only choice.

"We're not giving up Joe," Kayl reiterated.

"Understood."

I made my way out of the temple. The choices to come crushed my shoulders. A decision must be made—a simple one, yet oh so delicate.

This path would hurt me.

But I'd walk it.

Ben waited for me outside the Diviner temple. "Did you find what you were looking for, sir?"

I'd found a sodding headache. "Unfortunately. Let's return to the embassy. I need to pray to our Father."

33

You hear about that thief? The one who broke into Erosain's bar?
They gone and stole from his art gallery, didn't they? Proper wrecked it, too.
I ain't ever seen Erosain so mad. He was offering a bounty for information.
A Necro, so they say. Those pale freaks better watch their backs.
I'd sure like to earn myself a few extra bocs.
—Anonymous, *overheard in Sinner's Row*

I HUGGED DRU'S PILLOW and napped in her clothes. That was why I'd taken a Mesmer's form—to lose myself in unconsciousness and forget for a while.

Yes, I was ignoring my problems. I should have gone to Harmony straight away and let her know we were all potentially in danger, especially Joe. Quen wouldn't tattle our location, but his stupid-arsed betrothed would. There was also my twin sister locked in a room below, who I still hadn't visited yet because, quite frankly, I didn't want to. Let her scream and suffer for all I pissing cared.

Was I being a brat? Yes. Was I being irresponsible? Also yes. Was my apathy and ineptitude going to bite me in the arse later? Most certainly.

But fuck it. Dru wasn't here to drag me out of bed, so why should I bother?

I'd done enough. Whatever happened now was down to Quen.

Ambassador Arkey was retiring from her political career to pursue a life of extreme wallowing, napping, and chocolate bingeing. I dug out an unwrapped chocolate lime stuck to my pillow. One of my hairs clung to it, which I delicately peeled off before shoving the candy into my mouth. I was useless at most things, but wallowing? I was a natural.

YOU SHOULD HAVE TAKEN HER SOUL WHEN YOU HAD THE CHANCE.

If this is your idea of comfort, you can piss off. Not for the first time I wished I could block Corentine from my mind.

IS IT SYMPATHY YOU WANT, DAUGHTER?

No. I wanted Dru. *Is there any way to bring a mortal back from immortality?*

TAKE UNGHARD'S SOUL.

God's sake. I flipped onto my back, Dru's pillow resting on my stomach. She'd become an immortal. A saint, as Chime's high society referred to them. A slave.

Varen had once been in line to become a Winged Twilight. Valeria had gifted him wings as part of his 'ascension' but then changed her mind and ripped them off. Even Vesper considered it a blessing to become one of those horrific gargoyles. I'd always assumed Varen thought himself lucky to escape it. Varen was an idiot.

Immortals held their god's power. The only thing stopping them from turning into weapons against each other was the Covenant and the Gate itself. Immortals couldn't pass through. But did that mean Corentine could make them in Chime?

NO. WHILE TRAPPED IN MY PRISON, I LACK THE STRENGTH.

But you could? Did you make them before?

MY IMMORTALS BECAME GODS.

I supposed that made sense.

Frantic knocking pounded my door. Shit. Were we being invaded by Wardens already?

I staggered out of bed and smoothed down my wrinkled dress. Sinder peered around the door and burst in once he checked I was decent.

"It's Vincent. He hasn't come back—"

"Come back from where? What's happened?"

Sinder began pacing the room, steam coming off his glowing red face. "He's not been eating. Ever since those damn Mesmer caught him drinking from me, he's refused to feed. Wouldn't even entertain the idea of sneaking outside and doing it somewhere more private. He's been slowly starving himself."

Shit. I'd known he had issues, but I hadn't realized it was this bad. "Where's he now?"

"He said he was going to his temple to feed there—they have their own supplies for Necro to feed privately. But that was hours ago, and he hasn't returned." Sinder stopped pacing and faced me, fear burning in his eyes. "The crossing to Witheryn opens in an hour. What if he goes there? Or they take him? He—He told me they sometimes drag Necro through if they're a danger to Chime. If they've gone... feral."

My heart began to race. Vincent was smart—he wasn't the type to get himself kidnapped. Then again, he was arthritic and sometimes struggled to walk. If he was starving himself, then he'd be at his most vulnerable.

Gods damn it! I wasn't going to lose another one of my family!

I slipped on my shoes.

"What are you going to do?" Sinder asked as he followed me out of the room.

"Go to the damn Necro temple, of course. Give me your hand." Sinder did so, and my form changed to Ember. "I'll burn him out if I have to."

"Should I come with? Gods, I feel so useless—"

"Stay here and guard the temple in case he comes back."

"Will you be safe out there, darling? I should come with you—"

"I can take care of myself, remember?" I snapped my fingers and summoned a small flicker of flame. "I'll find him."

I didn't want to wait for Harmony to tell me how dangerous this was, not when Vincent's life could be on the line, and there wasn't any Dru to protect me this time.

There was no way I was going to sit and do nothing.

As I approached the Necro temple, I tried to keep a casual demeanor. We'd do this the easy way first, and the hard way if need be.

The Necro temple did nothing to calm my nerves. On the surface, it appeared to be a dilapidated, moody version of a Glimmer's stately home. The walls were made of stone, the windows blacked out, and not a single lantern shone around it, as though no one was in. But a Necro stood on guard by the gated door. A pale man in a dark suit.

He bared his fangs. A smear of blood stained his bottom lip. "Feeding time was an hour ago, bitch. Get outta here."

How charming. I could see why everyone in Chime considered the Necro so wholesome and cuddly. "I'm looking for a friend—"

"I don't care who you're looking for. This isn't the place for you."

We were going to do this the hard way, then. "My friend entered this temple a few hours ago. I want to make sure he's safe. Either you be a good boy and go check for me, or I'm going to burn my way through you and check myself." Flame rippled around my fists. "What would you prefer?"

"Go ahead. Burn me. As soon as you enter this temple, you'll have a whole nest of us at that pretty little neck. Now fuck off."

My fists flared. "You're not making this easy."

"You're not fucking listening. Unless you're a Warden, you're not getting inside. By the state of you, I'd say your pimp is probably wondering where you are."

Fuck him! I flipped him off and stomped away from his glare. With Witheryn due to open soon, I could wait around to see if Vincent came out of the temple and strike then, but if I knew Necro, they were subtle in their kidnappings and could likely escape under my very nose.

Personally, I didn't know any other Necro besides Vincent. Quen was obviously not a Necro, but if he had the authority to barge into the Mesmer temple, then surely the Necro temple would be no problem?

Did I have time to race to the embassy or his apartment? At this time of night, I had no idea if he'd still be at his desk or drinking tea with his betrothed.

And, honestly, I wasn't sure I wanted his help this time. Asking him to help me save Dru had worked out *so* well.

Once a Warden, always a bloody Warden. Though, he likely had no choice. His method of saving Chime was different from mine.

To a Diviner, sacrificing the few for the many was the logical choice. It wasn't like we *had* much choice when the gods were involved.

But I couldn't sacrifice more of my friends—my family. I couldn't.

Did that make me selfish? Perhaps in Quen's eyes.

Who did he have to lose? To sacrifice?

Shit. I didn't know what to do, but I refused to lose Vincent, too.

I'd run a few smaller operations on my own, missions Harmony thought I could handle, but for the bigger things, I'd relied on Dru more than I cared to admit.

Without Dru, I was useless.

YOU ARE STILL MY VOICE, Corentine said.

Fat lot of good that had been. *Fine. What do you suggest I do?*

GIVE UP.

Great advice, I wish I'd thought of that.

THE NECRO ARE TOO DANGEROUS TO TACKLE YOURSELF.

Well, she was right about that. If I dragged Quen or Harmony or Sinder into this, they'd likely say the same. Perhaps I should head on over to the embassy and throw my authority around. There was bound to be some poor Necro Warden I could coerce.

I shoved my hands into my pockets and leaned against a lamppost. Something dug into my palm. I pulled out a business card belonging to a Mr. M. Gast.

The Necro PI I'd met in Rapture.

Huh. It turned out I *did* know another Necro…

Returning to the Undercity was surprisingly easy.

I'd expected an alarm to go off as soon as I entered Central Station, or to be accosted by a Warden at the very least. But I made it onto the elevator going down without so much as a suspicious glance. Was I that inconspicuous with my Ember face? Or did the Wardens simply not care who entered the Undercity anymore?

If I'd known it was that easy, I would have returned weeks ago.

Riding the elevator down brought back all kinds of memories. The evening elevator used to be full of workers returning to Grayford, but with no Vesper to fill it, only a few Ember and Fauna stragglers swayed awkwardly in the empty space. An Ember male gave me a suggestive look, his eyes roaming up and down my body.

With my wrinkled dress and flushed face, he probably thought I'd lifted my leg in some dirty alley behind a pub. I ignored him, but if he got too close, I knew how to break thumbs.

The elevator lumbered down, and I soon caught a tram chugging its way to Sinner's Row. I'd not expected to return here anytime soon either, and I vaguely recalled some threat by Erosain to never step foot in his territory, but oh well. I was here now.

Sinner's Row remained exactly as I'd remembered it—all bright lights, gaudy paintwork, and fake smiles. The main street was full of Ember heading for a cheaper night out than Rapture. The Vesper pharmaceutical stores had been either boarded up or taken over by Ember with sunken eyes, clearly indulging in their own product. Fauna girls dressed in next to nothing loitered outside Tom Cat's Café, a well-known brothel.

A cat girl with ginger fur stepped in front of me. "Looking to earn some bocs, doll?" She waved a leaflet in my face. "We take Ember too, if you know how to use your hands. Ask for Trixie."

Was I really dressed that slutty? Still, if I wanted to find Gast in a hurry, she was likely the best mortal to ask. In her line of work, it paid to know who was who. "I'm looking for someone."

"You ain't gonna find anyone good here. For ten bocs, I'll point ya in the right direction." She held out her hand expectantly.

In my haste, I'd forgotten my purse, but as luck would have it, I found a crumpled twenty note in my pocket.

Ginger snatched it with glee. "Got no change, doll."

"Then don't spend it all in one place." I handed over Gast's business card. "Heard of him?"

"Oh, '*im*." She clicked her teeth. "Trixie has a soft spot for 'im, though fucked if I know why. Head into that alley, there, but keep an hand to your purse."

Well, I'd already been robbed once.

I followed her direction into one of the back alleys. Fortunately for me, Erosain's hired muscle didn't patrol these. Unfortunately, other undesirables did. I kept watch over my shoulder for any threats. A Diviner persona would have been better for this, but where would I find a Diviner here?

Damn it, Quen. This kind of operation needed him.

The alleyway was dark, dingy, and covered in litter. Grayford had always been a dank, dirty hovel, but this made it look respectable. Dirty-faced Ember and Fauna sat inside makeshift cardboard homes that stunk of cheap alcohol and piss. With Grayford abandoned, was this where Chime's poorest came to find sanctuary?

Gods. I wished I hadn't thrown away that twenty.

Light flickered from cracks within boarded-up windows, or the occasional aether-blue sign lit up to advertise a Necro surgery or medical store. I was clearly headed in the right direction—all the businesses here seemed Necro-owned.

And there, at the very end of the alley, was another aether sign that glowed with the words *Private Investigator*.

Gast's office didn't exactly inspire confidence. Its windows were boarded up, and the painted red walls were peeling. But a line of light shone from a crack in the doorway. Someone was in.

Footsteps echoed behind me. Shit! I'd been followed.

I hurried on down the alleyway. Gast's office suddenly became a holy sanctuary.

A door swung open into the alley, a foot from Gast's.

"Looking for something in particular?" said a raspy voice.

A slender Necro male slid out of a surgeon's clinic. He looked me over with bloodshot eyes, the blue veins prominent on his pale face. A dirty lab coat hung off his bony build.

I tried to brush past him. "If you'll excuse me, sir—"

He stepped in front of me, blocking my way. "You're a pretty young thing, aren't you? In the market for a touch-up? I could lift those delicate cheekbones."

"Are you in the market for getting burned?" I summoned a small flame to emphasize the point. "I'd be happy to oblige."

Those bloodshot eyes turned predatory. "Please do. I enjoy working on burn wounds. The way they smell of meat. The pulpy charcoal flesh." He licked his lips.

Coming here was a bad idea.

I TOLD YOU SO.

Save your nagging for when I'm dead.

"I don't think the lady's interested."

We both turned to Gast, who was leaning by his open office doorway.

"My apologies." The Necro surgeon bowed as he slunk backwards into his office, slowly closing the door behind him.

"Friend of yours?" I asked.

"Not when he keeps scaring away my clients. So, you got intel for me, or are you here to buy me that drink?" Gast was dressed in black trousers and a creased white shirt, the sleeves rolled up, exposing his pale skin and the blue veins stretched across it. Once again, I was taken aback by how ruggedly handsome he was. But that was Necro for you. All charm. All danger.

In fact, Gast was *exactly* my type. Rough around the edges with that bad boy aesthetic, and a heart of gold hidden underneath. Except I was attracted to Quen, and sure, he had the heart of gold, but that bad boy vibe? Quen?

Which was something I shouldn't be thinking about when I had Vincent to save. "Actually, Mr. Gast, I require your help."

"Then you better step inside." He gestured to his office.

I entered a shabby room. Cigarette smoke drifted across the ceiling, swirling around a chandelier where only half the bulbs gave off light. I approached a threadbare couch and desk, which had seen far better days. A stack of files teetered precariously on the desk, next to an ashtray with a lit cigarette and a half-empty glass of blood.

"Noct!" yelled Gast. "Get out here. We got company."

A Seren boy flew out of the back office dressed in a gray suit and holding a clipboard. His face was a pale blue, his hair black—if it wasn't for his wispy white wings, I'd almost mistake him for a tiny Vesper. "Is this your art thief?"

How many mortals knew I'd stolen from Erosain?

"That's her." Gast slumped into a worn leather chair and reached for his cigarette. "Take a seat, lady. What's the case?"

The Seren hovered over Gast's shoulder, his pen poised over his clipboard.

I sat on the creaky couch. "One of the Godless has gone missing. A Necro by the name of Vincent Holcroft. He was last seen entering the Necro temple. I need your help getting him out."

Gast wasted no time in grabbing his jacket and rushing me out of his office. Thankfully, he understood the urgency of my request. Soon, we were running to catch a tram, then the elevator, and another tram back across to the Temple District. I didn't know what time it was until the clock tower called quarter to six.

My entire jaunt underground had cost me a whopping forty-five minutes.

"You smoke?" Gast waved a cigarette packet at me.

"No, thank you."

"It'll take the edge off whatever cravings you get."

"I'll manage." I'd taken a Necro form before stepping out of his office, transforming once again into Nadine. I wouldn't get inside the Necro temple wearing an Ember's face, though I hoped the charming guard didn't notice any resemblance—or the exact same dress we wore.

Gast, to his credit, hadn't batted an eye when I'd suddenly changed. Then again, he and his Seren assistant seemed to know an unnerving amount about me.

"Suit yourself." He popped a cigarette into his mouth and walked up to the guard.

"Morty Gast," announced the guard. "What are you doing back here?"

I stifled a giggle. "Morty?" I whispered.

"It's short for Mortimer," Gast mumbled. "You know me. Working a case as usual."

"Yeah? And who's your friend?" The guard glanced at me. "Her face looks familiar."

"May I introduce the famous Nadine Noir."

"*The* Nadine Noir? The one who stole from Erosain?"

I gave 'Morty' a look. Just what *did* the Necro know about me?

Gast cleared his throat.

It was lucky for him that I knew how to put on an act. "I wouldn't lower myself to common thievery. Rather, I consider myself a redistributor of His Excellency's finest assets."

The guard hacked a laugh. "You're a living legend in here, you know? Not many would dare fuck over Erosain."

"I think Erosain has been losing his grip on reality for a while now, don't you? It's time for Sinner's Row to bring in some fresh blood."

"You said it. Oh, if you're here for a feeding, you're a little late. We're out of the fresh stuff until we get a delivery from the Asylum."

"Supply problems?" Gast asked as he took another drag on his cigarette.

"Had a couple of ferals who drained our supply dry. Fucking nobodies."

"Are they inside? These ferals?" I asked.

Gast gave me a warning look. Shit, had I asked the wrong thing?

The guard didn't seem to notice my ignorance. "Nah, it's quiet enough in there, if you want to head in, though you'll find more action in a Glimmer temple. You looking for a feral or something? For your case? Didn't realize Morana hired you back."

"She hasn't," Gast said. "I like to keep tabs."

"I wouldn't bother. Morana's already left for the crossing with a bunch of ferals. She seemed particularly interested in one of 'em, though. Escorted him personally."

Shit. I didn't know for sure if that was Vincent, but my gut said it was. "Anyone famous I should know?" I leaned close to the guard with a conspirator's grin. "Forgive me, but knowledge is my currency, and I can't resist a secret."

He checked over his shoulder and returned my grin. "You didn't hear it from me, but he's an ex-Warden. A fella named Holcroft."

My heart would have skipped a beat if my Necro blood were pumping. "And he went feral, you said?"

"Saw it myself. Blood-starved. Happens sometimes with these Wardens. They don't like to eat on the job. Makes 'em look bad, you see? But then the cravings hit, and they lose their job anyway. Makes us all look bad."

"When did they leave?" Gast asked.

"About fifteen minutes ago, I reckon."

The clock tower struck six. If we hurried now, we'd have time to cross into Witheryn, find Vincent, and hopefully drag him out before time was up.

Not that time was ever on my side.

"You heading in?" The guard gestured to the door. "I know someone who is dying to meet you."

I'll bet. "What do you say, Gast? The night is still young."

"You're right. Think we'll go stalk the streets for a bit. We'll come back when the blood does."

The guard nodded. "I'll save a bottle aside. Nice to meet you, Miss Noir."

"Likewise." I hid the disgust in my voice and joined Gast as he headed for the tram. "Who's this Morana?" I asked.

"Our ambassador."

Oh yes, I remembered her now from the Council meetings. She always dressed in black and hid her face behind a veil.

Why would the Necro ambassador take a special interest in Vincent?

I didn't like it. "You've worked with her before?"

"On a case. When an ambassador knocks on your door, you can't exactly turn her down." Gast stopped me before we reached the tram platform. "You sure you want to do this, lady? Witheryn is no picnic. This friend of yours worth it?"

"Vincent is worth it to me. He's family."

"If your friend has gone feral, he could be dangerous."

"Vincent wouldn't harm anyone."

"He might not realize what he's doing. That's why we call them ferals."

I'd never had a reason to fear Vincent. I wasn't about to start now. "If you're trying to dissuade me, you're doing a piss-poor job of it. Are you going to help me or not?"

"The things we do for family." Gast tossed his cigarette to the gutter. "Just so we're clear, I charge an hourly rate."

"Is that so you can pay off your fines? Littering is a criminal offense, Mr. Gast."

"Tell it to a Warden."

"I'm no tattle, though are you? Nadine Noir? Who came up with that?"

"It's like that idiot said—you're an urban legend among us Necro. A thief who not only stole from Erosain, but wrecked his fancy little art gallery too? Erosain was raging about that for a whole month."

"I had no idea the Necro hated Erosain."

"Sinner's Row is one of the few places that let Necro set up shop and be ourselves. But he charges extortionate rent and protection taxes. We'd be glad to be rid of him."

His wish may soon be granted.

We boarded the tram and headed for Central Station.

Truth be told, I had no desire to visit Witheryn. For all the stories I'd heard of Eventide, the ones I'd heard of the Necro's home domain were far worse. It was a nightmarish land. A world so devoid of hope, even Vincent shuddered when speaking of it.

Which was why I had to follow after him.

Perhaps I was walking into danger—I definitely was—but I refused to lose any more of the Godless.

As it turned out, I was useless at wallowing.

But entering domains and fucking shit up? Oh yes, I was a natural at that.

34

*As anyone will tell you, Witheryn is one of the most dangerous domains.
Chime's citizens are cautioned from crossing, but that caution also extends
to Wardens. If you have a legitimate need to cross into Witheryn, then
speak with their ambassador first.*
*If you must travel, then do so armed and with a guide. Do not wander. Do
not turn your back on the local populace. Do not eat or drink anything
offered. If you require the services of a Necro, I recommend seeking a
Warden-approved business within Warden HQ or the Golden City.*
—Q. Corinth, *Warden Dossier on Witheryn*

WITHERYN WAS AS DARK and dreary as the Necro.

Gast and I had made the crossing at quarter past six, and somehow, I'd
entered a world far gloomier than Chime at night. Central's streets were lit
with a mixture of silvery-blue aether lamps and golden oil lanterns that gave
the city a welcoming atmosphere. But here, the air bit with frozen fangs.
Color leached from the land as though I'd walked into a black-and-white
painting.

As though this domain had no soul.

"Stay close and watch your footing," Gast said as we entered a town
square.

Gray buildings encircled us. They resembled the fancier estates of the
Golden City, only a far bleaker version. Each had sharp turrets and
columns, and seated at the top were grotesque statues that reminded me of
the Winged Twilights of Eventide.

Even Witheryn's Gate was a crumbling gray stone arch.

White powder covered the square in a blanket of cold. It frosted over
the windows and hung from the rafters in sharp icicles. Wispy flakes fell
from the sky, and I caught one in my hand. It was cold to the touch, but in

my Necro form, the cold didn't numb me. "Is this snow?" Vincent had once described it to me.

"That it is. Keep away from the yellow variety."

"What's so bad about yellow snow?"

He gave me a grim smile by way of an answer.

The Gate was still open behind us, yet no one followed. In fact, the square was empty. I realized that was what made Witheryn so eerie.

It was deadly quiet.

"Where is everyone?" I whispered, unsure why I was whispering.

"Most mortals make the morning crossing. It's safer."

It had just occurred to me that I'd gone and entered one of the most dangerous domains with a complete stranger. I didn't think Gast was the type to lure young maidens to their doom, though one never knew. This wouldn't be the first time I'd been kidnapped or incarcerated, or indeed threatened with torture or death, and such adventures did grow tiresome after a while.

I hadn't let Sinder or Harmony know I'd decided to visit Witheryn of all pissing places, which meant if I *was* to be kidnapped or whatever, there'd be no one to rescue me.

Of course, if they'd known I planned to come here, they'd have probably knocked me out and tied me to a chair in the first place.

AT LEAST THEY HAVE SENSE.

I have to live up to my chaotic origins somehow.

Gast gestured to a parked carriage. It was steam powered like the carriages back on Chime, and it puffed out gray clouds of smoke that merged with the dancing snow.

"Where are we headed?" I asked as I wobbled over a slippery stone. Our path had been trounced into dirty gray slush.

"If your friend has gone feral, then there's only one place they'd have taken him. The Asylum."

"Is it as cheerful and charming as the rest of this place?"

"It's so welcoming, those who enter rarely leave."

"You make it sound like a correctional facility."

"You'd rather be locked inside a correctional facility. Trust me."

"If it's that bad, how do you intend to help me rescue my friend?"

"Easy." He tapped his nose. "We break inside."

Great. This rescue attempt was now official, and Vincent was my damsel in distress. I supposed that meant I couldn't get myself kidnapped, then.

Besides, I'd left behind my chivalrous gentleman in his tan suit and brass eyeglasses. Oh, what fun Quen was missing out on! A chance to actually play the hero.

The carriage driver was a Necro man in a top hat who waved as we approached. "What's your destination?"

"The Asylum," Gast said. "We've been called in for clean-up duty."

The driver shuddered. "Rather you than me."

We climbed inside the carriage. The entire interior was dark, like entering a cavern.

I made myself comfortable on a black velvet cushion. "Is color offensive to your domain?"

Gast sat opposite. "We love all kinds of colors. Our favorites are white, gray, dark gray, very dark gray, very very dark gray, an even darker gray than that, and black. Oh, don't forget red. We *love* red."

That explained why Vincent adored Sinder. Besides Sinder being a complete slut, anyhow.

The carriage rumbled to life. Gast lit another cigarette and stretched back against the cushions. Honestly, he looked *too* relaxed, and I got the sudden urge to light up as well. I'd tried smoking a few times in Grayford, but I'd never liked the taste. Drugs were easy to come by in the Undercity. I'd seen firsthand how they'd stripped mortals of their last bocs, and everything else—their agency, their dignity. Their last shred of mortality.

"So what are ferals? I've never come across that term before." Vincent had certainly never mentioned it.

Gast blew out a line of smoke. "You've probably not heard it because we keep it on the downlow. It means what you'd expect—a Necro's urges get out of control, and they become a danger to mortals around them. Hunger is different for our kind. It can send us mad. Make us violent. And when that happens, Ambassador Morana and the Wardens step in and forcibly remove the afflicted Necro from Chime before anyone's hurt. Or, more likely, they cover up whatever unfortunate incident has transpired, pay off the family or domain of whoever got eaten, and ensure no one blames our domain."

That actually sounded plausible. "How often do these unfortunate incidents happen?"

"More than you'd ever know about."

"If Necro are that much of a threat, then why do the Wardens let your domain into Chime at all?"

"Because we're useful. Who else can heal injured Wardens as well as us? Or provide accurate passport tattoos? And the Golden City couldn't live without our beauty parlors. They don't care if a Necro goes wild, so long as their victim is from the lower levels."

Again, that was painfully plausible. "Can Necro who have gone feral, as you call it, fully recover? Be rehabilitated?" If Vincent had lost his mind through hunger, then surely that could be fixed?

"It depends. With the right diet and self-control, yes. But many are too far gone. Others are locked away forever depending on their crimes and their victims. Generally, if one of us is struggling with our urges, it's best to fix the problem rather than risk being sent to the Asylum. Your friend should have known that."

I chewed my bottom lip. Vincent was no fool. In all the years I'd known him, he'd not publicly struggled with his urges, and he'd never given me reason to be concerned. Not until we'd entered the Mesmer temple...

All because, like Quen, he was a chivalrous arse. Vincent had always described his kind as monstrous. Had always disliked that aspect of himself. After Eventide, I could relate to what it meant to be a monster.

I contained monstrous power in my fingers. The ability to steal souls. To damn entire domains. Of course, I didn't get the urge to devour souls, not in the same way a Necro was compelled to eat flesh or drink blood, but if I did? I'd do all I could to suppress it, too.

Oh, Vincent. He may be a monster, but so was I.

The Godless had been my lifeline. My family. That meant we helped each other. I'd lost Reve. Lost Dru. I'd be damned if I lost Vincent.

As the carriage spluttered on, I pulled aside the curtain. Snow flurried past, so thick I could barely see beyond. We'd left the gloomy town and ridden into a landscape full of rolling white hills and leafless trees that twisted like shadowy creatures. Occasionally, we passed an iron fence guarding a stony estate or mansion, but the relentless snow hid most of Witheryn in terrifying obscurity.

"Do you feel urges like that?" Gast asked, and waved a lazy hand at me.

"I haven't been a Necro long enough to know. But I do remember liking the smell of blood. Is that normal?"

"As normal as a Mesmer and their candy. Just checking you're not going to go feral on me."

"I'll let you know if I'm feeling particularly peckish." Which, truth be told, was all the time. Dru was always chiding me for my appetite, but snacking was one of my favorite hobbies, up there with spreading discord and making Quen blush. "While we're getting to know each other, do you often whisk maidens off on deadly adventures?"

"When they're paying. I assume an ambassador keeps a fat wallet."

"Oh, so you're a whore for bocs?"

"Aren't we all? It's a funny thing, being mortal. The Covenant promises a life of liberty and freedom, from conception to old age and eventual death, but how many mortals actually die of old age? I could say I'm saving for retirement, but I've got no illusions."

"What are you saving for?"

"Good times, because there aren't many left."

"This seems like a risky way to earn an honest living. Have you considered becoming a paperboy for the Courier? There's less chance of death."

He smirked, exposing a fang. "You'd be surprised. Look, lady, I know what you are. It's pretty obvious when you can change faces like that. So I figure you're the one mortal in Chime who can help me find the fuck responsible for Eventide. I'll scratch your back if you scratch mine."

That was how we did things in the Undercity. A favor for a favor. Gast knew more about Chaos than he let on, and maybe I was foolish for employing his help. He sought answers to a question I wouldn't be able to satisfy. But I'd worry about that when it came to it.

He finished off his cigarette and flung it out the window. I watched it disappear into the flurry, and squinted at a dark mass ahead. It grew taller as the carriage neared, twisting into a large stone castle. Only white lanterns burned outside, floating in the snow like misty aether creatures.

"Here we are," Gast said.

"*That's* the Asylum?" It was a towering monstrosity decorated in statues of faces, for some godsforsaken reason. A barred metal fence surrounded it. "How are we supposed to get inside that thing?" There weren't any guards outside—the entire Asylum looked locked tight.

"There's a service entrance around the back. I passed through it last time I broke out of here."

"You've been locked inside before? Did you go feral?"

"I pissed off the wrong mortals. Happens in my line of work."

The carriage came to a slow stop. I followed Gast out as he paid the driver, and the carriage wasted no time in abandoning us. Gods know how we were going to get back to the Gate before it closed. I hoped Gast had a plan.

We trudged through the snow toward the looming castle. It was difficult to view the Asylum in detail as I battled the growing blizzard. Even as a Necro, I struggled against the howling wind. I buried my face in the collar of my coat. My boots weren't exactly equipped for this weather, and it was tough work pushing through the inches of snow around my calves.

Eventually, we found shelter against a stone wall. Gast pulled out a pocketknife and shoved it between the hinges of an iron door. It creaked open, revealing some sort of storage room.

Gast beckoned me inside, but I didn't need to be told. I huddled in the dank space and shook off the clumps of snow sticking to my legs. Somehow, it was even colder than the storm outside, and it smelled awfully rotten.

"Where are we?" I whispered. "It stinks!"

"An abattoir. It's where they collect blood for feeding."

"Are you joking?" I searched his bloodshot eyes in the dark and saw no sign of amusement. Gods. "Where—Where does the blood come from?"

"Never mind that. The abattoir connects to the lower cells. The whole Asylum is built on multiple levels with different wards depending on what ferals are used for."

The way he described it made my teeth grind. "What *are* ferals used for?" Why bother keeping them locked up here? Why wouldn't The Nameless One dust them out of existence and be done with it?

"Experimentation, mostly. The Nameless One likes to keep a fresh stock."

Shit. "We're getting Vincent out *now*." I stepped around a crate.

Gast grabbed my arm. "Hold it, lady. We can't just run up there. For one, this place is huge and well-guarded. I don't fancy getting caught and trapped in a cell, do you?"

I shrugged from his touch and scowled. "So what's your plan, *Morty*?"

He met my scowl with his own. "Only one woman calls me that, and you ain't her. New ferals are kept in the first-floor cells, but if your friend's an ex-Warden, I bet they'll want to question the poor bastard first. There's an interrogation room in the basement. It's risky, but we need to head down."

"How do we do that?"

"Carefully. Last time I did this, I had a Vesper helping me out. Can't do that anymore." He started rummaging through a laundry trolley.

Once again, I wished I'd retained my original Vesper form to make sneaking into death traps a lot easier.

"Here." Gast pulled out a bloodstained laboratory coat and threw it at me.

I almost dropped the ghastly thing. "Really? You couldn't think of a better plan?"

He exchanged his jacket for another stained lab coat. "Anyone we encounter will think we're part of clean-up. It's expected of all Necro to volunteer at the Asylum when called. Your friend likely did." Gast buttoned up the coat. "Stay close and act natural."

Act natural? For a Necro, that was the complete opposite of what 'act natural' meant. I donned the hideous coat and followed Gast's lead.

Together, we made our way out of the storage room and into the main abattoir. Blocks of ice and piles of snow filled the room. I soon discovered why.

Flesh hung from hooks on the wall. Arms. Legs. Chunks of someone's torso.

Gods. Was this what became of ferals?

No. Some of them weren't pale Necro flesh. Among them were Ember-red limbs. Golden Glimmer calves. Tiny Seren hands. Most were frozen, but some dripped with fresh blood, staining the ice beneath pink.

Fuck. I was going to be sick.

Gast pushed me. "Don't look," he whispered. "Keep moving."

"Is this what your domain does? Lures mortals to Witheryn and chops them up?" My voice was rising hysterically, but gods, oh gods, I wanted to get out of here.

"How do you think we eat?"

Shit, shit, *shit*!

Mortal bodies faded at death, which meant these were still alive, somewhere. Alive without their limbs or hands. The Necro could heal—they could very well keep a mortal alive in such a condition to feed on them.

No wonder we hadn't faced any resistance so far. Who would willingly step foot into this place? They were butchering mortals, and I'd happily come here!

Could I even trust Gast? What if he was leading me inside only to pissing eat me?

Or to throw me up on a hook?

He knew I was Chaos. What if he blamed me for Eventide?

What if this was some cruel game of revenge?

I should never have come here. Gods, I'd never sleep again.

"Get a grip," Gast said with a snarl. "We're here to rescue your friend, remember?"

Vincent. We needed to get Vincent.

I hurried out of this damn room as quickly as I could. Thankfully, it remained quiet, and we slipped out into a stone hallway lit by wispy white lanterns.

Footsteps and groaning echoed off the stone walls, but I couldn't tell from which direction.

"Don't look at the cells," Gast murmured.

I swallowed a lump in my throat and forced myself forward. Iron bars lined both walls. Cells. So many of them. My eyes were pinned to the gloom directly ahead. All I could hear was that awful groaning, joined by clicking, sighing, shuffling, and... sniffing?

"Meat?" whined a male voice from one of the cells. "I smell... meat."

Something clanged against the bars, and I jumped out of my skin!

In the dim light, a naked Necro man pressed against the bars, his teeth bared as he tried to reach me. Gods. His entire skin was covered in weeping sores of blood and yellow pus. The stench was unbearable.

LEAVE, Corentine urged. *TURN BACK NOW BEFORE YOU JOIN THEM.*

What's wrong with these mortals? What's The Nameless One doing to them?

THE NAMELESS ONE IS THE GOD OF DEATH AND DISEASE. HE EXPERIMENTS ON HIS MORTAL SUBJECTS TO CREATE NEW MEANS OF DECAY.

That's disgusting. Why would you create such a god?

ASK DOR. DEATH IS THE CONCLUSION OF TIME. TO BE BORN, TO AGE, AND TO DIE. END TIME, AND YOU END DEATH. THE NAMELESS ONE WOULD LIKE TO GET HIS HANDS ON A CHILD OF CHAOS.

I'm not leaving. Not without Vincent.

I couldn't bear to leave him in this place for another heartbeat.

Gast nudged me on. My legs were shaking so badly, I almost tripped over my own damn feet.

Finally, we stumbled upon a staircase. The air grew more frigid as we descended.

"I don't like this," Gast whispered. "It's too quiet."

Well, it wasn't like me to walk into a trap, was it? "Where's the interrogation room?"

"Straight ahead. Follow the blood."

I wasn't sure what he meant at first, but my Necro senses soon caught the metallic tang in the air. It led to an iron door at the far end.

Gast checked the coast was clear and slowly eased the door open.

I glanced over his shoulder and swallowed a scream.

A single metal chair was bolted in the center of the room, and chained to it was Vincent. His head lolled to one side, and blood stained his shirt. Shit. It reminded me of the soul-splitting machine.

I shoved past Gast and ran inside. No one else was in the room, and I ran to Vincent's side. He was unconscious, but still alive. Thank the gods!

"Careful," called Gast. "He could have gone feral."

I lifted Vincent's chin carefully. "Vincent? Can you hear me?" Please, let him be okay.

His eyes snapped open.

Before I could blink, he tore himself from the chair and knocked me to the ground. My palms scraped the hard stone, and I tried to shuffle back.

Vincent bared his teeth and pounced on me.

"Wait! It's me! It's Kay—"

He shoved my head down *hard*. Pain splintered through me, and I saw stars. I couldn't get up—he'd straddled me and had me pinned completely. No matter how much I pushed at his chest, I couldn't shake him.

Silvery-blue light burst from skin. Shit! I'd reverted to my Chaos form.

My palms tingled, and I instantly removed my hands from Vincent's chest. The last thing I wanted was to take his soul!

He pushed my head to one side.

And then his fangs sank into my neck.

I gurgled a scream. Sharp pain stabbed through my skin. The warmth of my own blood dribbled down my front.

Gods. He was drinking me!

Gast yanked at Vincent's arm, but he wouldn't budge. He pulled out his pocketknife.

"No," I moaned. "Don't hurt him."

Gast's eyes were wild. "He'll drain you dry if I don't!"

"Vincent, please," I whispered. "It's me. It's Kayl. You're going to kill me if you don't stop."

But Vincent continued sucking at my neck, his lips slurping as he lapped my blood.

TAKE HIS SOUL! Corentine yelled at me.

No. I could never damn his soul. Even if he drained me dry, there were worse ways to go.

My eyes fluttered. I relaxed as my life's blood flowed from me. "It's okay, Vincent. I forgive you. Get back to Sinder. Tell him... I love you all."

Vincent suddenly pulled back. Blood smeared his lips and teeth. His eyes opened wide in horror. "What have I *done*?"

Gast shoved him aside and was on me in an instant. "Hold still." He placed his hand over my throat, and warmth flooded through me.

I gasped a breath, which choked off into a cry.

"You're all right, lady. I've patched up your neck, but you've lost a bit of blood. You're going to be woozy for a while." Gast pulled me up into a sitting position. A wave of dizziness made the room spin.

The bitter cold hit me like a slap to the face. In my Chaos form, the climate of Witheryn showed no mercy, and my hands were shaking.

"I'm sorry, I'm so sorry." Vincent was slumped in the corner of the room, his knees bunched to his chest as he rocked back and forth. "I didn't mean—I'm so sorry."

I felt too light-headed to stand, so I crawled over to his side. He flinched as I approached. "Vincent. It's okay. We need to get out of here—"

"I can't." Tears streamed down his face. "I'm a danger to you—to everyone—"

"We can help you, all right? Sinder needs you." I tentatively placed a hand on his knee. "I'm not leaving without you."

"I hurt you." The pain on his face broke my heart.

I squeezed his knee. "Sometimes family hurts. It doesn't make me love you any less. Though you got blood on my dress, so I'm expecting you to buy me a new one."

He wheezed a smile, though his despair didn't entirely go. It was something, at least.

"At last. Our guest has arrived," said a familiar female voice.

The Necro ambassador stood at the doorway with two Necro guards. She was dressed in her extravagant lace outfit, a veil over her face.

Gast stepped back and brandished his knife. "Morana."

"Mortimer. You do keep finding trouble, don't you? Did you miss me that much?"

"What would my life be like without you to stab me in the back?"

"A lonely one, I daresay."

The two of them exchanged stares that spoke of years of history and resentment.

"If you two are planning on catching up, would you mind if my friend and I slip out the back?" I said.

Morana lifted her veil, and I swallowed a gasp. Raw lesions and sores covered every inch of her face, like the caged man upstairs. She smiled at me, a twisted thing that cracked her lips with a sheen of blood. "You're our special guest, Ambassador Arkey. Or should I say Nadine Noir?"

I leaned against the wall and slowly stood. "I don't recall receiving an invitation."

"I tried. But Ambassador Corinth wouldn't allow me. We needed a reason to entice you to Witheryn, and one so happened to present itself."

Vincent looked horrified. She'd kidnapped him, used him as bait to lure me here, but why? "What do you want from me, Ambassador?"

"It's not what *I* want. It's what my master wants."

A thick fog filled the room, swallowing me whole. With it, the temperature dropped so rapidly, all I could see was my own breath.

The fog lifted, and I blinked.

I spun, almost falling, as I searched for Vincent or Gast, but I was alone in what appeared to be another abattoir.

Gods.

Naked bodies hung from the ceiling off lines of hooks. Necro. Mortals from other domains. They jerked and twitched, groaning as the hooks pierced through their torso, shoulders, or arms, keeping them in place so all they could do was dangle uselessly. Blood ran down their skin and stained the floor.

Their limbs were intact, but... their faces had been peeled off, revealing pulpy flesh and bone underneath. Fuck.

I hastily stepped back, and my feet squelched through puddles of blood and flesh. The metallic scent made my lungs constrict. I ran past the bodies, bending sideways to avoid brushing against them, but there was no end to the rows.

No walls. No door.

I bent over and heaved, coughing up bile and spit.

You've got to help me! I cried into my mind.

WHAT A BEAUTIFUL FACE YOU HAVE, a soft melodic voice replied.

Shit.

Fucking shit.

The swaying bodies parted like a curtain of some obscene play, and a figure emerged from between them. It was a large black void in the shape of a hunched-over mortal, though it had no legs, and seemed to glide instead of walk. Multiple tendril-like arms branched from its torso. Atop that was an oval head bearing a white mask.

The Nameless One.

I'd only shit myself once in my life, after a dodgy Vesper mushroom, but I was mere seconds away from ruining my dress.

DO NOT BE AFRAID, The Nameless One crooned, in the same way a Necro would reassure their unwilling victim.

"Holding me against my will breaks the Covenant!" I yelled with as much courage as I could muster. Every child of the Undercity had heard tales of The Nameless One—that they liked to collect faces, for some unholy reason. I'd always assumed it a tale meant to scare, but it appeared the tale had some semblance of truth.

NOW WE SEE THAT THE DIVINER SPOKE TRUE. CORENTINE HAS CREATED NEW MORTALS. YOU HAVE HER FACE. THE FACE OF OUR BEAUTIFUL CHAOS.

"What do you want with me?"

THE DIVINER WISHED TO BARGAIN. WE OFFERED THEM TERMS, BUT THESE WERE NOT ACCEPTED. WE OFFER THEM TO YOU.

Quen hadn't mentioned this. Truly, I had no idea what they were rambling about, but at least when they were talking, they weren't murdering me or eating my face. "What terms?"

WE OWN MANY FACES, BUT WE MISS OUR MOTHER'S FACE. YOUR FACE. IT WOULD BRING US COMFORT AND PLEASURE TO OWN HER FACE ONCE MORE.

I stumbled back and almost screamed when I bumped into a female Umber swinging behind me, her skin a pale green.

She reminded me so much of Dru, it made my heart squeeze.

"I'm sorry, but I'm rather attached to my face."

The Nameless One's mask changed to the face of the Umber behind me, and they laughed. *WE ARE INFORMED YOU HAVE A TWIN. HER FACE OR YOUR FACE. IT MATTERS NOT TO US.*

Shit. What would The Nameless One do with Jinx? Rip her apart and torture her in so many ways as Vincent had once described. Jinx may be a pain in my arse, but there was no way I'd submit her to that fate. "How about I bring you a face mask instead? A little bit of mud can do wonders for your complexion."

IF YOU DO NOT VOLUNTEER YOUR TWIN, THEN WE WILL SIMPLY KEEP YOU.

"And break the Covenant?"

WE DO NOT CARE FOR THE COVENANT.

"Your mortals do! How will you get new faces if your access to Chime is revoked?"

THEY PALE IN COMPARISON TO CHAOS. YOU WOULD GIVE US ALL THE FACES WE DESIRE. UNTIL THEN, WE WILL KEEP YOUR COMPANION, AND THEN WE WILL EXCHANGE.

Shit, no! I wasn't letting this freak keep Vincent!

Gods damn it, I was caught in a bind. I either sacrificed myself, sacrificed Jinx, or lost Vincent. If Quen were here, he'd think of a way out.

Wouldn't he?

He hadn't been any help with the Lioness of Obituary, nor Dru. No, Quen would kiss the arse of whichever god held him by the balls. I'd assumed he was Godless like me, that he had no choice in bowing and scraping, because what choice did any of us mere mortals have?

What if... What if he did have the choice?

Would he give up a mortal to appease The Nameless One? Was a bargain with the Necro god really worth it?

Would he give up Vincent?

But no. He'd refused to bargain. Refused to bring me here. I'd come here of my own foolish volition, and now this was my mistake to own. And I'd gone and dragged Gast into my nonsense, but at least he knew this domain. He'd escaped the Asylum before...

Hrm. He had, hadn't he?

"Fine. We'll bargain. You can keep Vincent—I don't need him. So long as I can return to Chime with Morty."

The Nameless One tilted their head, and their mask changed to that of a Necro man's face. *YET YOU CAME TO OUR DOMAIN TO SAVE VINCENT HOLCROFT.*

"That prick owed me fifty bocs, what of it? Vincent's no use to me if he's gone feral. But Morty? He came all this way for me and saved my damn life! So if you could, drop me back off at the Gate with him."

This was a gamble, I knew. But The Nameless One wouldn't let Vincent go otherwise, and could I really trust a god to honor a bargain?

Their face changed to that of a Seren. *YOUR JUVENILE ATTEMPT TO TRICK US IS AMUSING. WE SHALL KEEP THEM BOTH.*

Two new hooks appeared out of nowhere. The sharp end pierced through the shoulders of two naked Necro.

Vincent and Gast.

Blood ran down their chests as their bodies idly dangled, their limbs twitching. Their faces were still intact, but contorted in silent agony.

"No!" I screamed and ran for them.

RETURN WITH ONE OF CORENTINE'S CHILDREN AS AGREED, AND THEY WILL BE RELEASED.

Thick fog wrapped around me once more. When it lifted, darkness pressed in on me, only now snowflakes tickled my cheeks.

I was standing in front of the Gate.

"*Vincent!*" I screamed until my throat went hoarse. "Give him back!"

My feet staggered through the frozen slush of snow. I needed to get back to him. I needed—

A clock in the square rang out seven o'clock.

The Gate blipped out. Trapping me here.

But then the Gate suddenly reappeared. Snowflakes started to fly *up*.

Someone was reversing time. The Nameless One?

I squinted at a figure stepping through the Gate.

Quen!

Time paused as he made a path straight for me, his face absolutely red with fury. Shit. I'd never seen him so angry before. Those silver eyes were as cold as Witheryn's snow. They flickered to my bloodstained neck.

"It's Vincent!" I yelled. "The Nameless One has him—"

"We're leaving. Now." Quen grabbed my hand.

"Not without Vincent!"

"There's nothing either of us can do for him if we're trapped in Witheryn for twelve hours. Come back with me, and we'll fix it."

Tears froze to my cheeks in the cold air. I couldn't leave Vincent, but what else could I or Quen do for him?

The Nameless One wanted me or Jinx.

At Quen's touch, my form changed to Diviner. His fingers were curled around mine tight, as though he was afraid to let me go.

Then he was pulling me through the Gate. Away from Vincent.

Time slipped back to the present as we left the numbing cold of Witheryn and arrived safely in Central Station. Zephyr brushed past us, ready for Tempest to open at any moment.

The clock struck seven again. I'd left Vincent behind, but also Gast— no, I'd fucked him over. The sight of them dangling on hooks would haunt me forever.

"May I have a private word?" Quen asked, though by the look in his eye, it was more of a command.

I nodded, too tired for words. My feet instinctively took me to the old bench with the broken streetlamp, and I sat before my legs failed me.

The entire trip to Witheryn had drained me, in more ways than one. A mixture of exhaustion and adrenaline shuddered through my veins. I'd be having nightmares for the rest of my life. I tucked my hands in my lap to stop them from shaking.

Quen sat beside me, and the coldness of his eyes softened a touch. "Why, in all that's holy, did you enter Witheryn?"

"The Necro ambassador kidnapped Vincent. I had to get him back."

"So you thought to enter *alone*? Why didn't you come to me with this?" Hurt strained his voice. "You could have waited until morning, or flagged down a Warden. Anything! Do you understand how dangerous Witheryn *is*?"

I hugged my chest, the cold still biting through my skin. "I'm sorry. But it was Vincent."

"If you enter domains without me, then you risk undermining everything I've worked for—"

"And that's all you care for, is it?" I snapped. "Your damn plans and bargains—"

"I'm trying to save you!" He squeezed his eyes shut. "Chime. I'm trying to save Chime."

A single drop of blood ran from the corner of his left eye. I caught it with my finger. "What is your god doing to you?"

He opened his eyes. There wasn't anger there, but fear. Sadness. "What he must."

My palm cupped his cheek, and he rested his own warm hand on top of it, pressing my hand in further. Savoring my touch.

It hit me like a blow to my stomach.

He was risking everything for me. Sacrificing everything for me. And I, in my ignorant selfishness, hadn't seen the pain I was causing him.

Was I really worth his bloodied tears? Was I worth losing Dru? Vincent? Hurting my friends and family? Hurting *him*?

I wanted to pull away. To stop this.

But I couldn't.

"Are you still my Quen?" I whispered.

"Until the end of time."

I choked back a sob. "I know what you're doing, and I'm not worth it."

"Kayl." He breathed my name like a prayer. "You're my salvation."

His lips pressed against mine with sudden desperation. Aether burned through my blood, melting away the pain and stress of the past few hours, and I returned his fervor as though this were our last night in Chime.

It was a domain-shattering kiss.

I wanted it to steal my soul and destroy me.

Quen was the order to my chaos. The logic to my madness. The dawn to my dusk. And yet he was none of those things.

He was a trapped soul. A Godless caught in the machinations of the gods. Bowing to their whims, but never completely. He fought to be free.

He fought for me.

He suddenly broke contact and yelled out in pain. His hands went to his head.

"Quen!"

"I can't—"

"Quentin," Pendula called out.

Oh shit!

We were surrounded by Diviner Wardens, with Quen's betrothed and Ben at the forefront. I hadn't heard them approach. Ben looked visibly concerned, but Pendula was all restrained anger. How much had she seen?

We were fucked now.

"You're needed," she said. "It seems Ambassador Gloria is ready to bargain with us."

Quen broke away from me like a guilty student who'd been caught reading naughty books in the library. "Right." He avoided looking at me. "Ambassador Arkey, if you could return to your domicile? Ben will contact you when we are ready."

The Wardens surrounded Quen and Pendula in a protective circle and left me sitting alone on the bench. Now they knew my not-so-secret meeting place, I couldn't use this for sharing information anymore.

But if the Glimmer were ready to bargain, then that meant the end of our adventure. Chaos would be given new lives. Corentine would be freed, somehow.

Quen would marry Pendula. What would happen to me?

WHAT DO YOU THINK WILL HAPPEN? Corentine said. *YOU THINK YOUR DIVINER CARES FOR YOU, BUT HE WILL BE OUR END.*

The future of the domains rested on our shoulders, and that was too much for mere mortals to handle.

Even in my Diviner form, I had no idea what time would bring.

But I did know who I was. A Godless.

And I knew who Quen was. A sinner, deep down.

Regardless of what Corentine thought, I believed in what we could be.

XXXV

THIS WAS THE MOST awkward train ride of my existence.

Ben had abandoned me, leaving me with Penny so we could speak privately—or so he'd said as he fled to the vestibule of the steam train. Though personally, I thought he'd run off to avoid the awkwardness, or to punish me for entering Witheryn without him. For a bodyguard, he certainly hadn't saved me from this unpleasantness.

For now, I avoided Penny's eye by stirring my tea continuously. Eventually I'd have to put down my spoon and face her, but saints, I was a coward.

A coward, a fool, and an utter bastard.

"Quentin," she said at last, her voice as sharp as a letter opener.

I wiped my spoon clean on a napkin. "Yes, dear?"

Oh, the look she gave me withered my soul, and damn near shriveled my testicles. "I expect my husband to be loyal and devoted to his wife."

I sank in my seat and wished it would swallow me whole.

My betrothed had caught me in the arms of another woman, our tongues firmly locked in a ballet that would shame most Golden City productions. Guilt curdled my stomach, for the pair of us would pay dearly for my mistakes, but it was Penny who'd carry the scars.

When a Warden had entered my office and alerted me that Kayl had made the crossing to Witheryn, it had sent me into a panic. I'd ignored both Ben and Penny's protests and raced across Central Station, missing the Gate closing by a minute.

A minute I'd yanked back through time without any thought for the consequence.

Kayl had stood there, frozen in her Chaos form. Blood stained her neck and the collar of her dress. With her in that state, I'd almost fallen to my knees, but I'd dragged her out, terrified out of my wits.

Lost in her eyes, I let all my carefully curated defenses fall.

She'd touched me. I craved that touch. I couldn't deny it.

I was a weak man. I should have been stronger. I knew what failure meant.

But I couldn't resist her.

Fuck. I was such a bloody fool. My idiocy could well damn us all. Everything I'd sacrificed up to this point, on the eve of success, could be wiped out by a single moment of stupidity. A single kiss.

Isn't that what the great poets say? That a kiss can devastate? Destroy hearts and lives and entire domains?

Yes, I was well and truly doomed. Goodbye soul. Goodbye tea and bourbon biscuits. Hello, eternal damnation.

I didn't want to damn Penny for my sins, but I could afford a little spite. "You should have informed me that Ambassador Arkey had left for Witheryn." Central Station's sensor had gone off when she'd first stepped foot inside. Penny had taken the report and chosen to ignore it until Kayl had made the crossing. We could have avoided this whole mess.

"Ambassador Arkey's brazen uncouthness was her own undoing. Is that what you enjoy in a woman? Is that how you'd like me to act? With uneducated vulgarity? Dressed in immodest clothing like some Undercity slag? Wanton, sinful behavior—"

"Stop it."

Penny sucked in a breath. "Are you loyal to me, Quen?"

"Should I ask you the same? You went behind my back to spy on her." I pulled out the remnants of her mangled pet bird and observed her reaction over the rim of my spectacles.

She examined the clockwork bird with an air of scorn. "Can I trust your judgement where Ambassador Arkey is concerned? She's a liar. A deceiver. A being made of chaos who is willing to destroy your own efforts to save them! Yes, I had her watched, because she cannot be trusted. She's a member of the Godless. She should never have been granted the rights of an ambassador. Did she seduce you? Or are you seduced by Chaos itself?"

"What do you want me to say?"

"That Chaos has seduced you—and that is why you have acted illogically."

Dor would need an answer. Was I in control of my own actions? Or could I blame them on the seductive wiles of a chaotic temptress and therefore exonerate myself?

While I'd credit Kayl's charms, my sins were my own. "You're right. Ambassador Arkey flaunted her irredeemable qualities, and I'm but an innocent boy—"

"Father teaches us to avoid sins of the flesh—"

"We all have our perversions."

"You are a Diviner. Act like one."

Right then. I'd been thoroughly chastised by my wife-to-be.

Though the lack of trust grated on me. Penny knew the Godless had made their base inside the Mesmer temple and hadn't informed me.

If I was an utter bastard, then what did that make her?

I took a sip of my tea. Gods curse it, I didn't want to return to the topic of Kayl, but time demanded it. "Ambassador Gloria visited my office earlier regarding our bargain. Did you inform her that a Glimmer was hiding in the Mesmer temple in exchange for offering Ambassador Arkey on a platter?"

Irritation flashed in her eyes at the mention of Kayl. "They want justice for the death of Lady Mae. Surely you must appreciate that we cannot rule the Council until Ambassador Arkey is brought forward to face judgement?"

We? I swallowed my immediate reaction—unbridled rage. "The Covenant provides protection for ambassadors, even those made of Chaos."

"I spoke nothing of punishment—"

"I know the Glimmer. They're quite vocal on their doctrine—an eye for an eye." Or a soul for a soul, in Kayl's case, though thankfully there were no soul-splitting devices left in their hands. "The Glimmer they sent me after? He's a man. You know what they'll do to him."

"There are no male Glimmer—"

"Now there are."

"Then he is an apostate. Why are we discussing this? Regardless of whether this Glimmer is male, female, neither or both, they've conspired with known heathens."

To that, I had no argument.

The windows went dark as the steam train reached its destination. Penny shuffled her files away into a folder. "We'll make arrangements for Solaris after our meeting."

Assuming we remained in any state to discuss it.

The station was busy for the ten o'clock crossing, even at night. Ben joined us, and we stepped off the platform and headed straight for the laboratories. Dor awaited me, but I wanted to check in on Doctor Finch and Ilona Burns while I retained my wits.

I hadn't spoken with them since that first time, and I could only hope they were getting along. But as I entered the stuffy lab to giggling, I realized my fears were unfounded.

The pair of them were seated on a bench. Ilona wore a headdress made of Zephyr feathers as the good doctor added more. As soon as they saw us enter, Ilona quickly yanked off the headdress and buried her face in a book.

Doctor Finch leaped to his feet and approached me. "Master Corinth! We didn't expect you so late."

Penny gave me a look as if it were *my* fault that everyone had suddenly lost their minds. She sat next to Ilona, her back to me. The interest Penny had in the Amnae girl worried me a little, though I couldn't place why. Perhaps it was simply overprotectiveness.

I shoved my hands into my pockets and walked with Doctor Finch back to his desk. "You're getting along, then?"

His feathers ruffled in embarrassment. "The girl couldn't sleep. I was merely offering a distraction from our work, which I believe is a logical solution to anxiety and fear."

He would know. Sadly, so did I. "Has she spoken of any particular anxieties?"

The doctor sat on a stool and picked up one of the aether collars as though he hadn't heard my question. "Allow me to update you on our progress, Master Corinth. We believe we have what we need to fulfill the operation's parameters. Our collars can block a mortal's natural abilities, with an unintended side effect—they also block the connection between a mortal and their god. We tested it on a Diviner volunteer."

A side effect we'd need to keep in the Diviner's hands only. The implications of its use were too dangerous to ruminate on. "How many do we have?"

"A handful. I've altered the biometrics to work with any Diviner fingerprint for mass production."

Mass production? A handful was all we needed to contain Chaos. But of course the Wardens would have an ulterior use for them. These collars would make incarcerating mortals of the various domains much easier.

I wanted to ask Doctor Finch more questions, but he was staring at me oddly. His head bobbed up and down, as though gesturing for me to sit.

Subtlety was not his forte. I sat beside him. "Please may you go over the technicalities of the collar for my benefit, Doctor."

He shuffled beside me and bent his head close, his voice dropping to a whisper. "You should have told me that your assistant was Hector Bezel's prodigy."

I glanced over my shoulder to where Ilona and Penny sat chatting. "That information is irrelevant—"

"I'm a scientist, Master Corinth. I work in the realm of fact and logic. Facts are, Hector's prodigy is projecting her own biases onto the girl. The same biases I witnessed in Hector, before his untimely departure."

"What biases would those be?"

"A fear of Chaos. I've overheard their conversations. I may not have wings, but my hearing is exceptional. The girl believes her father was killed by Chaos, that our work is designed to destroy it. Have our operational parameters changed?"

I swallowed a lump in my throat. Ben stood on guard by the doorway and watched me with an uneasiness I struggled to mask. "This operation is still under my command. Why would you assume otherwise?"

"Because your methods are illogical. I realize that sacrifices must be made in the pursuit of progress, but I cannot understand why such stringent testing is needed on Chaos mortals when the objective is to assist them. Even the girl is questioning your methods—"

"What methods are you speaking of?" Trust a Zephyr to spin an entire tale before getting to the blasted point.

"The testing! The girl shouldn't be subjected to it, nor burdened with the task of wiping those memories. She's a child." His feathers bristled. "There, I said it."

"Testing? On whom?"

"The Chaos mortal who came through the other day."

"I'm sorry, *what* Chaos mortal?"

Doctor Finch's beak tilted sharply. "You didn't authorize it?"

My unease brought my nerves to high alert. "Will you excuse me for one moment?" I left the doctor and strode for the connecting labs.

Dor's tower had space for a whole wing of laboratories where Diviner could research new technologies—I'd only been gifted the one for my own endeavors. It didn't take me long to find the observation room I was after. A group of Diviner in lab coats were standing outside it, scribbling notes on their clipboards.

I pushed between them and swallowed bile.

Chained to a chair inside that room was Chance. The Chaos mortal I'd so wrongfully assumed was safe and sound back at the Warden correctional facility on Chime. An aether collar was wrapped around his neck, and bloodstained bandages covered his wrists. A bruise bloomed under his right eye.

He looked pained. Uncomfortable. Exactly what I didn't want.

I snatched a clipboard out of someone's hands and flipped through the contents. They'd been thoroughly testing him. Taking his fluids, his vitals. Poking and prodding him every which way. I unleashed my ire on the scientists. "Who authorized these tests?"

One of them huffed. "This data is strictly confidential!" He reached for my clipboard.

I slapped his hand away. "I'm Ambassador Corinth, you pompous prat! This mortal is under *my* protection! Now, who authorized these tests?"

"Gentlemen!" Penny pushed between the scientists. "Leave this to me, please. Go take a tea break."

The scientists wandered off, leaving me to seethe. "Don't tell me this is your doing?"

She placed a comforting hand on my arm.

I shrugged her off. "I gave you no such authority! I explicitly stated that this mortal was not to be harmed. Look at him!" I pointed at the window. "This is barbaric—it is cruelty. You'll transfer him back to Chime *immediately*."

How could I marry a woman who would torture a mortal like this?

I'd sworn a promise he wouldn't be harmed. I'd *sworn*!

"These are our Father's orders," she simply said.

"Father never communicated this to me. I'm His voice—"

"And I'm your assistant. I know what's at stake—Father and I wished to avoid burdening you further. You would never have agreed—"

"No, I wouldn't!"

"For your plans to succeed, we need to test them on a Chaos mortal."

I grabbed my hair with both hands and paced. "How can I trust you when you make these decisions without consulting me?"

"I made these decisions so you wouldn't have to."

I stopped and stared at her. My future wife. She stood so casually, her cool silver eyes saying what she wouldn't dare speak aloud. I was weak, and neither she nor Dor trusted me to handle this operation. To make the difficult decisions.

In the twisted mind of a Diviner, it was logical to run these tests. Necessary. Damn the mortal who would be suffering under them.

This was my fault. I'd been too busy making bargains with gods, that I hadn't kept close watch over Chance. I hadn't noticed what was going on under my own damn nose. "No more. Do you understand? No more tests."

She dipped her chin. "As you command."

QUENTIN. Father's voice yelled inside my mind. *YOUR TARDINESS INSULTS ME.*

Apologies, Father. I counted my breath, letting calm wash over me. "We're needed."

Penny accompanied me as we strode for the elevator. So many of these meetings had me dragging my feet, trying to delay the inevitable punishments to come, but one could not delay a god of time.

I wanted it done with.

As we rode up, Penny became subdued. The gentleman in me wanted to beg for forgiveness at her knees. I'd wronged her so grievously, dishonored her—betrayed her—and I feared retribution. But she'd also wronged me, albeit not in the eyes of our god.

But... that was marriage, wasn't it, according to the great poets? Give and take. Pain and pleasure. Commitment and compromise. Witnessing and accepting the worst in each other. Cherishing the best.

We'd made a good start of it.

The elevator came to a halt. I forced myself forward, Penny dutifully by my side. She had a right to be angry with me when my actions harmed her reputation, and more besides. What was an appropriate remedy? Should I invite her for afternoon tea? Buy her flowers? No, flowers were wasted on Diviner.

An engraved watch was more fitting. Engraved with what? To Penny, with my love? That wouldn't be honest. To Penny, sorry for ruining both of our lives? Too honest.

The two Guardians opened the doors and stepped in after us. Always a bad sign.

One could afford to be flippant when reminded of one's frail and terribly squishy mortal body.

I entered the blinding light of eternity. The numerous clocks hung around me, quivering not with anxiety, but with a gleeful energy. Had we caught Dor in a good mood? Saints, I hoped so.

I kneeled in the center of His palm. "Forgive me, Father, for I have sinned."

YOU SUBMIT YOURSELF BEFORE ME, YET I DO NOT HAVE YOUR COMPLETE SUBMISSION. YOU CONTINUE TO SIN.

"I've made mistakes. I own them. To be mortal is to err—"

TO BE MORTAL IS TO OBEY.

Shame burned in my gut, and I lowered my eyes. "I beg your forgiveness—"

YOU UNDERSTAND THE CONSEQUENCES.

The two Guardians grabbed Penny's arms.

"Father, please! Punish me instead! Penny has done nothing but serve you—"

IT IS NOT I WHO PUNISHES YOUR BETROTHED. YOU DISHONOR HER, QUENTIN. IT IS BY YOUR HAND SHE SUFFERS.

Penny cried out as the Guardians ripped open her blouse, exposing her brassiere and the scar written above. Masturbation.

I tried to stand, but an invisible force kept me pinned to my knees.

Her silver eyes frantically blinked at me. Sweat already beaded on her brow.

I'm sorry, I mouthed. What use were apologies?

This was my fault. My shame. I should be the one to bear the brunt of our Father's anger.

This *was* my punishment.

The Dark Warden had failed to save so many mortals. Had damned so many to their gods. Elvira. Malkavaan. Dru. Vincent. Penny was just another in a long line of my failures.

Though unlike me, Penny was no coward.

Fear clouded her eyes, but she didn't beg for mercy as a Guardian lifted its finger to her cheek. The brass metal morphed into a tiny saw as the Guardian's other hand grasped her chin, holding her head still.

Saints.

The saw cut into her cheek.

Penny's screams drowned the tick-tock of Dor's domain. Blood dripped onto her chest, onto our Father's own hand. His blood. His flesh.

Time stretched with agonizing slowness, drawing out her pain.

I couldn't stand it!

"Stop!" I choked out. "Punish me, maim me, mark me for the sinner I am, but please *stop*!" My own bloodied tears fell to Dor's palm. "I'm sorry! I'm so sorry!"

YOUR APOLOGIES DISRESPECT ME. I BROUGHT YOU INTO EXISTENCE. I GAVE YOU LIFE. I GAVE YOU A PATH TO FULFILL YOU. I GIFTED YOU A WIFE TO BRING YOU HAPPINESS. YET YOU CONTINUE TO DISREGARD MY LOVE, AND FOR WHAT? FOR SIN. FOR PLEASURE. FOR CHAOS. IT HURTS ME, QUENTIN.

"I submit to you, Father. Your will is my will—"

YOUR ACTIONS OF LATE SUGGEST OTHERWISE. I OWN YOUR THOUGHTS. YOUR DREAMS. YOUR VISIONS.

"Then—Then you've seen what I've seen. The domains—"

ARE IN DANGER. I WARNED YOU WHAT ROLE CHAOS WOULD PLAY IN OUR FUTURE, YET YOU IGNORED THEIR SIGNIFICANCE.

"We've almost united the domains, Father! Then we can remove Chaos's powers and restore peace to Chime." My visions wouldn't have to come to fruition. I understood we were fighting against the forces of Chaos, but Father could surely rewrite the timeline to whatever He willed. He had that power.

THE FUTURE IS NOT YET WRITTEN, THOUGH I SHALL NOT INTERFERE WITH THE COVENANT. I AM PLEASED WITH YOUR PROGRESS.

Relief flooded my blood. I dared a look at Penny. Her screams had turned to muffled sobs as the Guardian finished its work. It stepped back, revealing the word now carved into her right cheek.

Deceit.

My heart skipped a beat.

DO YOU THINK ME HARSH, MY SON? I DO WHAT IS NECESSARY TO PROTECT OUR DOMAIN. TO PROTECT MY CHILDREN. I PUNISH TO CORRECT YOUR BEHAVIOR BECAUSE OF THE LOVE I HOLD FOR YOU. I WOULD SEE YOU FLOURISH.

"I understand, Father—"

THE GLIMMER MUST COME UNDER MY COMMAND. YOU WILL FULFILL THEIR DEMANDS AND HAND CHAOS TO SOLARIS. WHEN THE BARGAIN IS STRUCK, THEN WILL THE TIMELINE BE SAFE FROM CORENTINE'S CHILDREN.

He demanded I hand over Kayl.

My hands were shaking, and I pressed them against my thighs, my head still bowed.

REMEMBER THAT YOU ARE MY VOICE. I CAN ONLY AFFORD YOU SO MANY CHANCES TO PURGE YOURSELF OF YOUR DEFICIENCIES. SHOULD YOU CONTINUE TO DISPLEASE ME, YOU SHALL BE REPLACED. SERVE ME WELL, AND YOU SHALL ONE DAY BE IMMORTALIZED AS A SAINT.

A shudder ran down my spine. I understood what He was saying.

My replacement, whoever they would be, wouldn't serve Chime's best interests, and certainly not Chaos's. If I messed up like that again, then I'd lose everything.

But if I succeeded, then I would share the same fate as Dru.

In this task, I'd always needed to make the ultimate sacrifice.

It was never Kayl. Never Chaos.

It was me.

This was my path.

Like Kayl, I needed to wear a persona, and my chosen form needed to be that of Ambassador Corinth. But, like Kayl, I couldn't keep myself from switching between Ambassador Corinth, Quentin Corinth the Warden, Quentin Corinth the Diviner, the Dark Warden so many knew to fear and despise, and the many other versions of Quentin that Elijah and Walter had so carefully constructed.

The Quentin who had loved Elijah.

Who had killed for him.

And now, the Quentin who needed to be loyal to his future wife.

So many Quentins who had fragmented into pieces. Parts of myself I'd picked up, dusted off, and shoved into neat boxes to be ignored.

Underneath all those lay a boy, broken and scared, who'd once fallen inside Chime's clock tower and heard a voice no mortal was ever meant to hear. The voice of Chaos. And since then, Chaos had left its mark on his soul.

But that boy had always been falling.

It had taken one woman to catch him. To break his fall.

Only for him to fall again.

"I know what you're doing, and I'm not worth it."

At the bottom of my soul lurked the Dark Warden. The man who Elijah had wished me to be. That Quentin had pointed a pistol at Elvira Byvich's head. She'd stared with amethyst eyes, unafraid of what fate awaited her. She'd known a fundamental truth that wrapped itself around my bones.

Mortals belonged to their gods. Whatever mercies they granted us were a blessing we'd never earned.

Elijah had understood that when he'd ordered me to blast a hole in her head.

It was time to become the man he'd made me.

I stood on shaking legs and approached my betrothed. Blood ran down her face from that word. Deceit. A cursed word. I took off my jacket and wrapped it around her. "I'm sorry," I whispered. "This will never happen again. You're no longer my assistant, but my partner in all things. My equal." I brushed my lips against her head, a subtle touch of her hair that wasn't enough to trigger my abilities. "I will honor you, always."

She forced an uneasy smile.

I turned to my Father. My god. My very means of existence. Dor's form filled His domain. Forever old and wise. Never changing, despite the passage of time.

"I love you, Father. I thank you for all you have taught me, and all you have given. I see now that my deficiencies have brought you shame—have dishonored your domain. Please, forgive me. I am ready to do what must be done."

36

To sin is to feel shame.
But sin is nothing to be ashamed of.
Shame only exists because we decide something is shameful.
—Anonymous, *Godless flier*

I RETURNED TO THE temple alone.

Stares and whispers followed me as I staggered down Central's streets. I knew I must look a state—my clothes were damp, dirty, and stained with blood—but I didn't care.

Chime's stores had closed for the night, though there were plenty of mortals heading for the early evening cafés or bars. With the trams so busy, I avoided them entirely and sought solace in the shadows of Chime's alleys.

I'd wanted to merge with the shadows entirely and let darkness engulf me, but thanks to Jinx, I could no longer revert to my Vesper form.

Even the shadows had abandoned me.

My slow lumbering brought me back to the Temple District well after ten. Sinder waited outside the temple doors, his red skin aglow as he nervously sucked on a cigar. As soon as he caught sight of me, he tossed it aside, the movement sending a flush of guilt through my gut.

In my attempt to save Vincent, I'd damned Gast as well. Damned them both.

"No." Sinder breathed out smoke, and his eyes flared at the blood staining my neck. "Don't say it. Please. Don't say it."

"He's alive."

"*Where?*"

"Let's get inside."

I followed him into the reception area, where the Mesmer trio waited, their faces a mixture of anxiety and anticipation.

"Where's Uncle Vinny?" asked one.

"Is he okay?"

"Is that *blood*?"

Shit. I didn't need this right now. "Can you give us a mo—"

"That *is* blood!" the Mesmer—Cosmo, I presume—shrieked.

"Is that Vinny's blood?"

"Is he *dead*?"

"Will you fuck off?" Sinder yelled.

The three Mesmer stared in shock. I don't think anyone had ever shouted at them before.

I approached them and put a hand on one of their shoulders. "Sinder's upset right now. Can you give him a little space? Don't worry about Vin— Vinny. He's... on holiday, okay?" I ushered them to the door, and they reluctantly left us alone.

Sinder paced with clenched fists. "If he's in the Necro temple, we'll burn it down."

"He's in Witheryn."

He staggered against the reception desk. "With— No. How did he end up there? How do you know?"

"I followed him through. They said he'd gone... feral."

"You went to Witheryn on your own? And you *left* him there?"

My stomach clenched with the sudden urge to vomit. "I didn't have a choice! They locked him away and threw me out." I didn't want to blame it on Quen dragging me home. "And then the Gate closed. But we'll get him back. We'll bloody get him back."

"When? On the next crossing? How?"

"Quen and I will come up with a plan—"

"Because your last plan worked so well! What's your plan this time? That you and Corinth will politely ask The Nameless One to release Vincent over a steaming cup of tea? Will you even be awake at 6 a.m. to make the crossing?"

That stung. Sinder had every right to be angry, but we'd never fought like this before, and I didn't know how to proceed. "Quen needs to deal with the Glimmer and ensure the gods are working for him and Chime. Then we can go back to Witheryn."

Sinder's eyes opened wide. "You let The Nameless One take him. You sacrificed Vincent to save your own hide."

"You know I would *never* do that—"

"Do I? You've left him trapped in Witheryn for a whole twelve-hour cycle, and now you're saying you're going to leave him to rot because Corinth says so? Like you did with Dru—with Malk."

What had I done to Malkavaan? I couldn't remember! Heat rose to my face. "Don't you dare suggest I don't love my family—that losing Dru didn't cut me to my soul!"

"No. Maybe you had good intentions. But everything that's happened to us is because of you. We wouldn't even be in this temple if it wasn't for *you*." He shook his head. "Malk tried to warn us, didn't he? I should have gone with you to Witheryn, but I trusted you to know what you were doing! My big fucking mistake."

His words cracked through me. I reached for his arm. "Sinder, please—"

He yanked from my touch and stomped into the main temple, slamming the door behind him.

Shit. Fucking shit.

Sinder was right. This was all my fault.

I'd lost two of my family in one day. Dru. Vincent. And before then, I'd lost Reve and Malkavaan—a man I couldn't remember because of memories I'd lost! Even Quen was sacrificing himself for me. My actions were hurting him. If I pushed, I wouldn't just lose him forever. Dor could be torturing him in so many depraved ways.

And I could have lost Sinder. Not physically, but emotionally.

Would he ever trust me again?

THEY WERE NEVER YOUR FAMILY. I AM.

I couldn't be arsed to argue with Corentine right now. What would be the bloody point?

Why had I thought I could outsmart a god? I was stupid. A complete and utter idiot. Without Dru, without Quen, I was just some bumbling prat with no clue.

Jinx was my brain. I was her heart. Right now, my heart was broken. Useless.

Like me.

The reception door opened, and Harmony waddled out. "What the *fuck* is going on? I had Sinder practically barge past me, and the Mesmer are crying about Vincent. Where is he?"

"Witheryn?"

"*What?* How?"

"The Nameless One has him."

"You gave them Vincent?" Harmony stared at me in shock.

That she thought I'd willingly hand him over was a slap to the face. "Of course I didn't give them Vincent! I tried to save him—"

"I knew this was too much for you to handle." Harmony shook her head. "Fuck. I should never have allowed—"

"What else would we have done, Harm? Let the gods shit all over us? Let Jinx take your souls—"

"Like you took the Vesper?"

My heart stopped. "What?"

"It was you, wasn't it?" Harmony took a step back. "Tell me the *truth*!"

"I don't know the truth!" The words tore through me.

I thought I knew, but the memories were fuzzy. It was Jinx. She'd taken Valeria's soul. She'd destroyed Eventide. She'd ended the Vesper.

It had to have been Jinx.

Because if it wasn't her...

"Don't raise your voice at Harm," snapped Joe. He stood by the doorway. Shit, I hadn't heard him approach.

"Mind your own damn business," I spat back.

His golden skin glowed with a threatening aura. "Has schmoozing with ambassadors gone to your head?"

"I don't have to answer to you."

"Girl," Harmony warned.

"I don't need this. I'm done." I grabbed a spare jacket from the reception's coatrack. Vincent's jacket. I shrugged it on and headed for the doors. I needed to be anywhere but here.

"Kayl, wait—"

"No. I'm done."

Done with this temple. Done with playing ambassador. Done with being Godless.

Done with this shit.

Whenever life got me down, I'd always sought comfort in my friends. My family. Harmony always had a chore or two to keep me busy, as well as scandalous secrets from her day job at the Courier. Sinder was a gossip, too, and we'd do each other's nails or play cards with Vincent, who always had a wise word to share.

Dru kept me company during the rough days. We'd head to Grayford's night market and share a bag of chestnuts while bitching about whatever Glimmer boss we worked for that week. She was my rock, keeping me grounded.

And then Quen. He'd made time for me.

Where had all that time gone?

I'd had nowhere else to go besides the bench outside Central Station. It was late, with the Gate set to Kronos. The streets were largely empty, with only pubgoers wandering past, chatting, laughing, warming up for a night on the pisser. None of them would notice little old me sitting in the shadows under a blown-out streetlamp the Wardens hadn't bothered to fix.

Quen's betrothed could be spying on me, but I didn't give a shit anymore.

This was *my* bench. My only source of comfort. I should use whatever ambassador influence I had left to buy a plaque with my name on it.

Kayl Arkey.

CHAOS NEEDS NO FAMILY NAME, FOR WE ARE FAMILY, Corentine said, interrupting my thoughts yet again.

What family?

THE FAMILY YOU HAVE ABANDONED AND LOCKED AWAY.

Oh, here we go. Don't blame me for your damn problems! It's your fault the gods can't stand you.

YES, I ORCHESTRATED MY OWN IMPRISONMENT.

Ooh, Corentine was going to give me sass, was she? *We wouldn't be fighting if you and Dor kissed and made up.*

DOR CAN KISS MY CUNT.

I laughed. I couldn't help it. This whole situation was ridiculous.

Everything was shit, and I was somehow supposed to pull myself together?

I leaned back against the bench and closed my eyes, listening to the foot traffic marching into the station, the buzz of aether as the tram rode past, the clank of the Undercity elevator coming to a halt.

The bell of the clock tower striking quarter to whatever hour.

Exhaustion weighed on me, yet in the darkness, I saw Vincent hanging from that hook. I saw Dru's empty eyes as her immortal form forgot me. I saw Reve writhing and screaming, smoke drifting from his body. I saw Vesper collapsing into dust.

I saw Quen's body fading before me as I screamed his name.

And then, my thoughts fluttered away, a domain of its own lost to time.

My eyes adjusted to the darkness. Aether lights flickered around me, highlighting bronze panels. I'd been here before.

This was the maintenance tunnel inside Chime's clock tower that led to Corentine's prison. How in god's name had I ended up here? Shit—had one of my Chaos siblings kidnapped me and brought me back?

Soft whimpering echoed behind me, and I turned to see a man blocking the tunnel.

Quen.

He was dressed in his usual tan suit, his hair more of a vivid white than silver. He faced me with a finger against his lips. Gods. His eyes were ablaze with aether.

I cautiously slid to his side. "What's going on?" I whispered.

"He's just fallen," Quen said in hushed tones.

I glanced toward what he was speaking of.

A young boy lay on the maintenance platform, squirming in agony. A younger Quen. Corentine had shown me this vision before, but why was I here now? Why was the older Quen here?

"I'm dreaming again, aren't I?"

"You're dreaming. I'm watching history unfold. This is where it all began."

"Where what began?"

"My downfall. Your birth."

I'd almost forgotten. If it wasn't for Quen landing here and following Corentine's commands, she would never have shat me and Jinx out through the aether. I wouldn't exist at all. "I have a lot to thank you for."

Quen's arm slid around my waist, pulling me into the crevice of his body with practiced ease. "I have more reasons to be thankful." He gazed at me with eyes the color of aether. My eyes, I realized. "I'd kiss you right now, but I wouldn't want to disturb ongoing history. Doing so tends to have catastrophic consequences."

I placed my hand on his chest, over the flutter of his heart. "I can be quiet."

"I know from experience that you can't." His nose nuzzled close to my neck, his breath a caress that sent my toes curling in their shoes.

Gods. "And how would you know that, mister? Are you from the future?"

"I can't reveal all my secrets."

"How are we both here? *Why* are we here?"

He sighed against my neck. "I'm trying to find you. The future you. My Kayl. Let's say that the timeline is... complicated. Mesmorpheus knows this. They've brought you to me for reasons yet unknown to you."

"Could either of you be any more infuriating?"

He squeezed my hip and chuckled. "It'll make sense, I promise. I'll be taking my leave shortly. I just need to ensure events unfold as they should."

The younger Quen lay broken and hurting as we lurked in the shadows, watching. "Are you my Quen?"

"That depends on my past self. Right now, he's suffering at the mercy of Dor's whims. While Dor is in my mind, I have no choice but to obey his orders—to deny you."

"But you're here?" And whole?

"The timeline is fragile. This future is not set in stone. Whatever decisions you and Past Me make could change its path. I exist now, but should the timeline change, then this version of me will also change—or fade away entirely."

Everything had already changed. What if I ruined the future? What if Chaos or Jinx did? What if this dream was a remnant of a future that would never come to pass? "Then what future do you represent? What man do you become?"

His palm rested on my cheek. "I'm the Quen who adores you. Who will fight by your side for a future that glorifies all mortals."

"Does this version of you swear?"

He smirked. "He fucking does."

I grabbed his jacket and yanked him to my lips. His mouth opened in a promise of a future that was ours, and his arms wrapped around me once more, touching me again with the confidence of a man who knew how our bodies fit together. The implications of that sent aether burning through me.

This was *my* Quen.

He pulled from my grasp and placed a finger on my lips. "In time, my dear."

"How do I save you?" I breathed, my chest full and heavy.

"If you want this future, then you'll need to fight for it. I'm sorry. It won't be easy." He flipped open his pocket watch. "My time's up. But before I go, remember this: my past self has placed a sealed envelope under our bench. Don't forget it."

Light burst around him, and I shielded my eyes. "Don't leave me! I *need* you!"

"We'll meet again. You're my salvation."

There was that word again. Salvation.

In a single blink, Quen was gone. To where, I had no idea.

The younger version of Quen was still squirming on the platform. If this was a dream, then had Future Quen been real? Or was my mind simply fantasizing a version of him that I wanted? A version that likely didn't exist?

What did that say about me? That I wanted the suave Quen who knew how to handle me? Who would worship me? Kiss me?

There'd been so many versions of Quen through his memory loss, and now through future versions, that I'd always held on to my version. My Quen.

Deep down, he was Godless. A sinner enslaved to his god like every other damn mortal. I wanted to set him free. To set us all free.

What kind of man would he be then, without his shackles?

A man who kissed me.

I wanted that man.

Gods. Was I really going to seduce a man betrothed to someone else?

Yes. Yes I was.

Call me a sinner, call me a harlot. That was exactly who I was. And I loved it. I wasn't letting any god get in my way—not even the god of time. And I wasn't letting Quen escape me that easily, either. Not after I saw what he was carrying in his pants.

The younger Quen went through the motions of memory by following Corentine's instructions and allowing her that brief moment to create Jinx and me.

And there it was.

A silvery-blue spark flashed through the tunnel, lighting up the bronze panels with the radiance of aether. It happened so fast that any mere mortal would have missed it.

But I'd felt it. The static vibrated through my blood, as though it were a part of me.

Was me.

THIS IS HOW YOU WERE BORN. Mesmorpheus's voice echoed through the tunnel.

"You've seen this memory, haven't you?"

I WITNESSED THIS MEMORY THROUGH QUENTIN CORINTH'S DREAMS. I WISHED TO SEE IT FOR MYSELF.

"So why bring me here?"

TO TEACH YOU HOW TO WIELD AETHER.

If Corentine or Jinx couldn't teach me how to switch forms or summon pretty electric shields, then how could Mesmorpheus?

IF YOU ARE TO SAVE CHIME, THEN YOU MUST WIELD AETHER.

"What about Quen? Is there anything I can do to save him?"

WHILE DOR POSSESSES HIS SOUL, QUENTIN IS LOST TO YOU. HE CANNOT DEFY HIS GOD. YOU'VE SEEN WHAT WILL HAPPEN.

Shit.

Part of me had tried to deny the feelings I had for Quen. To lose him to Dor would break me. But I couldn't keep lying to myself.

What was the point in saving Chaos if I lost everyone I loved?

What was the pissing point?

The clock tower suddenly vanished, and I once again found myself before the Gate in a vision of Chime's terrifying future.

Color leached from the station. One by one, the figures of mortals began to crumble into dust. Just as the Vesper had faded on Eventide. I remained still, completely transfixed as the entire city fell apart into nothingness.

THIS IS THE CHIME YOU WILL BE LEFT WITH.

"Fuck it, then! At least if I no longer exist, I won't be forced to sacrifice my family one by one! I won't have to watch them suffer and feel it!"

YOU ARE EMOTIONAL.

"Congratulations on your almighty powers of deduction! And here I was thinking gods were hopelessly stupid."

Mesmorpheus materialized in front of me. Shit! I wish the Mesmer would stop bloody doing that! They stood as tall as me, wearing a classy tuxedo, their entire skin and face a rolling sky of stars. It hadn't bothered me before, but their faceless face reminded me too much of The Nameless One.

"Are you going to smite me? Join the queue! I'm sure there's a whole line of gods waiting their turn. Make sure Gildola gets a shot in first—"

WE ARE FAMILY.

"I—what?"

THE OTHER GODS CHOOSE TO FORGET. WE HAVE BEEN DISCONNECTED FROM ONE ANOTHER FOR MILLENNIA. THEY BELIEVE THEMSELVES UNIQUE IN THEIR POWERS AND DOMAINS. BUT WE REMAIN CORENTINE'S CHILDREN.

"And that's why you want to help Chaos?" Why the Mesmer had gone through so much trouble to help me?

I DO NOT ENJOY THESE POWER STRUGGLES. I DO NOT WISH FOR THE DOMAINS TO FIGHT. DOR CANNOT BE ALLOWED TO DESTROY CHAOS. NOR CAN CORENTINE BE ALLOWED TO DESTROY TIME. YOU AND CORINTH ARE OUR ONLY HOPE OF PREVENTING THIS.

"Quen, maybe. But I'm useless, and he's fucked while Dor is pulling his strings. Your biggest threat is Jinx, but I have her locked inside your temple. You're a god; go into her mind and rewrite it."

I HAVE TRIED TO ENTER HER MIND, BUT SHE DOES NOT DREAM.

Of course she didn't. That would be too normal for Jinx. "Isn't it about time the domains ended, anyway? I'm sure that's some Diviner philosophy. All things must end, et cetera."

YOU DO NOT BELIEVE THIS.

"Why does it matter what I believe? Dor will win. Maybe you should hand me over to the Diviner so you can stay on his good side." At least if Dor won, the domains would remain safe. Mortals would continue to live, albeit as mindless slaves with no sense of free will or imagination or creativity. Who needed any of that, anyway? Not when you could pore over spreadsheets and drink tea?

If Corentine won, we lost everything.

A mediocre existence was better than none, right?

Mesmorpheus continued to stare at me. Despite their lack of eyes and eyebrows, I could sense them judging me, the arsehole.

They could judge all they liked.

Being mortal was shit. Let the gods sort out their own damn problems.

I HAVE SEEN WHAT YOU WILL ACHIEVE.

"Thank you. That was an *excellent* pep talk. I'm feeling incredibly motivated to save the gods, the domains, and every bloody mortal through time and space. I may even have time for a quick cheese and onion pasty."

Mesmorpheus clearly wasn't impressed with my sarcasm. *YOU ARE RUNNING OUT OF TIME. ARE YOU WILLING TO LET THE GODS CONTROL YOUR FATE? OR WILL YOU TAKE CONTROL OF THE POWER WITHIN YOU AND LEARN TO WIELD IT? FORGET THE DOMAINS AND THEIR MORTALS. WHEN THE GODS COME FOR* YOU, *WILL YOU ALLOW THEM?* They held out their hand. *YOU ASPIRE TO BE GODLESS. I CAN TEACH YOU THE CHAOS NEEDED TO MAKE IT SO.*

Wow. *That* was a pep talk. Fine. If they wanted to risk me stealing their soul, then whatever. I grasped their hand.

Pain stabbed through my forehead.

It was aether—pure aether—ripping my mind apart! Splotches of color filled my vision. The dancing ballet of silver and blue.

"Stop!" I tried to yell, but the aether burned through me, shredding through my nerves, my blood, my bones. My living flesh.

My mortal body disintegrated, leaving me with the raw form of Chaos.

The aether became me. I became the aether.

Gods. It was beautiful.

In this state, I could somehow feel beyond the touch of my fingers. I breathed in electricity instead of air. My blood pumped with the rhythm of the cosmos. And when I opened my eyes, I saw the maddening swirl of cosmic energy. I floated within the heart of it.

Was this Phantasy? Had Mesmorpheus brought me to the stars?

THIS IS AETHER. EVERYTHING IN THE UNIVERSE IS BORN FROM THIS POWER. THE GODS. THE DOMAINS. EVEN YOU.

Shit. I finally understood what Jinx meant.

We were all made from aether.

AETHER FLOWS THROUGH YOU. IT CAN BE MANIPULATED IN THE SAME WAY A VESPER CAN SUMMON SHADOW. CHANNEL IT. USE IT.

I'd give it a go.

WE WILL SPEAK ONE LAST TIME, CHILD OF CHAOS.

"What do you mean?"

Darkness swallowed my words, and the stars blinked out, one by one.

"Shit!"

I sat up, my chest heaving. It was still dark—no, the streetlamps were on, I was still seated on the bench. The Gate was set to Memoria. How long had I been sleeping on this damn bench? An hour, my Diviner senses told me. It was five past one.

The itch of aether buzzed through my skin, waking me with a rush of adrenaline that got my nerves shaking. I'd never felt so alert—so alive—so eager to do *something*, whatever that something was.

I needed to get back to the temple.

As I moved, my skirt snagged against paper under the bench. A note?

I dug out an envelope that had been sealed with fancy silver wax. The Quen of my dream had instructed me to remember this, which meant it was for my eyes only.

Without Vesper vision, I wouldn't be able to read it. I tucked it into Vincent's inner jacket pocket and casually made my way across Central to an empty tram platform.

I checked no one lingered nearby and peeled open the seal, revealing a letter with Quen's handwriting.

"Kayl,

I trust you'll keep this letter in strict confidence. Please burn it after you've memorized the contents."

He had more faith in my memory than I did.

"Ambassador Gloria has invited us to Solaris to bargain. However, they refuse to negotiate unless they can bring Lady Mae's killer to justice."

Shit. Of course they were being hard-arses. Gloria had been after my head—or my soul—for weeks. But they must know Quen wouldn't bend to their ludicrous demand. I was an ambassador, for god's sake!

"Unfortunately, Dor is pushing for this. He wants the Glimmer brought under his thumb. I have no choice but to follow his command. Wardens will march on the temple in time for the afternoon crossing. I'm warning you in advance so the Godless can find alternative accommodation."

Fuck!

"As for you... We need the Glimmer on our side if I'm to save Chaos. I'm sorry. A sacrifice must be made."

My heart started racing. He couldn't mean...

"You'll prepare Jinx. Be ready."

Quen hadn't signed it. I crushed the note against my chest, my heart pounding.

He wanted me to sacrifice Jinx. To use her as a scapegoat in my place.

No wonder he hadn't delivered this damn news himself! Jinx was a pain in the arse, and yes, I could live my entire life without ever seeing her again, but to hand her over to the Glimmer? To do what? Kill her? Enslave her?

I couldn't do that to her.

Could I?

I leaned against the streetlamp, my mind reeling. I could run. Find somewhere to hide. Except there was no running, was there? If this deal with the Glimmer fell through, then Dor would order the Wardens to destroy Corentine—and Jinx and I would go with her regardless.

Quen had weighed up the options. This was the only solution he'd found.

To sacrifice my twin sister.

Jinx was the only thing standing in the way of Chime's future. I couldn't keep her locked up forever. If she got out, she'd still be a threat.

Shit. Fucking, absolute shit.

Handing her over wouldn't be a kindness, but... *Shit.*

SHE IS YOUR SISTER. SHE LOVES YOU.

Loves me? I could have laughed! *She tried to kill me. She zapped me and left me half-naked in a damn bush! What kind of sisterly love is that?*

ONLY BECAUSE YOU PUSHED HER AWAY.

No, she pushed me *away by trying to force me into genociding my family.* She'd lived in my head my entire life, seeing what I did. Feeling what I felt. And yet she didn't give a damn about Dru, or Reve, or any of them.

SHE IS YOUR FAMILY. GIVE HER A CHANCE.

Why should I? She never gave me a chance. If the roles were reversed, Jinx would damn me in a heartbeat.

And that was the truth of it. It was either me or her.

She'd killed mortals. I didn't forget the sight of bodies piled inside that Diviner watchmaker's. And who was to say I'd been the one to kill Lady Mae to begin with? Jinx had often taken over my body without my consent.

She was a murderer. Not I. She'd destroyed Eventide.

I'd sacrifice her, all right. But not to the Glimmer.

I'd do at least one good thing.

The Nameless One wanted a Chaos mortal. They'd get one.

Gods. Was I really going to do this?

For Vincent? Absolutely.

I'd make it up to him and Sinder. They were my family. I didn't give a shit about the Glimmer's thirst for vengeance or whatever.

And that meant I needed to act now. I'd have to drag Jinx somewhere before Quen and his Wardens turned up. The Necro temple. We could hide there. Dickface from yesterday may not let me by, but one quick word to his bitch of an ambassador would get me in.

Not even the Necro would deny their god.

It was time to confront my sister.

No one waited at reception as I returned to the Mesmer temple.

It was nearing two by the time I got back, but both the Mesmer and Godless kept a late schedule, thus I tiptoed my way through the corridors and downstairs to the padded cell. I didn't spot Harm, Sinder, or Joe as I snuck about.

It had been days since we'd locked Jinx away, and I'd not once visited to check up on her. For all I knew, she could have gone insane.

Well, she was already insane.

Her cell was unnervingly unguarded. I stepped to the window.

Jinx sat cross-legged on the floor. Her wrists were bound, and that collar was still closed around her neck. A faint buzz of aether hummed from it.

She gazed up at me with a manic grin. "You've finally come to betray me."

"Something like that."

"You were bound to show your true colors eventually."

"You betrayed me first."

Jinx shrugged. "You're my sister. I wanted us to be a family, but I wasn't good enough for you. Apparently sharing your mind for the better part of thirteen years doesn't count. Remember all those times I helped you? Advised you? Saved your ungrateful arse?"

"I didn't come down here to make a crossing to the domain of guilt."

Jinx stood, her chains clanging together. "Nope. You came here to cart me off to the domain of sunshine, daisies, and a bitch who wants us both dead."

How did she know about the Glimmer's demands? "Did Corentine tell you that?"

"It was obvious the Glimmer would demand one or both of us. So is that it? You hand me over to the Glimmer, and they join Corinth in his little prayer circle? Boring!"

"That's what happens when you shoot Glimmer in their own estate."

"That was your body."

"And your mind controlling my actions. Cut the shit, Jinx."

"You know what they say. A dead Glimmer is the best Glimmer. I have a friend who agrees with me."

Aether zapped at my back.

Searing pain rippled through my muscles. My limbs spasmed uselessly, and I collapsed to the floor.

Shit!

I forced myself to roll over, to see who had bloody shot me—

No.

Please no.

Sinder stood by the doorway, aiming a taser at me. "Sorry, dearest."

The door to Jinx's cell creaked open. She casually strode out, dropping the manacles from her wrists, and then she removed the collar. "Surprised, sister?" She licked her index finger. "Turns out these things only open with Corinth's fingerprint. They're quite easy to copy with a Necro's form."

"Wha—why?" I spluttered, letting drool run down my chin.

Jinx stood by Sinder's side wearing a shit-eating grin. "You fucked up. Like I told my new friend here you would. He's been passing me information, interesting tidbits to help me enact my plans. After our last encounter, I realized I needed to be patient and wait for the perfect opportunity. That's now, in case you're not keeping up."

No. I couldn't believe it—*wouldn't* believe it.

Sinder wasn't a spy. He couldn't be.

We were Godless. We were family!

Sinder avoided my eye. "I need Vincent. I can't—I'm nothing without him."

Jinx leaned against Sinder's shoulder, and the affection in it made me sick. "I promised to destroy Gildola for him. That's what I intend to do. When I have her soul, I'll have her power. Then we can burn through Witheryn together and save Vincent. Who's the hero now?"

"No!" I dragged myself to my knees. "If Jinx—all the Glimmer—like Eventide!" I spat out. "I can—can save Vin—"

"Like you saved the Vesper? You're such a dirty liar, telling everyone it was *me* who took Valeria's soul when it was *you* all along."

No. That wasn't true!

My form switched to Chaos as Mesmorpheus had taught me, and I let energy flow through my veins. Static built along my skin, writhing with blue and pink electricity. Gods, I was doing it! I was—

Another zap sent black dots over my vision. I blinked in and out of consciousness.

Something heavy pulled on my arms.

No. Sinder was locking the manacles around my wrists.

I grabbed his hand. He pulled from my touch, though not before my form switched to Ember. The effects of the taser had left me so out of it, I couldn't muster a single damn flame.

Tell her to stop! I called out to Corentine.

YOU HAVE OPENED THE DOOR. JINX WILL FREE THE GLIMMER FROM GILDOLA'S CLUTCHES.

No! We have a chance of freedom for you, for Jinx and all Chaos—

YOU PREPARED TO SACRIFICE YOUR SISTER. WHAT FREEDOM IS THAT?

She made her choice! Listen to me, Quen and I have united the domains. We're almost there! Don't throw this away, I'm begging you. If Jinx does this, then we won't get another attempt!

MY DEAR DAUGHTER. THROUGH YOUR EYES, I HAVE SEEN WHAT MY CHILDREN THINK OF ME, AND I WILL HAVE MY VENGEANCE. YOU ARE MORTAL. I FORGIVE YOUR TRANSGRESSIONS. BUT IF YOU CONTINUE TO FIGHT AGAINST ME, THEN I WILL HAVE NO CHOICE BUT TO—

"Let me do the honors," Jinx said.

My mind went silent as Jinx wrapped the collar around my throat.

Corentine?

There was no answer. The collar had cut her off as if I'd never had a god at all.

"Ah, so *that's* the trick," Jinx mused as she loomed over me. "I knew Corinth had a way to tell us apart, but I didn't realize he was such a devious bastard. There's a little dot in your pupil." She pressed a finger into my cheek. "So tiny, no one else would have noticed. But I know you as well as I know myself."

"Corinth had a Necro tattoo her *eye*?" Sinder asked from somewhere above me.

"Uh-huh. I bet he never even told you, did he, sister? Good thing I can imitate it. Did he ever tell you that he kissed me? He's a terrible kisser. All tongue and no bite." Jinx's face changed from that of Chaos to a Necro, and she gnashed her teeth. "Now let's get that dot out of your eye so Corinth doesn't get confused."

"Are you sure the Glimmer won't touch her?" Sinder's voice wavered.

"Relax. I won't let those golden fucks lay a finger on her."

"And you?"

Jinx switched to a Diviner form. "Do you want your Necro back or what?" She dug into Vincent's jacket pocket and pulled out the note Quen had left me. Shit! I forgotten to burn it! "Here's proof that my dear sister and her Time Boy planned to betray you all."

Sinder took the letter, his face expressionless as he read it.

"Sinder," I groaned.

"You've forgotten, haven't you?" Jinx leered. "Or someone has been fucking with your memories. You killed Valeria. You. Her soul is right in there along with *all* the Vesper." She nudged my chest with her foot. "Buried inside—"

"N—No," I spluttered.

"Think about it. If I'd taken Valeria's soul, I wouldn't need another, would I?"

Her words were a trick. They had to be.

And yet they squirmed inside my gut. I remembered entering Eventide. Chasing after Jinx. Entering Valeria's court, and Valeria crushing the life from me.

After that, everything had gone blank. I couldn't... I couldn't remember!

"We better gag her," Jinx said. "Can't have her blabbing her mouth and warning everyone we've switched places."

Sinder replaced Jinx in my line of vision. "I *am* sorry, darling," he whispered. "I almost backed out, but then Vincent..."

"Please—"

He carefully stuffed a cloth into my mouth and tied it around my head. "I love you. But I can't sit by the sidelines anymore. Don't worry. I'll make sure Harm is safe. I don't give a shit about Joe, though."

Shitting shit! I wanted to grab Sinder and shake sense into him, to scream in his face until my voice went hoarse, but my shackled limbs and the effects of the taser had rendered me useless. None of this was necessary! I could save Vincent!

Gods. I could save him.

All this time, Sinder had tried to make me believe Joe couldn't be trusted, and yet he'd been scheming with my twin behind my back.

Could I blame Jinx? For twisting him? Promising him the end of his woes?

When I'd failed to consider he was at melting point?

Shit. Just...

Shit.

Tears ran down my cheeks. Now Jinx had the means to take the Glimmer. To destroy them all. Destroy Joe. Destroy all attempts at uniting the domains and bringing peace.

Everything Quen and I had worked for was ruined.

And I'd been stupid enough to let it happen.

Once again, it was all my fault.

Part Four

XXXVII

Personally, I wouldn't bother with Solaris. Oh, it's very pretty, and full of wonderful teahouses, but the company is nothing to shout about.
Males are largely regarded as a nuisance and are often not given clearance into the Glimmer's domain. If you should be lucky, you'll be limited to certain streets and watched wherever you walk. The Glimmer themselves will ignore you. Some may hiss at you.
I recommend only entering Solaris if you have the required female parts. What, am I not allowed to write the truth?
—Q. Corinth, *Redacted Warden Dossier on Solaris*

THIS WASN'T HOW I'D expected my plans to conclude.

Wardens marched on Mesmorpheus's temple. Ambassador Reverie came out the entrance, her serene face more befuddled than angry.

"Is there a problem, Your Excellency?" she asked with her calm demeanor.

"Apologies. We have reason to believe the lawless group known as the Godless have been hiding inside this temple."

Reverie cocked her head. "Have they?"

"May we check inside?"

"Please do. Be mindful of my mortals. They scare easily."

I turned to the group of Wardens—a mix of Diviner and Umber—and nodded.

At my signal, they rushed into the temple. I stood with my hands in my pockets, watching events unfold. Ben and Penny flanked me on either side. Ben as my protection, naturally, and Penny, as she wished to be in charge of these proceedings. This operation was hers, after all. And thanks to my wonderful wife-to-be, we'd soon be on our way to Solaris.

Assuming our quarry hadn't made a run for it.

Exactly thirteen minutes later, a pair of Diviner Wardens came marching outside with the male Glimmer held tight between their arms—Joe Brightwell, if I recalled correctly.

An odd sight. As rare as Penny beside me. Dressed in a tight brown suit and with his hair cut short, Joe certainly was an eye-catching figure. That was Glimmer through and through—dazzling no matter their gender. He stood with his chin held high, making no attempts at resistance.

In those red eyes, I saw resignation. He knew his time had come.

My fingers tightened around the fob watch inside my pocket until it hurt. "Excellent work," I said to the Warden captain. "Please detain him in the correctional facility. Ambassador Gloria will decide what to do with him."

Penny nudged me. "If I may? Gloria would be pleased to receive him. We should bring him with us to Solaris."

"As the lady suggests. Use one of the collars. We can't have him burning through his restraints." Another odd sight to be arresting a Glimmer. A first, I was sure. But as Penny said, Gloria would be pleased indeed. Any Glimmer caught cavorting with rogues such as the Godless deserved whatever fate found them. "Were there any other mortals inside the temple?"

"No, sir. Only Mesmer."

Blast it. Where had the rest of them escaped to?

"No sign of Ambassador Arkey?" Penny asked.

"It was your assumption she would be here," I said.

"You wouldn't have prewarned her, would you, Quentin?"

"Of course not, dear. That would be undermining our very own operation."

"Don't get your knickers in a twist. I'm here."

Penny and I both turned to Kayl standing there with her sister, Jinx's limbs restrained by shackles, her neck wrapped in a collar, and her mouth gagged. Those aether eyes opened wide in a plea that caught in my throat.

I quickly compared sisters. Jinx wore the persona of an Ember and had donned a dress I was sure Kayl had worn before. Kayl, however, was wearing a Diviner form. The small birthmark I'd asked a Necro to add during her last passport touch-up was there. This *was* Kayl, though there were hints of anger in her eyes.

Considering everything she'd gone through, I could well understand.

"Ambassador Arkey." Penny addressed Kayl with forced politeness. "I'm to understand this is your twin?"

"You've got eyes. Good for you. I caught her hiding inside the abandoned Vesper temple. Ironic, I know. The Glimmer want vengeance for Lady Mae's death, and they'll have it. As Corentine's voice and a member of the Warden Council, I'm willing to hand her over in exchange for the Glimmer's promised cooperation."

"*She* is Lady Mae's killer? I was under the impression you were."

"We're twins; I can see how the Glimmer might make that mistake. This delightful creature"—Kayl yanked on the bindings holding Jinx, forcing her to stumble— "is Chaos personified. With her out of the way, Chime will be safe. Is that good enough for you?"

"Was it necessary to gag her?" I asked.

"You don't want her filthy mouth offending the Glimmer, do you?"

I supposed she had a point, but this whole situation unnerved me.

IT IS TIME CHAOS IS BROUGHT TO JUSTICE.

Yes, I understand, Father. This was a necessary sacrifice.

But I had to wonder... Did Kayl feel anything for her twin?

Anything at all?

"What of the other members of the Godless?" Penny asked. "Where are they? They were your acquaintances."

"*Former* acquaintances. I'm an ambassador. Why would I know where criminals go for tea and biscuits? Ask your lover boy."

Penny glanced to me. "Care to elaborate, *dear*?"

"We've already searched the temple at your suggestion."

"Then we'll have to question the, ah, Glimmer male. Have our Wardens properly bind and escort the Chaos creature," Penny ordered the Warden captain. "We must ensure she is secured for when we enter Solaris. Mistakes would be costly. Bind the Glimmer as well. We'll be bringing him with us."

"I'll handle the Glimmer, sir," Ben said.

I nodded. "Go ahead."

The Wardens carried out their orders with impeccable efficiency as Kayl watched on, her expression neutral.

I kept my distance by heading over to the Mesmer. Reverie stood outside the main temple doors, surrounded by the three Mesmer I'd met only yesterday. She shooed them back inside at my approach. Thank the gods for small mercies.

"I do apologize for the intrusion," I said. "I'll ensure you and your mortals are not implicated in any way."

Reverie closed the door behind her. "That would be appreciated."

"Are you still willing to lend us your expertise for when the time comes?"

"Mesmorpheus is eager to play their part."

"Wonderful. As soon as we've dealt with the Glimmer, we'll be ready to proceed."

Soon, my plan would come to fruition. It was hard to believe an entire week had passed already, and harder still to believe the domains would unite under Dor's rule. Assuming they honored their bargains. We still didn't have Faen's support, but the Fauna hardly mattered. Ambassador Morana had sent an early-morning telegram confirming The Nameless One's support, though I wasn't quite sure what had changed their mind.

All that was left was Gildola and her Glimmer.

Shouting came from one of the carriages. I ran over with a hand to my pistol and caught Ben dabbing a bloodied nose with one hand, and holding an empty pair of shackles in the other.

"The Glimmer—he escaped, sir."

"*How?*"

"I was adjusting his shackles and he walloped me good, sir, and made a run for it—"

"And you didn't think to pause time and stop him?"

He winced. "Sorry, sir."

Penny strolled over. "You've lost the Glimmer's bounty? Their return was part of our bargain!"

I pinched the bridge of my nose. "Yes, I'm aware."

HE LET THE GLIMMER ESCAPE, Dor said.

Obviously. Though we didn't have time to go chasing them across Central.

BENJAMIN SEASONS HAS BEEN ACTING IRRATIONALLY. YOU MUST DEAL WITH HIM. REMEMBER YOU ARE HIS MENTOR.

Once we're done with Solaris, I'll ensure he's adequately punished. An overnight stay at the Kronos correctional facility should sort him out. I'll flog him myself. That was how Elijah would deal with this. Punishment with a personal touch.

GOOD. SEE TO IT.

"We'll send some Wardens to look for Joe. We can't dally, or we'll be late for the crossing. Hopefully Gloria will understand. Ben, with me. Do try to pay attention from now on."

He lowered his head. "Yes, sir."

The Wardens were busy ushering Kayl and Jinx into a carriage. I caught Jinx's eye. She was a liability, even when under such heavy guard. I expected her to be angry. To be kicking and groaning in her captivity, fighting for freedom with every breath. Instead, she was subdued.

Those eyes held pain. Inevitability, perhaps.

Jinx had murdered mortals. Of course this outcome was inevitable.

Ben shifted uncomfortably beside me. "How do you know you've got the right one, sir?" he whispered.

"I have my methods."

Penny joined me, and together with Ben, we boarded a separate carriage. She sat opposite, her leg crossed over her knee while she checked a file, a parasol leaning beside her. The scar on her cheek was hidden under a layer of makeup. I wondered if Father approved? "Leaving Ambassador Arkey free goes against our protocol," she said without looking up.

"We need her cooperation for now. Then, we'll submit her to Doctor Finch's updated version of the soul-splitting device."

"And wipe her memory? Are you prepared to do that?" She met my gaze.

I didn't blink. "Whatever our Father commands."

The steam engine purred to life and then we were off, traversing Central's roads as the carriage rumbled its way to the Gate.

We made good time, and the ride was smooth, with no unfortunate complications. Two of the Godless remained unaccounted for—Miss Arabesque and Sinder—though I doubted they would interfere.

Jinx was the last of the Chaos mortals to enter our custody, those trapped within the clock tower notwithstanding. Corentine's reign would end today.

Our carriage arrived at the Gate as the clock struck four. The mournful dong of the clock tower sang a dirge to our destiny.

Solaris opened. We rode onwards to a future that was meant to be.

The domain of dawn was by far the most beautiful, though the constant sunlight could be hard on the eyes.

Solaris was an almost perfect replica of the Golden City. The same shimmering buildings, clean cobblestone streets, extravagant water fountains, and tailored bushes. Only the buildings were far grander, and you couldn't turn a street corner without walking into a cathedral or two. Oh yes, the Glimmer loved their holy buildings as much as they loved their fashion boutiques.

Ben was staring out the carriage window, a hand shielding his eyes from the unrelenting sun. Truly, Gildola's light reached every inch of her domain.

"Don't look at the sun, it'll blind you," I warned.

"Sorry, sir." He pulled away from the window. "There's so many sunflowers, Dru would—uh, never mind."

Penny raised a brow. I knew she expected me to discipline him, and I would. Though I couldn't fathom why Ben would willingly release our captive. Did he hold sympathy for apostates? I'd been there myself.

The Glimmer were right to punish them.

For an entire domain full of women, Solaris held an artistic charm Kronos lacked. The only men here were visitors from other domains, myself included, though they were placed under strict scrutiny, and the locals were largely forbidden from interacting with them. Ben and I would be watched, though Diviner knew to keep their hands to themselves. I had no such worries regarding Ben. Though I was glad we'd brought Penny. She would have much better luck negotiating with the Glimmer than I would.

Our carriage joined the traffic heading into the center of Solaris's holy quarter. We passed rows of town houses; their shutters closed to the never-ending light. Beyond stretched vast fields of golden wheat. These were one of the Glimmer's main imports into Chime, and formed the bland diet that Solaris's lower class ate. Gruel was a perfectly adequate meal for avoiding the temptations of sin.

Though that didn't stop the aristocratic Glimmer from indulging in afternoon tea.

The town houses were soon replaced with sprawling estates and mansions. All roads led to the center of Solaris; the grand cathedral.

Bells rang across the city, announcing our arrival. The carriage came to a stop outside the cathedral's green, and we stepped out, meeting with the second carriage.

The grand cathedral was magnificent in scope, even larger than the Academy back on Chime. Its structure was reminiscent of Valeria's castle, only the pointed spires were gold, and they reflected the sun with a dazzling brilliance. The walls were carved with intricate patterns of the sun, though it was the cathedral's stained glass windows that truly caught the eye. They were as tall as a tram, and each depicted the naked form of Glimmer in various golden, red, and orange hues. Though unlike the Ember's own artistic rendition of a mortal's body, these were tastefully done.

"So this is where all that workhouse money goes," Kayl said as she approached. "It's pretty. It would look even prettier as rubble."

"Do remember your place, Ambassador," Penny said. "If you wish to exit this domain intact, then I suggest you leave politics to the professionals."

"Is that a threat?"

Penny smiled and tapped the parasol over her shoulder. "Merely a warning."

"Ladies, please," I interjected. "Now is not the time to bicker."

They both scowled at me with equal annoyance. Goodness me.

A line of Glimmer waited for us outside the cathedral's main archway, headed by Gloria. She looked down her nose at both Kayl and Jinx. "The two Chaos sisters. But only one of them is in chains?"

"You get one of us, so don't be greedy," Kayl said. "This is the creature responsible for the destruction of Eventide, the death of Lady Mae, oh, and she shot you that one time, if you remember. You're welcome."

"Her Holiness will be pleased. Where is our agent, Brightwell?"

I pushed my spectacles up my nose. "Apologies. I'm afraid he got away. I have Wardens searching for him across Chime—"

"*Him?*" Gloria's face scrunched as though she'd tasted something sour.

"Mr. Brightwell has taken on the moniker of Joe—"

"Preposterous! There are no male Glimmer! Her Holiness would never debase her gift to the domains by creating a *man*. Brightwell must have been corrupted by Chaos, or perhaps by simple apostates." She shot a glare at Kayl.

Kayl shrugged. "Don't look at me. Men are all idiots."

"Yes, well. Her Holiness cannot locate Brightwell, therefore if he wishes to be a man, then we denounce him. There are no male Glimmer, and there never will be." Gloria touched a diamond necklace at her throat that held the golden symbol of Gildola in the middle. "Enough nonsense. Bring the Chaos creature. We are awaited."

The Glimmer took Jinx roughly by the arms and dragged her toward the cathedral entrance. I didn't expect she'd be shown any mercy inside— she'd committed both blasphemy and apostasy in heaps.

There wasn't anything I could do to soften her fate.

Not when I had my own fate to contend with.

Gloria gestured for us to follow. Penny lowered her parasol and entered first.

The clashing dongs of the cathedral's many bells vibrated under my feet as we entered the vestibule and dutifully made our way to the cavernous inner sanctum.

It wasn't the first time I'd stepped inside the cathedral, but each visit took my breath away. While the outside was a work of art to rival the Seren, the inside was stunning. Lines of pews surrounded the sanctuary altar on multiple levels and balconies, resembling a theater more than a temple. The glass stained windows cast a rainbow of light on the extravagant marble and gold furnishings that truly made full use of the Glimmer's fortune. If holiness was measured in wealth, then none would dare question the Glimmer's piety.

Above the altar, glass panes allowed Gildola's light to shine. It was so bright, it took me a few blinks to adjust my vision.

Gloria took her place by the pulpit. "You have been called to bear witness to the end of Chaos and a new dawn for Solaris! Today, even the god of time will marvel at the will of our Holy Mother. But first, we must cleanse the air with a baptism of the unworthy."

It was time to begin this travesty.

We passed docile Glimmer who filled the pews with their heads bowed, their hands clasped in murmured prayer. I'd expected Gloria to lead us somewhere private to discuss our business, but no, she apparently wanted an audience.

There were hundreds of Glimmer in attendance. Thousands.

I stopped short of the altar, Ben and Penny by my side, with Kayl and Jinx behind me. Incense wafted in the air with an unsettling sweet scent. That, and the constant whispered chanting behind, did nothing to abate my growing unease.

The Diviner and Glimmer had always maintained a partnership of sorts for Chime's sake. My presence here was mere politics. Yet despite the similarities we shared—our abhorrence for sin—our domains couldn't be more different.

The Glimmer held a penchant for theatrics. As they dragged a naked Glimmer onto the altar, the production commenced. The girl looked young. Terrified. Tears ran down her face as she struggled in the guard's grip. They tied her to a post while other Glimmer placed logs by her feet. Every sermon in Solaris began the same way.

With a spectacle.

"Looks like this party is finally heating up," Kayl quipped behind me.

She wasn't seriously making light of this?

"An apostate stands before you!" Gloria announced to her congregation. "A vile blasphemer who sought to reject Her Holiness's gifts. They will be judged under her eye."

Light flared above us. I averted my gaze as the light pulsated through the hues of sunrise and then shrank and formed a female body.

Gildola had graced us with her presence.

The god of dawn hung in the air, radiating heat. Her entire golden form was naked, except for crimson bangles wrapped around her wrists, ankles, and neck. Her long hair flowed behind her, glowing so bright that it merged with the light.

And those eyes burned with the power of the sun. Impossible to look at.

The Glimmer standing around us instantly fell to their knees, their heads bent in reverence. Penny did the same and dragged me and Ben down with her.

Kayl and Jinx, however, remained standing.

"You bask in the light of creation!" Gildola's voice filled the sanctum, stern and feminine. Gildola was not easily pleased, nor was she quick to forgive transgressions. Plus, she held a strong dislike of men, which made visits unfortunately awkward.

"Actually, you'll find that Corentine is the god of creation," Kayl said. "Without her, your pretty little domain wouldn't exist."

What in the saints' names was she doing?

Gildola's blazing eyes regarded her. "Children of Chaos. Misguided and woeful children. This universe is composed of many elements. Each are gifts from the gods to their mortal subjects. Gifts mortals cannot live without. Birth. Death. Time. Dreams. Memories. Duty. But some gifts are not needed. Worse, they seek to corrupt mortals. They do not need the sinful pleasure that Edana professes, for example. Nor do they need Chaos. A curse that encourages apostasy—"

"Chaos is bad, I get it. We didn't come here for a sermon."

"You came here to be judged for the sins of your mother. The sins of your tongue. But first, we shall deal with our own. Bear witness to the corruption of Chaos!"

Light appeared above the Glimmer tied on the altar, highlighting her for the congregation. The poor girl was trembling from head to toe. She could have burned her bonds and made a run for it, though she wouldn't get very far.

Sadly, this girl had likely taken Joe Brightwell's place.

"This mortal has chosen to deny my gifts." Gildola orated to her congregation with the dramatic flair of a stage production. "To deny the love I hold dear for my daughters. She fornicated with a male. An Ember. She debased herself with vile acts while speaking my name. But I am all loving, as I am forgiving. I will give you a chance to repent in the eyes of your sisters."

"I'm—I'm sorry!" the girl blurted out. "He—He did such—such despicable things to me. I never wanted any of it. Please, I swear—"

"I see your heart. Your lies. You wanted it. You enjoyed it."

"No! Please, Mother—"

"This is the effect Chaos has on mortal souls. They are tempted by sins of the flesh. They blaspheme. Once tainted, there is only one path a sinner can take to redemption. Only a baptism of fire can cleanse their souls."

I didn't want to watch—I *never* wanted to watch—but the girl was a blasphemer. A sinner. She must be made an example of. And I, as the voice of my Father, would watch justice unfold.

Flame took hold at the girl's feet.

"Stop!" she screamed. "I'm sorry! Have mercy! I'm sorry!"

"With blessings to Her Holiness!" Gloria yelled.

"With blessings," the congregation repeated in one long drone that drowned out the screaming.

The flame worked its way up with cruel sluggishness. I wanted to speed up time and end the girl's suffering, but this was Gildola's show.

She lasted minutes before her mortal body disintegrated.

When it ended, the scent of burned coffee replaced the incense. I hated that smell. I could taste the misery of it.

"The air has been purified," Gloria said.

"With blessings," the Glimmer chanted.

Gildola remained suspended in the air, her golden skin aglow. "Now we welcome a new dawn. The end of sin for every domain." She waved her hand, and the burned pyre was instantly replaced by a chair, light catching on the metal.

The soul-destroying device.

I shot a look at Penny, who merely nodded.

This couldn't be her plan? To support the Glimmer in ripping out Jinx's soul? I respected their desire for justice, but this went too far!

I shuffled close to Penny. "Tell me you didn't know of this?" I hissed.

"Of course I did," she whispered back with an exaggerated sigh.

"Then you knew they possess one of the devices? If Father knew—"

"Father knows. Why do you think we're here? To gather evidence of the Glimmer's wrongdoings. We both know the Glimmer are in defiance of the Covenant and our Father's commands."

"Then what is your plan?"

"To learn their intent. This is my operation. Let me handle it." She straightened the collar of my jacket with a smile and stood.

I ground my teeth and rose beside her. *Did you know of Pendula's plan, Father? Why am I only hearing of this now?* I despised being left in the dark when I was meant to be ambassador!

IT WAS PENDULA WHO LEARNED OF GILDOLA'S CONTINUED USE OF THE UNHOLY MACHINES. THE GLIMMER MUST BE HELD TO ACCOUNT.

I should be the one handling this. Penny wasn't a Warden—did she understand the risks of dealing with a god? We were going to be burned to a crisp!

PENDULA HAS PROVEN HERSELF COMPETENT WHEN DEALING WITH THE GLIMMER. THEY WOULD NOT REVEAL THEIR PLANS TO YOU. HOWEVER, PENDULA HAS INFILTRATED THEM WITH SUCCESS.

I knew Penny sought a way to prove herself to our Father, but this...

I didn't like it.

Nausea rolled through my stomach. That odious chair brought back memories I'd never forget—Walter burning as his soul was destroyed before my eyes. Me, helpless and squirming as Kayl was strapped in. I tried to catch her expression now, but she stared ahead at the device, her face devoid of all emotion.

What must she be thinking? Was she truly prepared to damn Jinx to this?

Could she do that to her own sister?

Saints. I'd shot my own lover in the head. Was it my place to judge their relationship, when my own had ended so abruptly?

To kill was justifiable. But to take their soul, wipe their existence away like an unwanted smear...

We'd done that together, hadn't we? We'd damned a Leander's soul. Was this any different? Jinx was a monster. The number of souls she'd destroyed was unthinkable.

Justifying it didn't make this any easier.

Gloria paraded around the chair as though unveiling an art piece. "We present to you the future. Isn't it beautiful?"

"How do you have this device in your possession?" I asked before I could stop myself.

Her smirk grew positively vulgar. "Let's not play games, Corinth. We both sought Doctor Zachery Finch for our own purposes. You seek a way of removing the power of Chaos, of rendering them harmless. A noble goal. We, however, have far grander plans." She scraped a nail down the chair's leather straps. "We discovered that severing a mortal from their god not only removes their powers, but also makes them completely docile. With this machine, we can free lesser mortals from the temptations of sin."

Docile? Could that be true? I searched Penny's face for horror, for disgust, but found none. Nor did Kayl react.

But Jinx—she was glaring at Gildola and straining against her bonds.

Was I going mad to find comfort in Jinx's rage?

"Have you tested this device works?" Penny asked.

"Naturally." Gloria clapped her hands twice.

Two Glimmer guards marched a group of mortals onto the altar. Three Ember, two Fauna. Their eyes were glazed over with an odd vacant look.

"You see?" Gloria stepped next to an Ember woman and slapped her hard across the face. The Ember's head snapped to one side, but she didn't cry out. Didn't react at all. "Completely docile, but still able to follow commands. Kneel."

The Ember sank to her knees.

Saints. This was what Father wanted me to do to Kayl. To all of Chaos.

That wasn't my plan! To remove the powers of Chaos, yes, but to then rewrite their memories and allow them a new life! This would turn them into slaves. Soulless living bodies.

I shoved my hands into my pockets to restrain my ire. "What do you plan to do with these mortals?" As if I couldn't guess.

"We'll create a new workforce of docile mortals. Mortals who are stripped from their god and free to be made anew—"

"If Edana or Faen learn of this—"

"These are no longer Edana or Faen's mortals. They're mine."

"Are you *insane*? You're inviting war with the domains! When the Council learns of what you're doing to their mortals, they'll be at your gate!"

"Will they? Or will the more prosperous domains see an opportunity to take advantage of the lesser ones? We'll gladly do business in exchange for stocking their own factories with willing workers. Ever since we lost Eventide, we've lost an advantage. Fortunately, the presence of Chaos has created divides. The domains will take sides."

Blast it, Gloria was right. Some of the domains wouldn't care if other mortals were being turned into glorified slaves, so long as it benefited them. And gods like Faen may not care enough to do anything about it.

Chaos may have created divides, but this would exacerbate it. "This breaks the Covenant!"

"As Dor has? Don't deny he won't do the same. Our ambitions are aligned—"

"He would never—"

"Dor is willing to compromise," Penny said. "Assuming that rules are adhered to."

I stared at her dumbfounded. *Father?*

Father didn't answer me.

Please, Father!

"We're willing to negotiate with Dor in exchange for Her Holiness gifting her power to Chime. That *is* what you wanted, correct? And in return, we'll offer a live demonstration of the device. Justice for the death of Lady Mae." Her gaze turned to Kayl.

Kayl was examining her nails. "Oh, were you talking to *me*? Sorry, you were doing that boring political dance, and I have to be honest, I didn't really give a shit."

"You will mind your tongue in Her Holiness's presence—"

"I've brought you a gift. Did you want me to kiss your arse as well?"

Gloria spluttered in outrage as shocked murmurs echoed through the congregation.

"Enough!" Gildola's voice shuddered through the sanctum. "Chaos stands before my daughters and speaks such wicked words, yet they desire my aid. Look at how small they are compared to our divine light. I have judged them undeserving of their mortality—"

"Ambassador Arkey has diplomatic immunity, Your Holiness," I interrupted, before Gildola saw fit to smite us all in another of her baptisms.

Her blazing eyes looked upon me with contempt. "Lady Mae's soul was taken from me. I am owed a soul in return."

"Relax," Kayl said. "It's this troublemaker here who wants to burn your entire domain to ash, not me." She took Jinx's chin and squeezed it. "Look at the hatred in those eyes. She's a real bitch, huh? Absolutely despicable. I'll let you have her on one condition—"

"You're in no position to be making demands," Gloria snapped.

"I want to be the one to pull the switch on my sister's soul. She's my twin. This is personal."

Gloria awaited her god's command.

"You may proceed," Gildola rumbled.

My heart was pounding as Kayl dragged Jinx to the chair.

Ben caught my eye, his expression one of unmasked concern.

Saints.

I knew a sacrifice needed to be made—that this was Father's will—but…

This wasn't right.

"This isn't necessary," I whispered to Penny. "These machines must be programmed wrong. We should return to Kronos and ask Doctor Finch to check them—"

"We've promised the Glimmer this as our end of the bargain," Penny whispered back. "And that Chaos creature is a risk to Chime. You know that. At least now she will no longer be a threat to us."

"Is that what you want for Chaos? To turn them into mindless workers? I can't—"

"This is what Father wants." Penny grabbed my wrist, her nails digging into my flesh. "Do you aim to disappoint Him *again*? To see me hurt? Be strong, Quentin!"

Jinx's muffled screams pierced through me. I watched on as Kayl and the Glimmer wrestled her into the chair.

I met Jinx's aether eyes. So like Kayl's. They were wild with fear, tears streaming down her cheeks.

Kayl glanced back at me and winked.

No. Gods no.

That wasn't Kayl.

Kayl was strapped to the chair.

I tore myself from Penny's hold. "That's the wrong twin! She's not Jinx, she's—"

Pain lanced through my skull. I collapsed to my knees. "Please *listen*!"

Penny placed her hand on my shoulder, pinning me down. "It'll be over soon, dear."

Father! That isn't Jinx! Jinx is free! Solaris is in danger—

DO WHAT MUST BE DONE.

Father, please!

THIS IS MY WILL, QUENTIN. YOU WILL OBEY ME.

No! I was wrong, so foolishly wrong, and now Kayl would pay the price. With Jinx free, Penny, the Glimmer—the entirety of Solaris was in danger.

And Kayl. No. She'd be subjected to a fate worse than death. Worse than losing her soul. I knew I shouldn't care, I knew she shouldn't mean anything to me, but I—

Agony burned through my muscles, forcing me to bend over and clutch my abdomen.

I could do nothing as Jinx grabbed the lever.

Who Say's I'm the Bad Guy?

*On my taking this assignment, Miss Bezel and Doctor Finch kindly
provided context. I'm not to concern myself with what Chaos is, yet to rewrite
their memories I will need to understand how they think. Up to now, I
assumed these mortals to be devious. Evil. An emotional sentiment rather
than a scientific one, but... They killed my father. Miss Bezel confirmed it.
Yet Zachery (he finds it annoying when I call him that, though he hasn't
asked me to stop) says that Chaos are victims of their circumstances. That is
why we're to give them a new life. I didn't believe him at first. Not until I
touched Chance and saw his memories. His pain.
I saw the thirteenth god through his eyes. Corentine. I saw the suffering she
and her mortals went through. And now... Now I'm not sure what to believe.
I wish my father were still here to explain it.*
—I. Burns, *Notes on Chaos*

CORINTH WAS SCREAMING BEHIND me, which was real fucking rude of him,
the noisy twat. Penny held him by the shoulders, her pretty little lips taut
in a grimace.

This was going to be *so much* fun!

My hand still clasped the lever. Golden bitch Gildola floated above me
like some sunny wraith. The cathedral waited in tense silence—the kind of
silence that sent tingles all over.

I was about to ruin everyone's day, starting with the bitch leering beside
me.

"Twice now we've tried to strap you in a chair." Gloria crooned over
Kayl as though she were some beloved pet. "You Godless have a tiresome
knack for survival. Now I know what you are... It makes sense. In the end,
I'm rather glad it came to this conclusion. Wiping your existence would

have been too easy. This way, I get to keep you as my personal attendant. My whip will treat you well."

"That's my sister you're talking about."

Gloria glanced at me. "I'd rather have you in that chair, Ambassador Arkey. But I'll keep it warm for you, for when the Council finally realizes exactly what you are. Shall we get started?"

"With pleasure." I wanted to giggle, and turned away to hide my delight.

This was already the best day of my new life so far, but my dear sister was not enjoying herself. I leaned close and whispered in her ear. "Do you really think I'd let Gildola take you? Funny, isn't it, how you were willing to sacrifice me, yet I'm going to save you. I guess that makes me the hero and you the villain."

Kayl's eyes opened wide.

Trust her to get into this situation. Well, yes, I had manipulated her close friend in order to betray her, but that's what siblings do.

Kayl wasn't the Glimmer's to take. She was mine.

I grabbed Gloria's arm and yanked her soul clean from her body.

"My daughter!" Gildola screeched. Gloria's empty body tumbled down the steps of the altar, landing faceup so everyone could see her socketless eyes.

I'd wanted to say something dramatic like 'behold the power of Chaos!' But I didn't get the chance.

Screams broke out among the congregation of Glimmer. They stumbled over each other in their haste to get as far away from me as possible.

"Compose yourselves!" Gildola's voice shook through the cathedral, causing the glass panes to wobble. The Glimmer paused in fear, their screams muffled into mumbling cries. "You are my holy warriors, and this *creature* is insignificant."

Sunlight burst from Gildola.

I had enough time to swap into a Glimmer form and raise my hands in a shield. The force of Gildola's power hit *hard*. If I were a mere mortal, it would have blasted me into smoke.

I was so much more.

While Kayl had been busy playing ambassador for the past week, I'd been preparing for the fight of my life. I'd collected a whole bunch of mortal souls so I could use their powers as I saw fit, bar the Vesper. Kayl didn't realize that taking the soul of another domain meant I could wear them at the drop of a hat.

With each soul taken, my strength had only increased. Not to godlike levels. Not yet. But enough to give this bitch a run for her bocs.

The light faded in an instant, and Gildola glared down at me. "You *dare* take the form of my mortals and use my own light against me?"

"Your light comes from Corentine—I'm here to take it back."

Flame curled around Gildola's form in some showy display that was supposed to intimidate me. "Corentine's reign ended millennia ago. I knew Chaos could not be controlled. Chaos is sin incarnate, born into every mortal soul. Only by eliminating your taint will mortals finally become pure. And I shall deliver their salvation. I am light. I am creation. I exist beyond chaos and time. I am—"

"Not the god of brevity, apparently." Because that was what villains did. Monologue and bluster when they should be murdering. Eh, maybe I was the villain.

"Everything touched by Chaos will be purged."

DESTROY HER IN MY NAME. GILDOLA'S LIGHT WILL END THIS HOUR.

For you, Mother. "Funny, I was thinking the same thing. I speak as the true voice of Corentine. She made you. I'll unmake you and return what is hers."

A streak of flame flew past my head and exploded against a marble column beside me.

Fuck!

More blasted in my direction, coming from all angles, and I threw another shield up. Gloria's Glimmer guards were advancing on me, but it wasn't just them trying to burn me alive. Members of the congregation were on the attack, flinging their flame with hopeless optimism.

Golden Girl didn't want to get her godly hands dirty, huh? Burning your enemies with holy light wasn't considered sacrilege inside Gildola's temple.

Kayl was thrashing in her seat and screaming behind her gag, which was honestly distracting.

"I'm a little busy here, sister." Flame lashed my shield, sending blinding ripples of light across the walls. I could do this all day, but I technically didn't have all day—I'd need to escape Solaris before the hour was up. And every second the Glimmer had me pinned here, I wasn't stealing souls.

The attacks suddenly stopped.

I lowered my shield. Wisps of flaming tendrils hung in the air, curling in a pretty pattern of golden hues. The Glimmer's angry faces were frozen.

Penny had paused time.

Corinth's bodyguard dragged him to his feet. "Your Holiness, please!" Blood ran down Corinth's cheeks, and he hastily wiped it away, smearing his face in a blush. "We've come here to negotiate peace, not start a war!"

Light once again flared from Gildola. "Do not take me for a fool—I know what moves Dor makes against me. He seeks to undermine my rule when it is *my* light that has grown and blessed Chime. Once again, he fears a woman who grows beyond him."

"Dor wishes to bring balance to the domains—"

"Dor betrayed his own Covenant! It was *his* mortals who created the soul-splitting devices to assert his control over the domains. Once, we bowed to his command, but no longer will we stand second to the Diviner. We will destroy Corentine ourselves and take our rightful place as Chime's rulers."

"I urge you to reconsider, Your Holiness!" Corinth looked stricken. Poor boy didn't realize his precious Covenant was a lost cause. "Chime cannot exist in peace while the domains are in conflict—"

"Dor has allowed sinners to pollute Chime! We will see it put to rights. We shall end the Ember's hold of Sinner's Row and purge the Undercity of sin. We—"

"*Boring!*" I yawned. "You two fucks can argue over Chime as much as you like, but that doesn't change the facts—Chime isn't yours. Nor the Diviner's. It never was. It's ours. And you're not welcome anymore."

Kayl screamed at me again. It was a good thing she was tied up, as she looked like she wanted to kick me.

"I am not without mercy," said the god who'd never shown mercy in her entire existence. "I will burn time's messengers quickly, and allow their souls to return to Dor so he may witness my words. You, however, will burn for an eternity."

Gildola raised her hands. Sunlight filled the cathedral, and the temperature started to rise.

Uh-oh. Now we were in trouble.

Time jerked forward. Penny fell back with a gasp, landing in Corinth's arms, while the hulking bodyguard stood there without a clue. The three of them stared open-mouthed at Gildola. Bloody useless Diviner.

The congregation was also raising their hands and began warbling some annoying choir hymn as sunlight continued to fill the room. They were going to fry us to death. Fantastic. I didn't care if Corinth and his lover got melted, but I couldn't let my dumb-arse sister join the aether.

I grabbed Kayl's collar. One press of Corinth's fingerprint etched over my own unlocked it. I yanked it off, sending it clattering behind me.

With her power now free, fire burst from her Ember form and melted through her bindings. She tore the gag from her mouth. "You bitch, Jinx! Look what you've done!"

"Get over it. If you don't want your Time Boy to get burned to a crisp, then I suggest you go help him in the next five seconds."

Smoke rose from Kayl's forehead with a glare so fierce, it rivaled Gildola. She shoved past me and ran for Corinth and Penny.

I quickly scanned the cathedral. Glimmer lined the pews and blocked the exits. It wouldn't take much effort for me to get through them, but I hadn't come here to run away now. That, and I couldn't leave my dear sister.

Corinth whipped out his pistol, as if the idiot could shoot sunlight.

"What now, sir?" the bodyguard asked.

"I'd suggest readying your final words. Try to think of something witty."

Penny opened her parasol. "Personally speaking, I'm not resigned to my fate yet."

"Really?" I jogged over. "A parasol?"

She gave me a look as haughty as a Glimmer's. "It's a reverse umbrella. It'll ward off the heat." With a click, mist sprayed from the parasol and cooled my face.

It was pleasant, I'll admit. "I don't think that's going to stop a god."

"No, but while you summon a shield, I'll keep us cool."

"Oh, you want *my* help? Kayl's an Ember, she can do it."

"I've never bloody done one before!" Kayl yelled. "What if I get it wrong?"

I rolled my eyes. "It's not that fucking hard."

"Ladies, *please!*" Corinth snapped.

"Looks like we're all gonna fry, then." I crossed my arms. "That's what you get for trusting my useless-arse sister to save—"

"Fuck you!" Kayl raised her hands and let flame flow out in a cocoon around us.

I added my sunlight to her flame, creating a bubble of dawn. I shouldn't be helping her, really, though even I'd struggle to protect all five of us against an entire cathedral full of Glimmer.

The heat didn't bother me or Kayl, but both Corinth's and his bodyguard's silvery skin had turned bright pink as sweat ran down their faces. They needed Penny's fancy parasol more than we did.

I enjoyed watching them squirm. The little gasps coming from Penny's parted lips were so delightful.

Maybe she should take off those clothes.

"Close your eyes!" Corinth said.

I didn't need to. In my Glimmer form, I could see through the light, though Gildola was barely visible. It was so intense, heat rippled in the air and melted the candlesticks on the altar into puddles, and then the candlestick holder itself drooped.

The heat turned into maddening tingles across my palms.

"Shit," Kayl muttered between clenched teeth.

The air started to burn. Definitely shit. "Don't let your shield down no matter what."

"I never wanted to come to Solaris! This is all your fault! You and Sinder!"

"Yeah, whatever."

Kayl whimpered but kept her hands up.

Fuck, this wasn't going well.

Hah! We might actually burn to death. I *knew* I should have brought sunglasses with me.

APPEAL TO GILDOLA'S SENSE OF HONOR, Mother said.

What honor?

GILDOLA HAS ALWAYS CARRIED AN INFLATED SENSE OF SELF-RIGHTEOUSNESS. SHE BELIEVES HERSELF TO BE THE STRONGEST AND MOST DIVINE OF THE GODS. PROVE HER WRONG.

I was going to prove it, all right. "Hey! Golden Girl! This heat is barely tingling my clit. I thought you were some all-powerful god, yet you're too scared to smite me yourself?"

"Are you trying to kill us quicker?" Kayl hissed.

"I think Her Holiness fears me, sister," I called out. "I've taken *many* Glimmer souls, and Gildola is nothing special."

The temperature dropped. I sucked in mouthfuls of hot air and caught the taste of burning flesh on my tongue.

Kayl and I released our shield.

Ash fluttered by, coating the marble furnishings and walls, which sizzled with steam. The Glimmer standing around us swayed unsteadily. Fuck. All were covered in horrific burns. Pulpy, raw red flesh across their bare golden skin, their clothes burned away.

So much for the mercy of gods.

"Kayl," Corinth whispered.

Kayl's hands were also red and blistered. Idiot didn't know how to shield her own fucking hands. Corinth took them carefully in his, and a bubble of time enveloped them. The blisters quickly receded, though the skin was still raw.

"What did you do?" Kayl asked with awe.

"Sped up the healing. You'll still need a Necro, but it'll do for now." Corinth cradled her hands with the tenderness of a lover. Pendula stood by. She wasn't harmed, by the looks of it, but the expression on her face had soured.

Fucking Corinth was ruining my moment of glory with his pathetic love life.

Gildola remained floating above us. Light radiated from her golden skin in fiery wisps. "I would not sully myself with lesser mortals." Her voice cracked in a blinding flash. "Though perhaps a demonstration is in order. My daughters shall witness your evisceration."

"Give it your best shot." I grinned.

Sunbeams shot toward me. I dove out of the way, and they headed straight for Kayl.

Fuck!

Corinth leaped in front of Kayl, using his own mortal body to protect her.

Then his bodyguard snatched Penny's parasol and wielded it like a shield.

The metal panes deflected the light, sending it bouncing off into the congregation.

A young Glimmer girl took the full brunt of Gildola's power.

How she was still standing, I didn't know. A singed hole had burned through the girl's torso. Blood and bits of her guts dripped onto the smoldering pew.

Penny covered her mouth.

"I—I didn't mean to," the bodyguard stammered, dropping the parasol.

The girl blinked. "Your—Your Holiness—"

Her body faded into a neat pile of ash.

"You bitch!" Kayl screamed. "You call yourself the god of creation? You're nothing but death!"

Gildola seemed unfazed. "I bring life to those worthy of it." The wounded Glimmer gasped as their burns and boils instantly receded. They fell to their knees, muttering prayers of thanks. "Those tainted by sin will be baptized in flame."

Sunlight rose from her skin in a bright display of dawn's beauty. The show-off.

I switched to my Fauna form and transformed into a magpie, leaving my dress to fall behind as I took to the air. Gildola's beam missed me by an inch, but then another one shot out, as fast as lightning.

I swerved to one side. Light singed the tip of my tail feathers.

"Jinx, stop!" Kayl called.

Corinth had his pistol out and was aiming at *me*!

That idiot. Didn't he realize we weren't leaving Solaris alive?

I was his best chance of keeping our mortal bodies intact!

And I'll be fucking damned if I was letting him or my sister steal this from under me.

Gildola was *mine*!

Sunbeams chased me around the cathedral as I flapped my wings hard and fast. They weren't reaching me, but they were preventing me from getting any closer to Golden Girl. Gildola's face glowed with amusement. She was toying with me—trying to tire me out so she could roast me into a meal.

Below, her Glimmer were rounding on Kayl, Pendula, and Corinth. He now aimed his pistol at them, and Kayl at least summoned her own flaming shield to protect her dumb arse.

Something shiny glinted in the sunlight and caught my bird's eye.

The collar I'd discarded earlier.

What effect would it have on a god? Would it work at all?

There was only one way to find out.

I swooped low, narrowly missing the sunbeams spiraling after me, and scooped up the collar in my claws. The damn thing was heavier than it looked. My wings ached heaving it up.

All I had to do now was get close enough to use it.

I flew for all I was worth at Gildola.

Sunlight shot right at me. I changed into an Umber form, and tucked the collar behind my back. Heat collided against my stone chest, but didn't slow me down.

I was going to barrel right on top of that bitch and knock her to the ground!

Air rushed against my naked body.

And then I stopped midair with a jarring pain around my neck.

Fuck! Gildola had caught me by the throat!

"Do you think me foolish, child?"

I spluttered a cough as she choked me. The collar fell from my hands and clanged somewhere below. I went to grab her arm and rip her soul out, but she took both of my wrists and pulled them apart.

Oh, that wasn't fair! She'd grown an extra fucking arm!

Fucking cheating gods!

I dangled helplessly, my legs kicking at nothing.

It was no use. She had me.

Her fingers tightened around my throat, squeezing air from my lungs until black dots crept across my vision.

No! I hadn't come this far to fail now!

I switched to a Necro form, and the pressure in my lungs eased.

"You're rather predicable for a creature of Chaos," Gildola mused as she turned me this way and that, as though admiring an object. "I shall take great pleasure in tearing you apart."

My heart pounded in my chest. What form could I change to? Fire wouldn't work against her, so I couldn't burn my way free. I could switch back to a smaller Fauna form and wiggle my way out, but she might crush me before I got the chance.

Fucking *fuck*!

REMAIN CALM, DAUGHTER. THIS IS YOUR BATTLE. I HAVE FAITH IN YOU TO WIN IT.

I've never been more fucking calm in my entire mortal existence!

"Careful, Your Holiness!" Corinth called out. "Jinx is dangerous. Return her to my care, and I'll ensure she is secured—"

"You brought this creature here for my judgement, and I exercise it freely. Your concern is touching, but unwarranted."

Light flared around me. Tingling shot up my arms and turned to a maddening itch.

And then it burned.

I thrashed in Gildola's grip. Flame bit into my skin, and I gurgled a scream.

Fuck! It *hurt*! It hurt worse than anything!

The pressure in my arms suddenly dropped, though the searing pain cut through my shoulder, my neck.

My arms were free, but...

No.

I couldn't move them.

Blackened stumps protruded from my torso. They dripped with ash and bits of charred flesh. I was vaguely aware of the smell, like burned meat, but they...

They weren't my arms. They couldn't be.

My arms weren't there anymore. Gildola had burned them off.

Searing agony radiated through me. I tried to use my Necro abilities to ease the pain, to heal whatever damage I could, but *fuck*, it was too much. Too much!

My entire body felt as though it had been torn in two—as if there were two of me, and both halves were on fire. Vomit spluttered down my chin.

Gildola sneered. "Disgusting creature. But as you can see, I have nothing to fear from Chaos." She held me up like a damn trophy. "Blessed be the light!"

Ringing buzzed in my ears. From somewhere, I could hear Kayl calling my name, and Corinth arguing.

It hurts, Mother.

I KNOW, MY DAUGHTER. IF I COULD TAKE YOUR PAIN AND MAKE IT MY OWN, I WOULD. BUT YOU HAVE STRENGTH BEYOND YOUR MORTAL BODY. MAKE GILDOLA PAY. TAKE WHAT IS OWED.

I'd waited my whole life for this.

To own a body. To move with my own limbs. Fuck with my own cunt. To feel: Pleasure. Pain.

The pain part was massively overrated, but still... This was *my* body. I decided what I'd do with it.

Fuck the gods. Fuck Gildola.

Laughter bubbled from my mouth.

"What amuses you, child?" Gildola asked.

I mumbled something incoherent.

"What was that?" She pulled me close to her ear.

I lurched forward and sank my teeth into her neck.

Gildola screeched.

She tried to wrench me away. I dug my Necro fangs in deep and swallowed mouthfuls of her blood.

And there it was. The tug at the end of my tongue.

I didn't need my hands to take her rotten soul.

Thousands of voices flooded my mind. The Glimmer. Living and dead. Many of them were mumbling prayers, their attempts at divine worship going ignored. Their emotions churned through me; fear, panic, anguish.

Save us! They called. Their voices cascaded over one another, begging, pleading.

It was maddening. Was this what it had been like for Kayl when I floated in her mind? I was only one voice—this was an entire domain.

I pushed them deep into my subconscious, leaving only a warm sensation to flow through my blood, dulling the sharpness that cut and stabbed from my shoulders.

Gildola tossed me. My ragged mortal body landed with a painful thud against the altar. I rolled over to my back.

Sunbeams burst from Gildola. She writhed as chunks of her flesh burned away. Ash rained on my face and tickled my cheek.

Kayl fell to her knees beside me. "What have you done?"

"I've solved your workhouse problem. You're welcome."

The Glimmer were screaming. They ran to the cathedral exits, rushing past Penny and Corinth, who would have been swept along with them if Corinth's bodyguard wasn't a wall.

"I am light!" Gildola shrieked. "I am creation! You cannot take this from me! You cannot—"

She exploded in a flare of dazzling light.

And then Golden Girl was no more.

"Do you realize what you've *done*?" Kayl's eyes were full of anger, but she pulled a handkerchief from her dress pocket and cleaned away the vomit and spit coating my chin. "The other domains will never side with us now! They'll war, and it'll be Chime's mortals caught in the crossfire. You've ruined their one and only chance of freedom!"

"That bitch burned my arms off, what did you expect me to do?" I nudged her away with my shoulder and rolled over to my stomach. It took a little effort to sit on my knees and then force myself to stand on shaking legs.

The cathedral had emptied, leaving Penny, Corinth, and his idiot bodyguard to stare at my naked armless body.

My form had switched to Glimmer after taking Gildola's soul, and now her power—*my* power—bloomed. It flowed down my shoulder and began to restitch what was lost.

This power *was* creation, and through it, I grew myself two new arms and gave Penny a hearty wave to check they worked as intended.

"How—How did you do that?" Kayl spluttered.

"It's easy when you understand how aether is connected to everything."

I'd done it. I'd won my first soul.

And now the rest of the domains would be *mine*.

I'M PROUD OF YOU, DAUGHTER. I NEVER DOUBTED YOU.

I did it for you, Mother.

"Uh, sir?" Corinth's bodyguard pointed to the ceiling.

Dust began to fall from the cathedral's walls.

"Time's up," Penny said. "I daresay Chaos has its uses." Makeup had run down her cheeks in the heat, revealing a scar that said *deceit*. What delicious irony.

"You know I'm going to destroy your domain next, right?"

She smirked at me. "Give it your best shot."

Cocky little cunt. I wanted to suck on her lips. Bite them. Taste her blood as she moaned my name and begged me to rip out her soul.

Fuck! Was I becoming as pathetic as Kayl, wanting to get into the pants of a Diviner?

They were such arrogant fucks. They deserved the obliteration coming their way. But here was a woman with ambition, like the Glimmer. Willing to do dirty deeds with the enemy to get what she wanted.

I wanted to do dirty deeds, all right.

I wanted to obliterate her with my tongue.

Corinth stared between us in disbelief. Working with a Diviner wouldn't have been my first choice, but both Penny and I had wanted the same thing—to destroy the Glimmer. I didn't care what her reasoning was—I assumed the Diviner had finally gotten fucked off with them to consider wiping their domain from the universe.

"We need to leave," Corinth urged.

He wasn't wrong.

Piles of dust already gathered by the cathedral door. Their souls belonged to me, now.

I was their hero. Their savior. One by one, I'd liberate the domains and end the reign of gods. This was only the beginning.

Two domains down. Ten to go.

39

*All mortals are made equal according to the Covenant, but how many
domains have actually earned their equality?
We believe in charity and helping the good citizens of the lesser domains,
but what do they ever do to help themselves? When domains like the Ember,
Fauna, and Vesper sin, what right do they have to the same basic luxuries as
the rest of us? Everything great about the Golden City was built through our
hard work. We've earned our place through our piety.
Poverty is a sin. It is a sign of laziness and apathy.
Our glory should not be diminished for the sake of lesser beings.*
—Ambassador Gloria, *The Golden Doctrine*

JINX GLOWED WITH THE power of a god.

Shit. Fucking shit!

Quen grabbed my wrist and dragged me away from the altar as the
cathedral crumbled around us in a sprinkling of gray dust. It was Eventide
all over again—it was Jinx's plan in motion.

I'd watched Gildola burn off her arms.

And then she'd literally sucked the soul right out of Gildola and grown
her bloody arms back!

Jinx had scared me before with the extent of her abilities—abilities I
either lacked or didn't know how to use properly—but this was worse.
Much worse.

Why she'd let me live, I didn't know.

"What about them?" I pulled on Quen's arm and pointed at the soulless
Ember and Fauna that Gloria had so ceremoniously paraded in front of us.
They were just standing there naked, staring at nothing. Not even reacting
to the craziness that had befallen. They'd been burned by Gildola's power,

and healed in front of my eyes, and yet… They hadn't reacted at all. "We can't leave them!"

"Forget them," Jinx said. "They're husks. They've got nothing worth living for."

"They're still alive! When Solaris goes, what'll happen to them?"

Quen doubled back. "We'll bundle them into a carriage, but we must hurry. Ben, with me!"

I ignored the incredulous looks on both Jinx and Pendula's faces and ran for the soulless with Quen and Ben.

Gods. Their eyes were vacant. Empty.

This was the salvation Quen had offered me and all Chaos mortals.

It was worse than death. Worse than having my soul churned through the aether.

How could they still be alive without a soul? The thought I could have become one of them sent me trembling. I had much to be angry about—Jinx, for putting us in this mess and damning a whole domain of mortals. Quen, for mistaking me for Jinx and handing me over. Sinder, for betraying me in the first place… But now wasn't the time.

I grabbed the shoulder of an Ember. It hurt to touch—my hands were painfully raw with burned skin and hastily healed blisters, despite Quen's quick thinking. "Listen to me. This domain is no longer safe. We need to run. Can you do that?"

They blinked at me with the spaced-out look of a Mesmer, completely unaware that the cathedral was now falling apart.

I tried to guide them out, but they stumbled and fell.

"Fuck's sake!" Jinx yelled. "We don't have time for this!" A beam of sunlight burst from her raised hand.

Quen yanked me away in time as Jinx's beam wiped through the soulless in an instant, leaving nothing but a smoldering smear of black.

"They were still alive!" I snapped.

Jinx's eyes flared gold. "I did them a fucking favor. Now, can we go?"

"She's right," Quen said. "We can't waste any more time."

I swallowed my rage and jogged behind Quen, Ben, and Pendula as they led the way. The cathedral was collapsing at a rapid rate, and I carefully stepped over piles of dust.

Gods. These had faded just as the Vesper had.

The irony caught in my throat with delirious amusement. I wanted to laugh. To cry. To scream.

The Glimmer had been my enemy for so many years, but I *never* wanted this.

Not this.

"Over here!" Quen called. He guided us to one of the steam-powered carriages and ushered us in. "Quickly now."

Pendula and Jinx both entered the carriage. I couldn't stomach being near either of them, and climbed up to the driver's seat beside Quen, forcing Ben into squeeze in the carriage instead. I hissed at the touch of metal on my palm, but that was the least of my problems.

Quen said nothing as he grabbed the carriage's levers and set us off down the main road of Solaris leading back to the Gate. I couldn't bear to look back. I knew what I'd see—the same devastation that had taken Eventide.

The carriage hurtled down the road. Glimmer ran for their homes and slammed their window shutters closed, but it wouldn't do any good. There was no hiding from this.

Above us, the perfect blue skies and golden sun were gone, replaced instead with gray. Even the beautiful golden buildings were being leached of color, and on the hills beyond, the yellow wheat fields were no more. Just... gray, empty space.

Nothing. As Eventide was nothing.

I wrapped my arms around my chest to stop the gray from leaching my own soul. "Did I do this?" I said, my voice shaky over the rattle of the carriage's engine.

"Jinx's actions aren't your own—"

"You were with us in Eventide when it... Who took Valeria's soul? Was it Jinx? Was it... me?"

He glanced at me with pain in his eyes. "I'm sorry. Valeria held you in her clutches. You did what you needed to do."

Then Jinx had been telling the truth.

I'd destroyed Eventide. The Vesper.

Screaming turned to a high-pitched whine. The light blurred into splotches of movement. I couldn't feel the carriage rocking beneath me. Couldn't taste the air that whipped past my face.

I was falling.

Gods, I was falling.

My mortal soul was disintegrating as surely as the world around me, turning to ashen nothingness. That was the color of my heart. Gray. Bloodless.

Grayford. The night market. The hurdy-gurdy players. The shadow puppet theaters.

Malkavaan.

I'd taken them. Ended them.

It was me. It had always been me.

"Stay with me, Kayl." Quen's voice was an anchor tethering me to reality.

"How... How do I face this? It feels like I'm falling."

"You do a little better each day. You find a reason to try."

"What reason? Eventide is gone. Jinx has taken Solaris—"

"Then you have ten more reasons to try."

I sucked in a shuddering breath. Quen was right. Ten domains remained. I needed to hold it together, at least until we escaped Solaris. "Was this your plan?"

"No. I never meant for any of this to happen."

Hadn't he? Pendula sure looked pleased with herself. The way she and Jinx acted like best buddies was almost out of mutual respect.

Could they have planned this from the beginning?

Did you know? I asked Corentine. *Did you and Jinx plan this behind my back?*

THE DIVINER WERE NEVER GOING TO GRANT OUR FREEDOM.

Then why make me your voice? Why let me carry on with the charade?

THROUGH YOUR EFFORTS, DAUGHTER, I NOW KNOW WHICH DOMAINS WILL SIDE WITH US IN THE WARS TO COME. WE WILL GAIN ALLIES TO REBEL AGAINST DOR'S RULE.

You used me? Despite everything I warned you against?

IT WAS NECESSARY.

Necessary? I gave up everything for this! For you! I sacrificed Dru, Vincent, maybe even Sinder—

NOW YOU UNDERSTAND WHAT I HAVE SUFFERED.

Fuck you! I knew I shouldn't have trusted her word, and I was an absolute bloody idiot for ever agreeing to become Corentine's voice.

And now Jinx had a god's soul, which meant Corentine would gain even more power.

Why had Mesmorpheus trusted me to save the domains?

Surely they must have seen this outcome in a vision?

In what future was *any* of this good?

Bells rang across the city, tolling Solaris's fate. Quen concentrated on the road ahead as Glimmer darted to false safety, their screams in time with the bells.

"Please, Gildola! Hear my prayers!" one of the Glimmer cried as she held a young girl at her hip. The woman gasped as her child disappeared from her arms, turning to dust.

She wailed a bloodcurdling scream.

And then she too was gone.

Would Jinx even care? Gildola may have been a raging bitch, but her mortals didn't deserve this! No mortal did!

"We're almost there," Quen said between clenched teeth. "Blast it!"

Shit! The Gate was in view, and Glimmer were rushing toward it in a mad panic. A crowd was blocking the way, literally climbing over each other in their haste to escape. It wouldn't matter. Those in Chime would still fade to nothing.

But they'd block our escape before that happened.

"What time is it?" I asked Quen.

"Quarter to the hour."

"Shit. What do we do? Plow through them?"

He shot me a horrified look.

"They're already doomed, Quen. There's nothing we can do to save them."

He swallowed a lump in his throat and nodded. "Hold on!" he called to the others.

I clenched my seat until the remaining blisters almost popped.

Solaris's main square was utter chaos. While most ran for the Gate, others were sitting on the cobblestones in prayer circles, muttering desperate prayers with clasped hands. Panicked Glimmer carried their crying children, but they couldn't fight through the mob.

"Your Holiness! Blessed Lady! Hear us!" they yelled to the sky. "Save us!"

My chest ached at the fear and pain laced across their faces. Their god was dead. No one was answering their prayers.

"Out of the way!" Quen yelled. He honked the carriage's horn, but didn't slow as we drove straight for the Gate.

Glimmer spun around in horror. Some dove out of the way, but many more were trapped in the crowds and either couldn't or wouldn't escape. The carriage plowed through them. Glimmer fell underneath the carriage's wheels, and I held my seat tight as we bumped over them. Their screams were cut off by a sickening crunch. I swallowed bile.

A young woman bounced off the front, her neck twisted.

I chose not to look at her.

The carriage flew through the Gate at alarming speed. Quen slowed time around us, and the carriage casually slid to a stop against a barrier.

We'd made it, but...

Shit.

The Wardens were expecting us.

Barriers had been erected all around the Gate, and behind that were lines of Wardens filling Central Station. Diviner, Umber, Leander. All armed with pistols and tasers, but they weren't aimed at us.

The Glimmer who had managed to escape Solaris were now swarming the barriers and frantically climbing over. The carriage shook as more stampeded past us, knocking each other down and scrambling over the fallen to get as far from the Gate as they could.

"Let us through!" they yelled.

"By the mercy of your gods, help us!"

"Get back!" yelled a Leander. He fired a warning shot into the air, but its blast was lost among the writhing and screaming Glimmer.

Some of them began to glow, their power aimed at the barriers.

The Wardens readied their pistols.

The Glimmer charged.

Shots echoed through the station, but the Glimmer faded before they could reach the Wardens. Their bodies disintegrated into a puff of dust, leaving nothing but their clothes to float onto the concourse in one final gasp.

The Glimmer were gone. All of them.

And Solaris was nothing more than a blank gray canvas.

"Saints," Quen breathed next to me.

The clock struck five, and the Gate switched to Arcadia.

What? How?

When Eventide had met its end, the Gate had effectively crashed, giving Corentine and her mortals a chance to attack Chime.

But the Gate remained powered on and continued its cycle as usual.

What had changed?

The carriage door flew open, and Pendula stepped out, flanked by Ben. A clockwork bird was perched on her shoulder. Despite almost being fried to death and running for her life, she didn't appear any the worse for wear.

"You look confused, Ambassador Arkey," she said. "Were you expecting us to open the clock tower to others of your kind? I'm afraid we're well prepared for all eventualities, including this one. The Gate will remain on no matter how many domains fall, and with it, Corentine will remain trapped."

"You planned this, you sick bitch!"

"Language, Your Excellency! Please set a good example for your mortals. Oh. Now I understand why they're so desperate and depraved." She smiled with such sweet innocence, yet the ugly scar across her cheek emphasized what a deceitful cunt she was. "Chaos has once again destroyed another domain. They are a liability and can no longer be allowed free reign. Quentin, my dear? Arrest her."

I swiveled around to Quen.

His fists shook by his sides. He fought internally, but by the despair in his eyes, I knew he'd lost the battle.

Shit!

"Quen, please—"

He grabbed my arm.

Fire exploded from inside the carriage. It split in half, sending me tumbling down. I landed on my elbow in a pained heap as Quen rolled to his feet, his pistol out.

Jinx rose from the burning wreckage, her naked form aglow with gold. "This is the domain of Babel! Of Chaos! And you're not welcome." She flung a beam of light at the Wardens. They quickly scrambled for cover.

Her beam bounced off an Umber male.

"Almighty god!" he cried out.

And then his entire body faded to nothing.

She hadn't done that, had she? Umber were strong enough to deflect flame—was Jinx now that powerful?

Confused murmurs ran through the Wardens. Another Umber suddenly popped from existence. Then another. And another. Umber were disappearing from thin air!

"What did you do to them?" I yelled at Jinx.

She looked baffled. "I didn't do shit."

"It's Unghard," Quen gasped. "They're recalling the Umber."

What? No!

More Umber vanished. Whole waves of them. Their discarded clothes joined the Glimmer as though Heartstone had also been ripped from the cosmos. Screams echoed beyond the station—it wasn't just Wardens being taken.

They all were.

The Wardens broke out into a panic.

Jinx flung up a wall of fire between me and Quen. "Now's our chance!" She landed beside me.

"To do *what*?"

"To get the fuck out of here, idiot! Or would you rather take a one-way trip to Kronos?" Jinx grabbed my wrist and dragged me through the crowd of remaining Diviner and Leander Wardens, throwing bursts of light at anyone who got too close.

I stumbled after her. We slid past the barriers and emerged into Central Station's waiting area. More Wardens stood here, but their numbers were dwindling.

"No!" a Leander growled. "Lionheart, please—"

They vanished, dropping their pistol.

Shit! Leander were disappearing too!

The Diviner remained in one piece, and were trying to command order, but the Umber were gone, and the Leander were now popping out of existence one by one.

"Let go of me!" I snarled at Jinx, and yanked my arm free.

"Oh, you don't want me to save your arse?"

"*Save* me? This is you—this is all *you*!"

Her eyes flashed in irritation. "Please. Don't act like you cared about the Glimmer. I did you and your worthless Godless a fucking favor."

"Is this what you wanted?" I pointed to an empty uniform that had once belonged to a Warden. "What in god's name have you *done*?"

"Don't blame me just because the gods are getting angsty—"

"Because of you! They're zapping their mortals away because they're scared of *you*!"

She grinned. "They should be scared."

Gods damn it! I clenched my fists to stop myself from knocking her to the ground.

"Stop!" called Quen.

Shit. He was climbing over the barrier, his pistol aimed at us. More Diviner Wardens followed.

Great. Just great. How could this day get any pissing worse?

"You still trust your lover boy?" Jinx taunted.

"More than I trust you!" I bolted for the station's exit.

Jinx swore—her anger drowned out by the buzz of tasers firing. I didn't dare look back as heat flared behind me.

Gods. I hoped she hadn't hurt Quen, but I needed to get away from both of them for my own damn safety.

JINX WILL PROTECT YOU FROM THE DIVINER.

Pull another one!

IF YOUR DIVINER IS SO TRUSTWORTHY, THEN WHY RUN, DAUGHTER?

Quen wasn't acting himself. Of course he wasn't! Not when Dor was pulling his strings. There was little I could do to help him now. Unfortunately, Jinx *was* acting herself.

I ran as fast as my legs could take me to the station's exit.

And came to a sudden stop.

Piles of clothes were scattered everywhere. Mortals ran in a panic, attempting to flee the station. The trams had stopped, Seren flew overhead, and many of the Glimmer-owned businesses had been abandoned, their doors swinging open. So many Glimmer made their home in Chime—it was impossible to think of how empty the streets would be. The Golden City, especially.

This was chaos—except there were no aether creatures snatching souls this time. The gods were seeing to that themselves.

"Halt, in the name of the Wardens!"

Shit!

Wardens were closing in on me. I hunched over and drew in ragged gasps. My calves were already aching, and while they wouldn't be able to stop time to grab me, they could still bloody shoot me.

"Kayl!" Harmony called my name.

Oh, thank the gods!

Harmony waddled across the square and tapped her ear.

At that signal, I slapped my hands over my ears, and Harmony began to sing.

"*Turn back, turn away. Leave us to our own devices. Turn back, do as I say. We want no ugly surprises.*"

The line of Wardens stopped suddenly, their blank faces confused. They slowly turned around and headed back into the station.

"What are you doing here?" I spluttered.

"Never mind that, girl." She jogged for the crowds running out of Central, and I followed. "What's happened to Solaris? What have you done? Joe's dead!" Her voice cracked with an emotion Harm never let out. She paused for a moment and pulled one of the aether collars from her handbag. "He found me here, wearing this thing. He... He turned to dust in front of my eyes!"

"Solaris is gone," I said. "Same as Eventide."

"*How?* Did you—"

"It was Jinx." I probably should have dropped Sinder in it, but I couldn't stomach the argument right now. "Quen is after me. He brought Wardens to the temple this morning. Do we have somewhere else to hide?" We'd lost our last safe refuge.

"Corinth's betrayed us?"

"Yes and no. It's complicated—"

"Why did none of you tell me? I had Sinder dragging me out of the damn temple this morning. Wouldn't tell me where you'd both gone. I tried to serenade it out of him, but he ran off—"

Someone screamed above us. A Seren flapped erratically and then fell from the air. Shit! I held my arms out to catch them.

Their clothes fluttered into my hands.

No. *No!* I stared as Seren began to disappear.

"What's going on?" Harmony's gaze darted around Central. "Why are they—fuck!" Her diamond pupils turned to me, wide with fear. "It's Serenity! They're taking the Seren!" She wrapped her arms around my waist. "Kayl, don't let them take me. Please. You can't let them take me back!"

I crouched and clenched her tight. "I've got you, Harm. I'm not letting you go. I'm not—"

Harmony vanished from my arms. I fell forward onto my knees.

My fists were still clutched around her blouse.

Not Harmony! "Bring her back, you bastard!" I screamed.

I was rocking on my heels, tears streaming down my face.

How could the Godless exist without Harmony?

How could she leave me like this?

We needed her! *I* needed her!

It took a moment for me to realize the screaming had stopped. Silence hung over Central. The same devastating stillness from my dreams.

I slowly pulled myself up, Harmony's blouse still in my hand.

The square was empty.

All that was left were clothes. Evidence of hundreds of mortals who had suddenly been snatched from existence. Every domain. Even the Diviner had vanished.

They were gone. All gone.

After everything, Jinx had gotten what she'd wanted. I'd failed in stopping her.

Chaos had won.

"They're gone?" came a male voice behind me.

Sinder.

He staggered between the piles of clothes as though drunk. His wild eyes landed on me, aflame with despair. "That's not—please don't say that's Harm?"

My fingers tightened around her blouse. "Why did you do it?"

"Kayl, please—"

"You knew what Jinx could do!" I stomped toward him and grabbed his waistcoat. "You knew what she was capable of, and yet you helped her—betrayed everything the Godless stood for—for petty *revenge*? I thought you were better than that!"

Tears hissed down his cheeks and instantly turned to steam. "She—She promised to help me save Vincent—"

"Don't give me that. You'd been spying for her ever since we entered that damn temple. I could have helped Vincent, but you didn't give me the chance! And now look what she's done! *Look!*"

Sinder couldn't meet my eye. "I'm sorry—"

"Sorry isn't going to fix this. How are you still here?" The Ember were gone. All of them.

He wiped his cheeks with the back of his hand. "Edana—she didn't want me. She's taken them all... but me."

"Congratulations. You've survived the purge. Welcome to a Chime with no Glimmer. Was it worth it? Was all of this *worth it*?" Rage and disgust roiled in my gut. I couldn't stand to look at him and shoved him away. "This isn't why I started the Godless. This isn't what we stand for! But it doesn't matter now, does it? It's over. You've lost Vincent. You've lost Harm. You've lost me."

"Please!" His voice broke. "I can't—I can't do this alone."

"You should have thought about that before you sided with a psychopath!" I yelled.

Thanks to him and Jinx, Chime was no more.

Empty.

Soulless.

How could he stand there and plead for mercy? Had I not tried to help him all these years to get past the Glimmer? Was his vengeance worth *this*?

I'd loved Sinder like family. How could he do this to his family?

THEY WERE NEVER YOUR FAMILY.

Piss off! I never want to hear your voice ever again!

Sinder picked up a pistol discarded on the street.

My heart leaped to my throat. "Sinder—"

"You're right. I can't—I can't fix it. Not without Vincent. Not without you." He put the barrel of the pistol against his head.

"No!" I wrestled the pistol from his grip. "You don't get to take the easy way out!" I threw the pistol aside. "You're no use to anyone dead."

He collapsed to his knees and sobbed. "What do I do? Tell me what to do—"

"You—"

A shot blasted across the square. It pierced Sinder's head, splattering his brains across the cobblestones.

His body tipped over and faded before it hit the ground.

Ringing filled my ears, turning into the harsh buzz of aether.

I screamed and fell backwards, tripping over a pile of clothes.

"Kayl."

Quen stood over me with his pistol in hand, a wisp of smoke floating from the barrel.

He'd shot Sinder. Killed him.

One of Pendula's clockwork birds fluttered over his shoulder, its many cogs and gears whirring with a satisfied click. That thing had led Quen to me, and a group of Diviner Wardens congregated behind him. I'd thought they were gone too, but no.

The Diviner still ruled Chime, until Jinx got to them.

Ben approached Quen's side, his expression devoid of emotion. He picked up the discarded aether collar and handed it over.

"Please don't run." Quen spread open the collar.

I didn't have the strength to run. Where would I even go?

I'd lost my friends. My family.

It was over.

Everything was over.

My skin changed to the silvery-blue of Chaos. My true self. I hadn't forced the change—still didn't quite understand how to do it. In my despair, my body had simply reverted to the state I'd been born in.

A child of Chaos.

Of destruction. Of nothing.

Quen crouched over me. I met his silver eyes. They were unfathomable pools. Domains of emotion cascading into one another behind a hardened shell. Dor had imprisoned his body, his mind, but not his soul. The real Quen remained hidden in those silver depths.

My Quen.

DO YOU STILL TRUST HIM, DAUGHTER?

As Quen wrapped the collar around my neck and cut off Corentine's voice once more, I wanted to scream into the aether so she heard me one last time.

Yes.

XL

Apostasy is the greatest sin of them all.
I would never expect a Diviner to deny the love of our Father. However,
apostasy comes in many forms. To reject His advice, guidance, and wisdom.
To reject His gifts.
To reject the path He foresaw of your future.
To curse your own body and the weaknesses it may present.
Your failings are tests of His faith. Do not question them, but instead
overcome your insecurities to become the man He wishes you to be.
—E. Karendar, *Commandments for the Diviner*

I DIDN'T KNOW WHAT I was meant to feel, so I reverted back to my old Academy days and decided to feel nothing at all. Logic trumped emotion. Logically speaking, I had a task to complete. As ambassador to the Diviner, I would carry it out with due diligence and impeccable grace.

Emotion wasn't needed. It wasn't welcome. Emotion simply got in the way.

Logic, then, demanded the facts. Solaris was gone. The Glimmer were no more. In order to protect their mortals, the remaining gods chose to withdraw them from Chime, effectively rendering the city empty. This was not an outcome I desired. In fact, it completely spat on my plans. But at least mortals were safe from Chaos.

The Diviner remained in Chime, or at least trained Wardens did. The city was effectively under our control now. We controlled the Gate. The clock tower. The trams.

This was what Dor wanted.

Corentine remained trapped. Kayl was in my custody. Jinx had escaped, and now that she was powered by Gildola's soul, she was more formidable than ever.

But we held Chime. It wouldn't take long to find her.

Oh yes. Everything had worked out wonderfully.

Absolutely wonderfully.

We'd arrived in Kronos ten minutes ago, and I wasted no time in taking the elevator up to Father to report to Him while Penny checked in on Doctor Finch and Ilona Burns and Ben ensured Ambassador Arkey was properly secured in a cell.

My heart fluttered from the adrenaline of it all, pounding faster as the elevator made its ascent.

It opened with a sharp *ping*.

Who would power the elevators of Chime now? Would there be any point in operating them? Or the trams? Diviner would still need to get around, I supposed.

Maybe now I could finally retire. Operate a tram with few customers.

The brass Guardians waited by the door as usual and dragged it open at my approach.

I slapped one of them on its cold metallic shoulder. "Good work, chaps."

Their cogs whirred in silent acknowledgement.

Blinding light welcomed me back into Dor's domain. Not many Diviner had the opportunity to bask in our Father's presence. For this opportunity, I was grateful.

I bent onto one knee and bowed my head, staring at the line on His palm. "I have returned at your command, Father."

The clocks floating around Dor's visage hummed with animated glee. *YOU HAVE SERVED ME WELL, QUENTIN. I AM PLEASED.*

"Forgive me, Father, but... this was not what I planned. Solaris is gone. The gods have withdrawn their mortals from Chime. I failed in my assignment to unite them."

YOU DID NOT FAIL. I FORESAW THIS OUTCOME.

"You... foresaw it?" Then why had I been forced to traverse the sodding domains and bow and scrape this past week?

FOR MY OWN KNOWLEDGE. WHEN CORENTINE AWOKE, I KNEW THE OTHER GODS WOULD CHOOSE THEIR SIDES.

THROUGH YOUR EYES, I HAVE LEARNED WHO WOULD BETRAY ME.

My heart fluttered anew. "You let Chaos destroy Solaris."

Negotiating with the Glimmer had been Penny's operation. I'd thought it a disaster from the start, but no. It was Penny's doing. All of it. Somehow, she'd known Jinx had swapped places with Kayl and planned to launch an attack.

Penny had let it happen.

Saints. She'd orchestrated it.

THE GLIMMER HAD BEEN ASSERTING THEIR AUTHORITY OVER CHIME FOR YEARS. THEY SOUGHT TO UNDERMINE US. NOW, WE NO LONGER HAVE A THREAT TO OUR RULE.

I sat back on my heels. All those mortal lives... Gone. "I understand Gildola was problematic, but we've handed her powers to Chaos." To Jinx. Surely Father could see that giving her this advantage on a silver platter would be to our detriment?

THIS WAS MY DESIGN TO SEND A MESSAGE TO THE OTHER GODS. THEY MUST UNDERSTAND THE TRUE THREAT OF CHAOS. THEY MUST REJECT CORENTINE AND REMEMBER THEIR PLACE.

Damn it, I'd been trying to unite the domains! "What happens to Chime now?"

CHIME IS OURS. IF THE OTHER DOMAINS WISH TO GAIN ACCESS, THEY WILL OBEY OUR RULES.

"And if they don't?"

THEN WE SHALL WAR.

A war between the domains—between the gods—would be unfathomable.

Who would refuse Dor's rule? Lionheart, certainly. The Leander lived for the challenge. Edana, most likely. Diviner rule would be too puritanical for them.

Would the rest fall in line? With the Glimmer gone, they stood to gain.

If they didn't... Chime would never be the same again.

I refused to give up on Chime. Mortals needed it—*I* needed it!

KRONOS IS YOUR HOME. YOUR LOYALTY IS TO THIS DOMAIN.

"Yes, Father. I understand, but someone will need to oversee its rule. What will happen to Chaos?"

THEY WILL BE DESTROYED.

"You promised—"

THROUGH YOUR EYES, I HAVE TESTED CORENTINE'S MORTALS, AND THEY HAVE FAILED. THEY CANNOT BE REHABILITATED. I GAVE THEM A CHANCE, AND THEY ARE CHAOTIC. VIOLENT. DESTRUCTIVE.

Jinx, perhaps, but Kayl—

I HAVE SEEN YOUR VISIONS, MY SON. I KNOW YOU FEAR HER. CHAOS IS A THREAT, AND I WILL NOT HAVE THEM HARM YOU.

My mouth went dry. Of course Father would have seen my visions, my dreams. Of course He would be concerned.

TO SAVE YOUR SOUL, YOU MUST DESTROY THEIRS. SUBMIT THEM TO THE DEVICE. RENDER THEM AS HUSKS.

He wanted me to force Kayl back into that odious chair.

To grant her a living death. A bullet to her brain would be kinder.

Chaos couldn't be allowed to remain. They were sin. They were destruction. Chaos had destroyed Eventide, and now Solaris.

Yet the thought of damning mortals tore through my chest and squeezed my heart.

I couldn't do this. Saints, I couldn't.

THIS IS MY WILL. YOU WILL PERFORM THIS LAST TASK, AND THEN YOU MAY REST. PROVE YOUR DEVOTION TO ME. ABSOLVE YOURSELF OF YOUR MORTAL SINS.

And if I couldn't?

YOU WILL MAKE THIS DIFFICULT CHOICE, AS I DID. CORENTINE WAS MY HEART. IT WAS OUR CONNECTION THAT BIRTHED THE GODS AND THEIR DOMAINS. IT HURT ME TO SEE HER LOCKED AWAY, BUT IT WAS NECESSARY TO

PROTECT OUR FUTURE. DID YOU EVER WONDER WHY I BURDENED YOU WITH THIS TASK, MY SON?

"To test me? Purge me of sin?" Punish me?

I SEE MYSELF IN YOU. I SEE MY DESIRES. MY STRUGGLE. I SEE THE PATH I MUST TAKE AND THE DECISIONS TO BE MADE. I WISH FOR YOU TO BE AS STRONG AS I AM. TO FACE THAT SAME CHOICE AND MAKE THE CORRECT ONE.

Mortals were born in the image of their god, but to assume that mortals compared to their gods was blasphemy. "I could never be as strong as you, Father."

YOU ARE MY VOICE. MY WILL. YOUR THOUGHTS ARE MY THOUGHTS. YOUR DESIRES ARE MY DESIRES. I WILL GIVE YOU THE UNIVERSE. BUT YOU MUST BE WILLING TO DO WHAT MUST BE DONE.

DESTROY CHAOS. FREE YOURSELF FROM ITS CLUTCHES.

I tucked shaking hands into my lap. It had to be me, if only to grant Kayl the kindness of a friendly face one last time.

Then I'd find the peace I surely didn't deserve.

I kissed my Father's palm. "I will do what must be done."

This was the end.

When I stepped outside, Ben was waiting for me by the elevator, his face grim.

"You need to learn to mask your emotions better," I said.

He bowed an apology. "Yes, sir. Sorry, sir. We've secured Kay—the Chaos mortal in one of the reflection chambers. Miss Bezel is waiting for you there."

"Right you are."

We entered the elevator, and the shift of gravity churned in my gut. Beside me, Ben wouldn't stop fidgeting, like a man in dire need of a confession.

I needed to find time to punish him, amid destroying Chaos, securing Chime, and a whole host of other problems. "Why did you let the Glimmer male escape?"

His fidgeting suddenly stopped. "They would have burned him alive, sir."

"And you cared for this male?"

"That's what Wardens are meant to do, sir. Protect and serve."

"Don't be so insolent."

He glanced toward his shoes. "Sorry, sir."

I rubbed the bridge of my nose. "Don't be. You're a good Warden, Ben. Thank you for your service. Would you mind if I touched you? The future concerns me. I'd like to verify it."

"Begging your pardon, sir, but I'd rather you didn't. There're parts of me I'm not ready to let anyone see."

"I understand. There're parts of me too I'd rather hide."

"You love her, don't you, sir?" He spoke the words so quietly I barely heard them.

"She's my future wife. I care about her deeply."

"You would do anything to protect her?"

I met Ben's silver eyes. "Yes."

I was about to make the ultimate sacrifice for her.

The elevator came to a halt.

Ben stopped me before I could exit. "There's something I think you should see, sir. Before I take you to the reflection chamber." His words were solemn.

"Lead on."

The reflection chambers and cells were a little further, but Ben headed for the laboratory. I had wanted to check in on Doctor Finch and Ilona, if only to ensure they were safe from the happenings in Chime.

Shouting came from inside the lab.

I ran on ahead, a hand to my pistol, and burst inside. Two Wardens pointed tasers at Doctor Finch, who was on his knees, an aether collar wrapped around his neck. Beside them, another Warden struggled to hold Ilona back—she, too, wore a collar.

"Release them at once!" I demanded.

"We can't, Your Excellency," said one of the Wardens. "We caught the Zephyr attempting to sabotage one of the devices."

"Because I've seen what they can do!" the doctor squawked. "The devices aren't fit for purpose! We tested them on the Chaos male, and it—it—he wanted to be a Zephyr! Like me!"

"I'm sorry, Doctor," I said.

"You knew? Then... You said I wasn't a prisoner!" He grasped the collar and tried to pry it open with his talons.

A taser fired, hitting him square in the chest. Doctor Finch fell into a fit of spasms that sent feathers flying.

"Don't hurt him!" Ilona screamed.

The door on the other side of the lab opened, and Penny waltzed out. "There's no need for these dramatics. He's quite safe, Miss Burns. We mean neither of you harm—"

"Then why are we wearing collars?" Ilona's chest was heaving rapidly—we needed to calm her down before she suffered an asthma attack.

"For your protection. You're tired. Why don't you take a moment to rest?" Penny turned to the Wardens. "Please escort them to their rooms and ensure they're made comfortable."

"I'll take them," Ben offered. He helped Doctor Finch up, who sagged in Ben's arms, his beak opening with a moan.

"Master Corinth, please!" Ilona begged as a Warden moved to grab her.

"Go with Ben. He'll get you something to eat and drink."

Ben flashed his best smile. "You can tell me about Memoria's plants, miss. I've always wanted to learn more."

The fear in her slitted eyes hurt me down to my core, but she nodded, and followed Ben and the doctor out of the laboratory.

I waited until the door closed behind her to exhale a breath. "Why are they wearing aether collars?" I asked Penny while trying to keep my voice neutral.

"You know why. Zyclone and Anima would have claimed them."

"So you thought to imprison them instead?"

"Doctor Finch tried to destroy his own work and turn Miss Burns against us. He's no longer an asset—"

"The machines—they've been tested on Chance?"

"While we were in Solaris, yes."

"And it... worked?"

"He's currently unresponsive."

The way Ben had grimaced sank in my stomach. He'd told me to come here. He'd known what had transpired in my absence.

I ran out of the laboratory and headed for Chance's room.

"Quentin, wait!" Penny called as she chased after me.

Chance wasn't in the same room as when we'd last spoken. Nor was he in any of the others. As I passed more empty cells, panic trembled through me.

Scientists wielding clipboards were marking notes beside a window.

I barged them out of the way and stared through the glass.

My breath caught in my throat.

It choked me until my body threatened to fade into unconsciousness.

Chance was laid out on an operating table in his Chaos form, not Zephyr. His limbs chained down. His head half obscured by a breathing apparatus.

Those aether eyes were vacant, yet still alive.

His entire torso had been cut open.

Surgeons dressed in bloodstained gowns were rummaging through it as though Chance were some toy that could be taken apart and pieced back together.

No.

I staggered against the glass and slid to my knees. My breath came in quick, shallow gasps. Sweat itched under my arms, and my chest heaved with the effort of taking in air.

"No!"

Penny crouched and grabbed my shoulders. "Easy now—"

"I told you not to!" I tore off my spectacles and rubbed blood from my eyes. "I told you—"

"He's Chaos. You know our Father's orders. Chaos must be destroyed."

"*By cutting him open?*" My voice sounded hysterical.

"It's vital we learn more about our enemies."

Our enemies. That was what Chaos was and always had been to her.

They'd killed her second father. Taken Hector Bezel's soul. No wonder she went to such extreme lengths to destroy Chaos.

I should never have made her my assistant. "This is revenge for you?"

"It's many things. Our Father wants Chaos to end. I serve Him in that endeavor."

"I can't... I can't do this."

She cupped my cheek and lifted my face until our eyes met. "You must. If you don't, Dor will punish me again. Is that what you want? To see me hurt?"

"Of course not—"

"Then do this for me. For us. For our future commitment." Her forehead rested against mine. "I want to help you, Quentin. When you've fulfilled your promise to our Father, to me, then step back. I can take your place as ambassador."

"You would?"

"I'll take that burden off your shoulders." She took my hand and placed my palm on her stomach. "Then you can be free to give me a son and help raise him."

Such an intimate touch. My hand rose with her every breath and helped calm my own. "I wouldn't have to be a Warden?"

"If you don't want to be."

"Well, I... Chime's trams need refurbishing, I couldn't abandon them—"

"I'll make sure your proposal goes through."

"Could I... drive them, perhaps? I know it sounds silly, but I've always wanted to be a tram driver."

"If that's what you want." She smiled. "Our new Chime will need drivers."

"And you'll look after Chime?"

"For you, my dearest Quentin. But there can be no future for Chime while Chaos remains. You need to do this. For me. For our future son. Please."

Her beautiful silver eyes held the promise of a future. A peace we could champion. Diviner had always ruled Chime, and now... Now we could remake the city into a haven for mortals with no Glimmer to abuse them.

We could do this. I could.

"I... I think I'm ready."

"Good." She kissed the top of my head. "Ben, can you help him?"

In my anguish, I hadn't noticed Ben return.

He grabbed my bicep and hauled me up. For the first time, Ben's expression was impossible to read.

Together, the three of us walked in silence through the sterile white corridors to the reflection chamber where Kayl was held.

I couldn't pretend this wouldn't be difficult. We'd met in the Undercity and known each other for only a short span of time, yet that time had felt much longer. We'd faced danger together. Had shared tea and biscuits together. Sorrow and joy in equal measure.

We were partners.

But today, our partnership would come to an end.

I had a future to strive for. A city to rebuild. A woman to marry. A child to raise. None of that could be achieved while Chaos existed.

I believed that now.

Truly, I would need to make it up to Penny. She was a wonderful woman. Intelligent. Beautiful. And not afraid to place herself in danger to serve the cause. Our son would be a product of Diviner logic and civility.

A future worth fighting for.

We reached the cell door. "Ben, may I have your taser?"

"Certainly, sir." He didn't hesitate in handing it over.

I weighed the heft of it in my palm. "A precaution in case she tries to run. Ben, stay guard by the door, if you will."

Ben opened the door, and I stepped right in.

Kayl sat on a single chair behind a table, scowling like the first time I'd captured her at a Glimmer estate and brought her to Warden HQ. Though today her persona was that of Chaos, her skin an aether blue instead of the indigo of Vesper. Her hands were chained, though with the aether collar wrapped around her throat, she didn't need gloves.

Her powers no longer worked—she wouldn't be able to take my form or my soul. But she was still a formidable woman, much like her twin. Her size alone outmatched mine.

Chaos was dangerous, and I read the danger in those eyes.

I approached her as Penny slipped in behind me.

"So this is Kronos," Kayl drawled. "Can't say much for the view. Oh, that's right. My cell doesn't have any windows."

I tightened my grip on the taser. "My apologies for the disappointing accommodation, Ambassador Arkey. I'd like to escort you somewhere more suitable."

"Are we visiting a café? I figure you Diviner must surely have the best teahouses."

"I'm afraid time has caught up with us. There's no room for tea in our schedule."

"What's on the agenda, then? Torture, disembowelment, and having my soul ripped out? Are you *sure* we can't fit in a quick cup of tea and a scone? Facing mortal peril does whet the appetite."

"You know, mispronouncing scone is one of the unforgivable sins."

"Is that why I'm chained here and being sentenced to death? Perfectly understandable."

Penny cleared her throat behind me.

"Yes. Quite." I stepped closer to Kayl. "If you don't mind, I'll need to double-check that your collar is secure."

"Go ahead. I hope you design more comfortable ones in future. It tends to pinch on the skin."

I bent over her.

"Why did you kill Sinder?" Kayl whispered.

I froze. "A... mistake on my part. I meant to collar him and submit him to the device as per Warden protocol."

"Then thank you."

"For what?"

"For everything."

Her words winded me.

DO NOT BE FOOLED BY HER CHARMS. CHAOS IS DESIGNED TO TEMPT AND DECEIVE. YOU ARE STRONGER THAN THAT, QUENTIN.

Strength came in many forms. I'd never been much of a fighter, but I'd always wanted to do what was right. Perhaps it was stubbornness that made this journey so difficult.

Thank you for correcting my path, Father. Without your mercy and guidance, I would never have become the man I needed to be.

My hand slipped underneath Kayl's collar. It was secure.

BE BRAVE, MY SON.

I will. In all things, I will move forward knowing the man I am. And for that, Father, I would like to say... I utterly despise you.

With one press of my finger, the collar clicked open.

In the blink of an eye, I pulled it from Kayl's neck and wrapped it around my own.

QUEN—

Dor's voice cut off in an instant.

I could breathe.

Fuck! I could *breathe*!

"Quentin?" Pendula gasped.

I turned my taser on her and fired.

She fell to the ground in a fit of spasms, her limbs twitching rather satisfactorily. "Stop," she spluttered.

"I'm not normally one for drama, so you'll forgive me for indulging in some theatrics, my dear." I shot her again.

This time she slumped over, unconscious. What a bastard I was, shooting my own betrothed. I hoped she'd consider this notice of our separation. Alas, our impending marriage had been doomed from the start.

"Sir?" Ben blocked the doorway.

I aimed the taser at his chest. "I don't want to shoot you, but I will. Release Kayl. I won't ask twice."

Ben wasted no time in unlocking Kayl's bindings and allowing her up. "I'll cover your back, sir."

"If you help me, Dor will punish you—"

"He's already punished me, sir." Ben popped open the top button of his shirt, revealing a scar much like Pendula's, etched across his collarbone with the words...

"I am a Diviner?" Why would Ben need that reminder?

"You may think it silly, sir, but I've always felt that I was born to the wrong domain. The wrong god. Until I learned of Chaos and met Kayl and Dru, I thought... there was something broken inside me. But Dru, she made me realize who I am." He pulled a golden flower out of his inner jacket pocket and cradled it within his palm. Dru's flower. "My soul is Umber. It always has been."

Saints.

A year ago, I may have called him ridiculous, perhaps insane—Diviner could be gardeners, of course—but now that I reflected on our time together, it made sense. No wonder Dor had wanted me to mentor him—to punish him. He would consider such thoughts blasphemous.

It wasn't a sin to live your own truth. Or it shouldn't be. The fact that Dor had tortured him in this manner was utterly depraved.

How ironic that my bodyguard turned out to be an apostate! Dor should have known better than to allow Ben under my influence.

"Come with us," Kayl urged. "You're not safe here."

"She's right." If Ben remained in Kronos, he'd be in danger.

"You won't get out unless I cover you, sir."

I passed the taser back. "Then help me save Doctor Finch and Ilona. I'm not leaving without them."

"Already have, sir. I escorted them to the station. I assumed you'd be headed that way."

"I could kiss you! How did you know I'd turn?"

He smiled. A real genuine one that lit up his silver eyes. "I didn't, sir. I hoped. Now go. I want to help Chance if I can."

"Ben—"

"I brought him here, sir, even though I knew what Miss Bezel planned. Let me atone for that. Please."

It pained me to leave Ben and Chance behind, but I understood the desire for atonement more than any, and there was little I could do for

Chance now. I whipped out my pistol and carefully stepped over an unconscious Pendula. "Stay safe."

Kayl patted Ben's arm. "Dru would have been honored to call you a friend. Keep her flower safe."

He tucked the flower back into his pocket. "Thank you, ma'am. I will."

We bolted from the room, while Ben ran in the opposite direction, back to the laboratory.

"Do you have a plan?" Kayl asked as we hurtled down the corridor.

"Naturally."

I led her through a maintenance tunnel that opened out to the train platform. The steam train was there, prepped and ready to go as Diviner finished loading their stock.

There was no sign of Doctor Finch or Ilona.

I holstered my pistol and gestured for Kayl to quickly slide against the train.

"You're taller than me," I whispered. "If I lift you, tell me if you spot the doctor or Ilona. She's a young purple-skinned Amnae of about thirteen—"

"A *child*?"

"Don't ask." I bent my knee for her to stand on, and with a grunt, I hefted her up. She checked through the window and then carefully slid back down.

"I couldn't see them, but there's a stray feather by the bar. My bet is they're hiding behind that."

"Right. I'm going to uncouple this carriage and take over the train. Fetch them and meet me in the cab. Be quick."

She slunk away. I set to work decoupling the carriage. The lever took some effort, but as soon as the carriage was free, I drew my pistol again and climbed into the cab.

A single Diviner engineer stood by the engine. Before he could open his mouth, I shot him through the head.

When one's life was in danger, one didn't have time for mercy.

His body faded into a crumpled heap of oil-stained overalls.

Shouts echoed outside. I flipped a switch and glanced out the window. Armed Diviner were running down the platform.

Blast it!

"We've been spotted!" Kayl said as she squeezed into the cab with Doctor Finch and Ilona. Thank the gods they were unhurt.

"*You!*" Doctor Finch squawked. "You're the reason I'm wearing this damn collar!" He gripped it with his talons.

"*Don't* take it off," I warned. "The gods have recalled their mortals from Chime. Remove that collar, and they'll take you, too."

His head tilted sharply at the sight of a collar wrapped around my own neck. "Why should we trust you? And what about Chance? You're leaving *him*?"

Ilona was hiding behind him, sucking on a bottle of water. Her confident teenage bravado had been betrayed by her true age. She was a child. Just a child. And my responsibility.

I flipped another switch. "I'm sorry, Doctor—Ilona—for what you've been through. There's nothing I can do for Chance. It's out of my hands. But if we don't leave now, we're never getting out of Kronos. Help me with these bloody controls, will you?"

The doctor shrilled a high-pitched whine and joined me by the console. I grabbed the various apparatus, and with Doctor Finch's help, the steam engine roared to life.

Kayl held Ilona's shoulders steady as the cab lurched forward. "Do you know how to operate this thing?"

I glanced over my shoulder with my brow raised.

"Forget I asked. Fancy a drink?" She pulled a small bottle of whiskey liqueur out of her pocket. "I pinched it from the bar."

"And you deemed this vital to our escape?"

She popped it open and took a sip before handing it over. "Quite vital."

With one hand on a lever, I allowed myself a deep gulp. The amber liquid burned down my throat in a satisfying baptism that cleansed me from the inside out.

Oh *yes*. This was vintage stock, with the sweet taste of fruit and spices. The kind of liqueur Elijah would have banned from public consumption, yet indulged in behind closed doors. How could I have ever escaped Kronos without it?

The train made slow going at first as it lazily huffed its way out of the station. Diviner shouted outside. I placed Ilona by the console to help Doctor Finch—partly to distract her from the immediate danger, and partly to ensure we weren't being followed.

I leaned out the window and breathed in soot. Steam clouds obscured the platform, and my hair ruffled in the wind. This was what freedom felt like.

We'd make it. We had to.

Kayl slid her arm around my waist. "Are you my Quen?"

I breathed in the liqueur on her lips. "Until the end of time."

She touched the collar. "This is protecting you from Dor?"

"For now."

It was my future self who'd given me the schematics to design it, even though my colleagues had done all the work. Even they hadn't realized that, although its designed purpose was to trap Chaos, it was intended for me.

To grasp my freedom.

Dor would be furious, which meant there was no going back.

This was my path.

"You couldn't have done this before Solaris went down?" Kayl asked.

"I had no idea what Pendula and Dor planned. I still held some hope we could unite the domains. That was no lie." They'd both used me. Dor had strung me along to exert his authority over the domains and wipe the Glimmer away. Pendula had coveted my position as ambassador. She was welcome to it, assuming she survived Dor's wrath. "I'm so sorry. For everything. For Dru, Vincent, and Sinder—I had to shoot him. The Wardens would have taken his soul—"

"I know. I don't blame you." She rested her head against my shoulder. "I've lost them all. If the gods have recalled their mortals to their domains, how do we get them back?"

"I don't know." Truly, I had never expected this outcome, and it absolutely infuriated me. Dor had practically ripped the Covenant to pieces, had declared war against the domains without a single thought for the mortals who'd be caught within the battles to come.

He'd ruined Chime. My real home.

And hurt Kayl and the Godless.

For all that and more, I would *never* forgive him.

She squeezed my waist. "This makes you a real Godless, you know."

"I suppose it does." Her body was pressed against mine, its warmth a balm to every horror Dor had inflicted. I wanted to bury myself in the crevice of her neck, to soak in her scent, to taste her skin with my mouth.

I wanted to sin with Kayl in oh so many depraved ways. To kiss her, right now, as we fled for our souls. But not in front of Ilona. Not while she and Kayl remained in danger.

And not while Malkavaan lay forgotten. I had to at least put that to rights.

The train hurtled out of the tunnel into a sight I'd never seen. A storm rolled over the city, blackening Kronos's skies. Peeking above the clouds was Dor's visage itself. His silver beard merged with the storm. His eyes flashed with lightning as his presence dominated his domain.

His hands, the size of skyscrapers, reached toward us.

"Oh shit." Kayl pointed to the sky.

"It's Dor," I gasped. "He's not best pleased."

"Really? I hadn't noticed!"

Thunder groaned, shaking the entire cab.

And the train began to slow.

"We're losing power!" Doctor Finch yelled.

I grabbed Kayl's shoulders. "You need to create an aether shield. I can't protect us against Dor. But you can." Since returning from the aether, I'd known that Corentine's power rivaled Dor's—that Chaos was the only force capable of stopping time.

In that, I had faith.

Her eyes widened. "What if I blow up the damn train?"

"Better that than Dor getting his hands on us."

"Well, when you put it like that." She positioned herself in the center of the cab and spread out her arms. Static electricity buzzed around her fingers.

"That's it! Keep going!"

"Are you *mad*?" Doctor Finch screeched. His feathers ruffled from the growing static. "Playing with aether will interfere with the electronics!"

"I'm trying to save our lives, Doctor," Kayl said through clenched teeth.

"Like when you dropped me in a *lake*?"

"You survived, didn't you?"

Static burst around us in a glowing bubble of blue and pink hues. Kayl radiated with pure aether. Swirls of energy pulsed from her skin with cosmic life. Saints.

She was the universe and everything in it.

The hairs on my body stood on end. I double-checked the collar was still working.

"I did it!" Kayl laughed. "I pissing did—"

Something landed on top of the train with a *thunk*.

"What the shit was that?"

I ran to the window. One of Dor's Guardian's had landed on the train and was climbing over the carriage toward us.

Another Guardian materialized out of nowhere and landed beside the first.

Oh wonderful.

I should have finished off the whiskey. "Ilona, get behind me. Kayl, keep your shield up!" I whipped out my pistol. "We have company!"

The train jolted forward. Kronos's main station was coming up fast, but not fast enough. I drew in a breath and aimed at the window.

A Guardian swung down. Its brass hand reached through to swipe at me.

One shot blasted a hole through its head. It screeched with the grinding of gears and fell backwards onto the track. A quick cock of my pistol's barrel revealed three bullets left.

We couldn't afford a shootout.

"Master Corinth!" Ilona screamed.

The second Guardian was forcing its way through the opposite window and reaching for the doctor, who was frantically trying to duck while operating a lever.

I took aim. The train rattled. My damn shot went wide and hit the steel wall.

The Guardian tore its way through the window. Its full height reached the top of the cab and towered over me as the clockwork monstrosity I'd feared as a child. The whirring of cogs and gears were meant to soothe Diviner, but as I caught my pale face reflected in its mechanical brass, I understood why so many domains thought us emotionless monsters.

Its metal hand grasped my wrist with a bone-crunching grip. I chewed my lip as I tried to pull free.

It snatched my pistol and tossed it out the window.

"That was my prized possession, you oversized box of bolts!" I rammed into the blasted thing with my shoulder. The Guardian didn't move an inch. I may as well have run into a sodding wall.

Its head tilted, the cogs in its face whirring.

Then its hand shot out and grabbed my neck.

"The—collar!" I gasped, afraid the Guardian would try and break it. But as it choked the life from me, panic filled my chest.

It wasn't merely trying to stop me, but kill me.

Even with the collar, my soul would return to Dor.

And I'd be at his mercy forever more.

Rage pumped through my blood. I kicked at its metal body, flailing with the last of my strength, but it made no difference.

Aether from Kayl blasted the Guardian, but that too had no effect. Not on a being made from clockwork parts.

Black dots swarmed over my vision.

No! I hadn't come this damn far to return now!

My soul—my thoughts—were *mine*!

The Guardian's grip suddenly let up, and I collapsed in a heaving, spluttering mess. Sparks flew from the Guardian's head with the unmistakable scent of whiskey. The whirring cogs that powered it clicked and shuddered. It stiffened and crumpled into a heap. Lifeless.

Ilona stood over it. Clasped in her hand was the bottle of whiskey, now drained.

I choked down a laugh. Of all the things that could have defeated a Guardian, I hadn't expected that! "You wasted good whiskey. How did you know that would work?"

"I could smell the sugar content. Sugar is sticky. Amnae avoid it because it gets caught in our fins. What is this thing?" She tentatively nudged the Guardian with her sandaled foot.

"An immortal. Expect more."

"Oh no, oh no, no no no," Doctor Finch was muttering. "We're coming in too fast!"

I peered out the window. Kronos was mere meters away. "Yank on the brake!"

"I *did*!" he squawked.

I shoved him aside and grabbed the lever. It snapped in my hand.

That wasn't good.

The train wasn't slowing.

Oh bugger. It was speeding *up*!

Dor was going to let us crash into the station and wipe us out that way. Damn any mortals who got caught in the wreckage!

I grabbed Kayl's hand. "Take my form. You need to slow us down."

She gawked at me. "Are you joking?"

"I can't use my powers, not while wearing the collar. You've slowed time before. You need to do it now, otherwise we're going to crash."

"Shitting shit!" Her skin turned silver as her persona switched to Diviner. Dor would be able to reach us now, but it was a risk we'd have to take.

"Grab an invisible lever," I said calmly, despite my heart thumping so hard it was about to burst. "Pull it back slowly."

Kayl nodded and did as I instructed.

Time slowed around us. Even with the collar, I could still sense fluctuations battling against us. It wasn't just Kayl manipulating time.

QUENTIN! Dor's voice thundered above us.

Merciful gods, the train casually came to a stop.

"Run for the Gate!" I grabbed Ilona's hand and dragged her out of the cab. Kayl and Doctor Finch stumbled behind me onto the platform.

Time jolted forward.

The cab folded in two, as though an invisible hand had crushed it. Saints!

Another Guardian appeared behind us.

"The Gate's off!" Kayl yelled.

"I know! Keep running!"

We bolted up the platform. Diviner loitering about the station leaped back as we raced past them, expressions of pure horror on their faces.

Behind, the Guardian's footsteps thudded along the platform. It was gaining on us.

I didn't dare let go of Ilona. Dragging her at this pace would hurt her Amnae lungs, but the alternative was far worse.

At least six Diviner Wardens waited by the Gate. They stood guard by the circular brass portal that was our only way out of Kronos, their pistols aimed at us.

Blast it! I had no way of taking them on.

Ilona pulled on my arm, slowing me down. "I can't—I can't run anymore." She doubled over, her gills flapping erratically.

"Just a little further!"

The Wardens fired.

I scooped Ilona into my arms and ran to a metal bench for cover.

Sharp pain slammed into my shin.

I stumbled. Ilona tumbled from my arms.

"Quen!" Kayl screamed. She'd ducked behind a bench opposite.

"Run!" I pushed Ilona forward. If she could at least get to safety—

She was frozen with fear.

Blood dribbled down my leg. The bullet remained lodged inside, plugging the wound, though reducing my movement. I managed to crawl toward Ilona with nothing but pure adrenaline urging me on.

I didn't want to die. Not here, not now, not on my knees at the mercy of a cruel god.

But if my life protected Walter's daughter, then I'd gladly offer it.

I attempted to shield her.

Then Doctor Finch leaped over me.

"Doctor! Stop!"

He spread open his arms, as though they were the wings his god had denied. "Protect the girl, Master Corinth."

A bullet hit him in the chest.

"Zachery!" Ilona screamed.

The doctor staggered. Another bullet caught his neck, sending a spray of blood and feathers into the air. And then another. And another.

They tore him apart.

I took the chance he'd given and dragged Ilona behind the bench.

The Wardens aimed potshots, keeping us trapped. A bullet ricocheted too close.

"I have to help him!" Ilona cried, and tried to run out.

I pinned her against the bench and risked a peek.

The good doctor's body had faded. The collar fell atop his empty lab coat.

Only bloodstained feathers remained of Doctor Zachery Finch.

Another mortal I'd failed.

"Why didn't you let me help him?" Ilona shrieked and punched my chest.

"He died to protect you. Don't waste his gift."

"What now?" Kayl yelled.

"Do what you did before, but in reverse!"

"You want me to speed up time?" Her voice was hysterical. "I thought that was a bad idea?"

"I'm out of good ones." The Guardian still lumbered its way up the platform. "Do it!"

"Shit!" She reached for an invisible lever. This time, she slammed it forward.

Time shuddered around me, as though displeased that an interloper was forcing it against its will. Various clocks clanged together throughout the city in one high-pitched tone. Hands of the clockface above the station were spinning out of control. It would have been humorous, if a Guardian wasn't charging right for us.

"When I say go, you run behind me," I whispered to Ilona. "No matter what happens, you run. Stay close and don't look back."

Tears rimmed her slitted pupils. Walter's eyes. "I want to go home."

"We'll get you home. I promise." I squeezed her hand with a gentle reassurance.

My goodness.

I held her hand and hadn't experienced a vision of her death. The collar had blocked all my abilities. Where had this technology been my entire sodding life?

The shock of pain in my leg made me nauseous. I hastily tore off my bow tie and shrugged off my jacket. There wasn't time to bandage the wound.

Seconds painfully ticked by.

And then the Gate burst into life.

"Go!"

I leaped over the bench with the intent to charge at the Wardens.

It wasn't my best plan. Pain radiated through my bloody shin, and I instantly sank onto one knee.

Ilona came to my side and hefted me up. She barely had the strength, but with her support, I half ran, half hobbled my way to the Gate.

A bullet whizzed past my ear.

The Wardens tried to slow time and aim their shots. Kayl's manipulations disoriented them. Those damnable fools couldn't properly aim without cheating.

That was one of the first lessons I'd learned during my Warden training.

Don't rely on time to save you.

I let go of Ilona and barreled into the nearest Warden. My fist smashed against his nose with a satisfying crunch. He fell hard.

Kayl collided with another, knocking the poor sod on his buttocks.

One of them pointed their pistol at Ilona.

No!

I dove for his wrist and wrenched the pistol free. With a quick flick, I placed the barrel to his head and pulled the trigger.

His blood splashed my spectacles. Chunks of flesh and brain matter dripped down onto my waistcoat. He collapsed at my feet as an empty uniform.

Once a brother. A colleague. A mortal with a name.

Now nothing but a memory I'd deign to forget.

"Quen!" Kayl yelled.

Another Warden swung at me, his fist connecting with my cheek.

My head snapped back with a flurry of stars.

"You filthy blasphemer!" The Warden readied another strike.

Kayl grabbed his neck. A pulse of aether passed between them, and the Warden stiffened before collapsing. His eye sockets empty. She'd taken his soul.

"Shit, I didn't mean to—"

QUENTIN! Dor's voice rattled through the station. *YOU HAVE DEFIED ME! YOU ARE MY MORTAL. YOU WILL DO AS I COMMAND.*

His hands broke through the clouds and reached for me.

I shoved Ilona toward the Gate. "*Go!*"

Kayl switched to her Chaos form and flung a rippling shield of aether around us.

The remaining Wardens ran for cover. I sent them off with a few potshots of my own, and then took aim at Dor.

His hands collided with Kayl's shield.

Electricity spasmed through the shield, sending sparks flying in all directions. Aether collided with the station's lamps in a storm to rival Tempest.

The power of a god pressed down on Kayl, yet she stood tall. Defiant. Sweat dotted her brow, and a streak of blood ran from her nose.

Her entire body shook.

She was giving everything.

"He's not yours!" she bellowed to the sky. "Quen was never yours and never will be!"

Static clung to my skin. My hair. All I could do was stare at her in reverent wonder. A mere mortal standing against a god.

I'd often thought fate was the realm of time, but no, it belonged to Chaos alone.

In a war between time and Chaos, Chaos would win.

And my soul would rest in peaceful damnation.

Dor's hands suddenly vanished.

And the Guardian stomped through Kayl's shield.

I took aim at its head. The pistol locked up. The bullet had bloody well jammed! Blast it! I tossed the useless thing aside.

Kayl wrapped her arm around my waist and dragged me with her. Together, we ran for the Gate. The wound in my leg slowed me down, my leg threatened to buckle.

We wouldn't make it.

"Run ahead," I groaned.

"Not without you!"

"Now isn't the time to be stubborn—"

"Too bad!"

The Guardian lunged.

My leg gave way. I fell arse over tit and landed face-first, my spectacles clattering to one side.

I rammed them back on. We were in Central Station.

Oh, thank the gods! We'd made it into Chime!

The Guardian's brass claws reached through the Gate.

What? That wasn't possible.

Immortals couldn't pass into Chime! And yet this Guardian was clearly stepping through the Gate, coming after us.

I shuffled backwards. "Speed up time!"

Kayl's skin instantly transformed to a Diviner persona. Time jerked forward. The Gate switched from Kronos to Memoria, cutting the Guardian in half.

It clicked with the painful stutter of a trapped gear and fell apart before me. The changing portal had burned through half its torso, leaving the brass metal molten red.

The whirring cogs that made up its face slowed to a stop.

"Where's Ilona?" I gasped as Kayl helped me to my feet.

"Don't move!" yelled a Diviner.

No.

A line of Diviner Wardens were waiting for us in Central Station. One of them held Ilona in their arms, the barrel of a pistol placed against her head.

41

Your life is but a beat on the timeline of existence.
Thousands have come before you.
Thousands more will come after you.
And you will be forgotten to time.
—H. Bezel, *Philosophy for the Young Diviner*

WARDENS POINTING THEIR WEAPONS at me was beginning to get old.

This day was turning into the longest of my life, and my feet were starting to cramp. Only this afternoon had I been betrayed by Sinder, kidnapped by my twin sister, dragged all the way to Solaris, threatened to be turned into some soulless slave, then escaped a god who wanted to fry us to death, burned my hands in the process of protecting myself from said god, witnessed the destruction of another domain, the death of my friends, the end of Chime as we knew it, escaped *another* god who wanted to see me obliterated from existence...

I drew in a breath.

I still had Quen. My Quen. My partner.

Until the Wardens killed us, anyhow.

Quen stood unsteadily on his injured leg and opened his hands in a placating gesture. "Good evening, gentlemen. If you don't mind, please release Miss Ilona Burns. Ambassador Arkey and I must escort her back to her domain—"

"Stop and raise your hands!" The Warden aimed a pistol at Quen. "We have orders to detain you both."

"Worth a try." Quen slowly raised his hands.

I had no choice but to do the same. There were at least twenty Wardens, all Diviner. Quite a force for three mere mortals. Clothes were still scattered around Central Station as far as I could see, and I swallowed the unease lodged in my throat.

Chime was quiet. Too quiet.

The urge to collapse in a fit of sobs threatened to take over me, but falling apart now wouldn't save Ilona or Quen. There'd be time to scream and grieve and plan later.

Quen had suffered as much awful shit as I had. Worse shit, even.

One of the Wardens produced an aether collar as another two whipped out handcuffs.

Between Quen and I, we couldn't stand against this many. Memoria stood at our backs. We could make a run for it, but not while they held Ilona hostage, and well, I didn't fancy seeking sanctuary in the home of another god who'd likely abuse me.

Wonky aether shield it was, then.

I wasn't confident on how well my new ability would deflect bullets, and so I readied myself to potentially get shot a hundred times and switched my form to Chaos.

Sunlight suddenly flared from out of nowhere. I cringed and turned away.

The Wardens shrieked. A heartbeat later, their screams were replaced by the hiss and crackle of flame.

Smoke sizzled from a charred black smear across the platform.

The Wardens had been reduced to ash.

Poor Ilona stood in the center of it. The girl was unharmed, but trembling from head to toe, her chest heaving with gurgled breaths.

"Jinx," I gasped.

Jinx stood admiring her work. She'd dressed in another crimson gown—her favorite color, I assumed—to pair with her glowing Glimmer form. "I heard you switched sides, Corinth. Finally realized that Dor is nothing but a conniving twat?"

"She's an Amnae, you arse!" I yelled. "You can't use flame around her—"

"She's still alive, isn't she? You're welcome, by the way."

Ilona ran for the Gate.

Quen lunged to catch her, and fell to one knee with a pained gasp. "Ilona, wait!"

The Amnae girl didn't look back. Her sandals slapped against the platform as she carefully avoided the remains of Dor's clockwork immortal and dove into Memoria.

I ran after her and skidded to a halt.

The Gate rippled. Memoria switched back to Kronos.

Oh shit! It was pissing switching back and forth!

An army of Diviner marched through. I doubled back.

Shots blasted across the station. A bullet narrowly missed my head.

Shit, shit, *shit*!

Balls of sunlight pooled in Jinx's hands.

"You can't kill them all!" I yelled.

"Fucking watch me!" Light burst from her outstretched hands.

"Stop it!" I rammed into her, knocking her off-balance.

Her aim went wide and scorched the clock tower. "What is your damn problem?"

"They're mortal!"

"So?"

More Diviner entered from Kronos, but this time they moved to one side.

One of the clockwork immortals stepped through the Gate, its hulking form bending to fit through the portal.

That couldn't be right.

I helped Quen up. "You said that thing was immortal?"

His weight leaned against me. "They are."

"Then how is it in Chime?" How could it make the crossing? The Gate was supposed to prevent them from entering!

"Rules of the game have changed." Jinx rubbed her hands together with sickening glee. "This should be fun."

Fun! Oh my fucking god!

YOU CALLED? Corentine drawled in my mind.

How can an immortal enter Chime?

DID YOU TRULY BELIEVE THAT THE GODS WOULDN'T BE ABLE TO ENTER CHIME? THEY HAVE ALWAYS HAD THE ABILITY TO TRAVERSE THE DOMAINS. THEY ARE GODS.

But—the Covenant!

THE COVENANT IS A GUIDELINE. A RULE TO CREATE PEACE BETWEEN THE DOMAINS FOR THE SAKE OF THEIR MORTALS. DOR HAS BROKEN IT, THEREFORE IT NO LONGER APPLIES.

The implications of that meant nothing good. War truly could become reality, with Chime as its battleground.

An outright war between the gods and their mortals and immortals.

Shit! *This is all your pissing fault!*

WHOSE SIDE WILL YOU TAKE, DAUGHTER?

The ground shook as the clockwork immortal's feet clanged onto the concourse, one shuddering step at a time.

"We need to run!" Quen urged.

All this running was wearing me out. I hadn't eaten in hours and was fueled only by the desire to *not* end up strapped to another bloody chair.

I let Quen wrap his arm around my waist as he hobbled. We made slow progress in our escape from the station. "Where do we go?"

"Anywhere," he ground out through clenched teeth.

Anywhere indeed. Chime was completely empty now, and I almost tripped over a pair of abandoned shoes—a fact that made me want to vomit, and I likely would have if my stomach wasn't so empty, and Quen didn't need me to remain upright.

He looked a right state. Blood bloomed through his trousers, and more stained his waistcoat and face. Our bodies were pressed so close together, I could smell the metallic tang of the dead on him.

We needed a Necro for his leg, but...

There were no Necro left.

"I lost her," Quen mumbled. "She didn't trust me, and now I've failed Walter."

"We'll get her back."

We'd get them all back.

"Where are you fucks going?" Jinx shouted as she caught up with us.

I snapped a glare over my shoulder. This was all her damn fault as well—Jinx and Corentine! And she had the gall to act like we were on the same side?

I wouldn't forgive her for *any* of this.

"Oh, don't be like that." She pouted. "I'm trying to help you."

"How? By ruining my life?"

"I can save your Time Boy."

Quen spun to face her, almost falling as he did so.

I snarled. "If you so much as *touch* him, I'll wring your neck."

Jinx rolled her eyes. "I could have taken his soul at any time, but I haven't, have I? I know how he can free himself from Dor. You want the secret? Then follow me." She jogged into an alleyway.

Quen and I shared a glance. Knowing Jinx, this was likely a trap. But she was leading us away from Central Station—from the clock tower. Moving through alleys would be the quickest way to lose our pursuers.

Chime was our home, and we navigated Central's backstreets with efficient familiarity, though not efficient speed. I should have asked Jinx to take on a Necro's form and heal Quen's leg, though she didn't offer, and truth be told, I didn't want her hands anywhere near him.

For all his suffering, Quen didn't once complain. "You're leading us to the Temple District?" he asked.

"Clever boy," Jinx said.

Not just the Temple District. Jinx led us directly to the Glimmer temple.

Really? "*This* is your new hideout?"

"Why not? I own Gildola's soul. Everything that was hers is mine."

I stepped over a pile of dust and entered the temple's foyer.

Shit.

The entire corridor was full of dust, more than in the Vesper temple. I had to be careful where I placed my feet. The temple resembled Gildola's cathedral back on Solaris, though a much smaller and more compact version. Gaudy gold and marble furnishings filled the foyer as light filtered in through the stained glass windows.

"Sorry about the mess," Jinx said. "I'll do some sweeping later."

I scowled, and she winked at me.

Quen took a moment to lean against the wall and catch his breath. "The Wardens will likely check here." He took off his eyeglasses and cleaned them on his shirt, smearing a streak of blood. "You're best off finding less assuming accommodation."

"What, like a watchmaker's? Tried that." Jinx headed further into the temple.

I followed as Quen limped behind. We entered a round sanctum. This too resembled the cathedral, with stone pews arranged around an altar, only this altar had a gleaming golden statue of Gildola looming over it; her burning eyes were huge red rubies.

Every seat was filled with dust piled atop clothes.

I hugged my chest. None of this felt right.

Jinx leaned against the altar and ran a nail through a line of dust. "You're still upset about the Glimmer?"

"They deserved better."

"No, they didn't. Stop acting all righteous."

"What do you want, Jinx?"

"The same thing I've always wanted; to end the reign of the gods."

"Good luck with that! In case you hadn't noticed, the Diviner are now in charge. Thanks to you, Chime is empty! The gods have won!"

Flame flashed in her eyes. "Chime belongs to Chaos, as it should. As for the Diviner, I'll be kicking them out, don't you worry." She pushed herself from the altar. "Here's the deal. I'll teach you a trick, and in return, you'll give up Valeria's soul."

Only this afternoon had I realized I actually owned Valeria's soul. I crossed my arms. "No deal."

"Nah-ah!" She waggled a finger. "Wait until you see my trick." She stepped before the statue of Gildola. "You think I'm a monster. The Diviner think we Chaos are creatures bent on destroying everything."

I snorted. "Aren't you?"

"Chaos is more than destruction. We're also creation. Chance could have told you that, if those Diviner fucks hadn't ruined him. Oh well, guess it's down to me to play teacher. Now watch carefully, sister." She spread out her arms in a parody of some theatrical performance.

Light flared, taking the shape of a man. I blinked away starlight.

And then... Gods!

Joe appeared before me—very alive, naked, and very male. Only, his skin wasn't the golden hue of a Glimmer, but the silvery-blue of Chaos.

He looked confused—terrified, even—and quickly ducked behind a pew to hide his nakedness. "What—What's going on? What have you done to me?"

"You're reborn," Jinx said, matter-of-fact. "Go enjoy your new life."

Joe grabbed an abandoned pair of slacks and dashed from the sanctum with a whimper.

"My goodness," Quen gasped. He leaned against a pew as though about to faint.

I rubbed my eyes. This couldn't be real. Could it? "How did you do that?"

Jinx examined her nails. "I told you. Everything is made of aether. The souls you take aren't gone—they're inside you, ready to grant their power. To be reborn again. You took Valeria's soul—the soul of a god. Her powers are yours. Her mortals are yours."

I was reeling. Absolutely reeling. I didn't know whether to pass out, vomit, piss myself, or all three. "You're saying I can bring back the Vesper?"

"Don't you see, sister? If we take the gods, we take their mortals. We can remake Chime. We can bring your precious mortals back—rebirth them as Chaos! Even your pathetic Godless. *If* you know what you're doing, which, no offense, you don't. Give Mother Valeria's soul, and she can bring back the Vesper for you."

This was a trap. It had to be. "Why tell me this now?"

"Because you can save me," Quen whispered.

I met his silver eyes. "No, Quen—"

"You can save me. *You.*" He staggered toward me and grasped my arm. "I can't wear this damnable collar forever. I have no idea how long the effects will last, and should the Wardens catch or kill me, I'll return to Dor."

"What are you saying? That you want me to take your soul? I can't do that!" I'd barely learned how to summon a shield! How was I supposed to resurrect an entire soul? What if I fucked it up? That would be par for the course, wouldn't it?

I may have Valeria's soul, but that didn't mean I knew what to do with it!

"You can. I've seen it. In my visions. My entire life has led to this—"

"You dreamed of me killing you."

"I dreamed of this moment." He cupped my cheek with warm tenderness. "Please, Kayl. Dor, he… I'd sooner risk losing my soul than go back to him. Do you understand? I'd sooner face my end than become his agent of death."

Tears stung my eyes. Could I really do this? There had to be a better way.

"Please," he urged. "You're Godless. Do what you swore to do. Save me from my god."

I rested my forehead against his. "What if I lose you? What if—"

"Then I will go into the aether blessed to have known you. And I'll be free."

YOUR SISTER SPEAKS TRUE. CHAOS CAN BE USED TO CREATE. TO RESHAPE SOULS.

Why did you never tell me this?

I DID. YOU CHOSE NOT TO LISTEN.

My entire world was falling around me.

I'd lost my family. Reve. Then Dru, Vincent, Harmony, and Sinder. Even though he'd fucked me over, I missed Sinder.

And Malkavaan.

I wanted them back. I wanted Quen beside me. How could I do this alone? Make this decision alone?

Everything had been turned inside out.

Quen was hurting. I knew Dor had tortured him, but did he really want to risk his mortal soul on Jinx's word?

There was no malice in her eyes.

"It's easy," she said. "You saw me bring back Joe. Take Corinth's soul and then rip it out again. You've got Valeria's powers, remember? You can do everything I can. We're twinsies."

Easy? Fucking gods. It certainly didn't feel like I held the power of the Vesper, let alone the power of gods. How was I meant to tap into abilities I'd forgotten?

I WILL GUIDE YOU.

Why? Why help me?

BECAUSE YOU ARE MY DAUGHTER.

You betrayed me, used me—why should I trust you? Why help Quen? A Diviner?

I RELISH THE OPPORTUNITY TO TAKE DOR'S CHILD FROM HIM. TO HURT HIM, AS HE HURT ME.

That reason was actually believable.

Quen wanted this. I would do it for him, and he alone.

But who would he be when I was done?

My Quen?

A true Godless?

Quen fell to his knees. His arms wrapped around my legs. "Please. If you have any love for me at all, then do it." Bloodied tears ran down his cheeks.

Dor had done this to him, and I couldn't bear it.

I'd failed my family, my friends. I wouldn't fail Quen.

Those silver eyes were so full of hope. He'd named me his salvation. He trusted me to deliver it. But we'd both swallowed salvation before and knew it tasted bitter.

I bent and kissed him. A soft kiss that stretched time for eons.

My heart ached for him. No, my very soul.

I broke the kiss with a gasp. "Don't leave me, Quen. Don't you dare. I'm not done with you yet."

He stole another kiss. One filled with stars and static.

I placed my hand on his neck, above that awful collar.

"Thank you," he whispered.

The tug tingled in my palm. Instinct compelled me to follow that tug, to take Quen's soul for myself. Aether zapped through my blood.

Quen's body slumped to one side.

His eye sockets were empty. His mouth open. Lifeless.

Dead.

Oh gods. I placed my hands on his chest. There was no breath. No heartbeat. "How—How do I bring him back?"

Jinx smirked. "You don't."

What? "But—But you said! You—" I stood on shaking legs. "You said I could bring him back? I haven't—gods, I haven't..."

No, I couldn't have. No, no, no, I couldn't!

"One less Diviner in the universe is no loss."

I stared at Jinx. At my twin. My mind for thirteen damn years.

Mother? I called into my mind. *How do I bring him back?*

NOW YOU REFER TO ME AS YOUR MOTHER?

Please, tell me what to do. What do I do? I haven't killed him? Tell me I haven't killed him?

YOU ARE MY DAUGHTER. I MUST PROTECT YOU FROM MAKING THE SAME MISTAKES I DID. YOU WON'T FIND LOVE IN A DIVINER.

No.

No, no, *no*!

My lungs squeezed the life from me. Each breath cut, as though my own soul was made of glass that had now shattered into pieces.

I was drowning. Gods, I was drowning.

And Jinx was standing there smiling as I fell apart.

"I fucking *hate you*!" I slapped her across the face, forcing her to stumble back.

The shock in her eyes twisted into quivering rage. "You know what? Fuck you! I wanted to help you. I wanted to bring you back to our mother. You can die alone for all I care. I'm done with you!" Jinx shoved past me and stomped for the temple exit.

Sobs racked through my chest. I covered my mouth and collapsed to my knees. Slowly, I crawled over to Quen and lifted his head onto my lap.

My tears landed on his eyeglasses.

I'd killed him.

Not only killed him. I'd destroyed his soul. Wiped his existence.

"I'm—I'm sorry!" I rocked back and forth.

This couldn't have been what he wanted?

I'd failed him. He'd done so much for me, and I'd failed him.

Just as I'd failed everyone.

My wretched tears turned to screams.

"Fuck you!" I shrieked, my voice echoing off the temple walls. "Fuck the gods! Fuck Dor! Fuck my goddamn fucking sister!"

Fuck you as well, you heartless bitch! No wonder Dor locked you inside a clock tower. You deserve one another.

DAUGHTER—

I used Quen's finger to unlock the aether collar and wrap it round my own neck, cutting Corentine off. I never wanted to hear her voice *ever* again.

Maybe Jinx was right in her desire to destroy the gods. What did I have left to live for?

Dor had destroyed everything. Corentine too.

I was going to rip their souls apart.

"She's here!" called out a male voice.

Shit! Wardens had found me! Two Diviner ran into the temple, kicking through the dust of the dead Glimmer without a single thought. They aimed tasers right at me.

I was a pissing idiot. My screaming had led them right to me.

Run, a voice said inside my mind. Shit, it sounded like Quen's voice. I must be going mad at long last. *Get out, Kayl. Run!*

The Diviner's silver eyes bulged at the sight of Quen's body on the ground. One approached me with an expression of absolute rage. "You're done for, you unholy whore." He raised his hand to slap me.

A bullet pierced his brain, splattering blood across my skirt.

The remaining Warden spun, and another blast echoed in the temple.

Their bodies faded, their clothes crumpling to the ground as their souls floated into the aether.

I squinted at the figure approaching me.

"It appears I've arrived in time."

No. It couldn't be. This wasn't fair! "But you're—you're *dead*!" My eyes darted between Quen on the ground and the man standing in front of me.

It was Quen. Another Quen. He stood in the tan suit I'd seen him wearing in the Mesmer temple, his eyes aglow with aether, his pistol the same my Quen had lost.

What. The. *Shit?*

"I've died quite a few times now, actually. It doesn't get any more pleasant." Quen—Future Quen, or whoever the fuck he was—peered over his own body and grimaced. "Oh my, what a state I'm in. I best not get too close. Paradoxes and all that. Can you walk? Or are you going to faint?"

"You're an arse!" I scrambled to my feet and thumped his chest. "You've just *died*, and you're standing here joking about it?"

"I'm not joking. But we *are* on a tight schedule."

"*What* are you talking about?"

He pulled out his pocket watch. "Wardens are on their way, and worse besides. You've met the Guardians by now, haven't you? Immortal creatures. Best we don't tangle with them. You're carrying my soul, and I need to get it out."

"I—what?"

He tapped my head. "In there. Hello, Past Quen."

Hello, Future Quen.

You've got to be joking! You're in my mind*? It* was *Quen's voice!*

Apparently so, Quen said. *It's rather odd, I'd agree. Is this how Jinx lived before she got her own body?*

I choked back a sob. *I thought I'd lost you. Did you truly believe I'd save your soul? That this would happen?*

Well, honestly, I expected you to destroy my soul and that would be the end of it. All my visions pointed to that outcome. I'm... not sure what happens now.

You absolute arsehole! You let me take your soul knowing I might have actually destroyed it? Were you going to let me live with that guilt for the rest of my life?

I'm sorry. I didn't mean to hurt you. But if Dor got his hands on me, he'd only use me to get to you, and I'd sooner die a thousand times than let that happen.

The relief that flooded through me far outweighed any irritation I might have at these impossible circumstances. I had Quen inside me, and not in a way I'd expected. *You're a pain in the arse, you know.*

I'm aware.

The other Quen—Future Quen—cleared his throat. "Time, please."

"So why are you here? What's your plan?"

"I thought that was obvious." He examined his pistol. "Follow me but stay close. We need to get into the Mesmer temple."

"Why there?"

"You'll see."

"I don't know why I trust you."

His lips quirked. "We're both grateful you do."

Future Quen checked it was clear and then beckoned me out with a finger to his lips. I held my breath as we slipped out.

A tram full of Wardens had pulled into the Temple District station. Shit.

We slunk behind the Glimmer temple as they marched in our direction. More were headed for the other temples, likely to search them. These were all Diviner, all male, all wearing their neat black-and-bronze Warden uniforms. And all armed.

There were four temples between us and the Mesmer's. We moved in a pattern of quick sprints and stops, waiting for the Wardens to turn away or look elsewhere.

Thankfully, the bulk of the Wardens headed into the Glimmer temple.

"Over there!" one of the Wardens called.

Shit! We were only feet away from the Mesmer temple.

"Go now!" Future Quen said.

I bolted for the door. The Wardens charged after us.

Shots blasted in our direction. Future Quen took aim, sending a few of his own bullets back, and a few left pockmarks in the hourglass statue within the center of the Temple District green. The noise alerted every Warden in the area, and soon an entire army was marching after us.

I ducked into the alcove of the temple door. We'd made it to the temple, but what then? We'd be trapped inside and easy pickings for the Wardens.

Future Quen shuffled beside me. "Close your eyes!"

"Why?"

A wall of sunlight burst from the ground. I cringed from its brightness as it completely surrounded the temple entrance, cutting us off from the Wardens.

Had Jinx returned to finish off her work? But no!

Through the flames, I could make out the figure of Joe. Gods! He flung light at the Wardens, sending them scattering. He stood topless, wearing only the slacks he'd stolen earlier. "Whatever you're doing, do it!" he yelled over the roar of his power. "I'll cover you!"

Thank the gods for Joe! Future Quen and I slid inside the temple.

Together, we dragged a few chairs to block the door. Joe wouldn't be able to hold off the Wardens for long. They knew we were here—or that I was here, at least. I'm sure they didn't expect to meet another Quen stalking Chime.

I suddenly burst out laughing.

Future Quen arched his brow at me.

I slapped a hand over my mouth. "That wasn't me!" I said, my voice muffled. *Did you make me laugh?*

Sorry. I like the sound of your laughter. I wanted to hear it.

You're a dork. Most men in your position would be undoing my bra and copping a feel.

I'm not most men. Though I'd rather use my tongue. Ah. Did—did I think that out loud? His embarrassment bloomed through our shared bond, heating my cheeks.

Yes, Quen, I can hear what you're thinking. Though now I have you at my mercy—Jinx told me you kissed her. Did you?

This is your concern right now?

I want a straight answer.

I felt Quen internally sigh. *Jinx kissed me. I reciprocated because I thought she was you.*

Giddiness fluttered in my stomach at the implication. *So does this mean we have a connection?*

We're sharing a body. I don't think we could be any more connected.

I could think of a way.

"Focus now," Future Quen said as he led us deeper into the temple. "The two of you will have opportunities for frolicking later."

Opportunities indeed.

Clothes were scattered around the corridors beside empty candy wrappers and spilled drinks. Gods, the temple was a mess. Without Dru or the rest of us to look after them, it appeared the Mesmer had reverted to their slovenly ways.

But they were gone. The temple was empty. Only their clothes had been left behind to prove that Mesmorpheus had taken them back to Phantasy.

We passed Vincent's old clinic, and a pang ached in my gut. "Why are we here?"

Future Quen shushed me and kept walking.

I followed him downstairs, past the padded cell where Jinx had been kept, and to the storage room where Future Quen had hidden previously.

He produced a key. "Trust me."

The door opened to a dark room, and not the storage room I'd been expecting. Lights in the ceiling flickered to life, illuminating a single chair in the center.

One of the soul-splitting machines.

"What is this?"

Future Quen approached a console and began pressing buttons. "You can't remove my soul from your body without help. Reverie recovered this device and rebuilt it to my specifications with Mesmorpheus's guidance. Please. Take a seat."

He intended to split Quen's soul from me in the same way Karendar had taken Jinx.

I kept a wary distance from that damn chair. "Jinx was able to bring back Joe. Why can't I do the same?"

Future Quen glanced over his eyeglasses. "Jinx didn't tell you everything you needed to know. She has the power of Gildola. A god. Without that same power, any souls you take will remain inside you."

"But—I own Valeria's soul, don't I?"

"You do. However, Anima rather conveniently blocked you from accessing Valeria's power, which is why you're struggling to remember certain details. They're buried in your subconscious where you can't reach them."

Conveniently? That fishy twat! Anima must have done something to me when I was in Memoria. And here I'd been blaming myself!

The derailed tram in Central before you entered Memoria, Quen said. *Was that caused by... my future self?*

"Yes, I caused the crash," Future Quen answered, as though reading my mind. "That was my—your—abilities you felt, Past Quen."

Shit. "It was you who told me to enter Memoria knowing Anima would fuck with my memories. Why?"

"Because if you'd retained Valeria's powers, then this moment in the timeline wouldn't have been possible."

He—I—cost mortal lives! Quen raged.

"Sacrifices had to be made," Future Quen said without remorse.

Is that the man he—I—become? Like Elijah?

"Stop being so dramatic. We're nothing like Elijah."

"I forgot the truth of Eventide," I said. "Of Malkavaan."

"And I won't apologize. You'll both understand why soon enough. Now, I must reiterate that we are on a *tight* schedule. This is the only way I can save you." He gestured to the chair.

Do you trust yourself? I asked my Quen.

It was my future self who gave me the schematics for the collar.

"You're wondering if you can trust me. Unfortunately, I don't have time to fully alleviate your fears. Just know that if your Quen dies, then so do I, and I'm not feeling particularly suicidal right now."

I can't remain trapped in your body forever, Quen said.

Jinx and I made it work. Sort of. I knew I was being selfish, but if we did this, then I could lose Quen for good. I'd lost him too many times already. *We could remain together. As partners.*

Partners with some caveats.

The caveat in this case would be life-changing. If Quen didn't have his own body, I wouldn't be able to fuck him.

You do know I can hear your thoughts, too?

I've never been shy about my intentions. Though yes, I did enjoy the privacy of my own thoughts. *All right. Let's sort you out, then.* Hopefully this was worth the risk.

I trusted Quen. Both Quens.

I tentatively sat in the chair. The first time I'd had my arse in one of these hadn't been pleasant, and now I was sitting in it voluntarily.

Future Quen attached the headpiece, but didn't bother strapping me in. "We'll need to take this collar off so it doesn't interfere." He detached it from my neck and set it aside. "You know what to expect."

Yes, and I wasn't looking forward to it. "I've taken multiple souls since—since Lady Mae. How do you know Quen will pop out?" And not the Diviner Warden whose soul I'd accidentally stolen earlier?

"Those souls are safely tucked away in your subconscious. Past Quen is not."

"And what makes him so different?"

"You share a connection." Future Quen returned to the console and pressed another button. The humming coming from the chair grew louder.

It was that simple, was it? "So when my Quen gets his body back, are you up for a threesome?"

He flashed a wicked grin. "Unfortunately, that *would* create a paradox. As soon as I pull this lever, I'll be gone."

"Gone where?" I didn't understand any of this time travel nonsense.

"The future. I must ensure events unfold as they should."

"If you're really from the future, then what do I have to look forward to?" If I knew what dangers were heading my way, I could attempt to avoid them—or prepare for them, at least.

"That would be spoilers."

"You can't give me some hint?"

"To impart any more than I already have would interfere with the timeline, and we can't risk that. The path ahead will be difficult, but I have every faith in you both. May the gods leave you to your fate." He yanked on the lever.

Static crawled up my arm. I could taste the aether in the air, and it howled with a mournful screech I hadn't heard since Eventide.

I strained my head around. Future Quen had vanished, as promised.

What madness awaited me in the future? War, certainly.

This was only the beginning.

The static turned into an itch. I braced myself for the pain.

You're wonderful, Quen said inside my mind. *For facing this and more.*

If we get through this, you can buy me cake.

If we get through this, I'll buy you an entire bakery.

Promises.

Aether burned through my veins.

My nails dug into the metal of the chair's armrests. I ground my teeth and tried to ride out the electricity rippling through me.

It hurt. Gods, it hurt.

Screams tore from my throat.

You can do this, Kayl. Quen's inner voice crooned my name in a soothing caress. *I want you to know that I—*

I felt Quen being pulled from my body.

Quen? Quen!

Silvery-blue light filled the darkened room with the dazzling brightness of stars. I clenched my eyes shut as the machine quieted into the hum of aether.

"Kayl."

I slowly opened my eyes.

Quen stood naked before me in the form of Chaos. His skin was the same silvery-blue, the tips of his fingers a light pink, and—gods! He even had pointed ears! Without his eyeglasses, he looked different. Though no, it was his eyes that were odd.

They were the same color as mine.

Pure aether.

Gods. He'd been reborn not as a Diviner, nor Vesper, but as Chaos.

As me.

I tore myself from the chair. "Are you my Quen?"

He examined his hands. "I don't—"

Then he suddenly disappeared in a puff of smoke.

"Quen!" I swiped through the air to grab him, but he was gone. Utterly gone.

What had happened? Had the device failed?

Had I lost him *again*?

HE IS CHAOS. HIS SOUL BELONGS TO ME, DAUGHTER.

No. Shit, no! *Give him back! Or I swear, I'll tear down that damn clock tower—*

PLEASE DO. THEN I WILL BE FREE.

Fuck you! Give him back*!* I paced the room and chewed on a nail. How had Corentine been able to take his soul when she couldn't take me or Jinx? She was trapped! She shouldn't be able to do *anything*!

BRING ME VALERIA'S SOUL, AND YOU MAY HAVE HIS IN TRADE.

Of course that was what she bloody wanted. She and Jinx had probably colluded to trick me again, and I'd fallen for it.

Except... Future Quen had encouraged me to do this. Whose side was he on?

Fucking shit! I kicked the damn chair.

Something banged on the door. "Come out with your hands up!"

Great. The Wardens had broken into the temple. Was everyone out to get me?

YOU ARE NOT SAFE HERE.

"Shit!" I screamed as Mesmorpheus appeared where Quen had stood a moment ago.

That was it. I'd truly lost my mind. This entire day was a horrific dream, because of course it was. I'd fallen asleep in the Mesmer temple after eating too many damn chocolate limes, and one of the trio was fucking with me because a god *could not bloody materialize in Chime*!

YOU MUST COME WITH ME. Mesmorpheus's voice echoed as it had so many times in my dreams.

"Oh, really? To where? The domain of candy and cakes? Are we going to fly there on edible clouds that taste like blueberry and then frolic among the candy grass and candy trees?"

Mesmorpheus waved a hand, and a portal opened inside the room.

"You've got to be joking." It looked exactly like the Gate's swirling portal, and through it lay Phantasy. "Do you have any idea how the Covenant works?" Or was supposed to. Hadn't Corentine said the Covenant was more of a guideline, and the gods could do as they wished?

I dreaded to think how the gods would act now they no longer followed their own bloody rules.

The storage door shuddered, and the hinge splintered. One more bash like that, and the Wardens would be in.

COME WITH ME, AND I WILL EXPLAIN.

Oh, fuck it. "Why not? I can't see how things could get any worse."

Famous last words. I regretted uttering them immediately.

Rule one of the Godless: things could always get worse.

The door crashed open. "Halt!" a Warden yelled.

I leaped into impossibility, and the portal closed behind me.

42

Phantasy can appear tempting to a Diviner—its observatory beats ours back on Kronos, and the very mechanisms used to control its apparatus is akin to an Ember's heavy bosom. Alas, therein lies the danger. Phantasy is full of dream parlors and curious Mesmer who don't understand that touching mortals without their consent is considered rude.
I would caution all Wardens against entering Phantasy. If one is not careful, one may lose their mind, and all the secrets contained within.
—Q. Corinth, *Warden Dossier on Phantasy*

OF ALL THE DOMAINS I'd had the pleasure or displeasure of visiting, Phantasy was by far the most impressive.

I stood inside the largest observatory in the known universe. A glass dome stretched above me, much like Memoria, only the sea surrounding it was more ethereal. A glorious number of stars swirled in trails of pink and silvery-blue dust, glittering like gems against the void of night.

In the center of the observatory was an odd construction made of spherical brass shapes that rotated around each other. It seemed to move like clockwork in patterns that reflected the stars above. And built within it was a giant telescope. It almost seemed Diviner in design, but Phantasy certainly wasn't as dreary as Kronos.

Gods. Had it really been only a few hours since I'd escaped that awful place?

I rubbed my eyes and pinched myself three times to check I wasn't dreaming, but no. This was harsh reality. I'd stolen Quen's soul, churned it through my mind, and spat it out again, only for Corentine to steal him from under me. Solaris was gone. Chime had emptied.

And I'd pissing walked through a portal directly into another domain.

Everything I knew and held holy had been scrunched up and thrown over my shoulder.

Jinx was right. The rules of the game had changed.

"It's Kayl!" squealed a familiar voice.

The Mesmer trio bounded over. They looked well, dressed in their black suits with matching faces and hairstyles, only the female one—Celene, or Celina—now wore a pink bow in her hair.

They stood at a polite distance. "We were worried for you!" Pink Bow said.

"We saw the Wardens take you!" said the other.

"I was so scared I wet the bed!" said the third.

I held up my hands. "It's been a day. I'm rather tired, but I'm fine." Though I looked a state. My makeup had run from all the crying and screaming, and my skirt was torn and marred with dirt and blood.

How would I buy a new outfit now that Chime's stores were closed?

"What about Uncle Vinny?"

"And Sinder?"

"And Harmony?"

"And Dru?"

"Give her some space," said Reverie, who glided out of nowhere. "She's Mesmorpheus's special guest."

"Yes, Auntie," the three of them said in unison. They slunk away, though kept shooting me curious looks.

"You're their aunt?" I asked.

"That's what they call me. Please, follow me. Mesmorpheus is waiting."

Reverie led me away from the open observatory into what appeared to be a hotel foyer decorated with flowery wallpaper and brass furnishings and lamps. That same sickly-sweet lavender incense from the Mesmer temple drifted through the air. There was no reception and no stairs, but a whole line of elevators stretched down a never-ending hallway.

Mesmer loitered around the foyer, either waiting for an elevator or napping on the couches spread generously throughout. Some were staring into space and drooling. Others were staring into space while eating from a bag of candy. Another picked their nose while reading a book. Lovely.

I examined a plaque listing various floors; memory parlor, library, restaurant, candy factory, spa, and… "A soft play center?"

"Mesmer like to play, but they fall asleep so easily. We need to ensure their play centers are well protected."

"Uh, right."

We entered one of the nondescript elevators. There were no buttons inside. "How does this thing work?"

The doors slid closed as I said it, and then we were moving up.

"Mesmorpheus controls the elevators," Reverie explained. "They sense the need of each individual Mesmer and ensure they arrive at the right place without getting lost."

"That's quite a hands-on approach. How do they manage hundreds of mortals?"

Reverie blinked. "Mesmorpheus is a god."

Well, that was me told.

The elevator traveled up in silence for an agonizing age and then came to a sudden stop with a cheerful *ping*.

The doors opened. I stepped out into a pure black room.

No, it wasn't black. It was night.

The elevator vanished, leaving me to stand on nothing. Literally nothing! Stars twinkled below me, and even further down, a golden speck shone. The observatory that I'd traveled from.

"Don't be afraid," said Reverie, who stood with her hands clasped in front of her as though waiting to be served tea.

"Is this the *sky*? How am I breathing? Am I even conscious right now?"

"You are awake."

Gods. I really wished I weren't.

THIS IS THE REALM OF POSSIBILITY, said Mesmorpheus's voice from all around me. *EVERY STAR IN THE SKY IS A DOMAIN. A UNIVERSE AND GOD OF ITS OWN. MILLIONS OF WORLDS, ALL WITH THEIR OWN STORIES AND SECRETS. SOME ARE NEWLY BORN. SOME ARE DESTINED TO DIE.*

A cluster of stars came together and formed Mesmorpheus's body. They floated in front of me in their perfect black suit, their hands and face made of purple nebulae.

"I have a *lot* of questions."

FIRST, I WOULD SHOW YOU A VISION.

Gods and their bloody visions.

An image bloomed like a portal I could step through. On the other side, there were skyscrapers and a gray sky. Kronos.

Two figures walked down a cobblestone street, arm in arm. A male and female.

Shit. The woman had my face and took the persona of Chaos. She wore a flowing silver dress and carried a blue parasol over her shoulder.

The male wore a pinstriped suit. His face... Gods. It was Quen, minus the eyeglasses, and with a rather handsome goatee that curled at the tip.

THIS IS DOR AND CORENTINE BEFORE CHIME EXISTED. WHEN THE GODS ENJOYED A TIME BEFORE CONFLICT.

I knew mortals were made in the image of their gods, but this was ridiculous. "Why show me this?"

HISTORY REPEATS ITSELF. THEIR LOVE BIRTHED THE GODS AND THEIR DOMAINS. OUR UNIVERSE EXISTED IN BALANCE. UNTIL DOR WITNESSED A VISION OF THE FUTURE. THEN THE GODS WARRED. MANY DIED. SOME ESCAPED TO OTHER UNIVERSES. WE THIRTEEN WERE ALL THAT REMAINED.

"I know this already. Dor saw Corentine destroying the universe, and so he imprisoned her."

I EXAMINED THIS VISION. IT WAS NEVER CORENTINE. IT WAS YOU.

My heart stopped dead. "What?"

YOU WILL DESTROY THIS UNIVERSE.

Unfortunately, my heart wasn't dead, but hammering so hard against my chest I was about to collapse any second. "How—How could that be me? Are you mistaking me for Jinx? I don't want to destroy the domains!

In case you hadn't noticed, everything that's happened in the past twenty-four hours is *her* fault! She and Dor! I've been trying to stop it!"

The vision of Kronos vanished, though in its absence, the stars grew more vivid and sharp, as though reflecting Mesmorpheus's mood.

I HAVE SEEN MANY POTENTIAL FUTURES. TIME FLOWS LIKE A RIVER, CREATING NEW PATHWAYS. NEW FUTURES. SOME OF THESE WILL FLOURISH. SOME WILL SUFFER DROUGHT AND WITHER.

BUT KNOW THIS; THE RIVERS OF TIME DEPEND ON CHAOS. THE GODS, THEIR MORTALS—WE ARE ALL CHILDREN OF CHAOS.

"I get it. Time and Chaos are as bad as each other. If you know the future, then why not just tell me? Why string me along with these vague metaphors, which have been, quite frankly, absolutely useless in saving the domains?"

I COULD NOT REVEAL THE FUTURE AS I WAS UNSURE WHICH FUTURE WOULD COME TO PASS. IT IS ONLY NOW APPARENT. THERE IS ONLY ONE FUTURE WHERE MORTALS CAN BE FREE. A FUTURE WITHOUT GODS.

"I don't need a crystal ball to tell you that."

THE GODS HAVE CHOSEN THEIR SIDES. THEIR DOMAINS WILL WAR, BUT IT IS THEIR MORTALS WHO WILL SUFFER. YOU MUST TAKE CHARGE OF THEM.

"Look, I couldn't even stop my sister from taking Solaris. The Godless are gone! Finished! You can't possibly expect me to stop a damn war. You're a god—why do you need me to fight *your* damn battles?"

I HAVE SEEN THE EVENTS TO COME. CORENTINE AND DOR WILL FIGHT FOR THE DOMAINS—THEY WILL TAKE THEM IF YOU DO NOT.

"If *I* don't take them?"

YOU HAVE WITNESSED THE POWER OF CHAOS. AETHER CAN BE RESHAPED. REBORN. TO SAVE THE DOMAINS, YOU MUST TAKE THEM BEFORE CORENTINE AND DOR. THEN THEY CAN BE REMADE.

They weren't being serious? I glanced to Reverie to check I'd heard Mesmorpheus right, but she remained standing there like some pissing lamp. "I'm sorry. It sounded an awful lot like you're telling me to go steal the souls of the gods and destroy their domains."

THAT IS CORRECT.

Oh, fuck me! "Are you out of your godly *mind*? I know you live among the bloody stars, but honestly!"

IF YOU WISH TO SAVE MORTALS, THEN THIS IS THE ONLY WAY. IF CORENTINE TAKES THE DOMAINS, SHE WILL DESTROY THEM, AND THEIR MORTALS WILL BE LOST FOREVER. IF DOR TAKES THEM, HE WILL DESTROY CHAOS AND TURN MORTALS INTO SOULLESS BEINGS.

"You're asking the impossible. Surely there is some other way?"

I HAVE SEARCHED FOR ALTERNATIVE FUTURES. I KNEW THIS WAS THE ONE WHEN QUENTIN CORINTH CONTACTED ME FROM A DIFFERENT TIMELINE.

"Why do you care for mortal lives so much? You torture your own mortals with nightmares!"

NIGHTMARES ARE DREAMS. THEY CANNOT HURT.

"Do you remember Reve? I sure do. His nightmares drove him to suicide!"

The stars floating around Mesmorpheus dimmed. *I WITNESS THE DREAMS OF MY MORTALS. THEY SHOW ME HAPPINESS. PLEASURE. I WISHED TO SHARE THE BEAUTY OF LIFE WITH REVE. I THOUGHT I COULD HELP HIM SEE WHAT I AND HIS BRETHREN SAW. HE DID NOT. HIS DENIAL CAUSED ME PAIN.*

His death caused me pain, too. "You can't control what mortals do with their lives."

I WITNESS THE WONDERS OF THE UNIVERSE. THE MAKING AND UNMAKING OF THE COSMOS. I WISHED FOR MY MORTALS TO SEE WHAT I SEE, BUT THEIR MINDS CANNOT COMPREHEND ITS MAJESTY.

So that was why the Mesmer were doolally. "All right. Say I buy your reasoning—as mad as it sounds—how am I supposed to stop Corentine and Dor? I'm one mortal."

YOU ARE NO LONGER MORTAL.

Any more revelations and I was going to hang myself.

THE INSTANT YOU TOOK VALERIA'S SOUL, YOU TOOK HER POWER. THE POWER OF A GOD. WHILE YOU POSSESS THE SOUL OF A GOD, CORENTINE CANNOT TOUCH YOU. YOU ARE SHIELDED FROM HER INFLUENCE.

Wait. Was that why she couldn't take my soul, but had taken Quen's? "Why did no one mention this?" I'd met with gods on Corentine's side—Edana, Serenity!

NOT EVEN YOUR ALLIES WISH FOR YOU TO UNDERSTAND THE DEPTHS OF YOUR OWN POWER. WITH EACH SOUL YOU TAKE, THAT POWER WILL GROW. YOU WILL BECOME A DEMIGOD. THE GODS FEAR MORTALS WHO HAVE THE POTENTIAL TO ASCEND. THEY WILL NOT GIVE UP THEIR POWER READILY.

A demigod? Really? "But—I haven't been able to access Valeria's power." I couldn't feel it inside me at all, as though it were hidden behind a veil. "I can't even remember how to turn Vesper, for god's sake."

NO. ANIMA HAS BURIED IT DEEP IN YOUR SUBCONSCIOUS, BUT IT IS STILL THERE. TO REGAIN IT, YOU WILL NEED ANIMA'S SOUL.

Great. A trip to Memoria awaited me in my future. "So is that where I start?"

I CAN NO LONGER SERVE MY MORTALS. TO FACE THE GODS AND STEAL THEIR SOULS, YOU WILL NEED MY POWER. USE IT TO SHIELD YOURSELF FROM CORENTINE'S INFLUENCE.

"You—You want me to take your soul?"

I OFFER IT WILLINGLY. IN EXCHANGE, YOU WILL PROTECT MY MORTALS.

That was an almighty ask.

But now that Mesmorpheus's words had sunk in, I liked the sound of them.

All right, I didn't cherish the thought of battling against gods, nor confronting Corentine or Dor, but finally freeing mortals from their divine masters?

That, I was born to do.

I could face The Nameless One and free Vincent. Take down Serenity and save Harmony. Release Dru from her servitude to Unghard. Gods, I'd even save Sinder from Edana, despite everything.

I could save them. I could bring them all back. Even the Vesper.

Even Malkavaan.

Ten domains remained. Eventide had fallen because of me—I carried that guilt regardless of whether I remembered it. Solaris had also fallen due to my carelessness. Sure, Jinx was being Jinx, but she was my responsibility.

And so were the domains.

I couldn't keep blaming her for my mistakes. Nor could I do this alone.

I needed my partner. "How do I get Quen back?"

WHEN CORENTINE TOOK HIS SOUL, I PLANTED A DREAM IN CORINTH'S SUBCONSCIOUS. HE WILL UNDERSTAND EVERYTHING I HAVE TOLD YOU. HE WILL KNOW WHAT TO DO.

BUT BEWARE. THE COVENANT IS BROKEN. THE VEIL BETWEEN DOMAINS IS SHATTERED. CHIME WILL BECOME THE BATTLEGROUND OF THE GODS, AND THEY ARE NOT PLEASED.

I blinked, and I found myself back in the observatory. Mesmorpheus stood there surrounded by the Mesmer trio.

"We love you, Papa!" said one.

"We'll never forget you!" said another.

The third clung to Mesmorpheus's leg and was blubbering. "Do you have to go?"

Mesmorpheus patted their head. *LISTEN TO KAYL. OBEY HER WORDS. BE WELL.*

The trio hugged their god in a circle.

Shit. I'd never seen a god act with such affection for their mortals before. This wasn't fair. I'd finally found the one kind god among the thirteen, and now I had to kill them?

YOU ARE GODLESS. BUT WE ARE FAMILY. CORENTINE WAS ALSO MY MOTHER. I WAS THE ONE WHO TRAPPED HER IN SLEEP FOR A MILLENNIUM. I WOULD VISIT HER DREAMS TO ENSURE THEY WERE PLEASANT.

I AM GRATEFUL THAT CORINTH WOKE HER. A MORTAL ACHIEVED WHAT I DARED NOT, AS HE WAS DESTINED TO.

I dropped into a low curtsy before them—the most respect I'd ever grant a god. "Tell me when you're ready."

I AM READY.

The trio shuffled back. One of them cried as the other two comforted them.

Mesmorpheus offered their hand.

I took it with a firm grip.

DEATH IS BUT ANOTHER DREAM. I LONG TO JOIN MY MORTALS IN SLEEP. PROMISE ME YOU WILL END THE REIGN OF GODS.

"I promise."

Aether burned down my arm at the tug.

Then hundreds of voices filled my head. Most of them were complaints—how they were tired, their bed wasn't comfortable, their pillow was too lumpy, or they'd run out of candy. Gods. What had I gotten myself into now?

I politely nudged them into the back of my subconscious for later.

Dust crumbled from Mesmorpheus's body in a twinkle of dying stars. It was beautiful, in a sad way. They'd welcomed their end with grace.

My hand had turned the dark purple of the Mesmer. I opened my palm to a collection of black stardust.

Mesmorpheus was gone. Returned to the cosmos they loved.

They dreamed of a better future. I'd deliver it.

The trio stood around Reverie as she hugged them. They wore sad smiles, but none of the Mesmer panicked or ran.

Above, the observatory cracked, and dust rained from the night sky. The stars were winking out at an alarming rate, and the colorful swirls of galaxies had turned gray.

"You best leave through the Gate," Reverie said in her calm voice, despite her domain falling apart. "Your children will show you the way."

My children? Had I accidentally adopted the entire Mesmer?

If Dru found out, she'd find it hilarious.

When she found out.

I hurried to where the Mesmer were pointing, and they guided me back to the foyer. Piles of dust had already replaced the Mesmer who'd been loitering here, and I carefully stepped past them toward an open elevator.

Only it wasn't an elevator, but Phantasy's Gate, and Chime waited beyond.

Not just Chime. Wardens were there, waiting for me to make the crossing.

Shit!

How was I meant to get past a line of Wardens?

We'll help you, said a voice inside my mind. Celeste.

We'll teach you how to use our power! said Castor.

We promised Mesmorpheus, said Cosmo. *You can remake us.*

The trio. Funny. Now that they were part of me, I recognized them and their names instantly as if I'd always known.

What power did the Mesmer hold? Besides eating an ungodly amount of candy?

It didn't matter. If I stayed in Phantasy any longer, I'd be trapped.

I reached inside myself, searching for my inner power. There, humming with the nervous energy of aether, bloomed Mesmorpheus's soul.

The god of dreams.

Their power flowed through me. I wasn't entirely sure what I was expecting until it clicked in my mind.

We were all made of aether.

In a blinding flash, three identical-looking mortals tore into existence. They stood naked in the colors of Chaos, but just as quickly as they'd been 'born,' their skin morphed back to the familiar dark purple hues of the Mesmer, and they each grabbed clothes abandoned in the foyer.

Celeste wrapped her arm around mine. "It's time to go."

"We'll protect you from those Wardens," said Castor. The stoic one of the three.

"You're our Mama now." Cosmo's eyes widened with the sparkle of silvery-blue stars. "We'll do what you say."

"Then let's go find a candy store," I said. "I'm bloody starving."

We walked arm in arm into Chime.

The Wardens readied their weapons. "Stand down!" Really, they were *so* predictable.

The trio closed their eyes.

A dark veil descended over the Wardens. They had enough time to blink at their predicament, and then the entire lot of them fell asleep where they stood, dropping their weapons in a collective *clack*.

That was unexpected. I laughed out loud.

We possessed the power of napping! How exciting!

Behind me, Phantasy had been reduced to a blank gray canvas.

Three domains gone. Three gods dead.

Cosmo sniffed back tears. "I'm going to miss home."

Celeste hugged their shoulders. "It won't be forever."

"We'll make a new home," added Castor.

The clock tower rang. At the turn of the hour, the Gate changed to Kronos. "We better not loiter," I said, and guided the trio out of Central Station and into the cover of the nearest alley.

Diviner entered the station. Honestly, there was a never-ending supply of Wardens, though no doubt they needed to secure the Gate. Jinx and I were their biggest threat. With Mesmorpheus's power running through me, I could now block my chaotic bitch of a mother from my mind.

That put Jinx and I on even ground.

"What's that?" Celeste pointed at the clock tower.

My gaze followed the clock tower up. An aether shield surrounded the clockface, but that wasn't what made my stomach flutter.

Dor's massive hands floated outside it, as though trying to push through the shield and pluck Corentine out himself.

Shit. The gods really could materialize inside Chime.

The Diviner had taken over Chime, but this was *my* city. Not Dor's. Not Corentine's. Not Jinx's. Mine.

I'd win it back.

I'd fight the gods. I'd tear apart their domains. I'd remake Chime in their ashes.

A domain for mortals.

A domain for the Godless.

I'd always felt this burning inside me. An unholy rage that spurred me on. That had founded the Godless. Every instance of injustice I'd witnessed or heard while in the Undercity had only stoked those flames. Occasionally, it flared into temper, but for the most part it had simmered beneath my skin.

Losing Reve and then Eventide... These events had only stoked it further.

A part of me had hoped those flames weren't truly me, but Jinx, and she'd taken them with her. Wasn't she the crazy one? The violent one?

But no. That flicker had always been inside me. It had taken the soul of a Leander. Had threatened gods.

And now, I couldn't contain it anymore.

It wasn't an Ember's flame. Nor a Glimmer's righteous fire.

It burned far greater than that.

I was ready to unleash it and watch the domains burn.

It was time we heathens fulfilled our true purpose—to end the reign of gods.

But first, I needed to rescue my partner.

XLIII

Ambassador Corinth and I had returned to Kronos with the Chaos creature known as K. Arkey. Our Father's orders were to submit her to the newly configured device; however, I failed to realize Corinth was not within his right mind. He overpowered me and escaped with Dr. Finch and I. Burns. The former was killed in the line of fire. The latter was able to escape to Memoria. Warden B. Seasons was caught attempting to sabotage our research of the remaining Chaos creature. Seasons has been placed inside our correctional facility as he is displaying blasphemous inclinations. Wardens searched the Temple District and found Corinth's body. I examined it myself. Chaos has taken his soul. It was Corinth's refusal to discipline himself against temptation and obey our Father's commands that has led to his death. This has unfortunately left a power vacuum. Someone will need to take Corinth's place.
—P. Bezel, *On the death of Ambassador Quentin Corinth*

I AWOKE TO THE soft hum of aether.

One moment I'd been inside Kayl's mind, my heart beating with hers, her thoughts echoing mine. Then I'd stood with a body. A new body. And that too had been ripped from me. I now found myself lying naked on cold metal.

I sat up and rubbed my eyes. Without my spectacles, the sight before me was a blur. Cables stretched across the floor by my feet, and I heard, rather than saw, the soft patter of feet. Even reborn, my eyesight was still awful.

A hazy golden figure stood before me. "Finally awake, Time Boy?"

Jinx's face was distorted, but it was unfortunately her. "Where am I?"

"Don't recognize it? These may help." She dropped my spectacles in my lap.

I quickly shoved them on.

My goodness.

I was inside the clock tower.

The room was dark, lit only by the waft of silvery-blue aether drifting through the air. The clockface dominated the far wall. It was truly magnificent, though the size of it dwarfed me. The hands alone were taller than me. Through the glass, Chime glittered below. It was night, and the skyline was still illuminated by aether streetlamps, despite the emptiness.

I didn't know what time it was.

"I don't know what time it is!" I blurted with a hysterical laugh.

Jinx pointed to the clockface. "There's a clock right there."

"I see it, but I—I don't feel it!" All my life, I'd lived with the passage of time flowing through my veins and ticking with my pulse. But that sensation was no more.

I examined my hands.

They were the silvery-blue of Chaos.

Oh my.

I was no longer a Diviner!

The timeline of Quentin Corinth had ended exactly as my visions had foretold. I'd once fallen to this very spot and unwittingly rewritten my entire destiny. And here I'd fallen again, floating through the baptism of eternity to be reborn into something new. A whole new life without the curse of death following me. A blank page. A fresh beginning.

It was everything I'd ever hoped for and more than I deserved.

WELCOME, CHILD OF CHAOS.

The voice inside my mind was feminine. Familiar. And certainly not Dor. *Corentine?*

YOU WERE ALWAYS DESTINED TO BE MINE, QUENTIN CORINTH. DID YOU EVER WONDER WHY DOR GAVE YOU THAT NAME? TO MOCK ME AS A REMINDER OF WHAT I LOST, AND WHAT HE SOUGHT TO DESTROY. CORINTH WAS THE FIRST MORTAL. THE BLUEPRINT FOR YOUR KIND.

I... Saints, I'm not... him? I held no memories of a past life.

PERHAPS. CORINTH LIVED A MORTAL EXISTENCE. TIME AGED HIM. WHEN HE PASSED, DOR WOULD NOT BRING HIM BACK. HE THOUGHT MORTALS UNRULY AND IMPRISONED ME SO MY INFLUENCE WOULDN'T REACH THEM, BUT MORTALS NEED CHAOS TO EXIST.

IT WAS DOR WHO INVENTED SUCH CONCEPTS AS SIN, BLASPHEMY AND APOSTASY IN ORDER TO SUBJUGATE MORTALS. CORINTH'S DEATH INSPIRED THE COVENANT.

You're saying I was created as a joke?

EXISTENCE IS ONE BIG JOKE. YOU WERE DESIGNED TO DESTROY ME AND MY MORTALS. TO END CHAOS.

I mean you and your mortals no harm—

NO? YOU PLOTTED TO STEAL MY MORTALS.

To save them! You knew Dor wouldn't let them live! Though not even I had been prepared for the obscene depravity of Dor's actions. *He used me to get at the domains.*

YOU ARE A FAILURE, QUENTIN CORINTH. A SINNER. AN APOSTATE. DOR FORGETS THAT ALL MORTALS ARE TOUCHED BY CHAOS. BUT YOU... YOU EMBODY DOR'S GREATEST WEAKNESSES, WHICH NOT EVEN HE WOULD DARE ADMIT. HE COVETS CHAOS. AS DO YOU.

WELCOME TO THE FAMILY.

Silvery-blue eyes blinked in the gloom. It wasn't only Jinx and me trapped inside this little room. I stood, letting my eyes adjust to the dim light.

Four other Chaos mortals sat in the far corner. They too wore the colors of aether, and were similar enough to Kayl and Chance to share the family resemblance.

Saints. Chance. I'd abandoned him in Kronos to a cruel fate.

Of course there were Chaos mortals here. We'd imprisoned them to keep the Gate safe from attacks. These didn't look despondent at their fate, no. Two of the males played a dice game, while another read an old edition of the Courier, and a woman sat brushing her hair.

"Recognize anyone?" Jinx asked. "It was your Wardens who trapped them in here with nothing but Mother for company. It's enough to send you crazy, huh?" She giggled at her own joke. "That's Lucky." She pointed to one of the dice players. "That's Flux—"

"Ambassador Corinth?" asked one of the Chaos, lowering their copy of the Courier.

I recognized this one. Joe. The Glimmer—or former Glimmer—I'd been tasked with dragging to Solaris. And would have, if Ben hadn't released him.

He approached with surprise in his eyes. "What are you doing here?"

Jinx slung her arm around my shoulder. "Corinth is one of us now, so play nice."

I pulled myself from her touch. "I've found myself here due to unfortunate circumstances. How are you here?" The last I'd witnessed of the poor chap, he'd been outside the Mesmer temple. I could hazard a guess at what fate had found him.

"The Wardens shot me, and I awoke here. I've died twice this day, yet I never asked to be remade like—like this." Joe gave Jinx a wary look.

"I made you into the man you wanted to be," Jinx said. "What are you complaining about? Is your new cock not big enough?"

"You had no right! Only I should choose what I wish to do with my own body. You're no better than Gildola."

"Gildola was a bitch. Me? I'm a worse bitch. Show a little gratitude and sit the fuck down."

Joe glared, but returned to his place on the floor.

"You're an inspiration," I said. "Truly, the morale in here is motivating."

Jinx leered at me. I hated that she looked so like her sister. "You talk big for a man with no clothes. Though I still don't understand what Kayl sees in you. It must be the little things." Her gaze dipped.

I crossed my arms over my chest. "If you've brought me here merely to torment me, then you're wasting your time. Dor has already thoroughly shredded my mental and emotional health. There isn't much more you can do to me."

She prodded my cheek. "Don't be a bore. You're here because we've got work to do."

"Work? What work?"

"You think I'm satisfied with Gildola's soul? We're going to end the reign of the gods. Starting with Dor."

"As much as I detest him, killing Dor will have catastrophic effects on time." Having existed as both Chaos and Diviner, and died enough times to make it count, I'd come to realize a fundamental truth about the laws of the universe and the gods who made it. Corentine only confirmed it.

Time was order, but existence was Chaos.

One could not live without the other.

And both Corentine and Dor were foolish to try.

DOR DESERVES HIS END.

I don't deny that, but mortals cannot exist without time! Whatever disagreements you had in the past must stay in the past for their sakes!

YOU WOULD LECTURE ME ON MOVING ON FROM THE PAST? YOU KILLED YOUR OWN LOVER.

Yes, well. I'm mortal. We make mistakes. You, however, are a god, and thus above such pettiness.

THE GODS CREATED PETTINESS.

Of that I had no doubt.

YOU STILL HOLD LOVE FOR DOR, DESPITE WHAT HE HAS DONE. SEE FOR YOURSELF HIS CRUELTY.

Aether lights blinked behind me, illuminating a darkened section of the inner clock tower.

Pipes stretched across the walls, all connecting to a chair.

A soul-splitting device.

Strapped inside it was a woman as naked as me, her skin the color of pale aether. Smaller pipes fed into her black veins, pumping out blood and energy.

Her head lolled to one side, shaved completely bare.

Slowly, her head tilted up, and her blazing aether eyes met mine.

Kayl's eyes.

I fell to my knees.

This woman looked identical to Kayl and Jinx, but her body was gaunt, deformed and twisted from years—centuries—of being strapped to that odious chair. Her lips were pulled back in agony, and I saw it in those eyes.

Pain. Anger. Hatred.

Madness.

"This is what Dor did to my mother." Jinx's words contained that pain, that madness, and now I finally understood where it originated.

I was going to be sick.

Dor had committed so many foul deeds. Elijah, too, in Dor's name. But this... This was truly obscene.

This was the price paid for Chime. My city. My home.

But if the cost came at such—such atrocity, then... Chime shouldn't exist!

None of this should exist!

YOU UNDERSTAND.

Saints. I did.

I didn't believe the Diviner to be a lost cause, yet by fostering logic over emotion, we'd created evils such as this. It had to end, one way or another.

WITHOUT DOR, NO MORTAL WILL AGE OR DIE. THERE WILL BE NO MORE SUFFERING. NO MORE PAIN. WILL YOU HELP ME, QUENTIN CORINTH?

"What is it you wish for me to do?"

BRING FORTH THE END OF TIME.

Author's Note

Thank you for reading! If you enjoyed THE CHILDREN OF CHAOS, then please consider leaving an honest review. Reviews mean the world to me and help support your favorite authors.

Kayl, Quen, and Jinx continue their adventures in:

THE CRUEL GODS BOOK THREE

THE END OF TIME

WANT MORE FROM CHIME?

Not ready to leave Chime yet or want to know what other projects I'm working on? Then join my monthly newsletter and you'll receive an ebook copy of **TALES FROM ACROSS THE DOMAINS**, a short story collection set in The Cruel Gods world:

TrudieSkies.com/Newsletter

Visit my website for signed copies of my books, domain map posters, character art, appendices, pronunciation guides, and other extra goodies:

TrudieSkies.com

Acknowledgments

Writing a book is hard work. Writing a sequel is somehow even harder! There's a lot of pressure to deliver a sequel that is both the same as book one, but different, and also better. I'm convinced all authors are either masochists or insane. Perhaps a bit of both.

A big THANK YOU must then go to the many readers, bloggers, and friends who have encouraged me to finish this book. I didn't expect The Thirteenth Hour to be as loved as it was, but it warms my godless heart to know you've joined me on this journey. The Children of Chaos is for you, and I hope it brings you as much happiness as a book about cruel gods can!

Many thanks to my wonderful beta readers for helping me get there. Thanks to Olivia Hofer, Rowena Andrews, and Tyra Leann for your feedback and support.

Thank you to Nia Quinn for once again providing your amazing editing skills. You are truly a pleasure to work with!

Thanks to Soraya Corcoran for the incredible domain map that I will never stop staring at.

Thank you to James T. Egan of Bookfly Design for once again using pure magic to create the book cover.

Special thanks to RJ Bayley for bringing Chime to life. Your Seren singing will live on in infamy.

Thanks to my dogs, Ben and Butch, for making me go outside.

And thanks to Jack Roots for keeping me well fed and sane.

Last but not least, a very special THANK YOU to those who have reviewed and praised The Thirteenth Hour. There are too many names to mention, but I love and appreciate all of you. We indie authors survive on the support of passionate readers and bloggers. It is YOU who makes this journey worthwhile.

About the Author

Trudie Skies is a non-binary author based in North East England, though they have been living inside fantasy worlds ever since they discovered books and refuse to return to reality. Within Trudie's daydreams you'll find SPFBO and BBNYA finalist The Thirteenth Hour, a gaslamp fantasy described as obnoxiously British and best read with a cup of tea.

When not conjuring new worlds, Trudie spends their free time exploring the realms of indie books and video games, staring at clouds, and chasing after their fluffy companions.

Follow the Author:

TrudieSkies.com
TrudieSkies.com/Newsletter
Bookbub.com/Authors/Trudie-Skies

Also by Trudie Skies

The Cruel Gods Series

Adult Gaslamp Fantasy

Book One: The Thirteenth Hour
Book Two: The Children of Chaos
Book Three: The End of Time
Tales From Across the Domains: A Short Story Collection

Cruel gods rule the steam-powered city of Chime and demand worship from their mortal subjects, but when soul-sucking creatures prey on Chime's citizens, it'll take godless heathens to save them—before the gods take matters into their own hands.

The Chosen One Con

Adult Gaslamp Fantasy

A televised contest of mages to find the 'chosen one' in a world of designer enchantments and celebrity-branded potions.